Also by Ma Jian

Travel
Red Dust

Fiction
The Noodle Maker
Stick Out Your Tongue

BEIJING COMA

BEIJING COMA

Ma Jian

Translated from the Chinese by Flora Drew

Chatto & Windus
LONDON

Published by Chatto & Windus 2008

2 4 6 8 10 9 7 5 3 1

First published in Great Britain in 2008 by
Chatto & Windus
Random House, 20 Vauxhall Bridge Road,
London SW1V 2SA

www.rbooks.co.uk

Addresses for companies within The Random House Group Limited can be found at: www.randomhouse.co.uk/offices.htm

The Random House Group Limited Reg. No. 954009

A CIP catalogue record for this book is available from the British Library

Hardback ISBN 9780701178079
Trade paperback ISBN 9780701182670

The Random House Group Limited supports The Forest Stewardship Council (FSC), the leading international forest certification organisation. All our titles that are printed on Greenpeace-approved FSC-certified paper carry the FSC logo. Our paper procurment policy can be found at: www.rbooks.co.uk/environment

Mixed Sources
Product group from well-managed forests and other controlled sources
www.fsc.org Cert no. TT-COC-2139
© 1996 Forest Stewardship Council

Typeset in Goudy by Palimpsest Book Production Limited, Grangemouth, Stirlingshire

Printed and bound in Great Britain by
Clays Ltd, St Ives PLC

For my mother

Through the gaping hole where the covered balcony used to be, you see the bulldozed locust tree slowly begin to rise again. This is a clear sign that from now on you're going to have to take your life seriously.

You reach for a pillow and tuck it under your shoulders, propping up your head so that the blood in your brain can flow back down into your heart, allowing your thoughts to clear a little. Your mother used to prop you up like that from time to time.

Silvery mornings are always filled with new intentions. But today is the first day of the new millennium, so the dawn is thicker with them than ever.

Although the winter frosts haven't set in yet, the soft breeze blowing on your face feels very cold.

A smell of urine still hangs in the room. It seeps from your pores when the sunlight falls on your skin.

You gaze outside. The morning air isn't rising from the ground as it did yesterday. Instead, it's falling from the sky onto the treetops, then moving slowly through the leaves, brushing past the bloodstained letter caught in the branches, absorbing moisture as it falls.

Before the sparrow arrived, you had almost stopped thinking about flight. Then, last winter, it soared through the sky and landed in front of you, or more precisely on the windowsill of the covered balcony adjoining your bedroom. You knew the grimy windowpanes were caked with dead ants and dust, and smelt as sour as the curtains. But the sparrow wasn't put off. It jumped inside the covered balcony and ruffled its feathers, releasing a sweet smell of tree bark into the air. Then it flew into your bedroom, landed on your chest and stayed there like a cold egg.

Your blood is getting warmer. The muscles of your eye sockets quiver. Your eyes will soon fill with tears. Saliva drips onto the soft palate at the back of your mouth. A reflex is triggered, and the palate rises, closing off the nasal passage and allowing the saliva to flow into your pharynx. The muscles of the oesophagus, which have been dormant for so many years, contract, projecting the saliva down into your stomach. A bioelectrical signal darts like a spark of light from the neurons in your motor cortex, down the spinal cord to a muscle fibre at the tip of your finger.

You will no longer have to rely on your memories to get through the day. This is not a momentary flash of life before death. This is a new beginning.

'Waa, waaah . . .'

A baby's choked cry cuts through the fetid air. A tiny naked body seems to be trembling on a cold concrete floor . . . It's me. I've crawled out between my mother's legs, my head splitting with pain. I bat my hand in the pool of blood that gathers around me . . . My mother often recounted how she was forced to wear a shirt embroidered with the words WIFE OF A RIGHTIST when she gave birth to me. The doctor on duty didn't dare offer to help bring this 'son of a capitalist dog' into the world. Fortunately, my mother passed out after her waters broke, so she didn't feel any pain when I pushed myself out into the hospital corridor.

And now, all these years later, I, too, am lying unconscious in a hospital. Only the occasional sound of glass injection ampoules being snapped open tells me that I'm still alive.

Yes, it's me. My mother's eldest son. The eyes of a buried frog flash through my mind. It's still alive. It was I who trapped it in the jar and buried it in the earth . . . The dark corridor outside is very long. At the end of it is the operating room, where bodies are handled like mere heaps of flesh . . . And the girl I see now – what's her name? A-Mei. She's walking towards me, just a white silhouette. She has no smell. Her lips are trembling.

I'm lying on a hospital bed, just as my father did before he died. I'm Dai Wei – the seed that he left behind. Am I beginning to remember things? I must be alive, then. Or perhaps I'm fading away, flitting, one last time, through the ruins of my past. No, I can't be dead. I can hear noises. Death is silent.

'He's just pretending to be dead . . .' my mother mumbles to someone. 'I can't eat this pak choi. It's full of sand.'

It's me she's talking about. I hear a noise close to my ear. It's somebody's colon rumbling.

Where's my mouth? My face? I can see a yellow blur before my eyes, but can't smell anything yet. I hear a baby crying somewhere in the distance and occasionally a thermos flask being filled with hot water.

The yellow light splinters. Perhaps a bird just flew across the sky. I sense that I'm waking from a long sleep. Everything sounds new and unfamiliar.

What happened to me? I see Tian Yi and me hand in hand, running for our lives. Is that a memory? Did it really happen? Tanks roll towards us. There are fires burning everywhere, and the sound of screaming . . .

And what about now? Did I pass out when the tanks rolled towards me? Is this still the same day?

When my father was lying in hospital waiting to die, the stench of dirty sheets and rotten orange peel was sometimes strong enough to mask the pervasive smell of rusty metal beds. When the evening sky blocked up the window, the filthy curtains merged into the golden sunlight and the room became slightly more transparent, and enabled me at least to sense that my father was still alive . . . On that last afternoon, I didn't dare look at him. I turned instead to the window, and stared at the red slogan RAISE THE GLORIOUS RED FLAG OF MARXISM AND STRUGGLE BOLDLY ONWARDS hanging on the roof of the hospital building behind, and at the small strip of sky above it . . .

During those last days of his life, my father talked about the three years he spent as a music student in America. He mentioned a girl from California whom he'd met when he was there. She was called Flora, which means flower in Latin. He said that when she played the violin, she would look down at the floor and he could gaze at her long eyelashes. She'd promised to visit him in Beijing after she left college. But by the time she graduated, China had become a communist country, and no foreigners were allowed inside.

I remember the black, rotten molar at the side of his mouth. While he spoke to us in hospital, he'd stroke his cotton sheet and the urinary catheter inserted into his abdomen underneath.

'Technically speaking, he's a vegetable,' says a nurse to my right. 'But at least the IV fluid is still entering his vein. That's a good a sign.' She seems to be speaking through a face mask and tearing a piece of muslin. The noises vibrate through me, and for a moment I gain a vague sense of the size and weight of my body.

If I'm a vegetable, I must have been lying here unconscious for some time. So, am I waking up now?

My father comes into view again. His face is so blurred, it looks as though I'm seeing it through a wire mesh. My father was also attached to an intravenous drip when he breathed his last breath. His left eyeball reflected like a windowpane the roof of the hospital building behind, a slant of sky and a few branches of a tree. If I were to die now, my closed eyes wouldn't reflect a thing.

Perhaps I only have a few minutes left to live, and this is just a momentary recovery of consciousness before death.

'Huh! I'm probably wasting my time here. He's never going to wake up.' My mother's voice sounds both near and far away. It floats through the air. Maybe this is how noises sounded to my father just before he died.

In those last few moments of his life, the oxygen mask on his face and the plastic tube inserted into his nose looked superfluous. Had the nurses not been regularly removing the phlegm from his throat, or pouring milk into his stomach through a rubber feeding tube, he would have died on that metal bed weeks before. Just as he was about to pass away, I sensed his eyes focus on me. I was tugging my brother's shirt. The cake crumbs in his hands scattered onto my father's sheet. He was trying to climb onto my father's bed. The key hanging from his neck clunked against the metal bed frame. I yanked the strap of his leather satchel with such force that it snapped in half.

'Get down!' my mother shouted, her eyes red with fury. My brother burst into tears. I fell silent.

A second later, my father sank into the cage of medical equipment surrounding him and entered my memory. Life and death had converged inside his body. It had all seemed so simple.

'He's gone,' the nurse said, without taking off her face mask. With the tip of her shoe, she flicked aside the discarded chopsticks and cotton wool she'd used to clear his phlegm, then told my mother to go to reception and complete the required formalities. If his body wasn't taken to the mortuary before midnight, my mother would be charged another night for the hospital room. Director Guo, the personnel officer of the opera company my parents belonged to, advised my mother to apply for my father's posthumous political rehabilitation, pointing out that the compensation money could help cover the hospital fees.

My father stopped breathing and became a corpse. His body lay on the bed, as large as before. I stood beside him, with his watch on my wrist.

After the cremation, my mother stood at the bus stop cradling the box of ashes in her arms and said, 'Your father's last words were that he wanted his ashes buried in America. That rightist! Even at the point of death he refused to repent.' As our bus approached, she cried out, 'At least from now on we won't have to live in a constant state of fear!'

She placed the box of ashes under her iron bed. Before I went to sleep, I'd often pull it out and take a peek inside. The more afraid I grew of the ashes, the more I wanted to gaze at them. My mother said that if a friend of hers were to leave China, she'd give them the box and ask them to bury it abroad so that my father's spirit could rise into a foreign heaven.

'You must go and study abroad, my son,' my father often repeated to me when he was in hospital.

So, I'm still alive . . . I may be lying in hospital, but at least I'm not dead. I've just been buried alive inside my body . . . I remember the day

I caught that frog. Our teacher had told us to catch one so that we could later study their skeletons. After I caught my frog, I put it in a glass jar, pierced a hole in the metal cap, then buried it in the earth. Our teacher told us that worms and ants would crawl inside and eat away all the flesh within a month, leaving a clean skeleton behind. I bought some alcohol solution, ready to wipe off any scraps of flesh still remaining on the bones. But before the month was out, a family living on the ground floor of our building built a kitchen over the hole where I'd buried it.

The frog must have become a skeleton years ago. While its bones lie trapped in the jar, I lie buried inside my body, waiting to die.

A portion of your brain is still alive. You wander back and forth through the space between your flesh and your memories.

I stare into my mind and glimpse a faint sketch of a scene. It's the summer night in 1980 when my father arrived back home with a shaven head after he was finally released from the 'reform-through-labour' system in which he'd been confined for the previous twenty-two years. He walked into our single room in the opera company's dormitory block and flung his dusty suitcase into the corner as though it were a bag of rubbish.

My mother hadn't gone to meet him at the station, although she was almost certain that he'd be arriving on that train.

She gathered up the clothes, hat, belt and rubber-soled shoes that my father removed before he went to sleep that night, and threw them in the bin, together with his metal mug, face towel and toothbrush. She tried to throw away the journal he'd wrapped in sheets of newspapers, but my father snatched it back from her. He said he would need it for the memoirs he was planning to write.

My mother made him promise that the journal didn't contain the slightest criticism of the Communist Party or the socialist system. After my father assured her that it didn't, she agreed to hide it in the wooden chest under their bed.

My mother spent the whole of the next day scrubbing the room clean, trying to remove the smell of mould that my father had brought with him.

The celebratory supper we had that night was a happy occasion. My brother and I had glasses set before us, both filled with rice wine. My mother climbed onto a stool to change the low-wattage bulb to a 40-watt one. It was so bright that you could see the spider's web in the corner of the room.

My mother had curled her hair with heated tongs. She told my brother to clear away his homework. Once he'd done this, the table looked much larger. The four of us sat down together in front of a steaming dish of braised pigs' trotters. There was also a plate of fried peanuts on the table, and a bowl of cucumber and vermicelli salad that I'd bought from the market.

I used to hate my father for the misery that his political status had inflicted on us. Because of him, I was ostracised and bullied at school. When my brother and I were walking through the school cafeteria at lunchtime one day, two older kids flicked onto the ground the plate of fried chicken I'd just bought, and shouted, 'You're the dog son of a member of the Five Black Categories. What makes you think you have the right to eat meat?' Then they clipped me around the ears, right in front of my friend Lulu, who lived on the ground floor of our dormitory block.

My father raised his glass to my mother and said, 'May you stay young and beautiful for ever!'

'Haven't you learned your lesson yet, you rightist?' my mother snapped. 'What are you thinking of, coming out with bourgeois claptrap like that?'

He was sitting on a pillow at the edge of the bed. When he took off his glasses his eyes looked much larger. His face, which resembled a crumpled paper bag, glimmered with happiness.

His imprisonment in the reform-through-labour camps had caused us much hardship. He'd cast a shadow over our family, connecting us with the dark, negative aspects of life: the countryside, fleas and counter-revolutionary criminals. But on that summer night, it seemed as though all our misery was about to come to an end. I no longer felt shamed by his rough and dishevelled appearance. I knew that, very soon, I would once more have a father with a full head of hair.

He took a sip of rice wine, gazed up at me with a look of curiosity that I'd never seen in his eyes before, and said, 'How come you've grown up all of a sudden?'

He seemed to have forgotten that, when he'd visited us in 1976 just after the earthquake, I'd already reached his shoulders.

He asked me what I wanted to do with my life. In his letters he'd told me I should join the People's Liberation Army, so that's what I told him I wanted to do.

He shook his head and said, 'No. I only wrote that so that my letter would get approved by the camp leaders. You must learn English and do a science degree at university. Keep yourself to yourself. Then, if you get a chance, go abroad and become a citizen of the world. Did you know that British people can fly to America whenever they want, and that Germans can walk freely through the streets of Paris? Once you're an international citizen, you'll be able to travel the world.'

'Don't corrupt your sons with your liberal thoughts, Dai Changjie,' my mother said. 'All the activists involved in that Democracy Wall Movement last year are in jail now.' Then she glanced at my brother and said: 'You don't hold chopsticks like that, Dai Ru! Look: wrap your fingers over the top, like this.' She picked up a peanut with her chopsticks and placed it in her mouth.

'If you hadn't set your alarm clock to the wrong time, you'd be living in America now,' my father retorted. Glancing at me, he explained: 'Your mother's father bought her a ticket to New York, but she missed the boat by half an hour. If she'd managed to catch it, she'd be an Overseas Chinese now.'

'You made it to America, but you still came back in the end, didn't you?' A piece of peanut had stuck to my mother's lower lip. With her chopsticks she divided the two pig trotters into four unequal parts. She gave the largest chunk to my father, and pulled off the nail from my chunk to chew on herself.

'It was 1949. The Communists had just liberated China. Everyone was coming back then. Besides, in America I was only a rank-and-file member of an orchestra, but back here I could be principal violinist of the National Opera Company . . .'

'It's your arrogance that's been your downfall. After twenty years in the labour camps, you're still reminiscing about your past. You should have transformed yourself into a simple labourer by now – learned to make do with your lot, and live up to your responsibilities as a father.'

While my parents were busy talking, Dai Ru and I finished all the peanuts left on the plate.

My father spat out some bits of bone and gave them to me and my brother to chew on. I discovered one of his teeth among the shards. He'd lost most of the others already.

He grabbed the tooth from my hand and looked at it, rubbed his gums, then placed it on the table. 'I've waited all these years to return home, and by the time I get here, I've got no teeth left.' He turned his eyes to my brother and asked, 'What year are you in at school now?'

'Year Three. My teacher said that you're a bourgeois rightist. I said that you're a labour-camp prisoner. What is your job exactly, Dad?'

My father raised his eyebrows and said, 'The Party put that rightist label on me. I had no choice but to accept it. But don't worry, I will make sure you get into Harvard, my son. In winter, the campus is covered in a metre of snow. Squirrels scurry back and forth across it. The chairs in the classrooms have spring upholstery. Once you sit down on one, you never want to stand up again . . . Is it true that people are allowed to have sofas in their homes again?'

'Huh! I hate the snow,' I said. 'My feet get so cold.'

'Don't huff like that, Dai Wei, or you'll be miserable for the rest of your life.' My mother would always say that to me and my brother whenever we let out long sighs. Turning back to my father, she said, 'If you have back-door connections with factory bosses you can get hold of some springs and steel rods, then you can buy some man-made leather in the market and knock up two armchairs for under fifty yuan. Most of the soloists in the opera company have got sofas and armchairs now . . . Fetch the soy sauce from the corridor, Dai Wei.' My mother picked up a fan from the table and flicked it open.

'Sofa! I want an American sofa!' my brother shouted.

'We need a sitting room first,' I said. 'My classmates have sitting rooms, with televisions, washing machines and fridges.'

'All we inherited was this iron bed,' my mother said. 'I didn't even get a copper bracelet. When the compensation money comes through, we'll buy a television. If your dad gets in touch with his uncle in America, we'll be able to convert the cash into foreign-exchange certificates and buy a Japanese TV at the Friendship Store. Sit up straight when you're eating, Dai Wei!'

'See, the world has changed now,' my father said, smiling. 'Even you are prepared to admit that foreign goods are better.'

I too had realised that having a relation abroad was no longer something to be ashamed of. In fact, by now it had become almost a badge of honour.

'I support Deng Xiaoping's reform policy,' said my mother. 'I'm not one of those stubborn people who cling to the past. The Party has pledged to raise the country's living standards to a moderately prosperous level by 2000. It is giving us all the chance to live better lives.' My mother was speaking to my father in a warmer tone than she'd used the night before.

'I saw two foreigners in the street today, Dad,' my brother said. 'Their eyes were yellow.'

'I hope you weren't following them,' my mother said sternly. 'The neighbourhood committee called us in the other day and told us that if we see foreigners in the street, we shouldn't crowd around them and stare.'

'They were walking along the pavement as I was coming out from school. Their footprints were huge.'

'If there are foreigners walking down the streets of Beijing, it won't be long before Chinese people are allowed to travel abroad again. I'll write to my uncle in America tomorrow. He has two apple trees in his garden. In autumn, so many apples fall onto the grass, he has to leave most of them to rot.' My father picked up a slice of cucumber that my brother had dropped onto the table and popped it into his mouth.

'Dad, I still haven't seen a squirrel yet.' My brother always dropped food onto the table when he ate. My mother would smack him whenever it happened, but it never had any effect.

'Don't eat with your mouths open,' my mother said. 'You sound like dogs.' My brother and I quickly shut our mouths and continued chewing.

'Mum, Dai Ru threw stones at the pigeons again today,' I said, suddenly recalling the incident. 'The old lady downstairs got very angry. She had to come out and drag him away in the end.' I was always having to apologise to others for my brother's bad behaviour.

'You'll smash someone's window if you keep doing that, then you'll have to pay to get it repaired.' My mother glanced back to my father and said, 'Before people go abroad now, the government allows them to buy three domestically produced items tax-free. If you sell just two of them on the black market you can make enough money to last you a year.'

'We should all go abroad. I'll teach the violin, you can give singing classes, the children can both go to university.'

'Do you think you'll still be able to play your violin with hands like that? And anyway, I'm just a chorus singer now. How could I teach a foreigner? I've been singing revolutionary operas for the last twenty years. I've forgotten all my Western training.'

'You were the most talented soloist in the company when we first met. You had a beautiful voice. I'm sure that if you had a chance to sing Western operas again, all your training would come back to you. In America, the government leaves people alone. The rich are rich, and the poor are poor. Everyone just gets on with their lives. I've spent every day of the last twenty years regretting my decision to return to China. The only thing that kept me alive in the camps was the hope that one day I might go back to America. Without that hope, I would have committed suicide years ago.' My father was staring at his left hand. The little finger had been broken when he was beaten up in the camp. Although he was wearing a clean white shirt that night, when I looked at his shaven head and weathered features, it was hard to imagine that he'd once been a professional violinist.

'Don't praise foreign countries in front of the children. Now that you're back, you'll have to read the papers every day and make sure you keep up with the changing political climate. We can't let our family be torn apart again.'

'Mum, will you sing me that Li Gu ballad "Longing for Home"?' I said. The tune had been in my head all day.

'Li Gu's voice is weak and breathy. It has no revolutionary spirit. Our company received a statement from the Ministry of Culture today warning that her ballad has had a corrupting influence on young people and could lead to the ruination of the country. The radio stations aren't broadcasting it any more, so don't you start humming it like a fool.'

'You're behind the times, Mum. Li Gu's ballad is old hat. You can buy *The Best 200 Foreign Love Songs* in the shops now.'

'Stop making things up! Why am I the only one in this family to have a political consciousness? From now on the four of us must study the newspaper every night and bring our thoughts in line with the Party. Dai Changjie, tomorrow you must adjust our radio so that it receives only Chinese stations. Don't let that son of ours drag our family back down again. And from now on, Dai Wei, you're only allowed to play your harmonica inside this room.'

'When my compensation money comes through we can buy a television, then we won't have to listen to the radio again.' My father took another gulp of rice wine. Beads of sweat dripped down his face.

'Last year, the three popular things to own were a watch, a bicycle and a sewing machine, but we only managed to buy a watch. This year, there are three new things everyone wants to own. I can't keep up! We might not be able to afford a shelf unit, but I'm determined that we get a sofa . . . You shouldn't be drinking so much wine, Dai Changjie – you've got a weak stomach.' My mother pulled the bottle of rice wine over to her side of the table.

'I'm so happy it's all over. I can hold my head up now.' My father gazed at my mother with a look of contentment in his eyes.

My mother walked out and put another charcoal briquette on our stove in the communal corridor. A thick cloud of charcoal smoke wafted back into the room.

I picked up the thermos flask and poured some hot water into a pot of jasmine tea, inhaling the tobacco smoke that my father was exhaling. I was thirteen, and had already smoked a few cigarettes on the sly by then.

My father took a sip of the tea and said, 'Mmm, that tastes good!' He had a cigarette in his left hand and a pair of chopsticks in his right.

'I posted several packets of that tea to the Shandong camp.'

'You shouldn't have bothered. I had to give them all to our education officers. Drinking tea as good as this while undergoing ideological remoulding would have been considered an act of defiance.'

'Didn't you give violin lessons to one of their children?' my mother asked.

'That was down in Guangxi Province on the farm supervised by Overseas Chinese. Director Liu was a nice man. He moved back to China from Malaysia after Liberation. It was brave of him to ask a rightist like me to teach his daughter. He even invited me to stay for supper a couple of times. His daughter, Liu Ping, was very talented. With good coaching, she could have become a professional violinist. Once my rehabilitation has been sorted out, I'd like to go back down to Guangxi and pay them a visit.'

My father kept a photograph he'd taken of them pressed inside the pages of his copy of the *Selected Works of Mao Zedong*. Liu Ping was in a white skirt, and was standing between Director Liu and my father holding her violin in her arms. She looked about twelve or thirteen.

My mother shot me a glance and said, 'You mustn't repeat anything you hear in this room to your classmates.'

'I know, Mum. Dad, can you speak English?'

'*Of course!*' my father replied proudly in English. 'I'll give you lessons. I guarantee that you'll come top of the class in all your English tests.'

'Dad, Chairman Mao said that we must be "united, serious, intense and lively",' my brother exclaimed as he chewed on his last peanut.

'You shouldn't go around spouting Mao Zedong's words like that. Just content yourself with memorising them.' An anxious look flitted across my father's face.

'Anyway, you got the quote wrong,' I said to my brother. 'What Chairman Mao said was that we should "unite together, study seriously and intensely, then go home with a lively attitude".'

Suddenly, all the lights went out.

'Not another power cut,' my mother groaned.

I went to my camp bed in the corner of the room to fetch my precious torch. I kept it hidden under my pillow so that I could read my *Selected Stories from the Book of Mountains and Seas* after everyone had gone to sleep. When it was dark, the torchlight made the battered basket hanging on the wall look like the face of a mysterious ghoul. The dried sprigs of spring onion that stuck out through the holes were the ghoul's dishevelled hair.

'Hey, I wonder what happened to the company's stage designer, Old Li,' my father muttered. Back in 1958, my father and Old Li were both sent to the same labour camp in Gansu Province.

'You didn't hear? He was skin and bone when he was released from the camp. On his first night back, he gobbled a whole duck, four bowls of rice and downed half a bottle of rice wine. He went out for a walk afterwards and his stomach exploded. He collapsed on the street and died.'

'I lost touch with my fellow Gansu inmates after I was transferred to the Guangxi farm. We rightists weren't allowed to write to each other. In Gansu everyone thought that Old Li had the best chance of surviving the camp. After we'd been working on the fields all day, most of us would lie on the floor and rest, but he'd still be rushing around, full of energy. He once climbed into the stable and ate a bowl of horse feed and some seeds that had been soaking in fertiliser. His mouth swelled up horribly. Sometimes he'd even eat maggots he found crawling around the cesspit.'

'He was the best-looking man in the company. The soprano, Xiao Lu, nearly killed herself when he was sent away.'

'He was very ingenious. One day, three rightists who worked in the camp's cafeteria were sent to the local town to fetch a batch of yams. When they returned, Old Li waited outside the cesspit, and after the men went for a shit, he scooped out the excrement, rinsed it in water and picked out the chunks of undigested yam. He managed to eat about a kilo of them. He knew the three men were so starving, they wouldn't have been able to resist munching a few raw yams on the way back from the town. There were three thousand inmates in the camp. We'd been on starvation rations for half a year, but Old Li was the only one of us who managed to still look healthy. He even had enough energy to fetch water every morning to wash his face.'

The candle on the table shone into my father's blank eyes. The flames reflected in his pupils grew gradually smaller and smaller.

'That's disgusting!' My full stomach churned when I heard him speak of people eating excrement and maggots.

'If you kids mention any of this to anyone, you'll be arrested and made to live like that yourselves. Do you hear me?' My mother placed her hand over her mouth and whispered to my father, 'Don't speak of those things in front of the children. If any of it got out, our family would be finished.'

I shone my torch onto my mother's foot. Her big toes were splayed away from the rest of her feet, and moved up and down as she spoke. Under the white torchlight, my father's feet looked dark and wrinkled. Most of his gnarled toenails were cracked.

'We mustn't mention to anyone that we're thinking of moving abroad,' my mother continued. 'If the government launches another political crackdown, it might be enough to get us arrested. By the way, your brother's son, Dai Dongsheng, came and stayed with us for a few days a while ago.'

'What was he doing here?' My father pushed the red candle deeper into the mouth of the beer bottle.

'It was just after the responsibility system was introduced in the countryside a couple of years ago, allowing farmers to sell some of their produce on the free market. Your brother sent Dongsheng here with more than fifty kilos of ginger to sell. I took a bag to the opera company, and managed to sell ten kilos. Then I sold another five kilos to some friends. But, without telling me, the boy took a bag out onto the street and set up a stall. Not only did the police confiscate all his ginger, they also gave him a hundred-yuan fine. In the end, I had to pay for his train ticket back home.'

'So how is my brother?' My father had long since severed his ties with his elder brother who lived in Dezhou, our family's ancestral village in Shandong Province. During the reform movement in the early 1950s,when Mao ordered land to be redistributed to the poor and classified landowners as the enemy of the people, my grandfather, who owned two fields and three cows, was branded an 'evil tyrant'. My father's brother was forced to bury him alive. Had he refused, he himself would have been executed.

'Still not right in the head.' My mother didn't like talking about him either.

'He shouldn't have gone back to Dezhou during the land reform movement.'

When my cousin, Dongsheng, came to stay, I learned that, before Liberation, his father had been a lawyer in the port city of Qingdao.

'He wanted to make sure your parents didn't come to harm,' my mother said. 'You shouldn't blame him. The land reform work team made him do it. Forcing a man to kill his own father – what a way to test someone's revolutionary fervour! Wasn't it enough that they confiscated your father's land? And your mother didn't come out of it very well either, going off and marrying the team leader.'

My cousin told me that, when the work team held a struggle session in Dezhou, my grandmother jumped at the opportunity to denounce my grandfather. He had three wives, and she wanted to be freed from him. She married the team leader just a few hours after my grandfather was buried alive.

'That's not fair! She was forced to marry him.' My father hated anyone criticising his mother. But both he and his brother broke all contact with her after she married the team leader.

The noises in the room seemed much louder now that the lights were out.

In the darkness, my father turned to my mother again and said, 'You drew a line between you and your capitalist family as soon as the Communists took over, but you still haven't been awarded Party membership.' When my father's face turned red, he sometimes had the courage to stand up to my mother.

'That's because I'm married to you. If you hadn't been labelled a rightist, I would have been invited to join the Party in the 1950s. You ruined my life.' When my mother got angry all her toes splayed out, making her feet look much wider.

My father fell silent and tucked his feet under the bed. They'd only spent two days together, and already they were arguing.

'The Party may have treated you unjustly in the past,' my mother continued, 'but now that Deng Xiaoping and his reformers are at the helm, everything will change. The new General Secretary, Hu Yaobang, is determined to redress past wrongs. He's been leading the campaign to rehabilitate rightists. If it weren't for him, you wouldn't be sitting here with us today. Did you hear what I said, children? Hu Yaobang has saved our family.'

The lights suddenly came back on again. My mother stood up and barked, 'Turn the lights off. It's time for bed!'

A bundle of neurons sparkles with light. Perhaps they are disintegrating. Memories flash by like the lighted windows of a passing train.

Fractured episodes from the past flit back to me. My mind returns to that summer night when my parents were reunited. I can see my mother's angry face – the corners of her mouth twisting into a grimace, beads of sweat dripping down between her eyebrows. The red candle's flame flickered from side to side as my parents fanned themselves. My father used a piece of cardboard. Although the breeze it created wasn't strong, when it blew on my face my skin felt cooler. The images waver like scenes from an old, scratched film projected onto an open-air screen shaking in the breeze.

The next image is not of my father, but of Lulu, whose skin always smelt of pencil shavings and erasers. When her face first appears, I hear the sound of gunfire, then everything falls silent again. The streets are empty. A bicycle zooms past. There are red and yellow banners emblazoned with slogans strung across the telegraph poles flanking the road. Someone walks by, their arms folded across their chest, and spits onto the pavement . . . It's a cold winter day now. Lulu is skipping down the pavement, kicking a bottle-top along as she goes. The black plaits on the sides of her head and the satchel on her back swing from side to side as she moves. She's wearing blue trousers and a pair of padded corduroy shoes. She zigzags behind the moving bottle-top. When she loses her balance, she flings out her arms like a bird and wriggles her little fingers. She kicks the bottle-top as hard as she can, but because it's so flat, it never goes very far. I'm following her on the other side of the street. The cabbage I'm kicking doesn't travel very far either, and makes even less noise than her bottle-top. In an attempt to attract her attention, I kick the cabbage into a gate, and scrape my shoes noisily against the lower metal bar.

We are walking home after school. The sun is setting behind us. The long shadows of our bodies and of the trees lining the road stretch on the pavements before us. Then darkness falls and a terrible fear grips me. I leave Lulu alone on the street and race back home as fast as I can.

The night often caught me unawares. It would slip out from under tricycle carts and from around street corners, and blot out the dusk. I would have to grope my way home. But it always knew which route I'd take, and would follow behind me all the way. The further I ran the darker it became. Faces grew indistinct. My body seemed to shrink into the gloom. The entrance to the opera company's dormitory block opened its black mouth to me. I knew I'd have to drag myself through it in order to get back to our room. Sometimes there would be a light shining in the stairwell, so faint that all I could make out were the bicycles propped against the banisters and the Chairman Mao slogans painted on the walls. Usually there was no light at all, because the residents had a habit of stealing the bulbs when no one was looking, and since the batteries of my torch often ran out, I'd have to walk upstairs in the pitch dark. I hated the dark – that vast, untouchable substance.

Whenever I reached the entrance, my scalp would go numb, and I'd cry out: 'Mummy, Mummy!' If Lulu was back already, she'd poke her head out from her family's room on the ground floor – sometimes all I'd see were her leg and half her face – and make strange noises to frighten me. She knew all my fears and weaknesses. I hated her. Sometimes, I'd kick her door as I passed.

I remember when we were about nine or ten her mother, who worked in the opera company's accounts office, took her away for the whole summer. When I saw her again on the first day back at school her face was tanned. Her body had sprouted up like a needle mushroom after the rain, but her head was still the same size. It looked as though it had been planted onto someone else's body.

On the way to school, her longer legs allowed her to stride out in front of me. The red skirt that reached down to her knees, and her left arm with its Young Pioneer red armband, moved with great lightness. I'd watch the petals printed on her skirt shudder over her bottom. On the straight path that ran through the yard it was impossible for me to keep up with her. Whenever she heard me move closer, she'd quicken her pace. My only chance to catch up came when the path turned into the main road. She'd always stop there and glance back to see if I was still behind, and I'd take advantage of this moment to sprint over to her. One time when she turned round she tossed me a plum, but I didn't catch it. The purple fruit rolled down the path, then came to a stop. 'You idiot!' she cried out, taking a few steps towards me. 'No wonder you haven't been allowed to join the Young Pioneers.' When she spoke to me I could see her white teeth . . .

The images are as light and brittle as falling leaves. Cells drift through the fluids of your body, leaving no trace.

Lulu fades away, and all I see is a red plum rolling down a pavement . . . I remember the earthquake that shook northern China in 1976, a few weeks before Chairman Mao died. I was about to start secondary school. My father was granted a month's leave from the Shandong camp so that he could look after us in Beijing. Although the tremors in the capital had been faint, everyone was told to sleep outside for a month in case there were any aftershocks. The residents of the opera company's dormitory block moved into a large tent that had been erected for us in the yard. My parents, brother and I had to share a single camp bed. I slept so close to my father that our noses touched. One night, when the rain was beating down onto the plastic sheeting above our heads, my father glared at me, his eyes cold with fear, and whispered, 'Don't go over to the tree. The officers will take a note of your name. Remember, you're the son of a rightist – you must learn to live with your tail tucked between your legs.'

The tree he was referring to was about a hundred metres from our tent. A few days after Mao died, someone had hung dummies of the four leaders of the Central Committee from the tree's branches.

My father didn't know that on the way home from school that day, I'd squeezed into the crowd that had gathered around the tree and taken a look. There were three male dummies labelled Wang Hongwen, Zhang Chunqiao and Yao Wenyuan, and one female labelled Jiang Qing. They swayed back and forth in the breeze.

I can't remember much about that month in the tent. But I remember one meal we all had together. There was fried chicken and beer. My father cooked a large pot of braised rice noodles. He added to it some dried fungus he'd brought with him from the camp. It was full of sand, but it let off a delicious aroma that filled the tent. As he stirred the pot, he turned his red face to me and gave me one of his rare smiles.

When he'd returned home for a few days the year before, he'd slapped me in the face for tearing down a large, handwritten political poster.

It was during the weekly residents' meeting in the yard. He played a tune from the 'The Red Detachment of Women' on his violin, then another one on his accordion. All the kids sang along with him: '*The Red Detachment of Women are Chairman Mao's most faithful soldiers . . .*' I could hear my brother's flat tones squeaking above the other voices. A few minutes later, the chairwoman of the neighbourhood committee rose to her feet and said: 'Please can all parents ensure that their children attend the cultural activities we organise every Sunday.' Then she pointed to the large noticeboard beside the front gates and said, 'Someone has torn off the corner of that big-character poster criticising Lin Biao and Confucius. Who did it?'

'Me!' I blurted. Everyone's eyes turned to me, and then to my father.

I saw a look of terror flash across his face. He was sitting under a large tree. Everyone could see him. He lifted his hands from his violin and locked them tightly together.

'Why did you tear it?' my mother said, pulling me up onto my feet.

My father's frightened face grew sombre. No one could have respected a man who had such a cowardly expression.

'I was going to the toilet and I forgot to bring some paper with me, so I tore off a small corner of the poster.'

'I tore some off too!' admitted a boy who lived on the first floor. He dug into his pocket and pulled out a scrunched-up ball of paper, then showed everyone the Chairman Mao badge that was wrapped inside it. His grimy neck began to redden.

The chairwoman cleared her throat and spat onto the ground. 'Dai Changjie, as a rightist, you should be keeping a close eye on your children's ideological education to make sure they don't follow the same path as you,' she said, then glaring at my mother, added, 'And Huizhen, you must be stricter with your younger son. He's been spotted playing with the bells of the bicycles parked over there on several occasions.'

'I know that my ideology still needs some more remoulding,' said my father, twisting his fingers. 'I want to learn from people like you who have a high level of political consciousness.' Then he rose to his feet, walked over to me and slapped me in the face. Lulu, who was standing next to me, jumped back in fright. I began shaking uncontrollably. The noise of the slap shuddered through my body like a clap of thunder.

I hated him. My teacher had told me that even if my father gained rehabilitation, I would still be banned from joining the army. I wanted the police to arrive immediately and drag him back to the labour camp.

As you shrink back inside your body, your childhood fears flicker through your mind. All the feelings you've felt in the past have been sheltering inside your flesh.

I can see my body soaking in the hot pool of a public bathhouse. My memories seem as muddled and random as the contents of a rubbish bin . . . It was a cold winter night. With a padded jacket draped over my shoulders, I walked towards the bathhouse, carrying my soap and towel in a plastic string bag. I usually took my brother with me, but this time I was going alone. I'd made up my mind that tonight I'd lower myself straight into the hot water and wallow there for some time, rather than edging myself in hesitatingly before quickly jumping out again, as I usually did.

I glanced at the chestnuts roasting in the wok of a street stall outside the entrance, and breathed in their sweet fragrance. Just as I was about to enter the bathhouse, I caught a whiff of the mutton skewers cooking on the stall's charcoal grill. The smell was so mouth-watering that I turned round and went to buy myself one. I sprinkled the mutton with cumin powder and sat down to eat it on a wooden stool under the street lamp.

I paid for the mutton skewer with the money a shopkeeper had given me for returning our old bottle-tops. My mother had let me keep it. After my father passed away, she often gave me small amounts of pocket money.

A strong wind was blowing around that street corner. It never seemed to let up.

I stared at the lamp on the other side of the street. The parts of the road that it illuminated were busier than the rest. The food stall's awning rustled in the wind. The air below it smelt of hot brown sugar, mutton and charcoal smoke. People on their way home from work stopped off to buy punnets of dried tofu.

Behind me was a brightly lit shop window, pasted with wedding photographs. The peasant squatting below it turned up the sheepskin collar of his jacket and hunched his shoulders against the wind. All I could see of his face were his sparkling eyes. He was selling a basket of large, pink-fleshed radishes. The radish he'd sliced in half and displayed on the top of the pile was as red as a lamb's heart.

When I finished the skewer, I pushed through the large quilt that hung across the bathhouse's entrance, and stepped into the lobby. Immediately, my skin softened in the warm, humid air. There was a synthetic scent of moisturising cream which stung my eyes, and behind it, a fouler stench that reminded me of boiled pigskins. Having just consumed so much greasy mutton, I was struck by a sudden wave of nausea.

Two large portraits of Chairman Mao and Premier Hua Guofeng hung in the lobby. Below them was a freshly painted red box in which to post reports of political misconduct and bad behaviour. Next to the box, two women were gazing into a mirror, combing their wet hair. Some of the water dripped onto the ground, the rest ran down the backs of the yellow-and-white jumpers they were wearing. Women were queuing up behind them to comb their hair in front of the mirror. The men didn't bother to check their appearance. When they walked out into the lobby, they'd just shake their heads, run their fingers through their damp hair then stride outside into the cold.

After I bought myself a ticket, I took off my clothes and headed for the hot pool. White steam rose from its surface. I spotted a space close to the door, gritted my teeth and lowered myself in. I splashed the scorching water onto my face and shoulders in a calm and confident manner, trying to look as though I'd done this many times before. As expected, the other men in the pool shifted their gaze to me, eyeing me with curiosity as I edged myself deeper into the water. They stared at my legs, the strands of hair that had only recently sprouted from my testicles, then glanced at my small, pale nipples.

I had made it. I was an adult now, no longer a child who was afraid of hot water.

Two boys a year or so younger than me were sitting on my left. One of them splashed the water with his feet and said to the other, 'We call our teacher "Miss Donkey". When she gets angry, she swears her head off and stamps her feet like this . . .'

I ignored them. I was a grown-up now, and grown-ups always bathe in silence. I grabbed my bar of soap and rubbed it slowly over my chest.

When people are naked they say very little to each other. They are stripped of their identities. Usually one can guess a person's status from their hairstyle, but in the bathhouse everyone's hair is slicked back. The only props they have are the identical white flannels in their hands and their variously sized bars of soap.

Smells of urine and dirty feet rose into the steam above the pool. Occasionally a cold draught blew in from the skylight, allowing my lungs to open up a little.

The man sitting next to me stood up, his bottom wobbling, and climbed out of the water. His flannel had left red streaks across his body that was already scarlet from the heat.

The scrawny old man sitting opposite me was rubbing his hands up and down his thighs. His skin was the same colour as the legs of ham on the butcher's counter in the local market. When he squeezed his flannel, his expression relaxed slightly. In the typical manner of a regular visitor, he rarely looked anyone in the eye. He moved about with such confidence and lack of inhibition that the rest of us felt as though we were guests in his home. Soon he lifted himself out of the pool and went over to the large tub where the water was heated to an even higher temperature. He slipped inside it without flinching and soaked in the scalding water for several minutes, letting out a soft sigh occasionally to express his pleasure.

I looked down into the water below me and noticed that my penis had swollen. My whole body seemed larger. My feet appeared to have moved further away from my head. My skin stretched tightly over my joints. I knew that, just like my father, I had a large black mole on the small of my back. I was the replica he had made of himself to leave behind in the world after he died.

A crack opens in the darkness, allowing more noises to reach you. These sounds are clearer than the ones you heard before. Although your ears tell you that you've returned to the world, you're still wandering through the intersecting lanes of your memories.

'It's not that cold.' I turned up the collar of my woollen jumper. The air wasn't too cold, but the ground was freezing. The hard soles of my shoes made a lot of noise as we walked along the pavement. The evening wind blasted down the side of the road which had just been planted with trees.

Lulu whispered, 'Get off. Don't touch me. Your hands are freezing. Don't be such a hooligan . . .'

There were some large, concrete pipes lying on the pavement, waiting to be buried in a long ditch in the ground. We crawled inside one of them. 'I'd be frightened to come inside here on my own,' Lulu said, the wind whistling through her voice.

'The wind's dropped again.' My voice trembled in the cold air. 'You should have worn a coat.'

'Let's crawl a little further inside. I don't want anyone to see us.'

'So you're not going back home tonight, then?' I swivelled my legs round, sat down, and was relieved to find that there was enough headroom for me to sit up straight.

'No. My father hit me . . .'

'But he's not even your real father . . .' Lulu didn't react to this comment, so I asked, 'Did your mother see him hit you?'

'Keep your voice down. There are people walking past.'

I remember the sound of those footsteps treading over the grit and sand on the pavement. The footsteps would grow louder then slowly fade away.

'What happened to your real father? He was a percussionist, wasn't he?'

She squashed her head between her knees and said, 'My mum told me he was arrested and sent to jail.'

'What for?'

'The opera company's Party secretary accused him of leading an immoral and licentious lifestyle.'

I remembered that I was four years old when I first met my father. At nursery school, I was made to stand outside the classroom during the singing lessons. The teacher said that, as a son of a rightist, I had no right to learn revolutionary songs.

'You must promise not to tell anyone that my real father's in jail,' Lulu whispered. 'Especially not Suyun. She keeps trying to wheedle the secret out of me. The other day she told me that her father had gone to the cinema with another woman. I knew it was just a ploy to make me open up to her.' She lifted her face as she spoke. The white steam escaping from her mouth scattered into the cold wind.

Her body was a black shadow squashed inside the pipe. There was nothing girlish about the silhouette.

'Your mum is nice to you, though, isn't she? She took you shopping last week.'

'Did you see us?' Her face seemed to move, but I couldn't be sure, because it was too dark for me to see much any more.

The night was quiet and still. Inside the pipe, we could hear people cycling down a road a couple of streets away. Sometimes, when a car drove past, I'd see the shadow of a passer-by move through the light, then everything would go black again. The only constant light came from the window of a distant building, but when a curtain was drawn across it, that light disappeared as well. It was a four-storey brick building that was still under construction. A few residents had moved in ahead of time, hooked up lights to a mains electricity supply and fitted glass panes into the window frames. The half-finished building looked like a monster frozen into the night sky.

'Do you like me?' Her twisted face appeared to turn to me again.

'Yes, I like you.' My heart started thumping. I clenched my teeth together to stop my jaw trembling.

'You gave me two of your stamps, so I know you must be fond of me.'

'If you want, I'll give them all to you. I also have a metal box I want to give you. It has a little lock and key.' My voice sounded strange as it bounced across the interior walls of the concrete pipe.

'It's getting cold now,' she said.

I rose into a squat and moved closer to her. Inside my head I heard a pounding, then a crack that sounded like a block of ice being plunged into hot water. I touched her hair that smelt of fried celery, then put my arms around her.

She took a sharp intake of breath, smiled and pushed me back. I pressed her hands down and moved closer to her face. I was probably trying to kiss her.

'You can't do that,' she said, 'I'm too young . . .'

The steam escaping from her mouth as she spoke became my goal. I moved my lips towards it. She pushed me back again and we tussled for a while until her arms grew weak. When her face looked up at me again, I floated once more towards her white breath. I stroked her hair and her nose, then pressed my mouth over her lips and pushed my tongue between them until, with a sigh, she relaxed her clenched jaw. Her tongue felt warm and soft. She moved her lips and, like a fish, sucked the saliva from my mouth.

I remember my trembling hand reaching towards her thighs and my legs shaking as I undid her belt and touched her warm stomach. When I stretched my hand inside her knickers, the lower half of my body disconnected from me and performed a dance of its own . . .

'My hair's all messy now,' she said when it was over, clasping my hand. 'And I forgot to bring a comb with me. What if someone sees me like this?'

'Don't worry.' I let go of her hand and she sat up straight.

'You're such a hooligan,' she said, doing up her belt.

'No, I'm not. You're the first girl I've ever touched.'

'Did you notice that plastic grip Huang Lingling was wearing in her hair today? She doesn't come from an artistic family. Who does she think she is, trying to pretty herself up like that?' Then she moved close to me again and whispered, 'I'm going to tell you something about my name. I want to see if you can keep a secret. My name is "Lu", as in "road", because I was born on the road. My mother was in the countryside on a training programme to prepare citizens for a possible American attack. Her group were made to run for hours, then throw themselves onto the ground, as though enemy planes were dropping bombs overhead. The third time my mother threw herself down, she couldn't get up again. That's when she gave birth to me. Because she didn't complete the training, she was labelled a "backward element".'

'I promise on Chairman Mao that I won't tell anyone.' The sperm stuck to my trousers felt cold and sticky. I wasn't in a mood to talk.

During that moment of bliss, you were able to forget yourself and leave your body behind. That secret pipe was your road to a new home that felt both strange and familiar.

One afternoon, I climbed into Lulu's bedroom through the window. She had left it open for me so that I would escape the notice of her grandmother, who was in the bedroom next door removing the covers from the quilts. It was a Sunday, and her mother and stepfather were both out.

After my father's rehabilitation was confirmed, my family was able to move from the single room in the opera company's dormitory block to a two-bedroom flat in a large residential compound of four-storey apartment buildings. Lulu's family was moved into an apartment in the same compound, so we were still neighbours.

She locked her door and we sat on her bed, and I listened to her play the harmonica. She'd transcribed all the melodies from *The Best 200 Foreign Love Songs* tape. I liked listening to the noise of the instrument and the sound of her breathing.

I pulled from my bag the copy I'd made of the banned novella *A Young Girl's Heart*. I'd spent the previous three nights writing it out. She put down her harmonica and leafed through the twenty-seven pages of neat handwriting.

'Be careful!' I said to her. 'The glue hasn't dried yet.' The previous night, I'd chewed some noodles into a paste and used it to stick the pages together.

'Is it a dirty book?' She put it down on her bed and made me a cup of tea with an expensive-looking tea bag.

'I bet you could brew five cups from that bag. Apparently, in the hotels where foreigners stay, there are baskets of tea bags like that in all the rooms. You can help yourself to as many as you like.' I glanced at the photographs under the table's glass top and said, 'You've got lots of family photos.'

On the cabinet by the wall there was a radio, a bust of Chairman Mao and an inflatable plastic swan. A calendar issued by the local family planning office was pinned to the wall above.

'Wang Long's mother works in a foreigners' hotel,' Lulu said. 'She told me that foreigners are really wasteful. They throw away the tea bags after just one cup. And the tea isn't good enough for them – they have to add milk before they can drink it.' Then Lulu said that the police were knocking on people's doors and confiscating any hand-copied novels they found, so she didn't want to keep the book. She said that she was sure it was pornographic.

'Lots of our classmates have read hand-copied books,' I said. 'This one is quite short. There's another one called *Tidal Wave*, but it's over two hundred pages long. I haven't got round to copying it yet.'

'Don't you know what could happen to you? During that last mass public trial, a young man was executed for copying banned books.'

'But *he* printed hundreds of copies on a mimeograph machine, and so was accused of poisoning society. I've only made one handwritten copy to give to you as a present. You're the only person who will see it.'

'Those aren't family photographs,' she said, looking down at the table. 'I cut them out from a magazine.'

'If you don't want to read it, I'll take it back home with me.' I leaned back against the table, let out a long sigh and stared at the thousands of dust particles floating across a beam of sunlight.

'If you want me to read it, I'll read it. But don't tell any of our classmates. Where's the dirtiest passage?'

'On page seven.' After I'd copied that page out on the first night, I'd had to hide under my bedcovers and masturbate.

'I won't need that one then.' She tore out the page with her delicate fingers, folded it up and handed it back to me. 'Read me a bit, will you? If you get to a dirty passage, just skip it.'

I opened the book and read: '". . . Most eighteen-year-old girls are as pretty as flowers. At eighteen, I was enchanting. It's no exaggeration to say that my figure was at least as beautiful as any film star you could name. I had large, glistening eyes, shiny black hair, cheeks as smooth as eggshell and eyebrows curved like fine willow leaves. My pert, ample breasts juddered gently as I walked . . . It was soon after my eighteenth birthday that I fell in love with my cousin. He was twenty-two, and had returned to Fuzhou for the holidays. He was tall and suave, with a dark moustache which gave him a mature and masculine air . . . To be honest, what really attracted me to him was the magnificent cock that bulged from between his thighs. When I think about it now, my vagina becomes so hot and itchy that it feels as though some liquid is about to spurt from it –"'

'Stop!' she cried, turning her red face to the wall. 'That's disgusting!' Reading the passage aloud had made my heart thud with excitement.

I stopped reading and glanced at her out of the corner of my eye. Once I'd assured myself that she wasn't really angry, I pulled out my mother's hair tongs from the pocket of my padded coat. A smell of scorched hair instantly filled the room.

'Look, I've brought them,' I said, changing the subject.

'So that's what they look like!' She took them and weighed them in her hand. 'They're not that much lighter than my mother's charcoal tongs.'

These tongs were made of pig iron. If you heated them in a fire, took them out just before they turned red then wrapped them around a lock of hair, they'd produce a curl that would last four or five days.

'The Chinese actresses who play foreign women all use these to curl their hair. Look, this is how you do it.' I took a section of her hair and curled it around the tongs.

'Get them away from me!' she laughed. 'They're frightening!' I'd told her I'd pop round and give her the tongs when I'd bumped into her in the department store the previous day.

She took the tongs from me and turned them around, inspecting them carefully. I watched her fingers move through the beam of sunlight. Her nails turned a transparent red. The lines of dirt caught under the tips looked like tiny crescent moons. I walked over and put my hands around hers. Together we clutched the tongs, squeezing tighter and tighter. Our hands began to tremble. We moved closer until our lips were almost touching. We were both breathing very loudly. 'I want to kiss you,' I said.

She blushed and pulled her hands away. 'It's still light outside. Someone might see us.'

I wanted to hold her hands again, but she wouldn't let me. So I sat back down on the bed. Lowering my gaze to her thighs, I said, 'Make sure the tongs aren't too hot. You should test them with a piece of paper first. If the paper goes yellow, let them cool down a little before you use them.'

'We're still only fifteen,' she muttered, then turned her head towards me again and said, 'What happens if the tongs scorch my hair?'

I thought of how my mother's hair looked after she curled it. 'I'll do it for you. I promise I'll be careful.' I could feel myself blushing. 'We've locked the door. What are you afraid of?'

She sat down at the end of the bed.

'What about when I go to school? Will I be able to press the curls down?'

'You can hide them under a hat. No one will see them. If you want to get rid of them, you only have to wash your hair.'

'Things have become so much more open now. People don't say "you're nice" any more, they say "I love you".'

'I love you!' I blurted. The words came out very easily, because I'd been practising saying them all morning.

She fell silent. Her face went bright red. She tried to cover a part of it with her hand.

'If you want to love me, you must be faithful to me and never dance with other girls. Apparently a few of the older kids at school have been having dance parties at their homes when their parents are away.'

'I know. Suyun's been to one. She's still going out with that boy who works in the pharmaceutical company.'

'I forbid you to talk to her, or go to any dance party she invites you to. She's only fifteen but she already owns a digital watch. Her morals are definitely suspect. You must promise on Chairman Mao's life that you won't speak to her again.'

'I can't dance,' I said. 'And anyway, her watch is a fake. It doesn't tell the time . . .'

'I don't want big curls,' Lulu said. 'I want them to look natural.' She untied her two small plaits, dipped a comb into a cup of water, then ran it through her jet-black hair, slowly straightening out the waves. 'Does it look pretty like this? If I let it grow a little longer I'll have proper shoulder-length hair.'

'Only girls with loose morals have shoulder-length hair. Even adult women who go to work aren't allowed to grow it that long.'

'Ha! You're too conservative. The woman who played the Party branch secretary in that revolutionary opera we saw last week wore a shoulder-length wig, so it can't be that immoral.'

'Still, it's safest to keep it in a short bob.' I could feel my heart thumping again. I moved my distracted gaze to the window. Lulu lived on the ground floor, so by three o'clock, the sunlight would already begin to leave her room. Our flat on the third floor remained sunny for at least an hour longer. A crab-claw lotus plant in a terracotta pot was sucking the condensation from her window. The flowers looked moist and red. The petals I'd knocked off as I'd climbed through the window lay limply on the sill.

'I want to kiss you,' I repeated, as thoughts of her smooth stomach and warm vagina filled my mind again.

'You can't. It's not dark yet.' She walked over to the mirror. 'Your mother sings in the chorus. She must have an official licence to get a perm.'

'Yes, I could ask her to lend it to you . . . You have a lovely voice. You should go to music college after you leave school.' I touched my hair, which I'd smoothed back with some Vaseline I'd taken from a pot in my mother's drawer.

'I can sing Li Gu's "Longing for Home". Listen: "My *dreams are always of you! After this day ends, we may never meet again . . .*"'

I watched her black shoe, which was dangling over the edge of the bed, move in time to the beat. The laces were tied in a messy knot. My face felt hot. I looked up and stared at her long, pale neck.

'Did you like it?' She had suddenly stopped singing.

'Very nice. Do you like basketball?' I thought of the cool smell of the limewashed walls that enclosed the school's football pitch.

'I hate it. Accompany me, will you?' She pushed her harmonica towards me. I took it, but my jaw felt too stiff to play it. I reached for her hand, but she pulled it away. We both stared at the floor.

'I'd better go,' I said finally.

'All right.' Half her breath seemed to be stuck in her throat. She released it through the corner of her mouth, blowing her fringe into the air.

I looked at her regretful eyes and smiling mouth and couldn't make out what she was feeling.

Without another word, I walked over to the window, climbed over the lotus plant again and jumped out.

If the police hadn't interrogated Lulu and forced her to confess to our relationship, our secret love affair might have continued for years.

It all started a couple of days before we were due to break up for the summer holidays. We'd finished our last exams. On my way to school, I noticed that the note I'd left under her flowerpot the night before, asking her out for a film, had been removed. I assumed she'd taken it away and read it.

When I walked through the school gates my form teacher, Mr Xu, called me over and took me to a room where two policemen were waiting for me.

This was the first time that I'd experienced real terror. My stomach went cold, I felt nauseous, then my whole body began to shake.

The policemen asked me my name then said: 'You must come with us.'

Mr Xu stubbed out his cigarette and said, 'Dai Wei, you must own up to everything. This is the opportunity to move forward that you've been waiting for.' I opened my mouth, speechless with terror, and nodded. The roar inside my head was so loud I couldn't hear what the students outside were shouting.

I walked out of the school gates, my head bowed low, with one of the policemen in front of me and the other one behind. I wondered whether my legs were bent. I seemed suddenly to have become much shorter.

When I reached the police station, my skin was hot and sweaty, but my bones felt cold.

I quickly tried to think through what they might have found out about me. I thought of Lulu. Perhaps she had passed around the copy of *A Young Girl's Heart* that I'd given her, and someone had reported the matter to the police. Perhaps Shuwei, who'd lent me the book in the first place, had been detained, and was now locked up in the room next door. I didn't know what to do.

I was supposed to take my brother back home for lunch. It was twelve already. Police officers on their way to the canteen passed through the corridor outside holding their aluminium lunch boxes. An oily smell of deep-fried meatballs wafted into the room.

One of the officers who'd arrested me walked in and asked whether I had any money on me.

I searched my pockets and pulled out five jiao's worth of coins.

He looked at me and said, 'Go and get yourself some steamed rolls from the stall across the road, then come straight back here.'

I hurried outside and ran over to the stall. I had crossed that road hundreds of times before, but that day everything looked unfamiliar to me: the locust trees seemed taller and larger, the road looked wider too. A stream of yellow smoke rose from the chimney of the dressmaker's shop and hovered in the windless air. I didn't recognise any of the faces that passed by.

After lunch, the two officers returned. One of them said, 'Just own up to what you've done. It's easy to get into this place, but hard to get out.' Then he left the room.

'Come here!' said the other officer. He leaned against the table and lit a cigarette. I didn't know what he'd eaten, but I could smell chives in the air.

I stood in front of him, holding up my trousers. They'd confiscated my belt to stop me running away. When he looked down at the note he was writing, he reminded me of the electrician who worked in the school boiler room. Black hairs pricked through the pores above his mouth. He put down his pen at last and said, 'Do you know why we've brought you here?'

'No.'

He sat down and swung his feet up onto the table. He looked like he was about to take a nap. 'We gave you all morning to think things over. If you own up now, we might let you go. Just tell me what kind of shameful things you've been up to recently.'

'I read *A Young Girl's Heart*.' I had been standing up for hours. I longed to squat down.

'Who gave it to you?'

'Wang Shuwei.'

'Who's he?'

'He's in my class at school.'

'Who else did you pass the book to?'

'No one. I just read it myself.'

'Dai Wei. Look into my eyes. Who else read the book? There's no point lying. We have a list of names.'

I didn't dare reply to his question.

'Own up to what you've done.'

'I made a handwritten copy of the book.'

'So it wasn't enough for you to read it – you had to copy it out as well.' He got up and walked over to me. 'Who did you give the copy to?' He was shouting now. My legs trembled and I sank into a squat. He kicked me to the ground, grabbed my belt from the table and whipped me over the head. He hit me harder than my father had ever done.

'I won't do it again, I promise!'

'Where is the copy?' His leather shoe was pressed against my chin.

'I gave it to Lulu.'

'Who's she?'

'Zhang Lulu. She's in my class as well.'

'You seem to have been very busy lately. What else have you been up to? Let me prod your memory. Did you not recently wander through your compound singing "*You're a flower in bud. How I long for you to come into bloom*"? Eh?' He kicked me to the ground again, then picked up the thermos flask from the table. My mind flashed back to the Cultural Revolution, when a group of Red Guards pulled our neighbour, Granny Li, out of the opera company's dormitory block and ordered the rest of us to bring out our thermos flasks. Once we'd brought them outside, we had to stand and watch as the Red Guards poured ten flasks of boiling water over Granny Li's head.

'Tell me what else you've done,' the officer said, removing the lid of the flask.

I stared at him, rigid with fear and blurted, 'I'll never read another pornographic novel again, I promise, or sing any licentious songs, or smoke cigarettes . . .' I fell onto my knees and sobbed.

'Little hooligan! If we don't teach you a lesson now, you'll end up with a bullet in your head. Look at all these letters we've received about you!' He poured more water into his teacup then pulled out some letters from a file.

I couldn't see what the letters said, so I quickly racked my brain, searching for another crime that I could confess to. 'I groped Lulu,' I finally admitted.

'Where?'

'In a cement pipe.'

'Just the once?'

'Yes, I haven't touched her again since then.'

'Did you trick her into going there with you?'

'No. We were out on a date.'

'A date – my arse! That's not called a date, it's called having illicit sexual relations! Open your legs!' He gave me a sharp kick. I howled in pain and rolled onto the concrete floor.

'You must write down the details of every crime you've committed. I want names, places and dates. If you confess to everything, we might let you off. Don't forget that your dead father was a member of the Five Black Categories. If it hadn't been for Deng Xiaoping's Reform Policy and your good marks at school, you would have been executed ages ago, you evil son of a rightist.'

I sat down and started writing. I didn't want to bring shame upon my school. By nightfall I still hadn't finished. I heard screams and the sound of breaking glass as someone was being beaten up next door. I hated myself for not being as courageous as the Communist heroes in our textbooks. At the first sign of violence, I'd crumbled and owned up to everything.

The officer looked at my written confession and said, 'Which hand did you stick into her knickers? How long did you keep it there? Where else did you touch her? I want every detail.'

In the middle of the night I heard my mother shouting in the corridor: 'My son's still young. He's got a lot to learn. I promise I'll give him a good talking-to . . .'

I broke into tears. My groin was still aching from the policeman's kick. I felt as though I'd sunk into a hopeless black hole. I didn't know what punishment was awaiting me. I thought of the convicts I'd seen dragged onto execution grounds during public trials our class had been taken to, and how their bodies shuddered on the ground after the soldiers' bullets hit their heads. One time our class was allocated front-row seats. When the young convict with the shaven head stood before the firing squad, his eyes seemed suddenly to focus on me. After the bullets struck his head and he fell to the ground, his legs kicked in the air so long that one of his shoes fell off.

The police didn't let my mother into the room. All they did was pass on the two apples she'd brought for me.

I thought of Liu Ping – the daughter of the Guangxi farm's education officer whom my father had talked about so fondly. I imagined her in a white skirt, playing her violin like an angel. The image gave me strength. Then I remembered the time my mother and I went to visit my father in the camp in Shandong. We travelled there by long-distance bus. I slept curled up on my seat, my head resting on the canvas bag on my mother's lap. Inside the bag were gifts she'd brought for my father: a blanket, a jar of pig fat and a woollen hat

The officer kicked a leg of the table, stirring me from my doze.

'Wake up! This isn't a dormitory. I've had to stay here all bloody night for you. How many pages have you finished?'

I handed him my seven pages of densely written notes.

He glanced through them. 'There's still a lot of information that you're holding back.' He checked his watch, lit a cigarette. I breathed in the smoke. It made me feel a little less alone. 'I'll give you one last chance. You have until dawn. If you haven't written everything down by then, we will show you no mercy.'

I searched through my mind again, and dredged up every bad thing I'd done.

I'd once carved a pistol out of a piece of wood and painted it black. It looked very convincing. I'd attached it to my belt, like Li Xiangyang, the heroic leader of the guerrilla force that fought against the Japanese. My mother had told me that people used fake guns to commit robberies, and that it was against the law to own one. I gave details of the time and place of the crime, but there were no victims to report.

I'd killed a chicken with a slingshot, then run away. The victim was a female chicken.

I'd also smashed a window. I'd thrown the stone in an attempt to hit a cat. The only victim of this incident was the windowpane.

Dawn broke at last. I knew this, not because the room became any lighter, but because I could hear buses driving past on the road outside. I caught a whiff of disinfectant. It reminded me of the public latrines across the road from our compound. I hardly ever used them, because we had a toilet in our flat. But my mother often went there. We had to pay for our water now, which we didn't in the old dormitory block, so my mother preferred to run down six flights of stairs and use the latrines rather than waste money flushing our own toilet. At night, the latrines were the only place in the area where there was a light still shining. After I'd learned how to smoke, I often hung out there in the evening with my friends. When men went in to have a shit, they'd always light a fag and toss the stub onto the floor before they left. We'd quickly pick up the stubs and carry on smoking them. Sometimes we'd snatch the fags from the men's mouths while they were still pulling up their trousers. The worst they'd ever do would be to call us filthy brats.

One night, one of our gang ran over to me and said, 'Dai Wei, some of Duoduo's shit has splashed onto your footrest.' We'd each assigned ourselves our own hole, and if anyone splashed their shit onto the ceramic footrests of an adjacent hole, they'd get beaten up.

We chased after Duoduo and dragged him back into the latrines. He tried to break free, kicking the wall so hard that chunks of plaster fell off. But there were four of us holding him down, and we had him firmly in our grip. I pulled down his trousers and slapped his arse, and he got an erection. Everyone shouted, 'Let's see how big it can get!' I grabbed hold of his penis and rubbed it hard.

'Let go! Fuck off! Let go of me!' His contorted face went bright red. He squatted down, trying to pull his penis free. Tears poured from his eyes. At last he ejaculated. I relaxed my grip and wiped my hands on the wall. We laughed as we pushed him out onto the street. He ran away, holding up his trousers, his silhouette growing smaller and smaller.

Three people had hung themselves in those latrines. One of them was an old woman who'd travelled up from the countryside. When she arrived in Beijing, she visited our local police station and made enquiries about a Mr Qian who'd been imprisoned by the Communists in the 1940s. The police informed her that this Mr Qian had been executed shortly after Liberation. They later discovered that the woman was Mr Qian's wife, and had been incarcerated since the beginning of the Cultural Revolution. When she was released from jail, the village head had refused to allocate her any land, so she came to Beijing to look for her husband. After she heard the news of his death, she hung herself in the women's latrines . . .

I'd already refilled the fountain pen three times from the ink pot on the policeman's desk. I felt as heavy as a sack of concrete. My legs were shaking with exhaustion.

A few hours later, my mother came to take me home.

As soon as we walked through the gates of our compound, I heard Duoduo shout, 'You're a big shot now, young man! Spent the night at a police station! That's quite something!'

'Bugger off!' my mother yelled.

In that instant, all the fear I'd felt in the police station melted away. Although my swollen testicles had rubbed my inner thighs raw, I was still able to stand upright. Had the police turned up to arrest me again, I would have sauntered back to the station with them, whistling as I went.

When we stepped inside our flat my mother slapped me hard on both cheeks. 'You shameful little hooligan! How can I hold my head up now?' She pointed to my father's ashes in the box under her bed, and shouted at them, 'This is all your fault, Dai Changjie! I had to bear the burden of your crimes for twenty years, and now I'm burdened with those of your son!' I cried when I saw my mother sob, and when my brother saw me crying, he burst into tears too.

I promised my mother that I'd never read another banned novel, and begged her to let me go to sleep. She wiped her tears. I collapsed onto her bed and dozed off, my legs twitching with tiredness.

When I woke again it was already dark outside. My mother had removed my trousers and applied red ointment to the purple whip marks on my legs.

She told me that I'd slept for thirty-six hours. 'They let you off lightly. If they'd had any sense they would have wiped out the Dai line! Nothing good will ever come of the sons of a rightist!' She pulled a tray over. 'Here's some cake and milk for you.' Then she grumbled, 'I brought you into this world. I should be the one to decide how you get punished. They had no right to beat you up like that.'

The cake I was chewing dissolved quickly in my bitter saliva.

'Mum, I swear on Chairman Mao's life that I'll study hard from now on. So they didn't label me a "wrong-footed youth" then?'

'I don't think so, but you're on their records now. And because of you, your friend Lulu was taken in for questioning as well.'

My limbs went limp. I had betrayed her. I shouldn't have given her that copy of *A Young Girl's Heart*, or given her name to the police, or told them that I'd touched her. I felt sick with regret.

'You've grown up too fast,' my mother said, her expression hardening. 'Those decadent traits should have been knocked out of you long ago. Your father was poisoned by Western ideas. It's his fault you've turned out this way. There are so many bad people around today, corrupting society with their bourgeois lifestyles. They talk about sexual liberation, sexual freedom – their only aim is to poison the minds of our youth, allowing imperialist countries to change China through peaceful evolution. If you don't step up your political studies, you'll end up on the wrong path. That boy who gave you the pornographic book has been taken in too. I suppose you did a good deed, exposing his evil crime to the police. That must be why they treated you so leniently.'

My mind went blank. Everything that happened in the police station was a blur. But I remembered writing my self-criticism. I remembered that.

'I'm sorry, Mum, it's all my fault,' I said, feeling a sudden urge to open the window and jump out.

Memories flit through your head like a torch beam. The scene you've just recalled sinks into darkness and is replaced by another.

My mother has no idea how much I still hate myself for all the harm I caused back then.

Shortly after my sixteenth birthday, I dropped out of school and went south to the coastal city of Guangzhou, where China's market economy had just started to take off. I wanted to regain my peace of mind, and make a bit of money too. I peddled pornographic magazines for a while, then bought some electrical goods that had been smuggled over the border from Hong Kong and sold them outside a foreign-currency shop. I had a foreign cigarette filter dangling from my mouth and a digital watch on my wrist. Once I'd saved enough money, I began making trips back to Beijing, bringing cheap southern goods which I then sold at a high mark-up on the black market. In just six months I grew thirty centimetres. I looked like a man of the world.

During my second trip back to Beijing, my cousin Dai Dongsheng and his wife came to stay. His wife had fallen pregnant with a second child, in contravention of the one-child policy. Fearing persecution from their local birth-control officers, they'd left their two-year-old daughter with a neighbour in Dezhou Village and come to Beijing hoping to find a private hospital that would agree to help deliver the baby.

'Look how you've grown! You're a young man now,' Dongsheng said. On his previous visit, I'd had to raise my head when speaking to him, but now he had to look up at me.

'What do you expect? I'll be seventeen this year.' My voice was deeper now too. I handed him a cigarette.

He had the typical rough, gnarled hands of a peasant. Because he was the grandson of a rich landlord, he'd been denied a place at middle school, and had been forced to scrape a living off the land since the age of fifteen.

His wife sat on the sofa that my brother and I had constructed a few days before. The bulge of her belly was as round as a terrestrial globe. She had the pure, unaffected beauty that only women from the countryside have. Her expression was honest but slow-witted. Dongsheng had aged a lot since I'd last seen him. He sat awkwardly at the end of my mother's bed, his legs pressed together and his hands folded politely on his lap. At his feet lay a fake leather bag printed with the words LONG LIVE MAO ZEDONG THOUGHT. The salted carp and two balls of red wool that they'd brought for us were lying in the middle of the table. The room stank of fish, and the dusty, rancid smell of train stations.

My mother had fried some sunflower seeds and laid them out in teacups. When I couldn't think of anything more to say to the couple, I turned on the television set I'd bought for my mother. Their eyes immediately moved to the screen.

'Look, that foreign woman's wearing a gold watch and a gold necklace,' Dongsheng's wife said.

The news programme was reporting on Deng Xiaoping's meeting with Mrs Thatcher, and his proposal that Hong Kong should return to Chinese sovereignty. Dongsheng said, 'If Hong Kong is returned to China, we'll all be able to travel there soon.'

'You can go there now, if you want,' I said. 'I've seen lots of Hong Kong people in Guangzhou. They look just like us.'

The expressions of surprise on their faces gave me a pleasant feeling of superiority. I'd bought my first ticket to Guangzhou with the money my mother had given me to buy a bicycle. I didn't stay at a hotel while I was there. It was so hot, I was able to sleep on the streets. I wandered through the Western Lake night market every evening, and visited China Hotel's duty-free shop to look at the imported watches, cigarette lighters, ballpoint pens and multicoloured bottles of perfume. On my last day in Guangzhou, I only had thirty yuan left in my pocket. I went to a street stall and bought four packs of playing cards with photographs of naked women printed on the back. I brought them to Beijing with me, and made a fortune selling them outside our local cinema.

'How many children are Hong Kong people allowed to have?' the wife asked.

'As many as they like,' I said. 'Many pregnant women in Guangzhou escape across the border and give birth in Hong Kong, then return with the babies a few months later. And since the babies have Hong Kong citizenship, the families can travel back and forth whenever they want after that.'

'That's a good idea!' the wife said enthusiastically.

My mother came in from the kitchen and said, 'Don't listen to him. He's been to Guangzhou a couple of times, and suddenly he thinks he's grown up. The only thing that's changed is that he now goes around with that stupid cigarette filter in his mouth. He hasn't even had his first shave yet!'

'Yes I have, Mum.' Although my voice had deepened, it was still prone to tapering off into undignified squeaks, so I had to keep it constantly under control.

My mother sat on the sofa and asked the couple what plans they had for the future. 'When is the baby due?' she said.

'Middle of next month,' Dongsheng replied. 'Our county has been named a Family Planning Model County, so the birth-control officers are especially strict. If a woman becomes pregnant with a second child, they force her to have an abortion. My wife managed to keep her pregnancy secret. Before she left the house, she always tied a cloth around her tummy to hide the bump. Last month she vomited while walking down the street. We were sure someone would report us. That's when we decided to run away.' After he said this, he removed the cigarette from his plastic filter, held it between his fingers and sucked a last deep drag.

'We didn't dare catch a train from our local station,' the wife continued. 'We'd heard that birth-control officers patrol it, trying to stop women who've fallen pregnant illegally from fleeing the county. If they come across a pregnant woman who doesn't have a permit, they drag her off to the station's family planning clinic and abort the child there and then. Apparently, at the end of each day, there are two or three buckets of dead foetuses in the clinic.' When the wife spoke, her eyes were brighter than her husband's.

'If you don't have a birth permit for this child, the Beijing police will arrest you too.' My mother looked anxious. She didn't know what she could do to help.

'We can't go back,' the wife said. 'Our house has probably been ransacked. When the birth-control officers discover that a couple has gone on the run, they come with big vans and take away all the family's valuables: the radio, the mirror, the wooden chests. I've got a feeling that this baby's a boy. Whatever they say, I'm not getting rid of it.'

'If a couple manages to evade detection and give birth to a second or third child, the birth-control officers force them to pay a huge fine. They're brutal. If you can't afford to pay the fine, they beat you up.'

'Government regulations strictly forbid the officers to use force,' my mother said, trying to defend the Party.

'We heard that the police are less violent in the cities. That's why we came here. In the countryside it's terrible. The people's militia have guns, loaded with live bullets. In some neighbouring villages, if a woman gives birth without a permit, the newborn baby is strangled to death. Some families dig holes in the ground so that the women can give birth in secret.' Dongsheng's attention was drawn to the television screen again, and the clip of General Secretary Hu Yaobang's visit to the Shenzhen Special Economic Zone near the Hong Kong border.

'What if it's a girl?' I asked, lighting another cigarette. Ever since my mother had given up complaining about my smoking, I'd been able to get through a packet of cigarettes a day.

'An astrologer told us it's a boy,' Dongsheng said. 'We've given him a name already: Dai Jianqiang.'

'Look, another kick!' the wife said. 'He's been moving all the time these last few days. Girls never move this much.'

'You can sleep here tonight,' my mother said dejectedly. 'We'll come up with a plan tomorrow. Dai Wei, go and turn off the kettle.'

A smile passed over Dongsheng's face. His wife smiled too, and said, 'We're sorry to put you to so much trouble.'

'Who's looking after your father now?' my mother asked.

'His mind's unstable, but he's able to look after himself,' Dongsheng replied. 'If we have a boy, I'll pick up a job here, make enough money to pay the fine, then we can all go home and be together.' He paused and stared at the screen again. 'Look at those tall buildings in Shenzhen. How do people manage to live in them? You'd wet your pants before you had time to make it outside to the latrines.' He finished his cigarette and spat a glob of phlegm onto the floor.

'The buildings are equipped with lifts. And anyway, all the flats have toilets.' I glanced at my mother's face. She hated people spitting onto the floor.

'They're living in the sky,' the wife said, smiling. 'If they opened the windows, the birds could fly straight in.'

'Dai Wei will be going to university soon, I suppose?' Dongsheng said.

'I'm revising for my high school exams,' I said, wiping away his spit with the sole of my shoe. I didn't mention I'd dropped out of school. I hadn't been back again since the November morning when Lulu was called onto the stage during assembly.

We had just completed our mass morning exercise routine. The headmaster called Lulu onto the stage at the front of the football pitch. I watched her standing up there, her head bowed low. Her thin, pale neck looked beautiful against her red down jacket. We hadn't spoken to each other since the police had taken us in for questioning.

The headmaster told her to remove her hat. 'Look at this, students! A high school student wearing nail varnish and rouge! What a disgrace!' He ran his finger down her cheek, then removed his glasses and examined it closely, searching for traces of rouge.

Finding nothing there, he then rubbed Lulu's mouth, and this time, despite his poor eyesight, he was able to detect some colour on his finger. 'Red lipstick? This is a serious case of "bourgeois liberalism", young girl! How can you hope to join the revolutionary classes after you leave school if you put stuff like this on your face? And look at these waves in your hair. Are you trying to turn yourself into a curly-haired lapdog of imperialist America?'

I wanted to disappear into the ground. I'd never imagined that my actions would get Lulu into so much trouble. The thousands of students in the football pitch who were staring at Lulu's red lips opened their mouths and let out mocking cries of derision.

After my first trip to Guangzhou, I was able to buy a television, a new bicycle for my brother and a rayon coat and nylon umbrella for my mother.

After my second trip, I came back to Beijing with twenty pirated tapes of romantic ballads sung by the 'decadent' Taiwanese singer, Deng Lijun, and made more than two thousand yuan selling them on the black market. I also brought over a thousand cigarette lighters with pictures of naked women stuck onto them. They'd cost me five fen each in Guangzhou, and I was able to sell them for ten times the price in Beijing. I asked the vendor I'd bought them from to post me some more, but he was arrested for trading in obscene products and sentenced to five years in jail.

On my last visit to Guangzhou, I bought twenty copies of the Hong Kong edition of *Playboy* magazine, and posted them to Beijing wrapped inside a long cotton dress. On the train back, a man from Hunan Province who was sitting next to me was arrested for possession of pornographic playing cards. He'd hidden the cards in a shoebox. When two police officers strolling down the carriage spotted the box on the floor and asked him whom it belonged to, he was too afraid to speak. The officers opened the box, and after they saw what was inside, they put him in handcuffs and dragged him off the train. On his seat he'd left behind a copy of *The Book of Mountains and Seas* – the book I'd loved so much as a child. I put it in my bag then ate the packet of Silly Boy sunflower seeds that he'd also left behind.

Like a prisoner in an execution chamber, you look back on the life which could end at any moment.

The basal cells of my nasal cavity's olfactory organ begin to reconnect intermittently with the surrounding nerve fibres. I inhale slowly through my nostrils, and for a second catch a faint whiff of orange peel.

I listen intently for any noise that might help me form a clearer picture of my surroundings. When I first became aware of this hospital, I couldn't hear a thing. I felt as though I'd sunk to the bottom of the sea. Only the beat of my heart told me that my body hadn't finished dying yet.

I think back to the morning I left home to go to university for the first time. I woke up on the iron bed. Because I'd suddenly shot up to 1.8 metres, my mother had swapped rooms with me.

In just six months of private study, I'd completed the entire Year Twelve science course, and thanks to preferential treatment given to students with relatives abroad, I'd managed to gain a place at Southern University in Guangzhou City to study for a degree in biology. I'd visited the university on my last trip the city. Many students from Hong Kong and Macao studied there, and the academic requirements weren't too high.

My mother handed me a fried dough stick and said, 'You must study hard. There's no point going to university unless you get a graduation certificate at the end of it.'

I lay in bed, munching on the dough stick. 'I'm nearly seventeen years old, Mum. Dad said he wanted me to read his journal once I've left school. Let me see it.'

My mother's expression hardened. 'Dai Wei, although your father was rehabilitated, his outlook on the world remained skewed,' she said. 'The Party has learned its lesson from the way it treated people like him, and it won't make those mistakes again. You must remember that when you read the journal, and not look at things too negatively. I wanted to burn it, but it was his dying wish that you should read it one day. If I do give it to you, you must promise not to show it to anyone else.'

'Times have changed, Mum. There's no stigma to being the son of a rightist or a capitalist any longer. Now that Deng Xiaoping is liberalising the economy, people like you, who come from a wealthy background, are held in higher respect.'

Unfortunately for my mother, her family had no foreign connections. She had an older brother and a younger sister. I suppose they were my uncle and aunt, but my mother hadn't been in touch with them for decades, even though her sister lived in Beijing. The wife of my mother's uncle travelled down from Tianjin to visit us when I was eleven or twelve. She brought out a handful of peanuts, placed them on our table and talked about her life. It was then that I learned that my mother's uncle had been a Guomindang general before Liberation. When Communist peasants dragged him up a hill and were about to execute him, his wife went to his rescue. She shouted out to them that when the next political campaign came around, they'd have to pick a new class enemy from one of their own families. The peasants decided to let my great-uncle go, so they could use him as a target in any future campaign. During the land reform movement a few years later, he was brought out again to be an object of hatred, saving many lives in the village. After all the landowners and rich peasants of the surrounding ten villages had been executed, he was lent out to them to play the enemy in their campaigns as well.

'Dai Wei, when you get to university, you must focus on your political education. You must do all you can to gain Party membership.'

I didn't bother to argue with her. I wasn't particularly interested in my father's past. The country had changed now. My father's foreign connections may have ruined his life, but they had saved mine. Thanks to him, I was now about to go to university.

Dai Ru said goodbye to me and went off to school. He was fifteen, and as tall as I had been when I was detained by the police.

Your flesh and spirit are still alive, buried inside the coffin of your skin.

Southern University was on the outskirts of Guangzhou City. The campus was ten times larger than my secondary school. Mosquitoes danced through the dense leaves and sprawling branches of hundred-year-old trees.

Our dormitories were housed in two former hospital blocks that had belonged to the old Military Medical Academy. The two-storey, adjacent blocks were connected on the first floor by an open passageway which was probably built so that patients could be wheeled easily from one ward to the next. This passageway was the only place in the campus where you could enjoy a cool breeze. Everywhere else – in the dorms, classrooms, cafeterias and basketball courts – the air was hot and humid.

In April, I would begin to sweat, and for the next six months would remain drenched in perspiration from head to toe. The heat steamed my energy away. I understood why southerners are so small and thin. All the students suffered from the heat, gulping at the air like goldfish, but students from the north, like me, suffered the most. During lectures, the professors had even more sweat on their foreheads than us. At meal-times, our sweat would drip into our bowls, and we'd swallow it down together with the soup and rice.

At dusk, the few female students would emerge clean and dry from their dorms, having taken showers and combed their black hair. They wouldn't play basketball, rush off to the library, or read books under the lamplight like the boys. Instead, they would slowly stroll back and forth along the open passageway, walking in pairs, holding a handkerchief or a fan in their hands. The sight of them strolling along was as refreshing as a gust of cool air.

I felt like a fish swimming in water. I gradually grew accustomed to living in the sea of perspiration. Like any other animal, I had to adapt to my new environment. My pores enlarged so as to release more moisture. My feet, which had previously always been clean and dry, were now constantly drenched in fetid sweat.

The science block stood in a windless spot at the foot of a steep hill. In the afternoon, the windows and whitewashed walls became scorched by the sun. We grew drowsy as the electric fan on the ceiling circulated the hot air through the room. I spent my first term sweltering in that southern furnace, studying Darwin's theory of evolution.

I started reading *The Book of Mountains and Seas* again. As a child, I'd loved this survey of ancient China for its magical descriptions of gods and monsters. But now I began to read it for the interesting scientific data it provided. Over two thousand years ago, the anonymous author of the book set out to explore China's landscapes and myths. He travelled to the four cardinal points of the empire, and to the wildernesses beyond, and reported back on what he saw. Although modern scholars believe the book to be a work of the imagination, I was convinced that it was based on real experience. I decided that, after I graduated, I would follow in the footsteps of the unknown author, and compare the plants and animals I found to those described in his text. I wanted to identify the strange species he listed, and investigate their evolution. I suppose *The Book of Mountains and Seas* had become my favourite book.

Only at university did it occur to me that I could perhaps make a name for myself as a scientist, and no longer be brushed aside as merely the son of a dead rightist. As it turned out, my father's persecution and my arrest at fifteen helped raise my status among my classmates, who were also impressed that I'd peddled pornographic magazines on the black market. For the first time in my life, I felt a sense of self-worth.

We were a generation with empty minds. We thirsted for knowledge. Now that China had opened its doors to the West, we devoured every scrap of information that blew in. China had emerged from the catastrophe of the Cultural Revolution, and we were eager to build our country up again. We were fired by a sense of mission.

In my first term at university, the Hemingway craze was soon superseded by a craze for Van Gogh, which was fanned by the recent Chinese publication of his fictionalised biography, *Lust for Life*. Van Gogh's madness and creative individuality taught us our first great lesson in life, which is: believe in yourself. Everyone copied out quotations from the book and passed them around.

During a dissection class at the start of the second term, I met a medical student from Hong Kong called A-Mei.

Her face was smooth and almost expressionless, although sometimes she looked as though she were secretly smiling to herself. Her eyes were as clear as glass and as calm as water in a well. She was very different from Lulu.

Her mother was a professional folk singer, and when I told her that my mother was a singer too, we struck up a friendship. She was born in Zhongshan County in Guangdong Province. Her family had emigrated to Hong Kong when she was one.

I bumped into her one day in the library. She was wearing a white dress, and her clean black hair was coiled into a neat bun. She knew that if we wanted to read a newly published book, we had to submit a reservation card, then wait for months. So she said to me, '*Lust for Life* isn't selling very well in Hong Kong. I could easily get my hands on a copy. I'll buy you one next time I go.'

After that, she often brought back books for me which were hard to get hold of in mainland China.

Although your cells and nerves are no longer interacting properly, the signal transmission mechanism is still functioning, allowing physical traces of past events to reappear in your mind.

'Fuck you! Of course I know who Freud is! I read about him ages ago.'

Wang Fei was sitting on the bunk above me, dangling his legs over the edge. The pale skin of his calves was covered with fine, black hairs. His toes, which hung like fleshy hooks at the end of his feet, clenched whenever he spoke. He was born in Wanxian County in Sichuan Province. There was a rumour that he came from a peasant family, but he claimed he had an urban residence permit, and that his parents owned a colour television. He spoke with a thick Sichuan accent, and whenever he got worked up about something, he'd slip back into his local dialect. Like me, he felt great anger about the injustices of the Cultural Revolution, and he enjoyed speculating on the inside story of Lin Biao's conflicts with Mao's wife, Jiang Qing.

'Tell me which country Freud was from then!' Mou Sen replied, unconvinced. He ran his eyes down the index of the book in his hands and read out, 'The hat as a symbol of the male genitals . . . Being run over as a symbol of sexual intercourse . . . The male organ symbolised by persons and the female by a landscape . . .'

That was the day I first heard of Freud, his book *The Interpretation of Dreams* and the terms 'sexual repression' and the 'unconscious mind'.

'That sounds interesting! Let me have a look!' Wang Fei lowered himself off his bunk and plonked his foot on my bed.

If Mou Sen wanted to read something, that meant it was good. He had the largest collection of books on our floor of the dorm block. They were stacked up, two books deep, against the wall next to his bed. When he acquired new books and couldn't find space for them next to the wall, he'd stuff them under his pillow, or under the folded quilt by his feet. I never saw him without a book in his hands. His father had been a writer, and, like mine, had been denounced as a rightist and confined in a labour camp for twenty years. After his father was released, he forced Mou Sen to major in science, arguing that literature was a dangerous subject, but this didn't dampen Mou Sen's voracious appetite for novels and poetry. Mou Sen's great-great-grandfather had been a famous scholar during the Qing Dynasty, and had been granted the honour of flying outside his home a flag stamped with the emperor's seal.

Mou Sen had passed on to me *The Red and the Black*, *The Old Man and the Sea* and *One Hundred Years of Solitude*, and although I didn't have a deep understanding of literature, I enjoyed them very much.

Sun Chunlin was standing in the middle of the dorm. His shirt was buttoned to the top. The collar was too tight. He picked up a thermos flask and poured some more water into his cup of green tea. As he took a large gulp from it, sweat streamed down the back of his neck. He was too priggish to ever remove his shirt. I had no inhibitions, though. As soon as I returned to our dorm after classes, I'd strip down to my Y-fronts or wander off to the washroom completely naked. If a girl came in to talk to someone, I'd wrap a towel around my waist.

It was July, and the temperature had soared to forty degrees. I didn't have any appetite for lunch, so I just sprawled myself out over the reed mat on my bed. We had completed most of our exams, so the pressure had eased a little. Usually, you could hear other students in the building playing English language cassette tapes, or revising in the washroom or toilets. But today we were all lying on our beds, panting in the stifling heat like dumplings in a bamboo steamer. So when Sun Chunlin came into the dorm shouting, 'I've got a book here by Sigmund Freud about sexuality and the unconscious!' it startled us a little.

Mou Sen found another passage in the book that took his interest: 'He's saying that below our consciousness lies an unconscious level of desires and memories that are repressed by the conscious mind. Without this repression, our brains wouldn't be able to function . . .'

'I have an unconscious desire to beat up the head of the recreation and sports association,' said Wang Fei. 'The stupid wanker! He only joined the Party because he wants to get a good job after he graduates. He hasn't even read the *Communist Party Manifesto*!' Wang Fei spurted so much saliva when he spoke that one's eyes were always drawn to his mouth and chin. I made sure never to share a meal with him.

'Wang Fei, you switched the light on and off about a hundred times last night,' Sun Chunlin said. 'You only stopped when the cord broke. What unconscious motive was behind that, do you think?'

Tang Guoxian was in the bunk next to mine. He banged on the wall and cried up to Wang Fei, 'It was a girl you wanted to pull – not the light switch! Ha!' He was tall, high-spirited and sporty, and always liked to bash something when he laughed. If you didn't get out of his way in time, his big hands would land on your face.

'I definitely don't have an unconscious,' Wu Bin said from his bunk. He had a shaven head, scornful eyes and a thin black moustache. He was always rambling on about Hitler's SS, Soviet double agents, or Sherlock Holmes. He'd often go missing for a couple of days. A rumour spread that he was a spy planted by the local police. Whenever he was around, everyone watched what they said.

'If you didn't have an unconscious, where would you get all your ambition from?' said Wang Fei. 'Didn't you say you wanted to be a great detective one day? Ambition is fuelled by unconscious desires.' Wang Fei always spoke his mind, and often ended up offending people. The month before, he'd got beaten up outside the cafeteria by some political education students.

'Read us another passage, Mou Sen,' Sun Chunlin said. His bunk was nearest the door, so he was the first person to be able to enjoy a breeze when it blew in.

Wang Fei circled the room slowly, then leaned down and swiped the book from Mou Sen's hands. Sun Chunlin ran over, shouting, 'Don't break it!' then grabbed it back and began to read another passage: '"If the unconcious, as an element in the subject's waking thoughts, has to be represented in a dream, it may be replaced very appropriately by subterranean regions. – These, where they occur without any reference to analytic treatment, stand for the female body or the womb. – 'Down below' in dreams often relates to the genitals, 'up above', on the contrary, to the face, mouth or breast . . ."' When he reached the end of the page he said, 'Guangzhou Bookstore received only a hundred copies of this book. They sold out in an hour.'

'Dreams are no more than a chaotic series of nerve impulses. I never have dreams,' Wu Bin said, rubbing his triangular eyes. The week before, after his scholarship money had come through, he'd avoided us for days, afraid that we might bully him into taking us out for a meal.

'I dreamed of a man's corpse once. There was green moss growing on the skin.' Mou Sen smoothed his hair back. He was the only science student whose hair was so long it hung over the eyes.

'That signifies you have an unconscious urge to kill your father! Ha!' Tang Guoxian punched the wooden frame of his bunk and roared with laughter. The room's temperature seemed to soar again.

'Freud was a genius!' said Sun Chunlin, taking another gulp of tea.

'Be careful you don't get yourselves accused of spiritual pollution,' Wu Bin said, grabbing a bottle of lemonade someone had left on the table. 'If the university authorities call me in and ask me about this conversation, I'll tell them I didn't hear a thing.' Wu Bin was very selfish. If he wanted something – whether it was someone's comb, tiger balm or new pair of shoes – he'd simply help himself to it, without bothering to utter a word of thanks.

The only time he showed any generosity was when he stole a chicken that belonged to Mrs Qian who worked in the university cafeteria. He cooked it on a small electric hob in the corridor and shared it with everyone in our dorm. He'd killed the chicken after the university's governor called for a clean-up of the campus, complaining that poultry and dogs belonging to the university's staff had been fouling the paths and lawns. Mrs Qian didn't realise that the staff weren't allowed to rear animals on the campus.

A few minutes after Wu Bin ran into our dorm with the dead chicken, Mrs Qian turned up at our door. She saw one of us slicing up some ginger, and guessed that we were planning to make a stew out of her beloved pet. By then, Wu Bin had taken the chicken to the men's toilets and hidden it in the water tank. Assuming that her pet was still alive, Mrs Qian whistled and clucked, trying to coax it out from its hiding place. When there was still no sound from it after half an hour, she reluctantly gave up and walked away.

'See, you do have an unconscious after all, Wu Bin!' Wang Fei said. 'You're afraid that if you get into trouble with the university authorities, you won't be granted Party membership! I tell you, the Communist Party is a rotting corpse. Don't be fooled by the cloak of reform it's draped over itself. Underneath, it's still the same.'

'The book doesn't belong to me,' Sun Chunlin said, passing it to Mou Sen again. 'I'll have to give it back tomorrow. If we all squeeze up on your bed, we can read it together.' Sun Chunlin came from a privileged background. He was one of the few students who owned a bicycle. His uncle was head of the Municipal Department of Communications. He always had cash on him. The imported digital watch on his wrist sparkled whenever he walked past.

I ran over to Mou Sen's bed and squeezed in next to Wang Fei. The previous month, I'd had to wait until two thirty in the morning for my turn to read *The Second Wave*. I finished it in two hours, then woke Mou Sen and passed it to him. But Freud's book was much thicker, and looked as though it would take all night to read, so everyone was desperate to get their hands on it first.

'Ask your Hong Kong girlfriend to buy you a copy!' Wang Fei jibed, trying to push me off the bed.

'Shut up! You never read books, but as soon as you hear the words "sexual climax" you suddenly become interested.' I looked at the haircut

I'd just given him. After years of cutting my brother's hair, I'd become quite proficient at it.

'Why don't you just stick to *The Book of Mountains and Seas* and plan your expedition!' Tang Guoxian said, then roared with laughter. He was a champion marathon runner. Although I was as tall as him, I was much less strong. He was always pouring ridicule on my ambition to be an explorer.

In the end, Wang Fei and Sun Chunlin lost interest, so I read the book with Mou Sen. He'd planned to go to a private screening of *Casablanca* at the Guangzhou University campus, but soon changed his mind when he saw the book. He insisted that we read it on my bunk. He said that he found my pillow more comfortable than his, and was able to think more clearly when he rested his head on it, so I had no choice but to let him squeeze up next to me. We turned to the first chapter. Whenever he stopped to take notes, I'd read on to the end of the page, then close my eyes and wait for him to catch up.

Since the police had forced me to write the self-confession, I'd developed an aversion to writing. I rarely kept a journal. The only time I wrote anything now was when I copied Mou Sen's lecture notes.

It was getting dark outside. After an hour of having our heads pressed together, our ears were beginning to hurt. We decided to take turns reading the book aloud to each other. To save time, we lit just one cigarette and passed it between us. We kept going until five in the morning. Everyone else in the dorm was fast asleep behind their mosquito nets. When we could stay awake no longer, we nodded off, our heads resting on *The Interpretation of Dreams*.

I dreamed that, just as I was about to drown in a river, I discovered I could fly. I flapped my arms and soared into the sky, yelling at the top of my voice.

'Shut up!' Mou Sen hissed. 'I was in the middle of a good dream.'

'Stop kidding yourself – you'll never write a novel,' I mumbled. He was always talking about his dreams, and would jot them down as soon as he woke up. He said that dreams were where writers got all their inspiration from.

I liked Freud's ideas, especially his theories about the repression of memories from the conscious mind.

Your body continues to function, driven by instincts of its own. It doesn't need your assistance. As Freud said, 'The goal of all life is death.'

After reading Freud, I understood why I'd hated my father so much. Unconsciously, I'd viewed him as my enemy and oppressor. As long as he was around, I'd felt unable to hold my head up high.

I also understood why my mother remained married to my father, despite all the misery he caused her. As a young woman, she'd cut herself off from her 'bourgeois' family. When her father jumped off the roof of a tall building after the Communists appropriated his factory, she didn't even go to identify the corpse. To prove her loyalty to the Party, she abandoned her mother and siblings. But when my father got into trouble, she couldn't let go of him. She knew that if she lost him, she would have nothing left.

Around the time I met A-Mei, I picked up a literary journal in the library and read a translation of excerpts from Kafka's novel, *The Castle*. Mou Sen had told me that if you didn't read Kafka, you'd never grasp the underlying principles of biology.

When I finished reading the excerpts, I was reminded again of my father. The protagonist is a surveyor who is summoned to a castle to conduct a land survey. But when he arrives in the village governed by the castle, he finds that he's neither needed nor understood. Some of the villagers even suspect him of being an impostor. The surveyor strives to gain recognition of his status, but is thwarted again and again by illogical bureaucracy. He moves in with a barmaid he dislikes, hoping that her relationship with an important official will help him gain access to the castle. In his struggle to resist his fate he is forced to become cunning and base, but inside, his frustrated spirit is writhing.

My father was condemned as a rightist. Like Kafka's protagonist, he had no control over his fate or his status. My mother was his legal wife. The family she gave him enabled him at least to sense that he existed in society. But there was no love between them. Six years after my father returned from America to Communist China, he was no longer a professional violinist. He lost his identity. He knew that at any moment he could be executed for saying something the Party didn't like, or for carrying in his pocket an object they didn't approve of. He was as vulnerable as a rabbit in a laboratory. Cowardice and stuttering became his only skills in life. Even though my mother and I pitied him, we regarded him as an outsider. We never really knew what was going on in his mind. But I will never forget the look of terror that haunted his face so often.

I suddenly wanted to find out everything I could about my father.

I pulled out his journal from a pouch in my suitcase. It was an ordinary-looking notebook. When I'd skimmed through it the day my mother gave it to me, I'd wanted to fling it in the bin. I hated how he laced his notes on life in the camp with ingratiating remarks about the

Party. While writing his thoughts down, he'd been constantly terrified by what might happen if they were discovered. It had struck me as a very clumsy way to live one's life.

But now I began to read the journal more closely. In the last third of it, which was written in hospital, I discovered, to my surprise, that he'd secretly found faith in God. I understood now why he'd said how much he regretted not visiting a church or reading the Bible while he was in America, and why he'd asked me to bury his ashes in the graveyard of an American church after he died, pressing the address into my hand.

He wrote that he felt the spirit of God looking down on him. He believed that the suffering he'd endured in the camps had been a test of faith. On the last page of the journal, he wrote: 'Almighty Father, I've spent long enough in Hell. Rescue me now and lead me into Heaven.'

My father was treated like an animal in the camps. The only time he got to eat meat was the day Nixon arrived in China in 1972. Not wanting to be accused of mistreating political prisoners, the government ordered every labour camp to give its inmates pork dumplings for lunch. A few years later, conditions improved a little. The prisoners were issued with sheets of newspaper to wipe their bottoms with and so were able at last to read snippets of news from the outside world.

My father had returned to the motherland after Liberation out of patriotism. He'd wanted to help build a new China, and had no idea that, within a few years, he'd be reduced to total subservience. When he was finally released from the reform-through-labour system, he tried to find a place for himself in society, but discovered that he was an outcast, with no work unit or marketable talent. He spent all his remaining energy struggling to regain his urban residence permit. All he wanted was to be an ordinary citizen like any other.

I wondered where his God had been when he'd needed Him, and what right He had to test my father's faith in that way.

While I read the journal, I saw parallels with the passages from *The Castle*. In both texts, the spirits of people excluded and oppressed by a mad and irrational system become twisted and warped. Although I didn't say a word to anyone, something inside me had changed. I was determined that I would, at the very least, avoid my father's fate.

My father started his journal in 1979, while he was in the camp in Shandong Province. Mao Zedong was dead by then. I doubt that he would have had the courage to keep a journal while the Chairman was alive. Sometimes the entries were just a few sentences long, such as: 'Early November. Heavy snow. Chen Cun's been moved to another camp.' Or: 'We've discovered that you can make a porridge out of wild speargrass seeds. But you can't eat it while it's still hot, or your stomach will explode. That's how Wang Yang died.'

After his release, he became more courageous and began to write about his experiences in greater detail. One passage went: 'During the "airing of views" meeting at the opera company that day, someone mentioned the photograph that showed me shaking hands with the American guest conductor after our orchestra's performance of Beethoven's Eroica Symphony in the Beijing Hall of Music. He said that I'd humiliated the Chinese people by trying to ingratiate myself with American imperialist forces. I explained that, in foreign countries, it's customary for the principal violinist to shake hands with the conductor after a concert, and that besides, it was the American conductor who offered to shake my hand, not the other way round. The photograph had hung in the main meeting room for three years, as an example of a successful cultural exchange between China and the West. Everyone in the company had seen it. Our Party secretary accused me of gazing up at the conductor like a lapdog. I explained that the conductor was standing on a podium, so I had no choice but to look up at him . . .' If one searched through the newspapers of 1954, I'm sure one could find a print of this photograph that changed my father's life.

What used to annoy me most about my father was the way he ate. He didn't let one grain of rice slip his attention. If a scrap of food dropped onto the table, he'd scoop it up at once and toss it into his mouth. After every meal, he'd furtively sweep discarded bones and fruit peel into his lunch box. A few hours later he'd take the box into a corner of the room and quietly chew on the contents. My mother would try to hunt out his secret stashes, but never managed to find them all, so there was always a smell of mould and decay in the flat. But after I read the following passage of his journal, I forgave him his eccentric behaviour: '. . . There were some dried shreds of sweet potato and pumpkin pulp lying outside the pigpen today. As soon as we spotted them, we pounced on them and stuffed as much as we could into our mouths. The guard on duty was a young man. Nicer than most. At least he didn't beat us. He just sneered and said, "That's disgusting! And you call yourselves intellectuals . . ."'

I knew I couldn't tell my mother what I'd read. If she'd known that her husband had been reduced to living like a dog, it would have made a mockery of her efforts to join the Party.

A page of my father's journal was devoted to a fellow rightist called Zhang Bo. '. . . When I refused to beat up my friend Zhang Bo, the officers handcuffed my hands behind my back. They didn't take the cuffs off for a month. At mealtimes, I had to lick my rice porridge off a sheet of newspaper, like a dog. I couldn't lie down to sleep. I couldn't even wipe the shit from my arse. I wasn't a security guard. How could they ask me to attack my own friend? . . . Everyone knew that Zhang Bo was short-sighted. When he scribbled "Mao Zedong" on his matchbox he couldn't have seen the words "Bring Down Liu Shaoqi" printed on the other side. He was daydreaming at the time. It was an innocent doodle. The camp leaders accused him of urging the Chinese people to "Bring Down Mao Zedong". How ridiculous! . . . Even if it had been deliberate, it was a minor mistake. He certainly didn't deserve to be executed for it.'

My father listed the objects that Zhang Bo left behind: 'One pair of leather shoes; one checked woollen scarf; one fruit peeler, handle missing. His closest relative is called Cai Li. Address: Bureau of Cultural Affairs, Hongqiao District, Shanghai.'

My father had suffered a lot for refusing to beat up this man. He was clearly less of a coward than I'd assumed him to be.

I didn't dare mention my father's journal to A-Mei, either. The only person with whom I discussed it was Mou Sen. He said that the suffering our parents endured would cause our generation to question the autocratic system we lived under.

An impulse spreads through your damp heart, then moves up the nerve fibres of the brain stem to the central nucleus of the thalamus. A-Mei flows through your mind like a slow and beautiful lament.

A-Mei and I boarded a train to Guangxi Province. It was the first time we'd taken a train together, and the first time I'd travelled with a girl.

Southern University had broken up for the summer, and I'd decided to go to the neighbouring province of Guangxi to visit the Overseas Chinese Farm where my father was sent in 1963. When the Vietnam War broke out in 1965, the area was in the direct line of attack. The authorities were afraid that the rightists incarcerated in the farm might take advantage of the chaos to escape across the border, so they moved them to my father's native province of Shandong.

A-Mei wanted to visit her aunt in nearby Liuzhou, and I hoped to make a side trip to Guilin to visit Director Liu, who had been so kind to my father, and his daughter Liu Ping. In my mind's eye, Liu Ping had taken on the features of an angel, with her hair in bunches, her small, delicate ears, and her arms stretched out like wings. Besides, Guilin, with its green peaks and winding rivers, was a famous beauty spot, and I thought A-Mei would enjoy the trip.

A-Mei and I weren't officially a couple, but I'd taken her out for a meal at the small restaurant outside the campus gates. I'd ordered pigs' trotters braised in peanut sauce, which was a local speciality I hadn't tasted before. It was delicious. I'd also taken her swimming at the Guangzhou sports centre, and had held her hand while crossing the road.

After her first trip back to Hong Kong, she brought me a carton of Marlboro cigarettes. She said that everyone else was buying them in the duty-free shop, and she didn't want to miss out on a bargain. But I knew that she was just trying to help me make some money, because you could sell those cigarettes outside Guangzhou train station for fifteen yuan a pack, which was enough to buy me lunch for a week.

Whenever she went to Hong Kong after that, she'd bring me a couple of cartons. After her third trip, she gave me a cassette of Beethoven's Violin Concerto conducted by Karajan. Unfortunately I didn't own a cassette player. So many people borrowed it from me that, after a week, the tape snapped.

I suppose we were in what's called 'the early stages of courtship'.

The train carriage was packed full. We sat on the wooden bench, squashed up against the metal door. At each station we were bashed by the luggage of the passengers who squeezed in. When the men sitting opposite us tore the legs off their deep-fried chickens and opened bottles of beer with their teeth, grease and alcohol splashed onto A-Mei's sandals. She tucked her feet away under the bench and turned her face to the window. After a long and sleepless night, we finally made it to Liuzhou Town.

As soon as we arrived, we decided to set off for Fish Peak Hill. From a distance the hill looked more like a penis than a fish.

I took a picture of A-Mei with her instamatic camera. Through the viewfinder, I was able to stare straight into her eyes. I moved around her, trying to find the best shot, but she looked beautiful from every angle. When I held the camera still, she gazed back at me through the lens, raising her eyebrows to widen her eyes.

Halfway up the hill, we came to a cave. A cool breeze blew over us as we stood outside it. A-Mei told me that the hill had seven interconnected caves, like the seven orifices of a human head, and that, according to local belief, if you succeeded in passing through all of them you would achieve spiritual enlightenment. This was a very difficult task, though. Some of the holes were so tiny that only small children could crawl through them.

'Let's go inside,' I said. 'I love climbing into caves. What do you think this one is – the nose or the ear? It's lucky I've brought my torch.' I undid the top button of my shirt. On the train I'd undone all the buttons, much to A-Mei's displeasure. She was a very proper and well-brought-up girl.

'No – I'm frightened of caves,' she said. 'Let's just follow the path to the top of the hill. Apparently, if you make it to the peak, you'll enjoy years of prosperity.'

'Why are you Hong Kong people so obsessed with money and prosperity? You're such philistines.' Whenever I accused the Hong Kongese of being uncultured, there was nothing she could say, because she herself had told me that people in Hong Kong never read books.

A group of tourists stopped right next to us to enjoy the cool breeze blowing from the cave. I asked one of them to take a photograph of A-Mei and me. Fortunately, A-Mei didn't protest. After the photo was taken, we continued up the hill.

Later, when we were coming down the hill in the dusk, I put my arms around her and kissed her. She'd just paused to take a swig from her water bottle and I'd moved closer and asked for a sip.

At the bottom of the hill, we hugged each other again, but didn't kiss. She looked at me, with a slightly nervous smile, and said, 'Who are you?' Then she stopped speaking in her broken Mandarin and muttered a few sentences in Cantonese.

'I didn't understand a word of that,' I said.

'You weren't supposed to,' she answered slowly.

Then I said, 'I like you,' after which she bowed her head and stared at her feet.

I put my arm around her shoulder and she leaned into my embrace. We began walking again very slowly. A large lake stretched before us. The reflected peak of the hill behind us plunged straight down into the deep green water. I wanted to sink my hands and tongue into every cavity of her body. The only girl I'd touched since Lulu was a girl at a friend's birthday party. I'd danced cheek to cheek with her, and run my hand down her back when the lights went out.

There weren't many other tourists around, so I bent down and kissed A-Mei again. She stopped walking. Her body seemed to grow heavier.

'That's very daring of you!' she said with a smile, gently pushing me away. In the dim light, I watched her fiddle with a lock of her hair. Her delicate hands were paler than her face. She looked up at me and didn't move. I felt a sudden surge of love for this girl in the white skirt, who was so different from me. We were standing very close, staring into each other's eyes. I put my arms around her and licked her hair, fingers, nose, ears, hair grip, eyebrows. I didn't care what I kissed, as long as it was part of her.

From that moment onwards, she became the centre of my life.

The love you felt for her is trapped in a remote bundle of motor neurons, too distant for you to reach. All you can do is lie here and wait, as your body slowly calcifies.

We stayed in the spare room of her aunt's flat that night. After I turned out the lights, I sat on the edge of A-Mei's bed and put my hand between her legs. I sat there stroking her all night, until just before sunrise I saw the tiredness in her eyes, and returned to my bed to sleep.

In the morning I left A-Mei with her aunt and caught a long-distance bus that delivered me to Wuxuan at three in the afternoon. It was a bustling, crowded market town. The dusty road outside the bus station smelt of diesel engines and dung. Small street stalls were selling clothes, hats and fake leather shoes that had been bought in the markets of Guangzhou. The dirty, crumbling walls behind them were pasted with peeling posters of foreign women in bikinis and tigers leaping across rocky mountains. Hung from a cable suspended between a door frame and a telegraph pole, like a piece of skewered meat, was a poster of a blonde woman leaning on a limousine. I asked for directions, and soon found my way to the headquarters of the Wuxuan Revolutionary Committee, where I met up with Dr Song, an old university friend of A-Mei's aunt. Dr Song had been a surgeon at Wuxuan County Hospital, but during the national campaign to rectify past wrongs launched by the liberal-leaning leader Hu Yaobang, he was transferred to the Revolutionary Committee to research the history of the Cultural Revolution in Guangxi Province.

He checked my student card, read the introduction letter from A-Mei's aunt, and said, 'Why waste your summer holidays coming here? You could be visiting the tourist sites of Guilin. And why on earth would you want to visit a reform-through-labour camp?'

I told him that my father had come to Wuxuan in 1963 and had spent two years working in the Guangxi Overseas Chinese Farm nearby. I wanted to visit it, but didn't know exactly where it was.

Dr Song looked surprised. 'What was your father's name?' he asked, checking my student card again.

'Dai Changjie. He played for the National Opera Company's orchestra.' I didn't want to disclose that he'd been branded a rightist. It was very dark inside the low-ceilinged brick hut. I turned my eyes to the brightness outside the window. There was so much dust on the panes that everything looked blurred. Most of the sky was hidden by a row of brick huts.

'Was he the rightist who played the violin?' As the thought came to his mind, the wrinkles above his eyebrows twitched for a moment.

'Did you know him?'

'Yes. I remember many of the inmates of that farm. Your father came to visit me once, when he was ill. He had a stomach inflammation. He'd developed the condition in the Gansu labour camp. How is he now?'

'He died three years ago, from stomach cancer. Just a year after his final release.' After these words left my mouth, my throat felt sore and dry.

'Was his rightist label removed?'

'Yes, a few months before he died. Did you know Director Liu, the farm's education officer?'

'It's a good thing your father was transferred to Shandong,' Dr Song murmured, looking away. It was as if he was speaking to himself.

'Why?'

'He might have been eaten, eaten like the others.'

He spoke so softly that it was hard for me to fully understand what he was saying.

'They ate Director Liu,' he mumbled. 'When we went to inspect the farm last month, we retrieved two dried human livers from a peasant who lives nearby. He'd kept them all these years. Whenever he fell ill, he'd break off a small piece and make medicinal tonics with it. One of the livers belonged to Director Liu. Although it had dried out, it was still about this big.' He looked up at me and gestured the size with his hands

'They ate him?' I remembered a passage in my father's journal that described an act of cannibalism he'd witnessed in the Gansu camp: 'Three days after Jiang died of starvation, Hu and Gao secretly sliced some flesh from the buttock and thigh of his corpse and roasted it on a fire. They didn't expect Jiang's wife to turn up in the camp the next day and ask to see the corpse. She wept for hours, hugging his mutilated body in her arms.' As the image shot back into my mind, my teeth began to chatter.

'You're still young. You haven't seen much of the world. I shouldn't be telling you this.'

'I'm a biology student, and have taken courses in medicine, so I'm not easily shocked. But I just can't imagine how anyone could bring themselves to eat another human being. My father told me that, of the three thousand rightists sent to the Gansu reform-through-labour camp, 1,700 died of starvation. Sometimes the survivors became so famished that they had to resort to eating the corpses.'

Dr Song walked over to the locked cabinet, picked up the two thermos flasks that were resting on top of it, gave them a shake, removed the stopper from one of them and poured some hot water into an empty cup. Then he brought out a small canister of tea, scooped out some leaves, dropped them into the hot water and placed a lid on the cup.

'Thank you, thank you,' I said, taking the cup from him. I wanted to swallow a large gulp, but the water was too hot.

'Here in Guangxi it wasn't starvation that drove people to cannibalism. It was hatred.'

I didn't know what he meant.

'It was in 1968, one of the most violent years of the Cultural Revolution. In Guangxi, it wasn't enough just to kill class enemies, the local revolutionary committees forced the people to eat them as well. In the beginning, the enemies' corpses were simmered in large vats together with legs of pork. But as the campaign progressed, there were too many corpses to deal with, so only the heart, liver and brain were cooked.'

I couldn't believe what I was hearing.

I pictured my father's body just before he died, and was relieved to think that it had been intact and unharmed.

'There were so many enemies. If your father hadn't been moved to Shandong, he would have got eaten in the end, too. How old are you? Nearly eighteen? Well you would only have been about two years old at the time, then . . . On 3 July 1968, Chairman Mao issued an order calling for the ruthless suppression of class enemies. He wanted all members of the Five Black Categories to be eliminated, together with twenty-three new types of class enemy, which included anyone who'd served as a policeman before Liberation, or who'd been sent to prison or labour camp. And not only them, but their close family and distant relatives as well.'

'That's a lot of people.'

'Yes. Just think: the literal meaning of the Chinese characters for "revolution" is "elimination of life". See this collection of books my research team has just brought out: *Chronicles of the Cultural Revolution in Guangxi Province*. Look, it says here that, in 1968, more than 100,000 people were killed in Guangxi Province. In Wuxuan County alone, 3,523 people were murdered, and of those, 350 were eaten. If I hadn't been imprisoned in August of that year, I too might have been killed.'

The ten volumes were stacked neatly on the small wooden shelf. They looked much heavier than my mother's volumes of *Mysteries of the World*.

'So who were the murderers?'

'Who were the murderers? You could argue that the only real murderer was Chairman Mao. But the fact is, everyone was involved. On 15 June

1968, a public struggle meeting was held here in Wuxuan, during which thirty-seven former rich peasants were killed. After they were publicly denounced, they were made to stand in line, and were then beaten to death one after the other. When a peasant called Li Yan, standing second in line, saw the man in front of her being attacked with metal rods and howling out in pain, she broke free and tried to run back to her house. But the crowds that had gathered to gawk at the public beatings ran after her, and pelted her with bricks and rocks. She died in the doorway of a house not far from hers. It's on that main street you must have walked down after you left the bus station. They'd branded her a rich peasant, but all she owned was three cows. You ask me who the murderers were. The answer is: everyone! Our neighbours, our friends across the street.'

'We've got a girl called Li Yan in our class,' I muttered distractedly.

'After Li Yan was killed, her children and parents were murdered as well. Her whole family was wiped out. During those years, the PLA soldiers sent to Wuxuan County were stationed here in Wuxuan Town. They were meant to carry out the executions, and the inhabitants of the surrounding villages were only supposed to make the arrests. But the villagers were eager to show their commitment to the revolution, so they took things into their own hands, and started executing the class enemies themselves. Look at this passage. It's a speech that was given by the director of the Wuxuan Revolutionary Committee at the time: ". . . The masses at the grass roots of society are permitted to carry out executions, but they shouldn't waste bullets. Instead, they should be encouraged to beat the enemies to death with their own hands, or with the aid of stones or wooden sticks. This way, they will be able to draw greater educational benefit from the experience." When your father was sent down here, there were about a thousand people incarcerated on the farm. After a couple of years, the hundred or so rightists among them were transferred to other camps. Of the nine hundred labourers who remained, over a hundred belonged to the twenty-three undesirable types. All of them were killed. The corpses of the few who'd contracted diseases were buried, but the rest of them were eaten.'

'You're a doctor. What are you doing working here?' All I wanted was for him to close the huge book in his hand.

'This is just a temporary post. Once I've finished overseeing this project, I'll be sent back to the hospital. I wish I could get transferred somewhere else, though. It was very difficult returning to the hospital after my release. My mind kept flashing back to the summer day in 1968, when I watched the hospital staff line up the head, deputy head, and twenty of the best surgeons, gynaecologists, pharmacists and nurses against the wall and bludgeon them to death with bricks and metal rods. I saw our laboratory technician, Wei Honghai, lying on the ground. His head was smashed open, but his limbs were still shaking. A PLA soldier walked over and finished him off with a shot to the chest. They didn't like using guns back then. Whenever they shot someone, the victim's family was made to pay for the bullet.'

'So where were all those people buried?' I didn't want to prolong this conversation, but I couldn't find a way to change the subject.

'No one wanted to collect the corpses. When relatives of the dead were seen to cry, they were murdered for "sympathising with bad elements". A woman called Wang Fangfang from Wuling Village flung herself onto her husband's corpse after he was murdered and burst into tears. She had a young baby tied to her back. The peasants beat Fangfang to death, then hit the baby with a metal spade. Hundreds of people were killed during those months. The streets and rivers were strewn with corpses. There were flies everywhere. It was horrible.'

'A hundred thousand people were murdered in this province, and no one tried to stop it?'

'No. Sometimes, when the militia grew tired of carrying out the killings, they forced the class enemies to kill one another. Listen to this passage about Daqiao District: "After the struggle meeting, it was decided that the bad elements locked in Building Four of the commune should be killed. The bad elements were immediately tied up with rope and led to a disused coal mine 300 metres away. They were made to stand in a queue and push the person in front of them into a pool of water that was 10 metres deep. When the bad elements resisted, the cadres and militia took control, and started pushing them in themselves. One of the women had lived on a boat and knew how to swim. After she was pushed into the water, she was able to swim to the other side, so the cadres had to hurl rocks at her. In the end, a militiaman pulled her out and stabbed her in the neck . . ."'

I couldn't take any more. I felt stupid for having made so much fuss about being beaten by the police when I was fifteen. I looked at Dr Song and said, 'At school, the only thing they told us about the Cultural Revolution was that three million people lost their lives. But I never really grasped the scale of the horror. I was only ten when it came to an end.'

'We received death threats while researching this material. The national government told us to carry out this research, but the county authorities refused to cooperate because most of the people who organised the atrocities are now high officials in the local government. This whole project is a sham. Only five copies of these chronicles have been published. I doubt the public will ever get to read them. Once the victims we've listed have been rehabilitated, the chronicles will probably be locked away in the government vaults. None of the top officials will lose their job.'

Dr Song lifted the lid of my teacup and said, 'Drink up before it gets cold.' I pretended to take a sip. I felt too sick to swallow anything, or to leaf through the two volumes he handed me: *Chronicles of the Cultural Revolution in Liuzhou County*, and *Chronicles of the Cultural Revolution in Nanning District*. I longed to escape this dark and dismal office.

I thought of my father's journal which was lying at the bottom of my bag, but I didn't feel in the mood to take it out and enquire about all the people who were mentioned in it. All I could bring myself to ask was: 'Does Director Liu's daughter, Liu Ping, still play the violin? Is she still living in Wuxuan?'

'Liu Ping was only sixteen when they killed her. She was the prettiest girl on the farm. She could dance and play the violin. The night the militia killed her father, they raped her, then strangled her with a piece of rope. Once she was dead, they cut off her breasts and gouged out her liver, then fried them in oil and ate them.' Dr Song flicked to another page in the book. 'Look, here's a photograph of Director Liu's family. The printing is very poor. That girl in the white skirt holding the violin is Liu Ping.'

It was just like the photograph my father had shown me, but in this one Liu Ping's chin was raised a little higher. I was certain that my father had taken this one as well.

The sky outside the window was black now. My hands and feet were as cold as ice. I got up and said that it was time for me to go.

'You've missed the last bus back to Liuzhou, I'm afraid. You'd better spend the night in the county guest house. There'll be another bus in the morning.'

I didn't answer him. I couldn't think of anything to say. All I wanted was to feel some sunlight on my face. I'd grown up reading sheet after sheet of public notices containing lists of executed criminals: thousands of names written in black ink, each one marked with a red cross. But the horror of the deaths hadn't struck me properly until now. I remembered how after some school friends and I noticed the name Chen Bin on one of the lists, we ran over to our classmate who shared the same name, drew pink crosses all over him and cried out, 'Only your death will assuage the people's anger! Bang, bang!' But in Dr Song's office, I felt real terror, in a physical way that I hadn't experienced before.

I briefly flicked through the *Chronicles of the Cultural Revolution in Guilin District*, remembering that I'd planned to go travelling there with

A-Mei, then I got up, hurriedly shook the doctor's hand and left.

As I walked from his office to the guest house, the skin on my back went numb. I sensed that everyone around me – the people walking behind me, towards me, or milling around on the street, and even the legless beggar sitting propped up against the lamp post – was about to pounce on me and eat me alive.

The night passed very slowly. Dr Song's revelations had disturbed me so much that I didn't dare close my eyes. While stroking and kissing A-Mei the night before, I'd come three times, so I was weak with exhaustion now, shuddering like a plane spiralling out of control. But despite my tiredness, I didn't sleep all night.

The circular paths inside your body lead nowhere. There's no route that will take you to the outside world.

The next morning I caught the first bus back to Liuzhou and arrived in the afternoon in a confused daze.

A-Mei was surprised to see me, because I'd told her I'd be away a week. The only explanation I gave was that the people I'd intended to visit had died.

'How come you didn't know that before you left?' she asked.

'They were friends of my father's. I never met them.'

'When did they die?'

'In the Cultural Revolution.'

'Put that cigarette out. You shouldn't smoke so much. Your hair and clothes stink of tobacco.' Then she said that she was only a baby when the Cultural Revolution started, but when she was older, her parents told her that during the violent years corpses with bound hands and feet would float down from China into the harbours of Hong Kong every day.

I didn't want to talk about this subject any more. I told her I wanted to travel up to Beijing a few days earlier than I'd planned.

She stared at me blankly for a moment, and said, 'Fine. I'll go back to Hong Kong a bit earlier too, then.'

We decided that we'd set off for Guilin the next morning, stay there a few days, then go our separate ways.

I was aware that a change had taken place in me. I'd acquired that cold detachment one develops after experiencing a traumatic event. On the long-distance bus to Guilin, I didn't hold A-Mei's hand. I felt uncomfortable when her leg brushed against mine. A-Mei looked sad. I guessed that she thought I'd lost interest in her.

I hardly said a word during our time in Guilin, and she didn't say much either. The intimacy that we had so recently established seemed to have evaporated. I knew that any show of affection would seem false, so I didn't dare touch her, let alone kiss her. When I sat opposite her in a restaurant, all I was aware of was the oily stench from the kitchen. The neurons she'd brought to life in the emotional centres of my brain seemed to have withered and died. I felt out of kilter. The sunlight and the sky felt muggy and close.

On Guilin's Elephant Trunk Hill, I asked her if she wanted me to take a photograph of her. She said no. I was relieved, because I felt incapable of fixing my attention on her.

A crowd of foreign tourists poured out of a coach, their blonde hair glinting in the sun. They put on multicoloured sun hats and smiled as they stood waiting for their photographs to be taken in front of the scenic backdrop. I wanted to tell them to run away, because the bodies of 100,000 massacred people were buried under their feet. They had no idea that China was a vast graveyard.

The following evening we moved to a new hostel. The girl at reception wasn't very experienced, and let A-Mei and me share the same room. It was a large dorm with seven single beds. We were the only guests.

After I blew out the candle, A-Mei felt afraid, and so did I, so we squeezed up together on one of the single beds and held each other.

I started to cry. I told her that I was upset on my father's behalf. The people he'd wanted me to visit were dead. She said that after her grandmother died, she was so upset, she didn't eat or sleep for a week, so she understood how I felt.

I told her that this was the first time that I'd shared a bed with a girl. She said it was the first time she'd shared a bed with a boy. I felt a desire stir within me. In the dark cavernous room, her limbs were warm and alive. We rolled over each other on the bed. I couldn't seem to keep hold of her. Her soft skin slipped through my fingers. Now and then the smells of her body, her face cream, and the odour of sweat previous guests had left on the pillow and mattress would rise into the air between us and be drawn into our lungs.

She said, 'I love you.' I said, 'Me too.' I inhaled her breath then moved closer to her and sucked her warm tongue. My legs rubbed against hers, and before I knew it, I'd thrust myself inside her. The shuddering darkness became a wind that propelled me back and forth, shaking me into a trance. I felt my neurons charge into her bloodstream. My throat tightened and my eyes burned. 'You're killing me, killing me!' I cried, falling into an ecstatic stupor.

At last she pushed me away, moaning: 'You're hurting me . . . get out . . .' She pressed her hand against my thigh and I stopped moving. 'You're very bad,' she said. Her words hovered for a while in the darkness.

'You're very good,' I said. 'You're my woman . . .'

'There's nothing good about me now. You've broken me . . .' I could tell that she was talking through pursed lips.

Even with my eyes wide open, I couldn't see a thing. The whole room seemed to be sliding and flowing.

Men and women are dark fluids. It's only when they make love that they're able to flow out and fill the crevices between each other's bodies and souls. If the fluids stay locked inside for too long, they eventually dry up.

The hotel receptionist banged loudly on the door and told us we must sleep in separate rooms. She said that the police had come and checked the register at midnight, and informed her it was against the law for unmarried couples to share the same room. I grabbed my blanket, groped my way out and went to sleep in the dorm next door.

I fell asleep and dreamed that the giant Mao Zedong face that hangs in Tiananmen Square began to smile. A crowd of millions knelt below it, their heads bowed low. A couple of people courageously looked up and saw Mao waving his arms in the air and laughing wildly. Then the crowd disappeared and became a vast, empty desert.

Your white blood cells sweep away small blood clots and particles of fat, and begin to shroud those memories as a creeper shrouds a brick wall.

A photograph taken in our flat flashes before my eyes. At first it's a black-and-white image, then slowly the colours seep through. In the background are the ten volumes of *Mysteries of the World* lined up on the wooden cabinet. My brother is standing next to my mother in the foreground, with a forced smile on his face.

When I opened the envelope my brother sent me, this photograph fell out. I was sitting at a small wooden desk in my dorm at Southern University. My brother must have been sixteen by then. Now that my father was dead, I felt responsible for him. I picked up my pen and began to reply to his letter.

I remembered one night, when we were much younger, he refused to go to sleep after I turned the lights out, insisting that I explain to him why Chinese ants are red and American ants are black. He said that black ants, which bite people, are braver than red ants, so logically speaking they should be Chinese not American. I refused to answer him, so to punish me he stole a pair of my socks and hid them under his pillow.

In the envelope, there was also a letter from my mother. She wrote that, for the first time in more than twenty years, her company had been permitted to perform Western operas again. They were now rehearsing *Carmen*, and she'd been chosen to sing soprano in a four-voice aria. She was very excited about this, and had begun to go jogging every morning in an attempt to lose weight. 'Your father would have been very proud of me,' she wrote. 'My voice has improved so much recently. It's as good as it was when I was twenty. I can even reach a high C.' When she used a fountain pen, my mother's handwriting looked quite elegant.

I pictured her face going red as she trilled floridly up the scale, so in my letter I reminded her to keep drinking infusions of the dried arhat fruit I'd sent her. 'You should practise in the park,' I wrote. 'The air in the flat is too dusty. It will damage your voice.'

My mother always peppered her letters with political exhortations. 'You have high ambitions and ideals, but you must take care to align yourself with Party policies and keep up with the changing political climate. If you focus exclusively on your studies and fail to achieve any political accomplishments, you will suffer your father's fate . . .'

In my letter back to her I retorted, 'Dad didn't commit any mistakes. I keep telling you that, but you never listen. If he'd done anything wrong, the government wouldn't have rehabilitated him . . . What our country needs now is knowledge, not ideology. Half of the professors in our university are rehabilitated rightists. The era of class struggle that you still cling to is a thing of the past. The only students who want to join the Party now are a few country bumpkins who are afraid of being sent back to their villages after they graduate . . .'

In fact, I knew that my mother's desire to join the Party was motivated by thoughts of self-preservation. She was like those victims of natural disasters who instinctively seek safety in the hills.

'I think Dai Ru has got himself a girlfriend,' my mother wrote. 'I heard that he took a girl to see a fashion show. Only couples who are going out together do things like that. The tickets were very expensive. When I asked him about it, he denied that he'd gone. You must have a serious talk with him, and tell him where you went wrong. I don't want him to make the same mistakes as you did.'

I thought back to my interrogation in the police station in 1982, and realised how much society had changed. Back then, you could get arrested for copying out a book that contained a few erotic passages. But now, just two years on, pornographic films were being shown in privately run video rooms on every street corner. Although it was against the university rules for students to date each other, no one paid any notice. In the holidays, when the campus was much emptier, girls and boys would move into each other's dorms. Students from Hong Kong and Macao could afford to rent rooms in the town, which gave them more privacy. When you have money, you have freedom. The government had recently announced that in the Special Economic Zone of Shenzhen, citizens were allowed to buy their own flats. Private ownership had reared its head at last in Communist China. I didn't want to interfere in my brother's life. All I told him was that he should start making plans to study abroad.

I found letter-writing a chore, but my mother wrote to me every week, so, now and then, I had to take the time to reply to her.

Wang Fei was fast asleep on the bunk above me. He always slept with his leg dangling over the side. It drove me mad.

'Pull your leg back up or I'll chop it off!' I shouted. 'It's time you got dressed, anyway. We've got a class to go to in a minute.' The class I was referring to was going to be held in the laboratory. Students from the medical and science faculties were to observe the dissection of the corpse of an executed prisoner.

I'd planned to help A-Mei move into her new room before the class. She was transferring to a block the university had just built for Overseas Chinese students where the rent was five hundred yuan a term. But she'd changed her mind and decided to postpone the move until the afternoon.

On 1 October every year, prisoners on death row were executed in celebration of National Day. With the improvement of surgical skills and the liberalisation of the Chinese economy, any patient with enough money could now purchase themselves the organs of executed prisoners. The organs of the corpse that was delivered to us that morning had been used for China's first successful heart-lung transplant. There had been an article about the operation in the newspaper the previous day, and now the heart and lungs were working away inside the body of a Hong Kong businessman.

We walked into the dissection lab. The room was stuffy and smelt of formalin.

Professor Huang was a celebrated cardiovascular specialist. The successful heart transplants he performed were often reported by the press. His lectures were fascinating. Even the most squeamish of students would stay to the end.

This was the first time we'd been shown a fresh corpse. All the bodies we'd seen before had been preserved in formalin solution. Everyone was eager to take a close look.

The corpse lying on the wooden table before us was that of a young male convict. There were freckles on his nose. The bullet that had killed him had blasted one of his eyes out. All that remained of it was an empty socket splattered with black, congealed blood and gunpowder.

Professor Huang slipped on a pair of surgical gloves and said, 'This dissection will focus on the brain and spinal cord. We have to leave the rest of the body for the other departments to study. You must pay close attention. It wasn't easy getting hold of this corpse.'

My eyesight was good – approximately R:1.5 L:1.5. I could see the dandruff flaking from the professor's scalp.

'Look, here. Because they needed his heart and lungs for the transplant, they shot him in the back of the neck, not the chest. The bullet entered the medulla oblongata, giving the surgeons a window of fifteen seconds to remove the heart and lungs before the donor lost consciousness and died.' He twisted the corpse's neck around a little and pointed to the bullet wound.

'Agh!' the students cried.

'That wouldn't have given them enough time to even disinfect the skin,' said a student standing next to A-Mei.

'I don't believe they could do it that fast!' Mou Sen said, sweeping back his long fringe. 'It would take them at least ten minutes just to locate the aorta and pulmonary artery.'

'I haven't finished, students . . . Medical technology has developed very rapidly. As soon as the bullet hits the hindbrain, the trachea is tabulated, and intravenous drugs are administered to allow the donor to resume a normal heartbeat. The chest is opened. The organs are then swiftly removed and taken to the operating theatre, where the recipient's diseased organs have been removed and extracorporeal circulation has been established . . .'

'I didn't know that execution grounds are equipped with operating rooms,' Wu Bin said, his triangular eyes lighting up. When he talked about Nazi gas chambers, he would give us every detail, down to the dimensions of the doors and windows. It was as though he'd been in one himself.

'Last year's Ministry of Health guidelines allowed surgical operations to be carried out in ambulances parked outside the execution grounds. But the success rate of the operations was low. The demand for organs has risen recently, especially from foreign patients who can pay in foreign currency, which is good for our economy. So to improve efficiency and meet demand, the government has now permitted executions to be carried out in the hospital where the organ transplant will be performed. This has taken place at South China Hospital, near Number One

Military Medical College, as well as at the Military Science University Hospital.'

'I've heard people say that it's inhuman to remove organs from a living person,' said Tang Guoxian from the back of the room.

Wang Fei moved to the front. 'In the Nuremberg trial, Nazi doctors claimed that the Jews had participated in their medical experiments of their own free will,' he said. 'But the judges argued that prisoners who live in fear for their lives are incapable of granting free and voluntary consent.' When Wang Fei held forth, he always liked to speak at the top of his voice. He didn't care whether anyone could understand his Sichuan accent.

'Before the counter-revolutionary Li Lian was executed in 1971 for criticising the Cultural Revolution, four policemen pushed her face against the window of a truck, lifted her shirt and cut out her kidneys with a surgical knife,' Mou Sen said, his face stony and white. 'I think that removing the organs of convicts while they are still alive is too much. It completely contravenes medical ethics.'

'This is a dissection class, not a political meeting,' Sun Chunlin said self-righteously. In our dorm, whenever our discussions reached a critical juncture, he would always butt in with a negative comment that would kill the conversation dead.

Professor Huang didn't seem annoyed by these interruptions, but he was wearing a face mask, so it was hard to tell. He cleared his throat and said, 'Wouldn't it be a waste to cremate a corpse without making use of its organs first? We don't have much time left, so if any of you want to leave, leave now. And if you want to say something, put up your hand first.'

At this, Wang Fei turned and left. Mou Sen, who was leaning against the electric microscope, hesitated for a moment but decided to stay.

Professor Huang drew a line around the corpse's head, then pointed to me and told me to start sawing it open. The steel hacksaw wasn't large, but when I picked it up it felt very heavy. I pulled back the corpse's ear. It was the first time I'd touched a dead person. I sawed through the skin below the earlobe. The hair had been shaven, probably just before the execution. The scalp felt slippery when I pressed it. My hands trembled. I was so anxious, I didn't know in which direction to cut. I dragged the hacksaw back and forth a few more times, then gave up.

I turned to Wu Bin and asked him to take over. There was only one spare pair of rubber gloves, so I removed them from my hands and handed them to him.

Until now, we'd only performed dissections on preserved body parts.

I glanced at A-Mei through the corner of my eye to check how she was coping.

The male students went over to the corpse and took turns to saw around the head until at last the top of the skull was lifted off, revealing the pink, blood-flecked brain inside. It looked much spongier than the brains soaked in formalin that we'd been shown before. A fine mesh of red capillaries covered the outer membrane, and an intricate network of blue veins ran through the folds in the cerebral cortex below. Professor Huang asked the students to point out the frontal, parietal, occipital and temporal lobes, and explain their respective functions. Then he picked up his knife and made a vertical incision down the length of the brain.

'It's like cutting a birthday cake,' Professor Huang joked, but no one smiled. I glanced at A-Mei again. I'd bought her a cake on her birthday, but the cream had gone off so she'd had to throw it away. She was staring down at her notebook. She never looked up during the dissection classes. One time, she was handed a piece of human calf muscle to practise her dissection skills on, and was so horrified that she vomited on the floor. She didn't seem cut out to be a doctor.

In the past, I'd imagined Hong Kong as a debauched and corrupt city of capitalists and prostitutes, but after I met A-Mei, I realised that it upheld many traditional Chinese family values that we in the mainland had lost. A-Mei was very close to her family, whereas I didn't know the dates of my parents' birthdays, or even my grandfathers' first names.

One day, A-Mei had asked me why I'd only told her that I loved her after our first kiss. I said that once was enough, and that there was no need to repeat myself now that she was mine. My reply upset her so much that she burst into tears.

In fact, she'd forgotten that I'd repeated to her that I loved her just a few days before, while we were lying on top of a hill. It was a Sunday. The weather was beautiful, so we decided to take a bus to a nature reserve an hour's drive away. I reached the top of the hill before her, and lay down on the grass, panting for breath. When she made it to the top, she crawled over and lay down beside me. The plimsolls she'd bought especially for the trip were wet through. I took them off for her and watched her warm little toes wriggle and curl. I moved on top of her. She lifted her hips, then lowered them, and we soon dissolved into each other. When I closed my eyes, I felt I was floating through the blue sky with her. I cried out, 'I'm in Heaven!' then whispered in her ear, 'I love you, A-Mei . . .'

During an argument we had later, she told me that she had goals and ambitions, and didn't just want to be somebody's wife. She said that it wasn't enough just to tell someone you loved them, you had to give them support and encouragement every day. It's true that, before I met her, I knew very little about love.

Professor Huang went over to the electric microscope, then came back to the corpse and said, 'This thin, wrinkled outer layer of cerebral cortex is the most highly developed part of the brain. It's responsible for conscious thoughts, perception, language and long-term memory. It is divided into the neocortex, palaeocortex and archicortex. This section I've sliced off is from the frontal lobe.' He picked up the thin slice with a pair of tweezers and showed it to everyone. 'This piece here might contain information about the man's bank account, his dreams, the appearance of his mother or wife. It's just a few milligrammes of brain tissue, but it holds a universe that, despite advances in neuroscience, still remains a mystery to us . . . Sun Chunlin, please step forward and describe to us the function of the neocortex.'

'The neocortex is this region here. No – here. In evolutionary terms, this is the most recently developed part of the brain, and is associated with higher functions such as conceptualisation and planning . . . It's commonly accepted that geniuses and great figures in history have highly developed brains. Think of Lenin, Tolstoy, Karl Marx – they all had big foreheads.' The brain tissue Sun Chunlin was pressing was as soft and springy as tofu.

'Dai Wei, come and say something about the function of the archicortex,' said Professor Huang.

'The archicortex is basically the hippocampus, down here . . .' I said, my face beginning to redden. 'It's the older, primitive part of the brain and is connected with memories and emotions . . . If this part of the brain is damaged, the patient falls into a vegetative state.' A-Mei, who was standing to my left, tried to encourage me with a supportive glance.

I'm not in a dissection class now. I'm a vegetable. I cannot move, touch or see. I'm a spirit trapped in a dark room, a neuron searching for a way out, a pebble plunging through the vast universe.

Melancholy yearnings stir within you. Forgotten fears and hopes drip from your bones like dark marrow.

I remember standing beside A-Mei at the sink after the dissection class. Her face was ashen. I quickly cleaned my hands with the bar of soap before passing it to her, because it had been resting in the palm of a preserved human hand left over from a previous dissection. Instead of going to the canteen, we decided to have lunch in the small restaurant outside the campus gates.

It was doing a good trade. The manager had built a second storey above the original shack, and students from several surrounding universities now regularly went there to eat. I had a bowl of chicken and dangshen-root soup. A-Mei ordered a plate of cold mung beans, but couldn't eat much because the dissection class had ruined her appetite.

The restaurant was filled with mosquitoes. I asked the manager to turn on the electric fan. An old pop song droned from the battered cassette player on the counter. Time passed sluggishly.

A-Mei hardly said a word. I reached over and ran my hand through her hair.

'You want another cigarette, don't you?' she said.

I'd already had three, so I said no.

She told me that, in Hong Kong, criminals were put in prison for up to fifty years, but were never executed. She couldn't accept the notion that a government could order a citizen to be killed. She said that she hadn't wanted to study medicine in China. It had been her parents' idea.

I hadn't realised that Hong Kong didn't use the death penalty. 'What about murderers and rapists?' I asked her. 'If the government didn't get rid of them, they'd pose a threat to public safety.'

'But what if the judgement is wrong? How can one ever make up for taking the life of an innocent man? And anyway, it's not civilised to kill another human being, whether they're guilty of the crime or not.'

She said that, while she was on hospital training in the Chinese countryside, she'd seen a doctor kill a newborn baby by injecting alcohol into its head. The mother wasn't allowed to set eyes on it. In the afternoon, the mother slipped back into the delivery room, retrieved her dead baby from the rubbish bin and ran away with it.

'I hear stories like that all the time,' I said. 'My cousin's wife went on the run after she fell pregnant with her second child. She came up to Beijing to stay with us, but the police tracked her down and sent her back to her village. As soon as she arrived, local birth-control officers cut her belly open, pulled out the foetus and drowned it in a bucket of water . . . And after I said goodbye to you at the train station last time you went to Hong Kong, I saw a young couple being chased by the police. The woman was pregnant, but didn't have a birth permit. The man managed to get away, but the woman was too slow. The police caught her and flung her onto the ground. She fell on her face. There was blood everywhere. They tied her up like a pig and carried her away.'

'Stop it, stop it – I can't take any more,' A-Mei cried. 'I want to go to Canada and study business management, or music.'

I always felt nervous when I saw A-Mei frown. I pulled a cigarette from my packet.

Noticing my worried expression, she changed the subject, and said, 'Put that cigarette away. Do you want to go and see the exhibition in Yuexiu Park tonight? There's going to be a bonfire party, with traditional dances performed by some ethnic minority people from Yunnan.'

Although A-Mei's room in the newly built Overseas Chinese block was small, it had a balcony big enough to fit two chairs. Being able to sit out there made the city's sub-tropical heat a little more bearable. She asked me to move in with her. I said I would, on condition that she let me pay the following term's rent. She agreed, so at the beginning of the winter holiday I brought some of my stuff over from the dorm.

She'd decorated the room with bits and pieces she'd brought up with her from Hong Kong. I especially liked the pair of small foot-shaped rugs beside the bed and the fold-up plastic wardrobe. I hung up the topographical map of China on which I'd attempted to mark out the routes described in *The Book of Mountains and Seas*. She laid a bamboo sleeping mat over her soft foam mattress. The desk that we shared was crammed with her cassette player and piles of her books and classical music tapes.

It was the first time in my life that I had a bedside lamp of my own. I could decide whether to keep it switched on and read my books, or to turn it off and go to sleep. A-Mei's lamp, on the other side of the bed, had a shade she'd made from an orange, flowery material. When she turned it on at night, it made the room look cosy and elegant.

She decided that the next time she went to Hong Kong, she'd bring back her violin and start practising again. She asked me whether the noise would disturb me. I told her that my mother was a professional singer, and that I'd grown up listening to her belting out arpeggios.

It was also the first time I'd shared a room with a girl. It felt very strange. Her rubber sandals were half the size of mine. I was able to go to sleep with her, wake up with her, and watch her take off and put on her knickers and bra. I could observe her rubbing moisturiser into her face and lengthening her eyelashes with a tiny black brush. I could peer inside her make-up bag and twist up her tubes of lipstick. The room had an en suite bathroom, so when she went to the toilet, I could hear all the noises she made. I was able both to see and smell her blood-stained sanitary towels. I could no longer get away with flicking my cigarette stubs onto the floor and grinding them out with my heel. If I wanted a cigarette, I had to smoke it on the balcony, then neatly deposit the stub into the tin she'd placed out there. I also had to start brushing my teeth twice a day.

A few seconds after A-Mei went to sleep, she'd shudder a little, like the frogs we experimented on in the laboratory. She'd lie in my arms, the lamplight falling softly on her face. She often told me how much she liked falling asleep with her head on my chest. So whenever she did this, I felt very happy, and tried to make sure I didn't fart.

During the holiday, we attended many lectures hosted by the university. She'd sit on the back of my bicycle, and we'd ride off to the campus through a string of lanes and alleys. The month passed very quickly.

Our friends began to refer to us as 'the married couple'.

In the last week of the holiday, A-Mei announced that she was going to return to Hong Kong to accompany her mother on a five-day trip to Thailand.

The night before she left, we clung onto each other's clammy bodies that smelt of the same sweat. The damp strands of hair above her ears fluttered in the breeze blowing from the electric fan. She let her arms rest limply at her sides and said very slowly, 'We've become so close to each other. It's wonderful. I'm yours, all yours . . .' Then she rolled over and laid her head on my chest. Before I'd had a chance to light a cigarette, I fell into a deep sleep.

As you drift unconsciously towards death, you reach out for the fractured sentiments that float by, trying to find one that is in some way connected to you.

I thought we were in love . . . The chapter of *The Book of Mountains and Seas* entitled 'Paths through the Southern Mountains' talks of a Mount Brazen that overlooks the Western Sea. That's where I planned to start my journey. On its slopes grows a plant that banishes hunger. I wanted to eat some of its leaves, then set off to find the Black Tree of the Lost Valley, whose blossoms are so radiant that if you wear one in your hair, you will never lose your way. The River Li springs from the foot of the mountain and flows westward towards the sea . . .

I wonder why *The Book of Mountains and Seas* interrupted my memories of A-Mei.

I remember telling her once that, after I graduated, I wanted to set off on a long journey, following the routes described in the book. I told her that I'd start in the Southern Mountains, climb Mount Brazen, then make my way to the mountains of the west, north and east.

'Do you think you'll have enough years in your life to travel to all those places?' she said. 'The Southern Mountains alone stretch for nearly two thousand kilometres. Anyway, the book isn't a proper scientific text. It's full of myths and fables. You told me yourself that many of the place names are impossible to locate. Some of them probably never existed in the first place. And what about all the strange animals? Do you really believe there is a species of bird that has only one wing?' She raised her eyebrows and smiled at me.

I pointed to the map of China I'd hung on the wall and said, 'The more people claim something doesn't exist, the more I want to go and find it. The book was written two thousand years ago, so it's natural that the place names will have changed. I haven't identified many of the towns and rivers, but look, I've been able to mark out most of the mountain ranges.'

She gazed blankly at the wall for a moment then said, 'I've worked it out. If you want to travel all the routes mentioned in the book, it will take you at least fifty years. I'll be seventy by the time you return – if I'm not dead by then.'

'It was just a thought I had,' I mumbled. 'I know very well that it would take more than a lifetime to complete the journey . . .'

'So why did you bother hanging up that map then?' she said impatiently.

Adrenalin is the lubricant of life. It makes your heart race, your face blush, your breath quicken, and helps you recover from heartache.

Ten days passed, and A-Mei still hadn't returned from Hong Kong. She'd told me she was only going to Thailand for five days.

I didn't attend the compulsory lecture on the first Tuesday of term, in case she phoned while I was out. I stayed in the room and rifled through her suitcases and drawers, searching for something that might explain her prolonged absence. I discovered that she owned four white skirts and several different watches. The only thing that roused my suspicion was that she'd taken the two diaries she usually kept on the desk.

I stepped out onto the balcony and peered down at the corner shop on the other side of the road. It frustrated me that there was always someone using the public phone that was kept on the shop's windowsill.

On Wednesday evening, just before supper, someone shouted up from downstairs: 'Room 413 on the fourth floor! A girl from Hong Kong on the shop phone for you!'

Without bothering to put my sandals on, I charged downstairs.

I was in a bad mood. I picked up the receiver and said, 'What's going on? Have you lost all track of time? Do you know what day it is?'

A-Mei remained silent for a long time then finally said, 'I've told my mother about you. I showed her photographs of us together.'

'So what? I told my mother about us ages ago . . . You've been away two weeks now. Isn't it time you came back?'

'I don't think I'm coming back this term.'

'What do you mean? Why haven't you phoned me before?'

'I've tried to reach you every day. The shop phone is always engaged.'

'Well, we can talk about all this once you're back here. The line isn't very good.' I never liked to talk much on long-distance calls, because I was afraid of the expense. But A-Mei was calling me this time, so I only had to pay the shopkeeper a small fee.

'My mother doesn't approve, Dai Wei. She said –'

'The woman's never met me!' I said dismissively. 'What right does she have to tell you what to do?'

'Calm down, will you? I'm phoning you now because my parents have gone out. Listen: my mother wants me to break up with you. She doesn't want me to return to Guangzhou.' I'd never heard her speak so loudly before.

'So you do whatever your mother says, do you?'

'I'm trying to tell you what the situation is. Why won't you let me explain things?' She'd probably forgotten that I was standing outside the corner shop. There was a long queue of people waiting to use the phone, and they were all staring at my mouth and listening to every word that came out of it.

'I don't have time for all this waffle. Just get to the point.' I glanced at the strangers in the queue behind me, and drew a certain comfort from the attention they were paying me. If there hadn't been so many of them waiting there, I probably wouldn't have spoken so abruptly. I had at least a basic understanding of politeness.

'All right then,' she said. 'If we're going to break up, we might as well get it over and done with. There's no point in dragging things out.' When A-Mei became angry, she'd slip back into Cantonese, but I could usually get the gist of what she was saying.

'OK, if you want to split up, let's split up!' I was angry that she let her mother dictate her life in that way.

'Well, OK then . . .' she stuttered, then put the phone down.

A sense of peace came over me. It felt as though I'd rid myself of a troublesome problem. I left the corner shop, hurried back to the room, put some books into my satchel and went off to the library. A new edition of the *Science and Modernity Journal* was delivered to the library at the beginning of each month. It got passed around so much that if you didn't get your hands on it early enough, there'd be nothing left of it for you to read.

Even now, I'm not certain who exactly broke up with whom. Did I hang up on her? No, she definitely put down the phone first. I'm sure of it.

It was only when I returned to the room in the evening that it finally dawned on me that she wasn't coming back, and that everything was over between us. It occurred to me that, if she'd been the one to initiate the separation, then I'd be the jilted lover and, like every jilted lover, I'd feel sad for a while. But if I had broken up with her, then she would be the sad and jilted one. But since I couldn't work out who had broken up with whom, I knew I'd just have to wait and see what my reaction would be.

That was the first day of our break-up.

Before I went to sleep that night, I read the chapter from *The Book of Mountains and Seas* called 'Paths through the Regions between the Seas'. I was fascinated by the descriptions of creatures that were half-human and half-bird: humans with bird faces, and birds with human heads. I wondered whether these were purely mythical creatures, or strange hybrids that had long since mutated or become extinct.

When I finished the chapter, I pulled out my father's journal again, and flicked through a few pages, but I couldn't focus on any of the words.

A couple of weeks earlier, I'd looked through some old 1950s editions of *Liberation Daily*, and found a review of the performance of Beethoven's Eroica given by the National Opera Company's orchestra. As I'd expected, there was the photograph of my father holding his violin in one hand and stretching out his other to shake hands with the American conductor. He was wearing a Western suit, and looked young and vibrant. I saw how much I resembled him.

Wu Bin had taken a photo of the newspaper picture, and printed some copies for me. I'd posted one to my mother, and given another to A-Mei. Although I wasn't a musician myself, I wanted her to know that I was the son of a violinist.

I looked through my photographs of A-Mei, put them away, then took them out again and started noticing details about her that I hadn't spotted before. In a picture taken during a visit we made to the Guangzhou Friendship Store, she was wearing high-heeled shoes. I'd never realised she owned a pair. Then, in a close-up picture of her face, I noticed fine, downy hairs above her top lip, and a crease in her left eyelid. At three in the morning, I was still pacing around the room, muttering to myself, 'All right, let's split up then. You'll be sorry, though. You'll come back to me. I know it . . .'

By midnight, I felt a cold, heavy ache in my heart and had a premonition that it was I who was going to suffer, not her.

I tried to resist falling into despondency. On a piece of paper I listed her faults: 'Indecisive, inflexible, lazy, weak, sleeps too much, takes too long putting on her clothes and make-up, always hiding from the sun.' Then, at the bottom, I added, 'Nothing too serious, I suppose. No one's perfect.'

This helped me to get through the rest of the night.

The next day I attended lectures as usual, but when I returned to the room in the evening, I could feel her breath emanating from her orange lampshade, her desk, rubber sandals, teacup, nightdress, socks, the menstrual bloodstains on her sheets, the book lying open at the last page she'd read, the tomato she'd left in the mini fridge near the door, the Vaseline Intensive Care shower cream she'd bought for my dry skin. I couldn't press the electric fan's start button, because I knew that her fingers had touched it. I preferred to sweat in the still heat. Her breath hung in the room, and with each inhalation, I breathed her in.

With a cold shiver I had to acknowledge that I was the heartbroken one, not her. She was a lake, and I was drowning in her. I was a fresh-water fish swept into the salt sea. No – I was a sea fish simmering in an ocean that was becoming hotter and hotter . . .

Until she left me, I hadn't realised that love could be so perilous.

Seeds of heartache, buried deep in your flesh, begin to shift into your arteries and veins.

Alcohol and sleeping pills didn't help me forget her. She was my conjoined twin. I knew that, cut loose from her, I would die.

On the third day after our break-up, my left ribcage began to swell. I became breathless, my throat felt blocked. Only people rejected by the person they love know the true weight of the human heart. I was about to collapse. I heard crashing noises in my head. I stepped out onto the balcony and stared at the blue sky. It was as blue as it had been before she'd left me. But even the blueness seemed to belong to her now. I looked down and felt that I'd never be able to look at the sky again.

I wanted to gouge her out of me. I walked into the streets and circled the campus. When I passed the small restaurant outside the gates, I remembered the dark scar left on A-Mei's right palm by a door that had closed on her hand when she was a child, and how often I had kissed it, trying to wish away the reminder of that moment of pain. There were some new plastic stools outside the restaurant. Although we'd never sat on them, my heart sank when I saw them. The restaurant manager's dog and the two stones on the ground reminded me of her too. She hated the dog. She said it had a man's face.

I tried phoning her home in Hong Kong, but her mother would always pick up and tell me crossly not to bother her daughter again.

Wang Fei had wanted kill himself after he was dumped by a girl he'd dated for only two months. I'd been going out with A-Mei for a year. I wondered how I'd ever recover.

On the fourth night, I woke in the middle of a dream and scribbled the beginning of a letter to her: '. . . I'm like a bird that has lost a wing. Without your wing to help me, I'll never be able to fly . . .' When I went downstairs to buy some more rice wine, I thought of a maths student who'd committed suicide the previous summer after his girlfriend had dumped him. I knew that if I was to live, I'd have to erase all memory of A-Mei from my mind.

I wondered whether the break-up had been predestined. When I'd seen her off at the train station, I'd glanced around the large hall and said morosely, 'Here we are at the border again.' The Hong Kong tourists entering the hall were well dressed, with neat hair and tidy suitcases. They didn't seem to belong to the same planet as the dishevelled hordes of mainland tourists who were trudging wearily around the hall in their bare feet, with plastic bags over their shoulders.

I wasn't allowed to go where she was going. The notice above us read HONG KONG AND MACAO COMPATRIOTS ONLY.

'Don't be sad,' she said. 'I've read in the newspapers that Hong Kong will revert to China in 1997. And anyway, there are no borders between you and me.'

'The Chinese are going to adopt a "one country two systems" policy, so the handover won't change anything,' I said fractiously. I always felt distanced from her whenever I saw her off at the station. She could tell that.

'I'll think about you every day,' she said. 'Don't forget to bring in my skirt from the balcony when it's dry. You can hang it up by the mosquito net.' I could see tears welling in her eyes.

'Remember to get me some cigarettes in the duty-free shop.' The money I earned selling them to the street stalls covered most of our living costs. After her previous trip, she'd brought back a camera and two lenses, and I was able to sell them for a thousand yuan, which covered the entire year's rent for our room.

Each time I tried to forget her, my mind filled with images of her face that were so lifelike, I felt I could touch them. I saw the teeth she revealed only when she smiled and the dimples that appeared when she laughed. I remembered trivial and mundane images, like her empty bottle of shower gel which I threw into the bin after she left, and the trace of her lipstick on a teacup. It had only taken me a few seconds to wash the lipstick off, but I couldn't wash the image from my mind.

A few fragments of speech were still trapped in my temporal lobes: 'You must be tired. Do you want me to come over? . . . A Hong Kong fortune teller said that we were husband and wife in a previous life . . . If we're going to break up, we might as well get it over and done with . . .'

I continued to go to classes, eat, get drunk and sleep. But inside, I was dead, and everything around me was dead. I locked my doors, including the one that opened onto the balcony. I didn't want any of the love that still remained in the room to slip away.

A few days later, Mou Sen and Wang Fei rescued me from the room and carried me to hospital. I was put in a ward that had four – no three – cupboards, three beds, and three stools. The words GUANGZHOU UNIVERSITY HOSPITAL were painted on the bedsteads. The form clipped to the end of my bed read: 'Registration number: 0046, Department of Internal Medicine, South Block. Diagnosis: physical weakness and inflamed liver.'

Cortisol seeps into your cells, filling them with sadness and causing your memories of her to ferment.

Mou Sen told me that being dumped by a girl is like missing a train: there's always another one to jump onto. Sun Chunlin told me that I'd become too caught up in my emotions, and that I should strive to regain a sense of balance. Wu Bin said that I should smuggle myself across the border and go and look for A-Mei in Hong Kong. Wang Fei just told me to buck up and get over it.

In hospital, the days passed very slowly. The cement floors were washed with disinfectant every morning, and the strong smell would stay in the air all day. My bed's wooden legs were swollen with water, like the organs inside my body. A rag that had fallen from the mop lay coiled snakelike beside one of the legs. I stared at it for hours.

'Number 46! How come you haven't taken your morning pills?' the nurse cried.

'I feel nauseous,' I sighed.

When I was admitted to hospital, I had a temperature of forty degrees. I'd been drinking and smoking too much, and not getting enough sleep. My body was exhausted. I knew I was going under, and I wanted to sink right to the bottom. I was in no state to smuggle myself into Hong Kong.

I moved my gaze to the nurse's stomach. She was wearing a long red skirt. With her warm hands, she bound a length of cloth around my arm. 'Stick out your tongue. It's time for your medicine.' The nurse's breath stroked my face.

I glanced to the side and saw the ring left by a cup on my bedside table. The splashes of antiseptic lotion next to it matched the urine stains on my sheets. A fly that had lost a wing was crawling around the oily crumbs trapped in a crack in the wood.

The draught blowing in from the corridor smelt of soiled sanitary towels. I closed my eyes and remembered my mother telling me how she gave birth to me in a hospital corridor.

The corridor outside looked like the interior of a long cement pipe. Most of the light from the blue bulbs hanging from the ceiling was sucked away by the dark-green walls. There was a white spittoon on the maroon floor. The lacquer along the central strip of the floor had been worn away, exposing the grey cement underneath.

I lay in the damp bed, waiting for my body to recover. Five days went by. I tried not to think about A-Mei, but her voice kept coming back to me, repeating softly, 'If we're going to break up, we might as well get it over and done with.'

It was only when I developed hepatitis that her voice began to fade away, and my breathing was able to return to its normal rhythm.

There was a thin nurse who would flit by like a shadow. She stirred the air when she walked into the room. As the brightness of her dress changed in the moving light, I'd be reminded of the female scents I'd breathed in the past. I didn't have the strength to ask her not to walk so close to me.

In the end, it was my father's journal that saved me. When I remembered the misery and death he described, my suffering seemed trivial. During my last three days in hospital, I thought only of the angelic Liu Ping, and the monstrous men who'd carved her up and eaten her. And I murmured to myself, 'Dai Wei, you must stop wallowing in your emotions and do something with your life. Do something that will make this country a better place . . .'

Axons within the olfactory organ in the walls of your nasal cavity have sprouted new nerve endings, reconnecting to the surrounding nerve fibres. As you inhale the breeze, an electric signal darts up the new neural pathways to your brain.

My mother is talking to someone. 'Today is 4 February 1990,' she says. 'He's been in a coma for exactly eight months, officer. Even if he did wake up now, he'd be a cretin. He wouldn't be able to tell you anything.'

I must be back in the flat now. I presume my mother has put me on the iron bed. I have no recollection of being removed from the hospital. I wonder who carried me up the six flights of stairs.

'He's just pretending to be dead, the brat,' the officer says, tapping my face. 'He's afraid that we'll fling him in jail when he wakes up.'

The change of location seems to have had a beneficial effect on me. The noises around me sound clearer and my sense of smell has improved. I can smell the scent of tree-bark in the breeze blowing in through the window and the stale odours in the flat. These odours are the familiar smells of home: my father's ashes; the insoles, socks and gloves drying out on the radiator; all the things that have fallen behind the radiator, such as scraps of steamed bread, plastic caps of ballpoint pens, the bits of paper that once wrapped meat pies, fried chicken or pickled cabbage; my mother's clothes and skin, and the disinfectant she sprinkles over the floor.

'The bastards!' my mother says as soon as the police officer leaves the room. 'They turn their guns on innocent people, then brand whoever gets shot a criminal. What kind of morality is that?'

Images of the flat and its immediate surroundings fill my mind, pushing out thoughts of A-Mei, the Guangzhou hospital, and my vague recollection of the Beijing hospital I have just left.

I strain to catch distant noises. It sounds as though it's snowing. I imagine the cold, hard scene outside the window: the white ice on the ground streaked with yellow debris emitted from the tall chimney of the electricity generator. In the morning, before the ash has fallen from the roofs and the branches of the big locust tree in our compound, the ice is still slippery. Food hawkers from the suburbs fire up their woks in the street outside and sell fried flatbreads. Large green flies dart through the fragrant smoke rising from the charcoal embers. In the afternoon, the flies move to the crates of yogurt stacked on the street corner. Every day, the same two elderly men sit beside the crates, trying to catch some rays of sun. One of them neither talks nor smokes, but just stares blankly at the people passing by. Occasionally a van turns off the main road and drives down the street to collect rubbish or deliver soft drinks to the grocery shop, blocking the way of cyclists, who wait behind it in the freezing cold, ringing their bells impatiently . . .

If your brain produces a little more protein, the fluid that has been blocked will flow again, and you'll be able to return to the world.

'The police dragged him out of hospital last month. They'd found out he was involved in the student demonstrations, and didn't want news of his condition leaking out. He's been put under constant surveillance.

Two officers visit me every day to remind me to take him to the public security office as soon as he wakes up. Not even Tian Yi dares visit him any more.'

My mother is talking to Yanyan, an old friend of mine from Southern University.

'I'll get in touch with her . . .' Yanyan's voice takes me back to the autumn night in 1986, when she, Wang Fei and Mou Sen came round to this flat for a beer. They'd just arrived in Beijing. It's hard to believe that fours years have elapsed since then.

After my stint in the Guangzhou hospital, I managed to pull myself together and graduate from Southern University with distinction. Wang Fei and I came up to Beijing University to do PhDs in molecular biology. Mou Sen went to Beijing Normal University to do a PhD in Chinese literature. He'd found the courage to turn his back on science and follow his passion. Yanyan secured a job as a reporter for the *Workers' Daily*.

'Insects are always crawling into his ears and nose, so I had to buy these tweezers,' my mother says, touching my face. 'His arms are covered in red blotches. He looks like a sick fish . . .'

I remember setting up the amplifiers in the canteen one afternoon during our first term at Beijing University. Frustrated by the slow pace of political reform, the students had set up unofficial 'salons' to discuss the taboo subjects of freedom, human rights and democracy. Some fellow science graduates and I had formed a discussion group called the Pantheon Society, and had invited the renowned astrophysicist Fang Li to give a lecture on China's political future. He was an outspoken critic of the government. The students held him in high esteem. We nicknamed him China's Sakharov. The previous month, the Democracy Salon, a rival forum founded by some liberal arts students, had invited the respected investigative reporter Liu Binyan to give a speech. So our society felt we needed to invite someone of Fang Li's stature to gain the upper hand.

My first two months at Beijing University had gone well. I'd been assigned a tutor and begun preliminary discussions on my dissertation, 'Primitive Biology in *The Book of Mountains and Seas*'. In my free time, I pored over science journals in the library or helped organise the Pantheon Society's numerous open meetings.

I was looking forward to Fang Li's lecture, and had prepared some questions for him, such as, 'Why do the people of southern China have so little interest in politics, and has this political apathy been instrumental in their region's economic success?' But after setting up the amplifiers, I had to go and buy a winter supply of cabbages for my mother. I queued for two hours in the freezing cold, then hauled the twenty cabbages back to the flat and stacked them up on the landing outside our front door. By the time I made it back to the campus, Fang Li's lecture had almost finished. The canteen was packed. I stood outside an open window and caught the final words: 'If the government is serious about reform, it must grant us freedom of speech and freedom of the press. These are fundamental human rights. Although they are not everything, without them we have nothing!'

When the audience broke into applause, I tried to squeeze myself inside the door. I didn't want to be accused of shirking my duties.

'Give Fang Li a teaching post at Beijing University!' the students shouted over the applause. Wang Fei held up the banner he'd prepared beforehand and yelled, 'Give us freedom of expression!' Everyone stood up and echoed his cry. It suddenly felt very hot inside the canteen.

Shu Tong, the founder of our Pantheon Society, asked the students to shout after him, 'Up with Democracy, down with Tyranny!' then cleared his throat and said, 'Now, it's time for questions from the floor.' Shu Tong was a shrewd and canny physics graduate from Shanghai. He was plump and pale-skinned, with well-groomed hair parted on one side, and a faint moustache that hung below his nose like a fine-tooth comb. He liked to cultivate the appearance and demeanour of a top Party leader.

'Economic development isn't dependent on political reform,' Bai Ling said, rising to her feet. 'The success of the Shenzhen Economic Zone is proof of that. China needs to build up its economy. That's the priority now. It doesn't matter whether we call our system capitalist or socialist, as long as it raises people's living standards.' Bai Ling was a psychology major. I often spotted her at our open meetings. She was tiny. She'd cut her hair into a short bob, but it didn't make her look any taller.

'I haven't been to Shenzhen, but I've read a lot about it,' Fang Li answered, pushing his glasses further up his nose. 'Without a democratic political system in place, our economy will eventually flounder. The people's wealth will be eaten up by the corrupt institutions of this one-party state.'

'My name is Nuwa,' another girl called out. 'I'm an English literature major. Professor Fang, if we demand the right to elect our government and form opposition parties, won't that make us counter-revolutionaries – criminals conspiring to subvert the state?' She was a member of the university's dance troupe. I noticed that she was wearing pink lipstick today. She raised her eyebrows and added, 'Do you think you could give us a maxim and an aphorism?'

'The Chinese people don't want to be dictated to by the Communist

Party,' said Fang Li. They want to be able to elect their public servants and hold them to account. Beijing University has a great democratic tradition. On 4 May 1919, three thousand students from this university gathered in Tiananmen Square to protest against China's inability to stand up to the West. They argued that the only way to save the nation was to introduce democracy and science. The protest spawned the May Fourth Movement – the most intellectually vibrant period of Chinese history. Years of Communism crushed the May Fourth spirit, but I am confident that your generation will revive it, and bring China into a new age of enlightenment. For the first time in decades, students have been allowed to hold open discussions about China's future. You must take advantage of this new political climate, and put pressure on the government to speed up the pace of reform. Remember, democracy is not granted, but won . . . My maxim is: "Don't do to others what you don't want done to yourself". My aphorism comes from Confucius's *Analects*: "If I walk down the road with two other men, at least one of them will be my teacher."'

Then Old Fu asked a question. He was the general secretary of the Postgraduate Student Association. Although he was only five years older than us, he had a wise, statesman-like air to him, which was why we all called him Old Fu. 'I'm doing a PhD in physics, and have a very heavy workload,' he said. 'I'd like to get involved in politics and use my knowledge to help society in some way, but I don't have the time to attend all these discussions and seminars.'

'I'm a scientist too,' said Professor Fang. 'The future of our country is an issue that concerns every one of us, no matter which field of study we are pursuing.' At this, everyone broke into applause again.

Having been stuck by the door for half an hour, I finally managed to edge myself further into the canteen. I raised my hand to ask a question, but Shu Tong didn't spot me. What I wanted to ask was: 'Who exactly did the Communists liberate? After the so-called Liberation in 1949, the Party drove one of my grandfathers to commit suicide, forced my uncle to murder the other, and locked my father up in labour camps for twenty years. They claimed they liberated the peasants. But the only peasants I've ever seen have been so destitute they don't know where their next meal is coming from.'

It was another hour before the lecture finally came to a close. At the end of it, I felt more hopeful about China's future and our ability to bring about change.

We returned to our dorms in high spirits. I wrote a letter to Tang Guoxian, my loud, sporty friend from Southern University, and enclosed some of the Pantheon Society's political flyers. I told him that Mou

Sen found the atmosphere at Beijing Normal depressing, and spent most of his time hanging out in my dorm at Beijing University playing games of Mahjong that would last for two days at a time.

Tang Guoxian was still at Southern University. Wu Bin had taken up a research fellowship at the Wuhan College of Engineering. Sun Chunlin, who'd lent me *The Interpretation of Dreams*, had left academia and gone to make his fortune in the Shenzhen Special Economic Zone. Through his uncle's back-door connections, he'd managed to gain a managerial post in a road construction company there.

At the end of November, Sun Chunlin came up to Beijing on a business trip and took our Southern University gang out for an expensive meal. Mou Sen brought Yanyan, the *Workers' Daily* reporter, with him. He confided in me that she'd agreed to be his girlfriend.

You long to cast off your cocoon. Your mouth is a locked door without a key.

When the sun goes down, a sharp wind blasts through the winter night. It brushes over my skin, sucking the warmth from my clothes and blankets, and soon the room is freezing cold.

I imagine gazing at myself through the eyes of a bird. I see myself lying flat on the bed, my nose protruding pathetically from the centre of my face, and my mother sitting on the edge of the bed, with stiff hands and cold feet.

Then I fly out of the window, and from the rooftops I see the lamplight shining obliquely on a battered bicycle frame chained to the railings. I hear the refuse truck winch a metal bin up from the ground. As the chain twists around the cylinder, there's a bang, bang, bang like a burst of shots from a machine gun. When the bin reaches the open top of the truck and tilts down, scraps of rubbish fall onto the ground. The noises make the blood rush faster through the veins circling my rectum. The striated muscles of the external anal sphincter relax, allowing a stream of air cooler than my body temperature to slip inside me. Then there's a crash as the bin is flung against the inside wall of the truck, and the flapping of the metal lid as the empty bin is pulled up. The truck then drives away, leaving a stink of rotting refuse that lingers in the air for hours.

When I was a child, I once tipped over a huge rubbish bin, just for the fun of it, then bolted back home. Our flat wasn't far away, but it seemed as though I'd never reach it. A fear gripped the small of my back and spread through my entire body. In my dreams, I return to this moment again and again. I am running as fast as I can. Sometimes a huge rock pursues me from behind, but in front of me there's always our rectangular, red-brick apartment building, lying on the ground like a coffin.

As I listen to the sounds around me and the blood racing through my body like cars speeding down a motorway, I know that I'm unable to stop breathing and die, as my mother longs for me to do. I have no control over my life or death. I am a captive now, like a lungfish in a muddy bank, sleeping through the summer drought. But the lungfish's captivity is only seasonal. Before it sinks into its fake death, it knows it will come back to life when the rains return and fill the riverbed once more with water. Its death is a form of survival. It dies but doesn't rot.

But when I was alive, I made no preparations for death, whether real or fake. I was in my early twenties, studying for my PhD in molecular biology. My dorm was in Block 29. The window looked out onto the Triangle – a small yard lined with bulletin boards which was the liveliest spot on the Beijing University campus.

While thoughts and desires travel through your temporal lobes, you listen to the noises inside your body, trying to gauge where you are.

I remember the heavy snow that fell in late December 1986. It covered my dorm's windowsill.

I peered down. It was getting dark, but there was still a large crowd milling around in the Triangle. Earlier that month, student demonstrations had flared up in Anhui Province, then Shanghai, and today news had reached us that students of Beijing's elite Qinghua University had also taken to the streets, protesting at the government's slow pace of reform. A notice quickly went up in the Triangle urging Beijing University students to gather in Tiananmen Square on New Year's Eve to demand more freedom and democracy. But before anyone had time to read it, a security officer tore it down.

There was no one left in my dorm for Mou Sen to play Mahjong with, so he and I went to look for Wang Fei.

Wang Fei's dorm was next to mine. The radiator was on full blast. Through the thick tobacco smoke hanging in the air, I could smell his cheap cologne. He and the other guys in the dorm were debating whether to go to Tiananmen Square on New Year's Eve.

Ke Xi was perched on a table. 'Beijing University has always played a vanguard role in the past,' he was saying. 'But today more than three thousand Qinghua University students took to the streets. If we don't mobilise ourselves now, we'll be left behind!' Ke Xi was studying for a bachelor's degree in education. He was a truculent, smooth-cheeked eighteen-year-old. When he got worked up, his brow furrowed deeply and his eyes became as narrow as a hawk's.

'We must go to the Square,' Shu Tong said. 'The Party hardliners want to halt the reform process. Our demonstration will strengthen the reformers' position.'

'Don't waste your time helping those so-called "reformers", for God's sake,' Wang Fei spat. 'They're all members of the Communist Party. They're only pushing through the economic reforms to consolidate their power. They're not interested in democracy.' Wang Fei's Sichuan dialect had softened a little since our time at Southern University. But his eyesight had got much worse. His glasses were so thick now that you could barely see his eyes through them. Whatever the weather, he never took his blue windcheater off, even indoors. He was always coming up with wild plans which he never had the courage to follow through. When we were at Southern University, he often bragged he was going to return to Sichuan and instigate a peasant revolt, but none of us believed him, of course.

'What if they arrest us?' I said. 'It will get marked down on our records.'

'Don't be so pathetic!' Wang Fei sneered. 'If you're afraid of getting arrested then don't join the revolution!'

'Democracies aren't created through revolution,' said Old Fu in his calm and measured way. 'They have to be built up gradually. The important thing is that society continues to move forward. The reformers have already made great strides.'

Mou Sen sat back and huffed in disdain. 'We've had the chaotic decade of the Cultural Revolution, followed by this decade of muddled reform. The Communist Party creates huge disasters, and then spends years trying to extricate itself from them. We shouldn't be wasting our talents trying to save the Party. It's China that needs saving!'

My dorm mate Chen Di was there too. He spent most of his time in Wang Fei's dorm, only coming back to ours to sleep. 'The reform process has been like a boat without a rudder,' he said. 'It's smashed into so many rocks that none of us know where it's going.'

'If you do go to the Square, I doubt I'll be able to persuade anyone from Beijing Normal to join you,' said Mou Sen dejectedly. 'The place is run like a penal institution. The students are depressed and apathetic. The Ministry of Education has just named us a "model university". The shame of it!'

'If we're not careful, Beijing University will go the same way,' said Liu Gang, sucking on his cigarette. Liu Gang was a skilled organiser, admired by us all. He edited an unofficial student magazine called *Free Speech*.

'We must draw inspiration from our courageous predecessors. In the 1950s, a journalism student here called Lin Zhao openly criticised Mao's persecution of rightists. She herself was labelled a rightist and put in solitary confinement. She was beaten and tortured, but refused to repent. Eventually, she was executed on Mao's orders. We're grown men. We shouldn't be afraid of going to the Square. Our cowardice is shameful.'

'A Beijing University student was condemned as a rightist?' Ke Xi asked.

'Yes,' Mou Sen chipped in. 'I've read about her too. She was one of Beijing University's most gifted students. She edited a student literary magazine called *Red Mansions*.'

'Why don't we bring our Pantheon Society into the open?' Shu Tong said, turning to Old Fu. 'The university authorities know what we've been up to. We should ask for official recognition.'

'If we became an official organisation, we'd be infiltrated by spies from the Ministry of State Security,' Old Fu said. 'There are spies embedded in every department now.' He'd been at the university for four years already, so he understood it better than any of us.

'The government doesn't need to plant spies – the Student Union gives them regular reports on our activities,' Ke Xi said. 'There's no point trying to be furtive. Let's start organising the demonstration and choosing our slogans.'

'I want to know what our slogans will be before I decide whether to join the demonstration,' Old Fu said.

'Would you come if we shouted "Down with the Communist Party!"?' Wang Fei asked.

'No. But I would if we shouted "Down with corruption!"' Old Fu slumped back against the folded quilt on the end of his bed, like a wax figurine softening in the sun. He suffered from chronic liver disease, and was always taking herbal medicines for it.

'You're still stuck in the Democracy Wall Movement era, Old Fu!' Wang Fei said. 'Times have moved on. We must come up with a more radical agenda.'

I could see the two Chans rolling their eyes. We called them Big Chan and Little Chan because one was tall and one was short. Big Chan was a bit of a university heartthrob. He played the guitar. The wall next to his bunk was covered in photographs of pop stars. He hated dirt and mess, and was always washing his hands. He and his friend, Little Chan, who slept on the bunk below him, were inseparable. Little Chan spent a lot of time checking his hair in the mirror. Neither of them took much interest in politics.

'The Chinese don't care about freedom of expression,' said Mou Sen.

'They just want to make money. Their spirits are empty.' He smoothed back his long fringe as he spoke. He looked like a bohemian writer.

'And what's your spirit like?' I said mockingly. 'All you think about these days is Mahjong! What happened to that novel you were going to write?'

'You must have sold at least ten bottles of that 101 Hair Regrowth Lotion this week, Dai Wei,' Ke Xi said. 'So go and buy us some beer.'

'No, only three,' I lied. 'The science students don't seem to suffer from thinning hair. Do you want to try selling it to those bluestocking girls in the Education Department?' This little business of mine was doing quite well. I'd asked Sun Chunlin to send me the bottles from Shenzhen. He bought them wholesale for twenty yuan each, and I sold them at a five-yuan mark-up. The previous week I'd made a hundred yuan profit.

'The university authorities are going to set up a security office in the dorm area to keep a closer check on us,' Shu Tong said. 'We must show them that we won't be cowed.'

'We might get expelled if we go to the Square,' said Old Fu. 'Let's keep our protests within the campus, and call for more academic freedom and official recognition of our democracy salons.' Old Fu always looked away while he spoke, but as soon as he'd finished, he'd look back again and fix his beady eyes on you.

'What was the Democracy Wall Movement exactly?' I asked, thinking back to what Wang Fei had said.

'You're so ignorant!' Liu Gang piped up. 'It was that brief flowering of dissent from '78 to '79. Deng Xiaoping had clawed his way back to power after the end of the Cultural Revolution and was trying to oust the remaining Maoists in the Party. For a few months, he encouraged activists to post criticisms of Mao and the Gang of Four on a wall in the Xidan District. Wei Jingsheng was the leading light of the movement. You must have heard of him. He wrote a poster proclaiming that, without political reform, the other reforms Deng Xiaoping was introducing were meaningless. Deng realised that things had gone too far. Wei Jingsheng was arrested and sentenced to fifteen years in prison, and the wall was torn down.'

Cao Ming was standing at the door listening to our conversation. 'If we don't concentrate on our studies, how will we be able to serve the country?' he said sternly. He was the son of an army general. He had a short military haircut and a scar on his left cheek. He didn't mix much with the rest of us.

'Relax, will you?' Chen Di said. 'Our dissertations aren't due for another three years.'

'Liu Gang, the science students all look up to you,' Wang Fei said. 'You must galvanise everyone into action and make sure we don't lose face. The history students have prepared their placards and banners already.'

Big Chan and Little Chan walked back in. They'd just been to the washroom. 'You're not *still* planning to stage that demonstration are you?' Little Chan said, drying his wet hair with a towel. 'It's a stupid idea. If we want to change things, we should start by asking the university to stop locking the gates at 11 p.m. This isn't a prison, after all.'

'Yes, and allow us to get up and dance at rock concerts,' Big Chan said. 'I hate the way they make us stay in our seats.'

The sky outside was black now. All I could see was an occasional snowflake hitting the windowpane. The grubby plimsolls in the room smelt worse than the toilets. I snatched a lit cigarette from Mou Sen's hand and took a deep drag.

'If we march through the streets, the local residents will arrest us before the police have a chance to,' Cao Ming said. 'Their lives have just started to get better. They don't want us coming and messing everything up.'

'My mother would be the first to hand me over to the police,' I admitted.

'That's even more reason for us to go out onto the streets. If we don't inform people about what's wrong with society, nothing will ever change.' Wang Fei removed his glasses as he spoke and rubbed them with his handkerchief.

'This is China's most prestigious university,' said Shu Tong, lifting his chin in the air like an arrogant Party leader. 'We must take the lead and go out onto the streets.'

'I think that our Pantheon Society should recruit new members,' Chen Di said. 'We can bring in students from other departments, activists like Ke Xi for example.'

'I'm not joining you!' Ke Xi said indignantly. 'I'm setting up a society of my own for the education students.'

'You're going to lead the Women's Brigade, are you?' Wang Fei sniggered.

'Don't *you* talk about women, Wang Fei,' said Cao Ming, pulling off his socks and shoes and lying down on his bed. 'I'm sick of you inviting your girlfriend round. As soon as she turns up, you draw your bunk curtain and set to work. You're in so much of a hurry, you fling your half-smoked fag on the floor without bothering to stub it out. If you keep inviting her back like this, the security guards will come knocking on our door.'

'You're the one who keeps throwing your bloody stubs all over the place!'

Wang Fei and Cao Ming were always arguing about something. Wang Fei's current girlfriend was a zoology student. She'd met him while carrying out a survey. She asked a hundred students how many times a week they masturbated, and fell for Wang Fei after he revealed that his average was three times a day.

'We only smoke to mask the stench of your armpits, Wang Fei!' Ke Xi said. 'You smell like a fucking gorilla!' None of us could stand Wang Fei's body odour.

'No, you only smoke to hide your bad breath,' Wang Fei retorted, pointing to Ke Xi's tobacco-stained teeth.

'Hey, who's got the foot odour?' Mao Da said, walking through the door. 'Smells like someone's growing fungus in their socks! Mou Sen, I hope you've got a fat wallet. We're about to start a game of Mahjong. We're betting with food tokens tonight.' Mao Da was another guy from my dorm. He always liked to place small wagers on each round of Mahjong.

The dorm was packed now. Shu Tong had to shout to get himself heard. 'We've got many able activists in the Pantheon Society. We should split up into groups tomorrow and try to persuade students from every department to go to the Square. We can prepare banners with slogans calling for freedom of the press, but we'd better not start talking about an end to dictatorship.'

Mou Sen slapped his thigh and said, 'Great! I'll go back to Beijing Normal and rouse the workers there! I'll be like Chairman Mao whipping up that miners' strike in Anyuan.'

'Everyone who thinks we should go to the Square, raise your hand,' Liu Gang said.

Apart from the two Chans and Cao Ming, everyone put their hands in the air.

'Fine, that's decided then,' Shu Tong said, standing up. 'Liu Gang, I'll leave you to get in touch with the Qinghua University students . . .'

In the silence, you search for a noise, a tiny hum that might help connect you with the outside world.

Someone is unlocking a bicycle in the yard outside. The noise isn't coming from the footpath, but from beneath the tree to the right of our building's entrance. I hear the key turn, but not the prop stand being kicked up.

The bike I bought myself during my first term at Beijing University was stolen after just a month. It happened the day after the Qinghua students' demonstration. Students had covered the Triangle's bulletin boards with handwritten posters calling for more democracy. A large crowd had gathered to read them. I squeezed my way to the front, and while I was busy copying the text of a poster into my notebook, somebody nicked my bike. It was careless of me not to have locked it. After that, I had to travel by bus whenever I went home on a Sunday, changing three or four times. And I had a long walk at the end, because the bus stop nearest our compound had been removed to make way for a new building. The old blacksmith's shop behind the bus stop was torn down too, and replaced by a dumpling restaurant. Two large light bulbs above its doorway illuminated the trampled snow on the pavement and the metal washing-line suspended between two locust trees.

The blacksmith's doorway used to be crammed with battered sheets of metal, funnels and empty petrol cans. The cans were dark green, and had white foreign lettering on the front and a picture of a human skull on the side. In the summer, the old blacksmith and his apprentice would take their anvil and charcoal furnace onto the pavement, and right before our eyes transform a petrol can into a metal chimney. The blacksmith would cut through the metal of the can with his large scissors as easily as if it were a sheet of newspaper. At the end of each day, the apprentice would take all the tools and scrap inside the shop, leaving an empty patch of swept pavement behind. I'd search that patch for hours, but all I ever found were a few bits of melted lead and some rusty bolt heads. My friend Duoduo cut his foot on a scrap of metal there. It served him right for walking out onto the street in his slippers.

The new dumpling restaurant made the road look brighter and warmer. The old plastic goods factory across the road was still there, but was now also illuminated. During Spring Festival, red light bulbs were hung above its doorway to form the Chinese characters for Happy New Year, and a pink glow would fall on the snow-covered cabbages on the roof of the small shack next door.

When I moved back to Beijing, we replaced our charcoal stove with a hob that runs on gas canisters. We also bought an electric water heater which I fixed to the wall of the toilet. So whenever I came home and wanted a shower, all I had to do was slip a plank of wood over the hole of the squat toilet and attach a hose to the heater. After living in the south for four years, I'd got used to having a shower every day.

Our flat has two bedrooms: one a little larger than the other. When you walk through the front door there's a narrow passageway that serves as our sitting room. It's just large enough to hold a small sofa and a tiny fold-up table. The iron bed I'm lying on is too big to fit in the smaller bedroom, and takes up most of the space in this room. If my mother wasn't so sentimental about it, I would have taken it to the auction room years ago. My brother and I hated the bed because, as soon as you lie down on it, the metal springs start squeaking.

After we bought the gas hob, my mother dumped the old charcoal stove and smoke funnel on the landing outside the front door, next to an old aluminium pan, a stool with a broken leg and a pile of leftover charcoal briquettes.

When I came home, I usually chose to sleep in my brother's single bed. We'd made a room for him by covering over the balcony outside my bedroom. There was an electric socket near the headrest, so I could plug in my radio and listen to it while lying in bed. I preferred that to watching television.

In 1986, my brother went to study computing at the Sichuan University of Science and Technology. When he lived at home, I used to hate the way he hung around me all the time, but after he left, I felt something was missing. He was almost as tall as me by then, but a little thinner. He had my mother's wide nose, while I had a narrow, high-bridged one like my father's.

After Dai Ru left for Sichuan, I became the only person my mother could talk to. Every time I came home, we'd end up arguing. She was approaching her fifties, and probably going through the menopause. In the past, when she gave me a haircut, she used to keep quiet and let me read the newspaper, but now she'd use the opportunity to criticise and nag me.

I remember the row we had on New Year's Eve 1986. It was the night before our planned demonstration. In the kitchen, I muttered casually that Deng Xiaoping was trying to turn himself into a second Mao Zedong. My mother threw down the bean sprouts she was washing under the tap and said, 'Deng Xiaoping liberated the Chinese people from the tyranny of the Gang of Four, and has put the nation back on its feet. You should be grateful to him!'

I finished washing the hairtail fish, sat down on the sofa, dried my hands, and said, 'What do you mean, "liberated"? Who did he liberate? Did he liberate you or Dad? Tomorrow morning we're going to Tiananmen Square to demand some democracy for the Chinese people.'

I heard a metal spoon drop and my mother shout, 'Don't you dare take part in any demonstration! I'll send the police to arrest you! Have you forgotten that your father spent twenty years in reform-through-labour camps?'

This was exactly the reaction I'd expected. She still smelt of the tomatoes she'd cooked the day before. Every winter she'd buy a crate of cheap tomatoes and simmer them for hours to make a thick sauce. There was usually enough to fill five large jars.

'The government pays me a salary and has given us this flat. What more could I want? Do you know how many counter-revolutionaries they've had to execute in order to achieve the stable society we enjoy today? Do you really imagine that you and your little band of classmates are going to be able to turn this country upside down?'

'I don't understand. The Party drove your father to suicide and locked up your husband. Why do you feel you have to defend it? If the Communists hadn't taken over in 1949, you'd be a rich woman now, living in a big house.'

'Without the Communist Party there would be no New China. Without the leadership of Deng Xiaoping and Hu Yaobang, our family wouldn't be having the life we enjoy today.' She stepped back into the kitchen, wiping her wet hands on her trousers.

'My father was a professional violinist, but he was made to starve in labour camps for twenty years. You read his journal, didn't you? You remember that Director Liu, and his daughter Liu Ping, he used to talk about so much? When I was in Guangxi Province I found out they were both condemned as class enemies during the Cultural Revolution, and their bodies were eaten.'

'If anyone heard you speaking like that, they'd drag you to the execution ground,' my mother said in a hushed voice. 'Why can't you learn from your father's mistakes? The Party is encouraging people to get rich now. If you're clever, you can go down to Shenzhen and make your fortune. Lulu's bought herself a flat down there.'

'Shenzhen is a capitalist haven, but a cultural desert. The only thing people think about there is money.' I realised that my mother hadn't taken in what I'd told her about Director Liu and his daughter. The story was probably too horrible for her to contemplate. I hadn't mentioned it to anyone else, apart from Mou Sen and Wang Fei.

'You should start reading the *People's Daily* editorials every day. If you don't keep up with the latest developments, you'll get into trouble.' My mother raised her eyebrows and returned to the kitchen again. The vegetables in the wok were burning.

After supper, my mother let out a loud belch and said, 'Your great-uncle in America has sent another letter asking whether you still want to go there to study. His son, Kenneth, has agreed to be your sponsor. I think it would be best if you left the country as soon as possible.'

'My English still isn't good enough. I'll wait until I've finished my PhD.' I didn't check the expression on her face. I knew that it was she who really wanted to go to America. When my father was cremated, she placed her favourite foreign-landscape wall calendar inside his coffin. Since then she has built up a large collection of calendars featuring foreign landscapes or monuments. She buys four or five a year. In the living room, there are calendars of the Paris Opera House and Louvre Museum, and in the toilet there's a three-year-old one with scenes of the English countryside. She once told me that the reason she married my father was that he'd promised they would travel the world together and lay flowers on Marx's tomb. I know she still longs to go abroad and fulfil his wish to have his ashes buried in America.

Although my mother always gave me a good meal when I went home, I only went back about twice a month. As soon as I arrived, I wanted to leave. I much preferred the communal life on campus.

When my father didn't have much longer to live, he began reminiscing about his student days in America. I always took a few magazines to read when it was my turn to sit at his bedside. He liked talking about his white-haired violin teacher who owned three dogs. The teacher and his wife would often invite him over for lunch at the weekends. The first time my father went, he didn't realise that Western meals have several courses. When the soup was served, he assumed that this was the entire meal, so he filled himself up with five slices of bread from the breadbasket. Then, to his dismay, the main course arrived, and he had to eat his way through a huge plate of steak, potatoes and fried onions. Just when he thought the meal was over, a large slice of cake was placed before him, covered in a chocolate butter cream. On his way back to his lodgings, he had to stop and lie down on a bench. For the next three days, he couldn't eat a thing.

'They were so good to me,' he said. 'If you ever make it to America, you must promise to visit them. But perhaps they'll have passed away by then. Who knows? Anyway, this is the address. I know it off by heart.' Taking short gasps of breath, my father wrote the address down in my notebook. He hadn't lied to me. He really could write in English.

He told me about the time he gave his final graduation concert. It was freezing outside, and his fingers were so numb, he couldn't pick up his bow. But American universities have central heating, even in the toilets, so he was able to go to the men's lavatory and warm his hands on a radiator before his performance. He played the Brahms Violin Concerto that day, and was awarded the highest grade.

He told me he'd returned to China shortly after he graduated and was immediately accepted into the orchestra of the National Opera Company. Their playing style seemed stiff and spiritless, and after five years as their principal violinist, he felt that his musicianship had deteriorated. 'I played Beethoven's Violin Concerto with them countless times,' he said, gazing sadly at the window. 'Then one day, I heard on the radio an American recording of the concerto, and realised that for the past five years, I'd been playing it like an automaton. The day I returned to China, my spirit died.'

I leafed through the magazines while he talked, only looking up at him when he asked for a drink of water or told me he needed to go for a piss.

At the time, I still hated him, and longed to free myself from the stigma of being the son of a rightist. I'd spent my childhood like a bird without feathers, unable to flap its wings and left to scuttle about on the ground.

On that last day of 1986, I waited until my mother fell asleep before pulling out of my bag a piece of red cloth I'd bought, and the characters BEIJING UNIVERSITY SCIENCE DEPARTMENT that I'd cut out of paper. I was going to sew the characters onto the cloth to make a banner, but I was afraid that the noise might wake my mother, so I decided to take a needle and thread from her sewing box and make up the banner the next day.

I went to bed, but was too excited to sleep. So to pass the time, I thought about A-Mei. I remembered lifting her long skirt and seeing her soft toes, each capped with a smooth nail, clench for a moment, and then relax.

You watch your wound heal over and neural pathways reconnect, and wait for the rest of your body to recover.

'A woman-trafficking racket has been uncovered in Zhuang Village, Anhui Province. Five hundred residents of the village have been arrested for abducting young women and selling them as wives to peasants in neighbouring counties. So far, sixty-one have been sentenced . . .' My mother has turned the new radio on. She must have bought it especially for me. The sound is very clear. It probably has short wave, which means I could listen to Voice of America on it, if only she knew its frequency. If she keeps it on, I'll be able to keep track of the time and know what day it is.

An image of me setting off for the New Year's Day demonstration, with my red cloth and cut-out characters in my bag, passes through my occipital lobe. The neurons disconnect for a second, then reconnect and transmit the image to my temporal lobes.

At noon, I joined the crowd of students huddled below the steps of the Museum of Chinese History, and looked over at the vast Tiananmen Square spread before us. This enormous public space, the size of ninety football fields, was completely empty. The authorities had ordered it to be cordoned off to prevent our demonstration from going ahead. A few police vans were parked on the road separating us from the Square, ready to take troublemakers away. Police officers and undercover agents paced back and forth nearby, stamping their cold feet on the ground.

Behind them, in the centre of the Square, rose the granite obelisk of the Monument to the People's Heroes. When I was a kid, my class used to be taken to the Monument every year on Children's Day to lay wreaths to the revolutionary martyrs. Beyond the Monument was the Great Hall of the People, the home of the National People's Congress. The tawny concrete building sat on the eastern side of the Square like a huge shipping container. I looked north to the red walls of Tiananmen Gate, the entrance to the Forbidden City where China's emperors used to live. From a distance, the police vans parked beneath it looked like tiny beetles. In 1949, Mao stood on Tiananmen Gate and declared the founding of the People's Republic. His giant portrait now gazed down from it, and his embalmed corpse lay in a memorial hall to the south. The Square was Mao's mausoleum. I couldn't believe that we'd dared venture onto this sacred site to express criticism of the Party he created.

'I'd hoped we'd get a bigger crowd than this,' said Wang Fei, walking over to me. 'Did you bring the banner? I knew Mou Sen wouldn't have the balls to come!' He was wearing his usual thin blue windcheater. He looked as frozen as an ice lolly.

'I bought the cloth, and I've cut out the characters, but I haven't had time to sew them on yet,' I said, pulling the red cloth from my bag.

'Don't do it in front of the police. They'll confiscate it. It's mostly arts students here. Only about twenty science students have turned up. Chen Di took his binoculars out a minute ago and saw someone filming us from the Great Hall of the People. He panicked and ran back to the campus.' As Wang Fei spoke, the steam rising from his mouth condensed onto the lenses of his glasses.

'I should have filched those binoculars from him ages ago, and given him some eggs for them,' I said. 'Let's go and stand behind those trees. The police won't see us there.' I was wearing a down jacket. My chest was warm but my face was very cold.

As we walked over to the trees, I spotted Wang Fei's girlfriend, the zoology student. She and some other girls were standing snuggled up to each other for warmth, their arms tightly linked. They looked as though they'd been frozen together. Wang Fei said to me, 'I've made a horizontal banner. You'll be amazed when you see it.'

'I doubt there are even a thousand students here,' I said. 'Apparently over two thousand people turned up for the Qinghua University demonstration last week.'

'The numbers aren't important. All that matters is that the demo gets reported in the foreign press. Shu Tong said that he's contacted all the foreign correspondents and asked them to come.'

The organiser of the demonstration, an earnest sociology researcher called Hai Feng, walked up with a group of his classmates from the Social Science Department. 'We've made a flag, but we don't have a pole,' he said. Drops of condensed breath dotted the portion of his scarf that was closest to his mouth. I'd heard that the previous year, he and a few of his friends had taken dusters and shoe cream to Tiananmen Square and earned some pocket money by polishing the shoes of National People's Congress delegates before they entered the Great Hall of the People. It had made him the laughing stock of the campus.

'It's so annoying,' the tall law student Zhuzi said, joining our small group. 'I bought loads of poles with me and hid them in the underpass over there. But a plain-clothes policeman took them away. How many science students have turned up?' We called him 'Zhuzi', which means bamboo pole, because of his exceptional height. He was the star of the university's basketball team.

'About a hundred,' Wang Fei exaggerated, lighting a cigarette. 'But it looks like students from other universities have come as well.'

I sat down under a tree and quickly sewed the characters onto the red banner. Then I got up and surveyed the scene. 'Look at those two plain-clothes policemen standing behind the foreigner over there,' I said. 'They're about to snatch his camera. None of us has got a camera. Who will take the photos now?'

Uniformed and plain-clothes officers guarded the perimeter of the Square, pushing away any pedestrian or cyclist who tried to enter. Even the Chinese tourists from the provinces, dressed in their best clothes, were being pushed back as they attempted to get onto the Square to take New Year's Day photographs in front of Mao's portrait.

Shu Tong, Old Fu and Liu Gang came over.

'Three foreign journalists have arrived, so all is going to plan,' Shu Tong said authoritatively. 'If they don't manage to get photos, at least they can write articles. The BBC World Service reported that the Square has been cordoned off. Lots of students from other universities heard the news, and decided to come along.' Then he turned to a student from the Chinese Department and said, 'How come Yang Tao isn't here yet?'

Yang Tao was a co-founder of the Democracy Salon. Wang Fei told me that he was a talented strategist, and was always coming up with cunning plans.

'He got a telegram saying his father was critically ill, so he rushed back to Chongqing,' a student in a heavy army coat answered, stamping his cold feet.

'Damn!' Hai Feng said. 'He fell into their trap. He of all people! I got a similar telegram, but luckily I had the sense to make a long-distance call to my dad. It turned out he wasn't ill at all. The police sent the telegrams to all the ringleaders to trick us into leaving Beijing.'

'There's no sign of Ke Xi,' Shu Tong said, walking up the steps of the Museum of Chinese History to assess the size of our crowd. 'Probably chickened out at the last minute.'

'The arts students have definitely outnumbered us,' I said. 'Hey, look over there! The police are filming us from the van. We'd better get down from here.'

The untrampled snow on the empty Square was brilliantly white. A few police officers were now standing in the centre of it, next to a truck emblazoned with the words TRAFFIC SAFETY WEEK. They looked minuscule. The four loudspeakers on the truck's roof blared out the message: 'The municipal authorities are carrying out a large-scale traffic survey. No work unit or individual must hinder proceedings. All group activities in the Square are strictly forbidden . . .'

'If Yang Tao's been tricked into leaving Beijing, I doubt many members of his Democracy Salon have made it here,' Old Fu said.

We went to join the crowd of civilians that had gathered outside the police cordon. They were all wearing heavy winter coats. Some were casual passers-by, others had heard rumours about the demonstration and had come to witness the spectacle. A peasant in a padded Mao suit holding a bag of peanuts squeezed over to us and said, 'I've heard there's going to be a demonstration against corruption and official profiteering. I'd like to take part. In the countryside, our lives have been ruined by corrupt officials. I want to tell Beijing citizens about all the injustices we have to put up with.' I asked him where he was from. He said Shandong Province. I told that him that we were compatriots, as my father was from Shandong too. I advised him not to join the protest. Two workers in blue caps standing beside him said, 'You're here now, mate, so you might as well join in. If you speak out on behalf of the people, we'll support you. You can't just stand here and watch.'

The two workers asked me what university I was from, and who was coordinating the demonstration. They said they wanted to get involved. I told them I was from Beijing University.

'Give me a leaflet,' they said. 'I bet your bag's full of them. Who's in charge of your propaganda?'

'I don't have any leaflets, just this university banner,' I said. 'I think it's best if you watch from the sides. You can be witnesses to history. Some students will hand out leaflets once the demonstration gets going.'

Wang Fei came over and said, 'The university security officers have a list of all the activists in our department. I was followed by a plain-clothes guy all day yesterday.'

'Half the students here aren't from our university,' Old Fu said anxiously. 'I don't recognise any of them. What should we do?'

'Don't worry,' Zhuzi said confidently. 'I recognise them. They're from Beijing Normal and People's University. As far as I'm concerned, the more people we have the better. The law is powerless against a crowd. And it's good that the public want to join in. We're demonstrating on their behalf, after all. There's a group of holidaymakers over there waiting to take souvenir photos in the Square. I'm sure that as soon as we start chanting slogans, they'll rush over and take some shots of us.'

'Wang Fei, go and find out what slogans the other universities have come up with,' Shu Tong whispered.

Someone came over and said that the police had cordoned off the underpass that runs under Changan Avenue, connecting the Square to Tiananmen Gate. As we discussed what to do next, a crowd of arts students suddenly unfurled horizontal banners, breached the cordon and strode into the Square shouting, 'Down with dictatorship! We demand freedom of speech!'

We rushed over and followed behind them. While I was walking, I pulled out my red banner, but there were so many people around me, I couldn't display it properly, so I just held it up with one hand and shook it about a little. Wang Fei reached into his blue windcheater and pulled out a three-metre-long banner that read DOWN WITH DICTATORSHIP! LONG LIVE FREEDOM!

Before we'd gone very far, hundreds of policemen charged over and encircled us. Undaunted, we pushed our way through them and ran towards the Monument to the People's Heroes, yelling, 'Down with corruption! Long live freedom!' A horde of armed police then emerged from a bus and started beating students back with batons. Wang Fei dropped his banner and ran away in fright. The two workers who'd been standing next to me shouted, 'Hey, you've dropped your banner!' I scooped it up and kept walking. As I shouted something to Old Fu, a policeman struck me on the head with a baton. My skull seemed to explode and silver stars flashed before my eyes. There were so many people squeezed around me that I had no room to collapse. The peasant from Shandong flung his bag of peanuts at the policeman who'd struck me and yelled, 'Fucking bastard! How dare you hit a student?' Then he pounced on the officer, bringing both him and me to the ground. I crawled to my feet, but before I'd regained my balance, someone kicked me down again. Soon, everyone around me was being kicked to the ground or dragged off to the police vans, their arms twisted behind their backs. While my head was still throbbing, two officers grabbed me by the arms and dragged me to the Workers' Cultural Palace behind Tiananmen Gate.

In less than five minutes, our demonstration had been crushed.

Inside the Workers' Palace, the policemen pushed my head down and made me squat against the wall. There were seventy or eighty of us in there. The officers kicked and swore at anyone who wasn't squatting properly. A teenage boy who screamed, 'I didn't shout any slogans!' was punched to the ground. After that, he leaned back against the wall, rigid with terror, and didn't utter another word.

One of the older policemen yelled, 'Anyone who opposes the government is an enemy of the people, a counter-revolutionary! You'd better own up to your crimes. If you confess, we might be lenient. If you don't, we'll fling you in jail.'

I had a gash on my face, a bump on my head, and aching shoulders, but I wasn't seriously wounded.

I glanced around me and didn't spot anyone I knew, apart from Old Fu. The peasant from Shandong was squatting by the door. His padded Mao suit was ripped. He was so big that, even when squatting down, he was a head and shoulders taller than everyone else.

The charcoal burner in the middle of the hall was blazing. I was sweating in my down jacket.

A plain-clothes officer walked in and demanded to see our documents. All non-students were made to stand on the other side of the hall.

The Shandong peasant looked up and said, 'I came to Beijing to do a little business. I didn't intend to create any trouble. I'm supposed to be taking the train home tonight.'

'Don't act so innocent! Didn't you say you wanted to complain about the injustices you peasants suffer? That's why we arrested you. Keep your head down!'

It was only then that I recognised him as one of the two men in workers' clothes who'd told me I'd dropped my banner.

The non-students were dragged outside and shoved onto a bus. I could hear someone screaming, 'You've got the wrong person! I was just passing by!' and a woman shouting, 'Let me go home!' It sounded like she was trying force herself off the bus. I could hear her punching and kicking the metal sides.

The rest of us had to stay in the hall. In the evening they brought us some bread. I volunteered to hand it out. A young officer told me to step forward.

He looked about the same age as me. I presumed he was a new recruit. Having heard me speak in a proper Beijing accent, he said in a friendly tone, 'This isn't a very good way to be spending New Year's Day, is it?'

'You're right,' I said. 'I had no idea it would be so cold today. In weather like this, the best thing to do is go to Donglaishun restaurant and have a nice lamb hotpot.'

'If you lot hadn't caused all this trouble, I'd be at home now, enjoying a hotpot with my family.'

I wanted to speak to Old Fu. So after I handed out the bread, I went to squat down next to him. 'How come we're the only Beijing University students here?' I whispered. 'Do you think the others have been taken somewhere else?'

'I think those two girls over there are from our university.'

'Wang Fei ran away at the first sign of violence,' I said. 'He likes to play the great revolutionary, but it's all an empty show.'

'I wanted to run away too,' Old Fu said, staring blankly at the wall. 'It was my first instinct. But my legs wouldn't do what I told them. How come they can still charge you for "counter-revolutionary activities"? I thought the 1978 constitution reform got rid of that crime.'

'They won't execute us. The worst we'll get is a few months in prison.' This being my second arrest, I felt like an old hand.

Then the interrogation officers turned up.

Old Fu and I asked if we could go to the toilet. The young policeman escorted us outside, and the three of us pissed against the wall below Tiananmen Gate's eastern viewing stand. As the policeman unzipped his trousers, he said, 'I wanted to change things too when I was at the Politics and Law University, but I'm an officer now, so I've had to put all that behind me.'

My lips trembling with cold, I asked him if he thought we'd get released. 'There were so many of you,' he said. 'It's difficult to punish a crowd. The authorities suspect that more students might come to the Square tonight, to protest against the arrests. We've been ordered to work through the night. Let's just wait and see what happens.'

'Do you think they'll send us to prison?' Old Fu asked nervously. 'I wouldn't survive there. I've got hepatitis.'

'I don't know. But they won't let those civilians off. They're the chickens, you are the monkeys. The authorities will kill the chickens to frighten the monkeys.'

'We're not in Mao's era any longer, Old Fu,' I said, hunching my shoulders against the cold. 'At worst, you'll be assigned a post in the border regions after you get your PhD.'

Sure enough, later that night, students returned to the Square to protest against the arrests. I could hear them shout, 'Long live freedom! Release our fellow students!'

The slogans raised our spirits. Old Fu closed his eyes, let out a sigh of relief and said, 'I can hear lots of girls' voices out there. The police won't be able to handle this situation much longer.'

Dawn approached. The sounds of protest outside had dwindled. The fire in the charcoal burner had gone out and the hall was getting colder again. Most of the students in the hall had dozed off, the rest were talking quietly among themselves. Two policemen had crawled onto a large table in the middle and fallen asleep under their heavy coats.

Then it was my turn to be questioned. I'd been counting the number of students who'd been called in by the interrogation officers. I was the thirty-fourth.

Your blood races onwards. The pulmonary artery warms as it pulsates. As regularly as a ticking metronome, oxygen-rich blood spurts through the heart's aortic valve into the aorta.

My body carries me like a boat lost at sea . . . There is jade on the north side of the mountain, and animals that look like sheep but have no mouths. They live well without eating . . . As fresh blood flows through my motor cortex, scenes from the *The Book of Mountains and Seas* are replaced by images of Beijing University's smoke-filled dorms.

When Old Fu and I returned to the campus after our release from detention, we were greeted like heroes. We didn't have to pay for our food or drink for a week.

We two were the only science students who'd been forced to write self-criticisms. Zhuzi and some of his fellow law students were let off with a caution. But Hai Feng and ten social science students were detained in a suburban police station in Tongxian for three days. Shu Tong and Wang Fei regretted not being arrested. Chen Di was embarrassed by his cowardice. The night before the demonstration, he'd written WIPE OUT TYRANNY on his bamboo sleeping mat, but he'd been the first to flee the Square. Ke Xi claimed that he'd got stuck behind the police cordon outside the underpass exit.

Still fired with political zeal, we publicly burned copies of *Beijing Daily* featuring a biased report of our demonstration, and resolved to form an autonomous student union with its own independent magazine.

But a few days later, newspapers reported that Professor Fang Li, the dissident astrophysicist, had been expelled from the Party, together with the investigative journalist Liu Binyan and a poet called Wang Ruowang. Those three men were our spirituals leaders. They had dared to openly criticise the political system and call for change. Their courage had inspired us to take to the streets, but our protests had destroyed their careers.

Sensing a change in the political climate, the university authorities tightened discipline within the campus. Police vans were positioned around the Triangle. The posters on the bulletin boards were torn down. The university's Party Committee visited our dorm and warned that any student who dared create more trouble would be handed over to the police.

News then leaked out that the reformist General Secretary, Hu Yaobang, had been forced to resign from his post for sympathising with the students' demands. Deng Xiaoping, who was still the paramount leader, stated that the Party would take tough action against any future demonstrations and wouldn't be afraid of bloodshed. Overnight, our gang of activists turned from being heroes to pariahs. Students like Big Chan and Mao Da who'd opposed our demonstration, blamed us for Hu Yaobang's downfall.

A few days later, the *People's Literature* magazine published *Stick Out Your Tongue*, an avant-garde novella by a writer called Ma Jian. The Central Propaganda Department denounced it as nihilistic and decadent, and ordered all copies to be destroyed, then proceeded to launch a national campaign against bourgeois liberalism. The hardliners in the Party were fighting back. They wanted a more open economy, but not the demands for political and cultural freedoms that it inspired. The brief period of tolerance had come to an end. It felt as though China had been put back ten years.

What angered me most though was that, after our demonstration, the government let the students off, but persecuted innocent bystanders. The Shandong peasant I met in the Square was sentenced to ten years in prison.

We spent the rest of 1987 in a state of nervous unease. I promised my mother that if I scored over 500 in the TOEFL exam, I'd give up my PhD and go abroad to study. My arrest had lost my mother a pay rise, and any chance of being granted Party membership.

The failure of our protests created disillusionment and apathy. Shu

Tong said student politics were a waste of time, and that his plan now was to make some money, set up an independent university, and change China from within. Students went back to spending their spare time playing Mahjong, going dancing, or looking for part-time jobs. In the dorms, the girls talked about Italian shoes and Swiss watches, and the boys returned to discussing which of the female students were still virgins.

Your organs lie scattered inside your trunk like a disbanded army. Your body is a felled tree, decaying on the ground.

My mother is sorting through some objects on the end of my bed. The metal bedsprings creak and groan like a car engine that won't start. She sniffs the air and mutters, 'It stinks in here . . .'

I could never escape the stench of latrines at university. The only toilets in the block were right next to our dorm. There were just four squat toilets for the two hundred male students in the building. Day and night, people would traipse down the corridor to go and use them. I was always hearing the toilet doors being opened and slammed shut.

At Southern University, I used to sleep quite well. The nights there were silent. But at Beijing University, students would stay up late into the night listening to the radio or cassette tapes. My sleep was regularly interrupted by a muted babble of songs and news reports: '*When you come back to my small home town, how happy I will be* . . . The new General Secretary Zhao Ziyang has submitted the plan for examination and approval . . . The acclaimed director, Zhang Yimou, lifted into the air the shining Golden Bear awarded for his film *Red Sorghum* . . . *All I want is a home of my own. Doesn't have to be a palace* . . . China's first test-tube baby was successfully delivered at Beijing Medical University today . . .'

A peasant from Sichuan lived in our corridor. We called him 'the drifter'. He'd left his poverty-stricken village in the mountains and come to the capital, hoping to find work. One of the students in our block had taken pity on him at the train station and brought him back to the university. He sat in the corridor all day, drinking and swearing, and generally making a lot of noise. The student who'd befriended him had long since graduated, but those of us who remained felt obliged to continue giving him refuge.

At night the library and classrooms were locked up. The only place I could do some English revision in peace was beneath the lamp in the yard outside. I thought back longingly to my days at Southern University when I was able to share a private room with A-Mei.

'Not even that girlfriend of yours can stand the smell of you,' my mother grumbles. 'It's been months since she last visited.'

I have no memory of Tian Yi ever visiting me. Does that mean that there have been times when I've slipped out of consciousness?

The tree splays out its branches, letting the wind blow through. Slowly your skin begins to remember.

I met Tian Yi in September 1988. Having probably left the campus at the same time as each other that morning, we happened to board the same bus. It was packed. The passengers were, as usual, avoiding all eye contact by staring at the ceiling or the floor.

At the second stop, a few passengers got off. A space opened in front of me and I became aware of her presence.

Furtively, I squeezed myself over to where she was standing, staring blankly, as if lost in reverie.

Warm bodies pressed against me. Usually, when passengers are so cramped together that they can smell each other's sweat, hair and breath, they instinctively turn away from one another. But I turned towards her and, through a gap between two heads, stared at her profile.

She was looking out of the window, so I was free to gaze at her as long as I wished. But she sensed she was being watched. She turned her head to seek out her observer's gaze, and her face was revealed to me. She glanced at me for a second, as though by accident. She was standing so close that, before she turned her head away again, I could see the flakes of chapped skin flattened under her lipstick.

When the passengers standing between us stepped off the bus, I moved towards an empty seat beside her. I pretended to hesitate about whether to sit down. As I'd hoped, she glanced at the seat.

'Please take it,' I said, lowering my eyes.

'No thanks,' she said, turning away.

'Why not?'

She stared at my university badge and said, 'So you're a biology student?'

As I started babbling about how silly it was not to take an empty seat, more passengers squeezed onto the bus and suddenly I was pressed right against her. A man put his leg between us and wriggled into the empty seat.

'All right then,' she said, 'I'll tell you the truth. I didn't want to crease my skirt. Are you happy now?' Then she sank once more into a daze.

The metal badge pinned to her shirt juddered as the bus trundled along. All the other passengers seemed to merge into one. Whether they were tall, short, fat or thin, they all shook in unison, back and forth, from side to side, mirroring each other's movements as they tried to maintain their balance. As we shook, I watched her delicately shaped ear moving towards me, then away from me. It looked like a foetus embedded in a womb of black hair. The soft outer rim and inner folds curved elegantly around the dark hole in the centre.

After I had stared into the hole for some time, it began to resemble an open mouth.

She'd tied her hair back with an elastic band to reveal the nape of her neck. The loose strands that had escaped the band fluttered in the breeze. A-Mei often wore her hair like that.

She was standing perfectly still now. My heart was beating fast.

The bus had stopped outside a department store, and many passengers got off. I took a deep breath of the air around her and watched the alighted passengers disperse into the bright sunlight.

When the bus drove off again, I gripped the handrail, stepped back and looked at her more closely. I knew that her glazed expression was deliberate. It served as a camouflage, allowing her to disappear into her surroundings.

While she stared blankly out of the window, I focused on her nose, which seemed more beautiful the longer I stared at it. I observed the graceful downward slope, the curved tip, the perfect arch of the nostril. I noticed the blackheads on the wing of the nose, and the crack in her foundation at the bridge which deepened whenever her eyebrows moved. Sometimes her nostrils flared a little, which was perhaps a reflex reaction to a momentary sensation of being watched. When women sense an unwanted male gaze fall on them, their faces take on a more masculine appearance.

Before we reached the next stop, the bus jolted to a halt. I clutched the handle above me to stop myself from falling. Now that the bus was a little emptier, I could see the wooden slats of the floor, as well as her feet and her white strappy sandals. Her legs were bare, and she was wearing a white cotton skirt just like the one A-Mei used to have.

I looked away and stared at the hot, dusty street outside the window. From the corner of my eye, I felt her gaze moving towards me. It was intense, luminous, alive. I continued to stare out at the shifting buildings and trees, and the colourful crowds wavering in the dappled sunlight.

I silently counted how many stops were left: one, two, three, four . . . Reflected on the window I saw the two black buttons of her white shirt. When the bus shook, her breasts moved but her stomach remained still.

Her hand became translucent in the sunlight. It was clutching the handrail, right next to mine.

Very soon this unknown girl would brush past me, and I'd never see her again. In my sadness and frustration, I could tell that for the rest of my life her silent image would move through my mind, like the memories of A-Mei's toes and transparent eyes.

It was a hot day. I watched the humid heat spill through the hazy streets.

A fidgety child suddenly stuck his hand-held electric fan out of the window and switched it on. The green-and-red paper blades shimmered irritatingly as they whizzed in the sunlight. 'Do you want to lose your hand?' shouted the father. The boy turned and knocked into her. 'I'm sorry,' the father said. 'My son's got no manners.'

'Don't worry,' she said.

I looked away, trying to erase the image of her.

We both got off the bus at Xidan market. As she stepped onto the pavement, she glanced back at me. I looked up and met her gaze.

She said she was going to buy some notebooks, and that three of her psychology classmates were celebrating their birthdays on the 20th. The party was going to start at eight. 'If you want, you can come along,' she said. Then she turned round noiselessly and walked away.

I watched her hips, wrapped in the cotton skirt, swing from side to side then disappear through a dark door.

I made up my mind to go to that party. I had to see her again.

You listen to your leaping thoughts, your rumbling organs, those shining notes of music.

When I opened the door of the classroom in the Psychology block, I was hit by loud music blasting from a cassette player. It was too dark to see any of the faces clearly. All I could make out were patches of pale clothes and gold plastic flitting through the candlelight. Students in the middle of the room were swaying to the music. A few girls holding candles were chatting in the corners. Their illuminated faces looked beautiful. Two girls in long dresses danced with their arms wrapped tightly around each other.

I glanced around the room. I could sense that someone's eyes had focused on me, but I hadn't spotted them yet. I wondered if I'd ever find her. In the dark, everyone looked the same. The dissolving of differences made people feel safe, and gave them the courage to move closer to one another.

My eyes slowly grew accustomed to the dark. Beginning to feel a little awkward, I tried to boost my morale, telling myself, 'She'll know that I'll be looking for her, she invited me, she wanted me to come,' while all the time trying to remember what she looked like.

The students in the middle of the room were now hopping and whirling to a Taiwanese pop song. Their shaking limbs, mannered gestures and youthful energy seemed both exciting and tedious. There was a smell of dust in the air.

A girl glanced up. Our eyes met for a second and I knew at once that it was her. She was twirling around, always slightly behind the beat, her fingers splayed out in front of her or resting on her hips. Her hair bounced around her shoulders. There was perspiration on her forehead.

My heart beat in time with the music. I walked back towards the door and stood in the corner.

Most of the tables and chairs had been stacked neatly against the walls. On the one table that had been left out was a birthday cake made of cardboard, surrounded by candles and a small paper model of a log cabin which had a torch inside that emitted a dull yellow light. Four pairs of women's eyes, cut out from a wall calendar, had been glued to the ceiling. They looked like the organs of a dissected animal. I put my hand in my pocket and stroked the three glass pandas that I'd brought as birthday presents.

With her vacant eyes and half-opened mouth, her face seemed lifeless. I wondered whether she'd recognised me. I almost hoped she hadn't. But when the music changed, she squeezed past two or three people and walked towards me.

She said something. But her mind was still distracted, so the first sentence was merely a garbled echo at the back of her throat.

I guessed what she'd said was: So, you've come, then.

We stepped closer to each other. Her expression becoming more animated, she asked, 'Are you here to see me?'

'I just wanted to drop by. So, is it your birthday today?'

'No. What's your name?'

'Jin Mu,' I said, breaking into a smile. 'What's yours?'

She cupped her hand to her ear. 'Jin Mu? Meaning "gold wood"? Sounds like the name of a feng shui expert. Who are you trying to fool?' She laughed. And I laughed too. It felt good. We were having a conversation.

'It's my pen name. My real name is Dai Wei. My parents are originally from Shandong.' I put out my hand. She shook it, pulled her hand away briefly to slip into her pocket a small object she was clutching, then shook it again.

'What's your name?' I asked.

'Tian Yi.'

'Meaning "heaven-one", as in "first under heaven"?'

'No.'

'As in "heaven and man unite as one", then?'

'No! It's not "heaven-one", it's "heaven-cloth". You know – "cloth of heaven", as in "seamless like the cloth of heaven".' She was a head shorter than me, and had to raise her eyebrows when she looked up into my eyes.

'That's very original.'

'Not as original as your "gold wood" pen name! So, Mr PhD Student, do you like to dance?'

'I prefer to watch. It's less exhausting.'

'Do you regard people as books that you can look at as you please?'

'I only came here to look at you,' I blurted out without thinking. The music had stopped suddenly, so my voice sounded very loud.

Searching for something to say, she asked, 'Do you like to read? What is your favourite book?'

'*The Book of Mountains and Seas*,' I said quietly.

'Really? That's mine, too. Recite a few lines for me.'

I took a breath. '"There's a tree whose sap looks like lacquer and tastes like syrup. If you eat it, it will banish hunger from your stomach and worries from your mind. Its name is . . ."'

'Comrade Dai Wei, that's the modern translation, not the original classical Chinese text. Do you find that your scientific knowledge gives you a deeper insight into the book?'

'As it happens, I'm planning to go on a journey, following the routes described in the book, studying everything I find on the way: the flora, fauna, geographical features, astronomical events. I love maps. When I was child I dreamed that when I grew up, I'd wander around the country like that Ming Dynasty geographer, Xu Xiake.'

'You should be studying geography then, not science. There's a professor in the History Department who's an expert on *The Book of Mountains and Seas*.'

'I don't want to get bogged down in dry, academic study. It's the travel that interests me most . . . You're a psychology student. Where does your interest in classical literature come from?'

'I like stories about ghosts and mythical animals. Like the snake with nine heads, the ox with one foot, and the bird that tries to fill the sea with sticks and stones. I read *The Book of Mountains and Seas* for its literary qualities. After I graduate, I want to do a Master's in Chinese literature.'

'We could go travelling together in the holidays. I have an ancient map of China that we could use to plan our route.'

She looked at me for a moment, her chest rising and falling. Then she glanced at the group standing beside her and said, 'These are my dorm mates. Let me introduce you.'

She grabbed hold of the girl standing next to her. It was the tiny girl with the cropped hair who'd come to Professor Fang Li's lecture at the Pantheon Society.

'I already know Bai Ling,' I said. 'We've been at some of the same talks.'

'Yes,' Bai Ling smiled. 'You science students organised lots of interesting lectures last year.'

'And this is Mimi.' Mimi stepped forward and waved her hand at me. 'I don't think you know her, do you?' When Tian Yi laughed she looked like a different person. 'You don't have a fear of crowds, do you, Dai Wei? Come on, let's dance!' She walked off into the middle of the room, and as her hair swirled round I stepped forward and followed behind her.

You pass through a web of capillaries and enter the ascending colon. A tangle of nerve fibres blocks your path back to the thalamus.

The rain had just stopped. Tian Yi and I were standing in the middle of the campus, watching the sun sinking into Weiming Lake. She turned to me and said, 'A friend borrowed my electric hob. I'll have to go and fetch it.'

'I'll get some pickles and popcorn,' I said.

It was 27 November. My twenty-second birthday. Tian Yi had taken me to see a foreign film at a cinema near her parents' flat. She told me that she seldom went home. She didn't like her elder sister or her brother-in-law. They'd taken over the second bedroom of the flat, so whenever Tian Yi stayed the night, she had to sleep on a camp bed in the narrow corridor.

We met up half an hour later in her dorm. I gave her a quick haircut, then I plugged her two-ring electric hob into a socket, filled an aluminium lunch box with water and put it on to boil. We were going to cook some prawns and birthday noodles. When the water began to bubble, I dropped the prawns in and the room instantly smelt of the sea.

She washed her hair in a basin of warm water. I scooped some water into an enamel teacup and rinsed the soap from her right ear. When I saw the curved hairline behind it, each strand of hair growing neatly from her scalp, I couldn't help leaning down and kissing her earlobe.

She twisted round and looked up at me. Her face was bright red, but her eyes were as blank as those of a dead sheep.

I went to the sink at the end of the corridor to empty the dirty water, and noticed some strands of her hair caught between my fingers. 'Look how long these are,' I said, returning to her dorm and holding the strands up to the light. She was squeezing the water from her hair. I couldn't tell what she was thinking. I stared at her broad, somewhat masculine forehead, her motionless mouth, the delicate curve of her narrow nostrils. She was wearing a sleeveless black T-shirt. When I saw her bare arms, I felt the blood rush faster through my veins.

'Keep your hands off me! There are people about.'

'I didn't mean to,' I said. 'It's just that, I mean . . . I've never seen you wear black before.'

'I always wear black.'

'The first time I saw you, you were wearing a white skirt.'

'You must have been dreaming of your little white angel. I'm a black witch, didn't you know?'

Before I'd got round to putting the noodles in, the water boiled over onto the metal ring, the fuse snapped, and suddenly all the lights on our floor went out. We were plunged into darkness. Girls in the other dorms walked out into the corridor shouting, 'Which bloody idiot did that? Come on! Own up!' Some banged bed frames, tables, chairs; others slowly clapped their hands or stamped their feet. I couldn't tell exactly where the noises were coming from. In the dark, it's difficult to gauge distances between yourself and others. The shouting and banging resonated through the block.

I tried to remove the aluminium box from the hob, but it was too hot to pick up.

'Quick, hide it under my bed,' Tian Yi said, yelping as the tips of her fingers touched the box.

'Let's find a lighter first, so we can see what we're doing,' I said. She tutted impatiently, grabbed the lunch box and put it on the ground. Then she kicked it under the bed and there was a horrible metallic noise as it grated across the concrete floor.

People outside were shining torches onto the building. By now, Tian Yi had managed to hide both the lunch box and the hob under her bed. 'Get a match,' she whispered to me, blowing on her scorched fingers. I groped for some matches on the table behind and knocked over a lamp.

'I can't find any,' I said, afraid to continue my search.

She pressed a hand on my shoulder and got up. I heard a fumbling noise, the flick of a match, then saw a flame of light.

She was standing in front of me. She lit a candle, pushed it into the mouth of an empty bottle then sat back down on the edge of her bed.

I touched her hand, but she pulled it away saying, 'My fingers are burnt!'

'I'll put some soy sauce on them for you.'

'Does that work?'

A girl in the corridor was singing, '*Don't be sad, it's not that bad* . . .'

Another girl walked by with a radio that crackled and hissed.

'Don't worry. The fuses go out all the time here. And I'm not the only one who has an electric hob. Four girls in the dorm next door have one.' She dangled her index finger above the candle flame and said, 'Look, a souvenir of your birthday!' The big red blister on the tip of the finger didn't seem real.

I grabbed her other hand, rubbed her warm palm and found a strand of bamboo she must have torn from her sleeping mat. Tian Yi was always clutching something in her fist. Maybe it made her feel more secure.

I squeezed each finger, each knuckle, and pressed the pressure points on her palm. She sighed anxiously. When I pulled her close to me and put my hand on her breast, she trembled and sighed again. I reached into her skirt and touched her soft stomach. She pushed my hand up towards her hip. The skin felt colder there. I ran my hand down over the mounds of her buttocks, then slowly slipped my fingers into the cleft in between. As I moved my fingers in deeper, I felt the warm dampness that I'd been longing to touch . . .

After I came, my fingers were still in the same place, but motionless. 'Take your hand away,' she whispered.

'I love you, Tian Yi,' I murmured into her hair.

For a while she didn't say anything. She just shuddered and intermittently sighed. Then her body stiffened. At last, she pulled her legs away from mine, and muttered, 'Why does everything always slip out of my control?'

I thought for a moment, and said, 'When it comes to our biochemistry, we can't control anything. All we can do is stand by and watch.'

'I feel like I've fallen into a black hole.' She turned her face towards the wall. I wrapped my arm around her and we lay in silence for a long time.

We were the only people in the room. There was an unspoken agreement in the dorms that if someone was visited by a member of the opposite sex, everyone else would leave within ten minutes, saying that they needed to borrow a book from the library or collect a parcel from the post office.

Suddenly, we both caught a whiff of burnt rubber. Tian Yi jumped off the bed, crouched down and pulled out her sandals. They'd been blackened by the heat of the electric hob.

'Don't worry,' I said. 'I'll buy you a new pair.'

'What do you know about shoes? These were made in Italy.'

'Well, we'll go to Shenzhen next holiday, and I'll get you the best pair of imported shoes I can find.'

'With clothes, it doesn't matter if you wear imported ones or Chinese knock-offs – they feel pretty much the same against the skin. But shoes are different. You can never lie to your feet.' She took her sandals over to the candle and inspected them more closely.

Her face looked very bright in the candlelight.

'Your birthday's been a bit of a disaster, hasn't it?' she said. 'How did you spend it last year?'

'At home with the Southern University crowd – Wang Fei, Mou Sen, Yanyan . . . and my mother, of course.'

'Did you get any nice presents?' she asked softly.

'They clubbed together and bought me a front basket for my bicycle. But the bike was stolen a few weeks later, so I didn't get much chance to use it.'

'And does today feel any different from last year?'

'Of course it does – I'm with you.' I felt uncomfortable. I wanted to tuck some tissues into my pants to mop up the sperm. I presumed that she hadn't realised I'd ejaculated.

'We're like trees that grow new branches every year,' she said, stroking the nape of my neck. 'Each time a birthday comes round, we need to prune them back if we want to grow any taller.'

'Did you know that no two branches in the world are the same shape? Each one is unique.' I'd probably picked that up from Mou Sen.

'If we stay together, you'll lean against me,' she said, 'and as you grow, your trunk will bend. Then, one day, when there's a storm, you'll break in half and die.' She rubbed her shoulder against my arm.

'But I need you,' I said, inhaling her breath. 'You're my sunlight and soil.'

'You're too old-fashioned,' she said. I looked at her blank face, took a drag from my cigarette and felt my spirits begin to sink again. 'We're very different people, you and I,' she continued, turning to me. 'You can see from our faces that we could never be man and wife. Your face is square, mine is round. Your eyelids have creases, mine are smooth . . . Sorry, I shouldn't speak like this. It's your birthday.' She reached out to touch the flame of the candle. 'You're so normal. But I'm different. Everything always looks grey to me.'

I opened the window to get rid of the smell of burnt rubber. The air blowing in from the campus smelt of dry leaves.

Tian Yi looked out of the window and said softly, 'The leaves will soon fall from the trees, then they'll lie on the ground and become yellow and brittle.'

She was convinced we weren't right for each other.

I didn't tell her that according to a book I'd read on the traditional Chinese art of face-reading, we were in fact a good match. Taoist monks claimed that facial dissimilarities indicate emotional compatibility, because a good relationship depends on the harmonious union of yin and yang. I had reason to believe this theory, because A-Mei and I looked quite similar but our relationship lasted only a year.

The lights suddenly came back on. All the girls in the dorm block screamed, just as they'd done when the lights had gone out, but this time Tian Yi and I screamed too.

It was nice to be able to see things properly again. I stared at the shadow under Tian Yi's chin.

'Tell me what your wish is for this year,' she said, moving onto the bottom bed of the opposite bunk.

'That you'll come travelling with me,' I answered.

'All right. I agree.' Her voice sounded strange. It was a sheep-like bleat.

'We could start our journey at the source of Red River,' I said enthusiastically, 'then travel to all those other places mentioned in *The Book of Mountains and Seas*: the River of Golden Sands, Yalong River, Mount Measureless and the Mountain of the Sorrowful Dungeon. I saw some pictures of the area in a photography magazine. It's full of beautiful green mountains with terraced fields and small minority villages. It looked like an earthly paradise.'

'You must be thinking of the "Land Within the Seas" chapter, where it goes: "In the south-west, near the Black River, is a land where the hundred grains grow of their own accord, germinating and flourishing both winter and summer."'

'Yes. It's in Yunnan Province. And I have another wish, too: I want to set up my own laboratory.'

'To conduct that genetic research you were talking about, growing human ear cells, or was it eye cells?'

'Placenta cells. No, what I want to study is ways of postponing death for as long as possible.'

'Without death we'd lose all fear and ambition.'

'Russian scientists have successfully cloned a mouse from an embryonic stem cell. It won't be long before we'll see the first human clone.

Before you die, you'll be able to decide whether you want to come back to life again in another body.'

'So my soul will live on. Maybe I'll marry your grandson next time round.'

'You have a rich imagination.' I always found it an effort discussing scientific matters with non-scientists.

'If you're such a great scientist, try and find a way to cook those noodles.'

'Let's go to a restaurant,' I said, crushing out my cigarette. 'There's one opposite the campus gates that sells wonton soup.'

'You still haven't asked me what I've bought you for your birthday, you fool,' she said, handing me a book.

It was an illustrated edition of *The Book of Mountains and Seas*. 'How wonderful!' I exclaimed. Now I had pictures of the devious rabbit-faced man whose meat is succulent and sweet; the metal-eating creature that resembles a water buffalo, whose steely excrement can serve as weapons; the 'red-jade' grass which can put you to sleep for three hundred years. 'I love you, Tian Yi,' I said, then I took her in my arms and kissed her, licking her tongue and her teeth.

She clasped her hands tightly around my back and said, 'Sorry I spoke to you like that. I'm frightened, that's all. In psychology it's called cherophobia – fear of happiness. I'm afraid of getting hurt. Promise me you'll never leave me.'

'I promise,' I said wearily. Suddenly, the memory of Tian Yi's appearance the first day I saw her vanished from my mind.

The bioelectric current flowing through your body spurts and fizzles, like a faltering beam passing through the cathode-ray tubes of an old television.

I can see dead fish before me, and they keep changing size. Perhaps this is a sign of approaching death. The fish have black eyes and white scales, and are lying on a bed of ice cubes. A sweet, sour smell wafts from the fruit stall behind. Everything glimmers and glints: the half-eggshells on the floor, the shiny jars of salt, the crunched-up balls of paper under the stallholder's stool, the golden pagodas printed on the plastic shopping bags of passers-by. I can't work out the significance of this confused scene . . . Another three hundred li east lie the Di Mountains. Although many rivers and streams run through their valleys, their slopes are barren. A fish that resembles an ox lives on the mountains. It hatches in summer and dies in winter . . . I remember Tian Yi reading that passage to me. Her voice was lower and huskier than A-Mei's.

I see her walking towards me. I enter the scene, relieved to have a memory to latch onto.

By the time she arrived at Weiming Lake, the late-afternoon sky behind her was like a sheet of steel. Everything felt cold – the earth, the grass, the insects flying through the air. The fishy smell from the lake was less pungent than it had been at noon. Students were sitting in couples on the small patch of grass by the shore. They were all in the early stages of courtship, so their gestures looked stilted.

I'd come from a biology tutorial and was standing on the grassy slope staring at the bright sky and the path that stretched in front of me. I'd been watching people's legs as they walked towards me. The foot would move first, then the knee would bend and the whole leg would swing forward. These were living people, undissected bodies wrapped in clothes. Whenever I saw a moving leg, my mind turned to the human muscles that floated in the specimen jars in the science lab. As the light began to fade, the legs started moving more slowly.

A guy in beige trousers walked slowest of all. He was a foreign languages student who'd recently won the university's singing contest. He and two friends were heading for the dorm blocks, moving the muscles and bones their parents had given them. Students from the countryside, still not accustomed to wearing heavy shoes, took steps that were too large. Students from mountainous regions walked with their knees bent and chests tilted forward, as though climbing a steep slope. The drifter from Sichuan who camped in our dorm block always walked like that.

Then a pretty girl came towards me, and my attention immediately shifted to her.

Beautiful girls are used to being observed, and deliberately move their legs in a way they know will attract the male gaze. The girl who was approaching me was from the south. She was wearing denim jeans and was with a foreign student. She moved with the grace and fluidity typical of people from the coastal towns of southern China. From the sway of her hips, you could tell she was in love.

It was freezing by now, and Tian Yi still hadn't turned up. After the sun went down, the air turned stiff. I thought of the rabbit that the technician had just killed in the science lab. As it took its last breath, it stretched its leg out as far as it could. A second later, it was a corpse ready to be dissected.

Gao Hua walked up to me. Even though she was only in her late twenties, she was serious and matronly and treated us like her younger siblings, so we all called her 'Sister Gao'. She was studying for a PhD in philosophy. Apparently, her father was an important academic.

'Hey, Dai Wei!' she said. 'How many bottles of that hair-growth lotion have you got left? A guy in our research department wants to buy one.' She was dressed like a young professor. In fact she was a professor of sorts. Tian Yi told me that she'd given a seminar on contemporary philosophical research that had been well received.

'I've sold out, I'm afraid. I'll have another batch next week.' My friend Sun Chunlin had been away from Shenzhen for a couple of weeks, so had been unable to replenish my supplies.

'The Democracy Salon is organising a debate tomorrow,' Sister Gao said. 'Their new leader, Han Dan, will be chairing it. Your Pantheon Society hasn't been very active this term.' The books she was carrying looked very heavy.

'Han Dan? You mean that lanky guy from the Chinese Department?' I said distractedly. 'The Pantheon Society hasn't done much, but Zhuzi's Law and Democracy Research Society and Hai Feng's Social Research Student Club have been quite busy organising debates and lectures.'

The Pantheon Society had, in fact, done nothing since the summer, when Liu Gang and Shu Tong argued over how to react to the murder of a Beijing University graduate by a gang of local hooligans. Liu Gang believed that the incident provided a good excuse for launching another spate of protests. He gave speeches in the Triangle, demanding that the assailants be brought to justice, and made plans for a demonstration in Tiananmen Square. But when Liu Gang heard a rumour from Cao Ming's father that Vice President Wang Zhen had called for a ruthless suppression of student activists, and realised that no other Beijing college was likely to join our protests, he suggested that we should organise a stroll through Tiananmen Square instead of a demonstration. He and Shu Tong argued for two weeks, until they both scrapped the idea.

As a result of this attempted renewal of student activism, Liu Gang lost his Party membership, and Shu Tong was forced to write a self-criticism. Shu Tong spent very little of his time on campus after that. A rumour spread that he was going out with the daughter of a high-ranking Party official.

As I watched Sister Gao walk away, I spotted Tian Yi at last. She was standing with her back to me, waiting. My pulse quickened. The night before, we'd made love for the first time. She was wearing the black skirt she'd worn to her cousin's party. She'd worn black shoes too, that night. I'd noticed that many people of an artistic bent had taken to wearing black. The party had been thrown by her uncle. He'd organised a exhibition of his six-year-old son's paintings and invited friends and family over for a private view. The walls of the sitting room and corridor were covered with his son's childish pictures of trees, tropical fish, girls with red flowers in their hair, and yellow apples on white plates. Since the boy was so much younger than Tian Yi, he called her 'auntie', not 'cousin'. His breath smelt of deep-fried dough sticks. A professor from the Central Academy of Art stuck to Tian Yi like a leech all evening, which irritated me.

I walked over and stood behind her, and stared at her back, her hair and her arms until she sensed my presence and glanced round. She quickly turned away again and, without speaking, walked with me towards the library.

She often retreated into her own world like that, cutting me out completely. I found it unnerving.

We reached a campus restaurant that had a small stall outside selling wonton soup. At night, they'd bring out an electric light. Students who got bored of wandering through the campus often congregated there to chat. Tian Yi walked through the light in front of the stall then vanished into the darkness again.

A moment later, she stopped and leaned against a brick wall. Her eyes were black. Her hair was a mess.

She broke into tears and said, 'Don't do it to me again.'

It began to snow. The flakes hovered in the air.

'Are you afraid of getting pregnant?' I was three years older than her. I felt protective towards her.

She stayed silent and pushed me away. After we'd made love the night before, we'd clung to each for hours, our legs tightly entwined.

'Look, the wind is altering the structure of the snow crystals,' I said, noticing her staring at the flakes on the ground. In the two months that we'd been going out together, I'd found that the only times she didn't contradict me were when I talked about things she didn't understand. I knew very little about art. She often criticised me for being unable to discuss Schubert, Picasso or Shakespeare. 'Is there anything you *do* know?' she would say, staring at me blankly.

Whenever I sensed she was considering breaking up with me, I'd rush off to the library and leaf through the books she'd mentioned during our conversations. I had, in fact, read one of the books she'd talked about – *The Man Who Laughs*, by Victor Hugo – but had forgotten the name of the author. I also read the blurbs on the backs of Mou Sen's novels, to help fill the gaps in my knowledge.

'I don't want to take things any further,' she said slowly.

'You're worried the university authorities will punish us. They won't, I promise you. I'm not worried. Everyone on campus is having relationships. It's not as if we're renting a private room together.'

'It's nothing to do with the university. I just don't like this situation any more. And my grades are suffering.'

'I love you, Tian Yi, I want us to stay together,' I said, clasping her hand. 'It's raining now. Let's go to the library. We can talk about it there.' Again there was something in the palm of her hand. It felt like a piece of bark or bamboo.

'I just want to be quiet. I've felt so unsettled these last two months. I haven't been able to finish one book.' Her voice sounded cold. I saw tears glinting in her eyes.

'What do psychologists call this emotional state?' I asked. I wanted to tell her that this is how you feel when you're in love, but I thought it might annoy her.

'Why are you so normal?' she said, looking at me straight in the face. I knew that if she dared look into my eyes, there was a good chance that we'd make up.

'I could be a brother to you, rather than a boyfriend. Would you prefer that?'

'You really are too conventional,' she said, the corner of her mouth curling upwards slightly. She grudgingly allowed me to take her hand, and as we walked on again, she moved a little closer to me.

I once asked Mou Sen what Tian Yi meant when she said I was 'too conventional'. He said she meant I was too rational, and not dramatic or artistic enough. He said women like men to be witty and passionate. I knew I wasn't particularly romantic, but I was 1.8 metres tall, honest and reliable – the kind of young man that many women might consider attractive.

On the bulletin board outside the library entrance, someone had stuck a note with a line from a pop song: I'M STILL STANDING IN THE RAIN, WAITING FOR YOU TO COME . . . The lopsided characters of the official notice next to it resembled rows of toppled cabbages. We walked into the warm hall and headed for the reading room.

'Let's keep quiet and read our own books,' she said. 'I don't want to see you tomorrow.'

'Can't we have lunch together in the canteen?'

'If you don't do as I ask, I won't go to Yunnan with you in January.'

'All right. But I told Mou Sen and Yanyan that I'd go to a party tomorrow night at Beijing Normal. I thought you might like to come too.'

'Who's Yanyan?'

'A reporter for the *Workers' Daily*. She was at Southern University with us, but we only really got to know her when we moved up here.'

'Oh I know, she's Mou Sen's girlfriend, isn't she?' Tian Yi thought very highly of Mou Sen. She said he was like a walking library.

'Yes, but she likes to keep that quiet. She's from the south, so she's quite old-fashioned about relationships.'

'Are you implying that I'm too liberated?' Tian Yi asked, frowning.

I didn't answer. I was always afraid of saying something that might upset her.

'All right, I won't see you tomorrow,' I agreed reluctantly, then said goodbye and walked off to the science reading room on the third floor.

I was deeply in love with her by then, and felt very attached to her. She'd healed the wounds that my break-up with A-Mei had inflicted on me.

You've scattered into the darkness, like a grain of salt dissolving in the ocean. What troubles you now isn't that you can't see anything, but that nothing can see you.

I see myself standing on the sunny mountain top, my mouth wide open, and Tian Yi dancing beside me, her hair floating in the wind. It was the first week of our two-week holiday in January 1989.

I pointed to the dense rainforest, and told her that it was the Land of Black Teeth described in *The Book of Mountains and Seas*.

'How did people back then make it all the way down here to Yunnan? It took us three days by train to get from Beijing to Kunming, and then another three days on a bus to get here.' Her face was covered with sweat. She was wearing heavy leather shoes, a pale green shirt and blue dungarees.

As soon as we'd arrived in Xishuangbanna, the tropical tip of southern Yunnan Province, we'd booked ourselves into a hotel and set off straight away into the mountain rainforests.

'It would have taken them at least three years to ride down here from the ancient capital,' I said. 'They would have been lucky to make it alive.' I looked like an American soldier in my camouflage combat trousers. I was also wearing a Lee denim cap. Tian Yi had forgotten to bring a hat, so she kept trying to take it from me.

All around us were huge trees. We couldn't see the summit of the mountain we were climbing. We were walking in semi-darkness. I'd never been in a rainforest before. It didn't look real. I felt as though we were floating through an eerie landscape from the fables.

The narrow path was covered with human footprints and the hoof marks of cattle. Damp grasses growing along the sides arched over, almost meeting in the middle. Our trousers and shoes were soon wet through.

She slowed down. 'It's too beautiful,' she said. 'Are those lovebirds up there?' She pointed to a flock of birds that had just taken off from the branches of a tree.

'No, they're cuckoos. Look at the long tails.'

'Do you know why cuckoos have red breasts?' she said. 'There was a princess in ancient China who died of a broken heart, and was re-incarnated as a cuckoo. She sang a mournful song for days on end until blood dripped from her eyes and stained her white breast red.'

'Did you know that, after two lovebirds pair up, they stay with each other for the rest of their lives? They never fly out alone.'

'Look at those huge beans hanging down there!' She walked over and tried to pull one down.

'They're croton beans. Don't try to eat them, they're poisonous.' I lifted her up and she pulled off a curved one that was as large as an ox's tusk.

'It would look great hanging up in my dorm. Go on, take a picture!' She let the bean hang from her neck, and excitedly handed me her camera. 'Quick, take a photo! The air is so fresh. Ah! That grass smells wonderful.' She was smiling and laughing.

'The oxygen levels here must be very high.'

'I didn't ask you about oxygen levels, you egghead.' She was always telling me off for sounding like a textbook.

'The Bulang tribe live in these mountains,' I said, knowing this would interest her more. 'They dye their teeth black. They think it makes them look more beautiful. Perhaps we'll come across one of their villages today. I saw photographs of them in an exhibition in Guangzhou on the minority cultures of south-west China. In the Bulang tribe, when a boy and girl fall in love, they sit together under a tree and dye each other's teeth black.'

'Did you go to that exhibition with your Hong Kong girlfriend?' Ever since I'd told her of my relationship with A-Mei, she'd often get me to talk about her so she could make some sarcastic comment.

I didn't want to answer her question because, as it happened, I had been thinking about A-Mei at that very moment. Instead, I took a deep breath and raced further up the slope. Soon, I had a view of the rain-forest engulfing the hill in front, and stretching into the far distance. I spotted a path winding off into the mountains and wondered where it led.

I turned round and saw Tian Yi climbing up towards me, puffing and panting.

There was no sun or breeze on this side of the mountain. I noticed small red berries on the bushes at the feet of the dark-green trees. Nearer the ground, there were shrubs with blue, yellow and white flowers. I remembered that A-Mei always liked to have fresh flowers in her room. In the north, no one kept plants in their homes. My mother once said that keeping plants and flowers was petit-bourgeois and a sign of an unhealthy mind. So there were never any flowers in our flat.

Tian Yi staggered towards me, her face flushed. 'I can't go any further,' she moaned. 'What's the point of going to the top? We'll have to walk all the way back down again afterwards.'

Why are girls so feeble? I asked myself, stretching out my hand and pulling her up. 'This mountain really isn't that high,' I said. 'Let's keep going for a bit. Perhaps we'll come across an elephant.'

'Elephants in a rainforest?' she said, her eyes sparkling.

'Yes, there are several herds here, apparently. Look at those giant ferns over there. They're living fossils. They probably haven't changed for a hundred million years.' The ferns loomed over the undergrowth like open parasols. I walked over to one and pinched a curled frond. Although I'd seen this species in the botanical garden of Southern University, they were much smaller than these.

'I've seen photographs of them in a geographical magazine,' she said proudly. 'Stand there. Don't move. I'm taking a picture.'

I led her further up the mountain. Her small hand was wet with perspiration.

On the path ahead, beautiful yellow butterflies were sitting on a cowpat. As we approached, they flew away. Tian Yi tore off a clump of wild grasses that were yellow, green and grey. Each one was exquisite, but none as beautiful as her hand.

She was exhausted. Her breath smelt of the rice flour we'd eaten the day before. She was like A-Mei – they both hated physical exertion.

She was about to lean against a tree trunk and take a rest, but jumped back when she saw the ants crawling up the bark, so she leaned against me instead. She closed her eyes, put her hand on her forehead and said, 'I suffer from low blood sugar, and I probably have a weak heart as well. Pass me the water bottle.'

I grabbed her wrist and checked her pulse. It didn't seem too fast. I took off my cap and fanned her face with it.

'I love climbing mountains,' I said. 'When you reach the summit and look down on the peaks below, you get a wonderful sense of achievement.'

Without opening her eyes she answered, 'Mountain climbing is a form of megalomania. Men think they can conquer a mountain by climbing it. They climb for days, all the way to the top, but when they come down again, they're still no better than a miserable beetle.'

As she leaned against me, I glanced down at the pale breasts hidden inside her green shirt and said, 'Women's lives are controlled by their bodies. They have weaker muscles, so it's not surprising they don't like climbing mountains.'

'You have no right to talk about women's bodies!' she snapped, opening her eyes again. 'Men may have stronger muscles, but that only drives them to chase each other across a sports field all day to work off their energy. It's so tedious!'

I squatted down and lit a cigarette, and wondered whether Tian Yi's aversion to group activities was a symptom of mild depression.

When she seemed strong enough to continue, I stubbed out my cigarette and said, 'This forest is beautiful. It would be a shame if we didn't make it to the summit.'

'I need more time to rest. You always walk too fast. I like to stop and look at the flowers and trees.' She sniffed the wild flowers in her hand. One of them had four dark-blue petals circling a soft ring of yellow stamens.

I sat down next to her, and we leaned back against the tree and gazed at the grasses and branches around us. A few rays of sunlight filtered down through the leaves. Then a breeze stirred the dense foliage. It came from a valley to the north and smelt of warm grass.

'What have you seen now?' she asked, looking into the forest and ruffling her hair.

'There's a wild boar behind that tree.'

'I don't believe you!' she laughed. 'You're trying to frighten me!'

We rose to our feet again and continued up the path hand in hand.

Further on, near the summit, the trees thinned out a little, revealing patches of bare mountain rock. Through the gaps in the branches, we could glimpse blue sky.

I took Tian Yi in my arms and held her tight. We were alone together on this mountain. There was no one else around.

'Tian Yi, you're my angel,' I said.

Her clenched hand opened and the wild grasses fell to the ground. 'Your angel suffers from vertigo,' she said. 'She's afraid of flying. Do you understand?'

We lay down and kissed, and I slipped inside her as easily as a foot inside a soft shoe. I moved back and forth on top of her. She shook in time with me, and the rainforest seemed to shake too. Whenever I glanced up, I'd see the bright, white rock of the mountain's summit shining above me. We kept our mouths pressed together, until her legs quivered and she let out a soft cry.

It wasn't until dusk that we slowly began to make our way back down the mountain. This was perhaps the first time in my life that I had the experience of utter privacy. She let me put my arm around her. When we reached the rocky bank of a river, she asked me, 'Will you stay with me for ever?'

'Yes. For the rest of my life.' Although I was worn out, I felt a sudden desire to make love to her again.

'I don't know why,' she said, 'but when I'm with you, my mind is always somewhere else. You seem so heavy, like this big rock here.' She was staring at a white rock that was glimmering in the fading light. A grey seam ran through its centre. The silent river was slowly darkening. A bird hovered in the air, landed on the water for a moment, and flew off. 'Whatever happens to this country, we must stay together. You must promise me.' Her eyes were red.

'Tell me you love me.'

'I told you in my letter,' she said, tilting her head up. Her eyes became crescent slits. As she turned her head, I could see the marks my kisses had left on the nape of her long pale neck.

'I love you . . .' Her voice cracked and she blushed. I pulled her down onto the ground again and held her in my arms. The sinking sun cast a glow over our entwined bodies. Everything slowed down. Just as we were about to doze off, mosquitoes began swarming around us. We leapt up, pulled our clothes on and fled.

You move like a submarine through the sea of red-brown cells, and watch your pain spreading like a white net.

I see myself entering my dorm. Everyone was sitting on the lower bunks, drinking beer and eating chicken.

The room was brighter than usual. Chen Di must have put in a stronger light bulb. Whenever he did that, we usually had a couple of days of bright light before the caretaker found out and replaced it with a lower wattage bulb.

There was no room for me to sit down, so I decided to return to Tian Yi's dorm, but as I went to the door Chen Di dragged me back in.

'You know it's our turn to feed him this week,' he said, pointing to the drifter who was sprawled over Qiu Fa's bed. Qiu Fa was on the opposite bunk. He was very fastidious, and usually couldn't bear anyone sitting on his peony-printed cotton sheet. In the mornings, he'd spend ten minutes brushing his curly hair into place, then he'd fill a glass jar with hot water and use it to flatten the creases in his clothes.

'Yes, you can't just sneak off like that!' Mao Da added. 'Go and buy us some beer!' Mao Da was the chancellor of the student union and a Party member too. He spoke like a government cadre.

'Be careful of the food-coupon thief,' said Yu Jin from his bunk. 'He's been coming onto the campus again. I've seen him with my own eyes.' Yu Jin was always claiming to have seen things 'with his own eyes'. He was a short, sprightly guy. He liked to roll up his sleeves to expose his muscled forearms and digital watch.

The truth is, he hadn't seen any thief at all. A few days before, it had been my turn to go to the canteen to fetch food for everyone. I forgot to take my coupons with me and returned to the dorm empty-handed. To save me making a second trip, I pretended that a thief had stolen the coupons from my pocket.

The drifter liked to stride up and down the corridor with his hands behind his back and a cigarette in his mouth, in the manner of a local Party secretary. When tired of that, he'd slump onto someone's bed and fall asleep, snoring loudly. The caretaker tried to get rid of him several times, kicking him out onto the streets or even taking him to the police station. But somehow or other the drifter always managed to worm his way back to us. His reputation increased with each new assault, and he soon was the star of our dorm block.

The drifter had no name. We called him 'the drifter' not in a pejorative way, but as a mark of respect. Giving shelter to a destitute peasant appealed to our rebellious spirits. It was always an honour when he chose to eat in our dorm, and he agreed. 'You little scamps should consider yourselves privileged,' he'd declare in his broad Sichuan accent.

He spoke very little in the beginning, but after a student in the dorm opposite arranged for him to sleep with a female poet, he livened up. He told us that women with thick lips have thick labia, just as men with big noses have big cocks, and explained that when women take off their clothes, their breasts hang down to their waists.

We took turns escorting him to the shower block. When he wanted to go into town and see a film, we'd help him over the campus wall. I was the best haircutter on our floor, and charged two jiao a go. But I always did the drifter's hair for free.

He propped his head up on Qiu Fa's pillow and chewed at a drumstick. His hands looked dark and grimy as they gripped the pale meat and bone.

I sat down by his feet. Everyone was tucking into the food and chatting loudly.

The drifter turned to me and said, 'Come on, boy, down it in one!'

I reluctantly took the glass he offered me. 'I've just had a beer,' I said. 'This is Erguotou spirit. I can't drink that much.'

The drifter shot me a disparaging look. 'You city people are useless. Beer's as weak as piss. Real men drink *this*.'

'Yes, come on Dai Wei!' said Dong Rong. 'Friend or foe, down in one go!' I hated playing drinking games with Dong Rong. He'd always win. He was a terrible poser. He wore designer sunglasses all through the year, and liked to brag about the cost of his American trainers. But although he was always smartly turned out, he had the smelliest feet in the dorm.

The spirit made my stomach and face burn and my head spin. I'd just had supper with Tian Yi. All her dorm mates were there, so I'd decided to come back to my dorm and read the copy of *The Catcher in the Rye* she'd lent me. Mou Sen had already read it, of course.

The drifter was wearing Dong Rong's designer shirt. It made him look like the Party secretary of a rural commune. Embroidered on the chest was a logo of a horse-rider waving a polo stick. Apparently, this brand was even more expensive than the one with the crocodile logo. Dong Rong had worn the shirt during the campus protests that followed the murder of the graduate student and hadn't dared wear it again in case it incriminated him.

Xiao Li asked the drifter to tell us a story about women or ghosts. Xiao Li came from a poor peasant family. His living expenses were paid for by his elder brother. I never saw him buy any food. In the evening, he'd go out to gather vegetables that had been discarded on the street. The previous year, he'd bought a tube of toothpaste but couldn't afford a toothbrush, so used his fingers instead. This year he'd managed to buy a toothbrush, but his toothpaste had run out, so he'd take some from my tube when he thought I wasn't looking. I always pretended not to notice. And I gave him free haircuts too.

The drifter mumbled drunkenly, 'No, no, I've got no stories to tell you.' But it was clear there was something he wanted to say. Having drunk and eaten his fill, he sucked on his cigarette and smacked his lips contentedly, like a peasant in a market who's just sold his harvest for a good price.

Xiao Li lay on his bed and tuned his radio to a news broadcast: '. . . Following three days of severe disturbances, Premier Li Peng signed an order today imposing martial law on Lhasa. A handful of rebellious Tibetan monks have been . . .'

'Tell us about that time you swore at the policeman,' Yu Jin said, patting the drifter's shoulder.

That was one of the drifter's favourite stories. One day, he was caught short while walking down the street. He pulled down his trousers and was just about to pee, when a policeman walked up behind him and said, 'You can't piss on the pavement! Pull up your trousers!'

'Who pissed? Did this piss?' the drifter said, waving his dick.

'Why have you brought it out then?'

'It belongs to me, doesn't it?' the drifter answered. 'I'm just taking a look. Is that against the law?'

The policeman was flummoxed. All he could say was: 'Well, you've seen it now, so hurry up and put it away.'

The drifter hadn't shaved for months. His beard had grown so long that security guards had arrested him twice recently, suspecting him of being a dissident artist. It was during the week when a band of avant-garde artists put on a show at the Beijing Art Gallery which involved shooting guns into the air.

'Chen Di, get your binoculars out and show them to the drifter,' Yu Jin said loudly. 'They're our dorm's mascot. They were made in the Soviet Union.' Chen Di's binoculars were a type that was usually issued only to high-level military cadres. He wouldn't tell us where he'd got them from. Even Cao Ming, whose father was an army general, had been amazed by how powerful they were.

'Apparently there's been some trouble at Nanjing University,' Xiao Li said. 'A black student was beaten up by some Chinese students for taking a Chinese girl back to his dorm.' Xiao Li had drunk too much. His face was bright red. He was eighteen, but looked much younger. When Mao Da stood next to him, you would have thought they were father and son.

'Did you hear that, Drifter?' said Qiu Fa. 'A black student was beaten up for sleeping with a Chinese girl. Do you think that was right?' His curly hair was clean and tidy. He washed it three times a week, and brushed his teeth twice a day.

'Yes, tell us, do you think he deserved it?' asked Zhang Jie. This guy was so quiet and reserved, I often forgot he was there. When I glanced over at him, all I saw were his dark, glassy eyes and grimy shirt collar.

Mao Da was sitting next to Qiu Fa, chewing peanuts. He pulled off his khaki jacket and said, 'Of course the foreigner deserved it. Serves him right for bringing dishonour to the Chinese people.'

The drifter didn't know much about black people, but had enough of an idea to say, 'A black guy, as black as coal, dares lay his hands on one of our women? We've got men of our own to do that! What a scandal! Beat him up, I say, beat him up!' He flicked his hand in the air like a policeman, almost hitting Zhang Jie who was sitting beside him.

Everyone laughed.

'Dong Rong, your girlfriend just called,' said Wang Fei wandering into our room with a cigarette in his mouth. 'And have you heard? The students of Nanjing University staged a mass march today to protest against the preferential treatment given to foreigners. But they were also calling for political reform and human rights.' A couple of days before, Wang Fei had told me that we should take advantage of the row between Shu Tong and Liu Gang to reshuffle the posts in the Pantheon Society. I said that, even if there was a reshuffle, he wouldn't get a post. No one had a very good opinion of him.

'The reform process has reached a crucial juncture,' Mao Da said, in the flat tones of a government official. 'This isn't the time to take to the streets.'

'Yes, we caused enough trouble last time,' Chen Di moaned. Then he turned to Wang Fei and said, 'What are you smoking? Can I have one?'

Wang Fei ignored him and shot me a knowing look instead. 'You've been humping that girl again, haven't you?' he said. 'Just look at the state of you! Bet you shot at least two loads last night!'

'Fuck off, Wang Fei!' I said, feeling the alcohol in my blood flowing down to my legs. I didn't want the conversation to turn to me.

Of the eight boys in our dorm, Chen Di and I were the only ones to have brought our girlfriends back. Mao Da and Dong Rong's girlfriends lived outside Beijing. The previous week, Wang Fei had brought back a tourism student from Xian. She popped into our dorm, and after a few minutes chatting with us, became completely smitten with Cao Ming.

Outside, the nightly news report blared through the university loudspeakers: 'The State Council has issued an emergency notice calling for strict controls to be placed on migrant labour . . .'

'Shut the window, I don't want to hear that bullshit!' Wang Fei said, passing his cigarette to Yu Jin. 'Let's get sloshed tonight. Come on! Friend or foe, down in one go!'

When Dong Rong, Mao Da and Yu Jin got the pack of cards out, I knew the dorm would soon become a gambling den again, so I went next door and collapsed on Wang Fei's bed.

The wound in your temporal lobe quivers, your memories blur.

'A survey found that seven thousand out of the eight thousand girls who graduated last year had lost their virginity,' Wang Fei said, sitting on the edge of his bunk. 'Who would have guessed?'

'Let's turn the lights out and go to sleep.' When Shu Tong closed his eyes, his face became a pale, featureless blob.

I was spending the night in Wang Fei's dorm so that Chen Di could sleep with his girlfriend. Xiao Li, Dong Rong and the others had gone to a room downstairs. The male dorms weren't supervised as strictly as the female dorms. If a girl dared stay overnight, the rest of us would cooperate and leave the couple in peace. It was easier at the weekends, because the caretaker seldom came up to check.

'You've got it wrong,' Liu Gang said. 'The seven thousand girls in the survey only said they didn't disapprove of sex before marriage, they didn't say they'd indulged in it. They'd never confess to that!' His girlfriend was at university in Anhui Province. They wrote each other long letters.

'A survey conducted by the Maths Department found that 27 per cent of students had had sex before they started university,' someone else piped up from a lower bunk. When men lie in the dark together, their conversation inevitably turns to women.

The lights in the dorm had been switched off, but a glow from the lamps outside filtered through the window. I could see photographs of film stars torn from a calendar pasted to the wall behind Wang Fei. Their eyes stared intently ahead. In the dark, smoky air, the women looked like empresses from some mysterious realm.

Old Fu on the bed above me was listening to Voice of America. He took the TOEFL exam every year, and always got high grades. He was hoping to get a place at Harvard.

I could smell the steamed bun that had burned while being heated over an electric hob, and the jar of spicy fermented tofu that Wang Fei kept in his bedside cabinet.

I was lying on someone's empty bed. My mind was troubled, but I didn't want anyone to know. Something terrible had happened between Tian Yi and me, and I hadn't seen her for two days.

'You're the one who's been bonking all the virgins,' Shu Tong said to Wang Fei, tapping the side of his bed with a book. 'That girl you took behind your bed curtain last night, I bet she was another one.'

'Whatever happens behind this curtain is my own business,' Wang Fei called back. 'You should respect my human rights.'

'Was she a virgin?' Old Fu asked suddenly. Although he was older than the rest of us, he'd never had a girlfriend.

'You made so much noise I didn't sleep a wink all night,' Shu Tong grumbled.

Big Chan and Little Chan walked in. The dust blown in from the corridor always reeked of the men's toilets, and made you want a cigarette. Big Chan switched the lights on and Little Chan dumped a thermos of hot water onto the table. When Big Chan poured some hot water into his lunch box, I immediately smelt a whiff of bean sprouts. Everyone suspected that Big Chan had tricked the drifter into leaving the campus the week before, because it was his dorm's turn to look after him this week.

I thought about the application forms I'd sent off to various American universities a few days before. My academic results and TOEFL score were high enough to get me a place at a middle-ranking college. The day I sent them, Tian Yi said to me, 'Don't stay in China. You'll be much better off in America. And with your rich great-uncle, you won't even have to worry about getting a scholarship.'

I tried to go to sleep but my mind flitted back to the woods beyond the campus walls.

Two days before, Tian Yi and I had decided to leave the crowded campus and go for a quiet walk. We walked to the end of the football pitch, sneaked over an ancient red wall and entered the deserted grounds of the Old Summer Palace. There was spring blossom on the peach trees growing wild on a grassy mound. At the foot of the slope a stream flowed silently towards a distant lake.

Tian Yi was wearing a black dress tied at the waist with a red leather belt. The dappled sunlight fell on her neck and shoulders.

This side of the wall was darker and damper, and covered in thick creepers. The peach trees were ragged and unkempt. Against their pale-green leaves, Tian Yi looked like a celestial fairy about to take flight. I was amazed to find this rural haven hidden beyond our campus walls. Tian Yi and I lay down on the grass beneath the peach trees. I kissed the warm splashes of sunlight on her skin.

We hadn't had a chance to make love in the two months since we'd returned from Yunnan.

'You want to?' she whispered, pulling my hand away from her thighs. 'Then take your trousers off. I want to see it . . .' Her face was the same pale pink as the blossom on the trees above.

'Men's bodies aren't that great to look at, you know.' I unbuttoned her dress and watched the sunlight fall on her breasts.

She stood up and combed her fingers through her hair. There were blades of damp grass stuck to the top of her pale feet, and fine leaves caught between her toes. Her nails looked like fallen petals. She pulled off her knickers, climbed out of her dress then squatted down in front of me, her black pubic hair brushing against the green grass.

'Do you see? I've got my period . . .'

I stared at the dark flesh between her pale thighs, pulled her down and rolled on top of her, licking her face. She dug her fingers into my back and grabbed my hair. We writhed against each other. As I poured myself into her I felt her thighs shudder.

'Get up! Get up!' someone shouted, kicking my legs. Behind us were three men, bending beneath the low branches.

'Get up, you little hooligans! We're taking you to the Summer Palace police station.'

We hurriedly got dressed. 'She's my girlfriend,' I said, standing up. 'We're at university together.' The men were all shorter than me. Each held a wooden baton.

'You're hooligans,' said the fat officer who seemed to be in charge. 'We're arresting you now and you can talk later.'

'We have our student cards.' Tian Yi was clutching her bra and a clump of grass in her hand. Strands of hair were stuck to her damp cheeks.

'Hurry up now!' The fat officer grabbed the cards without looking at them. The other two impatiently tapped the branches with their batons.

'We're going out together, we're not hooligans,' Tian Yi said, once she'd buttoned up her dress.

'Don't you know that it's against the law to have intercourse before marriage?' said the fat one. Then he glanced at the officer in sunglasses and said, 'Take her away and get her to tell you all she knows about his family background.'

The officer in sunglasses led Tian Yi down the grassy slope. She was still clasping her rolled-up bra in her hand.

'What's her name? Tell us!' the other two shouted.

'Tian Yi,' I replied.

'What's her father's name?'

I knew that if I named her father and his work unit, Tian Yi's future would be ruined. I was determined to keep silent.

'You don't want to tell us? You want us to beat you up? We saw what you two were up to. We'll take you back to the station and examine your trousers. Any sperm, and you'll get at least five years!' He poked me in the thigh with his baton.

I panicked. 'I'm sorry, comrades. It was wrong of me to bring her here. Please let us go. We'll never come back again. We'll be good students from now on and study hard.'

'Let you go? Do you know where you are? You've illegally trespassed onto a state-protected heritage site and you've committed an obscene act. That's two offences. What's more, the university regulations clearly forbid students to have relationships during term time.'

'But we're in love, we couldn't help it. I give you my word that we won't do this again. We'll concentrate on our studies. Please let us go.'

'If you want to go back to the campus, you'll have to leave us a deposit of at least three hundred yuan. But I'll have to discuss it with my two mates first.'

I pulled out all the money from my pockets. Fortunately, the day before I'd gone home and collected 120 yuan to cover a month's living expenses. The fat officer took the notes from me without looking and stuffed them into his pocket. Then he lit a cigarette, inhaled, and let a puff of smoke escape through the gaps in his yellow teeth.

'This won't even cover our overtime pay. Squat down and don't move until we return. We're going to talk to the university's security office.'

I stared down at the dirty green weeds and the moving shadows of the branches. After a while, I raised my head and looked at the path Tian Yi had walked down. The grass on the slope was still. Now and then a bird cried out as it flitted between the trees. I wondered where they'd taken Tian Yi.

At last, I plucked up my courage, stood up and followed the wall downhill. When I reached the stream at the bottom of the slope, I saw her. She was alone, standing against the wall, shaking so much that she couldn't speak. I hurriedly gave her a leg-up, and we clambered back over the wall into the campus. There were fewer trees there, so it was much brighter. Students were kicking a ball about. Tian Yi was still shaking. She could hardly walk. I sat down with her on the grass. She bit her sleeve then sobbed into her folded arms.

For the next forty-eight hours, Tian Yi wouldn't speak to me. Her dorm mates told me that she'd come down with flu and needed to rest. When I went to visit her, she told me to go away. I wasn't brave enough to ask her what the police had done to her. I knew that even if I did ask, she wouldn't tell me. I hated myself for having taken her to that place, and for allowing the police to lead her away.

Then, when I was eating supper in the canteen, I overheard someone say that a gang of thugs had been prowling the grounds of the Old Summer Palace pretending to be policemen, extorting cash from students they caught having sex. They'd made a fortune from the racket, he said. Something in my memory exploded: policemen don't refer to their colleagues as 'mates'. How could I have failed to notice?

Apparently, the men were bicycle menders. One day they pounced on a foreign student who was having sex with an English major, and extorted two hundred US dollars. They paid backhanders to the police authorities at the Summer Palace. It was a good business. They caught an average of seven couples a day in those woods. We'd been duped by a gang of thugs. I didn't dare tell Tian Yi. I knew it would only make her feel worse.

Wang Fei's dorm was so smoky that, after dozing off for a few minutes, I woke up again with a sore throat.

'Well, next time you bring a girl back, just let us know first,' Shu Tong said, still annoyed at having been kept awake by Wang Fei's noisy shenanigans the night before.

'No, we should have a rule that girls are only brought back to the dorm on Sunday nights,' Old Fu said.

'But there are eight of us. If we take turns to bring a girl back on Sunday nights, we'll only get some action once every two months.' Wang Fei wasn't happy.

'What is this, a brothel?' I shouted, unable to restrain myself. 'It's one o'clock already, for God's sake!' My throat burned as I swallowed a sip of water.

The cells in your temporal lobes begin to vibrate once more. Neurons spread their dendritic branches, allowing warm memories to flow to your thalamus.

'Dai Wei! Can you hear me? It's your mother . . . My God! His eyelids are moving. They're really moving. I haven't been wasting my time. All those injections have paid off. My God! Let me put another pillow under your head!'

I too sense that I'm emerging from a deep sleep. I can feel my four limbs, the head that my mother is propping up, the drip attached to my arm. A strong smell of disinfectant charges into my brain. I can tell that my body is intact and lying flat on the bed.

Perhaps everything is all right now. Perhaps I can return to the world.

'You're a survivor, my son,' my mother says. 'Whatever happens, I'll do my best to get you out of this country. Listen, I'll sing you a song. I used to sing this to you when you were a baby. As soon as you heard it, you'd stop crying at once . . . "*Pick up your pen and use it as a sword! The Party is our mother and father. Whoever dares criticise the Party will be banished to the depths of Hell!*" Oh dear, you won't like those lyrics. Never mind. So long as you can hear your mother's voice . . . Today is 23 April, 1990. You've been back from hospital for a few months now. Although you probably had no idea you were there. The doctor said that people who sink into comas like yours are usually dead within six months. But look, you're still alive. I told you not to get involved in the student movement. Oh God, you'd be better off staying in your coma. The police said that as soon as you wake up, they'll come up and arrest you.'

My ears transmit the noise of my mother's sobbing and sighs to my temporal lobes. Then images and conversations that have passed through my mind slowly return to me again: Mao Da sitting opposite the drifter, chewing peanuts . . . 'Beat him up, I say! What an insult to the Chinese people!' . . . 'Not many science students have turned up. Did you bring the banner?' . . . 'Stick out your tongue and swallow these pills' . . . A-Mei's reflection in the mirror staring me straight in the eye . . . 'I've arrested lots of hooligans like you before, and they all get a good beating . . .'

The real world seems to grow distant once more.

There are no blue skies now, no bright universes. All the exits are blocked.

The bullet struck me in the head. I remember a line of soldiers holding guns, and A-Mei walking towards them. When the guns fired, she knelt on the ground. Then my head cracked open. That's how it happened.

So, is A-Mei still alive? Was it really her I saw? Did Tian Yi visit me in hospital the night I was injured? Yes, she stood by my bed. My skin remembers the touch of her hand. But what happened before the shot was fired? Was Mou Sen struck down? Did Wang Fei die too in a pool of blood?

Images dart through my mind. I see Wang Fei's bloodshot eyes. He opened the door to my dorm and shouted, 'I'm going to make some posters to commemorate General Secretary Hu Yaobang! His death is a terrible loss for the Chinese democracy movement!' He'd just picked up the news of his death from Voice of America. His headphones were dangling from his neck.

THE MAN WHO SHOULDN'T HAVE DIED HAS DIED, WHILE THE MEN WHO SHOULD BE DEAD STILL LIVE, he scribbled in chalk over the walls and tables of the dorm. Then he bit deep into his finger, and with the blood that dripped from the wound wrote THE PEOPLE . . .

'Damn!' he said as the flow dried up. 'Why's there so little blood?' Recently, Wang Fei had fallen for a trainee pathologist at Beijing Union Hospital. She'd gone out with him once, rather against her will, and had then left his calls unanswered.

'You're a cold-blooded animal, that's why.' Chen Di was lying on his bed reading a magazine.

'Shut up! Some of us are trying to have a nap!' I shouted. Since the incident in the Old Summer Palace I'd been tense and irritable. Although Tian Yi was speaking to me again, she wouldn't let me touch her.

'If you lot hadn't taken to the streets and demonstrated in 1987, Hu Yaobang wouldn't have been forced to resign from his post,' Mao Da said. 'And now the poor man is dead.'

The room fell silent after that, but I was still unable to sleep. In low spirits, I decided to call Mou Sen to ask how the students at Beijing Normal were taking the news of Hu Yaobang's death.

He said the news had startled them. He was sure the death would spark a new round of student protests.

When I left the science lab later that day, I felt like a shower, so I walked back to my dorm block to fetch my towel and soap. The white blossom of the locust trees lining the path filled the air with a sickly perfume. For some reason, this scent, when combined with the various odours from the dorm blocks' open windows, always made me want to masturbate.

'Have you finished class?' Ke Xi asked, walking up to me with a bundle of damp laundry in his arms. 'The Triangle's boards have been covered with eulogies. Go and have a look!'

'I've seen them,' I said. 'Someone's hung up a memorial couplet in the graduate hall already. It's sad that he's dead, but we really can't start demonstrating again.'

'You're wrong – this is the perfect time to remobilise,' Ke Xi said, placing his left hand on his waist. 'We can't let this opportunity slip.'

As we approached our dorm block I said, 'I still feel guilty about the 1987 protests. We didn't achieve anything, other than push liberals like Hu Yaobang out of their jobs . . .'

Your breathing becomes steadier. Oxygenated blood moves into your pulmonary vein and is carried up to your left atrium.

I long to speak, but the language centres of my cerebral cortex are damaged, and the words won't come out. I believe the medical term for this is 'expressive aphasia' . . .

I can see that single red brick which jutted from the lawn outside the lecture hall. Every time I came out of class, I'd give it a sharp kick. It had never tripped me up, so my hatred for it was unjustified. Still, I always longed to find a spade and dig it out.

The telephone rang as I walked into the entrance of my dorm block. The caretaker handed me the receiver.

It was my brother calling from Sichuan Province. He said that students at Sichuan University of Science and Technology were pasting up eulogies to Hu Yaobang, and that even members of the student union had got involved.

I told him that eulogies had been going up at Beijing University as well, but that our activities hadn't spread beyond the campus walls. Apparently, the students of Qinghua University and the Politics and Law University had already staged a memorial march through Beijing.

'Do you think this is the beginning of a new student movement?' he asked in the slight Sichuan accent he'd developed.

'No, of course not. Don't get overexcited. If you do anything that draws attention to yourself, you'll be the first to suffer when the police clamp down.' I glanced nervously around me. There were spies planted in every dorm block now. They'd report any subversive activity they noticed to the authorities and, in return, would be promised a job in Beijing after graduation. Everyone in our dorm suspected the quiet, reserved guy, Zhang Jie, of being an informer. Before he came to Beijing University, he'd been groomed for high office by the provincial government of Henan.

'Most of the students who dared write posters are children of former rightists,' my brother said. 'Some of my classmates threw sheets of white paper from their windows as a sign of mourning, but they didn't have the guts to write anything on them.'

'The police won't arrest you for writing eulogies,' I told him. 'Just don't join any unofficial organisations.'

Through the open door of the dorm behind me, I could hear the voice of a rock singer growling from a cassette player: '*The world is a rubbish dump. We are rats that pilfer and steal. We gobble up all that's good then spew out shit ideas . . .*' The thudding noise irritated me. I quickly finished the conversation and put down the phone.

Wang Fei wasn't around, so Old Fu and I went to the girls' block to see if he was in Sister Gao's dorm. Sure enough, there he was. He'd calmed down a little and was drinking and smoking with Chen Di. Bai Ling and Mimi were also there, preparing some snacks.

Sister Gao was the eldest woman in the girls' dorm block and, just like Old Fu in our block, played the role of wise elder. She'd gone out to a street stall and bought a pig's ear for Wang Fei to have with his beer. As we walked in, Mimi was slicing it up and dousing it with sesame oil and vinegar.

Although it was spring, the students in the dorm were still wearing jumpers and down jackets. I kept my jacket on but removed my gloves.

'Have you heard about the eulogies going up in the Triangle, Sister Gao?' Old Fu asked. 'Some students in the Creative Writing Programme have even composed a memorial couplet.' Then he turned to Shu Tong and said, 'What does the Pantheon Society plan to do? Didn't you say that 1989 would be a good time to launch another protest movement, it being the two hundredth anniversary of the French Revolution, and the seventieth of China's May Fourth Movement? Last month Han Dan's Democracy Salon put up some posters calling for the legalisation of independent student organisations. It looks like they have an action plan.'

'My parents were denounced during the Anti-Rightist movement,' said Sister Gao, 'and I was branded the daughter of capitalist dogs. When Hu Yaobang rehabilitated millions of rightists ten years ago, we saw him as our saviour. So I'm not against mourning his death, far from it. But you shouldn't use his death as an excuse to launch a new protest movement. You'd be falling into the government's trap. The university authorities have been told to remain on guard.'

'The memorial couplet was put up by the law students,' Shu Tong said, waving someone's tobacco smoke from his eyes. 'It seems that Haizi's suicide has stirred them into action.' Haizi was a poet who'd studied law at Beijing University. Despairing of China's future, he'd made his way to the railway line near the end of the Great Wall the previous month, and thrown himself in front of a train. 'We'll get some engineering students to take a memorial wreath for Hu Yaobang to Tiananmen Square tomorrow. We'll keep it simple.'

'Let's turn our minds to happier things,' Sister Gao said. 'It's Bai Ling's birthday today. I'm going to boil up some birthday noodles for her. So no more talk about suicides and memorials, all right? Dai Wei, don't think you can just turn up here and cadge a free meal from us. Go and get some beer from the corner shop, and some candles too while you're about it.'

'Yes, I'm very squeamish about death and blood,' Bai Ling said quietly. 'So please change the subject.'

'How thoughtless of Hu Yaobang to choose to die on your birthday, of all days!' Chen Di smiled.

'In 1986, a Beijing University philosophy student called Zhang Xiaohui was arrested for writing *A Marxist Manifesto for the Youth of China*,' Sister Gao said. 'He was accused of spreading counter-revolutionary propaganda and sentenced to three years in prison. If you have any sense you'll stop all this nonsense and concentrate on your studies.'

'Is it true that Han Dan's taking break-dancing lessons now? I thought he was supposed to be a serious intellectual. What a joke!' Wang Fei narrowed his bloodshot eyes. I could tell he'd got through at least three bottles of beer already.

'Was Hu Yaobang the President of China, or General Secretary of the Communist Party?' asked Bai Ling. 'I can never remember!' Bai Ling was tiny but well proportioned. She had large eyes, high cheekbones, and a defiant, stubborn air.

'General Secretary of course. Zhao Ziyang's taken over his post now. He's a reformer. He helped set up the special economic zones, and wants to make the Party more open and democratic. If you carry on with these protests, he'll be forced to step down too.' Mimi spoke in a measured tone. She was a Chinese literature student. She was even shorter than Bai Ling, and had to look up at people when she spoke. So often had her lower lip been pulled down by her neck muscles that her mouth was almost always half open. Her husky, masculine voice was very distinctive.

'Didn't you lot say that you wanted to establish a new government and ask Hu Yaobang to be the leader?' Bai Ling said, turning to Shu Tong. 'Well, it's too late for that now.'

'Your generation is supposed to be the great hope of our nation, and you don't even know who the General Secretary is!' Old Fu said, smiling at Bai Ling.

'Hu Yaobang was a distinguished reformer,' Shu Tong intoned, sticking his chin up. 'The hardliners drove him to his grave. We're to blame for his death as well. If we hadn't demonstrated two years ago, he'd still be in his post now.'

'If we want to mourn his death properly, we should lay memorial wreaths in Tianamen Square tonight,' Wang Fei said, waking up a little.

'Where did that sudden burst of enthusiasm come from, Wang Fei?' Chen Di chuckled.

'Don't put your lives at risk,' Bai Ling said. 'You think that if you get killed by the police, you'll become glorious martyrs. But your deaths wouldn't change anything. The government would still be in control.'

'Other students went to the Square this afternoon to lay wreaths and recite eulogies.' Shu Tong had become much more optimistic recently. He and Liu Gang had made up, and had even made a trip together to the Politics and Law University to plan the next stage of the student protests.

'Let's go to the Square then! Right now!' Wang Fei said, gobbling another slice of pig's ear. 'We can march all the way there. I've got the banners ready.'

'Calm down, Wang Fei,' Sister Gao said, dropping the noodles into a pot of boiling water. 'You received a disciplinary warning after the '87 protests. Do you really want to go through that again?'

'You're right,' I said. 'The rest of us might have got off without a warning, but our names were blacklisted, so there's no chance of our getting jobs in Beijing after we graduate.'

'I hear that you've been sent an enrolment letter by the American university you wrote to,' Bai Ling said to me. Tian Yi must have told her.

'No, I sent off ten applications, but I haven't had any answers yet.'

'This country will grind to a halt soon,' Mimi said, fixing her cold gaze on me. 'Everyone's making plans to go abroad.'

'This time we must organise a massive demonstration!' Wang Fei seemed to have got over the distress of being dumped by the pathologist.

I didn't want to stay for the noodles, so when no one was looking, I slipped out and went to Tian Yi's dorm.

The light in the cold corridor was flickering, as it always did when someone was secretly using an electric hob.

Tian Yi opened her bed curtain. All the other curtains in the dorm were drawn. I couldn't tell if there was anyone behind them. I hadn't taken Tian Yi back to our flat since Chinese New Year. My mother asked me why. I gave her an evasive answer. I hoped that, with time, Tian Yi would forget what happened in the woods and we could return to how we were before.

She was lying on her bed reading a book. When she looked up at me, I saw a sudden warmth in her eyes, and breathed a sigh of relief. 'Bai Ling is having a small party,' I said casually. 'You should have come over and wished her happy birthday.'

'I was waiting for you to turn up,' she said calmly. 'Dai Wei, don't get involved in this round of protests. You don't want to get arrested again, do you? It's not worth it. I want to live a peaceful life. Promise me that you'll remain a neutral onlooker this time.' She was lying under her quilt, staring into my eyes.

I sat down by her side. 'All right, I won't get too involved,' I said, then leaned down and kissed her. She didn't turn away. She kept her eyes fixed on me and switched her lamp off.

My heart pounded. I lifted her quilt, and soon our bodies were pressed together. She let the book she was holding fall to the floor and whispered, 'What if you disappeared one day, and I couldn't love you any more? What would I do?' She leaned over me and closed her bed curtain.

'Nothing's going to happen to me, I promise. And when I finish my PhD, I'll take you to America – the safest country in the world – and buy you your own private garden.'

'Don't talk nonsense,' she said, then whispered, 'You must promise never to tell anyone about what happened in those woods.' Then with her left hand, or perhaps her right hand, she slid a condom sachet onto my stomach.

We trembled silently on her single bed, inhaling each other's breath. Her body became hotter and hotter, and seemed to slowly sink into her mattress. Each time I pushed into her, the bunk would groan, so I tried not to move too much. I could hear another couple making love on a bunk near the window. They'd put on a tape of American music to try and cover the noise. '*When evening falls so hard, I will comfort you. I'll take your part. When darkness comes, and pain is all around, like a bridge over troubled water, I will lay me down . . .*'

After my penis softened, the condom slipped onto her leg.

'The tape on my English for Beginners cassette has scrunched up,' Tian Yi said breathlessly, loud enough for the other couple to hear. 'Will you help fix it for me?'

'Yes, I'll flatten it with a jar of hot water,' I answered, feeling a cold draught blow through my limp body.

Molecules wriggle through your cerebrospinal fluid like rain running down the branches of a tree.

'He's waking up!' my mother cries. 'Look, he's trying to open his eyes . . . I must disinfect everything – his clothes, quilt and sheets – everything . . .'

A woman standing nearby says, 'You should use Brightness washing powder. None of the other brands kill bacteria.'

'It's a pity I covered over the balcony,' my mother says. 'If I hadn't, I could have given these quilts a good airing.'

'Have any of his friends from university come to visit him?'

'I don't like them coming round. It upsets me to see other people of his age. If they knock on the door, I don't let them in. See, I've installed an eyehole in the front door. It only cost two yuan. You can see who's standing outside, but they can't see you.'

'The police won't be happy about that!' The woman sounds like the National Opera Company's bookkeeper.

'I don't care. Everyone in this building has got one now . . .'

. . . I hear Mou Sen shouting, 'This is too much! What's the matter with you Beijing University students? Have you gone to sleep?'

Students had been pouring into Wang Fei and Shu Tong's dorm all day, saying that it was about time Beijing University students took some action.

Ke Xi had just come back from laying wreaths in the Square. 'A new student movement has begun!' he yelled. 'Thousands of wreaths have been placed in Tiananmen Square. Central Academy of Art students have hung a giant portrait of General Secretary Hu Yaobang on the Monument to the People's Heroes.'

'A thousand of my fellow students at Beijing Normal University have gone to the Square to mourn Hu Yaobang's death,' said Mou Sen. 'Even the leaders of the official student associations went along.'

Shu Tong shook his head solemnly. 'We must work out a strategy,' he said. 'We can't deploy all our troops at once. This time round, we should let Han Dan's Democracy Salon lead the protest. The Pantheon Society should play a peripheral role. That way, we won't get in so much trouble if there's a clampdown.'

'You're such a prevaricator,' said Liu Gang. 'Can't you be decisive for once?' I'd never heard such urgency in his voice before. He'd just been awarded a part-time post at the Research Institute of Beijing Academy of Social Sciences.

'I think it's time to take action,' Old Fu concurred. 'Tomorrow morning, we should go to the high-tech firms in Zhongguancun District and ask for donations. When we've collected enough cash, we can make up the banners for the demonstration.'

'If you're going to demonstrate, don't discuss it in this dorm,' Big Chan said, flicking through a magazine. 'I don't want to get entangled in this.'

'Yes, go and do your scheming in the recreation hall,' Little Chan said, sitting on his clean bed.

'You limp dumplings! If you're afraid to die, get out of here!' Wang Fei despised those two.

'This isn't your home!' Little Chan shouted. 'You think you can turn this dorm into some August First Uprising Museum? Well, you can't!'

'Dai Wei, someone downstairs has just shouted that there's a phone call for you,' said Shao Jian, returning from a trip to the toilets. He was a round-faced, mild-mannered physics student, and the only guy in Wang Fei's dorm who didn't smoke. He didn't have a girlfriend, but he'd often stand in front of the mirror in the evening, clipping his moustache, as though he was getting ready for a date.

I was afraid that it was my mother calling, but it was my brother.

'Mum's just phoned,' he said. 'She told me not to take part in any demonstration. She knows you've put up some posters, and that you're thinking of going on a march.' The line crackled and his voice broke up, but that was usual with long-distance calls.

'Tian Yi must have phoned her. She's afraid I'll get into trouble again. You'd better not join the protests . . . No, I'm not going to the Square. I only stood in the Square for two minutes in 1987, but it'll be on my record for ever . . .' I didn't want to tell my brother too much, because I knew it would get back to my mother. I wanted him to study hard and get a job in Beijing after he graduated, so he could look after my mother and I could go and study abroad.

A few moments later the line went dead. I walked back up to the first floor.

'Stop arguing! The minority should obey the majority!' Cao Ming shouted. Although he'd joined the Pantheon Society, he seldom expressed any opinion.

'We must call for the overthrow of the one-party dictatorship,' Ke Xi said, standing in the doorway.

'And the end of economic profiteering by corrupt government officials,' said Chen Di, who was standing next to him.

'Instead of "overthrow", let's just say we want to "put an end" to one-party dictatorship,' Old Fu advised. 'We should draft a petition, with a list of specific requests. For instance, we can ask the government to give a fair appraisal of Hu Yaobang's political achievements.'

'And to repudiate the campaigns they launched against spiritual pollution and bourgeois liberalism.' Liu Gang and Old Fu shared similar views.

Mou Sen fiddled with his long fringe. 'Will you give me a haircut, Dai Wei?' he asked. 'It's getting too long again.'

'If you want to start a revolution, you should shave it all off,' I laughed. Then I remembered he'd told me that his father had been forced to shave his hair off before he left for the reform-through-labour camp. Only political convicts from the high echelons of society were allowed to keep a little hair at the top of their heads.

'We must call for the right to publish independent newspapers, and an end to press censorship,' Shu Tong said, scribbling into his notebook. 'Our demands must be concrete.'

'Yes, and autonomous, democratically elected student unions,' Ke Xi said.

'Mou Sen, you have a good way with words, and Dai Wei, you have nice handwriting, so the two of you should write a petition setting out the Pantheon Society's demands.' Old Fu was in high spirits. His face, usually the yellow colour symptomatic of hepatitis sufferers, was now slightly flushed.

'Yes, and we must put up a notice in the Triangle urging students to join our demonstration,' Shao Jian said.

There was a guy playing the guitar and singing a love song on the lawn outside Block 31. He kept shouting out to someone in the girls' block opposite, then shrieking with laughter.

'Dai Wai, you've got the loudest voice,' Shu Tong said. 'Tell that wanker that cocks aren't allowed to crow at night.'

I poked my head out of the window and yelled, 'Fuck your grandad!'

Other windows immediately flew open, and people shouted, 'Fuck your grandmother! Fuck you!'

After I shut the window, I heard the guitarist shout, 'Come down here if you've got any balls! I'll beat you to a pulp!'

So I opened the window again and shouted back, 'If you've got any balls, come up here!'

The news of Hu Yaobang's death had left the students in an anxious state. A few guys saw this squabble as an opportunity to let off steam.

Some ran out onto the lawn, others threw tables and chairs out of their windows.

I didn't want to get involved, so I returned to my dorm and had a drink of water. When I looked out of the window, I saw Wang Fei fling off his jacket, set fire to it with a cigarette lighter and toss it onto a heap of wooden stools and brooms.

Everyone became excited when they saw the blaze. They opened their windows and flung rubbish and newspapers onto the flames. I grabbed Dong Rong's smelliest pair of trainers and tossed them down too. The fire roared and crackled. I fastened my shoes and ran downstairs.

The guitarist had long since gone. A large crowd had gathered around the fire. The girls were shouting from the windows of their dorm block. They couldn't get out because their front door had been locked at eleven.

Wang Fei yelled, 'Let's go and rescue the girls!'

About ten guys ran over to the girls' block and kicked wildly at the two front doors until they crashed to the ground. Immediately, a stream of girls rushed out, screeching with excitement. I tossed a stone at the window of Tian Yi's dorm. She and Mimi turned on their light and peered out.

Shu Tong suddenly yelled, 'Come on everyone, let's march to the Square!' A huge commotion swept through the dorm blocks.

'The man who shouldn't have died has died!' Wang Fei cried, throwing his shoes onto the flames.

Another student threw a bicycle onto the fire. Scraps of burning paper swirled in the breeze. Mou Sen rushed outside to make sure that the bicycle smouldering in the flames wasn't his.

Helped by some guys, the girls lugged the two front doors that had been cramping their lives over to the bonfire.

By now, Wang Fei had thrown most of his clothes onto the fire, and was wearing only a vest and long johns. 'Down with corruption!' he shouted. 'Oppose official profiteering!'

Every light in the dorm blocks was now switched on. Mao Da and the recipient of my free haircuts, Xiao Li, leaned out of our window and I yelled at them to come down and bring my jacket with them. They joined me a minute later, and we rushed off to the Triangle.

A ten-metre strip of white cloth was being unfurled from the window of the creative writing students' dorm on the fourth floor of Block 28. The words CHINA'S SOUL had been painted on it in black. Shu Tong told someone to pull it down. He said that we should hold it aloft as we marched to the Square, then drape it over the steps of the Monument to the People's Heroes.

We ran over and tugged the cloth. The creative writing students hauled it back up, but after some more tussling we finally managed to yank it down. Then we proudly held it up and circled the dorm blocks shouting slogans. Outside the Social Science dorm block we yelled, 'Practice is the criterion by which truth must be tested!' Reaching the PhD block, we shouted, 'Doctoral students, the time has come for you to use your talents!'

By the end of our tour, our numbers had doubled. Liu Gang and Old Fu were ready to muster the troops and set forth. Because of my height, I was put in charge of security. Before we left, I went to find Tian Yi to check how she felt about this. As I approached her dorm block, I saw Wang Fei standing in the entrance, chatting up a pretty girl with short hair. I tried to drag him away, but he grabbed the door frame and refused to budge, saying he'd catch up with me in a minute. He and the girl then retreated into the dark hallway. I recognised the girl. She was Nuwa, the English major who was a member of the university's dance troupe. I'd seen her perform the Peacock Dance of the Dai national minority.

I shouted up to Tian Yi's window. She stuck her head out and said, 'Don't shout. I'm coming down . . .'

Han Dan walked up, followed by a large crowd of arts students. He was wearing a beige jacket. Someone had clipped his hair, leaving a long strand at the front that reached the frame of his heavy glasses. He had the lanky gait of a high school student but the expression of a wise professor.

He and Yang Tao had just returned from the Square. He suggested that we circle the campus again, with each department marching as a block, and that we position the tallest students at the sides to act as security marshals. Once we'd amassed enough people, we could set off for the Square. He'd already managed to gather a crowd of two or three hundred.

'Let's get moving!' Zhuzi the tall law student said, walking into the Triangle with a large wreath over his shoulders. 'The students from the Politics and Law University have been on the Square all afternoon.'

'How many Beijing University law students do you think you can muster?' Old Fu asked him.

'At least two hundred, I should think. We've already got about eighty from our Law and Democracy Research Society.'

Two hours later, just as the blocks of marchers from the various departments finally linked up and set off for the campus gates, Shu Tong asked us about the petition. Mou Sen said that he'd only written the first line, and that he wouldn't have time to finish it now.

About twenty university security guards had lined up outside the main entrance. They'd padlocked the gates to prevent the students from leaving the campus and were refusing to unlock them. Zhuzi and I walked over and asked them to pass us the key. One of them, probably a cadre, said that the university rules stated that the campus gates should remain locked all night.

The students began pushing against the gates.

I shouted to the guards, 'If you don't open them, you'll have to take responsibility for any injuries that occur.'

Then I heard Ke Xi shouting, 'Beijing University is paid for by the people! For the sake of the people we will lay down our lives!' Then he yelled 'Charge!' and we rammed into the gates again. The gates and the lamps beside them shook. The girls crushed at the front of the crowd screamed in pain.

Shu Tong, Liu Gang and Han Dan moved to the front and tried to reason with the guards again. Old Fu arrived, brandishing a huge red Beijing University flag. He must have got hold of a key to the university's Communist Youth League committee office. When he unfurled the flag, everyone clapped, and the students who were pushing bicycles rang their bells.

Tian Yi walked up with Mimi. She was holding a camera. 'Aren't you afraid?' I asked.

'I just want to witness the event with my own eyes, and take some photos,' she said. As she seemed quite calm, I asked her to try to get Wang Fei out of the girls' dorm block.

Someone had managed to talk the guards round. The gates were opened, and we filed out into the street.

As we waited there in the dark, everything seemed frighteningly quiet. All I could see on the road ahead were some men squatting down playing cards in a pool of light under a street lamp.

Old Fu and Shu Tong called Ke Xi and Han Dan over to decide on the slogans to be shouted. Each chose one, and scribbled it on a piece of paper. Ke Xi had only gathered about ten education students, so his group was forced to tag along with the science students. He and Shu Tong were to lead the procession. As the appointed head of security, I was to supervise the front of the march, while Zhuzi, who was taller than me, was put in charge of the tail. I told the taller students that they must act as marshals, and form a human chain on either side of the column, protecting the students from attack and preventing outsiders from joining our ranks. Yu Jin walked briskly over to me, his sleeves rolled up as usual, and begged me to let him join my team. Although far too short to be a marshal, he was very keen, so I relented.

'All right then,' I said to him. 'I'll guard the front, Zhuzi will supervise the back and you can look after the middle. If anything bad happens, we must let each other know straight away.' Then I spotted Chen Di. He looked very pleased with himself, standing at the front of the crowd with his Russian binoculars hanging around his neck. I asked him to help me out, but he said that Old Fu had told him to lead the slogan-shouting.

I rolled a sheet of paper into a conical tube and shouted through it as I walked back along the column of students: 'Each department group must march behind its banner. Organise yourselves into rows of four, with the girls on the inside and boys on the outside.'

'We couldn't find a Social Science Department flag, so we made up this banner instead,' Hai Feng said, pointing to the red banner his group was carrying. Since his three-day detention for organising the 1987 demonstration, he'd concentrated on politicising his fellow social science students.

'How many of you went to the Square yesterday?' I asked him.

'About twenty. Most of them were graduate members of my Social Research Student Club.' The light from the street lamp was bouncing off the thick lenses of Hai Feng's glasses, so I couldn't see the expression in his eyes.

'Shao Jian!' I called to Shu Tong's dorm mate. 'You stay on the left, and I'll stay on the right.' I pulled off my red paper armband, tore it in two, then slipped one band onto my arm and gave him the other.

Old Fu came up from the back and said, 'We've got about two thousand students here now. Let's get moving. The board of governors will probably be coming down here any minute.'

Wang Fei turned up with Bai Ling. He was wearing a blue tracksuit.

Bai Ling said the computer she'd been writing her thesis on had just crashed, so she'd decided that she might as well join the revolution. Nuwa, with her boyish haircut, was standing next to her. Her T-shirt had a low scoop at the front. Her neck was even longer than Tian Yi's. She was the prettiest arts student in the university. I felt very uncouth standing next to her.

I told her to lead the slogan-shouting at the back and she said, '*OK!*' in English. Mou Sen walked over, pushing his bicycle. I borrowed it from him and rode up and down. The students seemed to have formed quite an orderly column.

Just as we were about to set off, Professor Chen from the Education Department came up and stood in front of us. He and a few other professors had been having a private discussion by the campus gates. He shouted, 'Students, your patriotic fervour is laudable, but if you walk out onto the streets, the authorities will look upon you in a very different way.'

Tian Yi glanced nervously around her. I said, 'Cao Ming's dad is an army general. If Cao Ming has dared join us tonight, it means that the authorities aren't about to take any strong action.'

No one wanted to listen to Professor Chen's advice. They shouted, 'Students from hundreds of universities are already in the Square. Don't stand in our way!'

'Ignore the professor!' Ke Xi yelled. 'We can't hang around here any longer. Let's go!'

Professor Chen got on his knees and sobbed. 'Students, don't stir up any more trouble, I beg you! If you march to the Square, it will be the end of the new liberal General Secretary, Zhao Ziyang.'

'Don't listen to him!' Wang Fei shouted. 'He's a neo-authoritarian!'

Shu Tong and Ke Xi grabbed the professor's arms and dragged him back inside the campus. Old Fu said to him, 'Just stay here, Professor, and think things over for a while.'

Mou Sen whispered into my ear, 'Perhaps the professor is right. Once we shoot this arrow, there'll be no going back.'

'The reform process has reached a critical stage,' Professor Chen shouted. 'Don't start demonstrating now, for God's sake! Let society progress peacefully.'

Chen Di began shouting the slogans. 'Beijing University is supported by the people! For the sake of the people we will lay down our lives!' A wave of excitement swept over us and we set off, echoing Chen Di's chants.

The dark, empty street stretched before us. Occasionally, someone returning home from a late shift would stop on the pavement and watch us pass.

At the Huangzhang intersection we saw two police vans parked on the side of the road. I became anxious. I knew that if I got arrested a third time, my mother would never forgive me. My detention in 1987 had denied her the opportunity of singing a duet in the opera company's annual gala.

But our chanting gave us courage. I joined the rest of the marchers in shouting, 'Oppose official profiteering! Down with corruption!'

Our procession surged forward like a train, rolling straight past the two police vans. The officers standing outside didn't try to stop us.

When we reached the gates of People's University, we shouted out to the students inside to join our march. Lights came on in the dorm blocks. Students opened their windows and shouted, 'We'll come with you, Beijing University! Just give us a moment to get dressed!'

'We can't wait for them, Dai Wei,' Zhuzi said, walking up to me. 'We must keep moving. They'll soon catch up with us.'

'Yes, we must keep going until we reach Tiananmen Square,' Cao Ming concurred. The khaki military suit he was wearing boosted our morale.

Yang Tao and Hai Feng, who'd been marching in the centre of the procession, ran over and said, 'Some of the students are already going back to the campus to get some sleep. We can't hang around any longer.'

After we crossed the next intersection, we saw about a hundred policemen and ten police vans blocking our path ahead. From a distance, they looked like a black wall. Light from the street lamps flashed off the windscreens and a few of the policemen's helmets. Chen Di climbed onto a rubbish bin, looked through his binoculars and announced, 'They're not holding electric batons. Their hands are empty.'

The procession immediately came to a halt. Han Dan, Hai Feng and the leaders of each department group stepped to the side and discussed what to do next.

'They've blocked us off before we've even reached the Square,' Cao Ming said. 'The university must have told them we were coming.'

'They haven't got guns, there's nothing to be afraid of,' Wang Fei said.

Nuwa's mouth was trembling with fear. 'We don't want to get ourselves arrested. It's the middle of the night. We should turn round and head back to the campus.'

Remembering my previous arrest, I too was nervous, but part of me wanted to keep going and put up a fight.

'Go and ask them if they'll let us through,' Ke Xi shouted, loud enough for the police to overhear. 'If they won't, we'll have to charge into them!'

As our procession began to march forward again, Tian Yi and Bai Ling retreated to the back. Nuwa was walking arm in arm with Wang Fei, so she had no choice but to keep moving. When we were just a few paces away from the police, we halted again.

The policemen remained silent. They didn't look as though they were planning to make any arrests.

Nuwa stepped forward and said, 'Dear officers, we citizens are acting in accordance with the constitution . . .' but was soon interrupted by Ke Xi, who shouted, 'Comrade policemen! Fellow countrymen! We have come out tonight, on behalf of students from universities across Beijing, to go to Tiananmen Square and lay memorial wreaths for Comrade Hu Yaobang on the Monument to the People's Heroes. As we're sure you can understand, we are very saddened by his death. We sincerely hope that you will let us through . . .'

The officers stared at him, saying nothing in reply.

We stood where we were and stared back at them, continuing to chant our slogans. Han Dan turned to me and said, 'Get the students at the back to come forward, so that we can line up facing the police. We'll stay here shouting slogans and singing songs until they get fed up and let us through.'

Local residents who'd been woken by the commotion poured out onto the pavements to see what was going on.

An hour went by.

Then Ke Xi went over to the policemen again and shouted, 'You are Chinese citizens, just like us. We are all grieving the death of Hu Yaobang. Please, comrades, let us pass!' The students behind him cheered and clapped their hands.

After a few minutes of silence, we heard a policeman announce through a megaphone, 'We were given orders to stand right here, so that's what we'll do.'

Once the crowd had understood what this meant, they laughed and cheered and moved forward, weaving their way past the officers and the vans. Some even chanted, 'The people's police love the people!'

I couldn't take this display of leniency at face value. I remembered how brutally the police treated us in 1987, and it seemed unlikely that their attitude could relax so much in just two years. I suspected that they were leading us into some kind of trap.

In the middle of the crowd, Nuwa waved her hands and cried, 'Beijing University students are fearless!' She really was the prettiest girl in the university. Tian Yi and Bai Ling were walking hand in hand. I promised myself that if the police started making arrests, I'd make sure that Tian Yi didn't come to harm.

Shu Tong turned to Han Dan, who was walking beside him, and said, 'What are we going to do when we get to the Square?'

'I don't know,' he answered. 'It was your idea to march there.'

'Well we must get a speech ready, and draft the petition. Old Fu, borrow a bike from someone and go back to the dorm to work on it. We'll wait for you in the Square.'

'All right,' Old Fu said. 'I'll call for a favourable re-evaluation of Hu Yaobang's career, and a clampdown on official profiteering. Mou Sen, will you help me write it?'

'OK. Give me that opening paragraph you wrote, Shu Tong.' Mou Sen grabbed the sheet of paper that Shu Tong handed him, then hurried back to the campus with Old Fu.

Your soul is this heap of flesh, or perhaps it doesn't exist at all. The internal landscape of your body is riddled with caves.

If only my mother would remove the incontinence pad that's fallen underneath my bed. She dropped it last week. Although it's almost dry now, I can still smell the urine. Ever since my sense of smell returned, the odours that have repelled me the most have been my own.

When dusk falls, I can smell the oil on my mother's sewing machine next door. Sometimes I can smell my herbal pills and the scent of washing powder on the damp clothes draped over the radiator.

I listen to the ringing of bicycle bells and the cooing of pigeons preparing to return to their nests, and long to hear, among those sounds, the metallic noise of Tian Yi's shoes clipping up the stairwell. I was with her when she went to the cobbler's shop on the lane outside the campus to have those metal plates nailed to the soles . . . I open my ears and nostrils and, like a shark that swallows draughts of sea-water hoping to catch a few small fish, I let all the noises outside flood into me. I heard my mother mention to someone that Tian Yi has made two visits, but I must have been unconscious both times, because I have no recollection of them.

Since I've been in this vegetative state, I have been able to re-experience smells and sounds from my past. These are the tiny details people generally store in the back of their minds and never get a chance to savour again.

Your flesh is enclosed in skin, your bones enclosed in flesh, your marrow enclosed in bone, but where do you fit in?

We reached the Square before sunrise. As we'd expected, it was filled with mourners and wreaths.

A huge black-and-white portrait of Hu Yaobang had been hung on the Monument to the People's Heroes at the centre of the Square. We trod through the paper flowers that littered the ground to the north side of the Monument, where seven wreaths had been laid. The largest was from the students of the Politics and Law University. We brought out our wreath and ceremoniously placed it next to the others, while Yang Tao read out the eulogy we had prepared. He was wearing a tight Lenin-style jacket and brown sunglasses. He looked like a newly qualified young professor.

Wang Fei and Nuwa walked over, hand in hand. They were the same height. I guessed that the blue tracksuit he was wearing belonged to her.

We climbed to the upper terrace of the Monument and formed a human ladder so that Hai Feng, who was the lightest of us, could clamber to the top of the obelisk and hang up the long white sheet daubed with the words CHINA'S SOUL. As the first rays of sun lit up the sky, the white cloth turned pale orange.

Hai Feng stood there for a while, addressing the crowd. 'We've made our three demands,' he concluded. 'Now let's see what more we can do!' His voice was still strong. But after shouting slogans for so many hours, I could hardly speak. I glanced around. The heavy rainfall a few minutes before had driven many students from the Square. Some had rushed over to the north side to watch the daily flag-hoisting ceremony. Others had wandered down to the south end to buy some snacks in the Qianmen market. There were only about two hundred people left in the middle.

I managed to find Tian Yi. I wanted to reassure her that I wouldn't take part in any future demonstrations. But when I opened my mouth, no noise came out. Chen Di had borrowed my jacket and my shirt was wet. I longed to change into some dry clothes and have a cup of hot tea.

Tian Yi laughed at me and said, 'Don't try to speak. You seem wiser when you're silent. You did a good job tonight. I never realised that you were such a good organiser.' She smiled. 'We should go to Hu Yaobang's private residence and lay some more wreaths there. It's only six o'clock now.' The v-neck jumper she was wearing under her waterproof jacket looked snug and warm.

'We've no more wreaths,' I croaked. Mimi picked up Tian Yi's camera and pointed it at us. I grabbed Tian Yi's hand. She squeezed it briefly then pushed it away. But when the shot was taken, I was still holding her with one hand and waving the university flag with the other.

She turned to me and smiled. 'Why is your expression always so wooden? Take off that mask!' She looked happy and relaxed. I felt proud to be standing next to her.

I could usually walk to the Square in two hours, but it had taken us double that time. After standing in the Square for another hour, we were so tired that we all sat down on the wet paving stones.

Liu Gang wandered through the seated crowd, asking the students if they were happy with the wording of the draft petition that Old Fu and Mou Sen had brought back. Hai Feng and Zhuzi encouraged everyone to chant slogans, afraid that they might lose interest and start drifting back to the campus. After a calm discussion, we settled on seven demands, which included an affirmation of Hu Yaobang's liberal views on democracy and freedom, a renunciation of past campaigns against spiritual pollution and bourgeois liberalism, pay rises for teachers and professors, an increase in press freedom and freedom of speech and the end of restrictions on demonstrations in Beijing.

Shu Tong placed his handkerchief on the ground, then sat on it and said, 'Good! At last we know what we're doing.'

'I saw you having a nap on the steps of the Monument just now,' Shao Jian said, lying flat down on the ground, too exhausted to sit up any longer.

'I hate going a night without sleep,' Shu Tong answered. 'Liu Gang, tell Old Fu to come over. We need to revise the petition and get more students to come to the Square. Tell him we're going to submit the petition to the government on the steps of the Great Hall of the People.'

Fortunately, a few tourists and local residents began trickling into the Square, making our crowd appear a little larger. Zhuzi and Chen Di said that everyone sitting on the ground should be in neat rows. I asked Yu Jin to help shout out the orders.

More and more onlookers gathered around us. Wang Fei suggested that we inform them of our goals. Having an audience cheered us up. They applauded us. Some even tossed us the dough sticks and buns they'd bought themselves for breakfast; others handed us cigarettes and money. Shu Tong told the students not to snatch the food, but everyone was so hungry they ignored him. Bai Ling caught a bread roll that was tossed in her direction and shared it with the rest of our gang.

A man who looked like a worker sat down next to us. He claimed to be volunteer teacher, and said that we were behaving irrationally.

Wang Fei lost his temper, and said, 'Do you know what the average teacher's salary is?'

'Do you imagine we're doing this for the fun of it?' said Nuwa. 'Last week the papers reported that China's investment in education is the second lowest in the world!'

'But things are changing now. Investment in education is going up, not down. And, look – you were able to march all the way from your campuses to the Square without getting arrested.' The man looked as though he'd just finished his morning jog. His hair was damp with sweat.

Wang Fei flung his half-eaten bun at the man and said, 'Whose bloody mouthpiece are you? I've had enough of hearing people say that things are getting better. It's bullshit!'

Ke Xi and Hai Feng persuaded the man to leave. Nuwa criticised Wang Fei for being too hot-headed.

When the rays of the morning sun reached the Monument's obelisk, we decided that Han Dan and Hai Feng should visit the reception office of the Great Hall of the People to discuss submitting our petition to Premier Li Peng.

Ten minutes later, they came out of the office and announced that the petition would be received by the deputy head of the State Bureau of Letters and Visits.

Wang Fei and Shu Tong said that this wasn't good enough. Cao Ming agreed that we shouldn't deliver the petition to such a petty official.

'It must be received by a member of the National People's Congress Standing Committee, at the very least,' Shao Jian said.

But Liu Gang and Yang Tao argued that the official's rank was unimportant. They said that if we managed to submit the petition publicly, in front of all the students gathered in the Square, we would have achieved our goal and could return to our campus in triumph.

I was handed a fountain pen and a poster-sized sheet of paper and told to start writing the seven demands we'd agreed on.

I glanced at Tian Yi's face. Her lips were pursed, but her eyes were calm. She didn't appear to object to what I was doing.

A universe circulates through your body. Noises pierce it like bolts of lightning. Sparks of light join, then disperse, like the head and eyes of a foetus on a sonogram.

I turned off my alarm clock and went back to sleep. I'd been up very late the night before, keeping watch over the posters in the Triangle. When I woke up again it was already six thirty in the evening.

On the table in the middle of the dorm were the strips of cloth Wang Fei had ripped from his bed sheet and daubed with the words DOWN WITH OFFICIAL PROFITEERING. His zeal seemed a little excessive. Tian Yi thought so too. She said that he was a narcissist and lacked the dignified air of a scholar.

I jumped out of bed and went to brush my teeth. Although the canteen would have already finished serving supper, I knew that Tian Yi would still be waiting for me there.

The entrance to our dorm block was splattered with muddy footprints. I guessed that it had been raining outside.

I took the short cut along a dirt track that passed through a patch of thick undergrowth. Overlapping male footprints marked the way. Girls instinctively avoided this patch of male territory, preferring the cement path that turned at a right angle. I was annoyed to see how tattered my shoes were. But at least I knew I could afford to buy a new pair, unlike Xiao Li who was so poor he had to play football in his bare feet.

The voice of the rock star He Yong blared out from a cassette player in one of the dorms: '*God bless the people who've eaten their fill. God bless the workers, the peasants, and the people's militia. Let those who want a promotion be promoted, and those who want a divorce get divorced . . .*'

Tian Yi was sitting alone in the canteen. 'I wish you wouldn't take the short cut,' she said as I walked up to her. 'Your shoes always get covered in mud.'

'I can't help it. I hate walking the long way round.'

'Hey, let's go and have a look at the posters in the Triangle.' Her white woollen scarf reflected a pale light onto her chin as she spoke. 'The politics students have put up lots of new ones today.'

'I don't like being a bystander,' I said, yawning. 'And anyway, I've only just got up and I haven't had a thing to eat yet.'

'I only want to read them. I won't write them down.' Although her tone was quite casual, I could sense that she'd had a change of heart and was now eager to get involved in the student movement. She leaned over and pressed a peanut sweet into my hand and asked, 'So which poster did you put up?' A draught blew in through the open door. The evening air felt clean and cold.

'I haven't put any up. You told me not to get involved, didn't you?' Remembering Tian Yi's dislike of sarcasm, I added softly, 'Let's go and take a look then, if you want. Just keep an eye out for any undercover agents.'

She glanced at me disdainfully and strode outside. I followed her out and looked beyond her at the large crowd of students in the Triangle. They were shining torches and candles onto the red-and-white handwritten posters pasted to the noticeboards.

Nuwa and another girl were about to stick their handwritten poster to a board. Nuwa's yellow down jacket looked very bright.

'Put it on top of that one!' someone shouted. 'What idiot wrote that?'

The poster said I'VE LOST MY UMBRELLA. WHOEVER SNATCHED IT FROM ME CAN KEEP IT. I DON'T CARE. THE CHEAP BASTARD!

I pointed to another that read AN HONEST MAN HAS DIED. THOSE WHO REMAIN ARE SWINDLERS AND LIARS! 'That's the one I put up,' I told Tian Yi.

'I thought you'd written an essay.' Tian Yi sounded a little disappointed.

'I'm not very good with words,' I confessed, looking her in the eye.

Another poster gave an account of our previous day's activities: . . . STUDENTS FROM OTHER BEIJING UNIVERSITIES JOINED US IN THE SQUARE THROUGHOUT THE MORNING. WE STAGED A SIT-IN, REQUESTING A DIRECT DIALOGUE WITH THE GOVERNMENT LEADERS . . .

'Why did they write it on a sheet of newspaper?' Tian Yi said. 'It looks so stingy.'

'Many departments have set up donation boxes,' I said. 'The tourism students have collected more than a thousand yuan already. They've bought an electric megaphone and a typewriter.'

'Put it up a little higher,' Nuwa said to her friend.

'My hands are shaking!' the girl said. 'We've only been here a few minutes, and I'm already scared out of my wits. Look, there's a surveillance camera pointing towards us. Hey, Dai Wei, will you come and help me put it up?'

I went over. As I helped the girl lift the poster, I caught a whiff of Nuwa's fragrance. It was a foreign perfume. I'd smelled it before in the lobbies of the luxury hotels in Guangzhou.

'How come you didn't get Wang Fei to help you?' I asked Nuwa.

'Why would I need him?' Nuwa said, turning the other way.

'Look at this one,' Tian Yi said, pulling me over. 'It says, "The Democracy Salon is staging a poetry reading in memory of Hu Yaobang. Everyone welcome."'

'Looks like Han Dan is getting busy again.'

'He seems very methodical.' Tian Yi glanced around her and said, 'Why isn't the lamp working tonight? Come on, let's go over there – it's lighter.'

'Someone must have smashed the bulb.' I didn't tell her about the fight I'd got into the night before. She hated violence. The university authorities had broadcast a series of announcements reminding students that they must return to their dorms by 11 p.m. Wang Fei suspected them of having some plan up their sleeves, so he and I slipped out and kept watch over the Triangle. Once all the students had left the area, four or five guys, who looked like security officers, turned up and ripped down all the posters. One of them smashed the Triangle's only lamp. We decided to follow him. When he realised we were trailing him, he tried to run, but I caught up with him, grabbed hold of his jacket and punched him in the face. Wang Fei swore, 'I'll kill you, you son of a bitch!' The guy confessed at once that the university's Youth League committee had told him to smash the lamp.

The university had already forbidden the small shops inside the campus from selling batteries or candles to the students. It was no longer possible to buy even a sheet of paper on the campus.

'Look how they've written "Emergency Meeting",' Tian Yi complained. 'The characters are a mess. Don't they know anything about calligraphy?'

My eyes fell upon another notice that read LOOKING FOR FRIENDS: I LIVE ON THE THIRD FLOOR OF THE ECONOMICS STUDENTS' MALE DORM.

I'M A LITTLE INTROVERTED, WITH NO PARTICULAR HOBBIES APART FROM READING. I WOULD LIKE TO MAKE FRIENDS WITH SOME MEMBERS OF THE OPPOSITE SEX, SO THAT I WON'T HAVE TO SPEND THESE PRECIOUS UNIVERSITY YEARS ON MY OWN . . . On the bottom right-hand corner someone else had scribbled FUCK OFF!

'It's too dark here. Look, someone's turned on a torch over there, let's go back,' Tian Yi said, dragging me away.

We squeezed our way into the crowd. Students at the front were reading out the posters to the students at the back. But there were so many people shouting that you couldn't grasp much. Students who were taking notes asked them to speak more slowly. Only a few fragments were audible to me, for everyone, male and female, was speaking at once, in different accents and at different speeds: 'Lost the hearts of the people . . . to the afterworld . . . boycott classes . . . resisted the police . . . from their filthy mouths . . . journalists should speak the truth . . . who shouldn't have died . . . let the wind carry him away . . . if we follow these suggestions . . . consign to the flames . . .'

I could hear Bai Ling's voice cutting through the din. It was clearer and faster than the others. She read out a poster that urged students to boycott classes. But she spoke so fast that the students at the back asked her to repeat it. She shouted back to them that her candle had gone out now and that she couldn't see a thing.

Tian Yi grabbed a torch from someone and asked the students in front of her to pass it forward to Bai Ling. While it was moving from hand to hand, someone switched it on. The beam of light shuddered above the crowd, until at last the torch was placed in Bai Ling's hands.

A girl next to her was reading a poster by candlelight. Her hand took on the orange of the flickering flame.

I remembered a fire breaking out while Tian Yi and I were queuing for tickets at Kunming railway station. I was holding Tian Yi's hand and she was so terrified that she dug her middle finger deep into my palm. When the fire was extinguished, she looked at my purple bruise and asked blankly, 'Does it hurt?'

As we squeezed our way out of the crowd, Tian Yi said, 'Did you hear that one? A law student wrote it. It was very cogent.'

Sister Gao and Old Fu were approaching us. Sister Gao hadn't brought her notebook this time. 'What are the students hoping to achieve with all these posters criticising the government hardliners?' she asked.

'They're just frustrated,' Tian Yi said. 'They need to let off some steam.'

'The posters are getting too personal,' Old Fu said. 'We can't start pointing our fingers at Premier Li Peng. How are we to know whether he's a bad guy or not?'

'You're right,' Sister Gao said. 'Li Peng has only been in his post for a year. Besides, he's only Premier. Zhao Ziyang is General Secretary, so *he*'s the man in charge. If we want to crack down on corruption, we should start looking at his record first. I've heard rumours that his son has been involved in profiteering.'

Liu Gang joined us. 'The student movement has really taken off,' he exclaimed. 'We'll have to set up some kind of organisation, or there'll be chaos.' Then he turned to Sister Gao and said, 'You know lots of students in the Creative Writing Programme. It's important that we get them involved.'

'Most of them are government officials,' Sister Gao said. 'They're part of the elite. They won't want to risk their necks for us.'

'But they've produced the best posters,' Old Fu said.

'Zheng He wrote them all. The other writers stood by and watched.'

Liu Gang lit a cigarette and said, 'We need input from people like you in the Philosophy Department, Sister Gao. Once the movement gains momentum, you'll be our intellectual backbone. It will be like a second Boxer Rebellion.'

Tian Yi became bored with the discussion and muttered to me, 'Han Dan's giving a speech. Let's go and listen to it.' Raindrops fell on her fringe. She swept the hair away, exposing her broad forehead. 'Hurry up! If you don't want to come, I'll go on my own.' She was buzzing with energy that night.

All I wanted to do was find a street stall and have a bowl of wonton soup and a meat pie. So I said, 'I'm starving. Go on your own, and I'll join you once I've had something to eat.'

'Why are you so morose tonight?' she asked coldly, then turned round and walked away.

Her sudden change amazed me. After just one day in the Square, she had become a different person. Two days before, she'd told me to be careful what I said in public, because two-thirds of the students were government informers. Now she was fearless and couldn't care less who overheard our conversations.

After my meal, I went to keep her company. We didn't return to her dorm block until two in the morning. The caretaker had gone home by then, so it was safe for her to smuggle me inside. Someone had removed the bulb from the overhead light in her dorm, which was a sign that one or more of the other girls had brought their boyfriends back as well. Tian Yi and I had to grope our way to her bunk bed in the dark.

As you drift through your body, you see living cells charge through the darkness, crashing into each other, dividing and dying.

'Last week, in the early hours of 2 August, Iraqi soldiers invaded the Gulf state of Kuwait . . .'

'Is this door meant to be open, Auntie?'

'Tian Yi! How good to see you! Come in, come in! Leave the door open. It's too hot in here. How did you manage to get time off?'

'I've just finished my exams. We break up in a couple of days. It wasn't easy getting permission to leave the campus. It's guarded like a prison now.'

'Yes, I've heard. Hey, your skin's much darker, and your hair looks thinner too. When I last saw you, you had your hair in two thick bunches.'

Is that really Tian Yi's voice? I can't believe it. She's come: the girl I think about every day. She's alive, while I'm lying here covered in flies, as motionless as a corpse.

Memories of her face, her smell, even her love letters that I kept in a biscuit tin, come flooding back to me. My brain releases into my bloodstream the mixture of phenylethylamine and seratonin that is known as love.

She's in the sitting room. My mother has just finished massaging my feet and thighs.

'How's Dai Wei?'

'He's skin and bone now. I'm still giving him medication. As long as he doesn't suffer any more fevers or convulsions, his condition won't get worse. Every few hours I have to move his legs and feet about to stop his joints seizing up. He's in a very weak state, but somehow he just refuses to die.'

'I've brought some strawberries. Here, you eat them. They're fresh. I'll wash them for you.'

'Don't worry, I'll wash them. You go in and take a look at him.'

She walks in to my room. As she approaches, I smell the scent of sweat between her toes that used to excite me so much. I can hear leather rubbing against leather. It's her sandals.

She sighs and says, 'Dai Wei. I'm here again . . . Auntie, I'm going to put on the electric fan for him.' She presses a switch and the fan starts turning.

She isn't sitting on the bed, so I can't hear the sound of her breathing. I long for her to stretch out her hand and touch my face. I'm naked. Every centimetre of my skin is waiting for her touch.

She goes to open the curtains. She probably wants to get rid of the flies. I hope she'll take away the radio that's lying next to my head.

'Are these his medical records? From the look of this electrogram, it seems that his brain is still active.'

'Can you understand those notes?' My mother is breathing very heavily.

'No, they're full of medical jargon. This first paragraph says that he was admitted to hospital on 4 June 1989, with a bullet injury to the brain, and was suffering from numbness and paralysis. On 6 June 1989 the bullet was removed from his head under general anaesthetic.'

'Don't go on. Even if I understood what the notes meant, it wouldn't change anything. Tell me, how are things with you?'

'The police and the university are still investigating my case. The self-criticism I wrote hasn't been assessed yet.'

'My advice is to just do as you're told. The important thing is that you graduate. You don't want to end up like me, pestered every day by the police then staring at my son's face all evening. It's a living hell.'

'You must be patient. He might wake up one day.'

'Because of his political background, the hospitals are forbidden to treat him, so I have to pay private doctors to treat him on the sly. At first, the neighbours were sympathetic. They came round and told me not to worry, and said that the government would soon reverse its official verdict on the Tiananmen protests. But as soon as the police began to target me, they stopped coming. When I pass neighbours on the street nowadays, they look away in terror, as though they've seen a ghost.'

'Chen Di told me that the police visit you a lot.'

'They come two or three times a week. They tell me not to speak to journalists or leave the flat. They demand the names of everyone who comes to see me. But you don't want to hear all this! Tell me, have you applied to go abroad yet?'

'There's no point in applying. They'd never let me go. Dai Wei's old dorm mate, Xiao Li, committed suicide the other day. He jumped off the top of the dorm block. The university was forcing him to write a self-criticism. One of the crimes he was accused of was singing the national anthem in public. They said he endangered public security. The Chinese people aren't even allowed to sing the national anthem any more!'

'Yes, I remember him. He was that boy in Dai Wei's dorm who came from a peasant family. Perhaps he's better off dead than living like a convict. The leaders of the opera company wanted me to write a statement saying I supported the government crackdown. It made me so angry. I've stopped reading the newspapers. I've lost all interest in politics. I don't even want to hear about this guy Jiang Zemin who's taken over as General Secretary.'

So Xiao Li killed himself. I can't take it in. My head throbs. Who is left from my dorm now? I seem to remember Mao Da visiting a few months ago, saying that Wang Fei has been discharged from hospital and has returned to his parents' home. So at least Wang Fei is alive. But perhaps my mind is playing tricks on me, and Mao Da never visited. Tian Yi's voice sounds very real, though. It can't just be my imagination.

The radio is too close to my ear. The female presenter whines: 'Today's newspapers are crammed with spurious advertisements that ask: Do you want to gain a place at university? Travel abroad? Grow taller? Have whiter skin? Get your name into the *Oxford Dictionary of National Biography*? If you do, please send your money to . . .'

Through the noise, I strain to catch Tian Yi's words, and try to imagine what she's wearing. 'Beijing University has become like a military camp,' I hear her say, 'or a Communist Party Academy . . .'

'Dai Wei's great-uncle died a few weeks ago. His son Kenneth sent us the money that was left for us in the will. At first the police wouldn't let me collect it, but they relented in the end. Kenneth asked whether you still want to go and do a Master's in America. Will you write him a letter in English?'

'Yes, of course. But if he sends a reply to my home or university address, it probably won't reach me.'

'I'll get on with the supper. You just sit here . . .'

'No, don't worry, Auntie. I'm going to eat with my parents tonight.'

'You've come all the way here, so stay a little longer, please. It's nice for me to have someone to talk to . . . No one speaks to me any more. Dai Wei had a seizure a few months ago, and I knew I'd have to take him back to hospital. I called out for help, but my neighbours bolted their doors. Those Marxist-Leninists! They're terrified of stepping out of line . . .'

'Their devotion to the Party is an obsessional neurosis. No one living in a dictatorship has a healthy state of mind . . . You go into the kitchen. I'll read him a passage from *The Book of Mountains and Seas*. It's his favourite book.'

'Oh dear, I haven't seen that book for a long time. I think his brother might have taken it.'

'Don't worry. I'll recite him something from memory.' Tian Yi wants my mother to go away and leave her in peace for a while.

Her lilting voice stirs up agitated thoughts. Perhaps today a chink will open in the walls that enclose you.

'Dai Wei, can you hear me? You're as skinny as that strange creature in *The Book of Mountains and Seas* that has the face of a man and the body of a monkey. But unlike you, that creature could speak, and change shape.' She turns down the radio and continues, 'Do you remember how you dreamed of going on a great journey, exploring all the mountains and rivers described in the book? You can't go anywhere now, so I'll just recite you a passage and you can travel there in your mind. Hmm. Do you want to head north, south, east or west? I think I'll take you north . . . If you walk on for another 110 li, you reach Spring Border Mountain, where wild onions, peaches and pears grow. The River Stick springs from its foothills and empties into the Yellow River below. A wild beast with tattoos lives on the mountain. It often roars with laughter, but as soon as it sees a human approach it pretends to be asleep . . . Do you remember what that beast is called?

In my mind, I answer: it's wild sunflowers and chives that grow on the mountain, not onions and pears. And the River Stick flows into the Col Marshes, not into the Yellow River. But I can't remember what that creature is called.

'You know the jingwei bird I like so much? Do you remember which mountain it lives on?'

Mount Fajiu. The jingwei is the reincarnation of Nuwa, Emperor Yandi's daughter, who drowned in the East Sea. Every day, to punish the sea that drowned her, she picks up twigs and stones from Mount Fajiu, then drops them into the East Sea, vainly hoping to fill it up.

'Do you remember the manman bird? It has only one wing and one eye, and has to pair with a mate if it wants to fly. I'm like a manman bird now that has lost its mate. How will I ever fly again?' She falls silent.

I long for her to touch my hand, then I remember the cadaver that I am.

'I wish you were around to look after me. At university, it feels like we're guarded by wolves.'

I miss you, Tian Yi. As that phrase repeats through my mind, I begin to feel myself returning to reality.

'If I hadn't written a self-criticism, I'd have been kicked out of university. We've been forced to act like slaves again.'

We joined the student movement to break free from our prisons, but we've all had to return to them now.

'The university's police officers will interrogate me when they discover I've visited you. I didn't feel like talking to your mother just now. I didn't want to be reminded of what happened. I study psychology but it's I who need a psychiatrist. What's the point of life without freedom?'

I wish I could hug you, Tian Yi. I'm inhaling your breath. Until this moment, I wasn't afraid of dying. But now I know that you're here and will be leaving any moment, the thought of death terrifies me.

'Shall I put another pillow under his head, Auntie?' Tian Yi composes herself as she hears my mother approach. I imagine there are tears in her eyes.

'No, don't bother. This room smells horrible, doesn't it? Sit on this chair. It's where I sit when I massage his hands and feet. Look how clenched they are. If I didn't massage them, they'd be as stiff as dried mushrooms.'

Tian Yi stretches out her hand and touches my foot. She squeezes it, then tries to swivel it around at the ankle. Although she can't turn it very far, the touch of her skin gives me so much joy that I could faint . . . We pulled off our trousers and I lay on top of your soft body. I placed the washbasin over our heads to muffle the noise of our breathing, then I switched on the cassette player. It was the 'Nine Hundred English Sentences' tape. A clipped voice droned: *Alan, please take this gentleman to the nearest bus station* . . . Not so loud, you gasped into my ear. Through the washbasin, it sounded as though the whole dorm room was shaking. There was sweat on your neck. You trembled, then flinched suddenly like a rabbit touched by an electric wire. *Where do you want to go? To the Japanese garden* . . . Switch it off, I tried to say, but before the words came out you pushed your tongue into my mouth . . . *No, I am not Chinese, I am American* . . .

The blood rushes through your veins. The reproductive mechanisms expel sour fragrances through your pores.

Tian Yi helps my mother remove the drip from my arm, squeezes my hand softly then rests it on the edge of the bed. I imagine a rubber band or paper clip hidden in the folded palm of her other hand.

She gets up and leaves. She stayed for less than two hours. Perhaps the smell of the room drove her away. Or my mother's constant prattle, or the supper she prepared.

I picture my head as it must be: sunk deep in the soft pillow, and beside it a herbal cushion, some fallen hair and my mother's spectacle case.

I take a deep breath. Tian Yi left no scent in the air.

Irritating sparks of light flash across my closed eyelids. The lamp on the wooden chest at the end of the bed is probably shining onto the glass syringes. I know this room so intimately that when I breathe in I can see everything laid out before me.

My mother switches the light off, and again I become one with the darkness.

Your lungs inhale the world outside. Memories move through your liver.

It was drizzling outside my dorm window. I could tell there had just been a heavy downpour. The lawns were green and wet. In the distance, I could see girls standing in the grass by the lake. They were blots of red and black in a sea of green, with the pale grey sky behind.

Everyone was moving quietly through the damp air. Ke Xi looked conspicuous, waving his hands about as he delivered his speech on the lawn.

Big Chan and Little Chan stopped to listen as they walked back to the dorm with their lunch boxes, and were nearly knocked to the ground by a student who cycled up behind them.

A couple walking hand in hand wandered slowly towards Ke Xi. As the rain petered out, a few more students gathered round him.

Chen Di opened our window and cried out, 'Beijing University has lost its balls!'

'Stop shouting!' Qiu Fa said, lying on his peony-printed cotton sheet. 'And you'd better pay me back for those empty bottles.' Before we'd set off for the march, Chen Di had gone to the window and thrown out all the bottles Qiu Fa had been keeping under his bed.

'I didn't touch your bottles,' Chen Di said, snatching his binoculars out of my hands.

'Why couldn't you have thrown your tumbler out instead?' Qiu Fa moaned, removing a folded shirt from under his pillow. 'The shopkeeper gives me two jiao for each returned bottle, and I had seven of them.'

'You're such a liar! They were Erguotou bottles, not beer bottles – no one gives money for those.'

'I stick Yanjing Beer labels on them, and no one can tell the difference. So cut the bullshit and hand over the money. At least give me a couple of jiao . . .'

I went next door to wake up Wang Fei. A few minutes later we all went outside. There was to be a meeting to discuss the formation of an organising committee. We'd pasted up notices and were hoping that many students would attend.

'Ke Xi is a general without an army,' Wang Fei said, staring at him through Chen Di's binoculars. 'Look! He's standing there all on his own, shouting to the heavens. No one's paying any attention!'

I thought of the poet, Haizi, who despaired of China's future. If he'd known the students would rise again, he might not have thrown himself in front of a train.

'He doesn't want Shu Tong to gain the upper hand,' I said. 'He won't get much support from his classmates in the Education Department, though. Those girls are such conformists. Wang Fei, that girl Nuwa hasn't been to visit you for a couple of days. Why's that?'

'Because I haven't asked her to, that's why,' Wang Fei replied, sounding pleased with himself.

'You've gone and got yourself the prettiest arts student,' I said, my mind suddenly returning to Lulu, the girl I fell in love with in middle school.

'Jealous, are you? And the general consensus is that she's not just the prettiest arts student, she's the prettiest girl in the university.' Wang Fei had recently been spending more time in front of the mirror. He'd washed his hair twice and bought himself a new jacket at the farmers' market. It was a cheap tailored jacket made of dark-blue nylon and lined with face-mask fabric.

Students who were on their way to the library wandered over to the two tables on which Ke Xi was standing. Shao Jian arranged the chairs he'd carried out from the dorm block. Liu Gang pulled out a megaphone and explained to the students how crucial it was to set up an independent student organisation and launch a new wave of protests.

When the students broke into applause, hundreds of people streamed over.

By the time it was Old Fu's turn to speak, a crowd of about two thousand had gathered. Old Fu talked about the 1987 demonstrations, and said we should now set up an organising committee. He emphasised that it would only be a temporary body, and would be disbanded as soon as the student movement came to an end in order to prevent any opportunists from taking it over and using it for their own political purposes.

'The movement hasn't yet started and already you're talking about what's going to happen when it ends,' Zhuzi muttered into his ear. 'We managed to get a few rounds of applause a minute ago. Don't spoil the mood. Dai Wei, it's your turn to say something.'

I climbed onto the tables. I hadn't prepared a speech, so I spouted the first thing that came to mind. 'Fellow students!' I shouted. 'The government is very crafty, so we must organise ourselves if we want to put up a fight.' Then my mind went blank, and I forgot what point I was trying to make. I could hear people sniggering at the back. 'But of course, the government is very clever as well . . .' I quickly added, but that only made people laugh louder.

'Are they crafty or clever? Make up your mind!' students shouted, waving their lunch boxes in the air.

Before I had a chance to reply, Ke Xi intervened and said, 'The government is an unelected, illegal organisation. The official student bodies it has appointed are therefore illegal too. Who is in favour of forming a democratically elected student union?'

The crowd went silent. The question needed serious thought.

Fortunately, Tian Yi had left the campus to collect donations, so hadn't witnessed my humiliation. I swore to myself that I would never speak in public again.

Zhuzi jumped onto the tables and shouted, 'Fellow students! What we need most is rule of law. Only that is going to save China. When we say that we oppose dictatorship, that doesn't mean we want to overturn the government.' Before he had a chance to say more, the crowd broke into applause. As he stepped down, I shouted out, 'Give us rule of law! Down with corruption! Down with bureaucracy!'

Wang Fei asked to speak, but Chen Di complained that only the students from Sichuan would be able to understand his accent. This annoyed him so much, he jumped straight onto the tables and launched into his speech. He started off in standard Mandarin, but soon slipped back into Sichuanese. Although few of the students could make out what he was saying, they listened courteously.

'If you support these views, have the guts to raise your hands and volunteer to join our organising committee,' Old Fu shouted.

Two or three minutes went by without anyone raising a hand. They were talking among themselves. They were afraid. Joining an unofficial organisation was held by the government to be a counter-revolutionary crime. When we were arrested in Tiananmen Square two years before, the first thing the police wanted to know was which organisation had coordinated the protest. Fortunately, there were no organisations back then. The protests had flared up spontaneously.

Old Fu heaved himself up onto the tables and said, 'Let's ask the chairmen of the student union to lead this initial stage of the movement. If any of these chairmen are present, please come forward and speak!'

There were now about four thousand people. It was the largest crowd I'd seen on the campus, but there was no way of knowing whether any of the student union chairmen were present. Although Old Fu and Cao Ming belonged to various official associations, they were now only low-ranking members. Mao Da, who was chancellor of the student union, hadn't been seen for two days.

Ke Xi grabbed the megaphone and shouted, 'If there's anyone here from the student union, they should have the balls to stand up and take over the leadership! Students from People's University and the Politics and Law University have gathered at the Xinhua Gate of the Zhongnanhai government compound demanding that the Party leaders come out and speak with them. We can't delay any longer. The student movement is under way. It's here now. Those who fail to join it will be condemned by history!'

Liu Gang climbed onto the tables and said, 'Everyone shout after me: "Leaders of the student union, come up and give us your leadership!"'

The huge crowd shouted out in unison, but no one came up.

'All right, shall we disband those official unions then?' Liu Gang yelled.

'Yes! Disband them!' The crowd was growing larger and noisier all the time.

A group of students poured through the campus gates and walked towards us. Old Fu said they were from Qinghua University.

Zhuzi went to greet them. One of them was a dark, rugged guy called Zhou Suo. He said that no one at Qinghua University was prepared to lead them, so they'd decided to come and join forces with us.

'So are we going to set up our own student body?' Old Fu yelled impatiently to the crowd. The cheers became quieter.

Ke Xi shouted through his cupped hands, 'If no one else wants to step forward, then those of us who've spoken during this meeting will become the founding members of the organising committee. Do you agree to this?' The crowd cheered and clapped their hands.

'I hope you will all attend our meetings and lend us your support!' Old Fu shouted. 'I hereby announce that for the next two weeks our committee will lead Beijing University's democracy movement. After that, we must set up an independent student union and let it take charge.'

Although I hadn't intended to join any organisation, I was standing by the tables with the other speakers, so I had no choice.

Shu Tong returned from Xinhua Gate just as the meeting was drawing to a close. Ke Xi told me to draw up a list of the people who'd spoken. Not wanting Shu Tong to be excluded from the committee, I dragged him over and told him to address the crowd. Old Fu handed him a megaphone and pushed him up onto the tables, saying, 'Don't lift your chin when you speak. Keep your head down.' He was afraid the students might find Shu Tong's manner arrogant.

In his gravelly voice, Shu Tong told the crowd that thousands of students were staging a peaceful sit-in outside Xinhua Gate, the southern entrance to the Zhongnanhai compound in which the government leaders live and work. He said that the student movement had kicked off and would soon spread to the rest of the country, and he urged Beijing University to join it at once.

His description of the sit-in surprised the crowd, because a few hours before, the state television had reported that the students at Xinhua Gate had demanded to speak to the government leaders and that, when their request was refused, had attempted to storm the gate. The report showed shots of armed officers with blood pouring down their faces, and claimed that the students had hurled empty bottles at them. But Shu Tong insisted that the mood was peaceful, and accused the government of fabricating lies. He admitted that there had been some pushing and shoving and that a few students and officers had got hurt, but denied that the students attempted to storm the gate. He said all they wanted was to submit their petition.

When the meeting came to an end, Ke Xi asked Shu Tong to join our committee too. He agreed, but suggested that we change the name to the Beijing University Solidarity Student Union Preparatory Committee, to make clear our spiritual links with the Polish democracy movement.

But we stuck to the name 'Organising Committee of Beijing University Independent Student Union' and drew up a list of founding members: Old Fu, Ke Xi, Liu Gang, Wang Fei, Zhuzi, Yang Tao, Shu Tong, Shao Jian and myself. We appointed Old Fu convenor, made up a batch of armbands and began printing off flyers and leaflets. Yang Tao was sent to Qinghua University to help them set up a committee of their own. At ten o'clock we convened a meeting to formulate an action plan. Then most of the guys set off for Xinhua Gate to join the sit-in. I hadn't slept properly for two days, so I staggered back to my dorm and went to bed.

Perhaps the rain has stopped. Everything sounds calm outside. All you can hear is the swish of bicycle wheels that grows louder and then fades away again.

At five in the morning, I was woken by a loud commotion. I rushed out into the corridor and heard students climbing up the stairs shouting, 'We were at the sit-in at Xinhua Gate. The police beat us up. They attacked us with electric batons. Lots of students have been rushed to hospital!'

I flung on some clothes and followed everyone else out to the Triangle. Wang Fei was there. 'Hundreds of policemen charged at us,' he yelled, his voice as hoarse as a cockerel's. 'They pushed students into their vans, beating anyone who resisted. Girls who didn't manage to run away fast enough were kicked and beaten too!'

'At three o'clock, ten police officers rammed a student from Wuhan against the wall,' Shao Jian continued. 'They whipped him about the face with leather belts. There was blood everywhere. One of his eyes was beaten out. It was horrible.' His usually calm voice was shaking. He told everyone to shout with him as he cried: 'Boycott classes! Save our nation! Punish the violent assailants!'

'The students are innocent! Patriotism isn't a crime!' the crowd yelled. Students were waking up and joining us in the Triangle. There were hundreds of us gathered there now.

'We must stage a mass march to tell the public what happened,' I said angrily.

Although not all the members of Organising Committee were present, Old Fu gave the go-ahead for the march and Shu Tong agreed. I dashed off ten posters attacking the police violence and calling for a class boycott. Chen Di and I then stuck them onto the bulletin boards, the campus gates and even the sides of public buses.

Han Dan hobbled back, weak and panting for breath. He told us that undercover agents had infiltrated the sit-in. They had walkie-talkies. They stole some of the students' shoes and flung them at Xinhua Gate to give the police a pretext to attack the crowd. 'Punish the perpetrators of violence! Boycott classes!' he shouted indignantly. None of us could go back to sleep after we heard this news, so we set to work on organising the march.

Now that the student movement had taken off, we felt a weight of responsibility fall heavily on our shoulders.

At dawn we went to the corner shop and bought paper, black ink and a large roll of red cloth – long enough to make five ten-metre-long banners. Chen Di's girlfriend had collected two thousand yuan in donations, which was much more than Tian Yi had managed. Although the girl spoke with an annoying nasal twang, she had a persuasive manner.

I carried the roll of cloth to Sister Gao's dorm. Tian Yi and Bai Ling helped cut it into banners and armbands. I wrote PUNISH THE POLICE! and LET THE TRUTH BE KNOWN! onto the banners while the girls wrote slogans on the paper pennants I'd prepared.

Thousands of students gathered in the Triangle, ready to set off on our march. I rushed to the canteen with Tian Yi and wolfed down a plate of steamed dumplings, then raced back to Wang Fei and Shu Tong's dorm, which had now become the Organising Committee's stronghold. When I arrived, Wang Fei was arguing with Old Fu, who'd changed his mind and now thought that we should cancel the march and focus on building up democracy within the campus.

Only seven of the nine members of the Organising Committee were present. We took a vote. Liu Gang sided with Old Fu, but Shu Tong,

Han Dan, Wang Fei, Zhuzi and I voted to carry on with the march. Although I secretly agreed with Old Fu and Liu Gang, I didn't want the banners and pennants we'd made to go to waste.

'All we want is a bit of democracy,' Old Fu said. 'There's no need to stir up a popular movement.'

'If you want democracy, you must fight for it, not waste time spewing empty rhetoric!' Wang Fei tossed his cigarette stub onto the cement floor and stamped it out, then picked up the banner he'd made from a torn bed sheet.

'The Chinese people have been on their knees since 1949,' Han Dan said. 'It's time they stood up and stretched their legs.'

'You shouldn't dismiss my views,' Old Fu countered. 'Lenin said that truth often lies in the hands of the minority.'

'We've put up hundreds of notices about the march,' Zhuzi said disgruntledly. 'The students are waiting to set off. We can't back out now. You don't have to join us if you don't want to, Old Fu.'

'All right, then, I hereby resign from the Organising Committee,' Old Fu said, removing his glasses as sweat trickled down his forehead.

'You haven't slept much these last few days, Old Fu,' I said, pulling him out into the corridor. 'Your eyes are swollen. You should get some rest, give your liver time to recover, then reconsider all this when your mind's a little clearer.'

He moved closer to me and said quietly, 'I've written my suggestions on this piece of paper. Here, put it in your pocket. If you get a big enough crowd, go ahead with your march. But if the numbers dwindle, cancel it. As head of security, that's your prerogative.'

I told him to go and have a nap on my bed, and said we could talk about this later.

Wang Fei had returned from Xinhua Gate unharmed, so I suspected he'd sneaked away from the sit-in to avoid getting caught up in any violence. 'Hey, Wang Fei, I bet you fled as soon as the armed police turned up!' I smiled.

He wiped the thick lenses of his glasses and said, 'As I was leaving, a policeman stopped me. I told him I was a magazine editor and just passing by. But the bastard searched my pockets and found a bread roll, so he knew I'd been there all night. Before I had a chance to come up with an excuse, he kicked me in the bum and told me to get lost.'

'Bet you were shitting yourself!' I laughed.

'He was a big brute of a man. He could have broken me in half with just one hand.'

'Did Nuwa go with you?' I imagined that if Nuwa had been there, she would have been shocked by his cowardice.

'She went to a party at Jianguo Hotel,' Wang Fei said sullenly. 'It was some French guy's birthday.'

'Don't waste your time being jealous,' I said. 'There's nothing you can do. She's surrounded by admirers.' There was a sudden clap of thunder. The sky outside the window darkened.

Having heard that Old Fu had resigned from the Organising Committee, Ke Xi walked in and said, 'I'll take over as convenor during this march. When we get back, we'll hold a meeting and have a proper election.'

Shu Tong didn't look happy. I knew he wouldn't approve of Ke Xi taking over the leadership.

As I'd expected, he said, 'Given the current state of affairs, I'd like to hand in my resignation as well. I think you'll do a better job without me. And besides, I was never elected to this post.'

The meeting quickly broke up. I was surprised that Wang Fei hadn't objected to Ke Xi's plan.

Sister Gao, Bai Ling and Mimi arrived with curtain poles and the banners we planned to attach to them.

Bai Ling told me that Tian Yi had a stomach ache and wouldn't be joining the march, but that she wanted me to take great care.

The bright-red banners filled us with revolutionary fervour. Everyone grabbed an armband and slipped it over their sleeve. The ink characters on two of the long banners were still wet, so Bai Ling and I took them to the Triangle and hung them out to dry.

The waiting crowd drifted towards us. Some departments had prepared even larger banners than ours. Students everywhere waved their home-made pennants in the air. Ke Xi and Han Dan were both holding megaphones. Although I was head of security, it hadn't occurred to me to buy myself one.

Han Dan got up and explained the rules of the march. He told everyone to stick to the official slogans. He said a girl at Xinhua Gate had shouted 'Down with the Communist Party!' as she was flung into a van, which gave the police an excuse to attack the crowd. He asked the students who'd turned up with bicycles to put them away and join the march on foot.

Then he handed me his megaphone and told me to say a few words.

'You must walk in rows of ten,' I said. 'The stronger students should stand at the sides and hold up the banner-poles. Everyone else should hold hands so that no outsiders can infiltrate our ranks. Only students with ID cards can join us today. If you want to go to the toilet during the march, take a friend with you. There will be police everywhere.' As soon as I paused for breath, Ke Xi raised his megaphone and shouted,

'Fellow students! If the police try to block our path or cut us up, just stand firm!'

Then everyone sang the Internationale and set off for Qinghua University.

Mou Sen caught up with us on his bike, and told us that thousands of Beijing Normal students were waiting to join us when we reached their gates.

Local residents standing on the pavements applauded as we passed, and drivers who'd stopped at the intersections hooted their horns in support. Wang Fei and Yu Jin held up a bed sheet. Bystanders gazed at it in bewilderment, unable to understand the slogan GIVE ME LIBERTY OR GIVE ME DEATH! written in English across it.

The weather was not on our side. When we reached Qinghua University, it began to pour with rain. A voice blared from four loudspeakers attached to the roof of a jeep parked outside the main gate: 'Beijing University students, if you want to demonstrate, go back to your campus! The Qinghua students are attending lectures and don't want to be disturbed.'

A few people inside the dorm blocks opened their windows and looked out through the driving rain to see what was going on.

Ke Xi said, 'All the Qinghua activists have gone to the Square. The students who've stayed behind are conformists. They wouldn't dream of coming out onto the streets with us.'

'Shall we storm their campus gates?' Chen Di said, walking up to us. He was pleased to be wearing his binoculars around his neck again, and to be leading the slogan-chanting.

Turning his back on Ke Xi, Shu Tong said to Han Dan, 'No, let's see if the Politics and Law University will join us. Mou Sen, cycle over to your campus and tell your classmates we're going to be a bit late.'

So we headed for the Politics and Law University, and sent Shao Jian ahead to warn them we were coming.

When we reached the main gates, the rain became torrential. Many of our marchers ran off to seek cover in the shops lining the road. But the Politics and Law University students remained stoically at their gates waiting to welcome us. It was like the military forces of Zhu De and Mao Zedong uniting on Jinggang Mountain to form the Red Army. They told us to go and warm up in the canteen, where there was food waiting for us.

The leader of the Politics and Law University's Organising Committee was a good friend of Liu Gang's. He advised us not to march in the rain.

I was wet and cold, and wanted to go back and see Tian Yi. Yu Jin and Chen Di also said they'd like to return to the campus. Now that we were sitting comfortably inside the canteen, the idea of marching through the rain again wasn't appealing.

'The government will laugh at us,' Zhuzi said gloomily.

'We can't turn back halfway!' Ke Xi said, knitting his brows. 'There are thousands of students waiting for us at Xinhua Gate and Tiananmen Square.

Shu Tong didn't want to give up either. 'If we stay here any longer, the marchers will lose motivation. Let's push on while our spirits are still high. As head of security, Dai Wei, and a member of the Organising Committee, you must comply with the will of the majority.'

Han Dan came over and said that he was going to head off alone to the Square to read out an open letter, and that he'd wait for us there.

I pulled out the note from my pocket, and told Shu Tong that Old Fu had advised me to abort the march if our numbers dwindled.

I decided that, whatever anyone else said, I wasn't going to march in the rain, so I put on my wet jacket again and went back to the campus with Chen Di.

You're wrapped inside a body that you can't see, a prisoner in a jail you can't touch.

A cold snowflake falls onto my face. My mother has left the door open. Two chickens have scuttled in, and are pecking at the ground near my bed. Last night, when everyone in the building was asleep, my old dorm mates Mao Da and Zhang Jie carried me out of the flat on a stretcher, put me in the back of a taxi and brought my mother and me to this shack in the outskirts of Beijing. I never paid them much attention in the dorm, so it's surprising that now, of all my friends, it is they who have come to help me.

I hear Mao Da walking towards the door, saying to my mother, 'It's all arranged. You can take him in tomorrow morning . . .'

He and Zhang Jie shoo the chickens away, shut the door, then lift up my camp bed and move it next to the window. I can smell the wood shavings and rotting cabbage leaves lying in the corner of the shack.

'Did you speak to that Dr Liang again?' my mother says.

'Yes. He asked whether Dai Wei has had oxygen treatment before. I had to say he had, otherwise they would have needed a signature from the hospital's director. Things are very tightly controlled now. Any doctors found guilty of treating victims of the crackdown are immediately sacked from their jobs.'

'We've paid for a two-week course for Dai Wei,' Zhang Jie says. 'It only cost three hundred yuan. It's called high-pressure oxygen treatment. It uses the latest technology. They'll push him inside a big oven-like machine then use shock waves and electromagnetic waves to stimulate his brain cells and improve his body's immune system.' These are almost the first words Zhang Jie has uttered since he and Mao Da picked us up last night. I remember how, in the beginning, his quiet and reserved demeanour led everyone in the dorm to suspect him of being a spy.

'I've heard that, after just one week of this treatment, paraplegics have been able to walk again,' Mao Da says. He still speaks in the wooden tones of a government cadre.

My mother's voice sounds full of gratitude. 'Here, have a cigarette, you two. Go on! I really can't thank you both enough!' She always keeps cigarettes in her pocket now, to hand out to anyone who offers help.

'We rented this shack for you from a peasant,' Zhang Jie says. 'If someone comes and asks questions, tell them you're from Fangshan County. Here's the document stating that you supported the government crackdown. No hospital will treat you without it.'

'We left some lights on in your flat when we locked up for you last night, so that your neighbours won't get suspicious,' Mao Da says, then takes a puff of his cigarette.

'The police haven't visited us for almost a month,' my mother says. 'It's probably the winter weather that's kept them away.'

'You're only a kilometre from the hospital's north entrance here,' Mao Da says. 'We paid the peasant who owns this shack an extra three yuan so that you can use his handcart. You should be able to wheel Dai Wei to the hospital without being seen by too many people.'

'Have you got enough money and grain coupons, Auntie?' Zhang Jie asks.

'Last month, the wholesale markets were selling grain at knock-down prices,' Mao Da says. 'We probably won't be using grain coupons much longer.'

'The last bus back to Beijing will be leaving soon,' my mother says. 'You'd better hurry. I wouldn't want you to miss your classes tomorrow.'

'Our grades don't matter any more,' Mao Da says. 'We'll be given jobs out in the sticks whatever marks we get. I don't care. I've decided to go to Shenzhen next year, and look for a job in a private company. Here's Dai Wei's hospital card. Go to the brick building we took you to this morning and ask for the neurosurgery department. Your appointments are at five o'clock every afternoon. I registered him under my surname, so he'll be known as Mao Daiwei. Right, we'd better get going.

I'll visit you again in a couple of days. Dai Wei, hurry up and wake up, will you? Show those bastards that we won't be defeated!' He pats the blanket draped over my stomach. I'm freezing. All I'm wearing is a vest and thin cotton trousers.

Only when I'm wheeled inside the hospital's high-pressure oxygen room a few hours later do my limbs begin to thaw out. A male voice says, 'First we must check whether he has any metal objects on him.'

'I've removed them all,' my mother says. 'It's very hot in here! Please, have a cigarette.'

'No thanks, I don't smoke.' The man turns on some switches, taps the metal oxygen canisters, shuffles around the room for a moment, then pushes me into the chamber. 'As the pressure starts to increase, his ears might hurt and he'll feel a rise in temperature.'

'I've been told that already. Don't worry about the pain. He's a vegetable, after all.'

I know about these chambers. They help boost oxygen levels in the brain and control the spread of bacteria. When I read about them in the papers, I had no idea that one day I'd be pushed into one. If the pressure or heat become unbearable, I have no means of letting anyone know. What if my eardrums burst?

The door to the chamber is sealed shut. A pain develops in my ears that soon becomes excruciating. The wound in my head seems to catch fire. As the temperature shoots up, I feel myself lapsing into unconsciousness.

From the wound in your frontal lobe, you slip into the brain's central fissure, then travel down the vagus nerve to the noisy thoracic cavity.

It was Mao Da who woke me up the morning after the aborted march. His face was drawn and pale.

'That meeting you held last night – was it in this dorm?' he asked.

'No, Shu Tong's.'

'You reshuffled the Organising Committee, didn't you? Shu Tong resigned, Old Fu was sacked and Ke Xi was promoted.'

'Yes. Who told you?' I sat up and pulled on a T-shirt. I could smell Dong Rong's smelly trainers. His socks stank as well. Tian Yi always complained about the stench when she visited our dorm. Qiu Fa walked off to the washroom carrying his enamel basin. Xiao Li was still asleep.

Mao Da glanced around the dorm to check no one else was listening, then whispered, 'You are the only person I will tell this to. Listen, because I'm only going to say it once: the university's Party branch filmed your meeting last night with an infrared camera. I'm a Party member. They called me over and asked me to identify who you were. Your friend Mou Sen is in deep trouble. They've had people following him for days. They suspect him of being a Black Hand – an undercover conspirator working for a secret organisation. They've sent the tape to the Ministry of State Security. Let me remind you that the Party considers student demonstrations to be a form of "contradiction among the people", but views the establishment of independent organisations as a "contradiction between the people and the enemy", which is a much more serious affair. I strongly advise you to dissolve your committee immediately.'

'I would never have guessed that you were a spy, Mao Da,' I said, astounded by this revelation.

'I've chosen to tell you because I know you won't blow my cover. I don't want any of you to get into trouble. I didn't sleep all night. If you dissolve the committee at once, you'll be fine.' He folded his quilt, placed it neatly on the end of his bed, picked up his bag and left the room.

I was dumbstruck. My legs were shaking. The face of the executed convict we'd dissected at Southern University flashed through my mind. I remembered the dirty graze above his one remaining eye. He'd been condemned to death for setting up a group called The Young Marxists. In the past, we hadn't dared form an organisation. This time, we had gone too far.

I lit a cigarette. My throat felt tight. The bicycle that Dong Rong had bought two months before lay propped against the wall. He couldn't sleep at night unless he brought it into the room. He was worried that if he locked it up outside someone might steal it.

I stuck my head out of the window and looked down. I could smell the mud on the trucks driving into town from the countryside, and the sour scent of the discarded eggshells behind the street stall. Everything looked the same as it had the previous day. The only difference was that there were now two vans I'd never seen before parked outside our block.

Xiao Li woke up. I told him that the police were going to arrest us. He said, 'They won't do that. The most they'll do is monitor us to make sure we're not meeting with foreign journalists or dissidents.'

I passed him a cigarette.

After a couple of drags I felt a little calmer. I reminded myself that the authorities had reacted leniently to our New Year's Day demonstration in 1987 and the 1988 protests that followed the murder of the graduate student. And we were less vulnerable this time, because so many more students had got involved.

'Just make sure you don't go anywhere alone,' Xiao Li said, glancing out of the window. 'They can't arrest you if you're in a group.' I worried for him. His peasant background hadn't equipped him for a situation like this.

I wanted to warn Mou Sen at once that he was being followed, so I went down to the ground floor and gave him a call.

Fortunately, he was in his dorm. I told him go and stay at his girlfriend Yanyan's flat and lie low for a few days.

I could tell from his voice that he was scared.

'Yanyan's away at a conference. Where else can I go?' Although Yanyan was fond of Mou Sen, she was very ambitious and her job always came first. She was now an assistant social affairs reporter at the *Workers' Daily*.

'Move to our campus, then. You can be our resident writer. We science students are no good at writing petitions and speeches.' I pictured him rubbing his nose. He always did that when he was nervous.

'Oh God! I wrote a poster yesterday calling for workers, peasants, intellectuals and private entrepreneurs to support our class boycott. The government could accuse of me of counter-revolutionary subversion and send me to the execution ground.'

Both our fathers had been condemned as rightists. When we talked about their lives, it always left us with a sense of powerlessness.

I tried to reassure him. 'The government won't do anything until after Hu Yaobang's state funeral tomorrow. And who knows, the protests might have cooled down by then.' I saw Yu Jin approach, and quickly put down the phone.

I bought a couple of steamed rolls from the canteen then went to find Shu Tong. He was in the library, reading up on the American constitution.

'It's a bit late for that now, isn't it?' I said, sitting down and biting into a roll. The library was usually packed, but today half the seats were empty. I lowered my voice. 'The university's Party committee filmed our meeting yesterday. The tape's been sent to the Ministry of State Security. Don't ask me who told me.' I didn't want to betray Mao Da.

'I don't have to ask! That bloody informer. He's such a fraud. As soon as he's screwed his girlfriend, he shows her to the door then lies down and pretends to read Buddhist scriptures. Who does he think he's fooling? It's obvious he's monitoring our conversations.' He clearly assumed that the spy was Zhang Jie.

I changed the subject. 'Wang Fei told me that the Pantheon Society is going to set up a broadcast centre and publish an independent student paper called the *News Herald*.'

'Yes, we talked about it this morning,' he said, sticking his chin up. 'You're not really afraid, are you? My brother's an officer in the Beijing Garrison Command. He said there's no real cause for concern. Anyway, if you worry too much, you'll never achieve anything.'

'They're watching our every move. Your resignation has allowed Ke Xi to take control of the Organising Committee. If he creates trouble and forces the government to clamp down, every member of the committee will end up in prison.'

'Leaders emerge in times of chaos, and it's always the radical ones who gain the support of the people. We should encourage Wang Fei to step forward. He's the most militant science student. We should get him to take over the leadership of the committee, then keep him under our control.'

'Wang Fei isn't a good public speaker, and even when he's following your orders, he's not very competent. The question now is, should we strengthen the Organising Committee, or take the movement underground?'

'We can't go underground. After the graduate was murdered last year, some friends roped me into joining a secret organisation. Although I was trying to persuade them to go public, the university's security office drew up a file on me and interrogated my mother. Whatever we do, we must do it openly.' Shu Tong's mother was a Party official at the Beijing Commodities Bureau.

'Are you going to Tiananmen Square tonight?' I asked, calming down a little. 'The authorities have said they will cordon it off tomorrow for Hu Yaobang's state funeral. But the students who want to pay their last respects to him are going to attempt to get round the curfew by camping on the Square tonight.'

'Well, *you'd* better go, or you'll be out of a job, Mr Security Chief!'

'About 100,000 students are expected to turn up. All the flags and pennants in the fabric shops have sold out.'

'As long as you get to the Square before the curfew comes into force, you should be fine,' he said, tapping the copy of *The Constitution of the People's Republic of China* that he was holding. 'There's a notice outside the Great Hall of the People saying that the 38th Army has been called into the city, but Cao Ming's father, who's a top general, says they refused to obey the order. It seems that factional rifts are emerging within the army.'

When I had finished the steamed rolls, I left Shu Tong and went back to the dorm. Soon after, I received a long-distance call from my brother. He said that his fellow students at the Sichuan University of Science and Technology had made three memorial wreaths for Hu

Yaobang, but the authorities had confiscated them and burned them in a lane outside his campus. The students were furious, and wanted come up to Beijing to join our memorial activities.

'Stay in Sichuan,' I told him. 'Mum keeps telling me not to get involved. If you came to Beijing, she'd never let you out of the flat.' I didn't want him to join our student movement. He had no experience in politics.

'The student union members are leading our protests, so I'm sure we won't get into trouble.'

'Don't take them at face value. One of the guys in our dorm is the chancellor of our student union. We all thought he was on our side, but today he confessed to me that he's been spying on us for the government.' As soon as I said this, the line went dead. I waited for a minute in case it got reconnected, then handed the phone to the person waiting behind me.

Wang Fei panicked when I told him we were being spied on. He said he'd stay in the dorm from now on. He was terrified of being arrested.

'You have the heart of a wolf but the balls of a rabbit!' I laughed. 'You strode out into the streets yesterday and set fire to a copy of the *People's Daily*, but now suddenly you're quaking with fear.'

'Let's wait and see what happens after Hu Yaobang's funeral tomorrow,' he said through gritted teeth.

You listen to the juices flowing through the pancreatic duct and the blood cells rushing down the left gastric artery to the dark-red folds of the peritoneum.

'Let's sing it faster this time, and with more spirit: *The little white house with the pointed roof – that's my home . . .*'

My mother is giving a singing lesson. She took early retirement from the National Opera Company after the Spring Festival holiday, and since then has been preparing three students for the Central Academy of Music's entrance exam. It's Saturday today, and as usual she's locked the door to my room to make sure her pupils don't catch sight of me.

'Slow down a bit a here: *I open my window and gaze into the sky . . .* Now, much more emotion: *The sun shines onto my house, and the first sweet kiss of spring is mine . . .*'

The three students repeat each line after her, so loudly that the whole flat shudders. Even my intravenous-drip stand is shaking.

'Put more passion into the words when you hit the higher notes. Come on, one more time . . .'

'*. . . and the first sweet kiss of spring is mine!*'

One of the three girls has a deep voice that reminds me of A-Mei's. A-Mei always promised she'd sing to me one day, but she never did.

'I hear your father is a doctor,' my mother says.

'Yes, he works at the Friendship Hospital.'

'There's an imported drug I've heard about that's very effective in treating stroke victims. Apparently, you need the consent of a hospital director in order to get hold of it.'

'Write the name down for me, and I'll ask my father about it when I get home,' the girl says. I can tell from her voice that she's taller than my mother.

As soon as the three students leave, An Qi, who came round yesterday, turns up.

She lives just a few bus stops away from us. Her husband was shot by the army in the Xidan District just west of Tiananmen Square, leaving him with a shattered pelvis. He's had countless operations, changing hospitals each time to avoid being tracked down by the police. He recently contracted a virus following a blood transfusion, and no hospital will treat him now.

'Be careful he doesn't get conjunctivitis,' An Qi says, observing my mother clean my eyes with alcohol solution. 'You should wash them with medicated eye lotion, and apply tetracycline ointment every other day. Never use alcohol.'

'Really?' my mother says, continuing to wipe the alcohol over my eyes. 'I've always cleaned them this way.'

'If you carry on doing that, he'll be blind by the time he opens his eyes. You'd be better off sewing the lids together with a needle and thread. If he wakes from his coma, you can just cut open the stitches.'

'You've picked up a lot of medical knowledge. You sound like a qualified nurse!'

'If I hadn't read up on these things, my husband would be dead by now . . . How many drip bottles does he get through a day?'

'The glucose solution he's on now has added vitamins, so it's more expensive than the others. I've had to cut the dose down from six bottles a day to four.'

'My husband's needle wounds have blistered like that too. They look like lepers, don't they?'

My mother turns down the radio and joins An Qi on the sofa.

The young woman sounds as though she doesn't move her lips when she speaks. Who else do I know who speaks like that . . . ?

'I feel like I'm back in the Cultural Revolution,' she says. 'My neighbours stare at me when I leave my flat. When I come here, that old granny downstairs asks me who I've come to see, and what about.'

'Everyone's suspicious of us. Before I retired, the opera company forced me to write a statement expressing my support of the crackdown. They said that if I didn't, they'd turn me out of this flat. I had to write it three times. They kept complaining that it didn't sound sincere enough. It was just like those letters you have to write when you apply to join the Party.'

My predicament has caused my mother to question her political beliefs.

The two women sit on the sofa, talking away until nightfall.

'What kind of country is it that punishes the victims of a massacre, rather than the people who fired the shots?' my mother says again.

'I went to see that primary school teacher whose husband was shot near Muxidi. She told me that crematoriums are now forbidden from keeping the ashes of people killed in the crackdown. She had to collect her husband's box of ashes and bring it home with her. She's put it on top of her wardrobe.'

'Yes, I heard she told her mother-in-law that he's gone missing. She couldn't bring herself to tell the old lady he's dead. Apparently, the old lady isn't too concerned about her son's disappearance. During the Sino-Japanese War, she was told that her husband died on a battlefield, but a few years later he turned up at her house, alive and well.'

'You know that woman in Mahua Lane, well, she got so sick of being harassed by the police and having to care for her injured husband around the clock, she packed her bags and left home. No one knows where she's gone.'

'I feel like running away too sometimes. But it's helpful to be able to chat to you like this . . .'

'My husband spent five thousand yuan on health insurance, but the company has refused to pay up. They said they're not allowed to pay compensation to victims of the crackdown. What kind of world are we living in?'

As I listen to them talk, my mind drifts to *The Book of Mountains and Seas* . . . In the northern region, a wild beast called Qiongqi is devouring a man with dishevelled hair. The Qiongqi looks like a tiger, and has two wings on its back. When it eats a human it starts with the head, although some people say it starts with the feet . . .

You approach the jejunum and the fan-shaped folds of membrane that attach it to the abdominal wall. A web of veins covers its surface. Lymphatic tubes and arterioles hang down like ropes.

'All university representatives, hurry up, our meeting is about to start!' Ke Xi yelled, pointing his megaphone at the students camping out in Tiananmen Square. The black scarf he'd wrapped around his sleeve as a sign of mourning made his arm look shorter.

I was dozing on the stone steps leading to the lower terrace of the Monument to the People's Heroes, but Ke Xi's shouting woke me before I had a chance to sink into deep sleep. Shu Tong's face was right next to mine. His eyes were still shut. I turned his wrist around and checked the time on his watch. There was a bitter chill in the air.

I sat up and looked out over the tens of thousands of students and the red-and-white flags and banners surrounding the Monument. Jutting above them was a black banner emblazoned with the words HU YAOBANG, THE STUDENTS OF BEIJING UNIVERSITY MOURN YOUR DEATH! I felt a sudden panic, the fear that grips you when you wake up in a place that feels unsafe. The foreign and Chinese television crews that had filmed us when we'd arrived in the Square the previous night were nowhere to be seen.

The sky slowly brightened. Hu Yaobang's state funeral was due to start in two hours. The cold of the night, and the smells wafting from the thousands of sleeping bodies, began to dissipate in the morning sun.

A couple of hours previously, Wang Fei and I had succeeded in getting the students crowded in front of the Great Hall of the People on the west side of the Square to stand in neat rows. Wang Fei had marched confidently through the orderly ranks with a megaphone in his hand. At the front of our troops, we'd placed the law students' three-metre-high wreath of flowers, and a large poster proclaiming the citizens' constitutional right to protest. By the time we'd finished organising everyone, I was too tired to search for Tian Yi, so went to lie down on the steps.

'What are we going to do?' Ke Xi said, shaking Shu Tong awake. 'The authorities won't let us attend the state funeral, or even send any representatives.'

'Don't ask me! I've resigned from the Organising Committee,' Shu Tong said, opening his eyes and catching site of Ke Xi's black armband.

'The police have promised that as long as we don't cross their cordon, we won't come to any harm,' Ke Xi said. 'But they won't let us go in and see the body.'

'Have you had private discussions with the funeral officials?' I asked. I was afraid that Ke Xi's hunger for power would destroy our unity. During the night, we'd held new elections for the Organising Committee and made Han Dan its leader. Ke Xi had then gone off and set up a temporary coordinating group to supervise the rally, but he still felt that, since the Organising Committee had been his idea, he should remain in charge. I'd been worried he would butt in when I was trying to organise the students into lines in front of the Great Hall of the People. Two cadres had walked over and asked me to move the crowd back twenty metres so that the guests attending the funeral could drive to the entrance. I'd talked this over with Zhuzi, and we'd decided to do as they asked. Han Dan walked over holding a cassette player that was blaring out the Internationale and said to the two cadres, 'We're here to pay our last respects to Hu Yaobang. All we want is to see his coffin being carried in. After that, we'll leave the Square.' The cadres raised their eyebrows and walked away. It appeared that the government had resigned themselves to our presence, but I wasn't sure their nonchalance would last.

It had taken Zhuzi and me two hours to get the Beijing University students to move twenty metres back. I discovered that it was essential to tell the students where we wanted them to go while they were still standing, because once they'd sat down it was almost impossible to get them to move again.

I'd been given a megaphone with a square-shaped funnel. It was white and made a good noise. It looked great hanging around my neck.

'When the funeral is over, we will ask the government to send someone out to receive our petition,' Ke Xi declared loudly.

'Where can I go to have a piss?' Shu Tong asked me, opening his red, swollen eyes. He hated it when Ke Xi started holding forth.

I needed to go as well. 'The public toilets in Qianmen are too far away,' I said. 'Let's go behind those trees over there.'

'The science students have managed to collect about three thousand yuan in donations,' Shen Tong said, 'so I think we can afford to buy everyone breakfast, don't you?'

'Yes, we should sort that out straight away,' I said. 'Some of the students are already wandering off to find something to eat. We don't want the crowd to break up.'

'Who's in charge of logistics?' Shu Tong asked, looking more alert now, and stroking his chin as though there was a beard there to rub.

'I've forgotten,' I said.

We squeezed through the crowd and walked over to the trees. A banner hanging from the national flagpole read: WE ARE IN THE PRIME OF OUR YOUTH. OUR COUNTRY NEEDS US! Shu Tong smiled when he saw it. 'Someone climbed twenty metres to hang up that banner,' he said. 'That's quite something.'

I wanted to find Tian Yi. Mimi had told me she was with some students from the Chinese Department. I'd bumped into her before I left the campus. She told me she was going back to her dorm to get some indigestion tablets. She said she often suffered from stomach complaints in the spring.

The students on the steps were beginning to wake up and complain about the cold. A few couples had spent the night huddled up together, with banners wrapped around themselves for warmth. People stood up and skipped about, trying to warm their feet. Pop songs and funeral dirges began blasting from portable cassette players and radios. The group from Tianjin's Nankai University, who'd been the first to occupy the Square the night before, set off for a morning run around the perimeter. A guy in a red down jacket jumped up and down, trying to hit a ray of morning light with his head. His friends pushed him into the crowd. Everyone laughed. The girls he landed on shrieked, then quickly sat up again and smoothed back their hair. The confusion of noise began to shake the air above the Square, and make our hearts tremble as well.

'How many Beijing University students do you think we've got here?' Shu Tong asked me. The earth below the trees was steaming with warm urine. I was surrounded by thirty or forty penises, all shooting streams of yellow piss.

'About four thousand students left the campus. But when I organised everyone into rows a couple of hours ago, there were only about three thousand left. A lot of them must have returned to the campus to sleep. They won't be able to get back to the Square now, though. Look, the police have blocked off all the roads.'

Changan Avenue, which runs along the north side of the Square, and Tiananmen Gate, which lies beyond it, were completely deserted. It reminded me of the empty forts I'd read about that generals of ancient China used as a ruse to scare their enemies into retreat.

I glanced over at the Monument and saw Liu Gang and Shao Jian draping our banner over the white marble balustrades at the edge of the lower terrace. A large crowd had gathered around to watch.

'Look at that huge crowd of Qinghua University students,' I said, spotting them in the background. 'There must be about five thousand of them, and they're all sitting in orderly rows.'

'Yang Tao's responsible for that. They didn't have a leader, so he went over and took charge.' Shu Tong shivered as he zipped up his flies. I wondered where the girls went when they needed to piss.

Xiao Li walked up. He'd been reluctant to come to the Square, but I'd persuaded him. He'd brought over a young man in a blue woollen hat who wanted to speak to Shu Tong. The man shook Shu Tong's hand and said, 'We've both got a petition to submit, so I thought we should have a talk.'

'We've stuck a copy of our petition on the Monument,' Shu Tong said with a guarded look on his face. 'Go and read it, if you want.' Before the man had a chance to reply, he added, 'You do your thing and we'll do ours. It's best if we come up with different demands.'

'What I'm saying is, I think we should make our requests specific, like the workers who are demanding a five-mao wage increase.' He looked like one of those petitioners who travel up from the provinces to lodge complaints with the central authorities. I often came across them when I walked through Beijing. Some would wander around publicising their grievances on cardboard signs hanging around their necks. Others would gather in small groups and make public speeches about the injustices they'd suffered, until the police came and shooed them away. Most of them slept on the streets. A few built themselves makeshift shelters in quiet rubbish depots, pasting their complaints on the surrounding walls. On National Day, the police would round them all up and fling them into detention centres in the suburbs.

I turned to the man and said, 'Why not go and talk to Ke Xi? He's the leader of a coordinating group that's supervising the rally.'

Shu Tong brushed past the man and walked off, clearly wanting nothing more to do with him.

'I've heard that Premier Li Peng has agreed to meet with you . . .' the man said, trying to keep up with us. Then someone stood in his way, and we managed to lose him.

The students had converged around the Monument in the centre of the Square, and in front of the Great Hall of the People to the west, but the rest of the vast space was deserted. Occasionally, I saw lines of armoured police in khaki uniforms wriggle like caterpillars through the shade of the trees along the Square's eastern edge.

'We must stay vigilant,' Shu Tong said, glancing back at me. 'The police have sealed off all the entrances to the Square, so the only people getting through now will be undercover agents. They've asked workers and cadres to man the cordons, which is a good way of ensuring they won't join us. They're killing two birds with one stone.'

I heard a commotion break out near the Great Hall. The students from Beijing Normal had gone to sit in front of the Qinghua crowd, right inside the twenty-metre exclusion zone. The Beijing University crowd jumped up to see what was going on. I rushed over as fast as I could.

Han Dan and Ke Xi were struggling to persuade everyone to return to their original places. Hai Feng and some of his fellow social science students went over and tried to help them. In the mounting chaos, I lifted my megaphone and shouted: 'Student marshals, stay where you are!'

Mou Sen struggled to break free from the throng. I tugged him out and said, 'What are your students up to? We promised the officials we'd keep the road in front of the Great Hall clear. No one's allowed to sit down there.'

'They went over to the Monument a while ago to observe a minute of silence. When they returned, they found that their places had been taken, so they pushed through and plonked themselves at the front.'

'Whoever is commander of the Beijing Normal division, get your troops to move to the back!' I shouted.

Mou Sen was chairman of Beijing Normal's Organising Committee. He'd mentioned that the committee members didn't communicate well with each other. 'This is too much!' he said, trying to pick up the white flowers that had been knocked from the wreaths in the crush. 'I've no idea who our commander is.'

'There's no point trying to push to the front,' I said. 'We asked that the hearse make a circuit of the Square so that we can see Hu Yaobang's body before it's taken into the Hall, but it will probably drive in through a back entrance, in which case we won't see a thing.'

A few Beijing residents had also spent the night in the Square with us. They began jostling through the crowds like shoppers in a busy marketplace. I was very angry at the Beijing Normal students for causing so much disruption.

Hundreds of armed police suddenly charged out of the Great Hall. When the students at the front saw them approach, they tried to move back, but the crowd behind refused to make space for them.

Wang Fei yelled, 'You rushed to the front, Beijing Normal, and now you're scared! Don't move back for them, the rest of you! Just clear a passage in the middle and let them file out, if they want to!'

The crowd dissolved into chaos again.

I squeezed my way through to a lamp post, and stood on its concrete base, shouting at everyone to stop pushing. I told my student marshals to form a human chain around the giant wreath of flowers at the front, but the crowd continued to push past it, knocking more petals to the ground. Zhuzi and Hai Feng pleaded with everyone to stay still. The marshals with megaphones yelled angry commands. Compared to the lines of armed police standing in solemn ranks opposite us, we looked like an undisciplined mob.

When the funeral music came through the loudspeakers above us, the students finally stood still. The mood calmed down and we all began singing the Internationale. The students who were wearing baseball caps removed them out of respect, and suddenly a swathe of black hair stretched out before me.

Some of the students started to weep. Although I was sad, I didn't cry. I couldn't shed tears for a man I'd never met. I wondered whether my break-up with A-Mei four years previously had numbed my capacity to feel distress.

By the time the voice of President Yang Shangkun came through the loudspeakers announcing a minute's silence, I still hadn't had a chance to look for Tian Yi. This was a historic event. I knew she'd want to witness it. The day before, she'd donated three hundred yuan to the student movement, which was the equivalent of her annual living expenses.

The tens of thousands of people in the Square, the government leaders inside the Great Hall, and the dense lines of armed police in between, respected the silence together. For a moment, everyone seemed united in grief.

The funeral dirge gradually petered out. Some of the students looked indignant, others stared blankly. My mind flashed back to A-Mei. I remembered her saying to me, 'Think about it, just think about it for a while . . .' as we came out from a lecture one day.

The state funeral had come to an end. I looked over to the Great Hall of the People and saw delegates of the National People's Congress and government leaders walking down the steps and being whisked away in chauffeur-driven cars. Most of them chose to ignore the massive crowd of students sitting before them.

We stared at the two exits of the Great Hall and tried to guess which one the hearse might emerge from. After half an hour there was still no sign of it.

Yet more armed police trooped out of the Great Hall in khaki uniforms, leather belts and white gloves. They sat down on the steps in four orderly rows. From a distance, they looked like a neatly trimmed bamboo fence.

'Do you think the hearse has left through a back gate?' Shu Tong asked.

'It probably left through an underground passage,' Wang Fei said.

Old Fu jumped up, full of energy. He had spent the night asleep in his dorm, only returning to the Square just before the dawn curfew, so he wasn't as tired as we were. 'God knows what those Party leaders have been up to!' he said. 'Let's hurry up and submit our petition!'

'Come on, let's storm the Great Hall!' Wang Fei said, sticking his thumbs up. 'They must have taken the coffin away by now. If we don't take action now, the government will ignore us.' He'd put on a clean pair of jeans today, and looked very smart.

'We can't do that. The Great Hall of the People is China's parliament. America is a democratic country, but it still doesn't allow its citizens to storm the House of Representatives.' Old Fu was holding our rolled-up petition. He was wearing a clean white shirt under his jumper.

'It would be dangerous to storm the Great Hall,' Shu Tong said. 'We've just had a funeral, and emotions are running high.' He always ground his teeth when he was nervous, although you couldn't hear him do it.

'I don't think we should storm the building, but we can't let things end like this,' Shao Jian said, readjusting his collar and tie.

The students at the back of the crowd began chanting: 'Dialogue, dialogue, we demand dialogue!' Another column of armed police marched out and positioned themselves behind the wall of armed police in front of us.

Everyone had left the Great Hall. The only people remaining were the supervisors in white shirts standing on the steps.

'The guests who left from these gates were lowly officials,' Shu Tong said. 'Not one of their cars had a red flag. All the important dignitaries will have left secretly through underground tunnels.'

The police began removing the cordons from Changan Avenue. Beijing residents flooded into the Square and surrounded us, trying to see what was going on. The student marshals held hands and formed a protective ring around us, trying to push back the encroaching hordes. Soon the marshals on the western side of the ring were almost touching noses with the armed police.

'Ke Xi, didn't you say that Premier Li Peng has agreed to talk to us?' Han Dan said, pushing his way through the crowd.

'I never said that,' Ke Xi said, pouting his thick lips. 'It's a false rumour that's going around.'

'But everyone thinks that Li Peng has agreed to meet us,' Old Fu said. 'They think we've got an audience with him at one o'clock. They're very excited about it. What are we going to do?'

When a black crow cawed as it flew out from under the eaves of the Great Hall, someone shouted, 'Look, Li Peng's come out to see us!' and the crowd roared with laughter.

'If they refuse to discuss our demands, we'll have to charge through the police lines and storm the Great Hall,' Hai Feng said, pushing his way through to us. The black shirt he was wearing under his sleeveless pullover looked too small for him.

It was midday already.

'We mustn't be too heavy-handed,' Han Dan said, pushing his glasses further up his nose.

'Why not choose a wreath and take it up to the Great Hall,' said Liu Gang, surveying the crowd. He'd just arrived in the Square after being trapped behind the police cordons for two hours.

'That's a good idea,' Han Dan said, then he shouted to the students holding the wreaths to bring them over to us. His megaphone was very loud.

But the students holding the wreaths ignored his command and began charging into the lines of armed police. The wreath from the Politics and Law University was so large that the four people holding it had to ask the student marshals to help them pass it over the policemen's heads.

Liu Gang snatched the megaphone from Han Dan and shouted, 'We're in a face-off with armed police, so it's important not to raise the tension any further. Our plan is to take just one wreath up to the Great Hall of the People, and present it to the officials to convey, on behalf of all the students of Beijing, our deep sadness at the death of Comrade Hu Yaobang.' At last, everyone stood still.

Han Dan and Hai Feng took the petition and, after a brief discussion with the armed police, were allowed to pass through the first few lines. Wang Fei, Ke Xi and Mou Sen chose a medium-sized wreath and were also allowed to squeeze their way through.

The people who'd climbed onto the bases of the lamp posts cheered excitedly.

'We need another representative,' Ke Xi shouted to the students from Beijing Normal, the Politics and Law University and the Beijing Institute of Technology. 'Do any of you want to join us?'

'And who are you?' they cried, many of them never having seen him before.

'My name is Ke Xi,' he shouted through his megaphone from behind the lines of armed police. 'I'm the head of a coordinating group that represents students from nineteen Beijing universities.'

Wang Fei and Mou Sen passed through the second block of police, walked up the steps and carried the wreath and petition inside the Great Hall of the People, emerging with only the petition a few seconds later.

'Look, the officials have taken the wreath but refused to receive the petition,' Old Fu said, watching them walk down the steps.

Wang Fei and Mou Sen exchanged a few words with Han Dan, Hai Feng and Ke Xi, then all five of them climbed up the steps again. Ten plain-clothes officers rushed out of the Great Hall and stood in their way. Hai Feng suddenly dropped to his knees and lifted the white petition above his head. Wang Fei and Mou Sen stood beside him and hesitated for a moment, then they too decided to kneel down. Ke Xi looked a little awkward and stepped to the side. Han Dan swung his shoulder bag over his back and tried desperately to pull the three of them up. Hai Feng refused to budge. He lifted the petition higher in the air and began shouting something we couldn't hear.

The students yelled, 'Don't kneel down! Stand up! Stand up!'

Old Fu was furious. 'They're kneeling down like submissive subjects petitioning an emperor. It's an unhealthy legacy of feudal China!'

'What the hell are they thinking of, kneeling down like that?' Liu Gang said, squeezing himself in front of us. 'The Organising Committee didn't tell them to kneel. It's going to stir up a lot of conflict.'

I too thought it was unwise of them to be kneeling down, but I kept quiet. The students at the front became agitated, and jumped to their feet once more. The armed police stood up as well and both sides began ramming into each other. I soon found myself squashed between the police and the students. I lifted my megaphone and shouted, 'Sit down! Sit down! Student marshals – link hands and contain the crowd!'

Under the dense, oppressive sunlight, the Great Hall looked like an immense coffin. The national emblem fixed to the roof appeared to waver in the haze. As the police lines shifted back and forth, the crowds surged and retreated.

'Why won't the government leaders come out and take the petition?' the onlookers said.

'They're terrified, that's why! They don't have the guts to show their faces in public!' others shouted out.

Both sides continued to push and jostle. The students rushed to wherever the police pushed hardest and shoved them back with all their might.

Chen Di got the students to chant after him: 'Oppose police violence! The police have no right to attack the students!'

'Calm down!' Shu Tong shouted. 'Stay disciplined! Quickly Dai Wei, get everyone to sit down again!'

'Those three guys have been kneeling on the steps for twenty minutes,' Liu Gang said anxiously. 'If they don't get up soon, a riot's going to break out.' I yelled at the crowd to sit down, but there was so much noise, no one could hear me.

The Beijing residents who'd gathered behind us pushed forward again, pounding into the southern end of the police lines. Some of them swiped the officers' caps off and threw them into the air. The outer police line crumbled. As the officers scattered to the sides, the line of armed police behind them stepped forward aggressively, and the crowd of residents retreated in fright.

The students who were sitting on the ground shouted, 'Come out Premier Li Peng! We want dialogue with the government!'

The armed police focused on the Beijing University students and charged towards us. I presumed they were coming to arrest us.

'Hold hands everyone,' I shouted. 'Make sure the girls keep in the middle!' A white-gloved hand landed on my cheek and twisted my head back. I grabbed it and tried to tug it off. I was surrounded by police caps. The officer I was wrestling with had lost his epaulettes. He stared at me with his mouth wide open. He looked just like my brother. His lips and ears were bleeding. The buttons of his green shirt had been pulled off too. When it became clear that the police merely wanted to push us back and had no intention of arresting us, I removed my hand from the officer, and he let me go.

I shouted at my marshals to get the Beijing University students back in line. Shu Tong said through his megaphone, 'Fellow students, we must remain calm and rational.'

The armed police returned to their original positions and cordoned off the forecourt of the Great Hall with rope. A paper banner that had said THE STUDENTS OF BEIJING UNIVERSITY GRIEVE THE DEATH OF HU YAOBANG lay on the ground, torn and trodden to pieces.

'They're supposed to be servants of the people,' Xiao Li cried. 'Why are they ignoring us like this?'

'Zhuzi, some of the students at the back have got down on their knees too!' a law student shouted out. 'What shall we do?'

Zhuzi undid the top button of his khaki jacket and shouted, 'We can't ask for democracy on bent knees! Tell the bastards to stand up!' Fuming with rage, he pushed his way to the front of the crowd and yelled, 'Stand up! Stand up!' to the three students still kneeling on the steps.

The students behind us shouted, 'Stand up! Democracy shouldn't be begged for!' and moved forward, propelling the students in front against the swaying lines of armed police.

Through the shouting, I could hear people weeping.

'Stop kneeling, stop kneeling!' the students cried. The waves of noise rolled over the heads of the armed police and bounced off the glass windows of the Great Hall.

Then Bai Ling squeezed between the police and the students, held up the megaphone that Han Dan had handed to her, and cried out with tears welling in her eyes, 'Government officials in the Great Hall of the People, the students have been waiting in the Square for eighteen hours, please come down and receive our petition.' She was so short that all I could see was her forehead.

'Quick, Dai Wei,' she said, catching sight of me, 'tell the student marshals to form a chain.'

I was terrified she'd get crushed. I quickly yelled for the marshals to hold hands and told the students behind me to stay still.

Bai Ling was now stranded inside the ranks of armed police, sweat pouring down her face. She cried out, 'The armed police are the sons and brothers of the people! We mustn't let this end in a bloodbath . . .'

An officer standing behind the police lines passed a water bottle to another officer nearby, who twisted the lid off and handed it to Bai Ling. The students who witnessed this clapped their hands in appreciation. Bai Ling swallowed a few sips, then shouted, 'Thank you, brothers and sons of the people! The students are tired and hungry, and our tempers are frazzled. But we don't want any of you to get hurt. You are our compatriots, after all!' The students around her broke into applause.

The mood of the officers, who were sweating in the confused scrum, began to soften. Some of them even had tears in their eyes.

A middle-aged man rushed out from the Great Hall of the People and walked down to where the three students were still kneeling. He flung his arms around them and sobbed. We couldn't hear what he was saying.

'That's Professor Chen from the Education Department!' Chen Di said, observing him through his binoculars.

'Are you sure?' Liu Gang asked.

'How did someone like him get invited to the funeral?' Bai Ling said. 'He's a very lowly official.' Her face was flushed, and her short bob was in a mess.

'Even the vice presidents of the universities don't get invited into the Great Hall!' Yu Jin shouted. 'He must be a secret agent. No wonder he tried to hold us back when we set off from the campus gates the other day.' Yu Jin was wearing a sports shirt with a small embroidered logo of the Olympic rings. The white collar was squashed to one side.

At last Wang Fei, Mou Sen and Hai Feng rose from their knees. Then, still holding the petition above their heads, they came down the steps, followed by Han Dan and Ke Xi.

Liu Gang and the other members of the Organising Committee rushed over to them. Everyone burst into tears. Ke Xi sobbed, 'I didn't kneel, I didn't kneel!'

Zhuzi was so enraged with them he began hitting himself on the head with his megaphone. He was taller than everyone else, so no one could stop him. I handed my megaphone to Chen Di, then jumped on top of Zhuzi and grabbed hold of his hands.

'How could you kneel like that?' he howled, blood streaming down his head. 'You're a disgrace to the Chinese race.'

'They kneeled for forty minutes, and not one member of the National

People's Congress had the courtesy to come out and speak to them!' Chen Di shouted through his megaphone.

'A hundred thousand students have gathered here to mourn the death of a leader, and the government has treated them worse than dogs!' Xiao Li said, tears streaming down his face.

Throngs of distressed students cried out as they squeezed past one another. No one seemed to know where they were going.

Although Shu Tong and Old Fu had resigned from the Organising Committee, they went straight to Liu Gang and Shao Jian and suggested they lead the students back to the campus before the situation in the Square got out of control. They could then inform the Beijing residents of the day's events and start organising a class boycott.

Dong Rong tore off the sleeve of his white shirt and wrapped it around Zhuzi's wounded head. Han Dan announced through his megaphone that the Organising Committee had decided that, in order to prevent any untoward occurrences, the Beijing University students should return to their campus.

The students began moving towards the south-west corner of the Square. They were in a volatile mood, and kept cursing, 'So much for the bloody "People's Government"!'

'Phone every university in the country and tell them to organise an immediate class boycott!' Chen Di cried in his clear, melodious voice.

'Let's hold another big rally on 4 May!' Wang Fei bellowed, breaking out into a sweat. 'We will march through the streets of Beijing, calling for democracy and change, just as Chinese students did seventy years ago in the May Fourth Movement. We will protest against this corrupt government just as they protested against the corrupt warlords.'

'We can't just let it end like this!' said Mao Da, who was walking beside him with a look of despair in his eyes.

'So you had the gall to turn up, did you?' I said, wanting to punch the traitor in the face.

'If we stage a class boycott, we won't have to do those exams next week,' Yu Jin said, waving his hands jubilantly.

Our bedraggled troops left the Square and set off for the two-hour trek back to the campus.

'Did we do anything wrong?' Bai Ling shouted from the back.

'No!' the students roared.

'Did we have ulterior motives?'

'No!'

'We will lay down our lives 10,000 times for the sake of the Chinese people! When the emperor loses the hearts of the people, he will lose the empire!'

Some of the girls sobbed as they repeated the slogans.

Beijing residents standing on the pavements shouted out to us: 'We support the students! The government can cut our bonuses, if they want to! We will speak our minds!'

Another man shouted, 'Let the students be an example to us!' then lowered his head in embarrassment.

A teacher walked up to us and said, 'You're amazing! We would never have had the courage to do what you're doing now. This country is politically and morally corrupt, and inflation is out of control. The price of meat has shot up from eight mao to five yuan. I can't afford to buy myself clothes!' The jacket he was wearing was scruffy and torn.

We marched on for more than an hour, shouting slogans as we went. When I could go no further, I sat down to rest on the pavement with Xiao Li and Yu Jin. It was then that I caught sight of Tian Yi. She was munching an apple, her hair falling over her face. I went over, grabbed the apple from her and took a bite.

'That's so rude!' she said. 'And anyway, my gums are bleeding.' I looked down and saw traces of blood on the apple's white flesh.

'Where were you?' I asked her. 'We agreed we'd meet by the flagpole at sunrise.'

'I was at the back, with the psychology students.'

'I saw the Psychology Department's flag, but I didn't see you.'

'I was busy,' she said, tapping the camera hanging around her neck. 'Do I have to get your permission before I do anything?'

She liked to take photographs then stick the prints up on her wall. She once cut out a picture of herself and pasted it to the bottom of a photograph of the Statue of Liberty. She kept the photo we'd taken of each other in the rainforest of Yunnan in her private album. I never got a copy.

'Let's go to a restaurant,' I said to her, staring at the long road ahead. 'I can't walk any further. I haven't eaten for twenty-four hours.'

'The university sent out some vans to take us back to the campus, why didn't you hop on one?' she asked, waiting for me to say: how could I go back, when I hadn't found you?

'I'm not an invalid,' I said. 'I should be able to make it back on my own two feet.' The few bites of apple I'd eaten had taken the edge off my hunger.

'All right, let's go for a meal. It's not as if you're needed here any more.'

The purple blossom of the parasol trees lining the road looked like a band of cloud reaching into the sky.

'There's a restaurant near here that serves Korean cold noodles,' I said, taking her hand and glancing down into the dip between her breasts.

'What are you looking at?' she said, the skin below her collarbone turning red. 'You won't find your *Book of Mountains and Seas* down there, you know!'

The strong light piercing your eyelids becomes a field of sunflowers. One of the flowers is your father's eye.

It's another sweltering summer. My skin has broken out in a heat rash. My mother rolls me over onto my stomach and sprinkles prickly-heat powder over my back.

She mutters that the skin over my shoulder blades is rotting. But I can't feel a thing.

'Your friend Chen Di was only detained for three months. His foot was crushed in the crackdown. I suppose the authorities thought that was punishment enough. He's opened a bookshop outside the university's rear gates.' My mother has become used to speaking aloud to me as I lie here as listless as a hibernating fish. 'He said he'll come and visit you when he gets a chance. He's made a lot of money . . .'

I don't want my friends to see my rotting bag of bones. I don't want Tian Yi to come again either.

'The herbal doctor said that you're not ill. You're like a candle that's been blown out. All we need to do is light you up again. He's given you some herbs. I'll have to find a way to get them into your stomach.'

There's no point pouring herbal tinctures down my throat. They won't do any good. A switch has been turned off in my brain. You must press it down again if you want the light to return.

'Kenneth has sent us a thousand dollars from America. You're lucky to have a kind relative like that. With this money, I'll be able to bring you back to life, you lawless rioter . . .'

I have a raging fever. My thoughts seem to have disconnected from my body. I long for the cool air that wafts over me when my mother opens the fridge door. Although it smells of herbal medicine and sour leftovers, it feels as though it's blowing from a land of ice and snow.

My mother turns the radio back on, as she always does when she wakes from her midday nap. 'The Ministry of Public Security has announced that twenty-five Chinese cities and counties have been opened to foreign investment . . . There are now 11,000 Chinese students studying abroad . . . The Shanghai Women's Association, in conjunction with the local law courts, has set up a Divorce College, and already more than three hundred of the four hundred students enrolled have successfully managed to repair their relationships . . .'

The stifling temperature conjures up images of roads scorching in the sun, sunburnt skin, hot, shadeless pavements . . . In the northern region of the Land of Black Teeth lies the Scalding Valley, where the ten suns go to bathe. A large mulberry tree grows in the hot water at the bottom of the valley. When the suns take their bath, nine of them sit on branches below the surface of the water, and one sits on a branch above it . . .

The cells of your prostate gland absorb ribose, nucleic acid and protein but are unable to meld them together. Your capillaries become weak and limp.

'You'd better come down!' Xiao Li said, poking his red face round the door of the dorm. 'The Organising Committee is going to hold another election. Shu Tong's very nervous. He wants to get reinstated. Now that it's clear the government aren't planning to clamp down on us, lots of students are putting themselves up for election.'

Since I'd forced Xiao Li to join our rally in Tiananmen Square on the day of Hu Yaobang's funeral, he'd written a poster entitled 'My Utter Disappointment with the Authorities' and had become very involved in the student movement.

'I thought the Organising Committee was going to hold an oath-taking ceremony this morning,' I said. I'd been up all night with Tian Yi, collecting donations for the student movement outside the Dongzhimen subway exit, and had only just got back to the dorm.

'They've cancelled the ceremony and decided to hold the election this afternoon instead,' Xiao Li said, sitting down.

I called out to Chen Di, who'd been up all night playing cards in the television room. Then I checked in on Wang Fei and Shu Tong's dorm, but there was no one there apart from a couple of students who'd travelled up from the provinces.

'So how did the speeches in the Triangle go?' I asked Xiao Li.

'Wang Fei accused Han Dan of being a saboteur, then Han Dan accused him of being a spy. Most of the students who'd come to listen laughed and walked away. Wang Fei's new girlfriend, Nuwa, had persuaded lots of foreign journalists to attend. She was so furious about the argument, she threw down her microphone and stormed off in a huff.'

'So where's Wang Fei now?' I asked. 'The idiot!'

Xiao Li looked exhausted. 'He's probably gone to the election meeting,' he said. 'If we don't get the science students to cast their votes, none of us will make it back onto the executive.'

'This is the fourth reshuffle. Go and see if Old Fu is at the meeting. I'll do a tour of the science block and ask everyone to go and vote.'

I climbed up to each floor of the science block, shouting through my megaphone, but there was hardly anyone around. Since the class boycott had started, many science students had taken advantage of the chaos to return home or go travelling. The ones who'd stayed behind lay on their beds all day with their noses in their books.

By the time I'd managed to round up twenty or so science students to come to the meeting, there were already more than three thousand people packed in the history block's lecture theatre.

Sister Gao was chairing the meeting. She talked through the rules and procedures, explaining that the candidates would be called one by one onto the stage to give a five-minute talk about the contribution they could make to the student movement. When she finished speaking, a man jumped onto the stage. He said he was a crane operator on a nearby construction site, and had been sent by his fellow workers to convey their support for the students and appreciation for their efforts in building a new China.

Shu Tong, who was standing next to him, took a sip of water, thanked him cursorily then launched into his speech, setting out his vision for a three-stage democratic campaign. In the first stage, the students would focus on class boycotts, demonstrations and dialogue with the government; in the next stage, they would set up independent radio stations and newspapers. Before he'd finished explaining the third stage, which involved taking to the streets in October in a nationwide movement for democracy, his five minutes came to an end and he had to cut his speech short. He'd worked himself up into such a state of excitement that his face was dripping with sweat.

Then it was Old Fu's turn to speak. He said the student movement shouldn't be turned into a national salvation movement, and proposed that, during times of emergency, the members of the Organising Committee be granted absolute powers. He ended by urging the committee members to read the posters in the Triangle every day, to ensure they stayed in touch with grass-roots opinion.

His speech didn't go down very well. He'd sounded like a logistics manager. I doubted that he'd get many votes.

The next candidate walked up to the microphone. Zhang Jie, who was supervising the proceedings, asked to see his student card. The man replied loudly, 'I don't have a student card. My name is Shang Zhao.'

'Which department are you from?' Sister Gao asked. 'Who are your guarantors?'

'I don't have any guarantors. I study from home, so I seldom come to the campus.'

'Well you can't put yourself up for election, then,' Sister Gao replied.

'I was called up here because the students put my name forward. Isn't this supposed to be a democratic election?' It was true that he'd been nominated. His name was on the blackboard. But he didn't look like a student. He looked more like a professor, or a plain-clothes policeman. He delivered a dry speech about the need for the students to abide by the constitution and remain on guard against conspirators intent on using the movement to overthrow the state.

I scanned the audience, looking for the traitor Mao Da, and spotted him in the row below me. Of the three thousand students sitting in the lecture theatre, I guessed that about two or three hundred were government informers, and that they would vote for this guy called Shang Zhao.

Just as Wang Fei was about to start his speech, a student who'd witnessed the public row between him and Han Dan earlier snatched the microphone and said: 'So tell us, are you a spy or not?' The intervention created such an uproar that Sister Gao and Bai Ling had no choice but to ask Wang Fei to leave the stage.

Ke Xi displayed his usual oratory skills. He said that he was prepared to lay down his life for democracy and freedom. He claimed he'd already bid his last farewell to his parents, and was ready to fight to the bitter end. The journalists standing at the front quickly pointed their cameras at him and snapped away.

Liu Gang and Hai Feng's speeches were well received. Zhuzi had tied a white bandanna around his head. He introduced himself as 'one of the older graduate law students' and said that if he were elected onto the committee he'd be able to provide invaluable legal advice.

They began tallying the votes up on the blackboard. Old Fu and Han Dan were doing well. Fortunately about twenty more science students turned up at the last minute, so that after the final batch of slips was counted, Shu Tong came out with almost as many votes as Han Dan.

In the end, Ke Xi, Han Dan, Liu Gang, Yang Tao, Old Fu, Shu Tong, Hai Feng, Zhuzi and Shao Jian all made it onto the committee. Ke Xi came out top, and was appointed chairman. Sister Gao announced that the Organising Committee of Beijing University Independent Student Union had been democratically elected.

Shu Tong climbed off the stage, dripping with sweat, and said, 'That strange guy, Shang Zhao, was a government agent. He was three votes away from being elected. How did he get so many votes?'

'At least we managed to get four science students onto the committee,' I said. 'That's not bad.'

'They're going to assign the posts now,' Shu Tong said. 'I want to be propaganda officer. That way I can make sure that we instigators retain control of the movement. Quickly, go and tell Shao Jian and Liu Gang to nominate me.'

'Isn't anyone going to give us something to eat?' Wang Fei hissed through his gritted teeth. He was livid that he hadn't made it onto the committee.

'Just look at your face!' Chen Di laughed. 'Did you really expect people were going to vote for a villain like you?'

'If you hadn't had that big row with Han Dan, we would have got even more science students onto the committee,' Shu Tong said, glancing angrily at Wang Fei.

Shao Jian wiped the sweat from his forehead, turned to Wang Fei and me and said, 'Go back to the dorm and draw up a proposal for a speech unit, a donation collection unit, perhaps even a supervisory office. If they agree to setting them up, we can wangle some jobs for you two.'

'This class boycott is going to change the history of Beijing University,' Old Fu said, his face beaming.

'You should have turned up earlier, Dai Wei,' Liu Gang said. 'We could have nominated you instead of Wang Fei.' He had thick eyebrows and foldless eyelids which, according to the ancient art of face-reading, denote a man who would make an able prime minister.

'I only like doing the practical stuff,' I said. 'I'm no good at giving speeches.'

'Ke Xi is now chairman of this committee and of the Federation,' Liu Gang said. 'He's got too much power.'

The previous night, thirty student leaders from several universities had met in the grounds of the Old Summer Palace and formed a city-wide coalition called the Beijing Students' Federation.

'Well, that's your fault for giving him the job then, Liu Gang,' Shu Tong said. The rest of us fell silent as it dawned on us that Liu Gang was the behind-the-scenes orchestrator of that organisation as well.

I wasn't particularly upset about losing my position on the committee, but Wang Fei looked distraught. We headed back to Block 29, still discussing the ramifications of the election.

In the east corner of the Land of Big Heels is a place called the Cocoon Wilderness. A woman who has turned into a silkworm kneels on the branches of a tree there, muttering 'Cocoon, cocoon' under her breath.

I remember A-Mei saying to me once, 'It frightens me how time just seems to go on and on for ever . . .'

I didn't know what she meant. I turned my gaze away from her black plaits and said, 'Yes. God knows how long it will take me to travel to all those places mentioned in *The Book of Mountains and Seas*.'

'You should try listening to some Mozart . . .' she said, clearly annoyed that I'd got the wrong end of the stick again.

The smell of the mattress I'm lying on takes me back to the Guangzhou hospital I stayed in after my break-up with A-Mei. The smell seeps into my muscles, causing me to re-experience past distress as physical pain. Do all unhappy memories stay etched in our flesh like this, remaining with us until the day we die?

'Put a sheet over your brother's stomach, Dai Ru,' my mother shouts from her bedroom. 'I don't want him to catch a cold.' Whenever the fridge's motor starts humming, the heat in the flat becomes a little less oppressive.

'Why have you got so many plastic bags hanging up in the kitchen, Mum? They're not wall calendars, you know.' My brother's holiday is almost over. He's been back with us for a month. He's very lazy. He gets up late every morning then spends most of his time listening to music on his earphones.

'They're useful,' my mother says. 'I washed them this morning. When they're dry, I'll fold them up and store them in this sack. They take up very little space.'

The sack she stores the plastic bags in is made of stiff polythene. Whenever someone brushes past it, it makes an irritating crackling noise that sounds like dried beans tumbling onto a sheet of glass. My mother hoards rag cloths as well. There's always one hidden away in some corner of the flat, letting off a damp and mouldy smell. I've grown up surrounded by that odour.

I presume that the ten volumes of *Mysteries of the World* are still lined up on top of the wooden cabinet. They were given to my father after he was rehabilitated, as compensation for the possessions confiscated from our family during the Cultural Revolution. They'd previously belonged to the opera company's set designer, Old Li. My mother often talked about the valuable objects that were taken from us: the piano, radio and silk bedcovers, as well as the music scores, violin, silver tray and cutlery which my father brought back with him from America.

'Damn! My train ticket is for tonight, not tomorrow,' my brother suddenly cries out.

He's been sleeping in the tiny balcony room since he came back, and has hardly left the flat. Despite his laziness, he's been quite attentive to me. He's massaged my clenched feet every day. They're much less stiff now. He even carried me to the toilet once and gave me a warm shower. Last week, he put a tube down my throat and poured milk and orange juice into it, which improved my bowel movements. My mother has had to clean up so much excrement and urine, her fingers have become raw and infected.

'Tonight? Then you'd better not carry your brother out to the park today. I must go to the bank and get some money for you. What time is it now?'

'Dai Wei has pissed again.' My brother lifts my feet in the air, peers between my thighs and whispers, 'You're as good as dead. What are you doing getting a hard-on?'

I have no control over my genitals, and I often get erections. It's so embarrassing. Sometimes I get one when my mother holds my penis and tries to get me to urinate.

'Take off the incontinence pad before his skin goes red,' my mother says, rubbing analgesic cream onto her hands. 'Then turn him onto his stomach and clean his back with alcohol. When you're gone, I'll have no one to help me lift him.'

'Your hands are so rough, Mum. You should eat more fresh vegetables.'

'I hardly ever go to the market. I'm afraid to leave him alone in the flat in case he has another convulsion. Last time he had one, the veins bulged out on his forehead and his face went dark blue. Anyway, I don't have much of an appetite these days. When you're not here, I never bother to sit down and have a proper meal. I just pour hot water onto a bowl of rice, or boil up some instant noodles.'

'You must force yourself to eat. Those sores on your hands are a sign you're not getting enough vitamins.'

My brother has grown up a lot. He's begun to show concern for my mother. But in my mind, I still picture him as the fifteen-year-old boy he was when I left home to go to Southern University. Although we saw each other regularly after that, it was never for more than a few days at a time.

In the background, a male newsreader drones: 'Kim Il-Sung, the General Secretary of the Workers' Party of Korea and Chairman of the Korean People's Republic, arrived in China today on a state visit . . .'

'Turn that radio off!' my mother says. 'I'd like to smash it up. I only put it on for Dai Wei. I can't bear the way they're always painting such a rosy picture of things.'

Since my mother began to devote her life to caring for me, her view of the world has changed. I often hear her grumbling complaints about the government or the police.

If Bai Ling hadn't persuaded all those students to join the hunger strike, if moderates like Shu Tong and Liu Gang had managed to retain control of the movement, if the students had evacuated the Square on 30 May, then perhaps I wouldn't be lying here now . . . There is a place in the mountain called Warm Spring Valley, where the nine suns rise every morning. As soon as one sun returns to the valley, another one rises up. Each one is carried through the sky on the back of a three-legged bird . . .

Like a heap of fish scooped from the sea and dropped onto a conveyor belt, your cells move towards their death.

We all squeezed into Shu Tong's dorm. The night before, he'd come back from an Organising Committee meeting and reported that he was now propaganda chief.

His first mission was to transform his dorm into a news centre, from which he would publish an independent student newspaper and run a broadcast station. He gave me some money and a list of equipment to go and buy at the Haidian electrical store. I wanted to take Tian Yi with me, so I went to find her. I'd heard she was helping set up the Organising Committee's administration office.

I walked into the arts students' dorm block and saw a sign pasted onto the door of a ground-floor dorm that said BEIJING UNIVERSITY ORGANISING COMMITTEE: RECEPTION. Bai Ling was in charge of this office. When I entered the dorm she was speaking animatedly to a group of businessmen who'd hoped to have a meeting with Ke Xi. They wanted to offer him advice and financial support. One restaurant owner had arrived with a truckload of mineral water he wanted to donate to the movement, and was waiting for Bai Ling to find someone to help unload the crates.

Tian Yi was in the dorm next door. The sign outside said BEIJING UNIVERSITY ORGANISING COMMITTEE: ADMINISTRATION. She glanced up at me briefly, then returned her attention to the committee meeting minutes she was sorting through. Han Dan, who was now secretary of the Organising Committee, had appointed her his deputy.

Sister Gao had been appointed chairwoman of the security office and spokeswoman for the news centre, but she hadn't been allocated a room of her own yet, so she'd come to help Tian Yi sort out the freshly printed leaflets which were piled up on the bunk beds.

The occupants of the dorm had moved out, and taken all their belongings and photographs with them. All that remained were four sets of metal bunk beds which were now stacked with piles of white and red paper, and boxes of ink bottles and calligraphy brushes. Now that the room was almost bare, the grime and dust on the large windows was more noticeable.

Two students tore open some boxes and placed a typewriter and a mimeograph machine onto one of the bottom bunks. The room suddenly resembled a black-and-white photograph I'd seen of a rebel faction's den in the Cultural Revolution. I guessed that those machines had cost over a thousand yuan.

The sheets of white paper on the desk that Tian Yi was sitting at were even more neatly stacked than the ones on her desk in her dorm.

Just as I was about to ask her to accompany me to the Haidian electrical store, she grabbed the hand of a boy who was walking out of the room and said, 'When I said no, I meant no!'

The boy was holding a box of business cards that had been donated by sympathetic onlookers during the rally at the Square.

'But you can photocopy them if you want,' she said, sitting up straight. 'I'll get someone to help you.'

I felt obliged to come to Tian Yi's aid, so I said to the boy, 'Yes, those cards are for everyone. You can't take them away.'

'I collected them myself when I was in the Square,' the boy said.

'We're not asking you to give them to us,' said Tian Yi. 'We just need to keep the originals here, so that people can have access to them. They will be vital to the student movement.' She sounded like a female revolutionary.

'But I need them for the records office I'm setting up,' the boy retorted, holding the box tightly in his arms.

'That's very presumptuous of you! The administration office is supposed to be in charge of the records.' Tian Yi's tone was becoming sterner.

'You – you really are too bureaucratic,' he stuttered angrily.

It seemed ridiculous that an anti-bureaucratic struggle had already erupted in this half-hatched, illegal organisation.

'Well, let's get the leader to decide,' Tian Yi said, settling in to her new role.

They marched off to Ke Xi's room, Tian Yi striding ahead and the boy following behind her. I decided to tag along too.

Ke Xi was cleanly dressed and had just had a haircut. Instead of coming to me for a quick trim, as he usually did, he'd gone to a barbershop and had it clipped short at the back, in the conservative style of a Communist Youth League member.

He was pacing around the room, talking to his subordinates. 'You must be patient,' he said. 'As I've told you before, the students who are still attending classes are not our enemies. We need to bring them onto our side. Unity is strength. Set up picket lines outside the classrooms, and urge them to join the boycott. You're the core members of the student movement. This is the time to show us what you're made of!'

The guys he was lecturing to looked like computer science students. As they turned round and headed for the door, the people waiting outside swarmed into the room and occupied the vacated benches. Mimi was writing down every word Ke Xi uttered.

Tian Yi couldn't squeeze herself through the crowd, so I barged my way forward, tapped Ke Xi on the shoulder and said, 'Ke Xi, this student here is setting up his own records office. He wants to take away the business cards he collected, and he refuses to let anyone have copies. Can you try to talk him round?'

'What business cards?' Ke Xi said, moving his eagle eyes towards the boy. A student standing next to me handed Ke Xi a cigarette and lit it for him.

'I'm a history student,' the boy said, pulling a few business cards out of the box and handing them to Ke Xi. 'I collected these cards myself in the Square.'

Ke Xi passed the cards to me, glanced into the box and said, 'These cards should be kept in the records office, but the administration office should retain copies of them.' He sucked on his cigarette. 'That's the only solution.'

I flicked through the cards and spotted ones from the *Beijing Daily*, the *Hong Kong International Trade Bulletin*, the Beijing Bureau of Statistics and the Changsha Yellow Mud Street Bookshop.

'Is that settled now, then?' Tian Yi said to the boy. 'I'll photocopy them at the printers then return them to you.' Tian Yi grabbed the box back from the history student and squeezed herself out of the room.

'Dai Wei, how are things going your end?' Ke Xi asked me, ignoring the many visitors, including foreign journalists, who'd crowded inside to talk to him. He hadn't visited Shu Tong's dorm since the argument he'd had with Wang Fei a few days earlier. Both he and Han Dan supported the mass march planned for the 27th, but all the science students, apart from Old Fu, were against it. The Organising Committee was going to vote on the matter in the afternoon.

'I'm setting up a public-address system, so that we can have our own little broadcast station. We've raised enough money to buy an amplifier and some loudspeakers.'

'Great! You must make sure you broadcast louder than the university's station. This morning they were telling everyone to come out with flags and denounce the "troublemakers".'

'We won't be able to drown them out. They have hundreds of

loudspeakers, and lots of high-wattage amplifiers and transformers. We'll have to make do with the electricity source in our dorm, which will power only four speakers at most.'

'We can buy more equipment when we have more money. Make sure the receipts are made out to the Organising Committee, then I can sign them and reimburse you. The radio station will play a crucial role in our movement.'

'Yes, it will help keep the students on our side.' Ke Xi's smugness was grating on me.

'As a member of the supervisory office, I hope you'll keep a close watch on the committee members, and make sure they stick to the guidelines.' When Ke Xi took a drag from his cigarette, he looked like one of those dissolute youths who hang out in train stations.

I'd completely forgotten that I'd been appointed not only to the security office, but also the supervisory office, together with Wang Fei, Cao Ming and the creative writing student Zheng He.

Tian Yi agreed to accompany me to the electrical store. She packed the business cards and two rolls of film into her briefcase and said we could stop off at the printers on the way.

It was pouring with rain outside. We opened our umbrellas and walked out of the campus.

'Ke Xi has got a "histrionic personality disorder",' I said, using a term I'd seen in Tian Yi's lecture notes. 'He always has to be the centre of attention.'

She pretended not to hear me. A-Mei used to ignore me like that too. When a minibus drove up I said, 'Come on, let's take it. I don't want to have to fight for a seat.' The fares of this privately run service were expensive, but I had three hundred yuan in donations in my pocket, so I decided we could afford this small luxury.

We squeezed inside and sat at the back. She wiped the raindrops from her face, then stroked my damp hair and said, 'Are you disappointed you weren't invited to the secret meeting?'

'You mean the one in the Old Summer Palace where they set up the Beijing Students' Federation, or the Provisional Federation of Beijing Universities as we're supposed to call it? Liu Gang organised it.'

'Yes, do you feel left out?' she smiled.

'I'm not the ambitious one. In the beginning, you were telling me not to get involved, but look at you now! Don't you think you're taking that little office of yours a bit too seriously?'

'If I agree to do something, I'll do it well. We mustn't look like amateurs. If this movement is going to succeed, everyone must get involved. I can't understand those students who've taken advantage of the boycott to go on holiday. I want to stay in Beijing and be a witness to history.'

'Not all those students have gone on holiday. Sister Gao told me the Federation sent three hundred students to go and link up with the provincial universities and tell them what we're up to.' Liu Gang had persuaded Sister Gao to join the Beijing Students' Federation, and had appointed her deputy chairwoman.

'I've heard a rumour that half the members of the Federation have applied for passports,' Tian Yi said. 'They're working to save the nation, while secretly making plans to leave it. They really are suffering from split-personality syndrome.'

'Anyone who's scored more than 600 in the TOEFL exam is bound to have made plans to go abroad. It's not unpatriotic to own a passport, you know.'

'They all want to run away to graduate school in America,' she said, ignoring me. 'They have no ideals.'

Her hand was resting on my lap. The numbers she'd written on it with a ballpoint pen had been smudged by the rain.

'Didn't we agree we'd both go abroad next year?' I said. 'Don't change your mind now. I wouldn't want to go alone.' She'd previously hinted to me that she'd accompany me to America if I was offered a place at a university there.

'I'll have to think things through again. This student movement has changed everything.'

'I never think things through. I just seem to go with the flow. If my cousin Kenneth hadn't sent me that sponsor letter, I wouldn't have taken the TOEFL exam. When this student movement took off, I thought I might as well get involved. It seemed the honourable thing to do. But I'm not fanatical. If it were to end tomorrow, I wouldn't be disappointed.'

She turned her hand, pressing her palm against mine. It felt soft and cold.

'I've heard that someone's given the Chinese literature students a cheque for 40,000 yuan, but no bank will dare cash it,' I said.

'I don't know about the money side of things. I can't stand those economics students who run the accounts office. My psychology classmates aren't much better. A few days ago, they were only interested in playing Mahjong. Now they've all tied red bandannas around their heads and joined the revolution! How can you trust people like that?'

'Why did you encourage them to join the class boycott then?' I asked, feeling she was being a little hard on them.

She ignored my question again, and said, 'Which of the leaders do you think is most ambitious?' She suddenly seemed less intelligent.

'It's hard to say. Han Dan's supposed to take over the chairmanship of the Beijing Students' Federation next week, but I doubt Ke Xi will let him.' Liu Gang had decided that the Federation should have a new chairman every week, much to Ke Xi's annoyance.

'Ke Xi is deluded if he thinks he can stop Han Dan.'

'Yes, Han Dan and Yang Tao are the only members of the Democracy Salon on the Organising Committee, but they've managed to form a small clique.'

'I hate cliques,' she said. 'Your Pantheon Society has formed one too, hasn't it?'

'Well, you and I don't have to get involved in the power struggles. We can just stick to doing the practical stuff. The news centre wants to set up a printing room. They've sent two students off to Xinhua News Agency's printing works to see how it's done. Shu Tong said that once we've got the computer system set up, we'll be able to print off 40,000 leaflets in one night.'

The minibus filled with the smell of diesel fumes. We were stuck in a jam at an intersection. Cyclists weaved past us on both sides, ringing their bells. The rain had almost stopped.

'I recorded a Voice of America programme from the radio last night. It was about the situation of Chinese intellectuals. Look!' She handed me the transcript she'd made. The characters were graceful and fluid.

'No wonder you didn't come to see me last night,' I said, putting my arm round her shoulder. 'Once we've got the PA system working tonight, you can read this out to the students.'

She pushed my arm away and said, 'Don't touch me. I've got my period.' There were beads of sweat on her forehead. Her breath smelt sour. 'You must remind me to buy some more wax paper for the mimeograph machine. I'll have to go to the wholesalers. The government has banned shops in the university district from stocking it.' She blew away a few strands of hair that were dangling over her face and pulled up the collar of her red-and-grey striped jumper. 'We'll need to print off a lot of leaflets for the march on the 27th,' she continued, her eyes red with fatigue. 'At least enough to fill this minibus, I should think.'

As I listened to her talk about these things, I sensed a distance opening between us.

Suddenly the face of Lulu, the first girl I fell in love with, flashed through my mind. It took me back to that night when she sat next to me inside the large concrete pipe, her whole body shivering from the cold. I looked at the traffic outside and felt a wave of sadness sweep over me.

Just as a fish could never imagine being scooped from the sea, you could never have imagined that your love would end.

'Number nine dribbles the ball past two defenders, but is intercepted by Peterson. Five takes it away, passes to seven, who strikes, and – oh dear! – hits the goalpost . . .' The radio programme is so loud it drowns out the soap opera blaring from the television in the flat next door.

An Qi is pushing my head down so that my mother can cut my hair. She's been here for an hour, but her hands are still colder than my mother's.

'Do you clean his teeth every day?' she asks.

'Yes, with cotton wool,' my mother says. 'And I wash him twice a day with a wet flannel. He's completely incontinent. Look at all those pads I've hung out to dry. If I forget to put one on him before I take him out, it always ends in disaster.'

In fact my mother rarely bothers to wash me or clean my teeth.

'My husband has his bladder cleaned out regularly,' says An Qi. 'It costs three hundred yuan each time.'

'Can you put that plastic sheet around his shoulders? His hair's so thin now, there's not much for me to cut. Yes, block his ears up with the cotton wool. That's right . . . Look, that's the bullet wound, just above the ear. Feel how soft it is. The hair won't grow back.' An Qi presses the wound with her cold finger. 'The brain's right there under the skin,' my mother continues. 'There's no bone in between. It's freezing outside. I must put a woollen hat on him before we set off for the hospital.'

'You should rub safflower oil on his back,' An Qi says. 'It would help heal those bedsores, and bring his temperature down as well. It smells horrible, though.' An Qi is younger than my mother, but not as strong as her.

'Look how inflamed my knuckles are,' my mother says as she pulls the thermometer from my mouth. 'Mmm, still forty degrees . . .'

I wish the fever would shoot up and kill me. But as I listen to my blood circulate through my body, I know I have no control over my fate. If I could, I'd jump into a volcano. My existence brings only trouble to those around me.

'Shall I take him down now?' a voice cries from the sitting room. It's Gouzi, an electrician who works in the restaurant across the road. He came up to our flat last month to paint some walls.

'All right,' my mother says. 'Take the quilt with you. We'll join you in a minute. I just have to finish packing his bag.'

I'm draped over Gouzi's back now, inhaling the charcoal dust on his coat. My head swings from side to side as he carries me down the stairwell. My mother forgot to put a hat on me. A cold wind blasts through the scar tissue of my bullet wound and freezes the blood vessels beneath. I see a blur of white stars.

When he puts me down on a tricycle cart outside, the freezing air causes my frontal lobes to seize up. I sense a small crowd gather around me.

'Is he dead?' a man whispers.

'It's the guy from the third floor. He's a vegetable. He can't eat or drink. He's been like this for over two years.'

'Is he still breathing?'

'He was on a ventilator for a few months, but now he can breathe by himself. Maybe he'll open his eyes one day.'

The harsh light falling on my face is making me dizzy.

'Where are you taking him?' I recognise this voice. It's Granny Pang, the old busybody who lives on the ground floor.

My mother told me that, during the protests, Granny Pang sent her grandson to the Square to give water and rice porridge to the students, and that after the crackdown, she came up to our flat to comfort my mother, saying the army would soon leave the capital and everything would go back to normal. But after the security officers visited our compound and asked the residents to report any suspicious activity, she began monitoring our flat. If anyone visits us in the morning, when she likes to sit in the sun on a stool outside our block, she always informs the police. Sometimes she even asks our visitors to write down their names and work units. She's become a human guard dog.

'I'm taking him to the hospital,' Gouzi says, pushing my leg back onto the cart. 'Did you think I was taking him out for a meal?'

'He knows lots of state secrets,' a child says, running up to us. 'The police are waiting for him to wake up. My mother told me to stay away from him.'

'Go away, the lot of you!' my mother shouts as she and An Qi join us outside. She pulls the quilt over my head, but I'm still freezing. 'Here's two yuan, I've counted them,' she says, probably handing Gouzi some coins. If she'd got an ambulance to take me to hospital, it would have cost her five times that much.

Buses are hooting behind us. We're on the road now. Through the quilt, I can hear people on the street say, 'It's his birthday today . . . Give me that . . . Two kilos of bananas, please.' Someone's sawing a plank of wood. Someone else is shovelling snow off the pavement with a metal tray. Gouzi rings his bell continuously as he drives us along in his tricycle cart. When we reach a traffic jam, we slow down and a gust of wind smelling of boiled mutton, charcoal and snow shoots up my nostrils.

My mother and An Qi are sitting in front of me, blocking some of the wind. 'When people fall sick in America, an ambulance will take them to hospital free of charge,' my mother says to An Qi. 'They don't have to suffer like we do.'

The wind blows the quilt away from my face. I can feel my skin contract as the freezing air blusters down my neck.

'You forgot to put his hat on,' An Qi says, pushing the quilt back down onto my face again.

'Huh . . .' my mother sighs.

Darknesses pull you deeper into your body, where you lie as in a mountain cave.

The bright morning sun shone down on the green poplars lining the pavement, and on the green caps and uniforms of the armed police who were blocking the street ahead. The police had formed a human wall, about forty rows deep. From a distance they looked like a belt of trees on the edge of a city.

Local residents packed the pavements. Their cries of 'Long live the students!' echoed off the surrounding buildings and the pedestrian flyover. There was a sense that the student movement had become a people's movement. I was with the Organising Committee members at the front of the march, right behind the flag-bearer.

The day before, on 26 April, the *People's Daily* had published an editorial entitled 'We Must Take a Firm Stand Against Turmoil'. It described our movement as a planned conspiracy to overthrow the government. The university authorities relayed a broadcast of the text throughout the campus. It created an uproar. Ke Xi's Beijing Students' Federation decided to turn the march we'd planned for the next day into a mass, city-wide protest against the editorial. Using the PA system I'd helped Shu Tong set up, we urged everyone to take part.

'Long live the people!' we cried as we advanced towards the police. The residents applauded, and handed us cups of water. Ke Xi was wearing a white shirt. He shouted through his megaphone, 'Long live the people! Long live peace and understanding!'

We were marching in rows of seven, with student marshals protecting each side. Zhuzi was head of the security team, and I'd been appointed his deputy. I was responsible for crowd safety, while Zhuzi was in charge of discipline and ensuring no outsiders sabotaged the march.

Han Dan put his sunglasses back on and shouted through his megaphone, 'The municipal government forbade Beijing residents to offer us food or money, or to come onto the streets to watch us. It looks like they've failed, doesn't it!'

Wang Fei said, 'In a speech yesterday, Deng Xiaoping said, "We're not afraid of public reactions, international opinion, or the shedding of blood!" I think we should use that as our slogan!' After reading the editorial, he'd stayed up all night writing a fifteen-page letter of protest. It was the longest text that had ever been displayed in the Triangle.

'That was an internal speech, we don't have a written copy of it,' said Yang Tao. His previous leadership of the Democracy Salon prepared him well for his new role as head of the Organising Committee's political theory office. He was wearing black-rimmed glasses. His neck was long and spindly, his shirt collars were always clean and his hair neatly combed.

'We've inside information that the police won't arrest us today,' said Shu Tong, 'but if this blockade proves impenetrable, it would be best to return to the campus and continue the demonstration there.' He looked very glum. He hadn't been in favour of the march. Earlier that morning, he and Liu Gang had spoken with the university authorities, who'd promised that if the students called off the protest, they would act as mediators and persuade the government to establish a dialogue. Shu Tong favoured the deal, but the rest of the Organising Committee rejected it, which left him with no alternative but to join the march. Old Fu, who was now head of logistics, had stayed behind to keep watch over the campus.

'This blockade is much larger than the one at the Zhongguancun intersection,' said Hai Feng, looking like a village schoolteacher in his white shirt and beige jumper.

The blockade at Zhongguancun had only been four rows deep. We'd charged through it very easily. The officers had been unarmed, and had retreated to the sides of the road as we approached. Some of them even laughed and waved.

But as we neared this blockade, the police raised their megaphones and bellowed aggressively. We came to a terrified halt. I swallowed the last mouthful of my pork bun, and shouted, 'Student marshals – hold hands! Don't give the police an excuse to attack us!' The megaphone made my voice sound crisp and clear.

'Keep calm, everyone!' Zhuzi shouted out from his side. 'Remember – this is a peaceful march! We're not breaking the law.'

Wang Fei and I had cajoled many science students into joining the student marshal team. They were now moving to the front of the procession to fend off any police attack.

The New Year's Day march of 1987 had taught me the importance of maintaining order. If things got out of hand, the police would make arrests and accuse a 'small band of manipulators' of creating turmoil. During marches staged in Changsha and Xian the day before, local residents had taken advantage of the commotion to loot shops. Zhuzi and I had already decided that if there was any violence we'd immediately lead the marchers back to the campus.

Bai Ling and Sister Gao were standing at the front. This was the first march Sister Gao had joined. Since she'd committed herself to the movement, she'd worked harder than anyone else. As well as playing an active role in the Beijing Students' Federation, she'd drawn up new guidelines for the Organising Committee, ruling that Ke Xi shouldn't be authorised to sanction expenditures of over one hundred yuan, and that all committee members must attend the daily meetings.

The students at the head of the procession began to line up opposite the police blockade.

Ke Xi held up a copy of the *People's Daily* and shouted to the police: 'Comrades! In yesterday's editorial entitled "We Must Take a Firm Stand Against Turmoil" it says, "A small handful of opportunists bent on fomenting unrest took advantage of the death of Hu Yaobang to deliberately . . ."'

While he read out the editorial, two students lifted him up onto the rack of a bicycle so that everyone could see him. When he came to the end, he yelled, 'We must oppose slanderous reporting and let the public hear the truth!'

He then pushed his way over to the police and asked them to let us through. The night before, he'd written out a will, and repeated his vow to fight to the bitter end.

'Go back to your campuses!' the head of police shouted. 'The road is blocked. If you come any closer, we won't be responsible for the consequences!' He had white gloves and shiny gold epaulettes. His face was expressionless.

Shu Tong turned to Cao Ming and said, 'Let's retreat and try to get to the Square through the back lanes. If we charge, who knows what might happen?'

'You said the police aren't going to arrest us, so what are you afraid of?' Shao Jian said. He'd seldom disagreed with Shu Tong in the past.

Wang Fei waved his index finger. 'This wouldn't be the first blockade we've charged through. Let's give it a go. If it doesn't work, we can turn back.'

Liu Gang said, 'There are 100,000 students marching with us today. We can't lead them through the back lanes. It would take us hours to reach the Square. We must press on. All the other universities are in the same situation. The Beijing Normal students have just sent word that the Beitaipingzhuang intersection is blocked too.'

'The Politics and Law University's march was blocked at Xinjiekou,' I said, 'and they're trapped in a road to the north.'

'Let's get more students to line up opposite the police wall and start shouting slogans,' Wang Fei said, his cheeks turning red. 'We'll show them who's the strongest.'

'If we break up the ranks, there could be a stampede, and people will get crushed,' I said.

'We'll never get past that blockade,' said Chen Di who must have climbed a wall or a lamp post to get a better view. 'There are two walls of police, each twenty rows deep, and between them, a crowd of old women from local neighbourhood committees. If we breach the first wall, we'll be squashed in the middle like mince in a pie.'

Han Dan patted a marshal's shoulder and said, 'Go and tell the other universities behind us what's happening.'

The back of our column suddenly began pushing forward, unaware of the blockade. The students crushed at the front ran off onto the pavements. I could hear girls screaming.

The sun shone on the sea of student faces. The eyes of the policemen opposite us were hidden by the shadow of their green caps.

'Continue the class boycott! Demand a dialogue with the government and a retraction of the 26 April editorial! The people's police love the people! The police fight official corruption, not patriotic students!' The waves of chanting voices continued to roll through the air above us and crash against the buildings.

'The Qinghua students have joined the back of our procession, Han Dan!' Yang Tao shouted, squeezing his way to the front. 'There are thousands of them.'

'Good! We might just make it then. Who'll lift me up?'

Chen Di and I squeezed over and lifted Han Dan onto our shoulders. He shouted through his megaphone, 'Fellow Beijing University students! The Qinghua students have come to help us! We're about to turn a new page in our university's history. Let's march forward with our heads held high, for the sake of our motherland, freedom and the Chinese people!'

'Come on, fucking hell, let's charge!' Wang Fei yelled through his cupped hands. Within seconds, two officers appeared in front of him. One told him to step back. The other, who had an official badge on his sleeve, talked into a walkie-talkie, no doubt giving a description of him. Moments later they were both knocked aside by the surging hordes of students. Everyone screamed and yelled in the mad rush. Bai Ling, who'd fallen down and was crawling on her knees, poked her head out between the legs of two policemen. By the time we'd pulled her up, she could hardly breathe.

Students from the Beijing Aeronautics University came up behind us singing, '*March on! March on! Our troops march towards the sun, treading the soil of our motherland* . . .' The banner they were holding said IF THE OLD GUARD DOESN'T STEP DOWN, THE NEW GUARD CAN'T STEP UP!

I shouted for the girls to move to the back. Then I gave my bag to Xiao Li and my megaphone to Wang Fei, and together with some tall guys from the Physical Education Department, I pushed to the front to take charge of the assault. 'Marshals at the front link arms,' I shouted. 'Everyone behind us start pushing – now!' I squeezed my face into the ranks of armed police. My legs became trapped. If the students behind hadn't pushed me forward, I couldn't have budged.

We rammed into the police a few more times, and although we didn't break through, we managed to push them back a few a metres. Everyone was sweating now.

I squeezed over onto the pavement and climbed a tree to gain a clearer view of the scene. The first wall of armed police was now only eight rows deep. I was surprised to see some female officers among them. A few sergeants were standing beside the police vans parked on the side. They had handguns fastened to their belts and were speaking nervously into walkie-talkies.

By midday, the students were exhausted from the pushing and shoving, and sat down to rest.

Zhuzi came and said to me that he wanted to organise another attack. Ke Xi said we should put the flag-bearer at the front, but Zhuzi said that in a crush, the pole might stab someone. He also said that the four guys holding the long blackboard should move to the back. They'd taken the board from the university's lecture theatre, and had written across it Deng Xiaoping's famous quote: A REVOLUTIONARY GOVERNMENT SHOULD LISTEN TO THE VOICE OF THE PEOPLE. NOTHING SHOULD FRIGHTEN IT MORE THAN SILENCE.

Then Yang Tao suggested we ask the girls to stand at the front and chant slogans until the police surrendered. We thought it was worth a try. Yang Tao called Bai Ling over to decide on the slogans. I handed her my megaphone. She grabbed it and told the girls to shout out after her: 'Raise the social standing of the police force! Raise police incomes! The people's police protect the people!'

As soon as Bai Ling began to shout, the armed police relaxed. Even the sergeants broke into smiles. I suspected that if Nuwa had come out to shout, the blockade would have crumbled at once.

'You must be tired, comrades! The people will remember your kindness . . .' The chanting chipped away at the police's resolve and put them on the defensive. The crowd of onlookers was larger than ever.

'Let's charge again,' Ke Xi said. 'I think we can push through this time. I'll go to the front and hold the university flag. Dai Wei, you get the marshals to stand behind me and shove me forward.'

I took the megaphone back from Bai Ling and shouted, 'All you girls move back a hundred metres and let the boys attempt a final push. Anyone with a banner or a bike should also move to the back. The first police wall is only eight rows deep. Our wall is ten times bigger!'

There was so much noise now, hardly anyone could hear me.

'Oppose the *People's Daily*'s slanderous attack on the student movement!' cried a group of students at the back.

I yelled as loudly as I could, 'You in the white shirt – put that placard down, or go to the back! Anyone holding hard objects should move back now!'

'I've got something very hard, but I'd better not pull it out!' one guy shouted. Some armed police officers heard him and sniggered.

'Anyone with glass cups, bottles or backpacks must also move to the back!' Han Dan shouted.

Liu Gang grabbed a megaphone and yelled, 'You must be exhausted, comrade policemen. We've come onto the streets today to ask for justice and truth. We'd appreciate your support! The Communist Party is very powerful, but it's riddled from top to bottom with corrupt, money-grubbing officials who abuse their power for personal financial gain. We're not motivated by selfish interests. We've come out here today for the sake of our country's future, and to support your noble profession!'

I moved forward and shouted, 'Everyone behind the flag, pack together and when I give you the signal, push! Lift Ke Xi up, you two. Yes, you, and you in the red shirt. Everyone in the front row, keep your arms tightly linked. One, two, three – push! One, two, three – push! Let the students through!' Everyone began pushing towards the flag Ke Xi was waving.

In less than a minute, Ke Xi had been pushed through the first wall, which began to disintegrate in the middle. Shu Tong seized my megaphone and shouted, 'Quickly, let's widen the chink in their wall. Everyone hold hands!'

The students rammed forward in regular bursts, then charged at the chink, making it wider and wider until the whole police wall collapsed. With deafening cheers, the procession surged straight through and began attacking the second wall. Onlookers standing on the pavements and pedestrian flyover roared in support. The students merged into the morass of police caps which once more scattered to the sides.

The jubilant students cried out to the officers, 'Thank you, comrades! Thank you for your help!'

The onlookers applauded our victory and handed out bottles of Coca-Cola and lemonade.

The police stood impassively at the sides of the road. A few officers and students searched the ground for lost shoes, then flung them to one another.

I was drenched in sweat. My legs were shaking. An armed policeman standing beside me removed his steaming cap and said, 'Will you calm down a little now, my friend? We've had just about as much as we can take.'

'I can't make any promises, I'm afraid,' I said, panting for breath. 'It's all up to Premier Li Peng. We'll have to see what he does next.' I flapped my shirt, trying to cool myself down. The three top buttons and the surrounding patches of cloth had been ripped off in the scrum.

I saw a pretty young woman standing on the back of a flatbed tricycle that was crammed with bottles of lemonade, Coke, yogurt and beer, which she was handing out to the students free of charge. A large crowd had gathered round her, smiling and laughing. She said, 'There's no more food or drink in the shops around here. The local residents have bought it all to give to the students.'

As I tried to squeeze my way through the crowd to grab a drink, I looked up at the young woman again, and realised that it was Lulu. I felt the same panic that had gripped me when my bicycle was stolen in the Triangle. She looked at me and gave me the victory sign. I couldn't tell whether she recognised me or not. My heart started pounding and everything became blurred. I saw myself as a boy of fifteen being kicked onto the cement floor by a policeman, and the dark shadows inside the cold concrete pipe in which Lulu and I had hidden. Lulu lifted a bottle of Coke in the air and opened it for me. I glanced up and caught sight of her armpits. In the bright sunlight, they looked dark and mysterious and seemed still to be sheltering secrets from my past.

It was seven years since my confession to the police had got her into trouble. Our families hadn't spoken since then, but I'd found out a few things about her. I knew that she hadn't gone to university, her brother had joined the army, and her deaf grandmother had died. My mother had also heard a rumour that she'd made some money in Shenzhen, and had returned to Beijing to open a small restaurant.

I remembered going with her to buy one fen's worth of marshmallow. The stallholder usually charged two fen, so he gave us half the amount, and shorter bamboo sticks too. We handed him the money and went to stand under a tree. Lulu held one of her sticks in each hand and moved them in and out, stretching her brown lump of marshmallow so that it hung in a thin thread between them, then pushing it back into a ball again. I sensed her observing me through the corner of her eye, so I tried to stretch my marshmallow into a longer string than hers. But as I glanced back at her, my string broke in half and a strand became stuck to my sleeve. She laughed out loud. The string left on my stick was too dry to push into a ball again, so I popped it into my mouth and sucked it. Lulu continued to stretch her marshmallow until the fine thread turned white and twinkled in the sunlight. I knew that if she'd touched it with her tongue at that moment, it would have pricked like a needle. But she was sure she could do better, so she pushed the thread back into a ball and stretched it out again, and this time it was longer than ever. 'You can never pull it into such a thin strand when you buy two fen's worth,' I said.

'*Pull marshmallow between the sticks, and watch it turn from brown to white . . .*' she sang, pulling the sugary thread once more. The thread stayed still for a moment, then drooped in the middle and snapped. I pounced on the needle-thin strand as it fell to the ground and tossed it into my mouth. As she slapped my head, I grabbed the bamboo stick she'd dropped and popped that in my mouth as well. Clutching the remaining stick firmly in her hand, she said, 'You horrible boy!' then walked off in a huff.

Before Lulu and I could exchange a word, the surge of the crowd carried me forward. Everyone shouted, 'Long live the people of Beijing!' I joined their cries, tired but elated.

In the distance, I heard Mou Sen cry through a megaphone, 'We should make today Students' Day!' Everyone cheered in agreement. As I tried to push my way over to him, I spotted Yanyan. She was wearing round glasses and a white baseball cap. Her gentle, poised demeanour made her look out of place in the packed crowd of students. I called out to her.

'What a great day it is today!' she said, moving closer to me. 'You students are wonderful!'

'For the first time in Chinese history, the people have been victorious!'

I said. 'So, will you write something about this march for the *Workers' Daily?*'

'I'd like to, but I doubt it would get published. The chief editor is very conservative. Lots of the younger reporters and editors have joined the march, though.' Then she smiled at me and asked, 'And where's Tian Yi?'

'Back at the campus looking after the broadcast station. She doesn't like marches. She gets stomach cramps when she's trapped in a crowd . . . You must come and see us.'

I pushed forward and discovered that the People's University students had joined the front of our procession. They sang, '*No Communist Party, no New China!*' as they charged through the police cordons at the Liubukou intersection and Xinhua Gate.

As dusk was falling, we finally made it to Tiananmen Square and joined the vast crowd of Beijing students and citizens already gathered there. The noise and commotion were overwhelming.

Under one of the street lamps, a student waved a bloodstained shirt, and said he'd been beaten up by the police. Ke Xi climbed onto the Monument to address the crowd. As I sat down on the ground, crushed with exhaustion, Nuwa walked up and asked me whether I'd seen Wang Fei. She was wearing his blue windcheater. It seemed that I was always looking at my worst whenever she turned up. I tried to sit up straight.

'You and your team organised things very well today,' she said, looking down at me. 'It was a great march.'

At the western edge of the Great Wastes lies Lake Utmost. It is the home of Bingyi, God of the Yellow River. Bingyi often roams across the land in a cart driven by two dragons.

When spring arrives, I imagine pale-green shoots poking out from the grey walls and roof tiles as I inhale the smell of earth on the carrots in the market stalls and the smoke from our neighbours' charcoal stoves. Although this smoke is present throughout the year, in spring it smells different, because our neighbours open their doors and windows and let it warm in the sunlight along with all the other household smells.

I'm still lying on the iron bed. The lengthy conversation my mother is having with the policeman keeps disturbing my train of thought.

'What is your position on the events of 4 June?' Officer Liu asks my mother. He knocked twice on our door before he walked in. He's now standing in the corner of the sitting room.

'Do you want me to give you the truth, or the lies that you've asked for before?' My mother has been hassled by the police so often these last two years that she's lost all fear of them.

'The truth, of course.'

'The truth is, I still don't understand why the army opened fire on the students, and why, after my son was shot, I'm expected to apologise on his behalf, and say he deserved it,' my mother replies indignantly.

'That's all in the past now. Try to be pragmatic. If you apologise for his crimes, you will both be better off.'

'Look at him lying there on the bed. That's not the past! He's alive, and I'll have to look after him for the rest of my life. Take him away now if you want, and put another bullet in his head!'

'I haven't come here to listen to you moaning. Tell me what you plan to do on 4 June this year.'

'What do I know? I'm not in a fit state to make plans. Stop asking me.'

'It's Grave Sweeping Festival tomorrow. Is there anyone's death you plan to commemorate?'

'Officer Liu, you've known me for some time now. My husband is under the bed – look, there, in that black box of ashes. The purple box next to it is for my son's ashes, when he finally decides to die. My father killed himself shortly after Liberation and wasn't even given a gravestone. So whose grave do you suppose I'd sweep tomorrow?'

'You know I'm only following orders, Auntie. I just needed to remind you not to leave the flat tomorrow, or visit any public cemeteries. It's no big deal. Write a statement saying that you'll be staying indoors, and I'll leave you in peace.'

'If you hadn't come round, I wouldn't have known what day it was tomorrow. All right, you write the statement for me and I'll sign it.' My mother has become very strong-willed.

The clang of bicycle bells on the street outside rattles through your skull. In the room next door, you hear your mother twist open the cap of a plastic bottle.

I walked over to Tian Yi and tapped my spoon on her ear. I'd bought her a portion of stir-fried pork and celery. She was copying out a petition for the Dialogue Delegation, a group Shu Tong had founded to press for direct talks with the government.

'Listen to this,' she said to Shu Tong, taking the box of food from my hands without looking up at me. '"We request – One: official recognition that the student movement is a patriotic movement. Two: a speeding-up of political reform. Three: the promotion of democracy and rule of law . . ." Don't you think these demands could be a little more specific?'

'Yes, they are a bit vague . . .' I muttered, as I sat on a bed and munched on a steamed roll.

'There's no need to wear those sunglasses indoors,' Tian Yi whispered to me. She'd bought me the brown sunglasses I was wearing. When I'd tried them on in the shop, she'd said, 'They make your wooden face look a little more animated.'

Shu Tong's dorm was now the students' broadcast station. My dorm next door was the editorial office of our new independent newspaper, the *News Herald*. Over the past three weeks of 'turmoil', our floor had become the nerve-centre of the student movement. The corridor was pasted with inky-smelling posters and was busier than a train station at rush hour.

'Don't worry,' said Shu Tong. 'These three points will open up the debate. Once the dialogue begins, we can make more concrete suggestions.' He tried to sniff back the mucus that was dripping from his nose. He often suffered from congestion when he didn't get enough sleep.

'What's the relationship between your Dialogue Delegation and the Beijing Students' Federation?' asked Xiao Li. 'Will they come into conflict?' During the past week, Xiao Li had managed to teach himself how to prepare mimeograph stencils. When he cut the characters, he'd lean right over the drum of the machine. When I tried my hand at it, I tore a large hole in the paper.

'The Dialogue Delegation is a temporary organisation,' Shu Tong said. 'It will dissolve once the dialogue comes to an end. The Federation represents all the universities and colleges of Beijing, and will lead the student movement in the months to come.' He was wearing a short-sleeved shirt. His arms looked as soft and smooth as Tian Yi's.

'There've been so many coups and reshuffles recently, I don't even know who the Federation's chairman is now,' Nuwa said, emerging from behind the blackboard that separated the broadcasting area from the rest of the room. Her new short bob made her neck look longer and paler.

'All those coups happened before the 4 May march,' Shu Tong said. 'Old Fu had the gall to convene a meeting while I was having a nap in the printing room, and got me voted off the Federation. If I hadn't founded the Dialogue Delegation I'd be out of a job now.' The previous week, tens of thousands of us had marched to the Square again to mark the seventieth anniversary of the May Fourth Movement. Fired by the same patriotism as the students in 1919, we demanded democratic reforms and direct talks with the government.

'I thought Old Fu resigned from the Federation,' Bai Ling said, then winced as she took a sip of boiling tea.

'Really?' Nuwa said. 'I saw him in the Triangle this morning. He was asking students to sign a petition calling on the university authorities to award Gorbachev an honorary degree during his forthcoming visit to Beijing. He asked me to help him find a translator. He wants to discuss the matter with the Soviet ambassador!' Nuwa laughed, covering her mouth with her hand to hide the pieces of fried dough stick she was chewing. Her gestures were always graceful. As I watched her dig her big toes into the insoles of her red leather sandals, I breathed in, but couldn't smell the sweat on her feet.

'I expect Old Fu handed in his resignation in the middle of the night,' Yang Tao said, coming in to look for something to eat. 'When he gets tired, he does rash things which he totally forgets about the next morning.'

'Old Fu's done his week as chairman, so it was time for him to resign anyway,' I said, handing Yang Tao a steamed roll, which he devoured greedily. Han Dan and Liu Gang were muttering behind the blackboard. They'd just taken part in a broadcast discussion of Gorbachev's perestroika reforms, and it sounded as if they were having an argument. The room was incredibly noisy. We couldn't shut the windows properly because of the many electric cables hanging out. I decided that the next day I'd block off the broadcasting area with hardboard to diminish the din.

Han Dan suddenly raised his voice. They'd forgotten to turn off the microphone, so I rushed over and switched it off.

'Stop going on about the '87 protests,' he yelled at Liu Gang, so loudly that everyone in the corridor could hear. 'This movement is on a different scale. We've had petitions, sit-ins, marches, class boycotts, demands for dialogue . . .'

'That's the problem: we've been doing too much,' said Liu Gang. 'We should stop the marches and refocus on building up democracy within the campus.' Liu Gang had been chairman of the Organising Committee since the 4 May march, and Han Dan was now his deputy.

'If you're going to have a row, leave the broadcasting area,' Shu Tong said sternly. 'The cables are in a terrible mess. Can someone sort them out?'

'But we've reached an impasse,' complained Han Dan as he and Liu Gang walked over to the bunk beds. 'The class boycott hasn't achieved anything. The best option now would be to go ahead with a hunger strike. It would win us popular support and force the government's hand.'

A hubbub broke out. 'I suppose that means you'll want to get everyone out onto the streets again,' Shu Tong moaned.

'The Federation and the Organising Committee are both opposed to a strike,' Hai Feng said, 'and so is the Dialogue Delegation. We can't hope to negotiate with the government while at the same time exerting pressure through a hunger strike. They wouldn't listen to us.'

'Well, they haven't shown much sign of wanting to listen to us so far,' said Han Dan, rolling up his sleeves. 'If we don't use a more radical approach, they'll ignore us completely, and our movement will disintegrate.'

'Our efforts at securing a dialogue are progressing well,' Shu Tong said, his face turning red with anger. 'If we launch a hunger strike, our relationship with the government will break down. And besides, most of the students here don't support the idea. That graduate student in Block 46 who's gone on hunger strike is a crank.'

'Hunger strikes can be a very effective form of political protest,' Bai Ling said, coming to Han Dan's defence. 'They've achieved a lot of success in other countries.'

Han Dan slammed his fist on the table and said, 'The reformers in the Party have sent us messages telling us to step up our protests. They said, "the bigger the better!"'

A little nervously, Tian Yi stood up and said, 'We've received many notes supporting a hunger strike. You're not in tune with the mood of the campus, Shu Tong. The students are much more radical than you.'

'Yes!' exclaimed Nuwa. 'You've spent so much time locked up in meetings here, you've lost touch with what's going on outside.'

'Gorbachev will be arriving in Beijing on the 15th,' continued Han Dan. 'It'll be the first time a Soviet leader has visited China in forty years. The government will want to hold a big welcoming ceremony for him in Tiananmen Square. If we stage a hunger strike in the Square while he's in town it will force the government to compromise.'

'Well, if you want to go ahead with this crackpot plan, you'll have to do it alone and resign from the Federation and the Organising Committee,' Shu Tong said. He knew that the strike would destroy his Dialogue Delegation.

'All you lot do is talk, talk, talk,' Han Dan said, 'but what we need is action.' I'd never heard him speak so forcefully before. 'All right, I will hand in my resignation. Switch the microphone back on, Dai Wei. I want to make a public announcement.'

'You can't let the students know how disunited we are,' Tian Yi said.

'Don't worry, I know what to say,' Han Dan said, stubbornly heading back to the microphone.

'We're relaying the Beijing Radio news at the moment,' I said. 'Do you want to interrupt it? Old Fu will be presenting his *Democracy Forum* show soon. Why not make your announcement then?'

Han Dan agreed, and went off to the canteen with Yang Tao.

Bai Ling and Tian Yi said they'd be willing to go on hunger strike. I laughed and said they'd give up after a day.

Wang Fei and I went outside to play ping-pong near the Triangle. On our way there, we bumped into my mother. Many parents had been coming onto the campus to ask the professors whether their children had joined the protests. My mother had just visited the university's Party committee office and told them that she'd begged me to withdraw from the movement, but that I'd refused to listen, and that she would support any action the government chose to take.

In the middle of the wastes, where the River Sweet peters out, lies a mountain that is home to three kingdoms. The inhabitants of these kingdoms have feathers on their bodies and hatch from eggs.

My mother asks a passenger to help lift me off the train, then we wait on the platform for my cousin Dai Dongsheng to turn up. He arrives in a hired tractor and drives us back to his home in Dezhou, thirty kilometres away. It is the Dai ancestral village where my father was born. I have never visited it before. Although there are very few members of the Dai clan still living there, I still have a sense that I'm returning to my roots.

On the bumpy journey there, I think about Wang Fei's letter. It arrived a few days ago, and my mother read it out to me on the train. Wang Fei described how, after he was discharged from hospital, he was interrogated by the police for several months and told never to disclose to anyone that he'd seen army tanks crushing the students. When he refused to agree to this, he was told he wouldn't be allocated a job after graduation. 'I'm confined to a wheelchair,' he wrote. 'But I haven't given up on life. I recently took part in the third national games for the disabled . . . A friend's sister helped me find a job in Hainan Island . . . You and I got the roughest deal in the end, Dai Wei. We're worse off even than poor Mou Sen. What a bloody mess this world is . . .'

At last, the tractor's noisy diesel engine is turned off. We've arrived. Someone is flashing a torch on my face.

'Say "Hello Auntie"!' says Dai Dongsheng to a child who is panting beside him. I presume it's his daughter, Taotao.

'Don't worry, it's late now,' my mother says breathlessly. 'She can say it tomorrow.'

A shrill voice shouts out, 'I'll take my case to the emperor! A murder must be avenged . . .' This must be Dongsheng's wife.

When she and Dongsheng visited us in Beijing during her illegal second pregnancy, my mother was unable to find a hospital willing to help deliver the child. The police tracked her down after a few days and sent her back to Dezhou, where her belly was opened and her baby boy was drowned before her eyes. The loss of the child drove her insane.

'Can she look after herself?' my mother asks, sounding a little ashamed. After they left Beijing, my mother cut out a newspaper article on the social benefits of the one-child policy and sent it to Dongsheng, telling him to persuade his wife to have the child in a government clinic, then pay the fine. She never dreamed that the family planning officers would order the child to be killed. When the couple had told us stories of forced abortions and infanticides, my mother had assumed they were making them up. Dongsheng sold a tricycle cart, five pigs, a wardrobe and a television to pay for psychological treatment for his wife, but no one was able to cure her condition.

'She makes about fifty brooms a day, which pays for our rice and oil. But she still keeps flinging things out of the house. Look, she's torn everything off the walls. It's not easy living with someone who's lost their mind. She's even more unstable than my father was.' Then he adds, 'Have you remembered to bring the crackdown certificate saying that Dai Wei wasn't involved in the counter-revolutionary riots? You'll need to show it to the clinic before they'll agree to treat him.'

'Yes, I paid someone to forge one for me. It's valid for two years.'

'I didn't realise he was in such a bad way. Can't he speak at all?'

'In your letter you said that this Dr Ma can bring the dead back to life, and make paralysed people walk again,' my mother says, not bothering to answer him.

'Yes, he's very famous around here. Two years ago, he was a full-time teacher at our village primary school, and only treated a few patients in his spare time. But after the niece of the county Party secretary started taking his herbal medicine, his name began appearing in all the newspapers. He made lots of money, and was able to open a private clinic just down the road. He has an official car to chauffeur him now. Anyway, I've set it all up with him. Dai Wei can check into the clinic tomorrow morning.'

'If he could get Dai Wei to open his eyes or stand up, that would be wonderful. Here are some cigarette cartons for you to give as backhanders. And I've got some more things for you in this bag.' My mother lifts the bag onto her lap and opens the zip. I can tell that Dongsheng, his daughter and his wife are all staring at the bag now.

'We're family,' Dongsheng mumbles. 'There's no need for you to give us presents.'

'I've brought some dresses and jumpers for you.' Now I know why my mother spent so long rifling through the wardrobe last night. She has lots of clothes. Most of them are gifts I brought back for her from Guangzhou.

The wife doesn't take the clothes that my mother offers her. She stays rooted to the ground, muttering, 'I will take my case to the emperor! A murder must be avenged . . .'

'These leather shoes are from America,' my mother says. 'Try them on.' She hands Dai Dongsheng the shoes that were too small for my brother. They should be as good as new. He only wore them once.

'We make do with rubber-soled shoes in the countryside. These look like something a cadre would own. People will laugh at me if I wear them.' But despite the protestations, he tries them on. 'They're great!' he says. 'A perfect fit. I can wear them when I go into town to do business. I'll look like an official.' I can tell from his voice that he's very pleased with them.

'And this alarm clock is for you,' my mother continues, turning I presume to their daughter. 'What's your name again? My memory's getting so bad.'

'She's called Taotao,' Dongsheng says. 'Quickly, say "Thank you, Auntie"! Now go and put the kettle on. Fill it right to the top . . . She's the opposite of her mother, that child. She doesn't say a word.'

'How much did the tractor you collected us in cost to hire?'

'Twelve yuan.'

'Well, here's a hundred. You can keep the change. It's spring. I'm sure there's machinery or seeds you'll have to buy.'

'There's no need for this. We're family, after all. You've got Dai Wei to look after. It's not as if you're well off.'

'Things aren't easy for us, but we're still better off than you are out here in the countryside. Go on, take it.'

'I will take my case to the emperor! A murder must be avenged . . .'

Alone on your wooden ark, you drift along the endless stream of lymph fluids, continuing your wretched journey.

While Wang Fei and I were playing ping-pong, we heard Han Dan's voice blaring through the students' loudspeakers: 'I've resigned from the Organising Committee. I plan to organise a hunger strike and intensify our protests . . .'

We put down our ping-pong bats. It was getting too dark to play.

'He's right to call for a hunger strike now,' Wang Fei said, wiping his sweaty hands on his trousers as we walked back to our dorm block. 'But I'm not going to jump on his bandwagon. I proposed a strike weeks ago, when the movement first started. Now he's making out it's all his idea.'

When we reached Shu Tong's dorm, I said, 'I hope Han Dan and Old Fu's resignations won't destroy the Organising Committee.'

'Han Dan is too impulsive,' Shu Tong said. 'I don't trust him. He wants to use the strike to boost his authority.' His expression had relaxed since Han Dan had left the dorm.

Old Fu was about to interview the dissident novelist Zheng He, the most celebrated member of the Creative Writing Programme. We'd worked together in the now-defunct supervisory office. He was a serious-looking man with a balding head and thick glasses. One of his books had been made into a low-budget art film.

We filed out into the crowded corridor to leave them in peace.

'The students are getting very worked up about Han Dan's speech,' Sister Gao said, striding up to us. 'The boycott was a good idea, but who knows what a hunger strike could lead to?'

'If we launch a strike, the government will crush us, and there'll be chaos and bloodshed,' Shu Tong said, pacing nervously up and down the corridor.

'I agree,' Liu Gang said. 'As the executive chairman, I'd like to broadcast an announcement stating that the Organising Committee is opposed to the strike.'

'There's no reason why we shouldn't push for a dialogue and stage a hunger strike at the same time,' Wang Fei said, puffing on his cigarette. 'Perhaps if we attack the government from both sides, it will be forced to compromise. The question is: will Han Dan cooperate with us?'

Nuwa went to stand beside him. She'd changed into a short skirt. Her pale legs glowed in the smoky darkness of the corridor. She pulled the cigarette from Wang Fei's lips and took a quick puff. I couldn't understand how she could bear to stand so close to him. The stench of his sweat filled the corridor.

Bai Ling poked her head out from my dorm and said, 'Shu Tong, I think the Dialogue Delegation's petition needs to be rewritten. It's too long-winded.'

'I'm tired, I need to sleep,' Shu Tong said, closing his eyes. 'I'll leave it to you and Tian Yi.'

Tian Yi was in the corner with Sister Gao. 'The Communist Party emerged from the barrel of a gun,' Sister Gao was telling her. 'It's a brutal, rigid organisation. As soon as we stepped out onto the streets, they accused us of creating turmoil.' Ever since the 4 May march, she'd been advising us to wind up the student movement.

'Yes, and President Yang Shangkun is a military man too,' Tian Yi said, dazed from lack of sleep.

'So is Vice President Wang Zhen,' Sister Gao said. 'This country is ruled by the military.'

The corridor was getting too noisy, so we went to sit down in my dorm. Five volunteers were proofreading articles for the next edition of the *News Herald*. Half of the bunk beds were piled with banners, flags and boxes of stationery. Two students who'd travelled up from Nanjing were asleep on my bed. Chen Di and Dong Rong were folding up some freshly mimeographed pamphlets. Mao Da and Qiu Fa had become so fed up with the chaos they'd moved into another dorm.

When Tian Yi and Bai Ling had finished rewriting the Dialogue Delegation's petition, they turned to a transcript of the speech General Secretary Zhao Ziyang had just given at the annual meeting of the Asian Development Bank. 'Listen to this,' Tian Yi said excitedly. '"China will not fall into turmoil" and the students are "not opposing our fundamental system, they are merely requesting we rectify a few flaws".'

'That's fantastic!' Liu Gang said, standing up. 'We must broadcast it at once. Shu Tong, wake up!'

'That shows that Zhao Ziyang disagrees with the 26 April editorial,' Shao Jian said. 'He's on our side!'

Xiao Li walked in and read out an emergency proposal just posted by the hunger-striking graduate student in Block 46: '"Given the gravity of the current situation, we suggest that we: a) launch a mass hunger strike, time and place to be determined; and b) occupy Tiananmen Square during Gorbachev's state visit to China. If we don't escalate our protests, our movement is doomed." Shall I turn that into a pamphlet?' Xiao Li had been making mimeographed pamphlets from the most interesting texts he'd seen in the Triangle.

'No, don't,' Shu Tong said. 'If there's a hunger strike, what will be the point of a Dialogue Delegation?'

'But the whole purpose of the hunger strike is to force the government into holding a dialogue,' Bai Ling said, glancing angrily at Shu Tong.

'The Organising Committee has opposed the hunger strike, Bai Ling,' said Wang Fei. 'If the strikers make headway, they'll become the voice of the students, and we'll be mere supporters.'

'And what's wrong with that?' Nuwa said, slapping his shoulder. 'You're supposed to be fighting dictatorship, but deep down you all want to be little emperors.'

'It's all very well having General Secretary Zhao Ziyang on our side,' Shao Jian said, lighting another cigarette, 'but Deng Xiaoping still holds the reins, and *he* thinks we're dangerous counter-revolutionaries. Deng likes to portray himself as a reformer, but don't be fooled. He's sly. He was responsible for the Anti-Rightist Campaign, but he managed to make everyone believe it was Mao's fault.'

'The hunger strike might spread through the whole country,' said Sister Gao. 'If China falls into turmoil, it will be the end of Zhao Ziyang. Over the last few days, the police have retreated to the suburbs. Beijing is a ghost town. They're waiting for us to start smashing and looting, then they'll launch a crackdown. We must declare our support for Zhao Ziyang's speech. It will boost the morale of the students and stop them from doing anything extreme.'

'Who's going to replace Han Dan now that he's resigned?' Liu Gang asked impatiently. 'We'd better hold a meeting. Let's get all the department representatives up here.'

Wang Fei and Nuwa had left the room. Wang Fei had seemed irritated by Nuwa's criticism a few moments before. Their relationship was quite stormy. They often seemed to be on the verge of breaking up.

Everyone began wandering off. Tian Yi sat down in front of the typewriter and continued trying to teach herself to touch-type. 'These little keys are upside down,' she said. 'They're impossible to read.'

'Foreign authors write their books on typewriters,' I said. 'If you practise long enough, you'll get the hang of it.'

'Those foreigners have twenty-six letters to deal with, we have two thousand,' Tian Yi said, looking up at me. In the faint light of the room her face had a comforting glow.

As your cells struggle on inside your body, you feel, once again, that you have been buried alive.

'Ah, you're here at last, Dai Dongsheng,' my mother says. 'Come in and take a look at your cousin. He's had terrible diarrhoea since the treatment started and it's not getting any better. What can we do?'

'He should stay here a few more days. I've just spoken to a nurse. She said the non-surgical treatment he's getting takes longer to show results. He'll need at least two courses, I should think.'

'I can't keep him here that long. The Beijing police might get suspicious and come and track us down. And I'm not sure about that Dr Ma. I followed him last night. He went to the graveyard behind the clinic and tore off some clumps of grass then dug up some roots and insects. They didn't look like the ingredients of traditional Chinese medicine to me.'

'He knows what he's doing. The grasses and insects in the graveyard have supernatural powers. A fox spirit appeared to him in the graveyard a while ago and gave him some herbs to treat a woman's swollen liver. He made a tincture from them and told the woman to drink it. It gave her acute diarrhoea for three days, but after that, her liver disease was completely cured.'

'But if this goes on any longer, Dai Wei will be dead in a few days,' my mother says impatiently.

The herbal soup this folk doctor has been funnelling into my mouth passes straight through me and gushes out the other end. After the first dose he gave me, my eyelids twitched and my stomach and intestines clenched. Blood rushed to my brain, stimulating my motor neurons. For a moment, I felt I could have stretched out my hand and grabbed something, even though I knew my hands were as clenched as chicken claws. Unfortunately, I haven't had any such reactions to subsequent doses.

'I've come to give you some good news, Auntie. The county Party secretary has asked you out for a meal.'

'What for? And where would he take us? There aren't any restaurants in Dezhou.'

'You have relatives in America, don't you? The local government wants people who have family abroad to persuade their relatives to return to this county and invest in the local economy. If they succeed, they'll be rewarded with an urban residency permit. If you get Dai Wei's great-uncle to set up a business in Dezhou, Taotao might get a residency permit for the county town.'

'That old man is dead, and his son Kenneth is a professional musician. He wouldn't want to move to this backwater. And besides, what kind of business could anyone set up here?'

'A Taiwanese man has opened a noodle factory that employs more than fifty people. It's doing very well. There's a talc mine near here as well. So Dai Wei's cousin could set up a talcum powder factory or a drug factory, if he wanted to.'

'What use is talc to a drug factory?'

'Drug factories put talc in their pills. Didn't you know that? It's quite safe to consume in small portions. If they didn't add it, the pills wouldn't be white or heavy enough, and no one would buy them.'

Dongsheng removes his padded coat and the air fills with the smell of stale leftovers and oily pans.

'The government keeps urging everyone to go into business,' my mother says. 'My only talent is singing. I can't do anything else. So when I retired from the opera company, I decided to give private singing lessons at my home. But the police come round so often, checking up on Dai Wei, most of my pupils have been scared away. I've only got one left now.'

'Dr Ma, you've come!' Dai Dongsheng shouts into the corridor in a Shandong dialect.

My mother gets up from her stool.

I hear the doctor approach, treading over the pumpkin-seed shells scattered across the floor. I can sense there's a group of people behind him, standing in the doorway, blocking the small amount of the light that reaches this room.

'You've left it too late, I'm afraid,' Dr Ma says. 'If you'd brought him to me two years ago, he'd be walking about by now.'

'He's been having terrible green diarrhoea, and he's got a temperature of thirty-nine degrees,' my mother says, a beseeching tone creeping into her voice.

'He needs stronger medicine. I'll take him to the graveyard tonight, and ask the fox spirit to offer assistance.' Dr Ma pinches my earlobes then inspects my tongue. 'Help me pull him up, Dongsheng. I want to move him about a little.' He and Dongsheng pull me up into a sitting position, then push me back down. 'And up again, down again, up again, down again . . . One can't rely on medicine alone. He must do these exercises. The joints and ligaments need to be supple if the herbs are to have an effect.' They fold me up and stretch me out one last time, then leave me to rest on my back. A confusion of red and black blotches dances before my eyes. I feel as though I'm suffocating.

You remember sticking your head out of the window of the covered balcony one cold winter morning, and gazing at the few golden leaves still clinging to the branches of the locust tree.

The nights are very black in the countryside. They've laid me down in the graveyard and draped a blanket over me. My limbs are freezing. We've been here a long time, and still no spirit has appeared, although for a moment I thought I sensed the ghost of my grandfather, who was buried alive here by Dongsheng's father during the Cultural Revolution. Perhaps I have already consumed traces of his spirit in the graveyard herbs I've been fed. A few hours ago, Dr Ma placed a pile of paper money by my side and burned it, muttering, 'Come and help this man, fox spirit, and let him walk again. Show him your mercy . . .'

When my mother had to leave me for a while, she asked Taotao to stay by my side and make sure no dogs or pigs came and bit me. After we were left alone, Taotao whispered to me, 'Stop pretending to be dead!' then picked up a stick and hit my face, hands and stomach with it. Thanks to that beating, I am now able to feel cold and anxious. Perhaps tomorrow I'll be able to move my fingers.

After an uncertain lapse of time, I feel a bright light shining on my eyes and hear someone say, 'Dr Ma, the secretary of the county Party committee has ordered us to take this patient to the county Armed Forces department.'

'You'd better take him, then. What's the problem?'

'A patient receiving treatment for physical injuries must have their crackdown certificate stamped by the public security bureau. The clinic's stamp isn't sufficient any longer. The provincial authorities telephoned this morning to inform us about this new regulation.'

The torchlight flashes over my face again. A dizzying prism of black and white blotches floats before my eyes.

Your thoughts return to those glimmering locust-tree leaves, and to the beautiful moment of dawn when darkness merges into light.

I used to long for Tian Yi's visits, but now I dread them. I know that my cousin Kenneth has sent her a letter confirming he'll act as her financial sponsor in America. All she needs to do now is hand in her residence permit to the talent-exchange centre, then apply for a visa.

She walks into my room. She hasn't seen me for six months. My appearance must disgust her. My body is shrivelled and dry. There's a feeding tube in my mouth. A stream of saliva leaking from the corner of my parted lips is trickling down my neck onto the pillow. My mother has opened the windows and doused the floor with eau de cologne, but the room still smells of sickness. The odour seeps from my pores onto the mattress and is released into the air by the spreading mould.

She sits down next to me. 'You've lost more weight, Dai Wei,' she says. 'It makes me so sad.'

I breathe in and smell the scent of her freshly washed hair mingled with the strange smells wafting from under the bed. Somewhere beneath me is a bag containing her journals and photograph albums. Inside one album is the photo of Tian Yi and me in the rainforest of Yunnan – the one where she's leaning against me, exhausted after our walk, her mouth half open.

'I've come today because it's the third anniversary of 4 June. The streets are filled with police cars and the Square has been cordoned off.'

After she leaves, her image lingers inside my head for a while, then slowly breaks up and disappears.

'I was never able to develop my talents in the opera company,' my mother says. 'The other singers would laugh at me when I went off to do voice exercises. They spent all their time playing Mahjong, or sucking up to the leaders, trying to wangle a trip abroad or a new flat. Everyone was so corrupt. I had to leave . . .' She's talking to An Qi in the sitting room. Fan Jing is also with them. Last time she came, she said that after her son was killed in the crackdown, her cat died of heartbreak.

Your skin is as dry as a wheat husk. Your heart lies trapped inside damp walls, invisible and untouchable.

On the afternoon of 12 May, Han Dan and Ke Xi posted a notice in the Triangle calling for students to sign up for a hunger strike due to start in Tiananmen Square at 2 p.m. the following day.

In Old Fu's *Democracy Forum* show that evening, Bai Ling and Han Dan gave impassioned speeches, urging everyone to join the strike. Ke Xi, who'd gone into hiding for three days after hearing rumours of an imminent police clampdown, turned up again in the Triangle to welcome a delegation of Shanghai students who'd travelled to Beijing to submit a petition to the government.

Sensing the new mood of excitement in the campus, the Organising Committee realised it would be futile to oppose the strike. Hai Feng suggested we set up a support group and a first-aid team to assist the hunger strikers during their occupation of the Square. By now, nearly forty students had signed up.

Shu Tong climbed onto the windowsill, gazed down at the crowd in the Triangle and said morosely, 'They stir the masses into a frenzy, then say, "Listen to the voice of the people!" Everyone from Hitler to Mao has done it. The movement we've worked so hard to build up is being destroyed by these bloody upstarts.'

'You've had many chances to seize the leadership,' I said, 'but you've always let them slip. You prevaricate.'

'No, my belief has always been that if we push things too far, we'll be crushed. The Communist Party was catapulted to power through student uprisings, so it understands the threat we pose to the status quo.'

Only when the Shanghai students were taken off to the dorms at two in the morning did the Triangle finally quieten down. I told Mou Sen he could sleep on my bunk, then went to find an empty bed in Tian Yi's dorm.

Mou Sen had been appointed the new chairman of the Beijing Students' Federation. His university was tightly guarded, so he'd based his headquarters at our campus. Sister Gao was his secretary general. They'd organised a meeting the night before, but no one had turned up. A few members sent messages saying they'd returned to classes or were being monitored by the authorities. The Federation seemed to exist in name only.

When I reached the Triangle, I saw Bai Ling and Tian Yi signing up to join the hunger strike.

I wasn't happy about this. Pointing to the front page of the *News Herald*, I said, 'Look, this article says that the 27 April march was a victory for the students, but warns that if we take things any further, China will revert to the chaos of the Cultural Revolution. It's written by a professor in the Politics Department.'

'I wrote that article, you fool!' Tian Yi said.

'Just because you haven't the courage to sign up, there's no need to sneer at us,' Bai Ling said.

'He's so stiff these days,' Tian Yi gripped Bai Ling's hand.

'Have you gone out of your minds?' I said.

'We're psychology students, so watch what you say,' Bai Ling smirked. 'You're afraid to join the strike because it will make you conspicuous.'

'So Mimi's signed up too,' I said, spotting her signature. 'People will accuse her of doing it to lose weight.'

'Why are you so scathing? No one's forcing you to join the strike, so keep your mouth shut.' Tian Yi was angry.

'All right,' I said. 'If you go on a hunger strike, I'll give up meat.' Tian Yi glanced derisively at me then marched off to Shu Tong's dorm. Bai Ling and I followed behind her.

Bai Ling and Tian Yi began drafting a hunger strike declaration. I sat beside them smoking cigarettes. A few hours later, Mou Sen wandered in to have a look at the draft, and said, 'That won't do. It's got no style. I'll have to rewrite it.'

Mou Sen had had a change of heart. A few minutes before, he'd announced that he'd resigned from the Beijing Students' Federation in order to join the Beijing Normal's hunger strike team.

In the eastern region of the Great Wastes there is a corpse with shoulder-length hair. This is God Jubi. He looks like a man, but his neck is broken and he only has one hand.

'We entreat all honourable citizens of China – every worker, peasant, soldier, urban resident, intellectual, celebrity, government official, police officer, and all those who have branded us criminals – to put your hands on your hearts and examine your consciences. What crime have we committed? Have we created turmoil? Why are we holding class boycotts, marches, hunger strikes? For what cause are we sacrificing ourselves? . . .'

At eight the next morning, Bai Ling was broadcasting the hunger strike declaration that Mou Sen had rewritten. 'We endured cold and hunger in pursuit of the truth,' she continued, 'but the armed police beat us back. On bended knees we begged for democracy, but the government ignored us. As our student leaders press for a dialogue, they find their lives are now in danger . . . We don't want to die. We want to live. We're young, and we want to enjoy our youth and study hard. There is still much poverty in China, and we want to work hard to eradicate it. We don't seek death. But if one person's death can allow many people to live better lives, then . . .' By the time she reached the end of the speech, she was sobbing out the words.

I looked out of the window and saw a large crowd of students standing in the rain. They'd come out of the canteen to listen to the broadcast. Many of the girls were crying. After the speech, they drifted over to the noticeboard in the Triangle where the students were signing up to join the hunger strike.

I too had been moved by Mou Sen's words. I went to a street stall outside the campus and bought three bowls of wonton soup which I emptied into an enamel washbasin and carried back to Tian Yi's dorm. By the time I returned, Tian Yi was already awake.

'What time did you go to sleep last night?' I asked her. I felt guilty that I hadn't stayed up with her. She was still copying out Mou Sen's draft when I left. 'I've decided I'll go on the hunger strike with you,' I said, sitting on a stool beside her.

The girls in the top bunks climbed down and went to wash their faces. Other girls were already looking into the mirror, pencilling in their eyebrows.

'You keep changing your mind. How can I trust you? There are more than 10,000 students in Beijing University, but only fifty have signed up for the hunger strike so far. It's pathetic.' She took the bowl of soup that I ladled out for her and pushed her quilt back against the wall. I noticed the cracks in the dry skin of her heels.

'A crowd of people have gone to sign up. They've just broadcast the hunger strike declaration you worked on last night. It was very moving.' I went to sit by her feet. 'Wang Fei wants to join the hunger strike as well, but is reluctant to align himself with Han Dan, so he's in a quandary.'

'They broadcast it? That's great! Mmm, this soup is delicious. Lots of coriander.' She crossed her legs and blew the steam away from the soup, then cried out, 'Mimi, wake up! There's some wonton soup for you.' She looked up at her and laughed, 'It's the last breakfast we'll be having for some time!'

'Yes, you'd better fill up before you go to the Square,' I said. 'You won't be getting any food this evening.'

Tian Yi slurped the soup from her spoon, then smacked her lips and said, 'You should stick to sorting out logistics. Don't join the hunger strike.'

'The Organising Committee held a meeting just now to discuss how we're going to help you. I'll ask my student marshals to escort you all to the Square. The strikers will need a lot of backup support. Old Fu's gone to the university's clinic to ask for first-aid supplies.'

Tian Yi put down her spoon and picked up a small black flag on which she'd written the words HUNGER STRIKE. For a moment her eyes looked grey and lifeless. The night before, I'd begged her not to join the strike, but she accused me of being a coward. I wanted her to continue working for the *News Herald*. She was interested in literature and current affairs, and I thought that after she graduated she could go into journalism. The previous day's edition of the *News Herald* included some editorials she'd selected from the Anti-Rightist Campaign which shared the same dictatorial tone as the 26 April editorial. She'd spent two days in the library searching them out. Everyone congratulated her on the job she'd done.

'You've got a weak stomach,' I said. 'I'm afraid you might collapse after a couple of days without food.' I poured the remaining soup into a bowl and handed it to Mimi, saying, 'Careful, it's hot.' Mimi thanked me and produced a jar of fermented tofu. When she unscrewed the lid a pungent stench filled the room.

'Give me some,' Tian Yi said. The pitch of her voice always rose when she spoke to girls. 'You might be afraid, Dai Wei, but I'm not.'

'We'll surround you with a cordon of student marshals to prevent you getting crushed if the police attack.' I watched them pick up small cubes of the pink fermented tofu with their chopsticks.

Mimi left the room, sipping from her bowl of soup as she went and using her foot to close the door behind her.

'Do you promise you'll look after me?' Tian Yi said.

'I'll sit down next to you. If you collapse you can fall on my lap.' I gripped her shoulders and breathed the smell of her hair and the fresh coriander she'd eaten. She pushed me away and stared blankly at the remaining soup in her bowl. Her nose was pinker and shinier than the rest of her face.

It was still raining outside. The dorm blocks looked like rows of featureless wooden boxes.

She sat on the edge of her bunk. Her right hand was resting on a table, almost touching a pile of books. She rubbed a coriander leaf between the ink-stained fingers of her left hand.

'Don't worry,' I said. 'You can give up the hunger strike if it gets too much. It's only for show, after all.'

'What if I die?'

'Adults can go without food for several weeks,' I said. 'You'll be fine so long as you keep drinking lots of water.'

'But what if I die?' she repeated, and closed her mouth.

'You won't die. If you pass out, we'll rush you to hospital.'

I seldom saw Tian Yi smile. I once asked her why she was always so serious. She said happiness felt unnatural to her.

'I must go and brush my teeth,' she said, standing up.

I went to my dorm to wake Mou Sen and ask him to help me draft an announcement ordering my student marshal team to assemble. He scribbled a few lines then hurried back to Beijing Normal on his bike.

As soon as Chen Di had broadcast the announcement, the campus became as busy as it had been in the lead-up to the last march on 4 May. Everyone began to walk faster and speak with greater urgency.

I was repairing the megaphones when Tian Yi came in and said, 'I'm going to head off to the Square. I don't want to walk with the others. If I don't make it back, you can open this bag.'

I guessed that it contained her journals or photograph albums. I touched her hand. It felt cold with fear.

'What if your stomach plays up? You must take your medication with you.'

'I've got it. Look inside my satchel. I've packed *Selected Essays on Modern Western Fiction* and Kafka's *Metamorphosis*, stomach pills, my camera and a torch.'

On the ground next to her satchel was also a travel bag containing a plastic soapbox, a roll of toilet paper and a blue plastic visor stuffed between some shirts and trousers.

Next door, Chen Di was broadcasting the rules of the hunger strike: '. . . Three: You can take water and soft drinks into the Square, but no food or sweets, unless you're not planning to join the . . .'

'I wish you'd change your mind,' I said, staring into her eyes.

'I should set off now. Take care.' She was always telling me to take care. I pulled her close to me. She bowed her head and said. 'No,' but didn't push me away. Her body was stiff.

'Don't worry. The strike will probably only last a day or so – that should be enough to scare Premier Li Peng.' I stared at the darkness between her rows of neat white teeth and inhaled the scent of toothpaste that flowed out. Then I took her hand and led her upstairs. When I found an empty room, I pulled her inside, shut the door and put my arms around her.

'You haven't locked the door . . .' she mumbled as I leaned down to kiss her.

We made love on the floor. As I lay on top of her after it was over, I felt her stomach rumble.

'It's raining now, so don't cycle to the Square,' I said as we quickly stood up again. 'You're better off walking. We'll bring the quilts out for you later. We've got two tricycle carts to transport things to and from the Square.' My voice cracked, as it always did when I became excited about something.

She combed the fingers of one hand through my hair, while tightening her belt with her other.

'I'm going now. Put my quilt in a plastic bag before you bring it to the Square.'

'Of course, and I'll bring your mattress and pillow as well.' I shuffled my foot over the pool of sperm that had dripped onto the concrete floor.

On the way downstairs she whispered to me, 'Take care of yourself.'

'You take care too,' I said, stopping on the landing of the first floor and taking a drag from the cigarette I'd just lit.

I listened to her footsteps disappear down the stairs. The white plimsolls she was wearing made almost no noise when they touched the concrete floor.

I felt as though I'd just dropped a porcelain vase. I crushed out my cigarette and returned to my dorm.

Shu Tong asked me to check on the Beijing University hunger strikers who'd gone for a 'farewell meal' at Yanchun restaurant, and report back to him on any developments. Before I set off, I told Chen Di and Yu Jin to get the student marshals ready.

By now three hundred Beijing University students had signed up for the strike. The restaurant was full. One girl was holding a placard that said I LOVE TRUTH MORE THAN RICE! I LOVE DEMOCRACY MORE THAN BREAD! Another student had written across his cotton vest I CAN ENDURE HUNGER, BUT NOT A LIFE WITHOUT LIBERTY! A tall student had a banner draped around his neck that said HUNGER STRIKERS WON'T EAT DEEP-FRIED DEMOCRACY!

Bai Ling's hunger strike declaration was blaring from the restaurant's cassette player: 'In this most beautiful moment of our youth, we must put the beauty of life behind us. Mother China, look at your sons and daughters . . .'

Most of the students were wearing white, black or red bandannas. As I moved over to a table, Han Dan and some other students stood up and began reciting the hunger strikers' oath: 'To promote democracy in the motherland, we solemnly swear that we will go on hunger strike and will persevere until our goal is achieved . . .'

The meal was hosted by some of the younger professors from our university. A bottle of beer was placed in front of every student.

After the oath was sworn, the students took souvenir photographs of each other beneath a banner on which the creative writing students had written THE HEROES ARE DEPARTING. WE AWAIT THEIR RETURN!

I ran back to the campus and told Shu Tong that hundreds of students had joined the strike and that the Organising Committee was definitely in danger of being sidelined. Shu Tong proposed filling the posts that had been vacated by the resignations of Bai Ling, Han Dan, Yang Tao and Shao Jian. Liu Gang took a puff on his cigarette, paused, and declared that we should just carry on with the five remaining members.

I mustered the student marshals and led them through the rain as we escorted the three hundred Beijing University hunger strikers to Beijing Normal, where we were to meet the other university groups before setting off together for the Square. Our paper banners and posters were so thin that most of them soon disintegrated in the rain.

I spotted a photographic shop on the corner and ran inside to buy two rolls of film for Tian Yi. On rejoining the march, I received a message from Shu Tong: 'The government has just agreed to hold a dialogue. It will take place tomorrow at the United Front Department. The Dialogue Delegation has been invited to a preliminary meeting this afternoon to discuss procedures. They're sending a car to collect us. Bring the hunger strikers back to the campus immediately!'

It was a bad moment. The hunger strikers had taken their oaths and were halfway to the Square. I knew that Han Dan and Bai Ling would never listen to Shu Tong, let alone me, so I stuffed the note into my pocket and kept quiet. After a while, I decided to go over to Han Dan and tell him about it. He stopped walking and said, 'Really? If only the message had reached us before we set off. But I'm afraid it's too late to turn back now.'

'You mean you too had doubts about holding this strike?' I asked.

'We chose to go ahead as a last resort. It seemed the only way of forcing the government to listen to us.'

'You and Ke Xi both belong to the Dialogue Delegation. You should go to the meeting at the United Front Department to represent the hunger strikers.'

'Let's talk about it when we get to the Square.'

'I must go back to the campus and update Shu Tong.'

Only Liu Gang was in the dorm when I arrived. He'd changed into a suit in preparation for the meeting. I told him of Han Dan's reaction and he said, 'I wish he'd come back and explain exactly what the hunger strikers' demands are. The government is terrified. If the hunger strikers are still in the Square when Gorbachev arrives the day after tomorrow, the Party leadership will be deeply humiliated.'

Just as we were walking out, Hai Feng ran up and told Liu Gang that a female journalist from abroad wanted to interview him. Liu Gang said there wasn't time. A car was already waiting to take the Dialogue Delegation to the United Front Department.

'Well, she can interview *me*, then,' Hai Feng said curtly.

To my surprise, Liu Gang turned round and barked, 'Members of the Organising Committee aren't allowed to have private meetings with journalists. It's against the rules!'

'I have the right to express my views!' Hai Feng retorted.

'Do you know why Wei Jingsheng, the Democracy Wall activist, was arrested in 1979?' Liu Gang said, stopping in his tracks. 'The government accused him of having private meetings with foreigners and betraying the country. Every foreign journalist in Beijing is trailed by secret police. It's dangerous to meet them in private.' Liu Gang was five years older than Hai Feng, and tended to speak condescendingly to him.

'I'll be taking some quilts to the Square soon,' I interjected. 'When I get there, I'll discuss all this with Han Dan. Perhaps when Gorbachev arrives, we can retreat into the underpasses below the Square.'

'That's a good idea!' Liu Gang exclaimed. 'If Han Dan agrees to that, send someone to the United Front Department to let us know. It will give us room to manoeuvre during our discussions.' Then he ran off to find Shu Tong and Sister Gao.

'What a wonderful idea,' Hai Feng said sarcastically as we walked down the stairs together. 'On the eve of Gorbachev's visit, the Square will be packed with students and red banners, and the next morning it will be deserted. That will really make the government shake in their boots.'

Let your aspirations slip into silence. Sit in forgetfulness, like the philosopher Zhuangzi. Leave your body behind and vanish like mist into the air.

Dong Rong knows his way to our flat. When he arrives, my mother is in the middle of giving a singing lesson.

'Sit down, I won't be much longer,' my mother says breathlessly. 'You and Dai Wei were at university together, weren't you?'

'We were in the same dorm. We've met before, Auntie, you've forgotten. I've come up from Shenzhen on a business trip. I don't think that old informer Granny Pang saw me this time.'

My mother puts him in my room then shuts the door. Now that there's no draught blowing, the smell of the dirty rags my mother has hidden around the room grows more intense.

'Dai Wei, it's Dong Rong,' he says, sitting down beside me. 'It's August 1992. I forget which day. I've come to see how you are. All our old dorm mates have gone their separate ways. Everyone's lost touch. In Shenzhen I bumped into Ge You – you know, your friend from Southern University. He was arrested after the crackdown and sent to jail in Guangdong for a year. We both work in the Shekou Development Zone now . . .'

My pulse starts racing. I'd forgotten that Ge You was in the Square that night.

Trying to fill the silence, Dong Rong continues, 'You've changed so much. You look like an Egyptian mummy. Can you hear what I'm saying?'

Of course I can, you fool. When people talk to me, they speak as though they're leaving a message on an answerphone. After a couple of sentences, their voices become stilted as they slowly realise they're talking to themselves.

My mother is playing a tape of a performance she gave of the drinking song from *La Traviata*. Her student is singing along with it. '*Let us drink from the goblets of joy, adorned with beauty* . . .'

'I hope you can hear me . . . Compared to some of our friends, I got off quite lightly. As you know, I've always tried to stay out of politics, but I had to come and see you, and bring you good wishes from all your old classmates who are now living in Shenzhen. Hey, did you hear about those other two friends of yours from Southern University, Wu Bin and Sun Chunlin? Well, after the crackdown, Wu Bin came down to Shenzhen and smuggled himself across to Hong Kong with Sun Chunlin. Sun Chunlin's uncle lost his job as head of Guangzhou's Department of Communication over it.'

Why would Sun Chunlin give up his successful business career to help out Wu Bin? They were never that close. I want to know more, but unfortunately let out a fart which drives Dong Rong out to the covered balcony. The single bed there occupies all the space, so there's nowhere for him to stand.

'No one apart from your mother would have the patience to look after you. She should hire a maid. I've left a thousand yuan on the table to help her with the cost. I'm leaving now. It stinks in here.'

I know you're very pernickety. You always insisted on wearing a clean shirt every day. But, damn it, can't you just stay a bit longer and talk to me?

If he is going, I hope he shuts the door behind him, because I can't stand it when my mother hits the high C at the end of the drinking song. The note pierces through my skin like a sharp knife.

Dong Rong didn't participate in the student movement much during the early days. The first time I really noticed him take an active role was when the hunger strikers entered the Square, and I spotted him standing among their ranks. If he hadn't come to see me today, he would have probably slipped from my memory entirely.

You imagine yourself standing by the window, your stomach pressed against the sill. You grasp the handle, push it down then swing the window open.

'The Dialogue Delegation is betraying the hunger strikers!' Wang Fei was shouting through his megaphone from the steps of the Monument to the People's Heroes. Dong Rong was beside him, holding up the Science Department's banner. 'They've dared to propose that we withdraw from the Square. Go and protest outside the United Front Department!' Wang Fei had been appointed the *News Herald*'s Tiananmen Square liaison officer by Shu Tong, but he considered this position too lowly, and was planning to set up a Tiananmen Square propaganda office instead.

'They're not betraying anyone,' said Sister Gao, rising to her feet. 'The dialogue is still in progress, and anyway, there are representatives of the hunger strikers in the meeting as well.' She'd just returned from the United Front Department with Shao Jian and Cao Ming to report on the progress of the meeting. They'd bought some crates of mineral water on their way back to hand out to the hunger strikers.

I sat on the steps of the Monument and looked out over the vast heaving crowd in the Square. Each university had its own protected circle of hunger strikers surrounded by flags and banners. The late morning sun turned the pale quilts and shirts a sepia yellow, giving the Square the appearance of a film set.

'The hunger strikers should be talking directly to the government,' Old Fu said, walking over to us. 'The Dialogue Delegation has no right to speak on their behalf.'

'You were against the hunger strike yesterday, Old Fu, and today you're supporting it,' Sister Gao said angrily. 'What happened?'

Old Fu fell silent for a moment and then replied, 'The hunger strikers are the true voice of the student movement now. You went back to the campus last night, but I stayed here in the Square, and I've seen the support they're getting. The situation has evolved very rapidly out here.' He was carrying a megaphone, an electric cable and a huge black poster with the words HUNGER STRIKE emblazoned across it in yellow paint. He was hoping to set up a broadcast station in the Square.

Shao Jian had just joined the hunger strike. He strolled over in his white bandanna and asked, 'Why is the Square in such chaos? Last night, everyone was sitting in neat rows.'

'The hunger strikers need to lie down,' I explained. 'This isn't a sit-in, it's an occupation. We're going to camp out here until the government agrees to our demands.'

'We must find some more blankets and quilts,' Sister Gao mumbled distractedly. 'I doubt if any of them slept very well.'

I looked over to the psychology students' camp, but couldn't spot Tian Yi. I'd checked up on her an hour before. She'd told me that, although she often skipped meals when she was feeling low, now that she was forbidden to eat, her hunger was unbearable. She said it felt as if there were millions of ants scratching at the walls of her stomach.

'It's getting very hot now,' I said. 'We must shelter the hunger strikers from the sun. I distributed the ten umbrellas we were given this morning, but we'll need many more. And we've run out of water too. Zhuzi and his marshals only managed to bring this one barrel of water. The students finished it in five minutes.' I tapped the sides of the empty barrel.

Pu Wenhua, a cocky young hunger striker from the Agricultural College, came over and said, 'The Dialogue Delegation has dared propose to the government that we withdraw from the Square. What right do they have to talk on behalf of the hunger strikers?' He was only seventeen, apparently, but looked even younger.

'The dialogue has been under way for two hours now, and the authorities still haven't broadcast it to us live, as they promised they would,' Han Dan said to Sister Gao, having just been interviewed by some foreign journalists. He sat down, removed his sunglasses and wiped the sweat from his face. 'Who else from the hunger strike is at the meeting?'

'Ke Xi,' said Sister Gao. 'He walked into the conference room holding the long banner that says, "I'm hungry Mum, but I can't eat."'

'Sister Gao, you're the general secretary of the Beijing Students' Federation, and you're opposed to the hunger strike, so it's probably best if you stay out of this,' said Bai Ling, crossly waving her limp hands.

'I *was* against the hunger strike, but it's started now, so there's no point opposing it. Last night, the Federation declared its support. I've come here to help you, not to control or criticise you. As it happens, many of the Federation's members have joined the strike too, so it's my duty to be here.'

Bai Ling was defiant. 'The Federation's role is to liaise between the Beijing universities, so you should return to the campus and get on with your job,' she said, no longer prepared to be bossed about by her older dorm mate. 'The hunger strikers are in charge of the Square now. We don't want to be dictated to by the Federation.'

'You and Han Dan haven't eaten for twenty-four hours, Bai Ling,' Old Fu said. 'You're not strong enough to look after the running of the Square. Why not let our Organising Committee or the Federation take over some of the administration?'

'We don't need their help,' Bai Ling said stubbornly. 'We can run things ourselves perfectly well.' When she'd arrived in the Square the day before, she'd founded the Hunger Strike Group and appointed herself leader.

Under the bright overhead sun, the hundreds of hunger strikers lying curled up on the Square looked like shrimps laid out to dry. The student marshals stood in cordons around them, keeping curious onlookers away. A hunger striker held up a will he'd written on a sheet of brown paper, and a crowd quickly gathered round to photograph him.

Yu Jin was wearing a checked shirt, with the sleeves rolled up as usual. He hadn't joined the strike, but had written the words FIGHTING FOR THE PEOPLE! on his baseball cap. I'd appointed him vice head of Beijing University's student marshal team. He enjoyed running about and making himself useful. A new batch of volunteer student marshals, sent from our campus by Shu Tong, had arrived in the Square, allowing my team a chance to snatch some rest. Even Big Chan, Little Chan and Zhang Jie had turned up to help collect donations.

'We'll only leave the Square if the government broadcasts the dialogue to us live, as they promised,' shouted a student from Nanjing called Lin Lu. He'd arrived in Beijing a few days before. Bai Ling had been impressed by speeches he'd made in the Triangle, and had asked him to help oversee the strike. He'd managed to persuade many students from the provinces to sign up. He seemed very competent.

'I'll go back to the United Front Department and check how the dialogue is progressing,' said Sister Gao. 'If the officials don't agree to start the live broadcast immediately, I'll tell the students to leave the meeting.'

'I don't trust you,' Bai Ling said. 'Whose side are you really on?'

'I'm not on anyone's side. I'm only trying to help. I came here to find out what you want, so that I can pass it on to the Dialogue Delegation.'

'We'll get some members of the Hunger Strike Group to accompany you,' Old Fu said. 'I'll set up a public address system. Dai Wei, go and find some hunger strikers to accompany Sister Gao.'

'We really must sort out the water problem,' I said. 'The authorities have cut off our supply. I've sent some marshals to buy more bottles of mineral water. But we can't stay in the Square much longer, Old Fu.' I was feeling fed up, but I didn't want Tian Yi to accuse me of not doing my job properly.

'The Square has divided into little kingdoms, each with its own student marshal team, each claiming to be the true representatives of the students,' Cao Ming said. 'The government won't need to break us up, because we're doing the job for them.'

I went to give Tian Yi her coat. I was worried about her. Even when she was eating properly, she suffered from hypoglycaemia and would often break out in cold sweats.

Tian Yi and Mimi were leaning against one another. Mimi was fiddling with a strand of Tian Yi's hair. Her red-checked skirt cast a rosy light into the air around her.

I asked Tian Yi how she was feeling. She said her head was spinning, and she felt she was losing control.

'You might start hallucinating soon,' I said. 'The nurses told me that you shouldn't be lying so close to each other. If one of you gets an infection, everyone will come down with it.'

'We'll be fine. So many local residents have come to the Square to cheer us on. It's worth going hungry for a few days just to see all this support.'

'Keep drinking lots of water. If you're not careful your kidneys could pack up because of your low blood sugar.' Although it was a swelteringly hot day, her hands were icy.

'Stop trying to frighten her into giving up,' Mimi said, wrinkling her brow. 'We're prepared to shed blood and sweat for this cause. With so much pressure from the public, the government will be forced to agree to our demands.'

'*Red dirt smeared across his yellow face, white fear in his black eyes. The west wind blows into the east, singing its sad refrain . . .*' A Taiwanese pop song droned from a cassette player. The batteries were running flat.

A hunger striker nearby suddenly passed out. Four marshals ran over, grabbed her arms and pulled her through the crowd. Voices shouted: 'Get out of their way! Let them through! Don't drag her like that. Lift her legs up!'

'Will someone hold the Psychology Department flag up for me?' Mimi asked. 'I want to take a nap.' She appeared to be wearing lipstick.

I took the flag from her and propped it up between two bags, but it wouldn't stay upright. Cao Ming shouted out, telling me to find Zhang Jie and ask him to accompany Sister Gao to the United Front Department.

You travel through the gall bladder and enter the hepatic artery. Drifting upstream, you catch sight of the heart, suspended in the darkness like a distant planet.

After queuing for two hours at the post office, I sent a telegram to my brother telling him not to come to Beijing or join the hunger strike. Then I went back to the Square.

During my absence, the dialogue with the government had collapsed. Mou Sen had been at the meeting and told me that Sister Gao had stormed in and shouted, 'Start the live broadcast right now, or stop the dialogue!' just as the Hunger Strike Group had asked. The meeting broke up at once. The Dialogue Delegation was furious and said that history would not forgive her. Hoping to regain their trust, she collected a dozen middle-aged intellectuals and brought them back to the Square with the aim of persuading the students to withdraw. By the time Mou Sen reached the Square, the intellectuals had been driven away by the enraged hunger strikers.

It was almost midnight. In the distance, I could hear Wang Fei shouting through his megaphone: 'We've reached a crucial stage. Do we go forward now, or do we retreat? . . . Citizens of Beijing, please stay in the Square with us and continue to give us your support! . . . The twelve intellectuals who spoke to us just now recommended that we agree to leave the Square on two conditions. We're grateful for their advice, but it's no use to us. According to them, our first condition should be that their "Urgent Appeal" is published by *Guangming Daily*. I've read that appeal. It's about freedom of the press, which might be their priority, but it's not ours! Their second condition was that Premier Li Peng and General Secretary Zhao Ziyang should visit the Square. Well, of course we'd welcome that. But we won't insist on it. We've seen enough of those two guys on our television screens!'

The crowd cheered and yelled, 'Yes! We will stay here until we get what we want!'

'We will not be moved!' Wang Fei shouted, and the crowd shouted out after him: 'We will not be moved! We will not be moved!'

Mou Sen disappeared into the throng. I tried to push my way over to the Beijing University camp, but couldn't find a path, so I headed towards the Monument. I wanted to tell Wang Fei that the hunger strikers needed to sleep, and that he should stop making such a racket.

'The government has asked us to vacate the Square in time for tomorrow's grand welcoming ceremony for Gorbachev,' Wang Fei continued. 'Well, we're not moving. They can hold the ceremony somewhere else, if they want to . . . We will use the power of the people to teach a lesson to the autocratic clique that's ruling our nation. We don't want to shed our blood, but if we do, we'll be able to write with it the most important page in China's history!' The crowd roared in support.

At last, I managed to make my way to Wang Fei's side. He was flanked by Chen Di and Xiao Li, who were both wearing hunger strike bandannas. Nuwa was sitting nearby, her black hair gleaming in the darkness. When I saw her there, I suddenly didn't feel like telling Wang Fei to shut up.

Chen Di offered me a cigarette. I took it, reminding him not to smoke while he was on hunger strike, then went back to look for Tian Yi.

Exhausted by hunger, she was fast asleep on the ground with a quilt draped over her. I touched her forehead, and was relieved to find she hadn't yet broken into a cold sweat.

Mimi was gazing blankly into the sky. The other hunger strikers were asleep. Not wanting to disturb them, I crept away quietly and returned to the Monument.

I found Mou Sen there. He was sitting with Sister Gao and Fan Yuan, a student from the Politics and Law University. Though not especially capable, Fan Yuan was very keen and had managed to insinuate himself into several powerful positions. He'd been chairman of the Beijing Students' Federation for a few days and was also a member of the Dialogue Delegation.

'Can't you go and tell Wang Fei to shut up, Dai Wei?' Sister Gao said to me. 'You're his friend, and the head of the student marshal team. It's the middle of the night. Everyone wants to get some sleep.'

'Nuwa's with him. I don't want to butt in.'

Mao Da came over to talk to Mou Sen. 'It's a pity you weren't here when the twelve intellectuals came. The reporter Dai Jing said that if we hadn't occupied the Square, the journalists would never have dared ask for freedom of the press, but then a second later, she begged us to withdraw. Old Fu was worried her speech might harm student morale, so he quickly played Bai Ling's hunger strike declaration over the PA, the one that brings tears to everyone's eyes. When the twelve intellectuals heard it, they knew they had no chance of persuading us to leave.'

Mao Da had arrived in the Square in the afternoon after Liu Gang had asked him to help with the security work.

'That was very unwise of Old Fu,' Mou Sen said. He, like me, was sorry to have missed the intellectuals' visit. Those writers and scholars were his heroes.

'You Beijing University students are in a mess,' Fan Yuan said. 'Bai Ling stopped the Dialogue Delegation from talking to the government, Old Fu stopped the intellectuals from talking to the students, and you, Sister Gao, keep confusing everything by jumping from one camp to another. How will this movement ever get anywhere?'

'I keep running back and forth, trying to help resolve conflicts, but all I get is abuse,' Sister Gao moaned. 'Now that it's clear the government aren't going to launch a crackdown, everyone's scrambling for power. It really is a case of "leaders emerging in times of chaos".'

Knowing that there was nothing more for me to do, I picked up a quilt, crossed Changan Avenue, and crept up onto one of the viewing stands flanking Tiananmen Gate. It was where state dignitaries sat to watch parades. Most students wouldn't have dreamed of going there. But I knew it would be quiet, and I'd be the first to know of police movements during the night, as the police station was in the courtyard behind.

You listen to the voices floating around you, as enviously as a tree trunk staring at falling leaves.

I woke up on the viewing stand with the sun streaming down on my face, and quickly climbed down to the Square. Gorbachev was due to arrive in Beijing in two hours.

'Did you see Yanyan last night?' Mou Sen asked me, then took a deep drag from his cigarette.

'No. Why? Have you had another row?' He'd mentioned they'd been going through a bad patch recently.

'No, no.'

There was a sudden burst of applause. I heard Pu Wenhua, the boy from the Agricultural College, shouting to the crowds, 'Let's show them! We'll stay here until the bitter end, until victory is ours!' Over by the hunger strike camps, I saw Beijing residents put on white bandannas and wave red banners as they posed for souvenir photographs in front of the fasting students.

'You shouldn't smoke when you're on hunger strike,' I told Mou Sen. 'The sugar and oxygen levels in your brain will be dangerously low now.'

'Look, Bai Ling's set up a Tiananmen Square Hunger Strike Headquarters on the lower terrace,' he said, his cigarette dangling from the corner of his mouth.

'When did she do that?' I asked. 'It wasn't there when I went to sleep three hours ago.'

'At five this morning. After a quick talk with that Nanjing student Lin Lu, she went to the PA system Old Fu set up and announced that the Hunger Strike Group is now the Hunger Strike Headquarters, and that she is commander-in-chief, with Lin Lu as vice commander.'

'What about Han Dan and Ke Xi?'

'She said that every member of the Headquarters must pledge to set fire to themselves if the army comes to clear the Square,' Mou Sen said, ignoring my question. 'It's too much!'

'That's barbaric!' I said. 'Everyone's coming up with more and more radical strategies in an effort to win the leadership of the Square. Who thought of the self-immolation idea? It couldn't have been Bai Ling.'

'It was Lin Lu's idea. He asked me to head their propaganda office. He knows I'm going out with a journalist, so he thought I could use her media contacts.'

'Does anyone know much about this Lin Lu guy?' I said, staring at the beams of morning light. Crowds of supporters were continuing to flood into the Square.

'He claims to be an undergraduate at Nanjing University, but he hasn't got a student card,' Mou Sen said.

'So many students have travelled up from the provinces, and once they get here they don't want to leave. The Square is packed now. I sent my brother a telegram last night telling him to stay in Sichuan.'

'Ke Xi asked the students to move to the east side of the Square just now, so that Gorbachev can at least lay flowers on the Monument when he arrives,' Mou Sen continued. 'He climbed onto the lamp post over there and shouted through his megaphone: "This is Ke Xi speaking. For the sake of our nation, I beg you to move to the east side. If you don't, it will be an insult to democracy." When Bai Ling heard his request, she burst into tears and threatened to set fire to herself. Then Lin Lu shouted he'd burn himself first.'

I looked back down to the hunger strike camps. Although a few of the strikers had passed out the previous night and had been rushed to hospital, hundreds more students had joined the fast. There now appeared to be about three thousand of them lying on the ground. Each camp was circled by protective rings of student marshals, who were themselves surrounded by crowds of onlookers. There were tens of thousands of people in the Square but no one was being crushed. Student volunteers walked among the strikers, checking for any signs of distress. Everything seemed to be in order.

'Sister Gao shouldn't have asked those intellectuals to talk to Bai Ling last night,' Mou Sen said. 'Bai Ling felt she was being patronised, which made her even more determined to continue the occupation.'

'Nuwa asked me about Yanyan yesterday,' I said. 'She knows she's your girlfriend.'

Mou Sen looked up. 'Why would she be interested in me?'

'Don't start getting any ideas! She belongs to Wang Fei.'

'You were the one who brought it up,' he said, looking down again. 'I've only met her a couple of times. We didn't speak much. But funnily enough, Yanyan got suspicious and asked me what my relationship with her was.'

'The Hunger Strike Group has really messed things up,' I said, then corrected myself. 'The Hunger Strike Headquarters, I mean. How long are you going to carry on with the fast?' I spotted Old Fu sitting on a cardboard box at the base of the Monument, smoking a cigarette. Sister Gao was sitting next to him, sipping from a bottle of saline water.

'Thirty hunger strikers from Southern University arrived last night,' Mou Sen said, crushing out his cigarette at last. 'They seem much more politicised than we were as undergraduates. Tang Guoxian brought them up here with a large group of students from Guangdong Province. Sun Chunlin's here too, on a business trip. He's staying in a luxury hotel. The bastard's made a fortune for himself in Shenzhen.'

'That's strange. Tang Guoxian was never interested in politics when we were at Southern University. Come on, let's go and speak to Liu Gang.' I pulled Mou Sen up and led him to the base of the Monument.

Liu Gang and Shu Tong were talking to Old Fu. They'd borrowed a van and brought three barrels of water to the Square, and were about to take away some sacks of rubbish.

'Our democracy movement has spread throughout the country,' Wang Fei said to us. 'It's like the fable of the Eight Immortals crossing the sea, joining together to reach a common goal.' He squatted down and stubbed out his cigarette on a polystyrene food box, creating a plume of acrid smoke. 'In times of turmoil, everyone wants to show what they're capable of.'

'Don't try and use the hunger strike to stir up trouble, Wang Fei, that would be too much,' Mou Sen said. 'You look exhausted, Old Fu. Why don't you go back to the campus and get some rest?'

Old Fu's eyes were red. He'd been up all night chain-smoking, unable to get to sleep. 'Gorbachev won't be coming here,' he said, gazing at the west side of the Square that was now almost empty. 'I'm sure the government has cancelled the welcoming ceremony.'

All the students and red banners had now shifted to the east side of the Square. A few students who'd refused to move sat in isolated groups between the Great Hall of the People and the Monument to the People's Heroes.

'Wang Fei, I sent you here to write articles for the *News Herald*, but now you're acting like some kind of leader,' Shu Tong said angrily. 'Look, it's nine thirty already. Do you really think the government would dream of holding a welcoming ceremony for a foreign statesman in front of a crowd of bedraggled hunger strikers? You lot thought you could hold the government to ransom, but they don't need to listen to you. They can hold the ceremony somewhere else if they want. There's no point in the students staying here any longer.'

'If we withdraw from the Square now, it will be an admission of failure,' Wang Fei said. He was very worked up. He kept raising his megaphone and shouting random slogans through it.

'Why don't you go to the Headquarters and sign up to burn yourself to death, then?' Sister Gao said.

'The Headquarters have just held their first meeting and decided to scrap that idea,' said Liu Gang. 'Their latest plan is to get the hunger strikers to lie down on Changan Avenue after the intellectuals' march this afternoon.' He seemed to have lost the enthusiasm he'd shown during the early days of the movement.

'Then they'll start calling for class boycotts, teachers' strikes, shop-keepers strikes, and before long, we'll have a revolution on our hands,' Mou Sen said, running his fingers through his hair.

'The hunger strike has ruined everything,' Shu Tong groaned.

'The reformist wing of the government wants our movement to progress peacefully,' Sister Gao said to Mou Sen. 'The hardliners want it to end in violence, so they can oust Zhao Ziyang from power. By continuing this hunger strike, we're playing into their hands.'

'Who's to say Zhao Ziyang and his lot are any better than the hard-liners?' Chen Di said. 'I've heard rumours that Zhao Ziyang's son has been using his power to buy colour televisions at low state prices then sell them for huge profits on the black market.' He'd written the words HUNGER STRIKE across his vest in black felt-tip pen.

'There's no hope of a peaceful settlement now,' Shu Tong said. 'The dialogue was going well, Old Fu. Why did you have to insist that it be broadcast live?'

'The hunger strikers didn't trust the Dialogue Delegation,' Old Fu said. 'They wanted to hear for themselves what was being said during the meeting.'

'Look, the west side of the Square is completely empty now!' Wang Fei said. 'The Dialogue Delegation made the same mistake as Ke Xi: they retreated first, then set out their demands, instead of only retreating once their demands were met.' The megaphone in his hand screeched as he fiddled with the switch.

'The hunger strike will test the government's resolve,' Mou Sen said abruptly. 'We'll see if they dare play with the lives of three thousand students. They'll have to respond to us by tonight. The fasters won't be able to continue much longer. Many of them are already in a critical state.'

Nearby, we could hear Nuwa's voice coming over the PA system: 'Some hunger strikers who passed out are being treated in the emergency care tent. They will only drink plain water. The nurses have tried to give them glucose solution, but as soon as they taste it, they spit it out and refuse to drink any more . . .' When she finished reading the statement, she repeated it in English. Her voice sounded beautiful. Mou Sen's gaze shifted to the loudspeaker she was standing behind.

'I heard that when the intellectuals came here last night, you grabbed the microphone from them, then shouted for everyone to leave the Square,' Mou Sen said angrily to Wang Fei. 'What were you thinking of, trying to steal the limelight like that?'

'We Beijing University students started this movement,' Wang Fei growled. 'We formulated all the demands. If you think you're so clever, go and start your own movement and see how far you get.' Wang Fei was convinced that he was the prime instigator of the student movement.

'We can't expect a corrupt government like ours to agree to our demands,' said Sister Gao. 'But if the leaders were to just come out and meet with us, we'd withdraw from the Square at once.'

'We're trapped between irrational politicians and irrational students,' Shu Tong said.

'Everyone's focused on the hunger strike now,' Old Fu said. 'We have no choice but to go along with it and lend it our full support.' He took a couple of liver tablets from his pocket and swallowed them without water.

'This is supposed to be a democracy movement, not a revolution,' said Shu Tong. 'If you take things too far, you'll be crushed in the end.'

'Our problem now is that no one person or group is capable of taking control of the Square,' Old Fu said.

Sister Gao wiped the sweat from her face with a paper handkerchief, then fanned her neck with her straw hat. 'Ke Xi has fainted again and been rushed to hospital,' she said. 'Even if he comes back, he won't stand much chance of regaining power. Han Dan has been sidelined. Your only option now is to negotiate with Bai Ling and Lin Lu.'

Old Fu shrugged. 'I'm only the Hunger Strike Headquarters' logistics officer, so don't look at me. You go and negotiate with them.' He leaned down and picked up a briefcase. 'I want to set up a proper broadcast station, Dai Wei,' he said, turning to me. 'The PA system is too primitive. Come and help me buy some equipment. This briefcase is full of cash. We put out four donation boxes on the Square and they were all filled within a few hours.'

I didn't feel like going shopping for electrical equipment, but I was desperate to find something to eat, so I picked up my bag and followed Old Fu out of the Square.

You are the earth dried by the hot sun, a tree abandoned by its soil.

There is a river between the mountains, but no grass or trees. The cliffs are too steep to climb. A wild animal that looks like a fox but has human hair lives in the valley. It has both male and female genitals, and can reproduce by itself. If you eat its meat, you will be cured of jealousy . . . This passage is probably from the chapter entitled 'Great Wilderness: West'. I'd hoped to explore those lands one day, but instead I've been forced to wander through the interior landscape of my blood vessels and organs.

My mother must have removed the empty bottle from my drip stand. I can hear her stick the tube into a new bottle of glucose solution. A few seconds later, a stream of antibiotics and vitamins flows through my veins and is absorbed into the hepatic lobules. The colon bacteria left on the needle by my mother's dirty hands also enters my bloodstream. The red blood cells it kills upon impact are pushed deeper into the hepatic sinus . . .

By sunset, Old Fu and I, with some help from Big Chan and Little Chan, had set up a broadcast station on the north side of the Monument. We installed the new batteries, amplifiers and microphones, and attached eight loudspeakers to the Monument's granite obelisk. When we broadcast the tape of the Internationale, everyone turned towards us, and the Monument became the focal point of the Square. Hai Feng brought over some plastic sheeting and constructed a shelter to protect our equipment from the rain.

Ke Xi hobbled over to us, a drip still attached to his arm, and said, 'I've appointed myself temporary commander-in-chief of the Hunger Strike Headquarters. Lin Lu and Bai Ling weren't elected to their posts. They have no legitimate authority.'

'You're all starving to death,' Old Fu whispered, trying not to disturb the discussion Mao Da was chairing. 'Where do you find the energy to engage in these power struggles?'

'The Headquarters is in charge of the movement now,' Ke Xi said.

'The Organising Committee and the Beijing Students' Federation must play subsidiary roles.' His pale face was covered in sweat. Two nurses were standing behind him, holding his bottle of IV fluid.

I wasn't in a mood to listen to them argue, so I went to test the new equipment.

A large crowd gathered round our new broadcast station and handed us ice lollies, bread rolls, telegrams, letters of support and pamphlets. In less than an hour, I received ten donations of cash. Some people pressed the notes into my hands then walked away without saying a word.

We taped up an empty cardboard box to make a new donation box. As soon as we put it down on our table, a middle-aged man who'd travelled up from the provinces took 10,000 yuan from his bag and said he'd give it to us if we let him broadcast a few words to the students.

We were dumbstruck. None of us had seen 10,000 yuan in cash before. We immediately put a microphone in his hands, then, since there were no chairs around, placed a sheet of paper over a large brick and invited him to sit down.

He spoke for almost five minutes, with tears streaming down his face, but his Fujian accent was too strong for most people to understand. In the end Old Fu whispered to me, 'We'd better cut him off. Everyone's wondering what's going on.'

I unplugged the microphone and politely asked him to leave.

A middle-school student from Guangdong Province walked up saying he'd come to Beijing to deliver seventy yuan his classmates had raised for us, but had lost his bag, and all the money, on the train. I gave him a hundred yuan and told him to catch the next train home.

Within the space of three hours, we were given a hundred telegrams from around the country. Nuwa, Mao Da and Chen Di almost lost their voices as they took turns to read them out to the Square.

I handed Nuwa a carton of orange juice. She wiped the sweat from her face and sucked the straw until it made a whistling noise.

'How do you think this will all end?' I said. 'Are you prepared for what might happen?' I'd wanted to ask her how things were going between her and Wang Fei, but felt that we weren't close enough.

The previous week, Tian Yi and I had gone out for a meal with her and Wang Fei at Kentucky Fried Chicken. She'd put her arm around Wang Fei during the meal, carried away perhaps by the restaurant's modern and relaxed atmosphere, but over the past few days, I'd detected a growing coldness between them.

She answered cheerfully, 'I don't think the government can ignore us for much longer. If we carry on with the hunger strike, and continue to be filmed by the foreign television crews, they'll start to worry about their image abroad. And besides, they have no real reason not to agree to our demands.'

Although Nuwa was sitting in a dark corner, I could see the dip between her breasts and the thin gold chain around her neck. She looked like one of the girls you see on foreign wall calendars. I suspected that this was why Tian Yi was always so frosty towards her.

'What do your family think of you getting involved in the movement?' I asked. 'Do they know what you're up to?'

Nuwa always claimed she was from Hangzhou City, but Tian Yi said this wasn't true, and that her family lived in a small town in Fuyang County, eighty kilometres away.

She laughed and said, '"The mountains are high and the emperor is far away," as the saying goes. I can do what I like. I don't care what they think.' Her voice was as smooth as her skin. Apparently she had a younger sister who was going to start university in the autumn.

'Listen to this,' Mao Da said, walking over to me. '"Deng Xiaoping's son, Pufang, is also guilty of official profiteering. His company, Kanghua, is one of the four most corrupt businesses in China." I don't think we should read out this pamphlet.' Mao Da had told me that the authorities had asked him to continue spying on the students, but that he'd refused to cooperate.

'I don't decide what material is broadcast,' I said, trying to get rid of him. 'I just deal with the equipment.' Then I turned back to Nuwa and said, 'You're very optimistic. I'm worried the government will refuse to compromise, and we'll have backed ourselves into a corner.'

'Don't be so gloomy,' she said. 'It will bring us bad luck.'

Then Xiao Li ran over and said, 'Hurry up, Dai Wei! Thousands of students are trying to storm the Great Hall, and a crowd of hunger strikers have gone to stand in their way. Come and help sort it out!'

It took me all evening to persuade the students to move away from the Great Hall, but when I got back to the broadcast station it was still swarming with people. Only at midnight did the crowds begin to thin a little.

The diesel generator donated by local factory workers was clattering away noisily. Sun Chunlin, who'd been chatting with me for an hour or so, handed me a five-hundred-yuan donation, then went back to his luxury hotel room.

I told Xiao Li to make sure that the broadcast station was well guarded. Pu Wenhua had come to the station hoping to broadcast an announcement that he'd taken over the Hunger Strike Headquarters and had appointed himself commander-in-chief, demoting Bai Ling to the post of propaganda officer, but Old Fu managed to push him away. I asked a volunteer to stay at the station to deal with any queries from the public, then went to find Tian Yi. She hadn't eaten for three whole days.

She looked older. There were wrinkles etched on her dry face, and her hair was like straw. I hated to see her in such a state.

'Listen, they're broadcasting the tape of Bai Ling reading the hunger strike declaration,' I said, pointing to the loudspeakers attached to the Monument.

'Did you record it?' Tian Yi said, leaning her head softly against my shoulder.

'No, Old Fu did.' I stared at the two empty bottles of glucose solution beside her feet, and decided not to tell her about all the wrangling that was going on at the Hunger Strike Headquarters.

'If we'd known the government had decided to hold the welcoming ceremony for Gorbachev at the airport, we wouldn't have had to move over to the east side of the Square. I feel nauseous. Even if I did eat anything now, I wouldn't be able to keep it down.'

I wanted to tell her that the students' dialogue with the government at the United Front Department the day before had ended in failure and that, according to Liu Gang, General Secretary Zhao Ziyang was about to suffer the same fate as Hu Yaobang, and that all that remained for us to do now was to wait for the authorities to launch a crackdown.

'I've sworn an oath to persevere until the end. I won't break my fast, even if the government flings me in jail.' Tian Yi sounded like a heroine from the Communist Revolution. I was exhausted, and didn't feel like talking. I took a swig of water and listened to Bai Ling's voice: 'As we hover between life and death, we want to look up at the Chinese people and see if we've stirred them out of their apathy . . .'

'The sound's not bad, is it? We've attached eight loudspeakers to the Monument and rented a high-power amplifier.'

'Who's looking after the broadcast station?' Tian Yi wasn't interested in electrical equipment. The only machines she liked were cameras.

'Shu Tong's still running the broadcast station back at the campus, and Old Fu and I are in charge of the one here. Mou Sen is chief editor tonight, but he's still on hunger strike, so he's having to chain-smoke to keep himself awake. Wang Fei's helping out too, and Zheng He from the Creative Writing Programme. Nuwa is the announcer. Chen Di and Xiao Li have been working flat out, even though they're still fasting. The broadcast station is the heart of the Square now.'

'Men are always fighting for power,' she said feebly. 'The provincial students don't like taking orders from the Beijing University crowd. They forced a revote and now a female student from Beijing Normal has been appointed co-commander of the Hunger Strike Headquarters along with Bai Ling.'

'So the two new commanders-in-chief are both women. How can you say that only men are obsessed with power?' I tried to speak softly, so as not to wake the hunger strikers who were asleep around us. Although Tian Yi was weak with hunger, she still knew everything that was going on in the Square.

She stared blankly into the distance. The bandanna she was wearing beneath her baseball cap was still drenched in the sweat that had poured from her head during the day.

'This blanket is quite warm, isn't it?' I said, after a long silence. 'I bought it in Guangzhou. It's made out of space fabric. It's very light.'

'A private businessman donated a truckload of blankets,' she said. 'They have horrible patterns on them.'

I wanted to tell her that the government couldn't care less that the students were starving themselves to death, but I didn't want to upset her.

'It gets so cold here at night,' she said. 'If there weren't any other students around, I'd sneak back to the campus to sleep.'

'Students aren't the only people here. There are lots of spies too. It's easy for them to slip through our cordons. We can't keep a check on everyone. Look at those two.' I pointed to a couple of men who were wandering about in front of us.

'They're not spies, they're hunger strikers. They've just got up to go to the toilet.' There was an empty barrel of water next to Tian Yi. I leaned against it and closed my eyes. My efforts to stop the mob of students and Beijing residents from storming the Great Hall had exhausted me. I felt my head was about to crack open.

'The university authorities have agreed to lend us two hundred camp beds,' I said. 'Hai Feng talked them into it. When they arrive, we'll give them to the girls first. And look at all those boxes of food stacked outside the broadcast station! A local shopkeeper donated them to us this afternoon.'

'Don't talk to me about food,' she said, looking away.

'Gorbachev was on television just now,' I said, changing the subject. 'He said that Zhao Ziyang told him that although Deng Xiaoping only holds a military post in the Party, he still makes all the key decisions in China. That information is supposed to be a state secret, even though it's common knowledge. Zhao Ziyang may be General Secretary, but he has no real power.'

'I just wish I could go and have a nice shower with my bar of foreign soap,' Tian Yi said, closing her eyes. She rested her cold face on my leg. Under the blanket, her body felt hot. She'd been sucking a throat lozenge. When she spoke, I could smell the mint on her breath. It took me back to the time in Yunnan when we lay down on the mountain together.

'The university's given me an authorisation letter, so I can apply for a passport now, if I want to,' I said. 'They've told me I can go to my local police station and fill out the forms.'

'The universities are issuing those letters to all the student leaders,' she said. 'It will be much easier for the government if you all leave the country.' Then she stared into the sky and said, 'When I look at the moon, I get an ominous feeling. It has shone down on so many atrocities. The famous reformer, Liang Qichao, got his head cut off sixty years ago, over there, by Xuanwu Gate.'

My thoughts turned to my father's student, Liu Ping. A band of villagers, who'd previously been like uncles to her, tore her father's liver from his body, then raped her and cut off her breasts. In the Song Dynasty, General Fen's army ate dried human flesh which they euphemistically called 'two-legged mutton'. They considered women's meat to be the most flavoursome, referring to it as 'mutton's envy'. But they only resorted to eating human meat because there was no other food available. The men who ate Liu Ping weren't driven by hunger, but by fear. The Communist Party had told them, 'If you don't eat the enemy, you are the enemy, and the Party will destroy you.'

'You should leave China at once and escape to freedom,' Tian Yi said, still resting her head on my lap. I couldn't see the expression on her face.

'I'll wait until the hunger strike is finished before I apply for a passport. I can't leave you alone now. And anyway, if I did leave the Square, I'd be branded a deserter.'

A new voice came through the loudspeakers on the Monument: 'I'm Dr Wang, from the Beijing University clinic. Many of you students know me already. I've come here to advise the hunger strikers to drink milk and soft drinks tonight. That's how Gandhi was able to stay on hunger strike for forty-five days . . .' When he finished, the deputy vice chancellor of Beijing University took the microphone and pleaded with the students to end their fast.

A recording of a Central Television news report was then broadcast. 'President Gorbachev arrived in Beijing this morning for the first Sino-Soviet summit in thirty years. We hope the students will respect this historic event, and refrain from doing anything that would harm China's national dignity or throw the country into turmoil . . . The leaders of the Central Committee and the State Council are concerned about the health of the hunger strikers, and hope they will call an end to the strike and return to their campuses at once . . .'

The students in the Square jeered with disdain. A few guys stood up in the murky light and belted out the Internationale, trying to drown the broadcast. One boy rose to his feet, wrapped in his blanket, and wailed, 'We're not creating turmoil! Retract that slur!' His voice was barely audible, but when the crowd echoed his words, the roar seemed to light up the night sky.

Yu Jin strutted through the crowd holding up a placard that said THE HUNGER STRIKE HAS REACHED ITS 60TH HOUR! accompanied by Zhang Jie who was wearing a black leather jacket.

The thousands of hunger strikers were bedded down on their quilts in neat rows. It reminded me of those two months after the 1976 earthquake when everyone in Beijing slept outdoors. Now and then, a few hunger strikers would wake from their sleep, and I'd see their hair or baseball caps popping up from under their blankets. The others lay motionless, occasionally stretching a foot or hand out from under their blankets or padded coats.

At three in the morning, the Square was still very noisy. Student marshals rushed past us on their bicycles to start their night shifts. Beijing residents arrived on tricycle carts piled with donations of woks and firewood. Beyond our line of marshals, a large white cloth daubed with the words SAVE THE PEOPLE swayed in the darkness. Below it lay ten hunger strikers from the Central Academy of Drama. Apparently they'd bought some petrol, and had vowed to set fire to themselves in the event of a crackdown.

Feeling a sudden pang of hunger, I pulled out a bread roll from my pocket and bit into it. A student lying beside me sat up abruptly and said, 'No one's allowed to eat in the Square.'

'What do you think you're doing?' Tian Yi said, jabbing me with her elbow. Mimi, who was lying next to her, sat up. 'A student marshal was shown on television yesterday eating bread in the Square,' she said. 'The reporter said he was a hunger striker. Look, all the students around here have put tape over their mouths.'

'I'm sorry, I forgot. I've got to get moving now, anyway. Some guys back at the broadcast station want me to cut their hair.' I stood up and walked away. I hadn't eaten a hot meal for two days. In fact, I'd hardly eaten any more than the hunger strikers themselves.

I felt dispirited as I walked away from Tian Yi. I was afraid that she'd fallen out of love with me. I hadn't dared join the strike. Like Wang

Fei, I didn't think I had the stamina. All my life, I'd dreamed of being an explorer one day, travelling around China like the Ming Dynasty geographer, Xu Xiake. But after three days of camping out in the Square, all I wanted to do was to lie down on a soft bed.

This is your body's dream, and you are trapped inside it. Like a universe gazing at the ravines of a small planet, you observe the undulations on the plasma membrane of a cell.

'Master Hu will now use his qigong to cure members of the audience. If any of you have illnesses you'd like him to treat, please come up onto the stage!'

My mother immediately pushes my wheelchair forward. All around us, people begin jostling and shoving.

'We'll come if you can give him a lift up!' my mother shouts, as everyone continues to dash to the stage.

'Master Hu's qigong skills have been praised by the government leader, Liu Ruihuan . . .' the female compère hosting the qigong demonstration says into the microphone. 'Central Television's *Eastern Horizons* broadcast a feature on him in which many of his former patients sang his praises . . .'

'I had to buy a ticket for my son tonight, even though he's a vegetable,' my mother says to the compère impatiently. 'I hoped that Master Hu might be able to cure him. I wouldn't have travelled all this way otherwise.'

'Please tell me sir, what illness are you suffering from?' the compère asks, not hearing my mother.

'Gastritis.'

'I see. And you?'

'Hepatitis.'

'Mmm. And you? What? Can you speak up please?'

'Bone hyperplasia and enteritis.'

'So you're suffering from two illnesses, then, madam.'

'I've got cholecystitis – let me up!' my mother shrieks in her soprano voice.

'Yes, you can come up,' says the compère, finally noticing my mother. 'And tell me, what is this young man you have brought with you suffering from?'

'He's been in a coma for three years. He's paralysed from head to foot. He suffered a head injury. He's a vegetable now.'

'All right, bring him up too. I will now ask Master Hu to banish the illnesses from the members of the audience up here on the stage. Let's give him a round of applause again to show our support! . . . The rest of you, please return to your seats. We have enough patients now. But don't worry, comrades, the qigong that Master Hu emits will spread right through the hall. If you close your eyes, you'll be able to absorb it. If you are ill, it will cure you. If you are well, it will protect you from falling ill. All right, close your eyes now. Master Hu will begin to emit his qi . . . See, this lady here is absorbing the energy. Her legs are shaking . . .'

As I listen to this woman speak, I remember Nuwa's gentle voice. It always reminded me of the sound of flowing water.

I've been lifted onto the stage in my wheelchair. I can sense waves of energy flow through my body, especially around my colon and spleen. Parts of my flesh begin to quiver.

'Look, that gentleman is smiling. Perhaps the qi has touched his funny bone. Please don't laugh, comrades. Compose yourselves . . .'

The laughter and chatter in the hall die down. The compère's high-heeled shoes click down the line of patients on the stage. For a moment I sense her attention focus on me. No doubt put off by my wooden expression, she quickly moves on to my mother. 'Look at this lady,' the compère says. 'She is clearly very sensitive to the waves of qi. See how she's rocking back and forth now . . .'

It's hard to imagine my mother, the loyal Communist, being willing to engage in this esoteric practice.

A garlicky smell of hot sour soup wafts from someone's mouth. A pager goes off. I feel like I'm in a busy restaurant.

'Master Hu is expelling the illness from her body. This young lady standing next to her, please make an effort. Close your eyes and let your arms fall loosely to your sides. Relax as much as you can. Everyone is reacting to the qi in different ways, depending on their illnesses. This gentleman said that he suffers from arthritis. Can you see how his knee is shaking now?'

I wish I could escape from this stage, and the thousands of eyes staring at me. Half an hour ago my mother was pushing me through the sunny streets. I heard the wind brush against my ear then whistle off into the distance. Now I'm sitting on the stage like an actor. The audience is waiting for me to open my eyes and stand up. But I know that I'm incapable of doing that, because the part of my brain that controls these actions has been irreparably damaged . . . To the north is the Land of Ghosts. The inhabitants have human heads and snake bodies, and only one eye . . .

A fierce wind brushed across my eyes. It filled the Square with blinding dust and dispelled some of the smells of broken medicine bottles, food-stained newspaper and rotting refuse . . .

You imagine your body hovering in mid-air, orbited by its memories.

The huge banner calling for HONEST DIALOGUE hung from the roof of the Museum of Chinese History, soaking up the bright sunlight. It was the fourth day of the hunger strike, and the crowd on the Square was larger than ever.

Han Dan and Yang Tao were the only instigators of the hunger strike who had not yet been taken to hospital. The previous night, Bai Ling had been carried out of the Square on a stretcher. A total of six hundred hunger strikers had passed out. Many of them rejoined the hunger strike as soon as they regained consciousness.

'The hunger is making everyone go crazy,' Han Dan said softly, tapping his ballpoint pen on a newspaper lying on the ground. His eyes were dark and sunken.

Sister Gao hurried over and said, 'A group of Beijing University professors have gone up onto the viewing stands and started a hunger strike in solidarity with us. They've been joined by thirty young professors from the Central Institute of Nationalities. Han Dan, you must decide how to respond.'

'I can only speak on behalf of the Beijing University students,' Han Dan said. 'Tell Mou Sen to write a letter of thanks and get the station to broadcast it. Apparently, the director of the United Front Department is going to visit the Square this afternoon to try to plead with the students to end the hunger strike. I'm in favour of ending the strike, but if Bai Ling and Lin Lu want us to persevere with it, there's nothing I can do.' Han Dan's only post now was head of the Beijing University Hunger Strike Petition Group.

'There must be at least 100,000 people on the Square,' Sister Gao said. 'And tomorrow, the professors want to organise a mass march through the city. With so much support behind us, how can you contemplate withdrawing?' Sister Gao appeared to have changed her mind again.

Two white ambulances drove into the Square, their sirens wailing, and sped down the lifeline that the marshals had cleared for them.

'Students from Beijing Medical University have come to discuss setting up a first-aid clinic, Han Dan,' Chen Di said, walking up. 'They're waiting for you at the broadcast station.' Chen Di had been surviving on milk and glucose solution for the last couple of days, and had broadcast many moving statements from other hunger strikers. Xiao Li was in a much weaker state. He'd passed out twice, and had been put on a drip in the emergency tent.

'Tell them to talk to Bai Ling. I can't speak on behalf of the Hunger

Strike Headquarters.' Han Dan's lips were dry and chapped. He was sweating so much that the black ink on his white bandanna was seeping onto his forehead.

'I can't go back to them now,' Chen Di said with a pained expression. 'I've just shat in my trousers. I've probably got colitis. I'm going off to buy myself some shorts.'

'I should put up a sign here saying: "Beijing University Hunger Strike Petition Group",' said Han Dan crossly. 'I'll only deal with our hunger strikers. The Beijing Students' Federation can look after everyone else.' He seemed perturbed that, by the fourth day of the hunger strike, his position had been usurped by more charismatic and radical students.

A large crowd came marching down Changan Avenue, holding a banner that said BEIJING CITIZENS' SOLIDARITY GROUP. A guy at the front shouted through a megaphone: 'We want to assemble a crowd of 10,000 residents and set off on a march. If anyone wants to take part, join the back of our procession!' They were dressed in blue overalls and red-and-white baseball caps. Some of them were holding spades or brooms, others had children on their shoulders. The colourful procession moved closer and spiralled slowly around the Square, progressing towards the Monument in the centre like fallen leaves and branches being drawn into a muddy hole.

'Dai Wei, where are your student marshals?' Old Fu cried out. 'I need them to protect the broadcast station.'

'They're guarding the Monument and the Beijing University hunger strikers,' I said as he came closer. 'Can't Xiao Li help out?'

'He's fainted again. The broadcast station is the mouthpiece of the students. If it isn't properly guarded, the Square will fall into chaos. You must recruit more marshals, then set up sub-units, each with its own leader, and give everyone a number. Go and buy some hats and armbands to distribute to your team.'

'Who are you representing now, Old Fu?' Sister Gao asked. 'The Hunger Strike Headquarters, the Beijing Students' Federation or our Organising Committee?'

'The hunger strikers, of course! They're sacrificing their lives for our cause. It's our duty to help them.' Old Fu was panting for breath. He sounded as though he'd just run a marathon.

'I thought you wanted to go back to campus, Old Fu,' I said.

'I can't leave now. Bai Ling has appointed me temporary commander-in-chief, and I've also got the broadcast station to look after.'

'The director of the United Front Department will be here in a couple of hours,' Han Dan said. 'Make sure the broadcast station is securely cordoned off by then.'

'He'll be wasting his time,' Old Fu said. 'The hunger strikers won't give up until the government agrees to our demands.' As I walked over to the broadcast station with him, he said, 'Everyone's trying to take control of the station. We should get all our guys over there now – Hai Feng, Zhuzi and Shao Jian – and come up with a strategy.'

'What about Shu Tong?' I was worried to see that the lifeline we'd cleared for the ambulances was now full of people.

'He's gone back to the campus again. He and Liu Gang opposed the hunger strike, so I doubt the students will let him return to the Square.'

'Han Dan and Ke Xi have continued with their hunger strike, but are both calling for a withdrawal. It doesn't make sense.'

'We Beijing University students must establish our authority, or we'll just get caught up in the struggles of rival factions,' Old Fu said.

'Those twelve intellectuals who came to the Square yesterday were trying to establish their authority too, but you thought they wanted to take over our movement,' I said, repeating a view that Mou Sen had expressed.

'No, they weren't trying to take control. They just wanted us to leave the Square in time for Gorbachev's welcoming ceremony so that the government didn't lose face.' Old Fu looked distracted. It seemed as though only half his brain was working.

As we walked into the broadcast station's tent, I said, 'I don't agree with you, Old Fu. The intellectuals knew the students had backed themselves into a corner. They were giving us a chance to withdraw from the Square with our dignity intact.' Mou Sen was lying on the ground writing a news bulletin, sucking deeply on a cigarette. I snatched it from his mouth and stamped it out. His face was like a sheet of grey paper, soaked in sweat. He looked as though he needed to be put on a drip.

'Some more Nankai University students have arrived from Tianjin,' Mou Sen whispered, not wanting to disturb the broadcast discussion Mao Da was chairing. 'They're stuck outside the Square's security cordon over there. They've got no food or blankets. It's too much. They're very angry.'

'Let them join our student marshal team,' Wang Fei said, waking from a nap.

Outside the tent, hundreds of students were queuing up, hoping for a chance to broadcast messages or statements.

'I sent some Nankai University students to guard the water barrels on the Monument's lower terrace,' I said, sitting down on a box of paper. It was quite cool inside the tent. I longed to hide in a quiet corner and sneak some food into my mouth. 'The Beijing University Youth League has come to the Square to support the hunger strikers,' Old Fu said to me. 'They've brought food and water. We've set up a supply station below the Museum of Chinese History. Can you send some student marshals over to guard it?'

'Ask Mou Sen to sort that out,' I said. 'I've got enough to deal with.'

'The Youth League has set up a telephone line,' said Wang Fei, lighting a cigarette. 'I think we should appropriate it. Hey, have you heard? The restaurant owners in Qianmen market are handing out free food to the students. If you show them your student card, they'll give you a box of provisions. It's just like the mutual aid teams that sprang up during the Cultural Revolution.'

'Many of the people on the citizens' march today work for government organisations. And they're calling for the same things as we are. The protests are ascending to a new level.' Mou Sen resembled the great writer Lu Xun in the famous photograph taken of him on his deathbed.

Mao Da walked over, grabbed Mou Sen's metal cup, took two sips from it, then returned to the debate he was chairing behind the stack of equipment. There were eight or nine people squeezed around the microphone.

'Let us resume the discussion,' Mao Da said. Now that he'd drunk some water, his voice was twice as loud.

'I'm an economics student. I'd just like remind everyone that no communist nation has ever had a successful economy . . .'

'I'm a second-year sociology student. The government keeps promising to provide universal English language education, but the majority of middle-school students around the country still fail to reach even the most basic level of English. What's the government doing with all our money?'

'I'd just like to say –'

'You must introduce yourself first,' Mao Da interrupted.

'Sorry, I'm a third-year geography student. I'd just like to say that I've never heard of a case where democracy has been created by a peaceful sit-in and a crowd of onlookers. If we want democracy, we must use more radical tactics. If we need to sweat, we must sweat. If we need to shed blood, we must shed blood!'

I could hear the huge crowd outside break into applause.

'I'm from Nankai University in Tianjin,' said a student in a yellow baseball cap. 'I arrived here two days ago. This morning, workers from Shougang Steel Plant marched to the Square to show their support. They held placards saying: "Don't worry, your brothers are here at last!"

. . . I have a sore throat, so I can't speak for too long. Thank you, everyone!'

I knew this student. The day before, he'd helped me reorganise the lifeline through the Square.

'Fellow students, I'm from Shanghai's Fudan University. I've queued up for hours for a chance to speak to you. I wanted to tell you that the students of Shanghai have taken to the streets, and hundreds have gone on hunger strike in solidarity with our fellow students in Beijing!'

Shu Tong walked into the tent, followed by Zhuzi. 'It took us ages to persuade the marshals to allow us back into the Square,' he said. 'Luckily, I had my student card with me. Where have all these new marshals come from? They don't seem to have any idea who I am.'

'The broadcast station back at the campus is better organised than this place,' Zhuzi grumbled. He was too tall to stand up in the tent, even with his head bowed, so he had to sink into a squat.

'We've brought some more cash with us,' said Shu Tong. 'Put it in a safe place, Old Fu. Hey, Dai Wei, I've heard your brother has joined the hunger strike in Sichuan.' He sat on a cardboard box. Sweat was pouring down the back of his neck.

'I haven't had a chance to phone him yet,' I said. 'My mother has been calling him every day, begging him to give up, but he won't listen.'

'So you've got a brother, then? Is he as tall as you?' Nuwa took a swig of Coke. Her hair was a little longer now. I could see the ends peeping out from under her baseball cap.

'Don't waste your time asking about him,' I said. 'I'm the tall, handsome one in my family!'

After this feeble attempt at humour, Nuwa looked away and didn't address another word to me.

'Apparently the Dialogue Delegation and Beijing Students' Federation set up offices in the Square this morning,' Shu Tong said. 'We've decided to shift the Organising Committee's focus to the Square too, and we'll be using this station as our base.'

'This station was set up to serve the hunger strikers,' Old Fu said, his eyes darting about nervously. 'You can't take it over.'

'But the Organising Committee paid for all this equipment,' Zhuzi said. 'We only sent you here to take care of logistics, Old Fu. Of course we should retain control of this place.' Since the police had left the city centre, Zhuzi had positioned teams of student marshals at various key intersections to supervise traffic, and had given them walkie-talkies so that everyone could stay in touch.

Wanting to defuse the situation, I said, 'The authorities have cut off our water again today. What shall we do?'

'You can get water in the men's toilets of the Workers' Cultural Palace,' Shao Jian said. 'I went there just now.'

'I've heard the student marshals haven't had anything to eat for hours,' Zhuzi said.

'I've just sent a group of them off to eat something by the Museum,' I said. 'The hunger strikers won't be able to see them there.'

'I stood with the marshals yesterday, protecting the lifeline,' Big Chan said. He was lying on a cotton sheet on the ground. 'Local residents came over and gave us food and drink. Some of them put cigarettes in our mouths and lit them for us. One old woman wiped the sweat from my face with a clean flannel. Then she took a fresh one from her bag to wipe someone else's face. It was very moving.'

'We printed 300,000 copies of the *News Herald* today, which is far more copies than any student newspaper printed during the May Fourth Movement,' Shu Tong said proudly, raising his chin.

'The *News Herald* has become the students' spiritual food,' Chen Di said. 'They go to sleep with copies draped over their faces.' He'd just run back to the Square after buying himself a pair of shorts in Qianmen market. His lips were dark purple and he was gasping for breath. Old Fu had told him to take a break from reading out announcements, and to go and lie down in the hunger strike camp. His girlfriend had passed out and was receiving emergency care in hospital.

'I have some good news,' Shu Tong said. 'Beijing University's chancellor has agreed to supply you with free food and transport while you're in the Square. Over a thousand students from the provinces have turned up at our campus since the hunger strike began. We've had to give them food and accommodation. They're sleeping in your bunks. There are two students in your bed, Dai Wei.'

'But I took the mattress off,' I said.

Realising that I hadn't seen Tian Yi for some time, I grabbed a bottle of glucose solution and went outside. In the hot sunlight, the Square looked like a sandy beach. It made me long for a sea breeze. As I stood in the centre of that vast arid space, I had an unsettling feeling that a heavy rain was about to fall.

I found Tian Yi lying next to Mimi. 'Look at that,' she said, pointing to a cut rose she'd placed in a plastic bottle of water. 'A local resident gave it to me. It will die in a couple of days. What a shame . . . Professor Xing visited us this morning.'

'What department is he from?' I sat down behind her and looked at her pale, thin face, and wondered how my brother was doing in Sichuan.

'He's from the Chinese Academy of Sciences. Very influential.' Tian Yi's forehead was covered in sweat.

'Did he say, "I'm sorry, I've come too late," like all the others?'

'He's eighty-seven years old. He said that the government was wrong to denounce our protests as "counter-revolutionary turmoil".'

'He only dared come here once he knew the government wasn't going to launch a crackdown.'

'They've just given me a 1000cc glucose transfusion,' Tian Yi said, stretching out her arm. 'If I'd refused to have it, they would have taken me to hospital. I feel as feeble as a piece of straw.'

I stared at her brown, hairless arm and the red bloodstain around her injection wound. Then I looked at her stomach and watched the folds of her shirt rise and fall as she breathed in and out.

The marshals guarding the lifeline began passing on a rumour that the director of the United Front Department had arrived in the Square. A few hunger strikers stood up in excitement. A voice cried, 'Sit down everyone! Stay calm!'

Other students yelled, 'Tell him to get lost. Chase him off the Square!'

Just as I'd managed to help Tian Yi onto her feet, everyone sat down again.

I suddenly remembered that Han Dan had asked me to ensure the broadcast station was cordoned off in time for the visit. It had completely slipped my mind.

Once the crowd had calmed down, I could hear Ke Xi's voice blaring through the loudspeakers. 'I'd like to start off by saying that Director Yan Mingfu of the United Front Department is an upstanding, reform-minded Party member . . .' Then I heard Han Dan give an update on the number of hunger strikers who'd passed out.

Buses rumbled past in the distance. The voices broadcast through the loudspeakers quietened the crowds, but from where I was sitting, I could only catch fragments of Director Yan's speech.

'. . . You must give up now, not for your sakes, or even your families' sakes, but for the sake of the country . . . Leave now, and I assure you there will be no political backlash . . . If you don't believe me, take me hostage . . . You shouldn't harm yourselves like this. The future belongs to you . . . The reformers in the Party are working hard to . . .'

Everyone seemed moved by the sincerity in his faltering voice.

'But we can't give up now!' Tian Yi yelled out. I was amazed. I'd never heard her shout like that before.

The Square fell silent. Tian Yi's eyes filled with tears. I watched her grubby fingers rub the leaves of her rose. The other hunger strikers around her began to cry too. A humid breeze moved through the Square.

'All we're asking for is an open dialogue, but the government leaders are too terrified to speak to us,' Chen Di shouted through a megaphone. 'They just send their lackeys from the United Front Department.'

'Don't tell us what to do, Director Yan!' Wang Fei shouted through his megaphone. 'We're not children!'

'Look at this!' Dong Rong called out to me, lifting his left arm. 'I was put on a drip for half an hour and it's swollen to double its size!'

The crowd became restless. Someone nearby shouted, 'What's the point of a United Front Department? We're all Chinese, aren't we? Who are we supposed to be uniting against?'

'Fuck it!' another voice shouted. 'I'm going to refuse all fluids from now on!'

Mimi was distraught. 'We're putting our lives on the line here, but the so-called people's government won't even bother to talk to us. They're a band of criminals!' She too had had an allergic reaction to the transfusion, and her arm was as red and swollen as Dong Rong's.

The atmosphere was tense. Finally, Lin Lu announced over the loudspeakers that Ke Xi had fainted again, and that Director Yan's speech would have to be cut short. He asked the university representatives to gather at the Monument for an emergency meeting.

Tian Yi's face was dripping with sweat. 'I'm not feeling good,' she moaned. I pressed her wrist. Her pulse was racing. She was trembling all over.

By the time Director Yan had left the Square, she'd calmed down a little, but she still looked very weak. I felt powerless. There was nothing I could do to help her. Zhang Jie and I cleared a space in front of the Monument for the meeting. After a long debate over whether to withdraw from the Square, Lin Lu announced that the Headquarters had conducted a survey and found that 2,699 hunger strikers were in favour of continuing the occupation, while only 54 were against.

The Dialogue Delegation and the Beijing Students' Federation had no choice but to follow the wishes of the hunger strikers, so the motion to leave the Square was rejected.

Sister Gao said despairingly, 'Of course the hunger strikers want to persevere until the end. But what about the other students? Who's representing them? They are the majority, after all.'

Shu Tong and Yu Jin set off to canvass opinion among the rest of the students in the Square. Then Yang Tao stood up, wiped the lenses of his glasses and declared loudly: 'Our only option now is to adopt the last of Sun Tzu's Thirty-Six Strategies: retreat. The situation in the Square is out of control. If we stay, our movement will be doomed. The only way to avoid defeat is to withdraw our troops immediately.' Yang Tao was an expert on Sun Tzu's *Art of War*. Since working in the

Organising Committee's political theory office, he'd acquired a reputation as a modern-day Zhu Geliang, the brilliant military strategist of the Han Dynasty.

Your body is a trap, a square with no escape routes.

Tiananmen Square was the heart of our nation, a vast open space where millions of tiny cells could gather together and forget themselves and, more importantly, forget the thick, oppressive walls that enclosed them . . .

'Is this young comrade a friend of yours?' asks Granny Pang from the doorway. She must be seventy by now, but she's followed our visitor all the way up from the ground floor.

'Hello, Auntie, I'm Yu Jin,' a voice says to my mother. 'I was at Beijing University with Dai Wei. I work in Shanghai now, for a financial company.'

I imagine him ignoring Granny Pang and walking straight into our flat.

'Yes, we've met,' my mother says. 'I just couldn't put a name to you. Please come in.'

'How long will you be?' Granny Pang asks. I'm sure she's put her foot on the threshold. Perhaps she's even stepped inside.

'Not long,' Yu Jin says. 'Have you hobbled all the way up here on your weak legs just to spy on me? Don't worry, I'll make sure I've left before you have time to report my visit to the police.'

'Who says I've got weak legs? I made it up six flights of stairs, didn't I? All right, you can have a quick word, but don't stay too long.' I hear her turn on her heel and prepare to leave.

'Careful you don't slip on your way down, Granny Pang,' my mother says sarcastically. 'Who would pay for your medical treatment?'

'All right, enough of your jibes,' she says. 'Just take care. I'm only doing this for you, you know. If the police were to come round, who knows what might happen . . .'

'Nothing's going to happen as long as you keep your nose out of my business. I warn you, I'm short of money. From now on, if you dare set one foot inside my flat, I'll charge you ten yuan.' My mother slams the door shut. 'That old bat's lost her mind,' she grumbles. 'As soon as anyone visits, she phones the police, then asks them to reimburse her for the cost of the call. Even *they're* fed up with her now.'

'Let me have a look at Dai Wei, Auntie.'

'Yes, yes. Come in. You were in the same dorm together. Mao Da mentioned you when he came round.'

I can feel Yu Jin looking at me.

A scent of tobacco and women's perfume drifts from his down jacket.

I used to tower over him, but now I'm lying shrivelled beneath him on this iron bed. I can't ask him any questions. I'll just have to wait patiently, hoping he'll tell me something I don't know, just as I did when Mao Da and Zhang Jie visited, and I learned that Old Fu and Ke Xi have set up a China Democracy Front in Paris and that Shu Tong and Lin Lu have been featured in a foreign television documentary and have had their memoirs published in America.

'Dai Wei! My God! How could you get like this? Back in '89, you were our great general. You kept us all in line. Huh! I can't believe it.'

'Sit down,' says my mother. 'I remember Tian Yi talking about you . . .'

'Don't mention her name to me! The photos she took in the Square got hundreds of us into trouble. The printers sent the negatives to Beijing University's Party committee. I know it was an innocent mistake, but many students suspected her of working for the government because of it.'

What a disaster! I remember taking those rolls of film to the printers for Tian Yi. I didn't tell them which university I was from. How did they know where to send them? They could have destroyed the negatives. They didn't have to pass them on.

'He looks dreadful now, I know,' says my mother. 'But for a couple of weeks in the autumn, he suddenly looked like a young boy again. His skin became smooth and soft. His whole face glowed. It was very strange.'

'He must have just had a visit from Tian Yi.' Yu Jin's voice hasn't changed. Voices always stay the same. When I first heard him speak a minute ago, I knew straight away that it was him. 'I'm sorry I haven't visited before,' he continues. 'I must be the last of his classmates to come and see you. But this is the first chance I've had. I was in prison for two years, with Zhuzi and Fan Yuan. After my release, I wasn't allowed to continue my PhD, so I moved down to Shanghai and got a job in a securities company in the Pudong District. I've just about managed to get myself together again. I never talk about politics any more. I've come up to Beijing on business. I arrived yesterday, and got your address from Mimi.'

So the little chap's a financier now, is he? I heard on the radio that the government has set up a Special Economic Zone in Pudong, similar to the one down in Shenzhen. Many graduates with a Master's or PhD have gone there to look for jobs in foreign companies.

'Mimi hasn't visited for months,' says my mother. 'Tian Yi only comes twice a year. Everyone's focusing on their careers. I suppose Dai Wei was lucky to escape with his life. But it's so hard looking after him, sometimes I wish he was dead. If his American cousin didn't send us money, we'd be out on the streets by now.'

Zhou Suo was jailed, but I don't know what happened to any of the other Qinghua University students. I know that at least thirty-six Beijing University students were killed. I'm not sure who all of them were, but some were definitely from the last batch of marshals I sent out to defend the intersections.

'I've brought a thousand yuan for you, to go towards Dai Wei's medical costs,' Yu Jin says. 'I haven't been in this job long, but it has good prospects. The Pudong Special Economic Zone has great growth potential. I've persuaded many of my old university friends to move down there.'

'I can't take that much money from you,' my mother protests. 'You haven't been out of prison long. You need to look after yourself. Are your parents both well?'

'Yes, they're fine. They live in Wuxi. They were both sacked from their jobs when I was sent to prison, though.'

I hear a phone ring. The noise startles me.

'Hello,' Yu Jin says. 'Yes. Fine. Seven o'clock, then. Get your brother to come too. Don't worry, it's my treat. We'll meet outside McDonald's on Wangfujing Street. Me? I'm at Dai Wei's home. Ha! All right, all right. See you later, then.' I hear Yu Jin press a button.

'What's that?' my mother gasps. 'It's bigger than the ones the police carry.'

'This isn't a walkie-talkie, Auntie. It's a cellphone. It's like the telephones you have at home, but you can carry them around with you.'

'Oh, I've read about them in the papers. They're called Big Brothers. Apparently all the rich entrepreneurs have them now. When they go out for a meal, they only have to plonk their phones on the table and immediately the restaurant managers grovel at their feet.'

'Pagers are old hat now. That's the way things go. Information is a commodity. If you don't have one of these, no one will respect you.'

'How much do they cost?'

'More than 10,000 yuan,' Yu Jin says breezily.

'I don't believe it! That's more than three times what it costs to get a landline connected. You've done really well for yourself. You're the first person I've met who owns a Big Brother.'

'It's no big deal. Lots of people in Shenzhen and Shanghai are using them now. Tell me, how is Dai Wei's treatment going?'

'Sit down. I'll get you a cup of tea. Here, you can sit on this chair.'

As I listen to my mother remove the bottles of pills from the chair and place them on top of the sideboard, I try to guess what the young financier Yu Jin looks like. I imagine him in a suit and tie, with clean socks and shiny leather shoes. His hair is short, or balding, perhaps. In the morning, he struts confidently into his office and nods a greeting to his colleagues, or shakes them firmly by the hand.

While my mother goes to pour the tea, I feel his eyes fix on me. After a while he says, 'Dai Wei, they may have split us up, but we must struggle on. When they arrested me, I refused to plead guilty. I just told them what happened. I said that you were the ringleader, of course. I knew you were in a coma by then, so you wouldn't get into trouble. Everyone with foreign connections has gone abroad. Those who've stayed have given up academia and gone into commerce. If you want to live your life with a bit of dignity these days you need to make money. Beijing University has lost its spirit. No one wants to study there any more. The students are forced to do a year's military training before they start their courses now, so it takes four or five years to graduate.'

What was wrong with our generation? When the guns were pointing at our heads, we were still wasting time squabbling among ourselves. We were courageous but inexperienced, and had little understanding of Chinese history.

You remember standing in the centre of the Square, the hot wind blowing across your face. The Square was like the room you are lying in now: a warm space with a beating heart trapped in the middle of a cold city.

Shortly before dusk, an announcement came over some new loudspeakers that had just been attached to the other side of the Monument. Yu Jin ran off to see what was going on, and returned a few minutes later saying, 'The Beijing Students' Federation and the Qinghua University students have set up their own broadcast station at the south-east corner of the Monument. They're calling it "Voice of Qinghua".'

Old Fu was talking to Mou Sen about establishing a new editorial system. They'd both been appointed vice commanders of the Hunger Strike Headquarters by Bai Ling. When Old Fu heard the news, he got up and said, 'Come on, let's go round and take a look.'

'Sounds like their equipment is at least three times stronger than ours,' Little Chan said. 'And they've got many more loudspeakers as well. Look, they're all stacked up there on the lower terrace.'

'It will be chaotic if we're both broadcasting at the same time,' Big Chan said, catching up with us. Since Big Chan and Little Chan had joined my student marshal team three days before, they hadn't left the Square. They took their jobs very seriously, and were now responsible for overseeing the security of the Monument area.

'I'm sure we can reach some kind of understanding,' Old Fu said calmly.

The Qinghua camp on the other side looked much better organised than ours. They'd erected a large white tent to shield their hunger strikers from the heat, and had cooled the stone ground in front of it with water and big blocks of ice.

Their broadcast station was a square lean-to shelter erected against the base of the Monument, just like ours. The door faced south. There were so many student marshals protecting it, I couldn't see inside. We tried to enter, but they blocked our way. Old Fu said, 'Please ask the station chief to come out. We've brought a tape for him to broadcast.'

Zhou Suo stepped out of the tent. He was the chairman of Qinghua University's Organising Committee. From his dark, weathered skin and rugged features, you could tell he'd grown up in the windy wastes of Shanxi Province's Yellow Plateau.

Yu Jin walked up to him. 'We're from the Beijing University broadcast station. I think we've met.'

'We've brought a tape for you,' Old Fu said, in a friendly but slightly condescending tone. 'It's very moving. You can use it if you like. We only broadcast to the Beijing University students. The people on this side can't hear us.'

'The Beijing Students' Federation decides what we broadcast, and you're not the chairman of it any more, Old Fu,' Zhou Suo said frostily.

A trace of embarrassment passed over Old Fu's face as he realised he'd lost his authority. 'Well, I'm still a member of its leadership committee,' he protested. 'Who else from the Beijing Students' Federation is here?'

'Fan Yuan and Sister Gao. You can ask them if they want to play the tape, if you like.' Zhou Suo clearly didn't want to have to take responsibility for anything.

We walked into their tent. It was very dark inside. I took off my sunglasses.

Old Fu spotted Sister Gao. 'You borrowed money off us,' he said, walking up to her. 'I didn't realise it was to set up a rival broadcast station!'

'The money I borrowed was to buy chocolate and biscuits for the hunger strikers who were taken to hospital. Cao Ming came with me when I handed the food out. If you don't believe me, ask him.' Sister Gao was kneeling on the ground, sorting through a pile of scripts.

'You only broadcast to the Beijing University students,' Fan Yuan said coolly. 'But the Federation has a duty to disseminate information to the broad mass of students and civilians in the Square. We didn't spend any of your money on this equipment. That generator was donated to us by the workers of Beijing.'

'We don't need the Federation in the Square,' Old Fu said, his expression hardening. 'You should go back to the campuses.'

'You're not chairman or commander-in-chief any longer,' Sister Gao said. 'You can't tell us what to do. The majority of the universities' organising committees supported this plan. They all supported us.' She often repeated herself when she was angry.

'If you carry on like this, no one will be able to hear our broadcasts back there,' I chipped in, seeing that Old Fu was now speechless with rage.

'Well, stop broadcasting then!' Fan Yuan said. 'All you do is get famous intellectuals to repeat that this is the gravest moment in our nation's history and it's our duty to take a stand. You're more of a celebrity show than a students' broadcast station.' Fan Yuan was wearing metal-rimmed glasses. From the side, he looked as thin as a plank of wood.

'We were here first,' Big Chan said. 'You're destroying student solidarity by setting up this rival operation.'

Their pretty announcer came over and said, 'Everyone's sick of your broadcasts. In the morning, they're sombre and depressing, but when the supporters turn up in the afternoon, they become light-hearted and optimistic. All those ups and downs are driving us mad.' She smiled as she spoke. The sound of her clear voice was as refreshing as eating an ice cream on a hot day. But she wasn't as beautiful as Nuwa.

'That broadcast you made just now wasn't very impressive,' Little Chan said. 'You were just reading out telegrams and petitions. Couldn't you come up with any better ideas?'

'Before you set up this place, it would have been sensible to discuss your plans with us,' Old Fu said meekly, aware now of his lack of clout.

'Without a broadcast station, we wouldn't be able to do any propaganda work,' Fan Yuan said. Then he paused and added, 'I think it would be best if you closed your station and let us get on with our job.'

'In that joint meeting we had a couple of hours ago, you didn't say a word about setting up this station,' Old Fu said.

'That meeting was about whether to withdraw from the Square or not,' said Sister Gao. She and Old Fu had been good friends in the past.

Realising that the argument wasn't getting anywhere, we turned and left.

'Our only option now is to buy a bigger amplifier and put up more loudspeakers,' I said on our way back to our station.

Nearby, someone had hung a small bottle over a placard that said THE PEOPLE OF SICHUAN INVITE YOU TO RETURN HOME, COMRADE DENG. This was clearly a pun on Deng Xiaoping's given name, which although means 'Little Peace' sounds identical to 'Little Bottle'. The people who gathered round it laughed as they read the message.

'When the Federation moved to the Square today, the Qinghua University marshals gave them access to the Monument's upper terrace,' Big Chan said.

'The Federation must have collected a lot of donations,' Little Chan added. 'Look, they've arranged a communication office and a finance office up there, and they're all wearing red neck-scarves. They look like a proper little army.' He and Big Chan were wearing the same brand of denim shorts.

Old Fu seemed suddenly to recover his authority. 'We must call a meeting of the university representatives straight away, and decide who is responsible for what. Let's get started. I'll clear a space in front of our broadcast station, and you go and notify the representatives, Dai Wei.'

I wandered through the crowds with the two Chans. We went to each university camp and asked them to send a representative to our meeting. Before long, we'd assembled more than a hundred people. When we returned to our broadcast station, I saw Sister Gao and Fan Yuan standing in front of it, with Lin Lu and Cheng Bing, the girl from Normal University who was now co-commander of the Hunger Strike Headquarters. Bai Ling, who'd just been discharged from hospital, was there too. Liu Gang, who'd trekked down from the campus to have a word with Old Fu, was sitting next to them.

The meeting kicked off with a discussion on how to manage the Square.

I scanned the assembled crowd. Ke Xi and Han Dan weren't there. They'd both passed out and were still recovering in hospital. Lin Lu and Liu Gang were the only people who looked composed. Wang Fei's face was bright red, as was Nuwa's, who was sitting next to him. He'd taken a table onto the Monument's lower terrace and fixed a sign to it that said TIANANMEN SQUARE PROPAGANDA OFFICE. As I looked at him, he stood up and shouted, 'If anyone wants to join the Propaganda

Suicide Squad, please sign up here. We'll set off tonight and reach Shougang Steel Plant before the first shift starts tomorrow morning. We'll give speeches outside the plant's entrance, informing the workers that our occupation won't end until our demands are met . . .' There were so many students from the provinces on the Square now that Wang Fei's regional accent no longer seemed out of place. Liu Gang stood up and proposed that the students return to their campuses, but was immediately shouted down.

A Beijing resident laughed and said, 'This movement's a farce! What can a bunch of amateurs like you hope to achieve?'

Shao Jian looked very frail. He stood up slowly and, wrinkling his brow, proposed that the students who weren't fasting take over the management of the Square.

But Bai Ling didn't agree. She was sitting on a wooden box, sweat trickling down her neck. Her face was gaunt and sallow. Two nurses in white coats were standing behind her, their hands resting on her shoulders.

'There are hundreds of thousands of people in the Square,' I said loudly. 'The government has pulled the police out of the city, so we are responsible for maintaining public order now. Hunger strikers are passing out every minute. We need to ensure the lifeline is well guarded so that the ambulances can reach them and take them to hospital. If everything is to run smoothly, we'll need a strong management team. How can you hunger strikers expect to supervise all this while you're in such a weak state?'

Chen Di's face was as rough and pale as hemp paper. He kept rising to his feet and asking to say something.

Mou Sen was lying on his side on a stretcher, holding a megaphone in his hand. He opened his eyes and said quietly, 'The Central Academy of Drama hunger strikers have announced they will refuse all liquids! We shouldn't waste time on these pointless discussions while students are on the verge of death.'

'The hunger strikers are in very fragile states,' said a young doctor who was attaching a drip to Mou Sen's arm. 'Don't say anything that might cause them unnecessary distress.' Three other student representatives were lying on stretchers next to Mou Sen, attended to by two nurses.

Hai Feng turned up and announced loudly, 'The hospital has informed us that several of the students who passed out are now in a critical condition, and some have even slipped into comas.' He moved over to where I was sitting and added, 'The Dialogue Delegation came to the Square this morning saying it wanted to join forces with the Federation.

But the Federation has fallen apart. When Fan Yuan convenes a meeting, he's the only person to turn up. What the Square needs now is some kind of central leadership.'

'How can you talk about such things . . . when we're struggling to keep ourselves alive?' Bai Ling said, having to pause in the middle to take a sip of water.

Crowds marching down Changan Avenue chanted, 'The students are starving themselves to death, while government leaders stuff their bellies with food! . . . If those corrupt officials sell off all their Mercedes, they'll wipe out the national debt in one fell swoop!' The noise was so loud that, for a moment, I couldn't hear what anyone in the meeting was saying.

'If you lot go on hunger strike, we'll stop our fast and look after the Square,' Cheng Bing said hoarsely. I'd heard she'd fainted from dehydration the day before. Although Tian Yi was very frail, she hadn't passed out yet.

'The 27th Army has already entered the outskirts of the city, for God's sake!' Hai Feng shouted, waving his hands about in exasperation. 'We need to get ourselves organised!'

'The students are collapsing from starvation, and all you do is continue your ugly scramble for power,' Lin Lu said with a deadpan face.

As the discussion shifted once more to whether we should stay in the Square or withdraw, Bai Ling suddenly fainted. The nurses shouted for someone to call an ambulance. No one was in the mood to continue the meeting. Liu Gang turned to Old Fu and said, 'Let's wind this up, Old Fu. We have a broadcast station. We should be using it to promote democracy in the Square and to inform the students of our various points of view.' He took two drags from his cigarette in quick succession, and watched the representatives get up and leave.

In the evening, groups of Beijing residents continued to pour into the Square to show their support. Whenever they passed a hunger strike camp, they'd yell, 'Long live the students!' Big Chan, Little Chan and I had to keep running over and asking them not to shout.

When I returned to the broadcast station, Mao Da turned up with Yan Jia and Bao Zunxin, two reform-minded intellectuals from the Chinese Academy of Social Sciences. Mou Sen and I invited them to sit down on the stools in front of the microphone. Mou Sen, who had great admiration for these men, said, 'Sorry about the strange smell. It's from this waterproof sheet we've just put up . . . I was very disappointed not to have been here when you visited the Square a couple of days ago. I've been reading your books and essays for many years.' He gazed into Yan Jia's eyes like a schoolboy thirsting for knowledge. I thought his obsequiousness was a bit over the top.

'I have an important piece of news to tell you,' Yan Jia said. 'Deng Xiaoping has resigned from his post. You students have done a wonderful job!' Yan Jia was a respected political scientist. He and his wife had written a ground-breaking history of the Cultural Revolution. I'd always assumed he was a young man, but in fact he was middle-aged. His thick-lensed glasses sat heavily on the flat bridge of his nose.

'Deng Xiaoping has resigned?' I said, barely believing my ears. 'My God! That means General Secretary Zhao Ziyang and his reformers have won the internal battle. Our movement has succeeded!'

'Are you sure this information is correct, Professor Yan?' asked Mou Sen, not daring to believe what he'd heard either.

'It is a piece of utterly reliable inside information,' Yan Jia said solemnly.

'We've brought a copy of our 16 May Declaration we've just written in support of your movement,' Bao Zunxin said. 'No one else has seen it yet.' Bao Zunxin was a researcher at the Academy's History Institute, a think-tank which supplied Zhao Ziyang's reformist wing with policy ideas.

Mou Sen stroked back his long hair. 'As luck would have it, we have a professional newsreader with us today,' he said. 'He's just the right man to announce this important news. Let me introduce you both to him. This is Mr Zhao. He works for China Central Television.'

'Yes, yes, I'm Zhao Xian – during the day, I'm the government's mouthpiece, and in the evening I'm the students' mouthpiece!' the TV newsreader said, chuckling to himself.

'When his voice comes over the loudspeakers, the students will think we're relaying a Central Television programme,' I said. I was surprised that in real life Mr Zhao spoke in the same clipped Mandarin he used when presenting the lunchtime news.

Mou Sen composed a short bulletin about Deng Xiaoping's resignation, and asked him to read it out. The news sent shock waves through the Square. Everyone cheered in celebration. Beijing residents let off firecrackers. Some people even set light to photographs of Deng Xiaoping. A column of students assembled outside the Great Hall of the People and prepared to march through the city, shouting, 'Long live Zhao Ziyang and his fellow reformers!' and 'Let Zhao Ziyang take over as Chairman of the Central Military Commission!' Lin Lu came over and told me to take a group of student marshals to Wangfujing Street, to make sure no one took advantage of the situation to loot shops. He didn't want any street disturbances to break out, in case the government used them as an excuse to clamp down on us. I was impressed by his foresight.

Although your nerves are numb, you can feel the memory of love juddering in your brain like a ticking clock.

That night, I dreamed that Tian Yi was running up to me with tears in her eyes, shouting for me to escape as soldiers came charging out towards us from narrow lanes. As soon as I woke up, I searched for her. Eventually I spotted her lying under her familiar flower-patterned quilt beneath a new makeshift shelter. The ground was covered with planks of wood donated by officials in the local government who were sympathetic to our cause.

I walked through the crowd of prone bodies and sat down next to her. It was the beginning of her fifth day on hunger strike. The psychology students were camped next to the Chinese literature students, so Bai Ling and Han Dan were both nearby. Our marshals had done a good job of guarding the camp. A few medics in white coats were the only outsiders they had let through. The ambulance sirens had woken up most of the hunger strikers, including Tian Yi.

I looked at her pallid face and cracked lips, and felt her freezing hands. She didn't just look old now, she looked as though she was dying. A cold breeze moved through the murky dawn.

'I'm so sorry I lost you last night,' I said. 'I had to take some marshals to Wangfujing Street to make sure the shops weren't looted and when I got back I couldn't find you. What's in that bottle you're holding?'

'Electrolyte in a saline solution. It smells like coconut milk. I kept wanting to retch yesterday, but there was nothing in my stomach to bring up.'

'It's very damp in here,' I said, rubbing her arms through her quilt.

'I hardly slept all night.'

'We were right to occupy the Square,' I said, trying to cheer her up. 'There's a new mood of optimism in the city. Everyone has joined our movement. Even the thieves and pickpockets have pledged to stop work in sympathy!'

'Look how feeble I am . . .' she said, struggling to raise her hands. 'Did you go back to your mum's flat last night?'

The sky was turning fish-belly white, and her face was almost the same colour.

'No, I've only been back once since we moved into the Square. I needed to fetch some clean clothes. She asked me why I hadn't brought you to see her for so long. She doesn't know you've joined the strike.'

'What does she make of our protests?' Tian Yi hadn't liked my mother until I took her to see her perform in *The Marriage of Figaro*. She was moved by her singing.

'She said we're right to oppose corruption, but she thinks the hunger strike is a step too far and will cause China to lose face abroad. She went on about my father again and warned me not to repeat his mistake. She said: "Don't draw attention to yourself. Remember, the bird that leaves the flock is always the first to be shot." But all the young singers in her opera company have come to the Square. It's the trendy thing to do.'

'There's not enough oxygen getting to my brain,' Tian Yi murmured. 'If I carry on any longer, I'll become a . . .'

'Have some of this milk,' I said, pulling out a plastic sachet I'd brought for her. 'The government is bound to agree to our demands soon. When the strike is over, I'll take you to the Muslim restaurant outside our campus gates and buy you a big plate of fried noodles.'

She tilted forwards and rested her frail arms on my lap. 'I hate the taste of milk . . .' she croaked. 'It reminds me of my childhood . . . My mother was six months pregnant with me when my father was condemned as a counter-revolutionary. The shock was too much for her. I was born prematurely and weighed only three kilos. She wouldn't breastfeed me. She was afraid that feeding the child of a counter-revolutionary would offend the Party. A few days later, she thrust me into my father's arms and ran away. My father bought two bottles of cow's milk and slowly brought me back to life.'

'If you don't want milk, I can get you something else.'

'My brain is jumbled . . . Trivial details keep returning to me. Just now, I remembered the red-and-white pyjamas I wore as a child. When you're alive you have to keep thinking about things. It's so tiring. I don't know if I can carry on.' Face downwards on my lap, she was now talking into the folds of my trousers.

'You won't die. When the body is starved, the cells work twice as hard. Your life force is strong.'

She grabbed my belt and tried to sit up. 'Why am I on hunger strike?' Her hands, so cold a few moments before, were now hot and trembling.

'You joined the Beijing University Hunger Strike Petition Group,' I said.

'I mean: who am I doing this for? Those government leaders? Do we really have to starve ourselves to death in order to get them to speak to us?' She closed her eyes again.

'There's no need to sacrifice yourself. It's not worth it. When the movement is over, we can go abroad and live our lives in freedom.' I wanted to put my arms around her but was afraid of hurting her frail body.

She looked up at me. The whites of her eyes were yellow. Her pupils reflected the dark outline of Tiananmen Gate.

I tried to open the sachet of milk. The plastic split and milk poured onto the quilt. It smelt sour.

'I suppose I'm doing this for my father,' she said. 'Ever since his father was executed by the Communists, he's lived in fear. When I was nine, he made me read the *Romance of the Three Kingdoms* because he wanted me to learn how sly and deceitful men can be . . . But he didn't realise the book would awaken in me a love for literature . . .'

The day before, Tian Yi had written a poem in classical Chinese. I'd given it to Mou Sen, hoping he would publish it in *Hunger Strike Express*, a newspaper he'd launched with some fellow classmates.

'In my childhood, I just saw my father as an old peasant who visited us every year,' I said. 'My mother brought up my brother and me single-handed.'

'I want to show my dad that you mustn't live your whole life in a state of docility and submission,' she continued. 'Confucius said that the three armies can be robbed of their commander, but the common man can't be robbed of his will. I don't want my father to spend the rest of his days in fear.'

'We're not asking for much,' I said. 'Personally, I'd be happy if they just granted us the right to have relationships while we're at university . . . Lie down now, Tian Yi, and try to get some sleep. I'll watch over you.'

'One day during the Cultural Revolution my mother put on a white face-mask,' she mumbled, resting her head on my lap again. 'Her bosses thought she was accusing the Party of starting a White Terror . . . She was summoned to a criticism meeting . . . The Red Guards stripped her and shaved off her pubic hair . . . She was so humiliated she killed herself the day after.'

'My mother was shaved by the Party and labelled a rightist's wife but she remained a devout Communist. Perhaps your mother had lost her faith in the Party.'

At that moment, a hundred motorcyclists known as the Flying Tigers roared into the Square, followed by a cavalcade of residents on bicycles and tricycles. They came every morning to deliver donations of milk, bread, fried dough sticks, hot porridge and pickles to the students who weren't fasting.

'So we're on Day Five now,' Tian Yi said, her eyes wide open. 'Why does my mouth feel so numb?'

I panicked. 'That's a sign that you've reached your limit. I'll take you to the emergency tent and tell them to give you a glucose transfusion. Then you must start eating again.'

It was getting very hot. A student was handing out ice lollies. I took one, and knowing that Tian Yi didn't have the energy to chew, I bit off a corner and put it in her mouth. 'I'll get some water to warm your hands,' I said, but suddenly her face went stony white. Her lips were motionless, her eyes glazed over. 'Nurse, nurse!' I shouted, 'Come here! My girlfriend has passed out!'

I removed the ice from her mouth and buttoned up her shirt. I was about to heave her onto my back when the nurse ran over and yelled, 'Don't lift her! Put her down flat on the ground!' She and I then placed Tian Yi on a stretcher and carried her to the emergency tent, where a doctor put her on a drip.

'Thanks for helping,' I said to the nurse, and sighed with relief when I saw the intravenous fluid trickle down the tube into Tian Yi's arm.

'You must be careful when someone faints,' she said. 'If you lift them by their hands and feet, it puts pressure on the heart.'

'Is she going to be all right?'

'She'll be fine after this transfusion. What subject are you studying?'

'I'm doing a PhD in molecular biology at Beijing University,' I said.

'We're both scientists, then. I studied pharmacology at Beijing Medical College.'

'Aren't you afraid you'll get punished for helping the students?'

'General Secretary Zhao Ziyang has praised your movement, and besides, the whole city has come out here to support you. The law can't punish a crowd.'

'What work unit do you belong to?' I asked.

'You sound like a policeman. All right, I'll give you my details. My name is Wen Niao. I work at the Beijing Pharmaceutical Research Institute. It's so boring there. When I first joined, I felt I was slipping into my grave.' As she looked up at me a few wrinkles creased her forehead. Her face was similar to Tian Yi's, but the bridge of her nose was a little higher, her eyebrows thicker.

'You're sure she'll be all right?' I said, glancing back at Tian Yi.

'Another fifty hunger strikers have fainted already this morning. They've reached the limits of their endurance. I hope that by tonight the strike will be called off.'

'If it is, then their efforts will have been in vain. The government still hasn't agreed to our demands.' Whenever I spoke to a nice girl, I tended to express opinions opposite to my own.

'They shouldn't put their lives at risk,' she said. 'You've already achieved a lot. You've shaken the government's authority and got the

Chinese people on your side. But if you continue this occupation any longer, things will go wrong. In June, the temperatures will soar, and you'll have epidemics breaking out.' Wen Niao had an annoying voice. It kept jumping from a high squeak to a low croak. Her neck was very slender so I guessed she had a narrow larynx.

'I could never go on hunger strike,' I said. '"Man is iron, food is steel, two missed meals and down he keels," as the saying goes.'

A male doctor came over and asked me, 'Does your girlfriend have any history of illness?'

'Why? What's the matter?' I said, panicking again.

'Her heartbeat is very erratic.'

'She suffers from hypoglycaemia. And she's claustrophobic as well. She fainted once when we were in a crowded train.'

'She shouldn't have joined the hunger strike, then. We'll have to send her to hospital. Wen Niao, go and call an ambulance.' Then, turning to me again, he asked, 'Do you know her blood group?'

'O. I'm O too. I'll go with her to the hospital.'

'Quickly, there's just once space left in the ambulance,' Wen Niao said, running back. 'Help me carry her over.'

You've been fasting for three years, motionless as a hibernating snake.

I remember pushing my brother onto the floor when we were kids. I see him sobbing on the ground, next to three bottle-tops, a comb and a small stick of chalk. Then I see my father towering over us, shouting, 'Shut up! Shut up!'

My mother is listening to the lottery results being announced over the radio while she tries to find space for the new objects she's bought. She copies the number of her lottery ticket into a notebook, and promises me that when she wins, she'll get a telephone line installed.

Someone knocks on the front door and my mother goes to open it.

'Have the police come round again recently?' asks Zhu Mei as she enters and sits down on the sofa. This is her second visit. Her husband was shot dead by the army on Changan Avenue.

'They're always turning up,' my mother grumbles. 'They saunter in here as though it was a supermarket, but they don't have the politeness to check their hats or bags in at the door. They're waiting for my son to wake up so they can send him to prison. He'd be better off dying in this flat rather than rotting in one of their jails.'

My mother has mentioned that the old covered market on the street outside has been turned into a supermarket. The food is wrapped in plastic, and customers can help themselves to the products they want.

The only drawback is that they have to check their bags in at the entrance.

'If he died now, the government would assess his case and label him a counter-revolutionary thug,' Zhu Mei says. 'After my husband was killed, he and I were both branded criminals. When the chairman of the Olympic Committee visited Beijing a few days ago, four security officers were posted outside my front door and my building was surrounded by police vans. You'd think I was a murderer or something.'

'The local neighbourhood committee keeps nagging everyone to support our Olympic bid. Apparently they sealed up the public latrines before the Olympic chairman visited the area, so that he couldn't smell the stench.'

A radio advert announces that big prizes are being randomly awarded to customers in Haidian Department Store. My mother has been visiting the store regularly for the last six months, buying things she doesn't need, such as lamps, mirrors, thermos flasks and hot-water bottles, hoping she might win a prize. There are twelve hot-water bottles under my bed now.

'So you went to the cemetery during Grave Sweeping Festival?' my mother asks.

'The police told me not to go. They warned me not waste money buying flowers or offerings, because the gates would be locked and no one would be allowed in. But I thought, damn them, and went anyway.'

'They came here too. They know that students killed in the crackdown have been buried in the cemetery, in contravention of guidelines. Last year, foreign journalists got in and photographed relatives burning paper money on the students' graves. The police told me that anyone entering a cemetery during Grave Sweeping Festival would be in trouble. If my son dies, I won't bury him in a cemetery. I'll keep his ashes under his bed.'

'I didn't see any foreign journalists there,' Zhu Mei says. 'So many people turned up, in the end they relented and let us in. But they'd only allow one family in at a time. They didn't want us to have private talks with each other inside. After I was let in, I ignored the plainclothes policemen wandering around, and went straight to my husband's grave, laid out the wine and roast duck, then knelt down and wept.'

'They let you cry?'

'I tried not to make too much noise. But while I was burning the paper money, I remembered how he'd cut his hand one night when he was building a coal hut outside our flat, and I let out a wail of grief. Seconds later, two police appeared and dragged me away.'

'You're lucky to be able to cry. All my tears have run dry.'

'But at least your son is still alive. Damn them! If they won't let me cry through my eyes, I'll cry through my nose and ears instead. See what they say about that!'

'These last years have been so difficult . . .'

'I know. The injustice we've had to endure. The injustice . . .'

The sitting room fills with the noise of Zhu Mei's weeping and my mother's attempts to comfort her. I feel my urine spread through my cotton sheet.

A smell of greasy meatballs lingers in the air long after Zhu Mei has left. It's a smell many visitors who've walked past the food stalls outside bring up to the flat. Sometimes, they also bring a whiff of those deep-fried fish fritters that crackle when you bite into them. My stomach has grown accustomed to hunger, but this morning I suddenly started fantasising about wontons – that delicious combination of flavours: rice vinegar, coriander, shrimp and preserved cabbage. Whenever I had a bowl, I'd always start by wolfing down a few of the tiny dumplings along with the broth they float in. Then I'd spoon out an individual dumpling, take a bite from it, pop a clove of raw garlic into my mouth and chew slowly, letting the pork and shrimp filling and paper-thin skin blend with the raw garlic and fresh coriander leaves. I'd grind them into a fine pulp that would slip softly down my throat. After each mouthful, I'd pause to inhale the fragrant steam wafting from the bowl. A sudden pang of hunger makes my stomach dilate and yearn for a morsel of food to digest.

Another image flashes past the wound in my brain. I see a single wing flap through the air, stirring up a breeze, then swooping into a mountain cave that becomes my empty stomach . . . The smell of meatballs and sesame oil still infuses the air. During the hunger strike, I often experienced cravings like this.

The tubular cells of your stomach lining come to life again and secrete gastrin into your bloodstream.

As the air began to warm, Nuwa's voice broke through the loudspeakers.

'Good morning, fellow students! The sun is rising to the glorious strains of the Internationale. This is the only broadcast station in the country that dares speak the truth. Our hunger strike is now on its sixth day. Who knows how many more hunger strikers will pass out today as we continue to fight for democracy and the future of our nation . . .'

I sat up and saw that my backpack was now buried under a pile of clothes, blankets and quilts that Beijing residents had brought for the students. Nuwa sounded as though she'd just woken up as well. Her voice was frail and husky.

I must have nodded off for about an hour.

There were four thousand hunger strikers camping in the Square now, together with tens of thousands of other students. Sleeping bodies, blankets, red banners and flags stretched far into the distance. Newspapers and cardboard boxes drenched in the night's rain lay sodden on the concrete paving stones. This must have been the largest mass hunger strike in history. The scene before me didn't look real. The students resembled extras lying on a film set, waiting for the cameras to start rolling.

Tian Yi was still in hospital. Although she'd regained consciousness and her condition was stable, the doctors wanted her to stay another day. The nurse, Wen Niao, and I had been up all night escorting sick hunger strikers to hospital.

Wen Niao said the fasters were driven by revolutionary zeal, and that this was dangerous. She feared that, if the strike continued any longer, it would become hard to stop, and many students would die. I told her the Communist leaders were wolves and didn't give a damn whether we lived or died.

I called over Zhang Jie, Mao Da, Big Chan and Little Chan, and set off with them for the morning inspection of our hunger strike camp. The Red Cross had advised us to check the fasters regularly. We discovered that seven students among the sleeping crowd had lost consciousness. Chen Di was delirious. His eyes kept rolling back. We put the sick students on stretchers and carried them to the ambulance parked next to the emergency tent.

'A student from Southern University has fallen into a coma,' said Mao Da, spreading his coat on the ground and lying down on it. 'His satchel and glasses are still on my bunk back in our dorm. He left them there for me to look after.'

'It can't be my old friend Tang Guoxian,' I said. 'He only joined the strike a couple of days ago.' I'd seen Tang Guoxian the day before. Wang Fei and I had tried to persuade him to give up his fast and help us with our work. We told him it was important that more students from the provinces became involved in the running of the Square.

'The marshals have been on duty all night,' Mao Da said, his eyes closed. 'Someone should go and give them some food.'

Old Fu's voice came over the loudspeakers. 'Another hunger striker has fainted. Clear a path for the medics.'

Then Nuwa's voice broke through again. 'Han Dan is about to chair an emergency meeting beside the black hunger strike banner. Can every university send a representative . . . Now I'd like to read out a letter we've received from some men who signed themselves "young generals of the Republic". "Dear students, your courageous actions have made the Chinese race proud. You're the most admirable people in the history of modern China. We would like to wish you all . . ."'

'Have you heard any news about Dong Rong and Liu Gang?' I asked Zhang Jie. They'd both been taken to hospital the previous night.

'No. Xiao Li is the only hunger striker from our dorm who's still in the Square. He passed out once, but he's carrying on with the fast.' Zhang Jie had an army water bottle hanging from his neck. Back in our dorm, he always had his nose in a book and hardly exchanged a word with anyone. But since the hunger strike, he'd begun to show more concern for others.

'Let's go back to the camp,' said Mao Da, standing up and patting the dust off his coat. 'I expect hunger strikers will be fainting every five minutes today.'

Dr Li, a surgeon at Beijing University hospital, ran over and shouted, 'Student marshals, go and protect the hunger strikers! They're being dragged away!'

'What's going on?' I said, standing up.

'Those guys from the Red Cross – there, in the orange vests – are trying to drag the hunger strikers off the Square. It's some kind of government ruse.'

I grabbed my megaphone and shouted, 'Student marshals! Form a tight circle around the hunger strikers and don't let any outsiders get to them!' We then headed for the guys in orange vests.

One of them walked towards me. 'Don't move,' I shouted. 'I'm in charge of security here.'

'We're from the Red Cross,' he said. He had a flat nose and spoke with a nasal twang.

'The Red Cross don't wear orange vests,' Zhang Jie said.

'We'll take them off, if you want. Are you just going to watch your classmates die, and do nothing to help them?'

'What do mean, do nothing?' Dr Li said. 'We've given them mattresses and blankets. We've moved the weakest ones into those shelters. We've cooled the ground with water and blocks of ice, and we've got medics on hand to keep watch over them day and night.'

'This is the hunger strike camp,' I said. 'Unless there's an emergency, no outsiders are allowed in.'

'We've come here to help the students,' the man said loudly.

Big Chan stepped forward. 'If you want to get involved with the emergency care work, go to the Monument and discuss it with the commander-in-chief of the Hunger Strike Headquarters.'

'We can't gain access to the Monument! You need a pass to get onto the lower terrace, but they're only issued on the upper terrace,' the man grumbled, then walked off in a huff.

I realised I'd forgotten to tell the student marshals that although Wang Fei had issued new passes giving members of the Hunger Strike Headquarters access to the Monument, the original passes Ke Xi had produced for the Beijing Students' Federation were still valid. I decided to go to the broadcast station and make an announcement.

When I entered the tent, I heard Han Dan say that the guys in orange vests were in fact medical researchers from the Ministry of Health, and not government agents as we'd assumed. Apparently everyone in their office had wanted to come to the Square to help care for the hunger strikers, so in the end they were forced to draw lots. They'd spoken with Lin Lu and advised him to bring public buses into the Square to protect the hunger strikers from the rainstorm forecast for the afternoon. But Old Fu had opposed the idea. He was afraid that if we moved the hunger strikers into the buses, someone might drive them away. I said it was a good proposal, and pointed out that if we wanted to stop the buses being driven away, we just had to deflate the tyres.

While you vegetate, your neurons race around, removing clots and dead cells, trying to clean the rusty networks of your brain.

A couple of hours later, Wang Fei and I went to a Beijing duck restaurant in the Qianmen district just south of the Square. Sun Chunlin, who was only in Beijing for three days, was hosting a lunch for our Southern University gang. He'd made a fortune from the road construction company in Shenzhen. Now he'd started a trading company and bought a villa by the sea in Shekou, next to the holiday mansion of the film actress Liu Xiaoqing.

Next to me was Ge You, a scrawny little guy who was always the last to get a joke. At Southern University he struck me as gauche, but he seemed a bit more confident now. He'd moved to Shenzhen after graduation and found a well-paid job in a tea company.

Sun Chunlin was talking to him. 'My uncle has just been appointed director of the Shenzhen Transport Bureau,' he said. 'I can use my connection with him to win a contract to build a twenty-kilometre stretch of road. If you join forces with me, I guarantee you'll be a millionaire within two years.'

'Really?' Ge You said, his eyes lighting up.

Tang Guoxian arrived with Wu Bin and helped himself to a duck pancake.

'I thought you were still on hunger strike,' I said.

'I'm the group leader,' he answered. 'If I carry on with the fast any longer, I won't have the energy to look after everyone.' He'd brought a group of five hundred students from Guangdong Province to join the hunger strike in Beijing.

Wang Fei took off his glasses and glared at Ge You and Sun Chunlin. 'You Shenzhen crooks!' he shouted. 'The whole reason we've been starving ourselves to death is to sweep away corrupt scum like you!'

'Don't pretend you've been on hunger strike!' Tang Guoxian sneered. 'I bet you couldn't even give up fags for an hour.'

Wu Bin had aged a lot since I'd last seen him. He had a goatee now, and his triangular eyes were less bright. He was halfway through his research fellowship at Wuhan College of Engineering. He'd arrived in Beijing that morning after Wang Fei had sent him a telegram urging him to join our movement.

The restaurant was full. The waitresses poured out tea for everyone. As soon as they heard I was a Beijing University student, they asked for my autograph. After I told them that Wang Fei was head of the Square's propaganda office, a crowd gathered round, offering him cigarettes and shaking his hand. In this new job, he was being pestered day and night by students wanting to make suggestions about the direction our movement should take.

'I have a great idea!' said Wang Fei, enjoying the attention he was receiving. 'I think our little gang here should establish a national student association.'

'I hear you've hooked up with a girl who's studying English,' Sun Chunlin said to him. 'What's she thinking of, going out with a peasant like you?'

'Fuck off!' Wang Fei spat. He'd asked Nuwa to join us for lunch, but she'd refused. They hadn't spoken for several days.

'Some Shanghai students talked to our group yesterday about forming a national association,' said Tang Guoxian. He grabbed a chicken wing from the dish that had just arrived. 'God, I'm starving! I'm not going on another fucking hunger strike for as long as I live.' He punched the table excitedly, just as he used to punch the walls of our dorm.

'Yes, if we want to seize power, we must do it now,' Wu Bin said, taking three long gulps from a beer glass.

'You haven't changed – still drinking from other people's glasses!' said Ge You, snatching his glass back.

'You've been going out with that girl for a year now, and I still haven't met her,' Sun Chunlin said to me. 'I hear she looks like A-Mei. How could you allow her to join the hunger strike?'

'She looks nothing like A-Mei,' I said, then wondered to myself whether they did in fact look alike. It had never occurred to me before.

'I bumped into an old dorm mate of A-Mei's on a student march in Guangzhou,' Tang Guoxian said. 'Shi Ye, I think her name was. She's studying at Guangzhou Teachers' College now. She's planning to come up to Beijing soon.'

'What, that short girl with glasses?' I said. After A-Mei broke up with me, I visited Shi Ye several times to see if there was news from her. A-Mei had asked her to post her belongings back to Hong Kong and forward the refund of her university fees.

'The Beijing Students' Federation wants to set up a national association as well,' Wang Fei said. 'We must keep our distance from them, and do our own thing.'

A young man walked over and asked Wang Fei to recommend some books to read, explaining that although he hadn't managed to get into university, he still wanted to improve himself. Wang Fei thought for a while, then wrote on a paper napkin *Jean-Christophe* by Romain Rolland and *The Confessions* by Jean-Jacques Rousseau.

Sun Chunlin tapped his cigarette on the rim of the glass ashtray, and everyone's eyes were immediately drawn to the gold Rolex on his wrist.

'If you'd had that watch when we were dorm mates, I would have nicked it and never given it back,' Wu Bin muttered. I remembered him blabbering on about Nazi gas chambers when we were at Southern University.

'It's not a fake,' I said, examining the watch more closely. 'It's a real Rolex.'

'How long has Mou Sen been on hunger strike?' Ge You asked, turning to me.

Suddenly the voice of a female newsreader rose above the hubbub in the restaurant. A waitress had turned up the volume of the television in the corner. 'Today, in the Great Hall of the People, Premier Li Peng and other top leaders met with representatives of the student hunger strikers: Ke Xi, Han Dan, Shao Jian . . .'

Everyone stood up and stared at the television screen in silence.

Li Peng was sitting stiffly on a red sofa, addressing the students in a stern and resolute voice. 'The government has never said that the broad masses of the students are creating turmoil. We have never said that. We have unanimously praised the students' patriotic fervour. Many of the complaints they have made are justified, and we are working hard to solve them. So the students' efforts have been positive. Nevertheless, events have taken a course of their own. Disorder has broken out in Beijing, and it is spreading to the rest of the country. Beijing is in a state of anarchy. The government cannot ignore the situation. We must protect the students and the socialist system. Factory workers, employees of government organisations and urban residents have gone to Tiananmen Square to encourage the students to continue their hunger strike. I do not approve of their actions . . .'

The next shot was of Ke Xi, still in his striped hospital pyjamas, upbraiding Li Peng. 'I thought there was no need to go over this again, but it seems that you still don't understand. So I will repeat once more: we will only leave the Square on condition that the slanderous 26 April editorial is revoked and the government engages with us in an immediate, open, equal, direct and sincere dialogue. If these demands aren't met . . .'

The newsreader then announced that the dialogue came to an end without any issues being resolved.

Loud debates erupted all over the restaurant. This was the first time in the forty-year history of the Chinese Republic that government leaders had engaged in a televised debate with a group of ordinary citizens. Everyone was astounded. The waitresses were so taken aback, they didn't bother to remove the empty plates on our table or bring us the remaining dishes we'd ordered.

'Ke Xi was very brave talking back to the Premier like that!' one of the waitresses said, jumping on the spot with excitement. 'It was amazing!'

'Bloody hell!' Wang Fei mumbled sullenly, 'Ke Xi's stolen the limelight. I knew I should have joined the hunger strike!'

'You students have really got guts, demanding to sit down with the government leaders as equals like that!' two customers shouted at us from across the room.

'Let's give a toast to the students!' customers on other tables said, raising their glasses. I quickly grabbed a glass and poured some orange juice into it. Everyone cheered and laughed, then gradually quietened down again.

We immediately started picking over the details of the broadcast.

Wu Bin rubbed his small goatee. 'Did you hear what Li Peng said at the beginning? He categorically stated that the students aren't creating turmoil! That's a big concession.'

'He's like a fox giving a New Year's greeting to some hens,' Tang Guoxian said, removing his shirt. 'Don't take his words at face value.' He'd clearly been keeping up his marathon training in the last three years. His chest muscles looked twice as large as mine.

'We must set up a national student association at once,' Wang Fei said, taking a deep drag from his cigarette. 'We here around this table will constitute its organising committee. If we're to have any impact, we must act now.'

'All right, I agree,' Tang Guoxian said. 'I can represent the Guangdong students, but who will represent the other provinces? The Beijing students won't want to join us, so I think we should call ourselves the Provincial Students' Federation.'

'I wouldn't make a good leader,' Wu Bin said. 'I hate giving speeches.'

'Well don't start having any regrets when others take over the leadership,' Sun Chunlin said.

'What will our relationship be to the Beijing Students' Federation?' I asked. 'I suppose they should be taking orders from us, since we're a national organisation.' I longed to go back to the campus and have a proper rest.

'Of course they'll take orders from us,' Wang Fei said, nodding his head confidently. I'd clipped his hair before we'd left the Square, but it was still uneven in patches.

'What financial resources do we have?' Ge You asked. 'It costs money to run an organisation.'

'I'd like to be the first to come forward and make a personal donation of a thousand yuan,' Sun Chunlin exclaimed loudly.

'I'll put out some donation boxes, and we'll soon have money rolling in,' I said. 'The Beijing Students' Federation's new finance office has collected hundreds of thousands of yuan already. Last week, they were so poor they couldn't afford to print any pamphlets and had to borrow money from the Hunger Strike Headquarters.'

'If we mobilise the students in the provinces and get the protests to spread through the country, this will become the most important student movement in China's history,' Wang Fei said excitedly. 'We'll establish our headquarters in the Square.'

'More students from Tianjin and Hunan Province turned up today,' Tang Guoxian said. 'It's like the Great Link-Up movement during the Cultural Revolution, when the Red Guards travelled around the country, exchanging revolutionary experiences.'

'I'll give each committee member twenty yuan to cover two days' living expenses,' Wang Fei said. 'After that, we'll have to live off donations.'

'That wouldn't even buy me a packet of fags,' Tang Guoxian moaned.

'The Beijing transport authorities have sent some buses to protect the hunger strikers from the rain, but there will only be fifty, instead of the eighty they promised,' I said. 'We can't stay in the Square for ever, you know.' I kept remembering Wen Niao warning me that if we remained in the Square any longer, epidemics would break out.

'I have to admit, I'm still not clear what the movement's goals are,' Wu Bin said, drumming his feet under the table.

'The goal of this movement is to strengthen our nation,' I said off the top of my head. 'Do you think America would be as powerful as it is today if it weren't a democratic country?'

'When General Secretary Zhao Ziyang met with Gorbachev, he confirmed that Deng Xiaoping is still China's paramount leader,' Wu Bin said. 'As Chairman of the Central Military Commission, Deng controls the army. And whoever controls the army, controls the nation. So shouldn't the first goal of this movement be to remove this power from Deng's hands?'

'I thought Deng Xiaoping resigned from that post,' Tang Guoxian said.

'That turned out to be a false rumour,' I said. Earlier that day, Sister Gao had received inside information that Deng Xiaoping was still very much in charge.

'I feel terrible stuffing my face like this while thousands of people are starving themselves in the Square,' Tang Guoxian said. 'Don't order any more food.'

I too felt uncomfortable. I wanted to get back to the Square. 'It's going to rain soon,' I said. 'We must move the hunger strikers into the buses.'

'What for? Where are you driving them to?' Wu Bin said, looking confused.

'I told you, the buses have parked in the Square to shelter the hunger strikers from the rain.' It occurred to me that Tian Yi might have returned to the Square by now and rejoined the hunger strike, which made me even more eager to get back.

'Apparently lots of the students have refused to board them,' Wang Fei said.

'We'll have to talk them round, then!' Tang Guoxian said imperiously, having eaten his fill. 'When the rainstorm hits this afternoon, the Square will be flooded. Let's go back and get some representatives from the provincial universities to join our association. Come on!'

You drift onwards through your cerebellum, weaving through the scaffold of a billion star-shaped glial cells.

'The police called me into the station this morning,' my mother says. 'They said that, if I promise not to speak to any foreign journalists or tell anyone about my son's injury, I can apply for a hardship allowance.'

She has three visitors today: Zhu Mei, who came round last week, An Qi, and another woman whose voice I don't recognise. All three of them have joined the 'Tiananmen Mothers', an underground group founded by a professor called Ding Zilin whose seventeen-year-old son was killed in the crackdown.

Zhu Mei has brought a box of hairtail fish. My mother is very pleased to have some fish. She seldom gets a chance to go to the market.

'How much will they give you?' asks An Qi.

'About ninety yuan a month,' my mother shouts from the kitchen as she drops the hairtail fish into a wok of hot oil. 'It will only cover two days' worth of his intravenous solution.'

'They gave me a one-off payment of two hundred yuan after my husband was shot,' Zhu Mei squeaks in her high-pitched voice. 'They said that now he's dead, I shouldn't speak about him again.'

A man and a woman are walking up the stairwell. I listen to the click of the woman's heels and the dull thump of the man's rubber soles as they hit the concrete steps. I'm terrified the police might turn up and discover my mother talking to these women.

'We've now found seventeen people who are prepared to state they lost relatives during the crackdown. Professor Ding said that we should submit a joint letter to the government demanding a public account of the killings.' This woman has never visited before. She sounds as though she's in her early thirties, and speaks in the breathy, monotone drone typical of bereaved women.

'Our local police aren't too bad,' An Qi says. 'They said that the government should have better things to do than pick on people like us. They advised us to move to a different town, somewhere no one will recognise us.'

'Don't be duped,' my mother says, coming in from the kitchen. 'Your personal files will follow you wherever you go.' The charred smell of the noodles she burned last night still wafts from her hair.

'Professor Ding wasn't allowed to attend the United Nations conference on human rights,' An Qi says. 'But the written statement she submitted at least exposed the suffering that relatives of the dead have endured.'

'My son's still alive,' my mother reminds them.

'So is my husband,' says An Qi. 'But that's no reason not to get involved.'

'Professor Ding sounds like a very brave woman,' my mother says. 'I should pay her a visit. Is that the list you've drawn up of people killed during the crackdown? How many names have you got?'

'One hundred and fifty-two,' the young woman says. 'The eldest victim was fifty-six, the youngest was only nine.'

'I can't see a thing without my glasses,' my mother mutters. 'Look how dry my hands are! I must rub some more Vaseline on them. Spring Festival's coming up soon. I wanted to repaint the walls and tidy the flat up a little.'

'Have we got a photocopy of the list?'

'I don't need one,' An Qi says. 'I've memorised every name, so even if the police confiscate the list from me, I'll still have a copy of it in my mind.'

'Huh, we're just a few middle-aged women. What can we hope to achieve?'

'Well, China lost its Olympic bid because of its human rights record. That shows our appeals haven't gone unheard . . .'

Memories spiral around me, sometimes crossing paths, sometimes colliding. I picture the dusty string of garlic hanging from a peg on the kitchen door; my father squatting down beside a washbowl, rubbing his bare legs with a wet cloth; a swathe of fallen bicycles sparkling in the sun like a field of wheat. The images float off into the air that is filling with greasy fumes and the smell of fried fish. Perhaps today is the day that my brain will stop thinking and my life will at last come to an end.

You want to climb onto the back of the Yingzhao beast – that winged horse with a human face – and fly through the Emperor of Heaven's grasslands.

Our broadcast station tent looked like an earthquake shelter. In the early afternoon, the sun beat down from overhead, and it became so hot and stuffy inside that everyone's faces turned scarlet. A heavy stench of diesel from the generator hung in the humid air, together with a faint scent of seaweed wafting from the box of sushi a Japanese woman had given us. The sushi was delicious. Although I was still full from lunch at the Beijing duck restaurant, I managed to gobble down five or six pieces. The rule about not eating in the Square seemed to have been abandoned.

Everyone was busy sorting out pamphlets and writing news scripts. I spotted Old Fu lying asleep on the ground with a cardboard sign around his neck that said COMMANDER-IN-CHIEF OF THE HUNGER STRIKE HEADQUARTERS.

'So you're back in charge, are you?' I laughed, leaning down and waking him up.

'Bai Ling's been rushed to hospital again. I had to take over the reins.'

'Lin Lu is Bai Ling's deputy, so surely he should have taken over,' I said, lighting a cigarette. 'And by the way, why didn't you and Mou Sen go to that televised meeting with Li Peng?'

'Neither of us were around when the officials came to collect the student leaders,' he said.

'There are rumours flying about that lots of the cash that's been donated has gone missing,' I said.

'Yes, it's a big problem. I'm only going to hand out money for food from now on. We must wait until we have a proper accounting system set up before we give money for anything else.' Old Fu sat up and stared at his feet.

Chen Di, who was sitting next to him, said, 'We'll need to buy some more broadcast equipment.' He'd given up his hunger strike, so he had more energy now to look through the scripts.

'There are donation boxes all over the Square, but the ones outside the two broadcast stations get most of the money,' I said. 'This place and the Beijing Students' Federation must have collected a million yuan by now.'

Mou Sen walked into the tent. 'It's no good,' he said. 'The militants are taking over. Lin Lu is reorganising the Square without bothering to consult the Beijing Students' Federation.' He'd been given a transfusion in the emergency tent. His left arm was red and swollen.

'I've just had lunch with our Southern University gang,' I told him. 'Wang Fei wants to set up a national student association.'

'That's a good idea,' Mou Sen said. 'We can't allow Lin Lu to monopolise things. He's behaving like a tyrant.'

'Wang Fei is a despot as well,' Chen Di said, filing away a script that had just been broadcast.

Nuwa walked out from behind the amplifiers. 'I wish you'd give up the hunger strike now,' she said, glancing at Mou Sen. 'There's no need to starve yourselves to death. The Beijing Medical Rescue Centre has told us that another five hundred hunger strikers have passed out. Most of them are suffering from diarrhoea and dehydration. I really think it's gone far enough now.' I was surprised she hadn't come to Wang Fei's defence after Chen Di had called him a despot.

'Broadcast that information at once,' Mou Sen said. 'If we don't, the Voice of Qinghua will, or the Voice of the Student Movement as they now call themselves.' Mou Sen was a very conscientious editor. He'd become much more cautious about what material he chose to air since he'd broadcast the false rumour about Deng Xiaoping's resignation.

'On the radio this morning it was reported that Zhao Ziyang and Li Peng visited some hunger strikers recovering in Xiehe Hospital,' I said.

'It appears the reformist wing and the hardliners are still engaged in a battle of strength.'

'Hey, Old Fu, there's a minibus parked over there,' Chen Di said, returning to the tent after popping outside briefly. 'I think it's been donated to the students. Shall I have it brought over here? It might be useful to us.'

'If we attach a loudspeaker to the roof, we could drive it around the Square and make broadcasts from it,' said Mao Da.

'Are you sure it's not one of the buses Lin Lu brought into the Square?' I asked. Lin Lu and Cheng Bing were still overseeing the arrival of the fifty public buses and getting them to park in neat rows along the north side of the Square.

'No, it's definitely a minibus,' Chen Di said.

'I'll go and take a look at it in a minute.' Old Fu stood up and straightened the cardboard sign hanging from his neck.

'We broadcast the intellectuals' 16 May Declaration, and now they've given us a 17 May Declaration,' Mou Sen moaned, glancing down at the document Nuwa had just passed him. 'We can't keep broadcasting this stuff, Old Fu.'

'Shut up!' Nuwa shouted at the noisy diesel generator that was banging away in the corner. 'No one can understand your peasant dialect. You make as much racket as that damn electric generator!'

'You don't seem to have any problem understanding Wang Fei's peasant accent!' Mou Sen said, smiling insolently.

'At least it's more intelligible than Yanyan's,' Nuwa said, having a dig at Mou Sen's girlfriend. Nuwa was wearing a short skirt. I could see the maze of fine capillaries under the skin of her thighs. As she walked through the tent, I watched her smooth knees wobble like the breasts concealed inside her bra, and glanced at her elegant calves that tapered softly towards her fine ankles and red leather shoes.

'This says "Down with Dictatorship!"' Old Fu said, reading the page that Mou Sen had just given him. 'I can't let that be broadcast.'

'It's too much!' Mou Sen cried, lighting another cigarette. 'We've had false rumours about Deng Xiaoping resigning, the government stepping down. We must vet the scripts carefully. Who knows what kind of rubbish will turn up next?' Then he looked at Nuwa and said, 'Have you noticed that whenever we broadcast a poem, the Voice of the Student Movement plays the Internationale? It's as though they're deliberately trying to drown us out.' Mou Sen had just been appointed the Beijing Students' Federation's deputy head of finance. All the expenses that Old Fu sanctioned now had to be approved by him and Sister Gao.

'You shouldn't smoke while you're on hunger strike,' said Nuwa, snatching the cigarette from Mou Sen's fingers. The short goatee he'd grown gave him the air of a scholar.

'I've never seen you try to stop Wang Fei smoking,' he laughed. Nuwa took something from her pocket and stuffed it into his mouth. I guessed it was a sweet or chocolate drop. Girls always carry little snacks around with them, and enjoy giving them to boys they like. I wondered whether she was having an affair with Mou Sen behind Wang Fei's back.

'Our tape of the national anthem is much more stirring than their Internationale,' Chen Di said. 'They can't defeat us. Hey, Mao Da's shouting to us. Let's go.' He pulled Old Fu to his feet and dragged him out of the tent.

I felt a wave of exhaustion sweep over me and went outside for some fresh air. As I stared at the two wooden school desks of the makeshift reception centre at the Square's north-east entrance, a Beijing resident walked up to me and said that her neighbour's daughter, who'd come to the Square to support the students, had been run over by a car on her way home. She wanted to appeal for donations to help pay for the girl's medical care. I wasn't sure whether she was telling the truth or not, so I didn't allow her into the broadcast station.

You watch the cerebrospinal fluid flow between the skull and the brain. The crooked microglia cells with quivering tails look like raindrops wriggling down branches of a tree.

I lay down on the ground, had a quick doze then returned to the tent.

'Look at all those buses parked out there,' Zhang Jie said as I walked in. 'That's Bai Ling's hard work.' He handed me the pile of paper he was holding. 'I've only been in this tent for ten minutes, and look how many reports and statements I've been given.' There was a tall girl standing next to him. I asked her what university she was from. She said she was a geology student, and had drawn a large map of the Square.

I told her I hadn't met many geology students before. She was holding the rolled-up map in her hand. She looked like an Overseas Chinese tourist in her baseball cap, brown sunglasses and clean, freshly ironed clothes. She'd just had a shower. We all looked dirty and dishevelled in comparison. Everyone crowded round her to look at the map she'd drawn.

'My name is Chuchu,' she said, taking off her grey windcheater, revealing a low-necked cotton blouse underneath. When she leaned down, the gold cross of her necklace dangled over the map. 'I thought that since this is a broadcast station, it must be the Square's command centre too. I'm leaving the country in a couple of days, and I wanted to give you the map before I left. I spent two days drawing it. Look, this is the Beijing University camp, and this is the lifeline for the ambulances.' She was taller than most of the boys in the tent.

'You've put in so much detail!' Mao Da said. 'It will be very useful to us when we need to reorganise the Square. We must make sure it doesn't fall into enemy hands.'

'Pu Wenhua drew a map, but this one's much more professional,' Wang Fei said, leaning over.

'But everything keeps changing,' I said. 'The buses have moved into this patch here, so this part needs to be redrawn.'

'The provincial students' camp won't be moving, and I was told that the finance office and propaganda office on the Monument are pretty stable too,' Chuchu said.

Big Chan patted Wang Fei's shoulder. 'This guy is the head of propaganda, and he's just told me he wants to move his office over to the Museum of Chinese History.'

Chuchu glanced at Wang Fei, who was considerably shorter than her, and continued, 'The map is of how things stand today. If there are any changes, you can amend it yourselves.'

'Which country are you off to?' Mou Sen asked, a note of envy creeping into his voice.

'England. I'm going to do a Master's at Manchester University.' Her face assumed the superior air of someone about to discover the excitement of foreign places.

'That's a great university, I think it's ranked number 8 in the UK,' Nuwa said, breaking into English. She didn't look at Chuchu when she spoke. She hadn't brushed her hair for several days, and was looking a bit scruffy.

'There's some important news here!' Hai Feng said, walking over with a newspaper in his hands. 'The official media have reported that Zhao Ziyang and Li Peng have visited some hunger strikers in hospital.' In his white tracksuit bottoms, he looked like a kid in summer camp.

'That's old news,' Old Fu said, wrinkling his nose. 'And anyway, if they'd wanted to speak to the hunger strikers, they should have come to the Square!'

'Still, it's a big concession for them to make,' Shao Jian said, having strolled calmly into the tent. His hair was neatly brushed. He looked as though he'd just stepped out of a hotel.

'You don't look like a hunger striker to me!' I joked.

'I'd like to see you give it a go,' he said, pointing to the needle prick on his swollen arm. 'I haven't eaten for five days.'

'There's a heavy rainstorm forecast for this afternoon,' I said. 'What are we going to do with all those boxes of supplies stacked outside?' I noticed that Chuchu looked a little crestfallen. Everyone had forgotten about her map.

'There's a long line of vans over there queuing up to deliver more supplies,' Big Chan said. 'Peasants from the suburbs have just given us a truckload of garlic and cucumbers, a food factory has donated a ton of sliced bread, and we've got four piles of woks over there.'

'It doesn't seem right to have these mountains of food here while the hunger strikers are starving themselves to death,' Little Chan said, looking up quizzically at Big Chan. They'd swapped watches with each other. The digital watch Little Chan was wearing had no night-light.

'Dai Wei, we've brought the minibus over,' Old Fu said. 'It's going to be our "broadcast minibus". I want you install a PA system. Spend whatever you need.'

'Don't worry, I'll do it,' Chen Di said, obviously thinking I wasn't up to the job. 'You stick to cutting hair, Dai Wei.'

'Well, let me know if you need any help,' I said, relieved to be absolved of the task.

Old Fu then turned to Hai Feng and told him to go back and tell Liu Gang and Shu Tong to move the Organising Committee to the Square and just leave a logistics office back at the campus. He'd forgotten that two days before he'd opposed the proposal to invite Shu Tong back to the Square.

'The weather's so hot now, our priority must be to prevent any outbreak of infectious diseases,' I said. Seeing that Chuchu was about to leave, I went over to her and said, 'Thank you so much for your map. I'm head of the student marshal team, so it will be especially useful to me.'

'It was no problem, I just wanted to help,' she said, turning to go. 'Goodbye, then.' She'd been standing on her own for ten minutes. Boys are always unwilling to speak to girls who are much taller than them.

As she left, a strong gust of wind suddenly blasted through the Square, sending plastic bags, magazines and paper boxes swirling into the air. The walls of the broadcast station's tent flapped up, and all the scripts and newspapers flew out. Our eyes became blinded by dust.

'My God!' Nuwa spluttered, crouching down in the corner of the tent. The canvas roof was bound to the bamboo frame with thick rope, and tied at both ends to the marble balustrades outside. I knew it wouldn't fall off.

'Damn, the rainstorm's about to arrive!' Chen Di shouted, pulling the blanket off the camp bed and flinging it over the electrical equipment.

'There are still a few hunger strikers lying outside, without shelter,' I said, helping to pick up the scripts scattered on the ground.

'I gave them umbrellas,' Old Fu said, squatting down and clutching his backpack. 'Dai Wei, muster your troops and go and make an inspection of our camp.'

'My marshals have gone to help Lin Lu get the rest of the hunger strikers to board the buses,' I said. 'The Beijing University hunger strikers moved into the buses a couple of hours ago.'

The wind was now howling. Zhang Jie and Mao Da staggered up with their hands over their noses and mouths. 'I thought we were getting eighty buses,' Zhang Jie shouted at Old Fu, 'but there are only fifty parked out there. Lin Lu wants you to go over and have a look.'

Hot gusts of dust swept through the Square, then the sky darkened and a torrential rain plummeted down. Half the tent's roof was lifted into the air and we were immediately drenched. Everyone squeezed into a corner, except Nuwa who hid under the plastic sheet covering the amplifiers. I watched the cardboard boxes of sliced bread outside collapse in the downpour. Cold, sodden students ran over to us, asking if we had umbrellas or raincoats.

When the rain began to seep through to the amplifiers under the plastic, we quickly unplugged them and shifted them onto the camp bed under the only remaining patch of roof. Then I moved the rest of the equipment over and began reconnecting the wires. Mou Sen told Nuwa to make an announcement. She grabbed the microphone for a second then decided instead to play 'The Five-Star Red Flag Flaps in the Wind' to ease the mood of crisis that had gripped the Square.

Although I had no umbrella, I decided to climb up the Monument to get a better view of the situation. I grasped a balustrade and pulled myself onto the lower terrace. The Square was enveloped in a thick grey haze of rain. I looked over to the fifty buses parked in neat rows to the north. The hunger strikers had rushed inside them as soon as the rain clouds had burst. Their abandoned camps looked like a huge empty car park now. Chairman Mao's portrait on Tiananmen Gate was a blur behind the sheets of falling rain.

The day before, I'd seen a Beijing resident march to the Square holding up a large photograph of Mao. He said he'd come to support the students. I asked him whether he knew of the Tiananmen Incident of 1976, when Mao sanctioned the use of force to quell a protest staged by tens of thousands of Beijing citizens against the Gang of Four. He said he'd never heard of the event. It wasn't his fault. For forty years, the Communist Party had worked hard at erasing history. If my father hadn't left behind his journal, I wouldn't have known the true horrors of the Anti-Rightist Campaign and the Cultural Revolution. No one is sure how many millions of people died under Mao's rule. Wang Fei told me that, after the madcap Great Leap Forward of 1958 to 1960, when Mao ordered peasants to abandon their fields and produce steel in small 'backyard' furnaces, twelve million people died of starvation in Sichuan Province alone.

At last the torrents stopped and the clouds were blown away by the wind. Water dripped from boxes, bags and plastic shelters. Newspapers, pamphlets, empty juice cartons, posters and banners floated on the shallow lake that covered the Square.

'Quick, broadcast an announcement telling everyone to clear up the rubbish that's floating about,' Cheng Bing said to Old Fu. Her hair was soaking wet. She looked very ill. I didn't know whether she was still on hunger strike or not.

'Do you have a script for me?' said Old Fu, treading through a puddle of ink-stained water. 'No? Well there's no dry paper here for me to write on. Why not ask a doctor from the emergency tent to make the announcement?'

Inside the tent, everyone was still busy sorting out the equipment. 'What a shame!' said Chen Di, scooping the map Chuchu had drawn for us out of a puddle. 'It's ruined before we even had a chance to use it.'

I had no dry clothes to change into, so I went to find Tang Guoxian, who was the same height as me, to see if I could borrow some from him.

When I returned to the tent, I suddenly remembered that I still hadn't sent a telegram to my brother who was on hunger strike in Sichuan, so I went in search of some students from his university to see if they had any news from him.

I walked up and down the maze of buses parked along the northern end of the Square. University banners started popping out again from the windows. The posters that had been stuck to the sides of the buses dripped their red and black ink onto the ground. Nurses in white coats were rushing back and forth, giving transfusions to sick students or carrying hunger strikers away on stretchers. Inside the buses, there was only enough room on the ground for three or four students to lie down. Most of the hunger strikers had to sit on the seats and rest their heads on each other's shoulders.

I finally tracked down some students from my brother's university. They'd got out of their bus and were preparing to climb up onto the roof. They hadn't been able to open their windows, and the stench inside had become unbearable. One of the guys knew my brother. He told me that Dai Ru had opposed the movement at the beginning, and hadn't even gone on the 4 May march. But since joining the hunger strike, he'd become one of their university's leading activists.

'I told Dai Ru not to join the movement,' I said. 'My mother only has two sons. If we both end up getting killed, there will be no one to look after her.'

'Your brother is a great orator,' the guy said. 'I heard his hunger strike speech.' He was wearing a white bandanna. The thick metal frames of his glasses flashed in the sunlight. The student standing next to him climbed into a cardboard box on which he'd written UNLOCK THE CHAINS OF TYRANNY. He stuck his head and arms out through holes he'd made on the top and sides then asked his friends to give him a leg-up onto the roof of the bus.

'That's hard to believe,' I said. 'He was always afraid of public speaking. By the way, the Provincial Students' Federation is going to be launched this afternoon. Make sure you send a representative.'

'That's good news. Students from the provinces have a hard time here. We keep having to beg the Beijing students for handouts. It's about time we set up our own organisation.'

'What do you think about this hunger strike?' I asked. 'Are you nervous it might provoke the government into using violence?'

The boy offered me a cigarette, took a puff of his own and said, 'The government won't dare use force. We've got the whole country behind us. Everyone wants democracy.'

'It's precisely because everyone wants democracy that the government will crack down on us,' I said. I walked away then glanced back at him and said, 'You shouldn't smoke when you're on hunger strike.'

After a long search, I eventually found Tian Yi. She was lying asleep on the floor of a bus next to Mimi, a folded quilt propping up her head and a drip attached to her arm. She looked contented. Not wanting to disturb her, I tiptoed away and returned to the Monument.

The cells of the pituitary gland at the base of your brain look like human bones scattered across a field.

After the downpour, the air smelt rancid. I was relieved that Tian Yi was safely hidden away in one of the buses.

In the distance, I spotted three girls from Hong Kong walking into the hunger strike camp with big red banners. Their hair was immaculately brushed, just as A-Mei's used to be. A pack of journalists waded through the puddles and photographed them as they passed.

I climbed to the upper terrace of the Monument. It was spotless. I assumed the rain had washed everything away. Then Shu Tong appeared and told me he'd got his student marshals to clean it up. He'd come to the Square to set up the Organising Committee's Tiananmen office.

Up until now, the Monument had been the territory of the Beijing Students' Federation and the Hunger Strike Headquarters. You needed a pass to get through the ring of student marshals guarding the base, another document to enter the lower terrace, and to gain access to the upper terrace, you had to have a special pass personally signed by Bai Ling, Lin Lu, Ke Xi or Han Dan. Despite this tight control, the terraces were usually filled with people.

But they were empty now, and there wasn't a speck of rubbish on the ground. Shu Tong ordered his student marshals to stand round the perimeter and link arms.

'It all looks so well organised now,' I said.

'You should have got this place cleaned up ages ago,' Shu Tong grumbled.

'I can only give orders to Beijing University students,' I said. 'No one else will listen to me. Students have flooded here from all over the country. It's a national gathering of vagrants!' I saw a banner in the distance that said GOD HAS DECREED THAT LI PENG SHOULD DIE! 'Look at that,' I said, pointing at it. 'Don't you think it's a bit extreme? We're pushing ourselves into a corner.'

'I thought you were one of the radicals, Dai Wei,' Shu Tong said. 'Why have you become so cautious? The hunger strikers have put their lives on the line. It's only natural that they should want to raise the stakes.'

'I thought you opposed the strike,' I said, feeling that it was he who had changed, not me.

'One must learn to adapt to evolving circumstances,' he said as we walked down to the lower terrace. 'The Square has become a battle zone. If Beijing University's Organising Committee doesn't get involved in the management, it will become marginalised from the movement.'

'How come you weren't at today's televised meeting with Li Peng?'

Before he had a chance to reply, Nuwa's distinctive alto voice poured through the loudspeakers: 'Everyone's shoes are drenched. If someone could get a batch of dry shoes and bring them to the broadcast station, we'd be very grateful . . .'

'Are you thinking of going back to the campus, then?' Shu Tong asked.

'I can't, not as long as Tian Yi is still here.' We walked down the second flight of steps and pushed our way through the security cordon at the base of the Monument.

'Beijing University students mustn't relinquish control of the Square,' said Shu Tong. 'Zhuzi has formed a secret action group with second and third echelon commanders who can take over from us in the event of our arrest.'

'Did you know that Wang Fei has set up a Provincial Students' Federation? He's already taken a group of his members to the Zhongnanhai government compound. He says the compound's a paper tiger, and that they should be able to storm inside quite easily.' I felt it was my duty to inform Shu Tong about these developments.

'Provincial students can't start trying to take control like that. Tell Wang Fei to stop all these dramatics and do something useful for once.' Then he patted me on the shoulder and walked off.

It was getting dark. I noticed that all the students entering the Voice of the Student Movement tent were wearing white T-shirts with the words BROADCAST STATION written in black pen. The sign hanging outside their entrance looked more professional than ours.

One of the three Hong Kong girls was inside the tent delivering a speech in Cantonese. 'The Hong Kong Student Association sent us here to convey our territory's support for your movement. We've been collecting donations from all over Hong Kong, and we've brought this money with us today, hoping that it will assist you. Tonight, as a show of solidarity, the three of us will join your hunger strike!'

The students outside who understood Cantonese shouted their appreciation. The girls' sharp intonations reminded me of when A-Mei would suddenly break into Cantonese when she was annoyed or excited, knowing I wouldn't understand much of what she said.

'Dai Wei, Chen Di needs you to connect the wires in the broadcast minibus,' said Lin Lu, walking up with a large group of students.

'Shu Tong's cleaned up the Monument,' I said. 'He wants to set up an office there.'

'I know, we moved out as soon as he arrived. We don't want to have to share that place with him.'

'You sort out the minibus – I'm not up to the job,' I said, then walked away sullenly. We were in danger of being arrested at any moment, but the student leaders were still caught up in petty, territorial fights.

A nuclear membrane caves in. The tubules lining the inner surface squirm like roundworms.

My room stinks of emulsion paint. Two workmen are sitting on the end of my bed having a fag. They're smoking the foreign '555' brand of cigarettes. My mother is having the flat redecorated so that it will look at its best for Spring Festival.

The window is open. The cold breeze that drifts in is tinged with the smell of stale gunpowder from the firecrackers that were let off last night.

'. . . So do you think they'll get nicked?'

'Depends what kind of backdoor connections they've got. That guy Zhang has a cellphone, so he can't be short of cash, but he still got flung in jail.'

'Wang's got two bank accounts. I'm sure he'll let us hide our cash in one of them . . .'

The sky outside the window is probably pale grey. The light beyond my eyelids was mauve this morning, but it's white now, and the room feels less oppressive.

The paint dripping from the ceiling has seeped through the sheets of newspaper the decorators have spread over me, and has soaked into the quilt underneath as well.

'So is this guy dead or not?'

'Look at this hand! It's just skin and bone. Those veins look like worms.'

'A vegetable – that's what they call people like this. His brain stopped working years ago. He just lies here like a plank of wood, with his eyes closed. He's still breathing, though.'

'I came up here once when I was a kid and asked if he'd let his brother play football with me, but he wouldn't. He sent him off to the market instead to queue up for winter cabbages.'

I realise who this guy is now. He's the grandson of Granny Li, the old woman I had to watch being scalded to death by the Red Guards during the Cultural Revolution. He was in the same class as my brother.

'He was quite a cool kid, though. He got arrested by the police when he was fifteen. He had a fling with that girl Lulu who runs that chain of bookshops.'

'You mean the girl who was sent to the re-education-through-labour camp for having an affair with a foreigner?'

'Yeah. She knows a top official in a publishing house and has managed to wangle a printing licence from him. She'll make a fortune from that. She's married to a Hong Kong property developer. They've got a villa in Shenzhen. I bet they're millionaires!'

'He smells disgusting. Let's put this blanket over him. Once we've finished touching up that bit behind the wardrobe we can get out of here.'

So Lulu is now the wife of a Hong Kong property developer. I didn't know she was sent for re-education through labour. It must have been when I was at Southern University. Her name card is probably still in my wallet. After I met her in the Square, I called her up and arranged to have a meal with her at her restaurant, but a power struggle broke out in the broadcast station that night, and I was unable to go.

Only in the second of silence before death will you be able to circumvent the bullet wound in your head.

I opened my eyes and stared into the empty night sky. I'd asked permission to go back to the campus for a rest, but when the time had come for me to leave I'd been too tired to move, so I'd lain down on the ground and fallen asleep. It was probably the announcement that woke me up. A voice blared through the loudspeaker: 'At noon on 20 May, the workers of Beijing will launch a twenty-four-hour, city-wide strike . . .'

Nuwa had left the Square for a few hours, and a student from the Broadcasting Institute was filling in for her. She was sitting on the brown rug in the corner of the tent. Her skirt was quite short. She kept pulling its hem, trying to cover as much of her bare thighs as she could. After every couple of sentences she'd pause to wipe the sweat from her nose. Mr Zhao, the Central Television newsreader, had turned up to help out as well.

Han Dan's voice suddenly came over the Voice of the Student Movement's loudspeakers. 'This is Han Dan speaking. Please can the Beijing University students stop broadcasting, otherwise . . .'

'What?' Old Fu said, jumping to his feet. 'Whose side is he on now?'

'Go and talk to him,' Bai Ling said. 'We can't allow the Square to have two separate power centres.' She was sitting in the other corner of the tent with a drip attached to her arm.

'If they can broadcast then so can we,' I said, trying to force myself awake.

'Make an announcement telling our Organising Committee, the Hunger Strike Headquarters and the Beijing Students' Federation to come to our broadcast station immediately,' Old Fu said.

'Dai Wei, your mother's here!' Wang Fei shouted, walking in.

'What new organisation are you setting up now, Wang Fei?' Old Fu asked angrily.

'No, no, it's Ke Xi who's setting up all the secret groups,' Wang Fei lied. 'I'm just going around telling people about the camp meeting tomorrow morning.'

'Still arguing at this time of night!' Bai Ling grumbled.

'Where's Nuwa?' Wang Fei asked, having noticed the girl behind the microphone.

'She's gone back to the campus to get some sleep,' Chen Di said. He was writing numbers on the baseball caps we'd bought for our student marshal team.

I stepped outside and spotted my mother's permed hair. She looked very staid and conventional standing in the crowd of skinny young students. She was the first parent to dare venture over to the broadcast station.

'What are you doing here?' I said curtly.

'Do you realise what crime you're committing?' she said. 'You're attacking the Party and the socialist system.'

'Who told you that? Even Premier Li Peng himself said that we're not creating turmoil.'

'A handful of people are stirring up unrest in order to overthrow the government,' she said, glancing from left to right. 'You're being manipulated by a small band of evil conspirators!'

'There are no evil conspirators here. The government's spreading false rumours. Please go home.'

'Listen, I've come here to tell you something. Our opera company was sent a transcript of a government leader's speech. They're going to impose martial law in the next couple of days. You must come home with me. I've been punished once already for being the relative of a counter-revolutionary. I can't go through that hell again.'

'Look around you, Mum. It's not just me here. The whole of China has risen up. The law can't punish a crowd.'

'Your father used to say exactly the same thing. Why are you so like him?' My mother's eyes were red. I could tell that she hadn't been sleeping well.

Wang Fei and Old Fu peeped out of the tent to see what was going on. I felt embarrassed.

'Dai Wei, is Bai Ling here?' Shao Jian said, walking up.

'She's inside the tent.'

'Can you call your marshals over? We're going to have a meeting.'

Then Zhuzi came out and said, 'If you want to express your views, Auntie, go and speak to the students at the reception desk. We need to prepare for our meeting now.'

'How dare you speak to me like that!' my mother shouted. 'This is my son!' Her face looked as worn as an old grey flannel.

'I can't go home with you, Mum. Tian Yi has been on hunger strike . . .'

'What?'

'Don't worry, she's stopped now. But she's still very weak. If she feels better tomorrow, I promise we'll come and visit you.' I knew that if I told her Tian Yi was still fasting, she'd insist on seeing her.

'Do you know how much damage a hunger strike can do to the body? She probably won't be able to have children after this.'

The remark sent a wave of panic through me. 'I know, I know, I keep meaning to send Dai Ru a telegram telling him to stop . . .' I mumbled, and immediately regretted it.

'What? He's joined the hunger strike too? My God! Why didn't you tell me? What kind of brother are you? How could you let him do that? Do you want to see him die?' She grabbed my arm. 'You're coming home with me now. It's not enough for you to bring shame on this country, after all the Party has done for you. You want to drive your mother to an early grave as well!'

I peeled her hand away from my arm and said coldly, 'This is Tiananmen Square. There are hundreds of thousands of students and residents here, fighting for democracy. It's reckless of you to speak like this. Not even Premier Li Peng would dare turn up here and say what you just said.'

In the distance I could hear a huge crowd bellow, 'Sell the imperial crown, and the people will have food to eat. Get rid of official corruption, and the people will have beds to sleep on!' It was so dark now that it was hard to tell which part of the Square the noise was coming from.

'We'll come here every day until Deng Xiaoping resigns!' a group of factory workers shouted as they marched towards us. Behind them followed two buses, each one equipped with two loudspeakers. The crowd roared. It seemed as though everyone in the Square was crying out in unison. I'd become so accustomed to the noise and commotion that I often forgot what a vast multitude of people I was standing among.

Zhuzi pulled me away. My mother looked frightened. She muttered under her breath, 'You're not my son any more. If you're killed, don't expect me to come and collect your corpse.' Then she turned and left.

Her visit put me in a bad mood. It reminded me of all the times she'd scolded and hectored me when I was a child.

In the south-western corner of the Land Between the Seas lies Mount Shu. The Lord of Heaven has captured a murderer on this mountain. He has tied the man's hair and hands to a tree trunk, and put his left foot in chains.

I sent my student marshals back to the campus to rest and replaced them with a new batch of volunteers. Then I returned to the broadcast tent, drenched in sweat, hoping to crash out for a few hours. I'd been on my feet all night guarding the lifeline and felt I couldn't stand up a moment longer. I lay down and shut my eyes, but the bright light bulb hanging from the tent's ceiling and the constant screaming of ambulance sirens made it impossible for me to sleep.

'So you've been to the emergency tent again?' Mou Sen said to Old Fu, noticing the needle prick on his arm. Mou Sen had just woken up. His head was resting on my folded coat. He turned to me and whispered, 'I can't carry on any longer, Dai Wei. I'm going to have to concede defeat. I'm not as brave as your father was.'

'I don't think you've reached your limit yet,' I whispered back. I remembered the night he read my father's journal at Southern University. The stories had disgusted him so much, he was unable to touch his supper. He'd sworn that, from then on, he'd give up student politics and do whatever the Party asked. What horrified him the most was that, in order to stay alive, the starving prisoners had had to resort to eating the flesh of people they'd known.

'I went for a quick transfusion,' Old Fu said. He was very pale. Although it was four in the morning and the broadcasts had stopped, the tent was still busy. People were streaming in and out all the time, delivering news reports and passing on information.

'Go and see what's happening on the Monument,' I said. 'There was a coup in the Beijing Students' Federation a couple of hours ago. They tried to sack Fan Yuan, but he refused to step down. He has re-appointed himself chairman and is going to give a speech setting out his plan of action.'

Shu Tong hadn't returned to the Monument since he'd cleared it up. Various student groups had moved back onto it, and the place was a mess again.

'They'll all power-crazy,' Old Fu said, sitting down.

Wang Fei charged into the tent and yelled, 'General Secretary Zhao Ziyang is in the Square!'

'I don't believe it!' everyone cried. 'Where is he?'

'He's just about to leave. He's in that coach over there. Premier Li Peng is with him too.' Wang Fei hadn't had time to put his shoes on. He'd been sleeping on a camp bed in the propaganda office.

'Shut up, there's no time to waste,' Old Fu said in a panic. 'Quickly, go and see if anyone took notes or made a tape recording.'

'Apparently a student jotted down his speech, but someone grabbed his notebook and passed it around, and now no one can find it,' Wang Fei said.

'So what did he say?' Mou Sen asked, his eyebrows puckering as he hurriedly lit a cigarette.

'He said that he'd come too late and had let the students down. And he said: "We are old men, but you are still young. You must think of your futures."'

Xiao Li, who had just walked in, said, 'I was standing beside the coach just now. Someone shone a torch onto Zhao Ziyang's face, and I saw tears in his eyes. Apparently he pleaded with us to end the hunger strike.'

'Tears?' said Mou Sen, sweeping his hair back. 'I don't believe it. He's a war-hardened revolutionary. He wouldn't be crying over this!'

'It's very brave of him to come to the Square,' I said. 'We must end the strike at once. If we do as he asks, it will give him more clout.'

'How long did he stay?' Old Fu asked.

'About ten minutes,' Xiao Li said, sitting down. It was his sixth day on hunger strike. He'd passed out once, but looked as though he could carry on a little longer. He was in better shape than Mou Sen. I rose to my feet and felt a jabbing pain in the small of my back. Earlier that day, I'd pulled a muscle while unloading boxes of mineral water from a van.

'Get Han Dan, Bai Ling and Cheng Bing over here at once,' Old Fu said.

'It's a bit late in the night to make an announcement, Old Fu,' said Mou Sen, noticing him switching on the broadcasting equipment.

'I don't care,' he said. 'The students must be told about Zhao Ziyang's visit. It changes everything. Xiao Li, you'd better stop your hunger strike. I'll need you to help look after the equipment. We can't afford for anything to go wrong now.'

When Bai Ling, Han Dan and Cheng Bing arrived, we all went to the broadcast minibus to speak to Lin Lu. Xiao Li then turned up with a transcript of Zhao Ziyang's speech he'd managed to copy from someone's notebook.

Mou Sen began to read aloud with a cigarette dangling from his mouth. Han Dan coughed loudly and said, 'Put that fag out!' Mou Sen reluctantly crushed it out, then continued: '"If you don't end the hunger strike, the hardliners will win the Party's internal struggle and it will be the end of all of us . . ."'

Cheng Bing looked at Lin Lu and muttered despondently, 'When you saw Zhao Ziyang on television a couple of days ago, you said he was brimming with confidence.'

'It's clear that the reformers have lost the fight,' Lin Lu said gloomily. 'I suggest that all members of the Hunger Strike Headquarters stop their fast.'

'Well, I'm not giving up,' Han Dan said sullenly.

Bai Ling had developed a high fever. She arched her neck, letting her head rest on her shoulder.

'Fan Yuan was about to give his inaugural speech as chairman of the Beijing Students' Federation just now,' Han Dan said listlessly, 'but when he heard that Zhao Ziyang had come to the Square, he resigned and ran away in terror. He's so spineless.'

'We must adopt a new form of struggle,' Yang Tao said. I hadn't seen him for a couple of days. I presumed he'd been in hospital.

'If anyone from the Headquarters ends their hunger strike they must resign from their post,' Cheng Bing said adamantly.

'We are fasting for the sake of the Chinese people,' Bai Ling said. 'We can't let them down.'

'Hu Yaobang lost his job for sympathising with us in 1987, and if we don't do as Zhao Ziyang asks, he's going to be sacked as well,' I said.

'Three police trucks joined a student march yesterday,' Han Dan said. 'I'm worried that if we surrender now, before we've achieved our goals, many people who've come out to support us will get into trouble.'

'If we end the hunger strike, we can still stay in the Square and continue our struggle,' Mou Sen said.

'We could set up a rotation system, with each student fasting for just one day,' Bai Ling suggested, furrowing her brow. 'We mustn't let the hunger strike fizzle out.'

'The Square's in such a filthy mess now,' Old Fu said. 'After yesterday's rainstorm, it looked like a refugee camp.'

We continued to argue for a while until Lin Lu brought the discussion to a close and said that we should hold a plenary camp meeting in the morning.

Mou Sen went back to the tent to tell Chen Di and Nuwa to broadcast an announcement about Zhao Ziyang's visit. The loudspeakers on the broadcast minibus hadn't been correctly plugged in yet.

Seeing that the sky was getting lighter, I left the minibus and went to find Tian Yi. I wanted to tell her to end her strike and convince her that it wasn't worth sacrificing her life just to get this bloody government to sit down and talk to us.

Tian Yi moves through your parietal lobe like transparent threads of mould spreading across the surface of a dank pond.

The noise of the fireworks outside causes a memory to resurface. Suddenly I recall the night Tian Yi came to this room to say goodbye to me before she left for America. How could I have forgotten that visit? I knew it was her, the moment I heard her measured tread on the stairs. My mother opened the door and said, 'You're covered in snow, Tian Yi. Come in and take your coat off. I'll put it on the radiator for you.'

'No, don't,' Tian Yi said. 'It's a wool blend. It will shrink . . .'

Psychologists believe that memories too painful to deal with are pushed into the subconscious by the brain's self-defence mechanism. The information is never lost, it merely becomes inaccessible. But it seems more likely that my lapses in memory are due to my brain injury rather than repression.

'I've brought you a wall calendar with photographs of the South Pole,' Tian Yi said to my mother. 'It's this year's most popular calendar.'

'It's beautiful. But where can I hang it? There's no room left on this wall.'

'Look, you can put it up there, next to that Châteaux of Europe calendar.'

They sat down on the sofa with their cups of tea and grumbled about rising prices. Tian Yi then told my mother that many of my old classmates had got in touch with her to ask about me. She'd brought a list of their names and addresses.

'You remember Shao Jian?' she said. 'He works for a big Beijing internet company now. Mimi was in the same dorm as me. She's opened a beauty parlour. If you have any problems, just get in touch with them.'

'Yes, Shao Jian. He came here with another boy. Now, what was his name? I'm getting so forgetful. He told me he knew Professor Ding, the woman who set up Tiananmen Mothers.'

'That must have been Fan Yuan from the Politics and Law University. Did he leave you his phone number?'

'I don't think so. But here's Kenneth's number. When you see him, don't tell him about the police harassment I've had. And remind him not to mention politics in his letters. In fact, it would be best if he sent his letters to Dai Wei's brother rather than to me.'

Tian Yi cracked twenty-nine pumpkin seeds between her teeth. I counted them. I imagined the empty shells hidden in the folded palm of her hand.

I try to remember what happened next, but my thoughts return to the moment I heard her ascending the stairwell. When she reached the landing outside our flat, I heard a thump followed by a long silence. I presumed she'd bumped her head on the leg of the stool perched on the tall stack of charcoal briquettes, and was glancing up to see what she'd hit. The landing is crammed with things my mother can't bring herself to throw away. Everyone in the building keeps piles of scrap outside their front doors as well, but my mother's pile is the largest. A moment later, I heard Tian Yi cough then knock gently on the door . . . I've lost the sequence again. My mind is so jumbled, it's hard to untangle the threads. Since my memories of Tian Yi are quite recent, her image is floating in and out of focus in the central regions of my temporal lobes. But A-Mei has spread through the entire neural network of my cerebral cortex. I have thought about her so often these last years that she's even entered my bone marrow.

Now I remember how Tian Yi's visit ended.

'Could I have a few moments alone with Dai Wei, Auntie?' she asked. 'There are some things I want to tell him.'

'Yes, go in. I'll close the door for you.'

At last we were alone together. The room was hot. I could hear mucus collect inside her nostrils, and sensed she was about to cry.

'I have something to tell you, Dai Wei,' she said. 'I don't want you to wake up and not know what's happened. I'm leaving the country. I'm going to America. For four years, maybe longer . . . I've brought you a tape. It's Mahler's Second Symphony – the Resurrection. I hope you'll listen to it sometimes.'

I remembered we'd heard that piece on the radio. I'd told her I liked it and she'd made a note of its name in her diary. But I knew that if she'd played the tape, I probably wouldn't have recognised it.

She slipped her hand into mine. After a while, I felt it move. She'd held my hand on her previous visit, but my mother had been in the room at the time, so she'd kept her fingers still. But this time she moved her thumb, slowly rubbing it up the palm of my hand to the mound below my index finger.

'I may never see you again,' she said, 'but I will always think about you, and the times we spent together . . .' Although I was locked deep inside my body, her voice sounded crystal clear. She began to sob quietly.

'I'd always hoped we could go abroad together,' she continued. 'I never gave you a straight answer when you asked me to go to America with you, but I'd secretly made up my mind that if you went, I would go too. I don't know if I'll ever be able to love another man . . .'

I knew that this separation was final. Even if I did wake up from this coma, I'd be a different person from the one she knew.

'Fate brought us together and fate has torn us apart. If you wake up one day, it's possible you might not even know who I am . . .'

She didn't realise that the changes she'd caused to my neuronal synapses during our time together were irreversible and that I could never wipe her from my mind.

She placed her other hand over mine. Her fingers were cold.

I felt blood rush to my groin and my penis begin to harden. Unfortunately, Tian Yi didn't notice this sign of life.

'After that last time we made love, near the Great Wall, I fell pregnant. I kept the foetus inside me for five months. I only got rid of it after I was told there was little chance of you ever waking up from your coma. It was a girl. I'm so sorry, Dai Wei . . .'

Those words are still hovering in my temporal lobe. If I recall them a few more times, they will enter my long-term memory and become fixed in my mind for ever.

She left very abruptly. I seem to remember her placing her hand on my cheek. The skin on my face was still numb at the time, but my instincts told me that the slight pressure I sensed was her hand pressing down. Then I felt a second pressure. Perhaps it was her lips, because I could smell her breath this time. Her face was very close to mine when she whispered her last words to me: 'Take care of yourself, Dai Wei.'

'Auntie, do you have my three notebooks?' she asked as my mother walked into the room. 'I remember Dai Wei telling me he'd brought them back here.'

'Oh, yes, there is a bag somewhere,' my mother said, kneeling down and rummaging under my bed. 'He came back one night to drop it off. He told me there were private journals inside, and I wasn't to open it.'

I'd also put some of my books and clothes in the bag. I'd decided to move them out of my dorm in case I got arrested.

'Yes – these are the notebooks,' Tian Yi said. 'How sweet of him – he brought back my mirror and tapes as well. This illustrated edition of *The Book of Mountains and Seas* is his favourite book. If you have time, you should read him some passages from it. He loves hearing about all those strange and fabulous creatures . . .'

'Oh, here's the journal my husband left for him. I've been looking for it for years . . .'

Then Tian Yi left. Ever since she disappeared from my life, I've thought of her as a clay figurine that keeps watch over me and that will accompany me to my grave.

There are no maps to help you find a path of escape. The road you're following leads only to the garden beyond the void.

At noon, we gathered outside the broadcast station, still shaken by General Secretary Zhao Ziyang's visit the night before. The Square was as squalid and messy as a football stadium after a big match.

'Let's replace the hunger strike with a sit-in,' Yang Tao suggested, squatting down and wiping the sweat from his forehead. 'If the government uses the strategy of "catching the thief by blocking the escape routes", we'll simply counteract with the empty-fort strategy.'

'The lifeline has broken down again, Old Fu,' said Xiao Li, walking up. 'The ambulances can't get to the hunger strike camps.' He helped himself to some strawberries a resident had just given us. I was glad to see he'd stopped his hunger strike. I put some strawberries into my lunch box to give to Tian Yi later, in the hope that I could tempt her to eat again.

'If the hunger strikers refuse to give up their fast, we should move them over to the Monument and get the other students to form a protective ring around them,' Yang Tao said. 'That way, if the government sends the army in, we'll have time to carry them out of the Square.'

'Hurry up and make a decision.' I was growing faint from the heat.

'Who's supposed to decide?' Old Fu said, exasperated. 'The Hunger Strike Headquarters, the Beijing Students' Federation, or the Provincial Students' Federation?'

'We're all in this together,' Yang Tao said, with an impatient flick of his hand. 'We must unite and reach a common agreement.'

'When will the meeting start?' Pu Wenhua asked. Although no longer a member of the Headquarters' standing committee, he still attended their meetings as a non-voting delegate of the Agricultural College.

'As soon as everyone turns up,' said Old Fu. 'It will be held in the public bus Lin Lu has transformed into a mobile command centre. You should get some marshals to place a cordon around it, Dai Wei.'

'The meeting must be held in secret,' said Yang Tao. 'If the hunger strikers find out we're considering ending the fast, they might attack us. They won't want to see their efforts end in failure.' With his constant strategising, Yang Tao was living up to his reputation as a modern-day General Zhu Geliang.

'I doubt many representatives will turn up,' said Zhuzi. 'Everyone's so dispirited.'

A procession of Beijing citizens in sky-blue shirts marched into the Square, beating drums. The men at the front were chanting, 'If the officials won't listen to the people, they should resign from their jobs and sell sweet potatoes!' Another procession passed them shouting, 'We can live without food, but we can't live without freedom!' The crowds in the Square surged back and forth. The light flashing from people's spectacles and plastic sun visors, or from the metallic paint of their bicycles, shuddered in the air. The ground beneath my feet was shaking too.

While you lie inside your silent dreams, your memories press into your flesh like iron nails.

Over seventy university representatives turned up to the meeting. We checked their identity cards and let them into the command bus. Once Fan Yuan and Han Dan had squeezed in, there wasn't room for anyone else so I shut the door.

It was five in the afternoon already. We'd covered the windows of the bus with newspaper so that no one could see inside. A few late-comers banged on the door, but Mao Da told me not to open it.

Bai Ling, as commander-in-chief, briefed everyone on the current situation, but was almost immediately interrupted by Hai Feng, who shouted out to both carriages of the articulated bus, 'I've just come back from the United Front Department, and have some very reliable inside information: General Secretary Zhao Ziyang has resigned from his post, and the hardliners have resolved to launch a crackdown. I propose we end the hunger strike. It will wrong-foot the government, and make any imposition of martial law look unnecessary and unjust.'

'Please stick to the proper procedures,' Lin Lu said loudly. 'Bai Ling hasn't finished her speech.'

Chen Di whispered to me, 'Lin Lu is so stiff and po-faced. I wouldn't be surprised if he was a government agent.'

Strong sunlight poured through the sheets of newspaper stuck to the windows, making the dark corners of the bus look even darker.

'I must remind everyone that this discussion is top secret,' Old Fu interrupted. 'If the students out there knew what we're planning, mayhem would break out and people would lose their lives.'

Liu Gang chipped in, determined to have his say. Over the previous couple of weeks, he'd been pushed to the sidelines of the movement he'd helped instigate. 'In 1976, Beijing citizens came to the Square to mourn the death of Premier Zhou Enlai,' he said, 'but we've dared come here to call for freedom and democracy. We've raised the nation's consciousness, which is what we set out to do, so we can now return to our campuses in triumph.'

'We've managed to get the people on our side,' Tang Guoxian said loudly. 'If we stop the hunger strike now, that support will crumble.' Since he'd set up the Provincial Students' Federation with Wang Fei and Yang Tao he'd assumed a new air of authority.

'If anyone dies, history will not forgive us,' Bai Ling said softly. 'We must ensure no one comes to harm.' Her voice was so quiet that most people couldn't hear what she was saying.

'You launched this hunger strike, Bai Ling, and now you want to end it,' Wang Fei said, tapping his megaphone. 'Is this all just a game to you?'

'The hunger strike will not end until every last hunger striker has passed out,' Mou Sen declared, staring at the dark end of the carriage.

'Or we could end it on Day Ten,' Shao Jian said, not wanting to concede defeat either. 'If we stop it now, the hunger strikers will feel betrayed.'

'Are you going to prolong the strike until every reformer in the government has been sacked?' said Sister Gao. 'We must end the hunger strike immediately and replace it with a sit-in. There will be 200,000 PLA soldiers turning up here soon, and we'll need to defend ourselves.' She lifted her arm to her face and coughed into her sleeve.

'As it happens, Han Dan, Ke Xi and I have ended our fast,' Cheng Bing confessed. 'We had some noodles in the canteen of the United Front Department a couple of hours ago.'

Everyone fell silent. The bus reeked of sweat and antiseptic. Occasionally, a beam of light shone through a gap between the sheets of newspaper and fell onto a NO SMOKING sign, a square of the yellow-painted interior walls of the carriage or a patch of someone's brown skin.

'You dared stop your hunger strike before the government has agreed to our demands?' Pu Wenhua said petulantly. 'How could you, after everything we've been through?'

'The hunger strikers from the Central Academy of Drama are refusing liquids,' Shao Jian said. 'I caught a glimpse of them through a gap in the crowd. All I could see were eight pairs of bare feet, lying completely still.'

'We're not cowards,' Lin Lu said. 'If the majority of students supported the strike, we would too. But the truth is, they don't.' Outside the bus, people were shouting and jeering.

'Students have flooded here from all over the country,' Wu Bin said. 'But they didn't realise that once they step into the Square, there's no way out.'

'We must take control of the situation and come to a decision, or people will die,' Old Fu said.

'I hereby announce that from now on, I will stop drinking fluids,' Pu Wenhua said. 'And if the government continues to ignore us, I'll set fire to myself.' He was very weak, and looked as though he was about to faint.

'Do what you want,' Han Dan said, wiping his glasses. 'But you'll be acting alone.'

'As I've said before, I think we should end the hunger strike but stay in the Square and submit a new petition,' Lin Lu said.

'The Beijing Students' Federation has called for an end to the fast,' said Sister Gao to Bai Ling. 'The Hunger Strike Headquarters must follow the will of the majority. If we keep fighting among ourselves like this, the students will lose trust in us.'

'Stop wasting time,' Mou Sen said. He too looked as though he was about to pass out. 'We can talk about our future tactics at the next meeting, but the question now is: do we carry on with the hunger strike or not? Let's have a show of hands.'

'Yes, let's have a vote,' said Lin Lu. 'Dai Wei, how many people are in the bus?'

'Ninety-seven.'

A vote was taken. Fifty-one students voted to end the hunger strike.

Students outside began bashing on the door again. Mao Da, Chen Di and I opened it and stepped out. A huge crowd had surrounded the bus. I spotted journalists and Beijing residents in the throng. A few people lifted their cameras and took flash photographs of us.

'Ke Xi wants to enter the bus, Dai Wei,' Big Chan said, squeezing over to me.

'He can't!' I shouted. 'Don't let him through!' I was afraid Ke Xi wanted to stir things up again.

'He's already pushed his way through the third cordon, and he's heading this way,' Chen Di said, watching Ke Xi approach.

I grabbed Chen Di's megaphone, switched it on and shouted, 'Please don't take flash photographs. The hunger strikers are very weak, and the flashes will disturb them. Please be considerate!'

A foreign journalist who was being pushed about in the scrum shouted in atonal Mandarin, 'Don't hit me! I'm not a dog! That's not friendly!' which made everyone laugh.

Ke Xi shoved his way up to us and said, 'I've heard there's an important meeting going on inside. Why won't you let me in?' He was accompanied by a doctor, two nurses and four students who were acting as his bodyguards.

'It's the rules,' I said, blocking his way. 'No one is allowed in once the meeting has started.'

'Ke Xi, you're here at last!' Zhuzi shouted from inside the bus, having overheard our conversation. 'Open the door quickly and let him in.'

Ke Xi moved feebly towards the bus. The two nurses fussed over him, shouting, 'Don't crush him! He could faint at any moment.' Although he'd eaten some noodles earlier in the United Front Department, he was pretending to still be on hunger strike.

Chen Di and I pushed Ke Xi into the bus then closed the door behind us.

'You're not a member of the standing committee, Ke Xi,' Bai Ling said sternly. 'You can only vote as an individual.'

'Cast your vote immediately,' Sister Gao said.

'What are we voting on? What's been happening?' Ke Xi was so squashed he could hardly speak. I was standing right behind him, almost choking from the stench of sweat and hospital disinfectant emanating from his body.

'We've decided to end the hunger strike,' Han Dan said. 'Do you agree or disagree with our decision?'

'Agree,' Ke Xi said, raising his hand in the air.

'Fine, then the meeting is now over,' Lin Lu shouted. 'In two hours' time, get the hunger strikers to gather outside the broadcast station, and we'll announce to the media and all the students in the Square that the hunger strike is officially over.'

'Is everyone clear now?' Shao Jian shouted through his cupped hands. 'We will end the hunger strike and replace it with a sit-in.'

'I'm going to storm Zhongnanhai!' Pu Wenhua said, banging the walls of the bus, tears streaming down his child-like face. 'It was my idea to launch this hunger strike! You have no right to end it!'

'The hunger strikers should decide themselves whether to stop the strike or not!' Tang Guoxian said. 'Students who haven't joined the strike have no right to vote!' But most of the students had squeezed out of the bus by then. A few students from provincial universities were getting their photographs taken with Bai Ling, Ke Xi and Han Dan, then asking them to sign their T-shirts and hats. It looked as if they were planning to head home.

'Who will announce the end of the hunger strike?' Liu Gang asked Old Fu, pulling him into a corner.

'Bai Ling, of course. She's the Headquarters' commander-in-chief.'

'All right, Bai Ling will announce the decision, then the Beijing Students' Federation will hold a press conference at 8 p.m.,' Liu Gang said solemnly.

'Zheng He has already written a Hunger Strike Termination Statement,' Mou Sen said, handing the text to Han Dan.

'Give it to Bai Ling,' Han Dan said, pushing it away.

'Let me read it first,' Old Fu said, snatching it from Mou Sen.

Lin Lu handed a scrap of paper to Mou Sen and said, 'This is the number of the State Council's general office. Call them up on the phone outside the Museum of Chinese History and tell them the hunger strike is officially over. We must get this message to them before they impose martial law. Hurry up!'

Lin Lu turned to the few students who were still inside the bus and said, 'Remember, this decision is top secret. Bai Ling must announce the news to the hunger strikers face to face. Before then, no one is to say a word. We don't want a riot to break out.'

Mou Sen opened the door, stared at the vast crowd outside and whispered, 'Will you help me squeeze my way through, Dai Wei?'

Tang Guoxian and Wu Bin stormed up to us and said, 'You Beijing students can stir things up as much as you like then run away scot-free. But when the rest of us return to our universities in the provinces, we'll all be thrown into jail.'

'Let's just see what happens,' I said. 'Anyway, no one should be heading home yet. This movement is going forward now, not retreating.' Then, wiping the sweat from my face, I took Mou Sen's hand and began pulling him through the crowd.

In the moment before death, there will be no time to climb the folds of your brain and gaze at the thoughts flowing by.

A long queue of people were waiting to use the telephone. I walked straight to the student at the front and told him we needed to make an urgent call. As Mou Sen grabbed the receiver, I glanced back and shouted, 'Please keep quiet, everyone. We're phoning the State Council.' The queue of people behind immediately quietened down and gathered in a close circle around us.

Mou Sen nervously dialled the numbers, put the receiver to his ear and said, 'Hello? We're phoning to inform you we've ended the hunger strike. I will now read out our statement. I will speak slowly, so you can write it down if you want.'

'There's no need. This conversation is being taped. Give me your name and your title.' The person on the other end of the phone sounded like a lowly secretary.

'My name is Mou Sen. I am the deputy commander of the Hunger Strike Headquarters . . .'

Although he tried to keep his voice down, several people caught snippets of what he said. After he put the phone down, a journalist from Xinhua News Agency edged forward and asked for a copy of the statement. I told him there would be a press conference in front of the Monument later, and that commander-in-chief Bai Ling would read out the statement in person.

Mou Sen and I sat down, took swigs from the bottles of water a student had handed us and watched the colour drain from the sky to the west. Mou Sen said it would be difficult to impose martial law in Beijing. 'When the government put Lhasa under curfew in March, they were able to cordon off the city and then attack the Tibetans away from the gaze of the Western media,' he said. 'But Beijing is filled with foreign diplomats and television crews. The whole world is watching us. The government wouldn't dare use violence.' Soon after he said this, his eyes rolled back and he collapsed in a sweaty heap on the ground. I pulled him up and took him back to the broadcast station to find him something to eat.

After I'd put him down on a quilt and given him some bread and peanuts, I went outside to organise the student marshal team. Rumours that the hunger strike had been called off had spread through the Square, and a large mob had gathered round the station, demanding to broadcast their views. Most of them were furious about the decision. The student marshals in yellow caps were struggling to hold them back.

'Look at this leaflet,' a sweaty man in his forties said, pulling me over. He looked like a government cadre. 'It says that officials in ten government organisations have decided to join the fast. It would be madness to end your hunger strike now! Let me through so I can broadcast this news to the Square.'

'Why not make copies of the leaflet and distribute them to the students,' I said. 'The broadcast station is packed at the moment.'

A woman with hair permed like my mother's walked up to me and said, 'If you end the hunger strike now, the government will assume you've surrendered and will crush you like flies once you return to your campuses.'

'This is the seventh day of our hunger strike and the government still hasn't responded to our demands,' I said, as she was joined by a young woman on a bike. 'In fact, we've heard rumours that they're about to impose martial law. A hunger strike won't be able to force any concessions from a government like this.'

'We're ending the hunger strike, but our protests will continue,' Chen Di explained to a middle-aged man in front of me. 'We're now going to hold a sit-in instead.'

Exhausted from the constant jostling and shoving, I stepped aside for a moment and asked Mao Da and Zhang Jie to tell the provincial marshals to collect their take-away suppers. Students from the Beijing campuses had been bringing meals to their classmates in the Square, which had created a lot of bad feeling among the provincial students, so Old Fu had given Big Chan and Little Chan 10,000 yuan to buy boxed meals for them.

Although the end of the hunger strike had still not been officially announced, many of the hunger strikers were starting to leave the buses. Some sat on the ground and stuffed biscuits into their mouths, others hobbled off to the emergency tent, propped up by medics in white coats. The ones who were too weak to move lay flat on the ground while doctors attached drips to their arms.

A man in a black shirt pulled me aside. 'You're the security chief, so that makes you one of the leaders, I suppose. In mid-June, there will be a meeting of the National People's Congress,' he said, pointing a big, grimy finger at the Great Hall of the People. 'If you're still in the Square when the meeting takes place, the government will never again be able to claim they represent the will of the people.'

'Yes, that's a good point,' I said. My red armband had the words SECURITY CHIEF written on it. I'd discovered the only way I could disengage myself from these irritating people was to agree with whatever they said.

A man nearby handed me a cigarette then walked away mumbling, 'The Chinese nation has reached the most dangerous juncture in its history, my friend!'

I continued to talk to the crowd, repeating that although the hunger strike was ending, our occupation of the Square would continue. My team of twenty marshals was struggling to keep the angry mob back. When the strain became too much, I sneaked back into the tent, sat down and fanned my face with my cap. My mouth was filled with ulcers, and it was painful for me to speak. I suspected that Tian Yi wouldn't be too upset about the decision to end the strike, but many other hunger strikers had taken the news badly and had had to be rushed to hospital.

Ke Xi walked in. I presumed he'd had another good meal, because he was standing straight as a rod now, and although he still had his two bodyguards with him, the nurses and doctor had gone. 'I've come to tell you that I've set up an Interim Command Centre,' he announced.

'That's a good idea,' I said. 'The Hunger Strike Headquarters should disband now.'

'And what's your Interim Command Centre going to do?' Mou Sen asked, gobbling a biscuit Nuwa had given him. The biscuits were a Hong Kong brand. The message MAY EVERYTHING GO AS YOU WISH! was printed along the side of the tin.

'It will take control!' When Ke Xi glared at you with his eyes wide open, he looked as if he suffered from a hyperactive thyroid.

'What will be your relationship with the other student organisations?' I asked.

'I will be commander-in-chief,' he said, ignoring the question.

'Will you be calling for the students to leave the Square or to continue the occupation?' Mou Sen asked.

'I will be commander-in-chief,' he repeated in a daze.

Mou Sen shook his head and sighed.

'You've lost your mind, Ke Xi,' I said, pushing him out of the tent. 'Go onto the Monument if you want to give a speech. We're in the middle of a broadcast here.' I watched him stagger away, then I sat down in the tent's doorway to stop anyone else coming in. I knew the broadcast station would become the focus of any new power struggle in the Square.

Ke Xi climbed onto the Monument's lower terrace and shouted through his megaphone. A large crowd of supporters gathered round him and cheered his every word. When he finished speaking, he passed his megaphone to one of his bodyguards and stepped down to shake hands with Beijing residents and sign the notebooks they thrust into his hands.

Mou Sen waved the Hunger Strike Termination Statement he'd been rewriting and said, 'That's it. I'm not making any more changes. Bai Ling can read it out at the press conference once she's announced the end of the hunger strike to the students.'

'They're only taking orders from Sister Gao now,' I said.

'Well forge her signature here and tell them she's approved it,' he said pointing to the corner of the page.

'Ask someone else to take it to them. I'm looking after this place.' I didn't want Nuwa to think I could be ordered around by Mou Sen.

It was nearly nine o'clock. Some of the hunger strikers had hobbled over to our broadcast station by themselves, others had been carried over on stretchers. But most of them were now gathered around the tent, listening to the tape of the Internationale and waiting for Bai Ling to make her announcement.

The hunger strikers didn't know about the threat of martial law that was hanging over us, so when Bai Ling announced that the hunger strike had been called off, many of them felt betrayed. Someone shouted, 'You've deceived us, you criminals!'

The crowd started pushing. If I hadn't brought another fifty marshals over to strengthen the cordon, the tent would have got knocked to the ground.

'Listen to the outcry!' Old Fu cried from inside the tent. 'We can't end the hunger strike. There'll be a riot.'

Lin Lu snatched the megaphone from Bai Ling's hand and yelled, 'Calm down, everyone! We need to change tactics. The army is preparing to enter the city. If we don't stop the hunger strike, we won't have the strength to defend ourselves.'

I stood up and surveyed the scene. Hunger strikers began drifting off to Qianmen market or going into quiet corners to have something to eat. Two ambulances became blocked by the moving crowds. Suddenly the feeling of common purpose in the Square seemed to dissolve.

Nuwa's jaw dropped. 'I've just realised there are three thousand hunger strikers who will want to eat now, but we haven't got any food to give them! What are we going to do?'

'Switch off the microphone and play some music,' I said. Nuwa knew how to operate the equipment herself now.

'This is too much!' Mou Sen said. 'Phone up the canteens of every Beijing university and ask them to bring us vats of dumplings and wonton soup.'

Old Fu looked outside and cried, 'You've betrayed the hunger strikers! Look at the crowd. Everyone's weeping.'

'Last week you opposed the hunger strike, but now you don't want us to end it,' Mou Sen said angrily. 'It's too much!'

'Listen to me, fellow students!' Old Fu shouted, grabbing the microphone. 'Ignore the announcement that Bai Ling just made. I now propose that we relaunch the hunger strike immediately.'

'Don't act like a despot, Old Fu!' Bai Ling wheezed. Since she'd read out the announcement, she'd been lying down inside the tent, gasping for breath. She still hadn't eaten anything. Old Fu's intervention angered her so much, she burst into tears. Her small breasts trembled like tofu. The nervous doctor at her side urged her to stay calm.

'You've destroyed this movement, Bai Ling!' Old Fu spluttered.

Pu Wenhua and a couple of other hunger strikers from the Agricultural College staggered into the tent and shouted, 'Now you've called off the hunger strike I suppose you'll be resigning from your post, Bai Ling.'

The doctor stood in Pu Wenhua's way and said, 'She's still on hunger strike. Don't upset her.' Pu Wenhua brushed him aside and lurched towards us. Lin Lu pounced on him while I wrestled with the other two.

'I've got some inside information!' Wang Fei said, rushing over. 'It's from Cao Ming's military contacts. Apparently, if we continue the hunger strike for just one more day, the hardliners' resolve might crack, and Zhao Ziyang could regain his authority. The reformist wing is in a precarious situation. Wan Li, the liberal chairman of the National People's Congress, has been detained in Shanghai, and won't be allowed to return to Beijing unless he supports the government's hardline approach.'

'We reached our decision through a democratic vote,' Mou Sen said to Old Fu. 'The minority should bow to the majority.' Apart from Bai Ling, everyone was standing up now.

'Why do you never broadcast any of the Agricultural College's statements?' Pu Wenhua said, pointing at Mou Sen.

'I make the editorial decisions here,' Mou Sen said sternly. 'I don't allow extremist statements to be broadcast.'

'Well, we'll have to take that power away from you, then!' Pu Wenhua told his classmates to grab Lin Lu's megaphone. Mou Sen and Old Fu tried to snatch it too, but Lin Lu swerved round and passed it to Bai Ling. Clutching it feebly to her chest, she went over to the camp bed and croaked, 'As long as I'm still here, I will remain in charge of this broadcast station!'

'We all know you're a government agent, Lin Lu,' Wang Fei said, pushing him back.

Pu Wenhua stumbled towards Bai Ling and tried to yank the megaphone from her. Too weak to fight back, Bai Ling sunk her teeth into his hand. Pu Wenhua was very frail too, so when Mou Sen gave him a light push, he fell flat on the ground. Mou Sen then slipped and tumbled on top of him, then Old Fu pounced on top of them both, and the three of them wrestled on the ground in a tangled heap.

I rushed over to the broadcasting area and switched off the microphone.

A large pack of foreign journalists waiting to interview Bai Ling were sitting outside among the baying crowds of students and residents. The doctors placed Bai Ling on a stretcher and carried her out of the tent.

'Get out, Wang Fei!' Nuwa spat, pushing him towards the door. 'Just go away!' Her face was red with fury.

'You think you're the stars of this movement,' Pu Wenhua screeched as I dragged him out of the tent. 'But just wait and see. Very soon I'll be more famous than any of you!'

'You haven't eaten for seven days,' the nurse shouted to Pu Wenhua. 'Your heart's very weak. If you don't calm down, you'll collapse and die.' She followed him out and urged him to drink a bottle of royal jelly, but he pushed her away. She fell down and burst into tears. I'd heard that her son was on hunger strike too. He was an undergraduate at the Beijing Institute of Science and Technology.

'It's too much, Old Fu!' Mou Sen said. 'The majority voted to end the strike. You have no right to overturn that decision.'

Having heard the commotion, Han Dan and Cheng Bing rushed inside to see what was going on.

Lin Lu pulled his shirt straight and said, 'Although I'm against ending the strike, the decision was reached through a democratic vote. What you're attempting now is completely unconstitutional, Old Fu!'

'We mustn't lose sight of the big picture,' Han Dan said calmly. 'We've got to stop squabbling and put this movement back on track.'

'Don't you feel guilty about letting down the thousands of hunger strikers out there?' Old Fu asked, still boiling with rage.

The doctors who were attempting to carry Bai Ling over to where she was planning to give her press conference were unable to squeeze through the crowd, so they brought her back into the tent to wait for things to calm down. I was glad to see that Bai Ling had a biscuit in her hand.

'Everyone's here now,' Mou Sen said loudly. 'We should start the press conference.'

Lin Lu and Han Dan agreed. Old Fu stormed out of the tent shouting, 'There's no need for you to sack me. I resign!'

'Old Fu's gone crazy!' I said. 'We must protect this broadcast station. If we lose this place, the Square will fall into chaos.' I pushed the large colour television some Beijing residents had given us over to the door of the tent to stop anyone else coming in.

Nuwa had brushed her hair and was preparing an English translation of the Hunger Strike Termination Statement.

'Apparently, a hunger striker who was taken to hospital had a stroke,' Mou Sen said. 'She's a vegetable now.' He took a handful of peanuts from his pocket and stuffed them ravenously into his mouth. I told him not to eat so fast. 'There's no more time to waste,' he continued. 'Ask the hunger strikers to sit down quietly, Lin Lu. And Nuwa, make an announcement telling the students that the doctors advise us to have wet towels and face masks at the ready in case the army use tear gas against us.'

'Can the Voice of the Student Movement tell everyone to come to the Monument, Han Dan?' Lin Lu asked. 'Your loudspeakers are stronger than ours. Once the government declares martial law, we must all stay by the Monument.' Lin Lu had already draped a wet flannel around his neck to protect him in the event of a tear-gas attack.

'Many of the hunger strikers are refusing to stop their fast,' said Wang Fei, standing behind the television. 'What should we tell them?'

No one paid him any attention, apart from Bai Ling who was now lying on the camp bed. 'I'm not in favour of ending the strike either, Wang Fei,' she said. 'But we have to go along with the majority decision.'

'There are hundreds of thousands of people in the Square, so it's vital we stay united,' Mou Sen said to Wang Fei. 'You and Old Fu have been in this movement from the start. How could you behave so badly at such a crucial moment?'

'I didn't go as far as Old Fu,' Wang Fei said. 'Still, I did act stupidly. I'm sorry, Bai Ling.' He'd calmed down a lot since Nuwa had shouted at him.

'All the university hunger strike groups have given up the fast,' Bai Ling said. 'The students who are carrying on are acting independently. We can ignore them. But we must take control of the next stage of the movement. You're head of propaganda, Wang Fei. Print up some copies of the Hunger Strike Termination Statement, so that we can hand them out at the press conference.'

'I've told the suicide squad to form a protective chain around the students, and have issued a first-degree combat order,' Wang Fei said, clasping his clenched fist.

'Just make sure we've got enough towels and face masks,' Bai Ling said. 'We'll need at least 50,000 of each.'

Chen Di walked in with Hai Feng and said, 'Old Fu's gone to the Voice of the Student Movement and announced that the hunger strike hasn't achieved its goals yet. He's using the strikers as hostages. He won't let them give up until the government has agreed to our demands.' Then seeing the look of fear on everyone's faces, he sneered, 'What's the matter? The moment you hear the words "martial law" you're reduced to shivering wrecks!'

Mou Sen stood up. 'I'll chair the press conference today. Dai Wei, can you help me set up the microphone?'

'I don't see the point of holding a press conference now,' I mumbled. But Mou Sen ignored me. He asked some of his Beijing Normal classmates to set up tables and chairs outside, and hang up a large poster behind that said WE WANT DENG XIAOPING'S FOUR MODERNISATIONS TO BE IMPLEMENTED WITHIN OUR LIFETIME.

I told Yu Jin and Xiao Li to fill in for me, then went to look for Tian Yi. I wanted to take her back to my mother's flat and make her some rice congee, or some other easily digestible food.

I was relieved to find her sitting on a quilt, eating a piece of a chocolate cake that a foreign student had brought for the hunger strikers who'd given up their fast. I told her that as soon as the press conference was over, I'd take her to my mother's flat and look after her. She wouldn't be able to rest back at the campus. The dorms were packed with students who'd travelled up from the provinces.

'Let's go to my home,' she said. 'I can have a shower there. All I want is a warm shower.'

'Hasn't your sister just had a baby?' I said. 'There won't be enough room for us all.' I lay down beside her, stretched my arms back and closed my eyes. 'I'd like to sleep for twenty-four hours. Old Fu and Bai

Ling had a big argument just now in the broadcast station, and they forgot to turn the microphone off.'

'Yes, I heard it.'

'Deng Xiaoping has secretly ordered the army to surround Beijing,' I said, my eyes still closed.

'You all look so frightened now. In the beginning, you were ready to cut off your heads for this movement.' She took a swig from a bottle. It was too dark for me to see what was inside.

'Berkeley has sent me a letter of admission,' I said.

'You have an escape route, then.'

'I still have to apply for a passport and a US visa, so there's a long way to go yet.'

'Don't try to fool me. You already have one foot in America now.'

The official loudspeakers attached to the hundreds of lamp posts dotted around the Square suddenly crackled into life. A recording of Li Peng's latest speech, given at a meeting of government and army cadres, echoed through the night sky: '. . . It is now clear that if we don't take firm measures to turn the situation around, our great nation, which was founded on the blood of revolutionary martyrs, will be in great jeopardy . . .'

Then the fiery voice of President Yang Shangkun declared, 'Beijing has been placed under martial law. The army has surrounded the capital. We have imposed new restrictions on the media, forbidding foreign journalists from conducting interviews within the municipality . . .'

'Shall we go back to the flat now, or do you want to stay for the press conference?' I asked Tian Yi, suddenly feeling breathless and trapped.

'Let's go to the press conference.' Tian Yi stood up. I held her arm, and slowly walked back with her to the Monument.

Soon we heard Bai Ling's voice cry out into the night. 'Fellow students, the hardline clique headed by Deng Xiaoping, Li Peng and Yang Shangkun has staged a coup, and General Secretary Zhao Ziyang has been sacked from his job. I implore all the hunger strikers to stop their fast, and for everyone to gather round the Monument so that we can prepare ourselves for martial law . . .' As she repeated the announcement, I could hear Wang Fei whispering in the background, asking her to read out the statement he'd just written.

Tian Yi's hand started trembling. Trying to calm her nerves, I said, 'Don't worry. If they really have imposed martial law, we'll return to the campuses. It's no big deal.'

'Zhao Ziyang was such a fine, upstanding politician,' Tian Yi said, clearly distressed. 'How could they just get rid of him like that?'

The crowds of students and residents in the Square were in uproar. Everyone was rushing about, crying and shouting.

'So much for the bloody "People's Premier"! What a tyrant!'

'Those hardline despots have no idea how to run this country!'

'Call every citizen of Beijing to the Square! We'll build a human Great Wall to keep out the enemy hordes!'

'Down with Li Peng's puppet government! Down with the corrupt military regime! Down with Yang Shangkun . . .'

Everyone was distressed and angry. People who didn't know each other became embroiled in loud debates. Girls hugged one another and wept. Nurses in white coats shouted, 'Calm down everyone!' then groaned, 'What kind of government treats its people like this?'

'It makes me sick to think we nearly starved ourselves to death for this rotten regime!' Tian Yi muttered, then walked off hand in hand with Mimi. I went to find some more student marshals to guard the broadcast station. I knew that if the martial law troops turned up, their first goal would be to destroy our tent.

The area we'd cordoned off for the press conference was already packed. I spotted a few fair-haired foreign journalists speaking into cameras. Their reports were being transmitted live via satellite to television sets around the world. Old Fu and Han Dan hadn't arrived yet. Mou Sen looked very cool with his shoulder-length hair, denim jeans and leather money belt. He held the Hunger Strike Termination Statement in his trembling hands and read it out on Bai Ling's behalf. By the time he reached the closing paragraph, tears were pouring down his face. Nuwa then read out the English translation, but her voice didn't sound loud enough. I regretted we hadn't used the Voice of the Student Movement's speakers.

Mou Sen took the microphone back and said, 'I now urge every one of the hundred thousand of us students here in the Square to begin a mass hunger strike.'

I couldn't believe my ears. A mass hunger strike? Had he lost his mind? There was a sudden blaze of light as thousands of camera flashes went off.

The crowd burst into applause and echoed Mou Sen's call for a mass hunger strike. Lin Lu prodded Mou Sen in the back and whispered something in his ear. A look of horror appeared on Mou Sen's face. He quickly raised the microphone again and said, 'I'm sorry, that was a slip of the tongue! I meant to say a mass sit-in, not a mass hunger strike!' The crowd jeered. Flustered and confused, Mou Sen groped his pockets for a cigarette, his face clammy with sweat.

Then Han Dan walked over. He had a damp towel tied around his arm, ready for a gas attack, but had removed his hunger strike headband. He took the microphone from Mou Sen and reminded the male students that it was their duty to protect the girls, and asked any middle-school students who'd come to the Square to go home immediately.

Bai Ling, who'd officially stopped her hunger strike, stood next to him with her back bent and a towel tied around her waist. As soon as she took the microphone, the journalists ran up to her with their cameras. Blinded by their flash bulbs, she closed her eyes and said, 'If the army drives us from the Square, we will seek refuge in the homes of local residents. Then when it's safe for us to go out onto the streets again, we will return to our campuses.'

Fearing the soldiers were about to turn up at any minute, the students panicked and ran about asking for wet towels and face masks to protect them in the event of a gas attack. The group of professors from Beijing University's Law Department who'd joined the hunger strike the previous day shuffled away despondently.

As soon as the press conference was brought to a close, Wang Fei grabbed some cash from Old Fu's bag and went off with Yu Jin to buy more towels and face masks.

While the air outside glimmers in the sunlight, your heart sleeps in the darkness and your lungs wait to inhale.

My brother is in the sitting room chatting to an old school friend about people they used to know.

'Yes, do you remember him?' he says. 'He used to sneak in here to watch television. He's a pop star now. Can you believe it? He's probably a millionaire.'

'Jiang Tie gave up his job at the research institute and went into business. He moved to Hainan Island last year and opened a software company. He's asked me to go into partnership with him, but I haven't got enough cash to invest.'

'I bumped into Hong Zhi the other day. You know, the girl whose hard-boiled egg you nicked on that Spring Festival school trip. She's running a clothes stall in Silk Alley now.'

'I thought she got into Qinghua University. I remember when our teacher asked us to swat flies, she killed enough to fill a whole bloody jam jar.'

My brother gets up and puts on the tape that Tian Yi gave me. I continue to listen to the conversation, but am soon lifted skyward by the choirboys' angelic voices. A violin plays softly, turning the sky a deep blue. Then a flute overlaps the melody and my numb mind begins to tremble. The orchestra returns and a contralto voice cuts through the strings. As a single, clear note hovers in the air, I feel a deep sadness which slowly subsides and merges into a sense of bliss . . .

Noises from my past return to me, bathed in gold . . . 'Look at my arm,' Lulu says, rolling up her sleeve. I'm standing in her room, my face warmed by a slanting beam of sunlight. 'I can't see any red spots, I promise you,' I say. She examines the skin closely. 'Well you'll have to check it again tomorrow.' She saw Momoe Yamaguchi in the Japanese television drama *Blood*, and has convinced herself that, like the heroine of the story, she too has contracted leukaemia . . . Now I see myself waiting for my brother outside the school gates. The girls skipping across the lane in the afternoon sunshine are singing '*Not as fragrant as a flower, nor as tall as a tree . . .*'

My brother switches the tape off and I slowly retreat back into my body.

I remember A-Mei saying that music could carry you to the heavens. At the time, I didn't understand what she meant. I don't want to listen to that tape again. If that music can affect me so powerfully, next time I hear it, I will be drawn through the gates of death.

'Do you want to go to that disco tonight?' my brother's old school friend asks, lighting a cigarette.

'Yes. I'm sick of spending my holiday staring at this bloody vegetable. If I stay in this stinking flat another hour, I'll fling myself out of the window.'

'He's your own brother, you bastard! He'll kick your head in when he wakes up.'

'He'll never wake up. Look at him!'

My brother sounds fed up. But I'm not angry. If I were going to attack anyone after I woke up, it wouldn't be him, it would be those lousy government leaders in the Zhongnanhai compound. But if I do wake up, I doubt if I would attack anyone. I'd probably want to forget about politics and concentrate on living a happy life.

My brother and his friend pour themselves some more beer. They have to wait for my mother to come back before they can go to the disco.

'I'd better turn him over. Come and help me lift him.' My brother walks into my room and takes my arm.

'I don't want to touch him . . . Look at those tubes attached to his mouth and dick. He looks like a fish tank.'

My brother crosses my legs, grabs my shoulders and waist, then pushes hard, flipping me onto my stomach. A light shoots through my brain as I turn. Then he stuffs the pillow back between my legs.

'Hey, you could get a job as a professional nurse . . .'

'Who would have guessed he'd end up like this? That day in the Square, he said to me, "Don't assume you're invincible. Remember: bullets have no eyes . . ."'

You long to cast off your body and escape this fake death.

The broadcast minibus drove round the perimeter of the Square, blasting out the national anthem and the Hunger Strike Termination Statement. It was very late, and the sky was pitch black, but the Square was still as noisy as ever.

Inside the broadcast station, a few students were writing articles by torchlight. Others were printing out pamphlets. Big Chan, Little Chan and I were distributing the new security passes that were stamped with a picture of the Monument. Our hands were covered in red ink.

The calm tones of Nuwa and Chen Di echoed continually through the Square. 'Everyone must have their face masks and damp towels to hand, in case the army let off tear gas,' Nuwa announced. 'You can use a strip of cloth, if you want, as long as it's wet . . . We've just received news that 450 army trucks, which were trying to enter the city, have been blocked by residents on the third ring road under Liuli Bridge. The citizens of Beijing are using their own bodies to halt the advance of the troops. Please can anyone with bicycles ride over there at once and offer them assistance . . .'

'This is an urgent announcement,' Chen Di said. 'Citizens in the western suburbs need our help. Can a hundred student marshals go there as soon as possible . . . The army has reached the Hongmiao intersection already, but has been halted by a wall of protestors. An old woman lay down in front of the trucks and shouted, "If you want to go any further, you'll have to drive over my dead body."'

I rushed back and forth, trying to ensure the broadcast station and the northern side of the Monument were well protected. Student marshals from Qinghua University and the Central Institute of National Minorities were guarding the south side. Dong Rong and Mao Da assembled a large band of students and went off to help man the barricades in the western suburbs.

Most of the students and hunger strikers had left the buses and shelters by now and had gathered round the Monument. Although no longer divided into distinct university groups, the crowd was well-organised, with the student marshals and male students on the outside, and the girls safely protected within.

Tang Guoxian and Wu Bin paced up and down waving their

megaphones and torches in the air. I was weak with exhaustion and could feel my eyes drooping. I went to find Tian Yi, hoping I could sit down with her for a while.

She'd just written a bulletin for the propaganda office, and was now lying down in a breezy corner of the Monument's upper terrace. Her face was as grey as a sheet of newspaper. Her camera was still hanging around her neck.

I opened her lunch box to check whether she'd eaten the strawberries I'd given her. They were untouched and covered in mould.

Nevertheless, she leaned over and said, 'Mmm, they smell delicious. I don't have to eat them. The smell is enough!'

'I've got some instant noodles for you, but there's no hot water.' The dirty pamphlets on the ground flew into the air as people walked by. I lay down beside her on the cold paving stones.

'Look, my hair's falling out,' she said, rubbing her head. 'Have you seen my bottle of conditioner?'

'Why don't you go back to the campus to have a shower?' I said, still struggling to stay awake.

'I'd be accused of desertion. Anyway, it's too late now. I wouldn't find a taxi at this time of night.'

'I can't help out any more. I'm exhausted. Ke Xi wants to be commander-in-chief again. I don't know where he gets his energy from!' I turned onto my side and glanced at my watch. 'My God! It's midnight. The government said the army would be here by now.' As I dozed off, the crowd's chants rang through my ears. 'You can cut off our heads or shoot us, but we'll never leave Tiananmen Square!' Nuwa then spoke over the loudspeakers, sounding as confident and carefree as a Voice of America presenter. 'The government wants to destroy our broadcast station. Everyone must protect it and make sure their evil plan doesn't succeed . . .'

Its cry sounds like a baby howling. It eats humans. If you consume its flesh you will be protected from evil spirits.

The wind slams the rain against the windows of the covered balcony.

I feel the damp enter the room and seep into the biscuits on the table, my father's ashes, and the old shoes lying in the corner. I'd love to slip my feet into a pair of damp trainers. But shoes are made only for upright bodies. Prone bodies must remain barefoot in bed.

The damp air from the landing also moves into the flat and absorbs the smell of the turnips rotting in the kitchen.

My mother begins the first day of April by breaking into song. She sings again and again, '*I say farewell to life, to life!*' struggling to hit the top note. In the past, she had no problem reaching that high C. Then she stops singing, and in her most theatrical voice begins to recite the telephone directory to me, reading out the numbers of everything from hairdressers to universities.

Has her yearning for a telephone driven her mad? She only submitted her application two months ago. Many people have to wait a year before they get connected.

My brother is moving to England. He has already booked his plane ticket. He's going to start a four-year degree course at the University of Nottingham.

'If this rain doesn't stop soon, our visitors won't be able to make it here. It's two o'clock already.' My mother closes the telephone directory at last and touches my forehead. Yesterday she cut my hair with a freezing pair of clippers. I can still smell the kerosene she lubricated them with.

I hear a soft knock on the door. It's someone with tact, not a rude policeman or an elderly busybody.

'Come in, Master Yao. Isn't this rain terrible? It hasn't stopped since last night!'

Master Yao tells my mother that he not only knows An Qi, but also an old friend of hers from the National Opera Company. It's hard to tell his age from his voice. His speech is clipped and precise.

They walk into my room and perch on the end of my bed.

'I can tell your son possesses the root of wisdom,' Master Yao says.

Last night my mother kept mentioning that she'd invited a qigong master of national repute to come and see me.

'This son of mine, he's so tall, so clever. He can turn his hand to anything, just like his father could.' I'm surprised to hear my mother speak well of my father, for once.

'It must be difficult, looking after him all on your own.'

'Yes, I'm sure you can imagine! A mother looking after a grown-up son – it turns the philosophy of *The Twenty-Four Filial Exemplars* on its head. I can never leave the flat for more than half an hour. I haven't had a good night's sleep for three years . . .'

I often can't tell whether I'm awake or asleep. My internal body clock doesn't function properly any more. When I sense light beyond my eyelids, more thoughts tend to come to my head. Occasionally, I have a gut feeling that it's morning or evening.

'Sometimes his hands go stone cold. I have to keep massaging him to stop his joints seizing up. Look at his left foot. It's been clenched for so long, the bones have bent.'

'There are associations for the handicapped. Haven't you got in touch with any?'

'Yes, and charities too: national ones, local ones. I've contacted them all, but none of them will help. I phone them up and they say they'll write to me, but they never do. If you don't have backdoor connections, you don't stand a chance. There are so many handicapped people begging them for help, why should they choose to help us?'

'I don't know how you cope. You should get a live-in maid.'

'Of course I'd like to, but I couldn't afford it. I have to ask my relatives to help pay for his medicine. I've spent over 100,000 yuan on him in the last three years. My neighbours used to be very nosy, always coming up and asking questions. But after I asked to borrow some money from them, they suddenly stopped visiting. When I knock on their doors now, they don't answer. They've even stopped reporting my activities to the local police.'

I was never close to my mother. I can't remember even touching her hand. When I cut her hair, the smell of sweat on her thick neck repulsed me. Now I have to endure the humiliation of her washing my naked body every day and removing my soiled incontinence pads.

'Where's the wound? Let me see.'

'Here. Feel it. It's soft. The piece of missing skull is still in the hospital's refrigerator.'

Master Yao rubs his cold finger over the wound above my ear. When he presses down, I feel brain tissue being pushed aside and a few nerves quiver a little. No matter how warm the rest of my head is, the wound always feels like the cold mouth of a cave.

I know I was shot in the head, and that the bullet didn't explode. And I know the shot was fired from a handgun by someone standing at eye-level to me on the pavement to my side. He must have been a plain-clothes policeman. A soldier wouldn't use a handgun.

'An Qi told me what happened to him. I don't care about politics. We qigong practitioners are only interested in performing good deeds. I can tell your son is a survivor. I'll do my best to help bring him out of his coma.'

'How lucky I am to have found someone as kind as you! I must admit, I still don't understand how the government could have killed all those students in cold blood. After the crackdown, I spent three days searching for his body. I went to one hospital after another. Each one was like an abattoir, with corpses everywhere. I feel sick just thinking about it.'

'I was still working at the Beijing Hotel at the time, in their accounts office. On the night of 3 June, plain-clothes policemen came and told all the hotel's shops and boutiques to close early, and asked the reception to give them the room numbers of every foreign journalist who was staying there. I knew something serious was about to happen . . . I'll start with some pressure-point massage. Once his channels are unblocked, it will be easier for me to transmit my qi to him. Look at these red spots on his nails. They're a sign of obstructions to the bloodflow in his brain. The darker the spots, the graver the problem. When they turn black, he won't have long to live.'

'You're right. His nails look very strange . . .'

'Can you open the window?'

'But it's still raining outside.'

'It doesn't matter. The room must be well ventilated when I transmit my qi or he won't be able to absorb it properly.'

Master Yao holds my foot in his hand, and with his thumb makes firm, circular movements on the back of my big toe. A pain signal shoots up to my head, causing the patch of dead cells around my wound to twitch, and for a moment I see a vision of my daughter. She's standing in the rain, clutching an umbrella with her small hands, her eyebrows exposed under her newly cut fringe.

Since Tian Yi told me about the abortion, I often imagine what my daughter might look like now, had she lived. She wouldn't be a miniature version of Tian Yi. She would have a round face, large eyes and two small dimples on her cheeks.

'People only care about money these days. If you don't bribe the doctors with red envelopes of cash, they won't bother to treat you . . .'

Just as Master Yao gets up to leave, Mimi and Yu Jin arrive. They're sitting on the sofa now, talking about Tian Yi.

'She sent me an email with lots of articles about new treatments for coma patients,' Mimi says to my mother. 'They're in English, but I can translate them for you.'

'What's an email? Do you mean a telegram?'

'No, it's a letter you can send through a computer. It arrives almost instantly.'

'How amazing. I'd like to learn how to send them.'

'As long as you can write Chinese in the Roman alphabet, it's very easy.'

'If you want to learn, I'll lend you a home computer,' Yu Jin says. He's sitting on my brother's bed in the covered balcony having a cigarette. I hear him kick his short legs as he speaks. I'm terrified the balcony will collapse and he'll plummet four storeys to the ground. My mother will never be able to learn how to use a computer. She has trouble switching on the radio sometimes. I used to spend a lot of time in the computer room at university, reading research articles stored on the large, cumbersome machines there. It's strange to think that, just a few years on, people now have computers in their own homes.

'Has Tian Yi got used to life in America?' my mother asks. 'I've heard Western food is very hard to digest.'

'Foreigners are like rabbits. They like to munch on raw lettuce!' Mimi always throws her head back when she laughs.

You want to fly through the dark like Hun Dun, the headless god who has six feet and four wings.

Mimi's jaw dropped when she saw Sister Gao walk towards us. 'We were told you'd been kidnapped,' she said. 'How did you escape?' There was a piece of garlic skin stuck to her lip.

'I don't know what happened. Someone dragged me off to hospital last night and put me on a drip. Can you pass me one of those cucumbers?'

Sister Gao sat down and wiped the sweat from her face with a tissue. We were on the Monument's upper terrace, having an early lunch.

'Well thank God you're here now!' Tian Yi said.

'The new student marshals nearly didn't let me up here,' Sister Gao said breathlessly. 'None of them seemed to know who I was.'

'You should have come up through your private entrance in the south,' I laughed, alluding to the power she wielded in the Voice of the Student Movement's tent.

'A plane flew over at ten this morning and dropped a bundle of leaflets into the Square,' Tian Yi said, then quickly put her hand over her mouth to stop herself from retching. She'd vomited twice since giving up her fast.

'All the student groups seem to have disbanded,' Hai Feng said. 'There's no one on duty at the Beijing Students' Federation's command centre. You lot had better take control, or we'll be in deep trouble when the army turns up.'

I glanced over to the Federation's command centre on the opposite side of the terrace. All I could see were a broken table and some empty cardboard boxes.

Below it, in the mid-distance, Bai Ling was leaning out of a window of the broadcast minibus, shouting, 'Fellow students, let us devote our lives to defending our constitutional rights . . .' Her mouth was too close to the microphone, so her words were muffled.

By now, we were broadcasting entirely from the minibus. We'd moved all our equipment into it, so that we could continue transmitting if the army came to drive us out. The broadcast tent was now only used for editorial work.

Zhuzi, who was sitting next to me, said that Bai Ling was a heroine, and that everyone in the Square looked up to her. But as head of security, Zhuzi was more powerful than her. He was in charge of all the student marshals in the Square as well as those guarding the major traffic routes of the city. In the event of a crisis, he would be able to take control.

'The government has cut off the water and electricity supplies to the Square,' Lin Lu yelled, taking the microphone from Bai Ling. 'This is an emergency situation! Comrade workers of Beijing, we need your support!' The white minibus then drove to the other side of the Square.

'You must be prepared for police violence,' I said. 'It's no joke being attacked with electric batons, I can tell you!' Earlier that morning, I'd accompanied Zhuzi on a tour of the barricades that residents had put up around the city. I could still feel the sweat of fear on my back.

Mao Da passed round some bread rolls then opened a can of luncheon meat. The cucumbers hadn't been washed, so I rubbed mine on my trousers before I took a bite. It was a delicious meal. Shu Tong had been in the Square all morning, reorganising Wang Fei's propaganda office. He'd asked some high school teachers to help write pamphlets and articles.

The Square was filled with people again. Columns of marchers poured in from all directions, followed by open-backed trucks crammed with protestors and placards. There must have been a million people in the Square now, talking and yelling. Loudspeakers wailed in unison: 'Oppose military control! Defend Beijing!' The multitude of human cries rose in waves that crashed against the Monument's central obelisk and rolled back into our ears. In this sea of noise, we had to shout to be heard.

'It won't be easy for the army to enter the Square,' Mao Da said, gazing out at the vast crowd.

'They didn't have much problem crushing the demonstrations in Lhasa a few months ago,' Liu Gang said. 'God knows how many Tibetans were killed. Did you see the images of Party Secretary Hu Jintao issuing the crackdown order in his army fatigues and helmet? He looked like a little Hitler.' He was lying on his back chomping on a cucumber, his face shaded by a straw hat. On our way to the Monument he'd told me he hadn't slept for two days.

'That massacre happened out in the sticks,' Mao Da said. 'This is Beijing. The army wouldn't dare open fire here.'

'Liu Gang and I saw about eight hundred riot police officers at Liuli Bridge,' I told Mao Da. 'They were beating up every student in sight.'

'Tear gas is very nasty,' Mimi said. 'It can frighten a crowd just as much as rubber bullets.'

'It's a miracle no student died during the hunger strike,' Sister Gao muttered. 'That night in the dorm when Bai Ling announced she wanted to launch the strike, I told her that if anyone died, she'd get her head cut off.'

Yu Jin walked over. 'We've received many reports. This one's from Dabeiyao Bridge, this one's from the Hongmiao intersection. The army has surrounded the city, from Changping District to the western suburbs.' In his red vest and red cap he looked like a turkey. He grabbed a bread roll from Chen Di, reached for a clove of garlic, then munched a cucumber, spitting the skin onto the ground as he ate.

'There are a million people in the Square now, and large crowds manning the barricades around the city,' Sister Gao said anxiously to Shu Tong. 'How will the Federation manage to keep everyone under control?'

'The Federation should hold a meeting,' Shu Tong said. 'The Hunger Strike Headquarters are having one right now over there. Pass me a clove of garlic.' He picked up his chopsticks and dug into the polystyrene box of fried pork and mustard shoots he'd brought from the university cafeteria. Near the Museum of Chinese History, student officers were handing out free boxed lunches paid for by the Hong Kong Student Association, but you had to queue for hours to get one.

Zhang Jie and Xiao Li walked over from the Headquarters' tent, looking for something to eat. They'd spent all morning supervising the student marshal teams.

'Hundreds of marshals have been guarding this monument for hours, not even taking time off to have lunch, just so that you lot can lie here and sunbathe,' Zhang Jie said, taking the cucumber Mimi handed him.

'So what decision have the Headquarters come to?' Hai Feng asked him.

'Bai Ling and Lin Lu have only just turned up,' he replied. 'They're discussing whether to call for a nationwide strike.' He grabbed two rolls, squeezed them together then took a large bite.

'The Square is swarming with plain-clothes policemen,' Sister Gao said to Mimi. 'If someone asks you what your name is, don't tell them.'

'Do you mean there are spies out here?' Mimi's voice had become much brighter since she'd stopped her hunger strike.

'Of course,' I said. 'When you're standing in the courtroom in a few months' time, you'll be shown videotapes of yourself eating cucumbers with Shu Tong.'

Mimi glanced nervously to her left and right. 'I can't imagine how it must feel to see men charging towards you with electric batons in their hands,' she said. She was wearing Tian Yi's blue plastic visor. The sunlight bouncing off it dazzled my eyes.

I stood up, shook the crumbs from my trousers and looked into the distance. I could see hundreds of students on the roofs of the buses parked along the north edge of the Square. Some were lying down on quilts, others were sitting up waving red flags. It looked like an elevated theatre stage.

'Ten portable toilets have been put up outside the Museum of Chinese History,' Hai Feng said.

'Make an announcement, otherwise no one will know they're there,' Tian Yi said, getting up. She and Mimi were planning to head off to Xuanwumen Hotel. The Hong Kong Student Association had established a liaison office in one of the rooms there. It was the turn of the Beijing University students to use the shower in its en suite bathroom.

'Look at the vast crowd we've got here,' Mao Da said. 'The martial law order hasn't been very successful, has it?'

'Have a look at these,' said Shu Tong, handing Mimi the pile of reports that Yu Jin had collected. 'If you find anything interesting, you can put it in your newscasts.'

'They're all about the citizens' blockades,' Mimi said, leafing through them and sorting them into three separate piles. 'We can use this one about residents forming a human wall across the street, and this one about soldiers violently forcing their way through a blockade. That should be enough.'

Tian Yi selected some other reports and knelt down to write a quick bulletin. When she'd finished, I picked it up and read it out loud. '"Armed police in steel helmets charged out of the Zhongnanhai government compound with electric batons and attacked the students who were staging a peaceful sit-in outside. The Beijing University students Liu Wei, an English major, and Gu Yanting, a post-graduate student in the Department of African and Asian Studies, both suffered head and chest injuries and have been taken to hospital."'

'I think it's best you don't broadcast any reports about injured students,' Shu Tong said, sticking his chin up.

'I don't want to hear that kind of news either,' Mimi said.

'Dai Wei, go and listen in on the Headquarters' meeting,' Shu Tong said. 'Once we know what they've decided, we can come up with our own plan.' He moved his lips about after he spoke, as though he were trying to remove a scrap of food lodged between his teeth.

'They wouldn't let me in. I'm not a member of the standing committee.'

'Don't worry,' Hai Feng said. 'It's a plenary meeting. You won't have to vote. Hurry up . . .'

In the Hunger Strike Headquarters' tent on the other side of the terrace, Ke Xi picked up a pamphlet and said, 'Look at this! It says it would be a grave mistake for us to leave the Square now!' The back of his shirt was drenched in sweat. He'd lost a lot of weight during his fast. The Headquarters' meeting appeared to be drawing to a close.

Wu Bin rushed inside, sweat pouring down his face. He'd been appointed head of the Headquarters' intelligence office, and was preparing to set up a KGB-style anti-espionage system. He complained that the marshals still didn't know who he was, and had tried to stop him entering the upper terrace. Whenever he finished speaking, he'd raise his eyebrows – or flex his eye muscles, to be more precise, since he didn't have any eyebrows to raise.

'If you walk up to them with a pair of pliers like these and say you've come to repair the cables, they let you straight through,' Shao Jian said, lifting his pliers. 'That's what I always do.'

Cheng Bing got up to speak. Her face had become much rosier since she'd given up her fast. Or perhaps the redness was caused by sunburn. The pink leaflet in her hand looked like a slice of raw meat.

Old Fu was having a quiet word with Lin Lu. His face was sickly yellow. He looked as though he was coming down with another illness. Mou Sen was in the corner, smoking a cigarette. His goatee had grown quite long. He looked like a bohemian painter now.

An official announcement blared through the government loudspeakers: 'While martial law is in force, foreigners are forbidden to participate in any activities which contravene the martial law edict. The military police have the right to use whatever means necessary to deal with any offenders . . .'

The crowds in the Square were still shouting and braying. One side of the Square yelled, 'Reinstate Zhao Ziyang!' while the other side shouted, 'Protect Zhao Ziyang!'

'If we're going to defend ourselves against the army, we must buy weapons and start military training!' Tang Guoxian said, punching the ground with his fist. He'd tied a red cloth around his wrist to protect his watch.

'It's against the law for citizens to use weapons,' Yang Tao said.

'We will wrest power from the government's hands, like the French revolutionaries who stormed the Bastille!' Wang Fei shouted through his megaphone. 'With our blood we will build a new Paris Commune!' The previous night, he'd managed to buy tens of thousands of towels and face masks. Bai Ling had been impressed, and had given him an appreciative hug.

The loudspeakers tied to the Monument's obelisk screeched again, and a voice cried out, 'This is Sister Gao speaking, deputy chairwoman of the Beijing Students' Federation. I have an urgent announcement. We want to send a hundred students to the barricades to try and persuade our comrade soldiers to turn back. Both male and female students are welcome to volunteer . . .' Her voice drowned out Wang Fei's speech. The members of the standing committee quickly appointed Lin Lu acting commander-in-chief, then brought the meeting to a close.

Two student marshals escorted three soldiers onto the upper terrace. The soldiers said they wanted to tell the students about their refusal to implement the martial law order. The brims of their caps were drenched in sweat.

'A soldier addressed the Square this morning,' Lin Lu said. 'He kept jabbering on about cutting up enemy forces and penetrating the adversary's camps. I couldn't make head or tail of it. Go and listen to what this lot are saying, Dai Wei. See if you can understand what they're going on about.' Lin Lu then asked Tang Guoxian to take him to the major entry points into the city to check the state of the barricades.

To the north of the Eastern Wastes lies the Land of the Nobles. The inhabitants have jade swords attached to their waists, and feed on wild beasts. Two tigers accompany them wherever they go.

The cold wind blowing outside the ambulance car I'm lying in makes me long for the streets of southern China – the smell of mosquito-repellent incense wafting from street stalls, the fluorescent light falling on plastic buckets and brooms hanging from windows and doors. Sometimes I'd sit on a kerb, drinking a bottle of Coke and slapping the mosquitoes that landed on my legs. When windows began to light up in the early evening but the sky was still bright enough to see the leaves of the distant trees, I'd close my textbook and think about where I was going to take A-Mei that night . . .

Fragments of various conversations I had with A-Mei float around my parietal lobes, but the locations in which they took place have become muddled. 'You go to the play, if you want,' she said. 'I don't like that actress.' I remember that we were sitting in a restaurant at the time. There was a window behind her. Through it I could see pedestrians and buses and the large branches of a banyan tree that was trapped between two buildings. But now I hear her saying these same words to me during a telephone conversation, so the memory of the restaurant must have been fabricated. My memories are like old tapes that have been recorded over in so many places that the original track has become incomprehensible.

My clearest memory of A-Mei is of her saying, 'What is it you love about me?' She was sitting naked on our bed when she said this, her brown nipples tilting to either side. But that question is all I remember of the conversation. Everything that came before and after it is a void.

'We agreed that if I gave you eighteen yuan, you'd take us right up to the emergency room!' my mother whines, sounding both congested and anxious. 'You can't just dump him at the hospital gates like this!'

I have a temperature of forty-two degrees. Apparently, my lips have turned blue. But I don't feel I'm about to pass out. In fact, my thoughts seem unusually clear at the moment.

'This is a professional ambulance car, Auntie! We should have charged you ten yuan just to carry him downstairs – especially since you live on the third floor – but we only charged you eight. And now you're trying to beat the price down even more. How do you expect us to make a living?'

'The Xicheng ambulance cars charge twenty yuan, but the drivers carry the patients to the car, then carry them all the way to the waiting room when they reach the hospital.' My mother had gone to a public telephone box and called many different ambulance companies before she chose this one.

'Rubbish. There are only two ambulance companies in Beijing, and we're the best. The drivers have medical training, and our cars are fitted with first-aid equipment.'

'Please, doctor comrades!' my mother cries. 'At least help me carry him to the hospital's entrance. It's only fifty metres away. I'll give you an extra two yuan. It's so cold outside. If you leave him on the street, how will I be able to drag him over there all on my own?'

'. . . You don't love me,' A-Mei murmured as she sat on her bed. 'You just have a longing to return to the womb. Like those fish that go back to their natal streams to spawn and die . . .' The bedside lamp cast a yellow glow over her bare stomach.

Feeling a sudden urge to have a smoke on the balcony, I sat up, reached for my pack of cigarettes and said, 'Yes, your body's a fleshy tomb. You want to lure me inside and keep me trapped there for the rest of my life.'

She stared at me with wide-open eyes, startled by my outburst, and remained silent for a long time, hugging a pillow to her chest.

The love you felt for her has spread through your cerebellum and seeped into the medulla oblongata at the base of your brain stem.

More than twenty hours had passed since the government had declared martial law.

Like deer gathering at a lakeside to drink, the students gathered at the Monument, unaware that the Square was a hunting ground and the Monument was the snare.

'If the soldiers are armed with real guns and real bullets, the government must have given them orders to suppress us,' Fan Yuan said to Bai Ling, who stared back at him blankly.

Everyone on the upper terrace was seized with a strange and horrible fear. We glanced about nervously, listening, waiting, harbouring suspicions about each other.

'The martial law troops have been sent to protect the capital and restore order,' Tian Yi said, too softly for anyone to hear. 'They won't attack us.' The night before, she'd gone to the emergency tent suffering from exhaustion, and had fallen asleep on the ground. The doctors assumed she'd passed out and sent her to Fuxing Hospital. But she'd returned to the Square in the morning.

'Premier Li Peng drew up plans to crush this movement on the first day of the hunger strike,' said Sister Gao, her face etched with anxiety.

'Of course he did,' said Old Fu. 'This Square isn't Speakers' Corner in London's Hyde Park, where you can get up and say what you like. It's the symbolic heart of the Communist state.' A large ring of keys hung from his belt. We were standing in the shade of the the Hunger Strike Headquarters' finance office which he headed. He'd bought a safe and got a marshal to sit on it twenty-four hours a day.

'There are a million people down there,' Lin Lu said with a deadpan expression. 'It's like being surrounded by a human Great Wall.' Han Dan was standing next him, his face filled with confusion. The two bodyguards flanking him were members of the university football team. One of them was wearing trainers that were at least size 43.

'This is the Deng Xiaoping era,' said Zhou Suo, the rugged Qinghua University leader. 'The government wouldn't dare use violence against the students.' He was wearing a grey tracksuit and had a knapsack slung over his shoulder. He gazed out at the Square with the same look of stubborn determination as a Shanxi peasant gazing at the dry hills of the Yellow Plateau.

'We were in Deng Xiaoping's era two years ago when Old Fu and I were arrested over there,' I said, pointing to the north side of the Square. I saw a BEIJING BUDDHIST SOCIETY banner flying there.

Monks in yellow robes sat in a long row in front of it, holding up placards demanding religious freedom. In the packed crowds, they looked like a line of yellow stitching running across a patterned tablecloth.

'But the citizens can't keep manning the blockades day and night. They've got jobs to go too.' Wu Bin pulled a cigarette from the pocket of his blue shirt, placed it between his lips and struck a match.

Tian Yi was crouching down, sorting through her brown leather bag. When she opened the front zip, a red ballpoint pen fell out and rolled across the terrace's pale paving stones.

'All right, let's just stay here until they come and arrest us!' said Sister Gao, losing her temper. The red sleeveless top she was wearing had been washed so many times it was covered in tiny balls of fluff.

'We should set up a military affairs office,' Wang Fei said. He'd just pushed away a boy who'd jumped onto the upper terrace hoping to take photographs. Students were constantly climbing onto the terraces, but the marshals were usually able to push them back down before they had a chance to reach us.

'I've heard rumours that student leaders have been pilfering money from the donation boxes,' I said. 'I thought we came here to fight corruption and embezzlement!'

'Yes, I've heard the Federation has stashed away 10,000 yuan, all in hundred-yuan notes!' Bai Ling said angrily to Fan Yuan. 'That's people's hard-earned money you're stuffing your pockets with!'

'That's a false rumour!' Fan Yuan retorted.

'If you lot hadn't started the hunger strike, we wouldn't be facing martial law now,' said Sister Gao. 'You've even told the students to set fire to themselves if the police try to arrest them.' She knew that Bai Ling's criticism of the Beijing Students' Federation was a veiled attack on her, and wanted to bring the argument out into the open.

'That wasn't my idea!' cried Bai Ling. She was much shorter than Sister Gao, but her voice was twice as loud. She had the forceful, insistent air typical of girls from Shandong.

'Well you claimed it was your idea in the newspaper interview that was published yesterday,' Sister Gao replied. 'Someone must keep a check on the finances. We're spending tens of thousands of yuan a day on food.'

'You should stop going out for meals at Kentucky Fried Chicken then!' Bai Ling screamed, her face bright red. 'The donations you're spending were for the hunger strikers, not for you lot!'

'Tell me how much money is donated to you every day!' Wang Fei shouted, pointing to Fan Yuan's nose. 'I want the exact figure.'

'It varies. We have two officers looking after the finances.' Fan Yuan seemed afraid that Wang Fei was about to turn violent.

'When we didn't have enough cash to buy face masks and towels, we asked you to lend us some money, but you only gave us seven hundred yuan,' Wang Fei said. 'You behave like little emperors!' Then, turning to Sister Gao, he said, 'I've heard you've siphoned off a million yuan that was donated to the hunger strikers.'

'Rubbish! Old Fu's been looking after the Federation's finances too, so if you don't believe me, ask him,' Sister Gao replied.

'Mou Sen knows more about the finances than me,' Old Fu said, sitting down on a plastic barrel.

'You're deliberately sabotaging our movement!' Bai Ling said, pointing her finger aggressively at Sister Gao, her little chest puffing with rage.

Tian Yi pulled me aside and whispered, 'I'm fed up with Bai Ling. She keeps flying off the handle. She never used to argue like this back in the dorm.'

We walked over to the marble balustrades at the edge of the terrace. Tian Yi raised her camera and was about to take a picture, but the huge crowd below made her feel self-conscious, and she quickly put it down again.

'Mou Sen's got a bodyguard as well now,' Tian Yi said. 'He's acting like a leader.' Her skin was sallow, and her eyeballs looked yellow too.

'As soon as students from the provinces turn up, he assigns them work and gives them money, so he's built up a big army of supporters,' I explained.

The workers of Beijing had formed an autonomous federation and erected a tent on the northern edge of the Square. Fragments of their broadcast blew over in the warm breeze: 'Many soldiers have already sneaked into the city in plain clothes . . . Tonight, five army divisions will be airlifted into the Square . . .'

I looked beyond their tent to Tiananmen Gate where Chairman Mao's huge face was gazing down on the crowds; then south to the Mausoleum where his embalmed remains were housed. The sight of that grey concrete building sickened me. I wished the students would storm inside, drag Mao's corpse out and fling it over the walls of Zhongnanhai. The two immense sculptures of revolutionary peasants and workers that flanked the Mausoleum were dotted with students. They perched like spiders on the marble shoulders, legs and outstretched arms. A few were even sitting on the heads, making the statues look like mythical creatures from *The Book of Mountains and Seas*.

'Let's go and have something to eat,' I said.

'I'll never be able to squeeze through that crowd,' Tian Yi said. She was wearing a necklace of coloured glass beads she'd bought in Yunnan.

'Walk behind me. I've got trainers on, so I can easily barge my way through.'

The restless, sweaty bodies below us suddenly resembled maggots wriggling over a lump of meat. We descended to the lower terrace and slowly pushed our way into the tightly packed crowd. It was almost impenetrable. When someone in front of us wanted to go to the toilet or look for a friend, a tiny crack would open, and we could follow behind them for a while. The people lining these narrow pathways, which coursed through the Square like veins, would instinctively raise a foot or shift their shoulders back to make way for us as we passed. If they happened to be sitting down, we had no choice but to climb over their heads. When someone shouted a new slogan, the crowd's focus would shift, and a new path would open for a second before quickly closing again, like a wound healing over. But there was always a circle of space around anyone holding a Communist Party flag, a national flag, or a Communist Youth League banner.

With great effort, we managed to climb over the metal railings that circled the base of the Monument, squeeze our way over to the Museum of Chinese History, push through the crowds under the trees and leave the Square at its north-eastern corner. By the time we finally disentangled ourselves from the throng, the biscuits in my bag were crushed to a pulp and my body felt like a broken abacus.

'Damn, my lens cap got pulled off,' Tian Yi sighed, her hair in wild disarray.

When the midday light slants onto your face, a smell of soap rises from your skin. You lie slumped inside your body, just as your body lies slumped on the iron bed.

I hear a pigeon flapping away the air as it lands on a branch of the locust tree outside, and for a moment I see the world through its eyes. The red-tiled roof of the apartment building behind is covered with dust and fallen leaves. The locust tree is dark grey. When the sun comes out, residents nail washing lines to the trunk, tie them to their windows and hang out their quilts to dry, making the tree resemble an open umbrella-frame festooned with damp cloths. When it rains, the tree's bark turns black and the leaves appear greener and paler. The tree is almost as tall as our building. At night, whether lights were shining in the windows, or a power cut had plunged the compound into darkness, I always felt safe when standing beneath its branches.

My hearing has become very acute after these years of living in the dark. I can distinguish the different noises from every flat in this building. The sounds are especially clear in the hour before dawn. It's the afternoon now, and I can hear the yelping lapdog a neighbour bought last week, and the clucking hen downstairs that will soon become chicken soup. In her flat on the ground floor, Granny Pang is saying, 'That boy Dai Wei hasn't got much longer to live. There was blood in his urine a couple of days ago.'

'He's not really in a coma – he's just pretending,' her daughter replies, pushing down on a creaking door handle. 'But he's ruined the feng shui of our block.'

The man in the flat next door says, 'She's lucky to have her son to sing to. No one else would put up with all that shrieking!' He can't stand my mother's singing, and I can't stand his son flinging objects against the walls. The constant bashing makes me think of the layers of bricks of this building pressing down on each other.

For a moment I leave my slumbering body and hover in the fusty air of the room. I see myself sprawled across the bed, not in pyjamas now, but in a shirt and trousers. I can feel the belt's brass buckle press coldly against my navel. Then I see myself getting up and walking down the street. I run over and pat myself on the back.

Having lost the battle, General Fu Yu drowned himself in a river. If he appears to you inside a house, the emperor will die. If you see him wandering through the wastes, a calamity will befall the entire empire.

It was just after three in the morning. The government had announced that the army would clear the Square at dawn. I felt as though we were trapped inside a wooden cabin, waiting for the wolves to turn up.

The leaders of the Hunger Strike Headquarters were having a secret meeting inside the broadcast minibus to discuss whether they should leave the Square before the army arrived.

'When the army gets here, they'll arrest us lot first,' said Bai Ling, her face pale with fear. 'I've heard there are regiments waiting inside the Great Hall of the People over there and in the pedestrian underpasses. Speak up now, everyone, and say what you think we should do.'

'Yes, what if one of us gets killed?' said Cheng Bing. She'd been arguing with Tang Guoxian when I'd gone to fetch her. He and some friends had been making primitive petrol bombs with beer bottles and kerosene.

Mou Sen lit another cigarette. Mimi yelled a slogan out of the window then turned to us and said, 'Don't smoke inside the minibus! The fumes will ruin these bottles of mineral water.'

'There are only about 10,000 students in the Square now,' said Old Fu. 'The army will be able to march straight in and round up all the so-called "troublemakers" – which includes me, and everyone else here in this minibus.'

'But a million people marched through Beijing yesterday,' said Shao Jian. 'In Washington, six thousand Overseas Chinese marched in solidarity, and in Hong Kong, members of the Basic Law drafting committee threatened to resign unless the government listens to our demands. With support like that behind us, we have no reason to be afraid.'

Mimi and Chen Di were sitting on the front seats, broadcasting news bulletins to the students, most of whom were now asleep: 'Many government leaders such as Wan Li and the Long March veteran, Xu Xiangqian, support our movement. Xu Xiangqian even said to the army, "I will kill any soldier who dares shoot a member of the public . . ."'

'Look at this bulletin, Old Fu,' Mimi said, turning round. 'It says the Voice of America reported that the President of the United States has declared unequivocal support for our movement. Shall we read it out?'

'No, I think you've read enough,' Old Fu said. 'It's nearly half past three . . . We should pack up and get out of here.'

'The Beijing Students' Federation can take over the management of the Square,' Bai Ling suggested.

'We should have a meeting with them first to let them know what we're doing,' Mou Sen said.

'The army won't come now,' Pu Wenhua said in his high-pitched voice. 'It's far too late.' He had a pair of what looked like toy binoculars hanging around his neck. He was sitting squashed up next to Wang Fei.

'All right then, I propose we leave the Square straight away,' said Bai Ling. 'Commander-in-chief Han Dan, and acting commander-in-chief Lin Lu can stay and hold the fort. The rest of us should go.' Bai Ling was in low spirits. The previous night she'd confessed to Tian Yi that she felt ready to quit.

'We could set up a new base in the Fragrant Hills, and ask messengers to keep us up-to-date with developments,' Wu Bin said. 'If the government can't locate our command centre, they won't bother sending the army in.'

'There are still some Federation members up on the Monument. They've got a liaison office up there.' Lin Lu's mouth didn't seem to move when he talked.

'I don't think we can skulk off without telling anyone,' Shao Jian said. 'The students would never forgive us.'

'Are you going to stay here and wait until the police fling us in jail?'

Old Fu said. He was shaken by a rumour he'd heard that the army was going to butcher its way into the city. An hour before, he'd said he wanted to go and hide in his parents' flat.

'The hunger strike is over now,' Bai Ling said hoarsely. 'If we want to keep the flame of the movement alive, we must leave the Square and go underground.'

'The students haven't left yet, so neither should we,' Shao Jian protested.

'I still have 200,000 yuan of donations in here,' Old Fu said, patting his leather briefcase. 'I've given the rest to the Beijing University Organising Committee. The Federation's cash is controlled by five treasurers. I've had nothing to do with it. I'll share out what's left here between us and we can use it as living expenses.'

'You have no authority to do that,' Cheng Bing said. 'That money belongs to the movement.'

'I heard the Federation sent its cash off to the Politics and Law University,' Pu Wenhua said.

'I've never handed out any money before, apart for a few small expenditures,' Old Fu said, frowning. I could tell he hated having to deal with money. The only reason he suggested sharing it out was that he didn't want to be caught red-handed with a bag full of cash if the army came to arrest him.

'I'm not a member of the core leadership,' I said. 'But in my opinion, all the students should leave the Square now, not just us.'

'Everyone in this minibus is a member of the leadership,' Old Fu said anxiously. 'When the army arrives, they'll have photographs of us all. They'll know exactly who to look for.'

'Let's hurry up and share out the cash,' Bai Ling said, desperate to get going. 'You can write out receipts, Old Fu. Call it a survival grant, or an escape grant. We must leave now before it's too late.' She closed her eyes. She looked as though she was about to pass out.

'You go if you want to, but I'm staying here,' Cheng Bing said. 'I'd feel guilty sneaking away like this. So don't give me any of that money.'

'Bai Ling has made the right decision,' Wang Fei said. 'The army have been ordered to drive the students from the Square and arrest the core leadership. If we escape now, we'll be able to keep our political struggle alive.' He put his arm around Bai Ling to stop her falling over.

'It's too much!' Mou Sen said. 'We can't creep away without telling anyone. We must make an announcement and explain our actions.'

'We're going underground and taking the movement out into the city,' Wu Bin said. 'Deng Xiaoping has mobilised a third of China's regular army forces. More than 300,000 soldiers have encircled Beijing.

That's a larger military force than was sent to attack Vietnam.' Ever since Wu Bin had been appointed head of the intelligence office, he'd become Bai Ling's one-man think-tank.

'Do you hear that?' Old Fu said. 'They'll crush us if we stay here. I'll distribute the money now. We can call it an emergency grant. Who's got a torch?' He pulled the cash out of his briefcase and glanced at his watch, but it was probably too dark for him to see what it said.

'Look at all that money!' Shao Jian exclaimed, staring at the wads of cash. Mimi and Chen Di switched off the loudspeakers and came over to take a look.

'Let's give everyone a thousand yuan,' Old Fu said, starting to count the money. 'That should be enough.'

'If we're going underground, we must have a plan,' Mou Sen grumbled. 'We can't leave without agreeing on a strategy.'

'All we need to do is keep the flame burning,' Wang Fei said. 'If we escape arrest today, we can set to work on launching a national campaign for democracy.'

'So, tell us, Wang Fei,' I said. 'Are you staying or leaving?'

'I think I'll go into hiding for a while,' Wang Fei said, glancing at Bai Ling.

I wanted to do the same, and take Tian Yi back to my mother's flat to recuperate properly, so I said, 'Let's all go into hiding, then.'

'Well, I'm staying here,' Cheng Bing said.

'Me too,' Pu Wenhua squeaked.

'All right, but the rest of us will leave,' Bai Ling said, standing up. 'When it's time to make the next decision, we can liaise with Lin Lu.'

'We should disguise ourselves a bit before we leave,' Wu Bin suggested, narrowing his eyes conspiratorially.

'I'll be staying in Beijing,' I said, taking the wad of cash that Old Fu handed me, 'so I can check on the situation back at the campus before I go underground.'

By the time Old Fu got to Pu Wenhua, there was only two hundred yuan left, which made Pu Wenhua very cross. Wu Bin reminded him that he wasn't a member of the standing committee, so he was lucky to get any money at all.

'We should leave the minibus one by one, and go in separate directions,' Wang Fei said in a hushed tone.

'What about Nuwa?' I asked, peering out of the window. 'I haven't seen her for ages.'

'Neither have I,' Wang Fei said, looking away. 'Maybe she's popped back to the campus.'

'All right everyone,' Old Fu said. 'Remember, this is top secret. None of you must tell anyone what we're doing. I'll go first. Goodbye!' He grabbed his empty briefcase, opened the door and jumped out.

Mimi switched on her torch and said, 'I don't know where to go.'

'Why not come with me?' Bai Ling said to her.

Wu Bin said he'd stay in a hotel for a couple of days to see how events unfolded, and that once the army had cleared the Square, he'd return to Wuhan.

We stuffed our cash into our bags and began filing out of the minibus.

'Wang Fei, you – you – deserter!' Pu Wenhua spluttered, waving his plastic binoculars in the air as Wang Fei and Bai Ling stepped off the minibus.

I followed them out, but as I walked away, something felt wrong. I knew it would have been impossible to get all the students to evacuate the Square, but it didn't seem right that the leaders were skulking away like this, especially since they'd been urging everyone else to stay.

Tian Yi was asleep in a tent with three other girls. I woke her up, led her outside and asked her to come home with me. I didn't dare tell her that the leaders had absconded. She said she wouldn't leave the Square until the army came and dragged her away. I told her the government was going to launch a crackdown, and the soldiers would shoot to kill, and that if she died, she'd only have herself to blame. 'Why not come home with me and wait to see what happens?' I pleaded. 'You can always come back here later if you want.'

'You go home,' she said. 'If the army takes us away, you must return and continue the struggle.' Then she crawled back under the sheet printed with a double happiness emblem that served as the tent's entrance curtain.

'There are too many mosquitoes in here,' she said. I could tell from her voice that she was lying down again. 'Can you find me some insect repellent? Or tiger balm would do too.'

I knew it would be impossible to change her mind. I saw a few lights glimmering inside the Great Hall of the People, and wondered whether there were indeed 10,000 soldiers waiting inside, ready to strike. I left the tent and climbed up onto the Monument's upper terrace. Fan Yuan and Hai Feng were there with hundreds of foreign and Chinese reporters.

I wondered how the army would be able to clear the sleeping students from the Square while the world was watching their every move. Two students stuffed a leaflet in my hand. I read it under the lamplight. It was a copy of a petition signed by over three hundred Beijing intellectuals and academics calling for the Standing Committee of the National People's Congress to impeach Li Peng. It said, 'In the current situation, only the sacking of Premier Li Peng will be sufficient to assuage the anger of the people . . .'

What a waste of time! I muttered to myself. Do they really think that the delegates of the so-called 'People's' Congress give a damn about the people's anger? They're all Party members, for God's sake.

I decided to stay in the Square. I knew I'd have to get rid of the money, though. I didn't want to be caught with it. I wandered off to the Science Department's shelter, hoping to get some sleep.

Xiao Li and Mao Da had put up a sign outside that said BEIJING UNIVERSITY SCIENCE STUDENTS and had hung a sheet over the entrance. A few of the bamboo poles holding up the canvas roof had split and been tied together again with chiffon scarves. There was a sheet of plastic on the ground. My quilt was still damp from the previous night's rain. I didn't want to lie down on it.

Liu Gang and Dong Rong were at the back of the shelter fast asleep. Yu Jin and Zhang Jie were sitting up drinking beer.

'You looking for volunteers again, Dai Wei?' Zhang Jie said, staring at his bottle of beer. 'I warn you, I'm so drunk I can't stand upright. When's the army coming to clear the Square?' He swallowed another gulp of beer. The shelter was pitch black and stank of dirty trainers.

'Stop drinking!' I said. 'You must sober up. When the soldiers charge in here with electric batons, you'll have to be fast on your feet.' There wasn't enough room for me in the shelter, so I rested my head on a satchel in the corner and lay down with my legs outside the entrance. I thought about the thousand yuan stuffed inside my pocket. If the army found it on me, they'd assume I was a ringleader. I pulled it out, wrapped it inside a sheet of paper that was lying about and slipped it under my back. Then I closed my eyes and started counting. One, two, three, four . . . Just as I'd begun to doze off, I heard Ke Xi's voice screaming out from the Voice of the Student Movement's loudspeakers: 'Fellow students on the Square, don't panic. This is Ke Xi speaking! Ke Xi! Stay calm. We are in an extremely dangerous situation. I'm therefore asking all of you to vacate the Square immediately and move to the embassy district.'

'What's he shouting about now?' Xiao Li said, waking up. 'We're trying to get some sleep here.'

'He sounds delirious,' said Mao Da, sitting up.

'When the army arrives, we'll just sit here in silence,' Dong Rong said. 'Why's he getting so worked up?'

'Is the army here?' a student behind me asked. 'Quickly, play that army song, "Three Rules of Discipline and Eight Points of Attention". It might stop the soldiers resorting to violence.'

I sat up too, my mind numb with tiredness.

The students sleeping outside began to stir like blades of grass in a wind. They stood up, beat the dust off their clothes and stamped their feet. Flagpoles fell to the ground. I could hear the reassuring sound of girls chatting and laughing.

Everyone inside the shelter was sitting up now, asking anxious questions. A few students went outside to fetch face masks and towels.

'Why does he want us to move to the embassy district?' Xiao Li said. 'Where's Chen Di?'

'Let's go to the Voice of the Student Movement broadcast tent,' I said, glancing down at my watch, not wanting to divulge that Chen Di had run away. It was already 5 a.m. I quickly slipped the wad of cash back into my pocket and got up.

Xiao Li and I weren't allowed inside the Voice of the Student Movement broadcast tent. I didn't recognise any of the student marshals guarding it.

'Must we really move to the embassy district?' the students cried. A huge crowd had surrounded the broadcast tent to ask for more information. A student pulled down a parasol from a police watchtower and detached the wooden pole to use as a weapon when the army arrived.

A new voice crackled over the student loudspeakers: 'Ke Xi has just fainted again. He's been taken to hospital. Please ignore the order he issued just now. It didn't have the backing of the student leadership. I am Lin Lu, the acting commander-in-chief.'

Then Han Dan took the microphone and said, 'This is commander-in-chief Han Dan speaking. No one has decided to leave the Square yet – not the Headquarters, nor the Beijing Students' Federation, nor the Provincial Students' Federation. So everyone must stay where they are . . .'

Someone shouted through a megaphone: 'It's six o'clock! The army hasn't come! Fellow students, we have triumphed! The people have triumphed! Quickly, play the national anthem!' It was Chen Di. He hadn't run away after all.

His announcement brought a smile to everyone's faces. A feeling of relief and celebration swept through the Square. I glanced into the distance and saw pale rays of light peeping above the horizon.

Your spirit drifts towards the River of Blood which carried you into this world.

My mother is jabbering into her new telephone.

'I got it installed two weeks ago, but I still jump every time it rings.

In the past, only top government leaders had telephones in their homes . . . Americans? I know they've all got phones . . . What, they even have them out in the streets? Aren't they afraid someone might steal them? If only you could come back to China, Tian Yi, we could sit down and have a proper chat. My wooden son here might not think about you, but I do . . . It's your birthday next week, isn't it? He wrote the date down in his journal . . . I'm sorry, I know his journal is private, but the doctor told me I should read it out to him. He said it might help him recover some memories . . .'

I hate my mother reading my journal, especially the passages about A-Mei and Tian Yi. There are lots of references to sex, but fortunately she can't understand most of them. When she came across the line: 'I want to die inside your beautiful, fleshy tomb,' she said angrily, 'Look at this! When you talk to a girl about love, all you're thinking about is death.'

'. . . Tell American journalists what happened to Dai Wei?' my mother continues. 'Imagine what trouble I'd get into! Well, I'll discuss it with the relatives of other victims and see what they think . . . Was her son killed too? What's her name? Fan Jing? Yes, I know her. She put her cat in the front basket of her bicycle and rode around the Square for hours searching for her son's body. She never found it. The cat was heartbroken. It refused to eat and ended up dying of starvation . . . Can you hear me? I'm sorry, I'll turn it down. I always keep the radio on for him . . .'

The telephone is in the sitting room. I can hear the murmur of Tian Yi's voice, but can't make out what she's saying.

My mother finally ends the conversation then slams the receiver noisily back into its cradle. 'Your girlfriend's doing very well for herself in America,' she mutters. 'She's passed her driving test, and has seen all the sights of New York. She's even gone up into the head of the Statue of Liberty. She said it's higher than Tiananmen Gate. See what a wonderful life she's having now! If only you had come home with me that day like I begged you to, you wouldn't have ended up with a bullet in your head. You'd be out there in New York with Tian Yi, studying at an American university. Why is it that all the bad things happen to me? Is anything ever going to change?'

I want to tell my mother that my heart has become numb since Tian Yi left, and that all that remains of me now is a pile of skin and bone waiting to crumble into dust.

When the telephone line was installed two weeks ago, my mother was so excited she spent all day on the phone. When she couldn't think of any more friends to call, she rang all the local shops, then leafed through the telephone directory and dialled numbers at random. But since a friend told her that each call costs a minimum of two jiao, she's hardly used it at all.

All memories are reconstructions. When my mother reads out the pages of my journal, memories that have crumbled into ruin are rebuilt in a different form. When she reads out my description of climbing the mountain in Yunnan, I see myself walking up with Tian Yi hand in hand, but from a vantage point that is above and behind. Although we did climb this mountain together, the scene I picture is a fabrication. How could I have seen myself from behind? And besides, the rainforest we were walking through was so dense, it would have been impossible to see us through the leaves. Who is that person who was looking down at me? Does a part of us leave our bodies and keep watch over our lives, transmitting images back to our brains like a satellite?

I picture a crowd, and search for my face. I'm probably wearing a white shirt, with a white vest underneath, and a grey jacket on top. Tian Yi was right. When I stand in a crowd of students, there's nothing particular about me that marks me out, apart from my height. My face has no expression, no superfluous fat. It's a face you could see a hundred times without it sticking in your mind. The only remarkable feature on it is the pair of sunglasses that Tian Yi gave me. They're black, and a little too large, but at least they add some character to my face. I knew she liked them, so I wore them all the time in the Square. I can also see myself from behind, placing my hand on her shoulder and saying, 'It's your birthday on the 28th. Why don't we pack a copy of *The Book of Mountains and Seas*, and go and climb Mount Tai?'

'Don't look so pleased with yourself,' she said, frowning. Bai Ling had just called off the hunger strike.

'Well, I did tell you the strike wouldn't achieve anything. And I was right. We're stuck in limbo now.'

'What makes you so sure?' I could smell that she hadn't brushed her teeth yet.

If the waters of life were to run through my dry channels once more, would she creep out from the silt and drag me back to our old life? Oh, never mind. Perhaps I'm better off lying here with my memories. Time has lost all meaning for me. Even if I did regain my lost memories and wake up from this coma, the only real change would be that my horizontal body would become vertical again.

The smell of Tian Yi's body slides past your bullet wound then mingles with the scent of leaves and rain in your frontal lobes.

It was almost dusk. Old Fu suddenly appeared from nowhere and shouted to Mou Sen, who'd returned to the Square a few hours before, 'What are these foreigners doing here? They can't attend the meeting. The government will accuse us of "colluding with overseas reactionary organisations"!'

'They're not journalists. They're members of the Hong Kong Student Association and the American Overseas Chinese Student Solidarity Group.'

Mou Sen, as the Beijing Students' Federation's general secretary, had convened a meeting of one hundred university representatives to discuss whether we should leave the Square. He'd gone back to the campus and had some sleep, and was now full of energy.

'I don't care,' said Old Fu. 'They can't stay.'

'Where did you go off to, Old Fu?' I whispered.

'I went to a friend's house and crashed out on his sofa.' He didn't ask where I went. He could probably tell I hadn't left the Square.

Mou Sen's girlfriend Yanyan was setting up the tape recorder. I'd bumped into her several times over the past couple of days. She'd become much more involved in the movement since the end of the hunger strike.

'It's too much, Old Fu,' said Mou Sen. 'I organised this meeting. The Hunger Strike Headquarters has disbanded now, so you have no right to tell me what to do.' Old Fu fell silent and skulked off.

I spotted Nuwa running up from the Monument's lower terrace. 'Has Wang Fei run away?' she asked angrily. She was standing on the stone steps now. When she looked up at me, her forehead became lined with wrinkles.

'I'm not allowed to disclose that information to you,' I said.

She turned to Mou Sen. 'I heard you all had a secret meeting in the minibus and decided to run away.'

Mou Sen had run away, but had phoned me in the late morning to ask how things were. I told him that everything was fine, and that the army never came in the end.

He didn't dare lie to Nuwa, because Yanyan, who was standing next to him, knew the truth, so he just mumbled, 'It was never my intention to run away.'

'So even Bai Ling absconded, did she?' Nuwa said, her nose turning red with fury.

'Mou Sen wasn't at the meeting in the minibus this morning,' I lied, trying to help him out. 'He drank a bit too much last night and had a hangover. The Hunger Strike Headquarters decided they should disband now that the hunger strike is over, so everyone went off to do their own thing. Wang Fei probably went to the campus to get some sleep. I'm sure he'll be back soon.'

Nuwa stepped onto the terrace and turned her anger on me. 'Don't try to hoodwink me with your sneaky little lies!' she shouted. 'The broadcast station has received reports about what went on. Look, I have one right here. It says that at three o'clock this morning, you had a secret meeting in the minibus and split all the donation money between you.' She glared at Mou Sen, swirled round then left.

'Well done!' Yanyan said angrily in her southern accent. 'You lot have really brought shame upon the movement!' I'd never seen her lose her temper before.

I knew that if the rest of the students in the Square found out about the secret meeting, we'd all be finished. Splitting the donations between us then going on the run – no one would forgive us. I imagined that what angered Nuwa most was that Wang Fei had run away without telling her. She was supposed to be his girlfriend, after all.

'They're taking this very badly,' I muttered to Old Fu. 'If you do decide to run away, I doubt you'll be allowed back.'

'Keep your voice down,' Old Fu said, glancing about anxiously. 'We don't want anyone to hear us. All I can say is that the situation looked very different to us earlier this morning.'

'I want to give my escape grant back to you,' I whispered.

'You should all be ashamed of how you behaved,' said Yanyan. She looked very downcast. I didn't know how much she'd seen of Mou Sen recently, but during the hunger strike, she'd visited him several times, bringing him books and antiseptic wipes.

To my surprise, Mou Sen suddenly lashed out at her. 'What gives you the right to stick your nose into our affairs?' he shouted, flinging his cigarette stub onto the floor. 'It's too much!'

Although Yanyan had worked as a journalist in Beijing for two years, emotionally she was still quite immature. After Mou Sen's outburst, she held her breath for a moment with tears welling in her eyes, then grabbed her backpack and left, sending the lighter, cigarettes and bag of leaflets Mou Sen had placed on top of it flying into the air. This argument took place under the full gaze of the students and academics who were waiting for the meeting to start.

Mou Sen snatched the bottle of mineral water I was holding and took a swig. I tapped his shoulder and said, 'You shouldn't have been so fierce with her. What she said was right.'

'We've had lots of rows like this before. She keeps telling me to step back from the movement and think about my future. But if I did that, I wouldn't achieve anything.'

'Stepping back isn't necessarily a sign of defeat. You're a chess player. You should know that.'

'But since we entered the Square, it's been impossible to step back. There are no escape routes. We're trapped here, in the spotlight. We have no choice but to stay and fight.'

The upper terrace was packed. The army's non-appearance had left us confused, and no one knew what to do.

Chen Di stepped onto a chair and shouted, 'Our latest slogan is: "Li Peng is a corrupt, incompetent ass. It won't be long before he gets the axe!"' The crowd roared with approval then chanted in unison, 'Arrest Li Peng first, then Deng Xiaoping. Once those two guys are gone, the world will be at peace . . .'

'Tell Chen Di to shut up!' Liu Gang hissed.

'Those slogans are far too militant,' Han Dan said. 'We're not here to overthrow the government . . .'

Lin Lu climbed onto a stepladder which a French cameraman had vacated, and launched into a speech.

The meeting went on for many hours. Late in the evening, Bai Ling and Wang Fei turned up looking bedraggled and sheepish. No one asked them where they'd been. Bai Ling gave a short speech then went to the broadcast minibus with Tian Yi and Mimi to have a rest.

Almost all the leaders who'd absconded at dawn had returned to the Square by now. Everyone tacitly assumed that the government had decided against launching a crackdown.

Zhuzi had brought a hundred new volunteers to join the student marshal team. I sent ten of them to guard the finance office, and positioned the others around the perimeter of the Monument's upper terrace, then I too sat down for a rest.

Zhuzi lit two cigarettes and passed one to me. Almost simultaneously we said, 'Fuck, I could do with a beer now!'

'We still haven't got enough marshals here,' I said, my back dripping with sweat. While I'd been showing the new marshals where to stand, a group of what I suspected were government agents dragged me down to the base of the Monument. One of them tried to punch me as I pushed him away. 'The Monument to the People's Heroes belongs to the people of China,' he yelled. 'What gives you the right to occupy it?' I was taken aback by the question, and couldn't think of an answer.

'How are things back at the campuses?' I asked Zhuzi.

'I've been building up a city-wide security network. Each university has its own security division. All the major roads in Beijing are now guarded by our marshals. Shu Tong has moved the *News Herald*'s editorial office to Block 31. Students have been printing pamphlets attacking the martial law order, and have been handing them out at the train station and airport so they'll get distributed around the country.'

'This Square is a madhouse,' I said. 'If Tian Yi hadn't been so determined to stay, I would have left days ago.' I'd taken Tian Yi home to rest for a while, but after a brief nap, she'd insisted on returning to the Square, and I'd felt it was my duty to stay with her.

'You're afraid she'll run off with another guy!' scoffed Zhuzi. After each drag of his cigarette, he'd lift his chin and exhale a large puff of smoke.

'Fuck off!' I muttered. Through the ribbons of cigarette smoke, the crowd looked like a sea of foaming blood.

'All the students have been sleeping around. There's a lot of shagging going on in those tents at night . . .'

It occurred to me that Tian Yi and I hadn't made love for weeks.

'You should come and take control of the Square's security, Zhuzi. The Hong Kong Student Association are going to send us some walkie-talkies soon. We'll be like real policemen.'

'That'll be great. Once we've got a proper communication system set up, we'll be able to control the whole of Beijing.'

'I think I'll lie down now and try to get some sleep.' I always found it easy to talk to Zhuzi, perhaps because he was a similar height to me.

Just as I was closing my eyes, Shu Tong walked over and handed me a telegram from my brother.

I sat up again and read it out loud. '". . . Students from fifteen Chengdu universities marched through the rain today, protesting against the military crackdown in Beijing. We carried eleven coffins on our shoulders to commemorate the eleven students who set fire to themselves in Tiananmen Square . . ." Who told them there was a military crackdown?' I skimmed through the rest of the text and laughed. 'Ha! They even think that Han Dan was killed!'

Shu Tong didn't smile, though. 'We were the chess players at the beginning, but now we're pawns, and we've no idea who's going to take us in the next move.' He perched wearily on a large battered samovar. He was usually asleep by this time.

In the tent area below, most of the students were still awake, listening to Simon and Garfunkel tapes, playing the harmonica or having games of poker. People wandered in and out of each other's shelters. It looked as bustling as a night market. I could hear someone snoring nearby. The noise made me want to crawl into a soft bed.

Wang Fei joined us. He crouched down and took deep, nervous drags of his cigarette.

'What's the matter?' I said. 'Have you had a row with Nuwa? She was furious you ran away without telling her.'

'No, no, I've just tallied the results of Sister Gao's poll,' he whispered. 'The majority of the students want to leave the Square. If this information leaked out, we'd have to withdraw.'

'Well, maybe that wouldn't be such a bad thing.'

'Keep your voice down,' he said, rolling up the sheets of paper in his hand. 'No one must find out about this.'

'Look at this newspaper the Hong Kong Student Association gave us,' said Xiao Li walking up excitedly. 'It's amazing! A million people marched through the streets of Hong Kong in solidarity with us.'

I grabbed the newspaper from him, eager to see the photographs. After A-Mei broke up with me, I gave my photographs of her to Shi Ye and asked her to post them to her. But A-Mei's image was still carved in my mind. I knew I'd be able pick her out at once in a crowd, even if she had her back turned to me.

'Are you looking for your lost love?' Wang Fei said. He could be unexpectedly perceptive sometimes.

'Shut up!' I said, punching his arm. 'She's not living in Hong Kong now, anyway.' I glanced at the photographs then handed the newspaper back to Xiao Li, my pulse racing.

A girl called Miss Li from the Hong Kong Student Association had told me her friend was studying at the same Canadian university as A-Mei. She'd smiled at me and said, 'You're the chief of security here. That's very impressive. I'll get my friend to tell A-Mei. I'm sure she'll be proud of you.'

'The provisions stall the Hong Kong Association set up over there is great,' Xiao Li said, having supervised the stall's security for the last hour. 'They're giving out food, drink, clothes, umbrellas. You should go and grab some of the stuff before it all runs out.'

'You're such a peasant!' I said tetchily. Zhuzi was lying down now, about to drift off to sleep.

My thoughts turned to A-Mei. Although I was in love with Tian Yi, the wounds from my break-up with A-Mei still hadn't fully healed. Now that the eyes of the world were focused on the Square, it was possible she might see my face on television or in the newspapers, and then try to get in touch. Unfortunately, I wasn't one of the prominent leaders, so I knew the chances of her spotting me were remote.

'Where's Bai Ling?' Mimi asked. 'She was here just a minute ago, and now she's vanished.' Mimi and Tian Yi couldn't sleep, so they were strolling around the terrace arm in arm to pass the time.

'No one knows where she sleeps at night,' Zhuzi chuckled. 'That information is top secret!'

'You must be exhausted,' I said to Tian Yi, as she walked away. 'If you want to go back to the campus to sleep, I could find a car for you.' When she walked with her back straight, her loose hair would bounce around her shoulders.

'Look at these mosquito bites,' she said, turning round briefly to show me her arms. Then she walked off again, her hips swinging beneath her skirt.

The eardrum and ossicles vibrate, striking the oval window of your inner ear, allowing the familiar tones of her voice to be carried up the cochlear nerve into your brain stem.

Tian Yi's voice sounds gravelly on the other end of the phone. 'New York is much colder than Beijing. It must be the huge windows. The apartments are as cavernous as churches . . . I know you'll wake up one day, Dai Wei. You mustn't give up hope . . . You were always so wooden and remote. It used to drive me mad. We could never have a proper conversation . . . It's noisy outside. I'll close the window . . . Did you hear me? I said that fate brought us together but then tore us apart. We weren't meant for each other . . . Do you remember the Land of the Black Thigh in *The Book of Mountains and Seas*? Its inhabitants wear fish-skin clothes and eat seagulls, and are accompanied by two birds that wait on them night and day. You used to say you wanted to go and live there one day . . . I must go now. Take care of yourself . . .'

Tian Yi can probably tell that my mother keeps taking the receiver away from my ear to listen to what she's saying. Her voice sounds a little strained. It's strange to think she's been in America for almost a year now.

Like an invisible thread, her fragile breath travels across the oceans and enters my brain's auditory cortex. Images assemble in my parietal lobes. I see rain streaming down the panes of a huge window . . .

Your mind dredges up memories which you snatch hold of then scatter into the air.

'There aren't many of us instigators left in the Square,' Old Fu said to me the next morning as we returned from the lavatories of the Museum of Chinese History. 'We must keep strong. It's very simple: all we have to do is stay here patiently until the army arrives.'

'The government sent the police to arrest us in the 1987 demonstration, but this time they're sending the army,' I said. 'It's war.' I glanced around the Square. There were now far fewer of the impassioned speeches and heated debates that had characterised the early days of our movement. Some students were sitting up, singing along to tapes of Taiwanese pop music, but most of the others were lying down chatting to each other.

'If the army turns up, we'll just sit still. They might use tear gas, but that won't be enough to drive us away. Would they dare use bayonets? I doubt it. Electric batons, perhaps, but not bayonets.' It seemed as though Old Fu had forgotten that just twenty-four hours before, he'd distributed the funds to the student leaders and fled the Square in a terrified panic.

'Old Fu, you change your mind three times a day. You keep coming up with plans, but never have the courage to carry them out. If it weren't for the fact that you're a few years older than the rest of us, no one would listen to you.' I had a sudden longing to brush my teeth.

The crowd was so much sparser now, I could see from one side of the Square to the other. A few groups of students were helping street cleaners sweep rubbish into plastic bags. Although the subway was up and running again, not many residents had turned up to offer support. Fewer students were arriving from the provinces, and many of those who were already in the Square were beginning to return home.

'The government is using the Taoist idea of controlling chaos with quietness,' said Old Fu. 'It was clever of them not to concede to our demands.'

'These constant discussions about whether to stay or leave are meaningless. The fact is, we're trapped here, like chickens in a cage. All we can do is wait until the army comes and slaughters us.'

'I thought you were one of the brave ones, Dai Wei.'

'I don't want to argue with you. Shu Tong and Liu Gang talked to you last night, and they weren't able to change your mind. Hey, someone from the bus company came to ask if we could get the students off the buses. They need them back now.'

'Tell them they can take them away. We must get rid of them before the army turns up, or they'll get smashed. Ask someone to broadcast an announcement telling everyone to vacate the buses immediately.'

Wang Fei walked up holding a megaphone. His black leather shoes sparkled in the sunlight. He wasn't wearing socks. His bare ankles looked very pale, even through the dark lenses of my sunglasses.

'I've just spoken to a journalist,' he said. 'Guess who he bumped into in the Workers' Stadium? Deng Xiaoping's son, Deng Pufang – you know, the one in the wheelchair. The journalist asked him what he thought of the student demonstrations, and he said, "The sky must remain above and the earth below. Whoever tries to change the natural order will perish."'

'Do you understand now?' I said, turning to Old Fu. 'The government thinks we're trying to topple the state, and they're determined to crush us. Let's pack up and go back to our campuses.'

'Don't surrender so soon,' said Wang Fei. 'This is the moment we finally force the Communist Party to hand over power to the people. Only the brave are victorious.'

'Apparently another of the students who went on hunger strike has fallen into a coma,' said Old Fu. 'Can you ask Tian Yi to find out who it is?'

'I've almost sunk into a coma myself!' I said. 'I'm so exhausted, I can't think straight.'

'I must find Bai Ling,' said Old Fu. 'We're supposed to be going to another meeting of the Capital Joint Liaison Group.'

'Han Dan went to the last one, claiming he was the representative of the Beijing students,' Wang Fei said, fiddling with the switch of his megaphone. 'He's as bad as the Communist Party. None of us asked him to represent us.'

'Will you look after logistics while I'm away, Dai Wei?' said Old Fu. 'A factory manager has donated more towels and torches. Get some volunteers to distribute them. Wang Fei, you need to print out more leaflets informing the students how to protect themselves against tear gas. Chen Di has got hold of a special antidote. If there's a gas attack, you just dip your towel in it and hold it to your face. Hurry up now, there's no time to waste.' Old Fu glanced at his watch then went to look for Bai Ling.

'There are only bread rolls for lunch today,' I said as I followed Wang Fei onto the upper terrace. The three students running his propaganda office were printing leaflets on the mimeograph machine.

You watch a cell disintegrate within the coffin of its plasma membrane.

Tian Yi was sitting in the broadcast minibus chatting with the Hong Kong students. Miss Li was there, her hair slicked back into a neat ponytail that was so shiny it looked wet. You could tell at once she was staying in a hotel. I remembered that A-Mei's hair was sleek and smooth like that. She used to wash it every day. Tian Yi and Mimi looked scruffy in comparison.

'Of course we won't be able to fend off 200,000 soldiers, but if we go back to the campuses now, we'll become scattered, and it will be easier for the government to arrest us,' Mimi said, repeating a view she'd heard Bai Ling express.

'Why do we have to use such boring methods?' said a Hong Kong girl called Jenny. 'There are more exciting ways of resisting violence than sitting on the ground!' She was chair of the Hong Kong Student Association, and spoke in a thick Cantonese accent. She was wearing baggy trousers that tapered at the ankle. It was a style that hadn't reached Beijing yet.

'Yes, we should organise a massive student carnival,' Mou Sen said, looking up from the stack of accounts he was checking through. Earlier that morning, the Hong Kong Student Association had handed over tens of thousands of Hong Kong dollars to him, or rather to the Beijing Students' Federation. He should have had bodyguards protecting him.

'You're right, you can't learn about democracy from books,' I muttered. 'We should be imaginative and think up strategies of our own.'

'Our only reference point is the Cultural Revolution, so there's always a danger this democracy movement will degenerate into a communist-style rebellion,' Mou Sen said earnestly to the two Hong Kongese girls, raising his head once more from his papers.

'I was only seven years old when the Cultural Revolution ended,' Mimi said. 'What influence could it have had on me?' Then she opened the window and yelled out, 'Hey, Old Fu! Come here! We've been given a pile of student ID cards that were found lying around in the Square. We couldn't broadcast the students' names in case there were government spies listening, so we just asked anyone who'd lost their ID card to check these ones, but no one's come over yet.'

'Well, just keep hold of them for the time being,' Old Fu shouted back, irritated by Mimi's lack of common sense.

Five military helicopters suddenly came crawling through the sky, so low that they almost scraped the tip of the Monument's obelisk. Everyone became agitated. The ground rumbled as the air overhead pressed down on us. Tian Yi stuck her head out of the window, gazed up at the helicopters and excitedly reached for her camera, but her hands were shaking so much she couldn't unzip the case. Earlier that morning, Chen Di had broadcast an announcement calling for students to fly kites or release balloons to prevent army helicopters airlifting soldiers into the Square. A shopkeeper had donated a box of large silvery balloons, but they weren't any use to us as we didn't have any helium.

The helicopters completed another circle of the Square, dropped a cloud of leaflets into the air then flew away.

'That's too much!' Mou Sen muttered. 'How dare the government drop leaflets when their own martial law edict strictly forbids such actions?' Then he jumped out of the minibus and, like all the other students in the Square, dashed around frantically, grabbing as many leaflets as he could.

The sky was so blue and clear after the helicopters left that when anyone walked across the Square that morning, their gaze was inevitably drawn upwards.

The winged dragon, Yinglong, lives in the north-east corner of the Great Wastes. Since he killed Ziyou, he has been unable to return to the heavens and make rain fall from the clouds. Whenever a drought sets in, the local people dress up as him and pray for the rains to fall.

In the afternoon, Hai Feng rushed over to the minibus looking for Old Fu. He said a large crowd had gathered below Tiananmen Gate because three men had just thrown ink-filled eggs at Chairman Mao's portrait. The crowd by the Gate had become very rowdy, and he was worried a brawl might break out.

Everyone was shocked by this news, and suspected that the culprits were agents provocateurs, deliberately vandalising the portrait to give the government an excuse to launch a crackdown.

'Old Fu and Bai Ling haven't come back from the Capital Joint Liaison Group's meeting yet,' said Mou Sen. 'Go and find out whether those three men are working for the government.'

'It's a government plot!' Wang Fei said, raising his index finger. 'No question about it! Come on, let's check it out.'

We ran over to Tiananmen Gate and looked up at the portrait. Chairman Mao's pale face was flecked with black ink and red paint. One large splat between his eyebrows had trickled down to his mouth. But the painting was so huge that the specks didn't diminish the Chairman's imposing air. Hordes of students and Beijing residents had gathered below the portrait to take a look. Some praised the vandals, others accused them of reckless stupidity, but most were too busy taking photographs to say anything.

Student marshals had detained two of the three culprits in a bus parked outside the Museum of Chinese History. When we squeezed inside it, we saw the two young men kneeling in the aisle.

'These guys are called Yu Zhijian and Lu Decheng,' said Zhuzi. 'They're not students. They've given us their ID cards. We have no legal right to interrogate them. All we can do is ask them questions.'

'They have harmed the integrity and good discipline of our movement, and we must deal with them accordingly,' Tang Guoxian barked, punching the wall of the bus. He was still as boisterous and loud as he'd been at Southern University, but since he'd joined the Provincial Students' Federation, he'd lost his joviality. He'd become quite ruthless, too. Although Wang Fei had founded the Federation, he'd had him expelled on the grounds that he was studying in Beijing.

'We should hold a press conference at once and make clear we have nothing to do with these men,' Wu Bin said, flaring his triangular eyes. 'Then we should hand them over to the police and let them deal with them.'

'You came here to sabotage our movement and give the government an excuse to crack down on us,' Wang Fei said, removing his glasses.

Yu Zhijian was the first to reply. He looked up and said, 'Our action was no more radical than the slogans you've been shouting in the Square.' His thick eyebrows buckled together in the middle of his unhappy, square face.

'To be honest, I've often thought of doing something like that,' Wang Fei said. 'I'd love to assemble a big crowd and go and drag Mao's body out of the Mausoleum. There are only two armed officers guarding the entrance. Tell us, who sent you here?'

'It was our idea to do this,' said Yu Zhijian. 'No one put us up to it. We're from Chairman Mao's native province of Hunan. We wanted to express our anger at the crimes he committed against the Chinese people.' He unzipped his beige blouson to let the sweat that had collected around the collar escape down his neck.

'Would you like something to drink?' Mou Sen said, squatting down. 'I know your motives were good, but your actions might turn the people against us. Many of the citizens who've come out to support us have been holding up pictures of Chairman Mao. He's still a hero to them.'

'We wrote a statement expressing our views but you refused to broadcast it,' Yu Zhijian said, passing a copy of it to Mou Sen. 'That's why we had to resort to direct action.'

'Yes, I read it,' said Mou Sen, handing the copy back to him. 'We can't broadcast any criticism of Mao now. We're trying to keep the army back. The soldiers waiting to march into the city worship Chairman Mao. They'd go mad if they heard us criticise him.'

'Do you know anyone here in Beijing who could verify your identities?' Wang Fei asked, softening his tone a little. 'How are we to know your ID cards aren't forged?'

'A Central Television reporter wants to do some interviews,' Wu Bin said, stepping back into the bus.

'Good,' Tang Guoxian said, lighting a cigarette. 'It will give us a chance to make clear we weren't responsible for this act of vandalism.' I'd never seen him smoke before. He seemed very anxious.

'Go and speak to the Hunan students,' Lu Decheng said. 'Maybe one of them knows me.' He was a short guy, with arched eyebrows and a thin goatee. The shirt under his black woollen slipover was grimy. He didn't look like a government agent to me.

The Central Television reporter stepped onto the bus. Wu Bin checked his identity card and said officiously, 'We can only spare you half an hour.'

Tang Guoxian walked over to Zhuzi and me and asked us to help organise a press conference.

'We're not a police force,' Zhuzi said disapprovingly. 'We have no right to arrest people. I think we should just let these guys go.'

'Mao may have been a tyrant, but you shouldn't have vandalised his portrait,' Hai Feng shouted at the two men. 'The government will treat us as enemies now. You've created a serious political incident here.' His face was so contorted with anger he looked as though he was weeping.

'This Square is a public forum,' Yu Zhijian said. 'Everyone should be free to come here and express their views. We were protesting against autocracy, like everyone else here.'

'I'd like to start the interview,' the reporter said, switching on his tape recorder. 'Would you mind leaving us alone for a while?'

As we moved out of the bus, we heard the young man called Yu Zhijian explain in a thick Hunan accent what he and his two friends had done. 'We arrived in Beijing the day before martial law was declared. We were excited to join the student movement, but soon became frustrated at the direction it was taking. The hunger strike didn't achieve anything. We knew we'd have to use more radical tactics if we wanted to continue pushing for political reform. Our original plan was to take the portrait down, but it's nailed very securely to the wall . . .'

'That guy's too pompous to be a government agent,' I said, listening in from outside.

'Can you call the journalists over, Mou Sen?' Tang Guoxian asked as he stepped off the bus.

'There's no need for a press conference,' Mou Sen said grouchily. 'We should just issue a statement saying the students had nothing to do with this act of vandalism.'

'Yes, me mustn't blow this out of proportion,' said Wang Fei, stamping his feet nervously, aware that he'd overreacted. 'They did go a bit far, but they were right to attack Mao. He symbolises all that's wrong with our country.'

Two men in their thirties walked up and said, 'Hand those guys over to us. We'll deal with them.'

I could tell at a glance that these were genuine government agents, but Tang Guoxian didn't catch on. 'Who are you?' he said loudly.

'We're from the security office,' one of them answered. 'We should be handling this matter.' He looked very much like the policemen who'd interrogated me in 1987.

'Before we hand them over to you, we must make sure they have no connections with the student movement,' Tang Guoxian replied.

'You're from the Tiananmen Police Station, aren't you?' I said. 'I've had a lot of dealings with Inspector Zhang.' Over the previous couple of weeks, I'd visited the local police station twice to discuss matters of security.

'What's your job?' the government agent asked me brusquely.

'I'm the Square's deputy commander of security. I must ask you to be patient. We can't afford to do anything that might jeopardise the safety of the students in the Square.' I could tell my authoritative tone had successfully bridled them.

'Well, you understand that this matter needs be sorted out, then,' they said. Not wanting to continue the conversation any longer, they turned and left.

'Now *those* are government agents,' I said.

'Maybe they're all in it together,' Tang Guoxian said, still misreading the situation.

'We must ask the Headquarters what they think,' Wang Fei said, running his hand through his hair.

'You mean the Hunger Strike Headquarters? That disbanded ages ago!' Tang Guoxian said, stepping back onto the bus.

Zhuzi and I went to the tent of the Beijing Workers' Federation to see what they thought should be done.

It was sweltering hot. It must have been at least thirty-six degrees. The Square had no shelter and was paved in concrete, so on a hot day the heat became overwhelming. Most of the students had drifted off to the sides of the Square to cool down in the shade of the trees. Beijing residents who'd turned up to offer support or merely observe the passing scene wandered through the almost empty Square shielding themselves from the scorching rays with sunglasses, sun hats and umbrellas.

'I don't think it was a government plot,' Zhuzi said, wiping the sweat from his forehead as we entered the Workers' Federation's tent.

As we'd suspected, Yu Dongyue, the third of the three Hunanese demonstrators, was there. He was sitting on a stool, his dirty shirt stained with flecks of black ink. Fan Yuan was asking him if he'd like a bowl of noodles. Zhuzi went over and said, 'Don't worry. Your two friends are with the Provincial Students' Federation. They're being interviewed by a television reporter.'

'You're in pretty deep shit!' I said. 'The students want to hand you over to the authorities and the secret police are onto you as well.' It was unbearably hot inside the tent. I pulled off my T-shirt and immediately felt much better.

'We'll take responsibility for our actions,' Yu Dongyue said. 'We won't shift the blame onto anyone else.'

'Well, you're free to leave now, if you want to,' Fan Yuan said. 'Here's your watch and your documents.' Fan Yuan had been helping out at the Workers' Federation since he'd been sacked from the Beijing Students' Federation for fleeing the Square during Zhao Ziyang's visit.

Yu Dongyue looked up and said, 'We won't run away. We'll see this thing through to the end.'

'They didn't break the law,' Zhuzi said. 'Why did you take his watch? You're not police officers.'

'The Dare-to-Die Squad confiscated it when they brought him over from Tiananmen Gate.' I'd often seen Dare-to-Die members running around the Square in their red armbands. The Workers' Federation had created this squad to deal quickly with any trouble that broke out in the Square.

'How old are you?' I asked Yu Dongyue. He looked very young.

'Twenty-two,' he said, taking a gulp of water.

'We're a couple of years older than you,' Zhuzi said. 'We're more experienced, too. I'm a law student. I know that if you burn the national flag, which is a symbol of the nation, you'll get three years in prison. So if you deface Mao's portrait, you'll probably end up with a similar sentence.'

'There's nothing in the constitution that says a person's portrait can be regarded as a symbol of the nation,' Yu Dongyue replied.

'What subject are you studying?' Zhuzi said.

'I studied Fine Art at university. I work for Changde Press now, in Hunan.'

Wu Bin marched into the tent, accompanied by four student marshals. He said he wanted to hand Yu Dongyue and his two friends to the national security police. His tone was very gruff. I advised him to phone up Changde Press to check Yu Dongyue's identity. But Wu Bin replied sternly, 'It's obvious they're working for the government. We can't let this event become another Reichstag Fire.' He'd never behaved so imperiously before. The vastness of the Square seemed to have inflated everyone's egos.

'Dai Wei's in charge of security in the Square,' Zhuzi said, sitting down. 'Let him deal with this.'

'He doesn't have any authority. The Hunger Strike Headquarters has been dissolved and the Beijing Students' Federation has broken up as well. The Provincial Students' Federation is the only student organisation left in the Square, so we should be controlling matters of security here.' Wu Bin delivered his lines like an actor on the stage. He'd recently been appointed the Provincial Students' Federation's vice chairman.

'You've no right to take the law into your hands!' Zhuzi countered.

'If you don't let these men go, you'll be no different from the thousands of plain-clothes officers already swarming through the Square,' I said to Wu Bin. 'If the Dare-to-Die Squad had flung ink on the portrait, would you have arrested them too?'

The leader of the Workers' Federation walked into the tent and said, 'The troops have surrounded Beijing. We can't give the government any excuse to launch a crackdown. If they were to take a hardline approach now, you students would get three-year sentences, but we workers would get locked up in jail for the rest of our lives.'

Wu Bin grabbed Yu Dongyue's arm and dragged him out of the tent.

'I'm a law student,' Zhuzi shouted angrily. 'I'm telling you, this is the most idiotic and dangerous decision you could ever make, Wu Bin.'

'There are so many different security teams now,' I said as we watched Wu Bin drag Yu Dongyue and his two friends off to the police station. 'Yesterday, the Lanzhou University students set up a squad called the Wolves of the North-West.'

'Most of the students in the Square now are from the provinces, so as chairman of the Provincial Students' Federation, Tang Guoxian has a lot of power,' Zhuzi said.

We wandered back to the broadcast minibus. Girls stared at us as we passed, whispering to each other, 'Look at those two tall guys. I bet they play basketball.'

When we were halfway across the Square, a strong wind whipped up, lifting plastic bags and scraps of paper into the air. The sky overhead filled with black clouds. There was thunder and lightning, then torrential rain drummed down. By the time we finally reached the minibus it was packed with people and we couldn't squeeze in.

The fifty buses that had been parked in the Square had gone now, so there was nowhere for us to shelter. The only objects surrounding us were the flags, posters and dirty mosquito nets that were being battered by the downpour.

A voice shouted, 'This storm is Chairman Mao taking his revenge!'

A chill ran down my spine. I turned back to look at Mao's portrait, but saw that it was now covered by a large sheet of cloth.

'He's right!' someone else shouted. 'Those three vandals will get struck by lightning.'

'Don't say that! It will bring us bad luck!'

A few students ran frantically across the Square, searching for an umbrella to hide under. In the distance, I could hear girls screaming in terror.

'Don't forget that Mao's corpse is lying right in the middle of this Square.'

'They dared throw ink on the emperor's face!'

'Fuck you, Chairman Mao!' Wang Fei shouted, standing stubbornly in the rain. The thick lenses of his glasses looked like two ping-pong balls.

A sense of menace pervaded the Square. It was cold and dark. Even during the biggest thunderstorms, I'd never seen the sky turn so black before.

But a few minutes later, the clouds left and the sky lit up again.

Tian Yi ran out of the minibus, pulled out her camera and began photographing the aftermath of the storm. Everyone was trembling with cold. We passed round towels and sheets of toilet paper, and tried to rub ourselves dry.

Tents, cotton sheets, quilts, wooden planks, banners and posters floated in the pools of rainwater that covered the ground. In a bemused daze, students began wandering over to the new Mao portrait the authorities had just hung up to replace the vandalised one.

It wasn't until an hour or so later, when a huge procession of Beijing residents came marching into the Square shouting their support for us, that the mood in the Square began to lift a little.

Local residents donated ten boxes of umbrellas and padded jackets. We distributed them among the crowd in the bright afternoon sun. It soon became so hot that we had to strip down to our vests. Bai Ling returned to the Square at last. She was furious when she heard that the three guys from Hunan had been handed over to the police. She took off her baseball cap and, fanning her face with it, said, 'That wouldn't have happened if there hadn't been a power vacuum in the Square. My plan now is to establish a group called the Defend Tiananmen Square Headquarters.'

I remembered the peasant I'd met in the Square in 1987 who was sentenced to ten years in jail, and suddenly felt ashamed that I hadn't done more to stop Wu Bin taking those three guys off to the police station.

'That's a great plan, Bai Ling,' Wang Fei exclaimed. 'We won't leave this Square until we achieve victory!' He and Bai Ling seemed to have struck up a close bond since they'd absconded together.

'You must persuade the Provincial Students' Federation to calm down and stop stirring up trouble,' Bai Ling said to him. Her large sunglasses had slipped halfway down her nose.

'I give you my word of honour!' Wang Fei said, saluting her theatrically. 'I can handle that upstart Tang Guoxian. No problem! He always took orders from me back at Southern University.'

'How did that university manage to produce such a cocky band of graduates?' Bai Ling said with a flirtatious smile, swiping Wang Fei's glasses off him.

'It really is time we left this Square,' I groaned.

'Stop being such a grump, Dai Wei!' Tian Yi snapped. She'd agreed to go home with me earlier, saying she'd get her films developed on the way, but after Bai Ling returned, she changed her mind and decided to stay.

Shrouded in the smells of herbal medicine and sour leftovers, your body moves closer to the earth.

'We're leaving tomorrow!' my mother says, walking back into the room.

The police, who've been monitoring our flat for the last week to ensure no one visits us during the fourth anniversary of the 4 June crackdown, have left now, and my mother has been telephoning friends and relatives trying to arrange our trip to Sichuan Province. Master Yao, the qigong teacher, has advised her to take me to Qingcheng Mountain to see a qigong healer who specialises in treating the varied and complex ailments of bedridden patients.

The doors and windows of the flat are open. The new plastic tiles my mother has stuck to the floor have been baking in the sun, filling the room with a pungent smell of glue.

'If only you'd hurry up and die! Can't you make a little more effort to control yourself and show your poor mother some respect? It's so humiliating having to clear up your mess.' My urine has overflowed again and dripped onto the floor. My mother pulls my catheter out of the full bottle of urine then inserts it into an empty one. The catheter attached to my bladder is emitting a warm, rubbery smell. 'What crime did I commit in my past life to deserve a fate like this?' my mother grumbles as she shuffles off to the toilet.

She forgot to switch on the radio today or to pull down the blinds. The blistering sun has been beating down on me all morning. I feel like the stinking rubbish bins baking on the street corner outside. A collage of shapes drifts through my head. At first, they look like slices of hard-boiled egg stuck to the steep walls of my brain. Then the central yellow cores expand and the intricate structure of the cells is revealed . . . I see A-Mei walk into my room in the Guangzhou hospital I was admitted to after our break-up. She emerges from the dark corridor, stands still for a moment in the bright light, then moves towards my bed. Her black dress hugs the gentle curve of her stomach then creases between her thighs. She leans over, her hair and hand touching my feverish face. 'I've been here for weeks,' I mumble, my eyes moistening. 'What took you so long?'

Although this episode never occured, it's stored in my long-term memory together with events that really did happen. Every time my temperature rises above thirty-nine degrees, it reappears before my eyes.

When I was lying in that hospital bed with a raging fever, the other patient in the room assured me that no girl in a black dress had come to visit me. He was suffering from a blocked intestine. The pain kept him awake all night, so he would have known if anyone had visited. I can still remember how he'd scrutinise my expression, like a dog gazing at his master, trying to determine what emotion he should be feeling. He had a thick chin and honest eyes, and teeth that glinted each time his mouth twitched. Every organ of his body seemed to be waiting to be told what to feel. I'll never forget the guilty glance he gave me after he screamed in pain so loudly that he frightened even himself.

My relationship with A-Mei is like a piece of uncut cloth. I'll never get a chance to make anything out of it. Perhaps she has already vanished into dust by now.

Inside my parietal lobes, I often rewind to those last moments before I was shot, trying to work out what I saw. But a few seconds before the bullet hits my head, there is a loud gunshot and the image of a girl, in what looks like A-Mei's white skirt, falling to her knees. Then the scene breaks off. Perhaps it wasn't A-Mei at all, just someone who resembled her. I haven't heard any news of her since. No one has mentioned her name. But as far as I know, no foreigner or Hong Kong citizen was killed during the massacre. If she had been shot, I would have found out by now.

The piece of my skull that flew off when the bullet struck is now lying in a hospital refrigerator. Although skin has grown over the gap, the medulla and nerve cells along the edges of the wound have died. Scavenger cells have eaten away at them, leaving behind tiny granules that lie scattered among the living cells like grains of sand in a bowl of rice, strengthening the wound tissue.

My mother's always forgetting to turn on the radio. The silence is a torment because it forces me to recognise that I am lying motionless on an iron bed. Whenever I contemplate this truth, I hurriedly return to the streets I used to walk down and try to hide myself in the crowds. After a while, my mind clears, and death shows its face to me. In fact, death has been lurking inside me for years, waiting to strike me down when a disease sends the signal. Most of the time, I pretend not to know it's there.

I'm on an aeroplane, soaring into the heavens. There's nothing in front of me, not even an angel with a broken wing . . . By the time a female foetus has grown to the size of a banana, it already possesses all the egg cells it will use in its lifetime. And inside each one of its egg cells lies another tiny angel . . .

'If this trip doesn't cure you, I won't bother bringing you back,' my mother mutters as she hurriedly packs our bags.

Those mythical lakes and hills are the flesh and blood of your body. You set off once more from the Western Mountains, that vast range of seventy-seven peaks, then travel 17,510 li to the . . .

Wang Fei walked into the propaganda office with Zheng He, the bald writer enrolled in the Creative Writing Programme. They were both wearing square, brown-framed glasses. Wang Fei waved a sheet of paper and said loudly, 'Here's a list of the members of the Defend Tiananmen Square Headquarters' standing committee. Hurry up and type out a copy of it for us.'

I took the list from him and read, 'Commander-in-chief: Bai Ling. Deputy commanders: Wang Fei, Old Fu and Lin Lu. General secretary: Hai Feng. Chief adviser: Liu Gang. Head of security: Zhuzi . . .' Sister Gao, representing the Beijing Students' Federation, also gained a place on the committee.

After Mou Sen looked through the list, he said, 'That's too much! What about Shu Tong and Han Dan? And why hasn't Ke Xi got a post either? They were the instigators of this movement too, after all.'

'Han Dan is the convenor of the Capital Joint Liaison Group,' Zheng He said. 'It's an important role. Type up the list then print out some copies – two hundred should be enough. Add a note at the bottom saying that our first task will be to unify the Square's security passes and student marshal teams.' His goldfish eyes sparkled behind the thick lenses of his glasses.

I was disappointed not to see my name on the list. When I'd returned to the Square that morning after spending the night at home, Miss Li from the Hong Kong Student Association told me she'd phoned A-Mei in Canada, and that A-Mei had been very pleased to hear I was the Square's security chief. She said that the Association of Chinese Students in Canada was sending a delegation to Beijing to support our movement, and that A-Mei might join them.

Spotting me in the corner, Wang Fei said, 'You can be deputy commander of security, Dai Wei. Zhuzi doesn't come to the Square very often, so you can still look after the Beijing students' camps, as well as the Monument and broadcast station area.' I pushed my sunglasses further up my nose and grunted my acceptance. Then he turned to Mou Sen and said, 'And I've appointed you deputy head of my propaganda office.' The musty odour of sweat wafting from his armpits smelt odd today. I suspected he'd splashed on some cologne.

By noon, I'd called the tallest student marshals to the Monument's lower terrace, given each one a baseball cap and a red armband, and informed them that the Headquarters had decided to take over the Voice of the Student Movement's broadcast station.

Mou Sen had set to work reorganising Wang Fei's propaganda office, which now belonged to the Headquarters. He was a much more competent manager than Wang Fei. He'd recruited a new batch of volunteers, brought back the mimeograph machine, stencil boards and wax paper that had been returned to the campus, and erected a new tent to protect the office from the sun and the rain. When I walked inside, it felt cool and well ventilated.

I told Mou Sen that if we managed to take over the Voice of the Student Movement's station, he could move his propaganda office into that tent, if he wanted. I glanced over at Nuwa as I spoke. As well as being the newsreader, she was now also the student press officer.

Everyone seemed to be enjoying this fresh burst of activity, especially Tian Yi, who was now editor-in-chief. She was sorting through a pile of documents in the corner of the tent, too preoccupied to talk to me. Hundreds of volunteers were running around the terrace, delivering boxes of stationery to the tent, distributing leaflets and security passes, and clearing away dirty plastic sheets and abandoned bicycles.

'It looks like we're heading for another big wave of protests,' I said glumly, treading on an empty tin of luncheon meat.

'We'll keep going for a few more days and see what happens,' Mou Sen said, looking up from the letter he was drafting. 'When we had that secret meeting in the minibus a couple of days ago, I was in favour of leaving the Square. But now I feel there's a possibility this democracy movement might at last take off and spread to the rest of the country. The Communist Party killed your father, and it killed my father too. Our generation has now got a chance to stand up and protest. We should make the most of it. It may never come round again.'

'We've given the government a fright. Isn't that enough?'

'No, it's not enough! We arrived in this Square waving the national flag and singing the national anthem. That shows how petrified we are of the government. You think you'll be safer back in your dorm room, but the police could easily drag you away from it if they wanted to. There's nowhere to hide in this country. Every home is as exposed as a public square, watched over by the police day and night. If we want to create a country in which everyone can feel safe, we'll have to do much more than give the government a fright . . .' He got up and went to talk to Nuwa, who was typing up a news script. When I glanced over at her again, I caught a glimpse of her cleavage and a small patch of her white bra.

A voice boomed through a distant loudspeaker: 'This is Bai Ling speaking. I am now commander-in-chief of the Defend Tiananmen Square Headquarters . . . I want to mobilise every Chinese person around the world to resist martial law! If the government can't succeed in imposing martial law after four days, then it won't succeed after ten days, a year, or a hundred years! . . .' When she came to the end of her speech, the crowds roared their applause.

You lie on your bed like a felled tree decaying on the ground.

The breeze blowing through the window smells of sour dates. The tart, puckery scent always reminds me of Tian Yi. Whenever I think about girls, various smells come to mind, especially those emitted from their feet and leather sandals.

Perhaps if I make it into the twenty-first century, scientists will be able to embed a microchip into my brain that will replace my wounded hippocampus. By then, the government will have created a Ministry of Memory which will produce silicon chips that mimic the pattern of the brain's nerve cells. Once a chip is inserted into my head, it will connect with my neurons, bypassing damaged tissue. I wonder whether the chip will be able to register the scent of Tian Yi's body and commit it to my long-term memory.

It's the rainy season, and I can hear the swollen wood of my mother's wardrobe crack in the humid air. It makes me think of when my father used to take off his shirt and go into the yard to saw up planks of wood. All the neighbours would wander out to see what he was up to. He'd set up a long workbench under the locust tree. No, it wasn't here that he did the carpentry – it was outside the dormitory block we used to live in. But there was a locust tree there too, I think. The local Dongfeng Watch Factory would put out their rubbish on Saturday mornings, and if you went there early enough, you could pick up metal coils and scraps of copper, but my brother and I always chose to stay with our father instead. When he shouted 'Tea!' I'd run up to our room and brew him a cup, while my brother swept up the wood shavings and handed them out to the other kids in the yard. In just three days my father was able to construct a wardrobe that was taller than him.

Although my father was a violinist, I never saw him perform in public. I prefer to remember him as a carpenter rather than a musician, and recall his strong, chapped hands sliding a wood plane across a plank, creating beautiful mounds of curled shavings . . .

Within the sea of dead cells, the surviving neurons reconnect, allowing the agitation and excitement of those days to appear once more before your eyes.

'You have no right to barge in here!' a skinny Qinghua student called Zhang Rui cried as we stormed into the Voice of the Student Movement broadcast station.

There were only about twenty marshals manning the security cordon outside the tent, whereas there were more than fifty of us, so we were able to push our way through quite easily.

When Wang Fei announced that the Defend Tiananmen Square Headquarters was going to take over the station, the Qinghua students inside the tent became incensed.

Mou Sen tried to reason with them. 'The Beijing Students' Federation, which you and your leader Zhou Suo belong to, has merged with the Headquarters,' he said. 'So it's only natural we should take control of your station.'

'People come here every day trying to take us over,' Zhang Rui said. 'How can we be sure you've been given authority to do this?' The two girls in the tent continued to read through their documents, and didn't bother to look up.

'This is a note from Sister Gao,' Wang Fei said. 'And here's a list of instructions from Bai Ling, our commander-in-chief. We've come here to carry out the transfer of power. From now on, everything in the Square must be managed in a planned and regularised manner.' His jacket was draped over his shoulders. He looked like the leader of a rough street gang.

'Will I be able to stay here and carry on with my job?' one of the girls asked, looking up at last.

'There's no need,' Wang Fei said. 'We have enough staff of our own.'

'We only take orders from the Beijing Students' Federation,' the other girl said stubbornly.

'I'd better write an announcement informing the students of the takeover,' Zhang Rui said, realising that his situation was hopeless.

'Wait a minute,' Wang Fei interjected. 'I'd like to go through this equipment with you. We'll give you a receipt for everything.'

'I must write the announcement first. Surely you'll let me do that?'

'Let him write it,' Mou Sen said, stamping out a cigarette butt he'd tossed on the ground.

Zhang Rui dashed off a statement in English, and said, 'Here, check it, if you want.' Wang Fei's English was poor. He took the sheet of paper and pretended to read it, then pointed to a word and said, 'What's that word mean, Dai Wei? Can you translate it for me?'

I took the statement and began to translate it for him. 'The student organisations in the Square have splintered into conflicting groups. We have been forced to . . .'

'There's no way we'll let you broadcast that,' Wang Fei interrupted.

Zhang Rui grabbed a megaphone and began shouting the statement to the students outside. Wang Fei pounced on him and tried to snatch the megaphone from him, but the rest of us swiftly pulled them apart.

'Quickly! Drag him out of the tent!' Wang Fei cried, panting for breath.

Fuming with rage, but knowing that his situation was hopeless, Zhang Rui broke free and maliciously pulled all the plugs out of the sockets. The two female announcers were alarmed and scurried out of the tent hand in hand.

'We know about electronics, so there's no point trying to break anything,' I said, grabbing hold of another student who was sneakily pulling out another lead.

Once we'd taken control, I sent half of my squad back up to the Monument's lower terrace, and kept the other half with me, in case the Qinghua student marshals attempted to storm in again. Then I asked someone to fetch Bai Ling so that she could assume command.

Two hours later, Zhang Rui and the others returned to collect their clothes and documents, then Mou Sen and his propaganda team moved in with backpacks and cardboard boxes.

'Look, there's a telephone!' Nuwa said. She picked up the receiver to check the line was working. 'We can make calls with it, but we won't be able to receive any, because we don't know the number.' Everyone was buoyed up by the excitement of moving into a new place.

But before we had time to unpack, a large mob of Beijing residents rushed over and surrounded the tent. A few of them marched in and announced they were taking over the station. They said we must be feeling very tired by now, and that perhaps it was time we returned to our campuses.

I said that if we handed over control to them, there were tens of thousands of students in the Square who would be ready to take it back again.

'Who do you represent?' Wang Fei shouted as one of the guys tried to push him onto the camp bed. 'Who's your leader? Tell him to come forward and speak to us!'

Mou Sen said the broadcast station represented every student organisation in the Square, and announced that its name was going to be changed from the Voice of the Student Movement to the Voice of Democracy.

The residents pushed Nuwa and Mao Da out of the tent. Outside, Xiao Li and Chen Di were speaking to the mob through megaphones, urging them to leave. I broke out in an anxious sweat. I wished I hadn't sent half my team back up to the lower terrace.

We continued to argue, each side refusing to budge. As two young men twisted my arm back and were about to fling me outside, Nuwa returned to the tent with three foreign journalists. The journalists took out their tape recorders and pointed them at the guys who were arguing with Mou Sen. 'Take their pictures!' Wang Fei shouted. 'Photograph them, so that the whole world will see their faces!'

The residents stepped back in fright. Tang Guoxian then turned up with a group of marshals who, when combined with the thirty guards I'd kept with me, allowed us to gain the upper hand. Wang Fei and I spoke through our megaphones, encouraging our side to remain firm. Realising they were outnumbered, the residents gave up their fight and shuffled out of the tent.

'This is ridiculous!' said Mou Sen. 'Who's going to try to seize power next? Hurry up and call Bai Ling over. We'll ask her to tell everyone to calm down. All she has to do is say, "Hello, this is Bai Ling speaking" and everyone in the Square will fall silent.' Mou Sen's sweat-drenched fringe clung to his forehead.

'We need more marshals around this tent,' I said. 'But where are we going to get them from?' I didn't recognise any of the marshals who were standing outside, apart from a small group of Beijing University chemistry students from Block 48.

'Yes, we'll need at least a hundred marshals guarding this station from now on,' Wang Fei said.

'Thanks for helping us out, Tang Guoxian,' I said.

'Well don't expect me to rescue you next time,' he muttered as he walked away, rubbing his sore fist.

'I told the foreign journalists we only needed them to help us defend the station,' Nuwa explained to Mou Sen. 'They won't mention the incident in their reports.' Then she turned to me and laughed, 'You didn't do a very good job of defending our station, Mr Head of Security!'

'The Zhongnanhai compound isn't guarded by a hundred soldiers, and it's the home of the government leaders!' I said. Wang Fei and I then stepped out and saw that the Beijing residents were now sitting in orderly rows. There were hundreds of them, all of them young men.

'Fuck! It's an army of secret police!' I spluttered. 'They'll probably wait here until it gets dark, then attack us again when there are fewer people around.'

'Call Zhuzi over and see what he thinks,' Wang Fei said, holding the frames of his glasses as he looked up.

'There must be a reason they didn't try to arrest us just now,' I said, as we hurried back into the tent.

'If they take control of the station, it will be easier for them to clear the Square,' Mou Sen said nervously.

'God, it stinks in here!' Mimi cried as she walked inside with Tian Yi. She'd become much more vocal over the past few days.

'Yes, it smells of urine,' Tian Yi said, wrinkling her nose.

'Who would have guessed that there was such an evil-smelling little den as this hidden in the Square?' Mimi laughed.

'Still, we can't let this place slip into enemy hands,' Wang Fei said. 'Dai Wai, make sure the marshals are standing firm.' He then went to speak to Bai Ling and Lin Lu who'd just walked in. There were so many people inside the tent now, I could hardly move.

'It's too noisy in here!' Nuwa shouted. She was speaking to someone in English on the telephone. 'This is an important call. Can you all step outside for a while?'

'Stop arguing, you two!' Bai Ling said, glaring at Wang Fei and Lin Lu. 'The Defend Tiananmen Square Headquarters has only been up and running for a day, and you're already quarrelling. If you carry on like this, I'll sack you both.' Then she pulled Wang Fei and me aside and whispered, 'I heard a rumour that the Provincial Students' Federation was planning to kidnap me. You Southern University graduates are a bunch of bandits!' Her forehead was covered in red mosquito bites. The insect bites on her neck looked like love bites.

'That can't be true,' I said, searching for a large piece of paper on which to write a VOICE OF DEMOCRACY STATION sign. 'Tang Guoxian and Wu Bin wouldn't have the guts to plan something like that.'

Everyone shuffled outside to let Nuwa continue her conversation in peace. The air was less suffocating than it had been in the tent. I felt too tense to sit down, so instead I walked around the security cordon, reminding the marshals that they had to ask my permission before they went off to the toilets.

As dusk began to fall, the army of secret police stood up and filed out of the Square. The red paper sign I'd attached to the tent flapped in the cool wind. The crowd in the Square was as noisy and bustling as those that gather outside temples during Spring Festival. As I gazed across it, I was startled to catch sight of Lulu. She was with a group of girls, listening to a Beijing resident's speech. I pushed my way through the crowd and shouted out to her. She raised her eyebrows and smiled.

'I wondered whether I might see you here!' I said, moving closer to her.

'Well, here I am!' Her newly cut hair blew softly in the breeze.

'You handed me a bottle of Coke during a march a few weeks ago. I didn't know whether you recognised me or not. Why didn't you say anything to me?'

'There were too many people about.'

'I heard you've opened a restaurant.' I felt as though I was looking into my past. Her face was a slightly enlarged version of the one she'd had at fifteen.

'I'm not as clever as you. I wouldn't have got into university.' She was wearing a purple dress and a gold necklace.

'Don't be so curt. It's not every day you meet up with an old school friend. And we weren't just school friends . . .' I was suddenly back in the present again. The awkwardness I'd always felt in her presence seemed to have vanished.

'I suppose you're right.' She raised her eyebrows again. Because I was so much taller than her, she was speaking to my university badge instead of my face.

'Do you still hate me?' I asked calmly.

'I never hated you. I just didn't like the way you let me take the punishment for something you did.' The corner of her mouth twitched for a second. It reminded me of how nervous she'd get when we used to sneak off alone together.

'It's a good thing we've joined this movement,' I said. 'These protests will help us get rid of all our pent-up anger.'

'This movement belongs to the people! You shouldn't be using it for your own selfish purposes. We're here to fight corruption, not to take revenge on people who've hurt us in the past.' She laughed, clearly pleased with herself.

I'd lost interest in the conversation and didn't know what to say next. I felt as confused as someone who enters a noodle restaurant full of excitement only to be told that there are no more noodles left. Fortunately, she quickly filled the silence. 'I'd better be off now, comrade student,' she said. 'We can have a proper talk next time. I come to the Square every day now to hand out steamed buns. I really hope you students succeed in changing this country. We're sick of the government bullying us all the time.' When she lifted her hand to flick back her fringe, I glimpsed the black hairs under her arm – those fine strands of my past.

'Where's your restaurant?' I asked. 'I might pop in for a meal one day.'

'Yes, do! I'll give you a 20 per cent discount. It's right opposite Fuxing Hospital. It's called Lulu's Café.' Then she waved goodbye and walked back to her friends.

I watched her legs and black leather court shoes disappear into the crowd, and breathed a sigh of relief. I remembered the first time she was allowed to buy herself an ice lolly. When the ice-cream seller lifted the quilt he'd draped over the ice box, pulled out the frost-covered lolly and handed it to her, her face glowed with pride. As she stood in the sunlight, waiting to put the lolly into her mouth, she looked like an angel. I was standing beside her, sweaty and sunburnt, poking my stick into the hot road then smearing the lumps of molten asphalt onto the trunk of the locust tree.

Neither Bai Ling nor Wang Fei dared leave the broadcast station that night in case there was another attempted coup. They seemed to have completely forgotten about the martial law troops standing in wait on the outskirts of the city.

Your organs try to halt the passing of time, whimpering and lashing out like dogs that have lost their owners.

'Shall I close the windows, Director?'

'Yes, close them all.'

The man sitting beside me presses my Greater Yang point. 'There's a piece of skull missing here,' he says.

My mother takes a deep breath. 'I know. It's in the refrigerator of the hospital where he was first operated on. He's as numb as a plank of wood. Do you think he'll be able to absorb your qi?'

'Wood can catch fire, don't forget. But even if he doesn't absorb my qi, I'll still be able to enter the root of his disease and examine his soul.'

'Here are his medical records, Director,' a young nurse standing next to me says.

'Please can everyone leave the room now, and close the door behind you.' The director speaks with the same Sichuan accent as Wang Fei.

Last night, my mother whispered into my ear that we'd arrived at Qingcheng Mountain in Sichuan Province. Although this is a small, private hospital in the middle of nowhere, the director is a member of the Chinese Qigong Association, and has even studied abroad.

He presses my soft wound again, transmitting a warm glow into my brain. As his fingers dig down, I can feel that one of them is longer than the other. He then prods the Eye of Heaven point between my eyebrows, and I see a bright flash of light. As his energy waves continue to pulsate through my skull, the neurons of my cerebral cortex begin to twitch, and light flashes through the tubules of my endoplasmic reticulum. Brain cells that have lain dormant for years jolt to attention, as though they'd just heard a school bell ring. Then, through a ball of white light, I see a man approach. He looks at me and says, 'You must imagine yourself as me. Only then will I be able to stimulate the subtle channels of your body and let my energy resonate at the same frequency as yours. Can you hear me?'

I remember reading a research article on thought-transmission a few years ago, but I've never experienced the phenomenon before.

My memories begin to swirl. His electromagnetic waves seep through my brain like wine. 'Relax, relax, as though you're drifting into sleep . . .' the director murmurs as his image flickers before my eyes. I can hear a patient, or a nurse, walking down a hospital corridor, but I'm not sure which hospital it is. Because I was born in a hospital corridor, I'm very sensitive to the sounds that echo through them. Perhaps the director has dredged up a long-forgotten memory of my first moment in this world.

'His skin used to be fine, but since the transfusions he's been having here, it's become blotchy and dry,' my mother says. I presume the director is staring at my chapped arm.

'What does he enjoy doing?' he asks my mother. At the same time, he enters my brain and asks me, 'What do you enjoy doing?'

'As a child, he liked making model warships,' my mother says. 'When he was older, he liked to read biographies of famous people, especially memoirs from the Second World War. One year, he spent the whole summer reading *The Book of Mountains and Seas*.'

I answer, 'I like to travel, and play football, and . . .' I rack my brain, trying to come up with another hobby, but can't think of one.

'Imagine you're sitting on a boat, the sea all around you,' he murmurs to me in my brain. 'You are eight years old . . .'

'No, I get seasick,' I reply to him. 'I like to climb mountains, though . . .' Although I don't recognise his face, there's something familiar about him.

'Try it, it's easy. It's like having a dream. You must return to your childhood, and start all over again.' His voice repeats through my brain: 'Think about your school textbooks, your stamp collections, the model warship you made . . .'

'No, it was a model aeroplane. What I liked most was making kites. I remember a huge sunbird kite I made . . .' My brain becomes warmer and begins to sweat. For a moment, the director disappears. All that remains is the echo of his voice, and the memory of his gaze, which was as intense as Mou Sen's.

Then I hear a loud crash and the sound of breaking glass.

'That was a wall exploding in your mind. It was blocking your memories. Everything's fine now. You can walk straight through. Think of a loud noise you heard as a child, then follow it and see where it takes you . . .'

I remember letting off firecrackers when I was a kid. The loud bangs they made left me deaf for days. I can see red and yellow paper from exploded firecrackers scattered across a pavement. I'm standing in a lane I used to walk down as a child. Further along, I spot a charred biscuit tin. When I press my foot into the paper ashes inside, they fly up and dance in the breeze. I walk on and come to a locust tree. On the grey wall behind I see the shadow of its branches swaying in the wind. An old man with a red armband is squatting beneath the tree. No, he's not squatting – he's sitting on a fold-up stool.

'Keep walking. You know these lanes very well . . .'

I keep going, turn right and arrive outside Lulu's window. The building's red bricks are dry and crumbly. All the plaster has peeled off, apart from one large patch that hangs on the wall like a piece of old cloth.

'Go back to your childhood. Go deeper and deeper. Keep going. Don't be afraid. Use your thoughts to ram your way through . . .'

I hesitate for a moment, because I know that Lulu's family moved out of that ground-floor flat years ago. I glance at the gap below the windowsill. I found an old key once and tried to sell it, but no ironmonger would buy it because it was made out of cheap metal, not copper. So I scraped out a hole underneath Lulu's windowsill and hid the key inside. I move closer to the gap, wondering if the key is still there.

'I can't stay with you much longer. My energy is running out. You must hurry up.'

I clench every muscle in my body then ram my head through the wall and enter a great blackness. As shards of my past spin around me, the face of Granny Li, who was scalded to death by the Red Guards, suddenly appears before my eyes.

'Look, he moved!' my mother cries. 'His mouth moved! Look, look! His lips twitched, at least three times.'

'I can't open his Eye of Heaven,' the director says, removing his hand from my head. 'He has very few memories left. I emitted strong electromagnetic waves, but the DNA of his pathological tissue is severely damaged. It will never be able to repair itself.'

'The *what* of his tissue?' my mother asks.

'The DNA – it contains the genetic information which determines how our tissues develop and function. Sometimes damaged DNA can repair itself, allowing the tissue to regenerate, but his injury is too severe. It will take more than just qigong to cure him.'

'But I saw his mouth move just now. That's the first time any part of him has moved since he fell into the coma.' My mother is even more excited than me.

'I know. But if he's going to make any further progress, he'll need to take specific medication to strengthen his cells' vitality. Unfortunately, the particular drug I'm thinking of isn't available in China yet.'

'He has a cousin in America. If you write down the name of the drug, I'll ask him to send it to us.'

'The drug can't be bought in pharmacies. It has to be prescribed by a hospital physician. So unless you take your son abroad, you won't be able to get hold of it.'

My mother falls silent.

Although the director has removed his hand from my head, my wound is still pulsating. The stimulated neurons there have packed into a tight ball which is emitting waves of light. I saw the director's face in my mind, but unfortunately it seems he didn't see me.

Everything goes dark. Granny Li and the hole below the windowsill disappear. Then a memory of me standing in a cold classroom wavers into focus. There's an arithmetic question on the blackboard behind me, and a heap of brooms and dustpans stacked next to the door. I stare at the rays of sunlight on the concrete balcony of the classroom. The balcony is so stark and empty, it looks like a black and white photograph. What is the meaning of this image? Without the director to guide me, it's impossible to decipher.

Blood from my brain flows into my limbs, then swishes back up again like the waves of a sea. My numb arms seem to want to move. I take a deep breath and, tense with excitement, try to wriggle my fingers.

Another male voice speaks. 'The last paraplegic the director treated was able to stand up after just one session. The director has cured hundreds of invalids. He's famous throughout Sichuan.' He sounds like the assistant doctor. He's wearing trainers, so I didn't hear him walking in. His hands smell of soap. He's pushing my chin down so that he can take a look at my tongue.

Without another word, the director gets up and leaves the room. How could he abandon me like this? He's the only person in the world I can talk to. There are so many things I want to ask him.

'But he could open his eyes when he came here, unlike your son,' the assistant doctor continues. 'There's no patient the director cannot cure. So don't worry. Your son will have another session tomorrow.'

Someone in the corridor cries out: 'Chunhua! There's a woman on the phone for you! You can take it down at reception.'

'Tell her I'm busy!' a nurse next to me shouts. Then she mumbles, 'It's probably my mother.'

'Don't touch that cable,' a younger nurse says. I didn't hear these two women walk in either.

'It's not all up to us, Auntie,' the assistant doctor explains, scribbling something onto a sheet of paper. 'Doctors are the broadcasting stations, and the patients are the radios. If the radios aren't turned on, they won't receive the broadcasts.'

'Do you feed him through a tube?' Chunhua asks.

'Yes, I've brought the tube with me. You won't need to buy him one.' My mother is always worried the doctors will add unnecessary expenses to her bill.

'The feeding tubes need to be regularly replaced, Auntie, or they'll become infected,' the assistant doctor says. 'They only cost seven yuan each. Why not let us buy him a new one? Here are his transfusion bottles. He will be given a daily dose of three bottles of glucose solution and six bottles of nutrition fluid. The products are made locally. It's a high-quality brand. It works out cheaper if you buy them from us rather than the pharmacy.'

'Let's have lunch at that Taiwanese beef noodle restaurant that's opened down the road,' Chunhua whispers to the young nurse.

'Pass me that box of needles. Yes, that one.' The young nurse moves closer to me and I catch the scent of her shampoo.

A voice calls out from the stairwell: 'Chunhua! Someone on the phone for you again. It's a man this time. Hurry up.'

'All right, I'm coming, I'm coming . . .' When Chunhua swirls round, a musky, feminine odour wafts out from between her legs.

Sensing my penis begin to enlarge, I quickly focus on the noises around me. The steel toecaps grinding against the concrete floor of the stairwell landing sound like metal spoons grating against a ceramic bowl.

My mother grabs a pillow and quickly pushes it between my legs to hide my erection from the young nurse.

'We're going to examine his cerebrospinal fluid this afternoon. We've put him down as an inpatient, so he'll get a fifty-two-yuan discount . . .'

The doctor and nurse walk out of the room, leaving behind a confusion of smells.

I'm still locked inside my head. I keep seeing those black paper ashes rising from the charred biscuit tin. It's a random image of little significance which, until now, has remained locked in some deep part of my brain. But if I can retrieve *this* lost memory, perhaps there are other more important ones which I can also reclaim.

The director told me that if I want to come out of my coma, I must make a deliberate effort to remember events I've chosen to forget. Before I return to my old life, I must first complete this inward journey into my past. Perhaps eventually I'll be able to return to that hospital corridor and push my way out into the world once more.

My mother hasn't shut the door. She's probably planning to go out for walk.

This small town isn't far from Wang Fei's home. I'd love to see him, or rather, I'd love him to come and see me . . .

The sunlight is warming the room, softening my skin and causing my pores to dilate and secrete beads of sweat. The pores on my back are squashed flat against the sheet by the weight of my body, and very little blood is flowing through the capillaries there. I can feel ants crawling across my bug-infested bed, transporting the breadcrumbs my mother dropped onto my arm back to their nest.

You keep returning to that moment, searching for the forgotten sound of the single gunshot.

In the afternoon, the sky above this small town in Sichuan fills with sparrows. Their loud chirping and the swish of bicycle wheels outside spin through the strange-smelling air in the room.

I hear a key grate in a lock on the floor below. It sounds like a child coughing.

My mother stomps around the room, her footsteps growing heavier and heavier. Whenever she passes the doorway on my left, the plastic floor-tiles squeak.

She scratches my scalp. When her hand brushes against my ear, I hear waves crashing onto a beach.

She gobbles and sucks a tangerine, and mumbles, 'Your dandruff is getting worse. Look, it's all over your pillow. Your father used to have terrible dandruff too.' This amounts to a show of tenderness. Half an hour ago she said, 'The treatments they've lined up for you are so expensive. It would be better for both of us if you died in your sleep.'

She picks up the newspaper lying on the bedside table and tosses the tangerine peel out of the window. A strong citrus scent darts through the air.

'Listen to this. Twenty-four Taiwanese tourists were killed in a pleasure boat on Qiandao Lake. Local bandits raided the boat, robbed the tourists of their money, locked them inside a cabin then set fire to the boat to destroy all evidence of their crime. How can people be so evil? . . .' My mother peels another tangerine and mutters, 'They're much cheaper here than in Beijing. The skins are a bit thin, but they're very sweet.'

My body is slowly contracting. My hair smells like rotting pondweed. The sweat between my toes has evaporated and my dry soles are beginning to crack.

You remember the pleasure of lifting your legs in the air, your tendons straining as you twirled your feet in circles. That sour twinge of pain, like a slice of raw lemon sliding up your bones.

Mosquitoes and moths flitted around the naked light bulb inside the Voice of Democracy broadcast station. Mou Sen and I were sitting outside having a cigarette.

'Look at all these people,' Mou Sen said, his eyes sweeping across the Square. 'As soon as danger strikes, you won't see them for dust.'

'You said this Square is our home, and the more guests we have the greater our prestige.' I glanced at the security office I'd just help set up on the lower terrace. I'd asked Xiao Li and Yu Jin to keep an eye on it. It was right next to Old Fu's finance office and Mou Sen's propaganda office. The Voice of Democracy broadcast station was directly below it on the south-east corner of the Monument. The Monument was the nerve centre of our movement. As long as it was securely guarded, we could keep the situation in the Square under control.

'No, as far as I'm concerned, the moment we entered this Square, we all became homeless,' Mou Sen said, rubbing his goatee. 'We have nowhere to go now. Tang Guoxian wants to turn this place into a semi-militarised zone. He's got guts, but he never takes the time to think things through. His recklessness is more dangerous than all of Wang Fei's weak-kneed bluster.'

'The government's trying to split us up,' I said, then remembered those nights at Southern University when Mou Sen and I would lie squashed on my bed reading the same book, our faces pressed together. Fortunately, he didn't have a moustache and goatee back then.

'Cao Ming's latest intelligence report says that Li Peng moved into the Zhongnanhai compound yesterday,' he said, scratching the red mosquito bite on his leg. 'He's in the villa Chairman Mao lived in before he died. I suppose he wanted to move closer to the action, so he can oversee the clearing of the Square.'

'The Beijing Entrepreneurs' Association has donated boxes of eggs and soap. They're stacked up over there. The eggs will go off in a couple of days.' We stubbed out our cigarettes and returned to the tent.

'The crowds are dwindling and the journalists will want to know why,' Nuwa said, glancing at Mou Sen as we walked in. 'Can you come up with an explanation? Someone told me you were planning to leave the Square to go and write a book.' As Bai Ling's spokesperson, Nuwa had to deal with a constant stream of questions and requests from the foreign media.

'So he's finally going to write his novel, is he?' I chuckled. 'We Southern University graduates are such bullshitters!' The tent reeked of garlic. Someone must have been chewing a raw clove.

'Mou Sen is the most talented wordsmith in the Square,' Nuwa said, turning her gaze to him. When she stepped forward, I noticed a small mosquito bite on her inner thigh, but otherwise her legs were smooth and unblemished all the way to her red-lacquered toenails.

'He should wait until the book's finished before he starts bragging about it,' I said. Secretly, I knew that, being such an avid reader, Mou Sen was probably more than capable of writing a novel.

It was past midnight and the broadcasts had come to an end, so the mood in the tent was relatively relaxed.

Wang Fei was sitting next to Bai Ling, staring at his shoes. 'The reason the crowds have dwindled is that many students have gone to help man the blockades,' he said, responding to the question Nuwa had asked Mou Sen. 'The battlefield has shifted to the perimeter of the city. If there are 200,000 soldiers surrounding the city, there must be at least 200,000 students blocking their advance. The Square is now the rear area of our operations.'

'There must be a mosquito nest in here,' Tian Yi said, numbering an audio tape and stacking it away. 'Can someone fetch some more insect repellent incense?'

'I've been bitten to death,' Mimi mumbled. She was lying on the ground with her eyes closed. I wondered whether she was talking in her sleep.

'There are a few coils left in that box,' Mou Sen said. He stood up, casting a dark shadow on the tent's canvas.

Tian Yi put a tape in the cassette player. The voice of the rock singer Cui Jian sang out: '*Let me cry, let me laugh. Let me go wild in the snow . . .*' The drumbeat was strong and insistent. In the shadows, Nuwa's hips began to move back and forth. I stared at her bottom shaking beneath her tight denim skirt for a while, then quickly shifted my gaze to Tian Yi. Earlier that day she'd told me she didn't approve of Nuwa painting her toenails red.

'When the soldiers drag us away, I hope you boys will behave like gentlemen and come to our rescue,' Nuwa said, still swaying her hips. Her lips were always shiny and red. Tian Yi's lips only turned red after she'd had a shower.

'We must muster a crowd of a million people and go on a . . .' Lin Lu muttered as he lay fast asleep on the ground.

'Go on a what?' Nuwa sneered. 'A night tour of Beijing?' She didn't like Lin Lu. She found him false and affected.

'Hey, Dai Wei, your brother just called you on the phone outside the Museum of Chinese History,' Liu Gang said, walking into the tent. 'He said he'll call back in an hour.'

'How did he know the number?'

'All the provincial universities call us on that phone when they need to get in touch with us.' Liu Gang handed me the note he'd scribbled for me and left.

The left pulmonary vein climbs up the heart's red cliff face, brushing past the right coronary vein on its way. The peritoneum clings tightly to the duodenum.

Behind the scent of tangerine blossom in the air, I detect a distant smell of rotting carcasses. Perhaps someone is cleaning the street, and the stench is from the muck in the gutters.

If I were to wake from my coma now, I'd go straight to a library and leaf through all the new books and magazines. No, the first thing I'd do is jump on a bus and visit Wang Fei.

I can hear people speaking in the room downstairs.

'Are you married?'

'Am I married, indeed! I've got a kid at school!'

The air slides across my face like warm water. When the sun leaves the room this afternoon, I hope the air will become colder and less fluid.

Someone down the corridor opens a window again and shouts, 'Turn right at the watchtower, then left after the Taitai Oral Liquid poster . . . What? If they won't give you a refund, just come straight back.'

Then another voice leaks into my brain. 'All right then, I'll tell you the truth. I didn't want to crease my skirt. Are you happy now?' It's Tian Yi speaking to me on the bus, the day we first met. The conductress shouts impatiently, the doors close, and the engine splutters as it revs up. It was a very ordinary remark, but as soon as the words left her mouth, I knew I was doomed to fall in love with her.

I imagine walking through the sunlight on the left side of a lane and looking up into the blue sky. As I remember my hair being warmed by the sun, I feel blood rush to my scalp. I like to gaze at the sky when I walk through the streets on a sunny day. It makes me feel giddy. Sometimes, when I look down to see where I'm going, then suddenly look up again, I forget I'm still walking.

How wonderful it feels to walk! When my feet touch the ground, clouds of dust lift into the air. I walk down stone pavements and asphalt roads that are sometimes soft and sometimes hard. I step over high kerbs and low kerbs, and stamp on empty cardboard boxes heaped in the corner of the street. Sometimes I tread on a shard of broken glass that hasn't yet been crushed into pieces. With one kick, I can make an old plimsoll that's been lying under a tree fly several metres into the air. I spot a pile of scaffolding rods stacked against a wall. If I climb up it, I'll be able see the tree's upper branches stretching into the sky.

By the time the sunlight has shifted onto the floor, my mother comes back from her lunch, smelling of oil and deep-fried fish. 'The prices keep going up. Even a plate of stir-fried tomato and eggs costs 1.8 yuan now.'

Someone knocks on the door and asks softly, 'Do you have any matches? . . . Is that your son?' It's a woman's voice.

'Come in and sit down, won't you? Are you in the room next door?'

'Yes. I can't stay. I'm having trouble with the kerosene stove I bought. It's a nightmare to light. I've gone through a whole box of matches in just two days.'

'Come on, sit down, just for a minute. Have you had lunch?'

'I really can't stay.' She nevertheless perches on my bed, pulls the sheet flat, then shifts her bottom about until she's found a comfortable position. 'Hmm, what a shame,' she says, sitting still at last. 'He looks so young. How long has he been like this?'

'Two years,' my mother lies. On the train down here, she told the attendant I'd only been in a coma for two months.

'What happened to him?' The woman is speaking towards my face. Her breath smells of garlic.

'He ran into a washing line while trying to cross a road and fell onto the ground.' My mother has told this story many times. The first time I heard it was in the hospital in Beijing.

'You mean he became like this just from a fall?'

'He was running very fast and the metal caught him here – right here.' I presume my mother is gesturing to her neck. 'He went flying backwards and landed head first on the concrete pavement . . .' Her sleeves make a rustling sound.

'Tss. I see what you mean. Head first, like an upturned leek . . .'

'What are you here for?'

'I've got tumours in my bladder.'

'How long have you had them?'

'Eleven months, almost a year. This is my third time in hospital.'

'Have you been operated on?'

'Yes. I've had two tumours removed already. I've spent over four thousand yuan on hospital fees. I sold all our pigs for this next operation, but only made half of the two thousand yuan I need. The doctor said that if I don't pay all the money upfront, I'll have to go home and wait to die.'

'It must be a complicated operation.'

'I've been here six days. They found strands of blood in my urine. They said I needed to be operated on at once.'

'Have you got someone to look after you here?'

'My husband is with me. He's had to leave all the work in the fields. I've told him to go back, but he refuses.'

'Oh, is he that tall guy who came here this morning? How many children have you got?'

'Two. They're both grown up now. My daughter went to Shenzhen three years ago. She works as a hair washer at an expensive salon. She's sent us more than two thousand yuan already. She even phoned our village leader once and asked to speak to us. I had a conversation with her. It was very strange. It sounded like she was standing right next to me . . .'

The room grows dark. A smell of fried rice travels down the corridor and escapes through my open window. The noises around me become muddled. I feel like I'm lying in the sleeping car of a moving train.

There's a train in front of me. It appears to be moving, but in fact it hasn't set off yet. I run as fast as I can, trying to grab hold of a handle.

Although I'm aware I'm chasing a stationary object, I know that however fast I run, I will never reach it. My tendons edge towards my skin's sense receptors, allowing me to gauge the position of my legs and experience a sensation of weariness.

The soles of your feet exchange longing glances. The large mole on the small of your back yearns to speak.

Flocks of sparrows settle on the roof of this hospital which was once a small government-run hotel. The loud chirps are accompanied by a scent of leaves. As the sparrows fall asleep, the mosquitoes fly out of their nests. Last night they covered my face with bites.

Someone in a room at the end of the corridor has put on a tape. '*I don't want to live alone. I want to meet someone new . . .*' The pop singer has a strong local accent. I haven't heard her before.

Another song blares from a cassette player in the small shop outside: '*If you want to go, go. But don't come back again . . .*'

When the door of the room at the end of the corridor is opened, probably to let out some of the smoke from the food being cooked on the camp stove inside, the pop song becomes much louder. '*This loneliness is unbearable. Marry me tomorrow and take me away . . .*' It's already dark enough to turn on the lights. Now that the heat of the day has subsided, everyone is rushing around again, making a lot of noise.

My mother is sitting quietly by my side, reading the newspapers and magazines she borrowed from the woman next door.

No one hears your silent breaths as despair waves its beckoning hand to you.

The evening is gloomy and damp. Moisture that evaporated during the day soaks back into my quilt, pillow and skin, and condenses onto the bedside table and floor. Everything in the hospital room becomes heavier. My mother and the furniture are sinking down. In fact, the whole building is sinking.

This is how every night begins in this small mountain town.

There's a horrible grating sound as my mother closes the window. The magazine she tossed onto my bed is slowly splaying its pages. Once the window is closed, the whiff of urine rising from the sheets grows stronger.

My mother walks to the door, bolts it shut, then returns to the chair.

'By the time I was your age, I'd toured the Soviet Union and sung the lead role in *Carmen*. If your father hadn't been labelled a rightist, I would have become a famous soloist . . .' My mother turns to another page of the magazine. 'Look, there she is again. Singing to foreign dignitaries. I don't know how she got to be such a big star. She never applied herself to her art when she was at the opera company. Too busy flirting with the baritones . . .' She flicks to the next page and sighs, 'Huh, if only I hadn't married your father . . .'

Rubbing off scraps of dried food stuck to her trousers, she continues, 'I was one of the prettiest girls in the opera company. When your father joined the orchestra, he used to knock on my door every day and give me an apple. They were very expensive back then. But I didn't allow him into my room. Then, a few months later, our opera company travelled to the countryside. The village was very poor. We stayed in an army barracks and were only given half a bowl of rice for supper. When we returned to the barracks after the performance, everyone was starving. Your father sneaked off to the kitchen and stole a bread roll for me. The police arrested him and made him write a self-criticism. If he hadn't stolen that roll, I might never have married him . . .' When my mother rambles on like this, she can talk herself to sleep.

Unfamiliar towns often smell strange and disconcerting. But new environments can stimulate the brain. Fish that swim to new waters every day are more alert and agile than those that remain in the same pond all their lives. Since the director gave me the qigong treatment on my second day at this hospital, I have become aware of the many unusual smells of this town. When the evening wind blows into the room, I feel them stimulating my nerve cells.

'Huh, I'm wasting my time talking to you. I might as well be playing the lute to a cow . . . If I don't get these medical fees reimbursed, you really will have to die. I can't afford to keep you alive any longer . . .'

My mother's words enter the ampullae of my inner ear. The body is a room with a locked door and an open window. Although you can peep in through the window, you can never enter the room or control what's going on inside. Your organs behave as they wish. They can knock you down at any moment and leave you paralysed for the rest of your life.

'Look at the prices they're charging! Ninety per cent glucose solution is nine yuan a bottle, and the atropine is double the usual price as well.' My mother is skimming through the hospital's cost sheet. 'Nursing only costs eight yuan a day, though, which is less than Beijing hospitals charge. If I can find another patient to share with you tomorrow, at least the room rate will be halved . . .'

The smell of dank earth blowing down from the mountain sticks to the walls of my trachea. It reminds me of the smell of death I detect on my breath after I've spent a week or more in hospital. I know the smell is just bad breath and that death itself is odourless, but I also know that a healthy person who falls sick is already in death's waiting room. After patients lie in hospital wards for more than a week they begin to reek of helplessness.

Sickness is worse than death, though. When the body begins to rot, you lose your dignity and self-respect. You have to lie down, exposing your weaknesses and failings to the world, and allow doctors to probe and inspect all your previously well-guarded orifices.

I was looking forward to the director's thought-waves entering my head again tomorrow, but the nurse has just informed my mother that he's fallen ill and has had to cancel the session.

I imagine the wind chasing after me. I am dry and hard. My shrivelled skin yearns to suck the moisture from my marrow, like deer in summer that yearn to drink from a lake . . . My cheeks must have caved in by now. I looked cadaverous even before my brother moved abroad. My mother took a photograph of him and me together, and gave him a copy to take to England. When he saw it, he said, 'I can't take this with me. It's bad luck to be photographed next to a corpse.'

You enter the mind of the man pointing his gun at you, and yell as he pulls the trigger. Those damaged brain cells will never repair. After you fall to the ground, you place your hand over the charred bullet hole, trying in vain to maintain some dignity.

I ran over to the telephone and waited for my brother to call back. There was a lot of noise around me. A group of students nearby sat huddled around a cassette player, singing along to a tape: '*Walk on, little sister. Don't look back . . .*'

As soon as the phone rang, I clamped the receiver to one ear and stuck my finger in the other.

'I just wanted to let you know that we'll be coming up to Beijing soon,' my brother said in a voice that sounded as mature as mine.

'I don't think that's a good idea,' I answered in a quiet monotone, hoping to dampen his enthusiasm. 'Everyone's fed up with the provincial students. They beg for handouts, then blow the cash on presents and fripperies . . .'

'We won't need your money. We've collected 100,000 yuan in donations.'

'Really? That's impressive. Most of the provincial students arrive with nothing. It's chaos here.'

'I know! What the hell's been going on? Three days ago, you lot told us the hunger strike had been called off and the students were going to leave the Square. So we ended our occupation of Chengdu's public square and returned to our campuses. But as soon as we got back, you sent us a message telling us to continue the struggle. So we returned to the square the next day. Then yesterday we heard you were planning to withdraw again, and we went back to our campuses. And now today we've been told to mobilise the workers and organise a mass industrial strike. Why do you keep changing your minds? Whose orders are we supposed to be following?'

'I'm not even sure myself. The Beijing Students' Federation, I suppose. Anyway, just stay where you are for the time being. Don't come to Beijing . . .'

After I'd hung up, I regretted dissuading him from coming. My mother had told me that my cousin Kenneth had recently got married and was planning to bring his wife to China for their honeymoon. He was hoping I could show them around Beijing. I realised that if my brother were in town, he could show them around instead, which would save me a lot of trouble. I decided that I'd leave the Square in the morning and go home to rest for a couple of days. I was so weak with exhaustion, I couldn't think straight.

I returned to the Monument's lower terrace and saw a banner that said RECONVENE THE NATIONAL PEOPLE'S CONGRESS, PROMOTE DEMOCRACY, SACK LI PENG, END MILITARY RULE hanging on the obelisk like a pair of old knickers. Four guys with long hair and steel-toed boots who'd formed a rock band called May Flower sat on the Monument's northern steps and performed one of their songs. A crowd of thousands gathered round them, clapping and cheering. I suddenly remembered it was Tian Yi's birthday on the 28th, and reminded myself to buy her a present.

On the lower terrace, students were lying asleep, or sitting up talking, flicking away the swarms of mosquitoes and moths flying through the air. Guys on the southern steps were having a smoke and trying to chat up girls. It was just like any other night in the Square.

When I walked inside the broadcast tent, a long-haired student from the Central Academy of Art was waving his hands animatedly. '. . . We're going to build a huge statue called the Goddess of Democracy,' he said. 'It'll be amazing.'

'To put up in the Square? How big will it be?' Bai Ling was having a phone conversation, so couldn't give her full attention to him and his friend. The phone she was using was a private line we'd set up for her. It was connected to a circuit we'd found in a metal box below one of the lamps in the Square.

'It will be a replica of the Statue of Liberty. Not as tall of course, but it will still look very impressive.'

'What do you think of the idea, Mou Sen?' Bai Ling asked. 'I think it could work.' Her eyes looked red and sore. She'd been up two nights in a row, speaking on the phone to student leaders, intellectuals and academics across the country.

'I love it!' Mou Sen exclaimed, searching his pockets for a cigarette. 'Artists always come up with the best ideas.'

'Yes, it will be brilliant! You can put it right in the middle of the Square, directly opposite Mao's portrait.' Nuwa's eyes sparkled as she clapped her hands with delight.

The other art student had a shaven head and was wearing a torn T-shirt. 'Millions of people will flood to the Square to look at it,' he said, 'which will make a mockery of the government's martial law edict!'

'You were horrified when those guys from Hunan threw ink at Mao's portrait,' Tian Yi said to Mou Sen, 'but you're happy for these students to erect a Goddess of Democracy. What's the difference?'

I couldn't stay awake any longer, so I stamped on a couple of cardboard boxes and lay down on top of them. My clothes reeked of sweat. I didn't dare remove my shoes because I knew my socks smelt worse. I hadn't brushed my teeth for ten days. I hoped A-Mei wouldn't turn up suddenly and catch me in this state. She was very particular about cleanliness. She could get through a whole roll of toilet paper in a day, using it to wipe dust from the furniture, windowpanes and cups. After she took a shower, she'd remove the water from her tummy button with a cotton bud.

Bai Ling sat down for a moment deep in thought. 'All right,' she said at last. 'Let's put up a statue then! Broadcast an announcement telling the students about the plan, then get Wang Fei and Old Fu back here to convene a meeting.' When she stood up, her toes splayed out, making her bare feet look much wider.

If you travel a further 5,490 li, you will see the god of Mount Zhu, who has the face of a human but the body of a snake. If you want to win his favour, bury a live cockerel and pig in the ground.

I can feel the grime of the hospital on my skin. This south-facing, first-floor room smells very different from the clean examination room downstairs. When people use the latrines next door, a sour scent of urine wafts into the room. In fact, I smelt urine the moment I was brought in here. The odour has permeated the wallpaper, together with the smells of fermented sunlight, herbal medicine, disinfectant and rotting fruit.

The lung cancer patient who's moved into the bed next to mine is moaning in pain. His breath smells of the Sichuan-spiced noodles he ate an hour ago. He eats about six bowls of noodles a day. After each one, he lights a cigarette and spits onto the ground.

During the hour after lunch everything quietens down, but the rest of the time the corridor and stairwell are filled with the noise of shuffling feet. I hear people walking up the stairs now. It sounds as if there are three of them. The footsteps are hurried and confused. This cheap concrete building is an echo chamber. Every noise is amplified.

Someone taps a glass on my bedside table and suddenly my hand seems to want to touch it. It's a tall, cylindrical glass, I think, half filled with tea that is probably lukewarm by now. I see my hand moving towards the glass through shards of light bouncing off the blue plastic tablecloth. When I touch it, the sensory receptors on the tips of my fingers inform my brain that it's cold and hard. But perhaps the sensation I'm experiencing is a remembered one, and my fingertips haven't touched the glass at all.

A nurse is cleaning my body with alcohol solution and sticking acupuncture needles into my pressure points. The director is sitting on a chair talking to my mother. 'He has no awareness of the world around him,' he says. 'His brain has stopped processing new information. It's like a piece of dead wood. I can't bring it back to life. I had a terrible headache after the session I gave him the other day. The best hope for him now would be to put him on this 20,000-yuan treatment plan. It includes a weekly session of UV light therapy and a course of drugs imported from England. The 10,000-yuan treatment would still give him the UV therapy, but the drugs are from a Sino-Japanese joint-venture company, and aren't so effective. This 6,000-yuan plan he's on now gives him just five of my qigong sessions, an acupuncture session and a course of Chinese herbal medicine. It only lasts twenty-four days. There's no way he will have come out of his coma by then.'

'I like the sound of that 10,000-yuan plan, but he had a month of UV therapy in Beijing last year, and it didn't seem to have any effect. Could you make up a plan for him that has the foreign drugs but no UV?'

'If you want to alter his plan, we'll have to get approval from each department then print out new documents, and all that will cost money.'

'It won't involve too much work, surely? How about we agree on an 8,000-yuan plan?' My mother's voice falters as she remembers how little money she has left.

Another doctor turns on the heartbeat monitor. 'It's a bit faster today,' the nurse says. 'Eighteen beats per minute.'

'Insert a two-centimetre needle into his Mute's Gate point. I can see that it's not only his upper head that's blocked. Both the Spirit Path and the Wind Pool points at the back and base of his skull are clouded too. That's why the qi isn't flowing smoothly through his body.'

'The test you performed yesterday proved he is sensitive to sounds,' my mother says.

The director stands up. 'He probably only has very basic hearing abilities. Many of his bodily functions are in a vegetative state. Strictly speaking, he isn't human any longer. He can't process thoughts and his nervous system is very weak. If you want to see any real improvement, you'd better go for the 20,000-yuan plan.'

'All right. But I brought him here for qigong. I didn't bring enough cash to pay for all these extra treatments . . .'

I can hear the water in the electric cup begin to bubble. The relatives of the lung cancer patient lying next to me put it on to boil.

An announcement hisses from the radio in the room upstairs: 'In December, a fire at the Friendship Theatre in Kelamayi, Xinjiang Province, took the lives of 325 people . . .' The dial is turned to another station. 'In this Year of the Dog, our canine friends have become a hot topic of conversation, especially since the Beijing government announced a strict ban on keeping them as pets . . . During a visit to a television factory in Shenzhen yesterday, Premier Li Peng said . . .'

Let your mind wither away, then lock its ashes in a box and watch the key slowly rust.

'*Arise, ye toilers of the earth . . .*' The Internationale woke me from my sleep before the sun had risen.

I glanced at my watch. I'd slept for almost two hours. Although my head was still pounding, at least I could move it from side to side now, and think a little more clearly. I turned over. Tian Yi and Nuwa were asleep on the camp bed next to me. Their bare feet were sticking out of the blanket. It was easy to tell whose feet were whose. Tian Yi's had very distinctive big toes that curled up at the end. Nuwa's feet were smaller. When I looked at them, I thought about her long, delicate fingers.

'The Workers' Federation are going to hold a press conference outside the Museum of Chinese History at nine o'clock,' Mou Sen said, waking up Nuwa. 'They want Bai Ling to be there. I offered to go instead, but they wouldn't have it. What shall I do?'

'Well if they don't want you, don't go.' Nuwa sounded different when she was lying down.

People had begun to gossip about Wang Fei and Bai Ling. They spent most of their time together now. Although Nuwa was upset, she tried not to let it show. When anyone asked her how she felt, she kept repeating that she and Wang Fei had never been more than good friends.

'I saw Wang Fei and Bai Ling chewing from the same spare rib,' Mou Sen whispered to her.

'Are you jealous?' Nuwa laughed, splaying out her toes.

'No, I was just worried that *you* might be.'

'Huh! No chance!' Nuwa said, tapping Mou Sen's hand, or perhaps his leg. Then either she pushed him, or he pulled her. When I saw her toes curl inwards, I looked away.

Yu Jin came over to speak to me. As I sat up, I saw Mou Sen drag Nuwa off the camp bed and lead her behind the wall of broadcasting equipment.

It made me uncomfortable to see them flirt. I knew Tian Yi would never be so fickle in her affections.

Chen Di came into the tent with Xiao Li, his binoculars hanging around his neck. 'The marshals who were on night duty have returned to the campuses. There's no one guarding the Monument.'

'The whole security system has collapsed, so it won't make any difference,' I muttered.

Mou Sen walked out from behind the equipment. I could hear the click of a brass buckle as Nuwa fastened her belt. The Internationale had come to an end, so it was time for her to read out the morning news.

I stepped outside to have a smoke. The other guys joined me, so I handed them each a cigarette. During the night, Lin Lu had stormed into the station, hoping to enact a coup, but we'd managed to kick him out. The small victory had created a new sense of solidarity among us.

'We haven't had a moment's peace since we took over this damn station,' Chen Di said, lighting his cigarette. The strap of his watch had broken during the fight.

The Square was blanketed in dawn fog. Everything was quiet. The nights were much livelier. Boys would sit back to back drinking beer. Couples would huddle in quiet corners humming love songs to one another, then sneak off into empty tents to make love. It was like a huge party. When Yang Tao had come to the tent the night before and proposed that we leave the Square and go home for a couple of weeks, he was met with stony silence.

'Lin Lu's quite harmless really,' I said to Chen Di. 'He's no spy. He's just a megalomaniac. It's government agents like Zhao Xian that we have to watch out for.' Mr Zhao, the Central Television newsreader who'd delivered some newscasts for us, took many of our documents home with him. After rumours spread that he was a government spy, he vanished from the Square and never returned.

'Can you give me a haircut, Dai Wei?' Mou Sen said, grabbing a comb from Nuwa. I glanced at his head and said, 'You've grown it out into a new style. I wouldn't know what to do with it.' But he'd already taken off his shirt and handed me some scissors.

'They're blunt,' I said. 'I can't use them.'

'Just give me a simple trim. It's too hot to have shoulder-length hair.'

As I combed his double-crowned head, I smelt wafts of hair grease and shampoo.

'Shave it off,' Chen Di laughed, expelling a cloud of cigarette smoke. 'He thinks he's so cool.'

I pushed Mou Sen's head down to trim the back. 'Careful,' he yelped. 'You cut my shirt collar last time.'

'Shut up!' I said. After a while, I noticed I'd taken too much off the right side, so I told him he'd look better with a crew cut. My hands were drenched in the sweat pouring from his scalp.

'I'll go to the toilets and rinse my head under the tap,' he said after I finished. His eyes were red with tiredness.

'Not so fast!' I shouted. 'Come back here and sweep up your hair before you go.' I clapped my hands loudly, hoping that Nuwa would hear me.

As your thoughts expand in the fermenting pool of your brain, you glimpse your cadaverous face reflected on the surface.

The nurse packs away some medical appliances and grumbles to the lung cancer patient, 'I told you to practise your deep breathing before the operation, but you didn't listen to me.'

His right lung has been removed. When he breathes in, he sounds like a bicycle tyre being pumped with air. His money will only cover one more night in hospital, so he'll have to go home tomorrow and wait to die.

'No one told me you'd cut out the whole lung,' he complains, panting noisily.

'You stay here,' my mother says to me. 'I'm going downstairs to have some supper. Your drip bottle won't need changing for another half-hour.'

She turns off the lights and everything goes black. As she shuts the door, I imagine myself crying out, 'Get me some bananas, will you?' I can smell bunches of them on the street stall outside.

The nurse who stuck acupuncture needles into me this afternoon said to my mother, 'He probably can't feel the needles go in. I'm stimulating his head and lung meridians. We've cured more than ten paraplegics with this treatment.'

I didn't feel a thing. Apart from the first qigong session the director gave me, none of the treatments have had any effect.

I see a yellow blob floating in the darkness. Perhaps it's a street lamp outside the window. I think once more about how it might feel to wake up from this coma. I imagine myself sitting up, opening my eyes, turning my head to the right, going to the door, pressing down the handle and walking out of the room.

Although I'm lying here like a silent ghost, the cancer patient's dying breaths sound so clear, I know I must still be alive.

In the toilet next door, I hear an enamel bowl clinking against the sides of a ceramic sink and a toothbrush rattling inside a glass cup.

Further down the corridor, someone opens a door and asks, 'Have you eaten?'

'Yes,' a man replies gruffly. The radio in his room is tuned to a discussion of today's television schedule. 'In tonight's episode of the drama series, *Tender Darkness* . . .' I'm fed up with these banal details burrowing their way into my brain.

Without bothering to wash her feet, my mother lies down crossways at the end of my bed and prepares to go to sleep. This saves her the expense of renting a camp bed. As she dozes off, she grinds her teeth and mumbles, 'Let them out, let them out . . .'

I presume she's dreaming about the fire at the Friendship Theatre in Xinjiang Province which killed 323 people, 288 of whom were children. This morning my mother said the twenty-five officials in the audience had insisted on leaving the theatre before the children, and should be severely punished. But the lung cancer patient said the officials were VIPs, and it was their right to leave the theatre first.

The cancer patient yells out in pain, waking me from my doze. His brother switches on a torch briefly then turns it off again.

Someone slips into a pair of slippers and shuffles off to the toilets. Someone else is pacing up and down the corridor in a pair of rubber sandals. Two people in the room upstairs are playing Chinese chess. One of them slams a chess piece onto the wooden board then lets out a dry laugh.

These irritating distractions slowly fade away, allowing me to drift back to sleep.

A corpse appears every night, its hands, legs, chest, head and teeth scattered across a field. Apparently it is the corpse of the murdered herder, Wang Hai.

The pre-dawn breeze smells of charcoal smoke. Occasionally, I hear a box being flung onto a flatbed truck, or something falling from the back of a moving cart.

Just before sunrise, the metal shutter that seals the hospital's entrance is pulled up. The loud grating wakes my mother. She rolls onto her side and sits on the edge of the bed. She takes my hand, pulls the drip stand closer to the bed, then inserts the needle into my vein. My muscles contract for a second. Usually, she clicks her tongue at this point, but today she remains silent.

At eight in the morning, I hear doctors and nurses exchange brief greetings as they begin their morning shifts. The noises and smells in the building are less complicated at this time of day. I hear a bird, which is not a sparrow, chirping on a tree in the hospital's backyard.

My olfactory receptors have become more sensitive. I can smell the fresh fish on the market stalls a few streets away. The tart, briny odour drifts through the air, leaving behind it a milder scent of the sun-baked sea.

Before the doctor walks in, my mother opens her handbag again. When she pulls out the plastic bag containing my medical records and bottles of pills, I smell the musty scent of the last hospital I stayed in.

'How are you feeling this morning?' the doctor asks the cancer patient. 'You must keep doing those breathing exercises. You only have one lung now. You can't rely solely on your oxygen canister. Oxygen is more expensive than rice wine, you know!' When he hears that, the cancer patient immediately pulls the oxygen mask from his face.

The doctor moves to my bed and addresses my mother in a standard Chinese accent. 'Remember to inspect his back every day for early signs of bedsores. They can be very hard to treat. The director is giving the mayor a course of qigong treatment. He'll be back in a couple of days. We've upgraded your son to the 8,000-yuan treatment plan, as you requested. So we'll need the extra 2,000 yuan by the end of the day, please.'

'Poor Auntie!' the nurse says sympathetically. 'You'll probably die from exhaustion before this son of yours kicks the bucket.'

When you stand on Mount Sublime, you will see Mount Immortal in the north, Love Marsh Lake in the south, the Hill of the Battling Beasts in the west, and the River Deep in the east. The Tree of Man grows on the mountain. Its fruit have supernatural qualities. If you eat them, you will become obsessed with the desire to continue your ancestral line.

'Come in and have a cup of tea, Master Yao,' my mother says, opening the front door for him. 'It's exhausting having to walk up here to the third floor.'

'I'm used to it. I live on the fifteenth floor of a block of flats. The lift operator clocks off at 11 p.m., so whenever I get home late, I have to haul my way up thirty flights of stairs.'

'Here's some tea. It's so hot today, isn't it? I bet your flat has piped gas. The buildings in this compound don't even have a proper electricity supply. As soon as the neighbours downstairs turn on their washing machine, all my lights go out. The local authorities are planning to pull this place down soon.'

'He looks a little better than the last time I saw him.'

My mother and Master Yao are standing on my left. I can hear them breathing loudly.

'He didn't have any wrinkles when I brought him back from Sichuan. But these three lines have appeared since then. He looks like an old man now. Well, he'll be thirty in a couple of years. How time flies!' She puts her damp hand on my forehead. The two of them are blocking the breeze from the electric fan.

'Let me look at his palm,' Master Yao says, then takes a gulp of tea. 'Here's the sky line, here's the man line, and here's the earth line. They are clear and strong, which is auspicious.'

'Oh, I forgot, would you like a canned drink?' my mother says, rushing off to fetch a couple of cans from the kitchen. 'They're cold. This one's a sports drink, and this is Coca-Cola. When you open them, a stream of bubbles comes out. Oh dear!' The cans fall from her hands. I can smell sweet carbonated liquid spilling across the floor.

As she and Master Yao squat down to pick up the cans, they bump into each other. My mother fetches a cloth, then silently kneels down again and wipes the floor. Master Yao stands up.

After a while he says, 'Your hair is still very black.'

'You haven't got many white hairs either.' My mother probably averted her gaze when she said this. Although the electric fan is very noisy, it produces only a slight breeze. There's a rustling inside my cochlea. An ant crawled into my ear last year and suffocated to death, and its corpse is still trapped there.

Master Yao grabs my hand and says, 'I'll give him a quick session,' then sits on the chair my mother has pulled over for him.

My mother paid a nurse to give me an acupuncture treatment yesterday. Before the woman left, she said to my mother, 'You must face the fact that your son might die at any moment, Auntie.' After showing her out, my mother sat on the sofa for a moment then came into my room and said, 'Just make up your mind. Do you want to live or die? I need to know. I can't go on like this any longer. I don't have the energy . . . I'm fifty-six years old now. No mother should have to bury her own son . . .' She walked off into the sitting room in floods of tears, then went to the toilet and blew her nose noisily on a tissue as she squatted down to piss.

Since the month of qigong treatment I had in Sichuan last year, my health has fluctuated. Sometimes I glimpse the key that will reactivate my motor neurons, lying just out of reach. But sometimes my heart stops beating, and I feel as though I'm drowning in a dead sea. Whenever that happens, my mother quickly calls an ambulance then makes me perform sit-ups, pulling me up then pushing me down again so many times that she weeps with exhaustion.

'I can feel him absorb a small amount of my qi,' Master Yao says quietly. But the truth is I haven't felt anything yet.

Despite the nutrition I receive from the IV drips and the liquid formulas poured into my feeding tube, my weight never rises above seventy kilograms. I'm very weak. The nurse was right. If I contracted a bacterial infection, I wouldn't have the strength to fight it.

Master Yao tells my mother to switch off the fan, then starts massaging my feet. He rotates them slowly then presses his hands into the arches. I feel a shot of electricity run up my legs. My body tingles and becomes warm. This is the second time this month that I've felt a connection to my body. His ten fingers send hot electrical waves to the motor cortex of my brain. Even my hair seems to be quivering in the current.

'The problem isn't only in his brain,' Master Yao says, pausing for a break. 'His blood isn't circulating smoothly and he has excessive levels of negative qi.'

My mother lowers a fresh cup of tea onto the cabinet, trying not to make any noise, but the lid still clinks. Master Yao places his hands above my head then moves them down my body all the way to my feet. It feels as though a hot thermos flask is rolling over me.

'Yesterday you performed the Grab of the Immortal Hand. What qigong set are you doing today?'

'This is called the Rejuvenating Hand of Buddha. I'm trying to push his negative qi downwards. Just now I performed the Devil's Palm exercise to locate the root of his sickness.'

A ball of heat trapped somewhere close to my navel is dispersing through my body. The nerves between my lumbar vertebrae and coccyx begin to shudder. I suddenly feel as though I've been plunged into a wok of hot oil, and that I will soon twist and contract like a deep-fried dough stick. But just as I sense I'm about to stretch out my legs, Master Yao pulls his hands away.

A fly buzzes through the room and lands on my sweaty forehead. I hear someone outside drag a gas canister off the back of a flatbed truck. My body seems to rise from the bed. I hear a bang, then someone shouting, 'Let us through! Let us through! A student's been shot! Those fucking bastards, how could they do this? Check if there's an ID card in his pocket. Take off your shirt and wrap it around his head.' There's a stream of muffled yells. All I can see before me is a faint light and a floating ribbon of cloth. The image is so transfixing, I forget to breathe.

'Open the door too,' Master Yao says.

I take a deep breath and feel the summer heat stream down my trachea.

'Have a rest, Master Yao. You've been healing him for three hours now. Why not wipe away your sweat?' I've never heard my mother speak so gently before.

Master Yao removes his hands from my Greater Yang point.

My mother taps the drip bottle, picks up the electric fan and goes to join Master Yao in the sitting room. Cool intravenous fluid flows into my warm vein. It's a pleasant feeling. My mother comes back to fetch her cup of tea then returns to the sofa.

'Your son's qi has been too severely damaged,' Master Yao says. 'I don't think I can help him.'

'What am I going to do? I'm getting frail. I won't be able to look after him much longer. He's been having problems passing urine. If they put him on a urine drainage bag, how will I cope? I have a life too, you know. I've been looking after him every day for the last five years. If only he could just open his eyes . . .'

I gradually revert to the state I was in before the qigong session. Since Master Yao thinks he's failed, I doubt he'll bother treating me again.

If only he'd persevered a little longer, something might have happened. I felt the capillaries in my brain wriggle with anticipation and my eyeballs rotate in a semicircle. But just as my eyelids were about to part, he pulled his hands away.

On Buzhou Mountain grows the jia tree. It has oval leaves, and flowers with yellow petals and red sepals. If you eat its fruit, you will forget all your worries.

'Someone told me that you were once a school teacher, Master Yao,' my mother says, enunciating her words clearly.

'I worked in a district education department. But I was in the finance office. I was never a teacher.'

'You've been practising qigong for many years, I assume.'

'More than ten. I took it up after I was demoted and sent to Henan Province.'

'You've been a victim of the campaigns too, then.' My mother pauses to take a sip of tea. 'Is your child working yet?'

'I've got two. A boy and a girl. They're both married.'

'And your wife, does she still work?'

'She passed away two years ago.'

'Oh.' My mother doesn't question him further, showing some discretion at last.

'She contracted an incurable disease,' Master Yao says quietly.

My mother is now thinking of him as an unattached widower, rather than a qigong master. She falls silent for a moment, no doubt mulling over this new information.

'Let me give you something to eat before you go,' she says.

'It's too early for me. I usually don't have supper until seven o'clock.'

'But it's so nice for me to have company. I can never be bothered to cook when I'm on my own.'

'All right, let's cook ourselves a meal then. I'm no great chef, but I can guarantee you won't be disappointed with my stir-fried kidneys and pig's liver.'

'That sounds delicious. I've got some hairtail fish and prawns in the freezer as well . . .'

For the first time in years, I hear my mother laughing. The new kettle she bought whistles loudly as it comes to the boil. While I listen to the irritating noise, it occurs to me that if I weren't lying in this coma, I might be exploring the Tianshan Mountains in the far-western province of Xinjiang. Those mountains are freezing, even in summer. Snow lotuses bloom on the ice-capped peaks. Tian Yi asked me many times to take her to Xinjiang. When I think about her now, I feel I'm staring out at a vast, silent desert.

My muscles have been softened by Master Yao's qi. The summer heat is stupefying. Usually, when my thoughts turn to *The Book of Mountains and Seas*, I can wander through the imaginary landscapes for hours, but today's sweltering heat has blocked all those mountain paths.

Your head is submerged in cold, fetid water, but you're still breathing.

'Get out! This is the girls' dorm!' Mimi cried as I lifted the curtain she and Tian Yi had hung across a corner of the broadcast station, blocking off a small area for their own private use. It had that sweet, damp smell typical of girls' bedrooms.

'We're preparing for the final battle, but we're not optimistic about the outcome . . .' Bai Ling said into the telephone. It didn't sound as though she was talking to a journalist.

I tapped her shoulder and said, 'The journalists outside want to know what you think of the demonstrations taking place around the world today.' I'd returned to the campus the previous night to get some sleep. The dorm was crammed with boxes and backpacks, and the corridor was littered with leaflets, discarded tea dregs and leftover food.

'I can't speak to them now, I need to go and have a word with Lin Lu,' she said, donning the baseball cap and sunglasses she always wore when she wanted to walk through the Square unnoticed.

'I don't know how you put up with Lin Lu,' Mimi said to Bai Ling. 'He's so cold and ambitious.'

'We need to bring him onto our side,' Bai Ling answered. She'd smeared tiger balm over her legs. Her skin was very susceptible to mosquito bites.

'If you were drowning in the sea, and there was only room for two people in the lifeboat, who would you chose to go with you – Wang Fei or Lin Lu?' Mimi asked.

The question seemed a little absurd but, without hesitating, Bai Ling answered, 'Wang Fei, of course.'

'Ha! So you really have fallen for him!' Mimi laughed. 'Hmm, this student movement is getting very interesting . . .' Bai Ling's face turned deep red.

'I spoke to a construction manager today, and he suggested that during our next campaign, we erect a vast tent covering the entire Square,' Tian Yi said, emerging from behind the curtain.

'You think there'll be a next time?' I said. 'If the government launches a crackdown, we'll all be spending the next twenty years in jail.'

'Can you get us something to eat, Dai Wei?' Mimi said, furrowing her brow. 'The bread rolls in that box are mouldy.'

'They look fine to me,' I said, picking one up. Mimi was standing in front of the equipment. The borrowed aertex shirt she'd changed into was far too long for her.

When you've stared at the past for so long that time dissolves, you'll be able to wake from your slumber.

Mou Sen was sitting with Nuwa beneath the English Department banner. He got up and strolled with me to the south side of the Square.

It was still early in the morning, and not many supporters had turned up yet. Professors from the Beijing Institute of Science and Technology were marching up from Qianmen brandishing brooms and holding banners that said SWEEP AWAY CORRUPTION! A student cycled past them waving a straw effigy of Li Peng.

'There are only three thousand students left in the Square now,' Mou Sen said despondently. 'We must withdraw.'

'I'm sure more people will turn up in the afternoon,' I said.

'The army has encircled the city. If we stay here any longer, we'll be doomed.'

'I'd like to leave too. I'm only staying because of Tian Yi.'

'Last night, I told Bai Ling we should leave, but she accused me of being a coward. If she doesn't decide to vacate the Square today, I'll resign.'

Just at that moment, Bai Ling walked up to us with Mimi.

'I didn't make myself clear last night,' Mou Sen said to her. 'The Square's in chaos. If we don't withdraw soon, it will fall into anarchy.'

'So you still think we should leave, then?' Bai Ling said, putting on her sunglasses.

'Yes. It's our only option. If you don't agree, I must resign from my post.' He reached into his jacket and pulled out a resignation letter he'd written earlier.

'I can't betray the students,' Bai Ling said. 'History would never forgive me.' She skimmed through the letter he handed her, signed her name at the bottom and walked off.

'I bet you didn't think *that* would happen,' I said, tapping his shoulder. 'You're out of a job now, Mr Broadcast Station Director.'

'I didn't really want to resign,' Mou Sen moaned. 'What a mess . . .'

We turned round and went back to the broadcast station. As soon as we walked in, Mou Sen announced he'd resigned and was planning to return to his campus.

'Let's all resign, then,' Xiao Li said. 'I wouldn't mind going home for a few days.'

'Here we are at the critical moment, and as soon as he says he's leaving, you bolt out of the door,' Old Fu said angrily. 'All right, go then! Both of you! The rest of us will cope well enough without you. But the tapes and documents must stay here. No one must touch them.'

'This will mean you'll finally be able to take charge of the broadcast station, Old Fu,' said Xiao Li, rubbing some dirt off his trousers.

'And what do you mean by that?' Old Fu snapped. Everyone knew he resented being logistics officer and that he thought that, since he'd set up the first broadcast station in the Square, he should have been appointed director of the Voice of Democracy.

'You keep to your logistics work,' I said to him, 'and let Wang Fei run the station.'

'I'm the one who's been holding the fort here!' he shouted. 'Without me, this station would have collapsed ages ago.'

The mood became so hostile that I felt obliged to resign as well, which angered Old Fu so much he hurled a cardboard box to the ground.

Nuwa came in and tried to persuade Mou Sen to stay. I told her that Bai Ling had approved his resignation.

Mou Sen picked up his denim rucksack and said, 'I'm off now. I'm going to visit the political scientist Yan Jia to discuss an idea of mine. I plan to set up a Democracy University, right here in the Square. It will be open to everyone. We'll invite guest speakers to give classes on politics and culture. Students will be free to jump up and challenge them whenever they want. I hope you'll all get involved.' He raised his hand triumphantly and left. Nuwa clapped her hands in excitement and followed him out of the tent.

In the western region of the Great Wastes, the headless corpse, Xia Geng, stands upright, holding an axe and a shield. It was the warrior Shang Tang who cut off his head.

'You can send letters to anywhere in the world with it, without having to go to the post office? No, I won't bother buying one. I'd have to register it at the police station . . . Last week, Haidian Department Store promised that any customer who spent more than a hundred yuan would be given a lottery ticket. I bought a pair of trainers that cost 120 yuan, but when I went to collect a lottery ticket, the woman behind the counter said the shoes were on discount, so I didn't qualify for one. Those sharks! They completely swindled me!'

My mother is chatting to An Qi, who has brought along a woman called Gui Lan whose son was sentenced to eighteen years in prison for setting fire to an army tank during the crackdown. She's brought a copy of the written judgement that was issued to her son. She keeps repeating she'll be dead and buried by the time he's released.

'I bought a thermos flask in the market last week,' Gui Lan says. 'I filled it with boiling water, and after just two hours the water was lukewarm. I tried to return it, but the stallholder said he only gave refunds within three days of purchase. But the sticker on the thermos says it's guaranteed for three months.' I can tell from her accent that she was born in Shandong.

'I bought a packet of frozen dumplings from a chain store today. There were stubs of ungrated ginger in the filling. I couldn't eat them, but my husband wolfed them down quite happily.'

'Have you seen all those new food stalls in the street outside? One of them sells deep-fried locusts.'

'The district office doesn't bother to send anyone to collect the rubbish. At night, there are so many rats in that street, I don't dare walk down it.'

'Sesame cakes cost two yuan each in the market now, and rice dumplings are three yuan a jin.'

'It's silly to waste money on expensive food. Whether you eat mung beans or lobster, it all looks the same when it comes out the other end!'

'On the last anniversary of 4 June, the police bought me a train ticket to my parents' village. They didn't want me to be in Beijing in case I did something to commemorate the victims of the crackdown. They followed me all the way there and all the way back, so it was impossible to relax. Whatever they say this year, I'm not leaving my flat.'

'The police took us to a guest house out in the countryside. They wouldn't even tell us the name of the village. We spent the whole week in our room, watching television all day.'

'Maybe they took us to the same guest house! They bought me a tomato and egg stir-fry one day. It was so salty, I spat it out.'

My mother takes a sip of tea, puts the cup back down on the radiator and says, 'This flat is guarded like a prison. Sometimes I long to run away.'

'What would happen to your son if you left?' says Gui Lan. 'You're lucky to have him by your side . . . I'll have to move home soon. Construction workers walked down our lane yesterday and painted the word "demolish" on every house. The government is planning to pull down the whole district.'

'How much compensation are they offering you?' my mother asks.

'3,000 yuan a square metre. So all I'll get is 18,000 yuan, which isn't nearly enough to buy a new flat around here.'

'Why don't you move to Tongxian?' An Qi says. 'It's only an hour away by bus. Our block is dilapidated. I keep asking the neighbourhood committee if it's going to be pulled down, but they tell me there are still no plans.'

'Don't worry. You live inside the second ring road. The government said that everything inside the third ring road will be demolished, so they'll get to you eventually.' My mother comes over to check whether the enamel basin my urine tube empties into is full. Although her constant jabbering is infuriating, I know that no one else would have had the patience to look after me like this for all these years.

'I hope I can move into a flat like this, with central heating and running water,' Gui Lan says. 'My room in the courtyard house gets so cold in winter. And I hate having to use the dirty communal toilets at the end of the lane.'

'We used to live in a traditional courtyard house,' An Qi says. 'We had to share it with eight other families. It was so cramped.'

'At least in those single-storey houses you don't have neighbours above you or below you,' my mother says. 'And there are no stairs to climb. When I get older and my joints seize up, I don't know how I'll make it up these six flights of stairs.'

'I'd like to live in one of those modern apartments with floor-to-ceiling windows, like the ones you see in the television adverts.'

'I read in the papers that the authorities are going to tear down all the ancient buildings in Beijing apart from the Forbidden City, and replace them with high-rise tower blocks made of concrete, steel and glass. It will look just like New York.'

It's dark outside by the time the two women leave the flat. The sound of them shuffling paper and cracking pumpkin seeds between their teeth still hovers in the air, together with the smell of the cucumber omelette my mother fried yesterday.

Your conversations with the past stir your muscles from their sleep.

In the evening, my mother sits on a chair at the end of my bed and rubs my clenched toes. Then she takes out my father's journal again. After flicking through a few pages she begins to read out loud. '"People who have beds to lie on are so lucky. They can dream their lives away . . ." Huh, that sounds just like him. Your father was very cocky as a young man. He kept bragging that he'd be a famous violinist one day. But look what a frightened little mouse he became in the Cultural Revolution. "People who have beds to lie on are so lucky!" Ha! He wouldn't say that if he could see you lying here now!'

The mirror frame my father never finished making is underneath this bed, together with a broken wooden chair he picked up on the street. I remember him saying it was a Ming Dynasty chair, and that people in America would pay a lot of money for it.

'". . . Everyone is sent to work in the fields, irrespective of age or rank. I'm so frail, I collapse from exhaustion after a couple of hours. The officers award flags at the end of the day, depending on how much soil we dig. We get an entire steamed roll for a red flag, half a roll for a yellow one, a quarter of a roll for a blue one, and only an eighth of a roll for a black one. We have to dig four cubic metres of earth to get a red flag. Very few people can manage it. If you dig all day, hoping to get a red flag, but end up with a yellow one, you faint from hunger. If you're very unlucky and only get awarded a blue flag, you could end up dead. The rightist Old Zhang died of starvation while sucking the tiny piece of roll his blue flag got him. He didn't even have the energy to swallow it . . ."'

My mother goes to shut the window. An insect on my shoulder flies into the air, settles back down again then crawls up my neck. I imagine lifting my hand and swatting it.

'No wonder he was like a hungry ghost when he returned from the camps, scavenging scraps of food from the rubbish bins,' my mother mumbles, as she picks up the journal again. '"Beethoven had a passion for life, and felt disgust for mundane, worldly affairs . . ." He insisted the orchestra play Beethoven's Eroica Symphony when the American conductor visited. It was so reckless of him . . . "Everyone should have the right to choose their own path in life . . ." Did you hear that? That's enough to get us branded "relatives of a counter-revolutionary" all over again!' She slams the journal shut. 'Why did your father never speak to me of these things?'

Perhaps tomorrow she will reach the page where he describes having to resort to eating human flesh. When she reads it, maybe she'll understand at last why he returned from the camps a broken man.

There's a knock at the door. My mother invites the visitor inside and asks him his name.

'My surname is Huang,' the man answers. 'Master Yao told me your son is ill, and asked me to see if I can help.'

'Oh, you're Old Huang. Yes, Master Yao told me about your special gifts. I've heard you can speak the Language of the Universe.'

'So many buildings around here are being demolished. Most of the roads are blocked off. It took me ages to find this compound . . . I studied medicine when I was younger. My ancestors were all doctors. Unfortunately, I didn't get very far . . . Let me take a look at the patient.' He and my mother walk into my room.

'His temperature is very low . . .' he says, turning my hand over. 'So many horizontal lines.'

'That's the sun line you're pointing at,' my mother says brusquely.

'This is his health line. He's clearly suffering from a serious case of exhaustion.'

'He's slept solidly for six years, and he's still exhausted?' my mother laughs coldly.

'He has a black line along the middle of his forehead.'

'That's just the light. There are no black lines on his face.'

'No, there's definitely a dark line. That signifies calamity is about to strike.'

'Well, he managed to survive a bullet in the head, so I guess he could probably survive anything.'

'But his complexion is quite good.'

'He looks worse than my husband did when he was lying dead in hospital.' My mother is losing her patience.

'What does he eat?'

'Nothing. I pour a glass of milk into him every day, and give him three bottles of glucose solution. He's barely more alive than a corpse.'

The man sits down, and I feel the metal springs of the bed contract.

'Look at the colour of this!' he says, holding my urine bottle up to the light. 'That is very fine quality urine.'

'Since I've been giving him the vitamin fluids, his urine has turned golden yellow.'

'I'd like to have a taste. Will you fetch me a cup?'

'*What?*' my mother gasps. 'That's too peculiar. If you're thirsty, I'll make you a cup of tea.'

'Don't worry. I've been drinking urine for ten years. I've tasted all kinds, but I can tell that his is top-quality stuff.'

'What do you mean, "top quality"? This is piss you're talking about, not alcohol.'

I chuckle inwardly to myself. Perhaps the three bottles of glucose solution that I'm fed each day have turned my urine into a sweet beer.

My mother continues to express reservations about his strange request, but is finally won over when he tells her that Chinese emperors used to drink the urine of infant boys for medicinal purposes. He says he drinks his own urine last thing at night and first thing in the morning, and that after years of doing this, his hair has become blacker and his mind more alert. He advises my mother to pour some of my urine into a glass of fruit juice and take a sip. He points out that, in the womb, foetuses drink some of the urine they pass out into the amniotic fluid. He says that urine is the body's vital essence, and has the power to cure a thousand diseases.

'Look at the little red spots on his nails,' my mother says. 'I've been told they're a sign that a virus is attacking his brain.'

'No, they just indicate blockages in his blood's qi. As long as they don't turn black, you don't have to worry. Fetch me a cup, will you?'

It is very late by the time my mother is finally able to say goodbye to this strange visitor. She shuts the door, sits down beside me and mumbles to herself, 'He's quite a character, that man . . .'

In the kitchen, I can hear water from a wet mop dripping into the sink.

You move deeper into the fleshy wall of the past, groping for objects and emotions that no longer exist.

In the early afternoon, Old Fu stormed into the tent and said, 'I told you, you're not to broadcast anything that might shake the students' morale.'

'Now that Mou Sen has resigned, we don't know who's supposed to be vetoing the scripts,' Tian Yi said, looking up at him.

'I read out that statement,' Nuwa said. 'What was wrong with it?' She'd just broadcast a statement from the Provincial Students' Federation announcing they'd decided to merge with the Beijing Students' Federation to form a National Federation of Students.

'You should think carefully before you broadcast sensitive news like that,' Old Fu said.

Sensing that an argument was brewing, I stepped out of the tent.

The sunlight was scorching. Everyone was wearing straw hats or baseball caps, apart from a few bare-headed peasants who'd travelled up from the countryside. I saw several new faces in the crowd outside. They stared at me and the tent like curious tourists. There were fewer people in the Square that day. The flags and banners were rumpled and frayed. As I stood in the sweltering heat, I could feel sweat pouring from my thighs and groin. I turned round and retreated back into the shade of the tent.

'Broadcast it again if you want to!' Old Fu said, pushing his way out. 'I don't care any more.'

'I'm not your damn mouthpiece, you know!' Nuwa shouted.

'Calm down, everyone,' Bai Ling said, walking in with Wang Fei. 'Wherever I go, people are having arguments.'

'We left the Capital Joint Liaison Group meeting early,' Wang Fei announced, sweat streaming down his face. 'Shan Bo, that teacher from Beijing Normal, proposed that Ke Xi should take over as the student leader. He said he's China's Lech Wałęsa.'

'What a wanker!' Wu Bin said. 'If Ke Xi became leader, our movement would disintegrate.' His eyes were as black and shiny as tadpoles. His shaved head was shining too.

'Ke Xi got up and bragged that all the students revere him,' Wang Fei said. 'It made my skin crawl.'

'He said, "I may not be as politically accomplished as you intellectuals here, but I'm the most famous student in the Square. And with Mr Shan Bo to guide me . . ." Bai Ling gave such a good impersonation of Ke Xi that Tian Yi chuckled, then I chuckled, and soon everyone was roaring with laughter.

'The intellectuals are as prone to personality cults as the Communist Party,' Chen Di said. He looked clean and fresh. He never seemed to sweat.

'They got into a futile argument about whether the movement is a momentary aberration, or belongs to China's long tradition of popular protest,' Wang Fei said. 'We couldn't take it any more, so we got up and left.'

'We mustn't let those intellectuals come to the Square and stir up trouble again,' Tian Yi said, fanning herself with a pamphlet.

'I'd prefer to be crushed by the army than destroyed by the Joint Liaison Group,' Wang Fei said, whipping off his sweaty vest.

'So who's in charge of vetoing the scripts now that Mou Sen's gone?' Nuwa asked. Her short hair was in a mess. There was a big tuft sticking up at the back.

'Well Tian Yi's chief editor, isn't she?' Wang Fei said. The jeans he'd borrowed were too short for him.

'I didn't ask you,' Nuwa said curtly. She'd been in low spirits since Mou Sen had left the Square.

'Hey, Wu Bin, I've heard you lot want to set up a special operations unit to control the Defend Tiananmen Square Headquarters,' Wang Fei said, then sucked his cigarette and blew out a ring of smoke.

'It's the Square we want to control, not you lot,' Wu Bin said calmly.

'The only students supporting the Provincial Students' Federation are from Wuhan Iron and Steel University and the Fushun Petroleum University,' Wang Fei sneered. 'What can you hope to achieve?'

'There are 100,000 students from the provinces here now, and fewer than two thousand students from Beijing. So it's inevitable we'll take over control of the Square sooner or later.'

'Over my dead body!' Wang Fei shouted, then took a large gulp of mineral water. The water he spilt collected at his feet like a puddle of urine.

I could tell that the Y-fronts I was wearing were rancid. I reminded myself that I should go to the shops and buy Tian Yi a birthday present.

You lie coiled on your iron bed like a sleeping serpent. The heaven you yearned for is no more than an epitaph carved on a gravestone.

My mother leans against my bed and tugs at a drawer of the wardrobe, but it won't open fully. She shifts to the side and tries to jam the drawer in again from a different angle. It must be the third drawer. It always used to squeak when I opened it. The wooden strips at the bottom have worn out and a few screws are missing.

'I should throw this damn wardrobe your father made onto a fire!' she moans. 'How could he just die like that out of the blue? He promised he'd take me to America one day. I've dreamed of going to America all my life. If it weren't for you, I'd be living there by now. Oh, what a burden you are to me!' She lifts my hand, probably to check the injection wounds on my arm. When she lowers it again, I feel the air stir a little.

In a wobbling vibrato, she sings '*Aaaah, she fell in love with you-ou-ou . . .*' dragging out the last note for as long as she can as she walks off to the toilet.

As usual, she doesn't bother to close the door. She feels no need to. As far as she's concerned, I'm merely an object lying on the bed.

Her urine hisses out in fits and starts. It's from those parted legs that I emerged into the world. She's standing on the footrests of the squat toilet singing: '*It's your birthday today, Mother. I've brought you a lovely bunch of flowers . . .*' Her voice sounds flat, even on the higher notes. She is conscious of this, so she repeats the line: '*A lovely bunch of flowers . . .*' a little sharper this time. I hear her pull up her trousers then flush the toilet with water from a plastic cup. She usually only bothers to flush the toilet after she defecates, and even then she will only use fresh tap water if the old washing-up water she keeps in a bowl has run out.

I remember my father often saying to her, 'You don't put enough emotion in your voice when you sing. It lacks feeling.'

My mother would reply, 'You once told me it was my voice that made you fall in love with me, and now you say you hate it.' Or sometimes she'd say, 'Before we married, you used to beg me to sing to you. But now, when my voice is so much better, you're always finding fault with it.' My father would fall silent. After he was released from the camps, my parents had conversations like that almost every day. I can't remember my father ever praising my mother. But perhaps she wasn't a great singer after all, because she never did achieve a solo career.

My father's eyes appear before me. There are three parallel lines on his forehead. When he speaks, the red tip of his cigarette and his smoke-filled mouth move up and down. The dirty collar he's attached to his shirt has left a streak of grime around his neck. He's sitting at the end of the table next to a pile of music scores and LPs. There's a mountain landscape painted on the bamboo brush-pot next to his ashtray. I can even see his saw propped against the wall behind him.

'*With a thousand arms to aid me, I could drive the mill wheels wildly . . .*' my mother sings out from the sitting room. If my father were still alive, he'd interrupt her now and say, 'That "*wildly*" was too loud . . .'

'*With the strength of the storm winds blowing, I could keep the millstones going . . .*' Her voice relaxes as it reaches for the top notes.

My father would say, 'That's Schubert's "Maid of the Mill", isn't it? I heard it performed in America.'

And my mother would say, 'Stop going on about America. We're in China now. If you like America so much, why don't you go back there?'

One night my father's violin slipped off the sofa and fell onto the floor. It probably cracked. He flew into a rage and yelled, 'Stop shrieking! You'll never get a solo role if you sing like that.' My mother stopped singing, and a few seconds later we heard a cup smashing to the ground.

It's the early afternoon now. My mother turns on the radio and coughs into her hand. Because of me, she'll never be able to perform on stage again. 'Last week, experts from seventeen provinces and cities held a conference to debate the ethics of euthanasia. Shanghai is currently conducting a trial programme . . . It has been reported that of the 100 million elderly citizens in China, 6 million have suffered various levels of abuse. One man in Wuhan placed his mother in a coffin while she was asleep and took her to be cremated . . .' The sky is overcast, so the radio signal is poor and there's a constant background hiss.

'If only you could die happily in your sleep like that old woman,' my mother says, patting my shoulder. 'Have you made up your mind to die yet? Why don't I sign you up for euthanasia? We could make a trip to Shanghai. What do you say? I tell you, I can't go on like this any longer.'

I remember a dream I had yesterday afternoon. My hair grew long and thick and became a lush forest. I stood on a treetop. The sky was blue. A field of sunflowers lay spread out below me. I began to float like a cloud. I looked down and tried to grab hold of someone standing on the ground, but I was so high up, my arms couldn't reach them.

While you wait to decompose, the iron bedstead creeps into your body, transforming it into a rigid tree.

When the sun began to set, the heat in the Square became less stultifying and a few lights twinkled in the pale grey sky. The Beijing residents were less afraid than they'd been at the start of martial law, and the shops and stalls of Qianmen market south of the Square were bustling with customers again. Tian Yi, Wang Fei, Bai Ling and I walked into a small privately-run restaurant there. I'd invited them to supper.

I looked at the menu. At the top were pork dumplings priced at two yuan a jin, and below that was a list of stir-fried dishes. I ordered spicy tofu and stir-fried tomato and eggs, which I knew Tian Yi liked, and two bottles of beer. I'd spent five yuan on Tian Yi's present, and only had twenty yuan left in my wallet, so I didn't dare order anything too expensive.

'And let's have three jin of dumplings as well, a plate of boiled peanuts and some cold bean vermicelli,' I said to the manager before he walked away.

'Order some Coca-Cola as well,' Tian Yi said. 'We'll need it on a hot day like this.'

'I didn't know you were inviting us for a vegetarian meal!' Wang Fei said, then called out to the manager, 'Hey, and bring us some braised pigs' trotters too!'

'Why are you ordering so much food?' Bai Ling said. 'This isn't the Last Supper, you know.' She was wearing a baseball cap and sunglasses.

'Come on, let me tell them,' I said, glancing at Tian Yi. 'It's her birthday today!' I was sitting next to Tian Yi on one side of the table, and Wang Fei and Bai Ling were sitting opposite us.

'Oh, how embarrassing!' Bai Ling said. 'I haven't got a present for you. I'll make it up when we return to the campus. So what did you give her, Dai Wei? Show me. I remember how you wheedled your way into our party last year, just so that you could catch a glimpse of Tian Yi.' When Bai Ling smiled, which didn't happen very often, you could see her two pointed canines.

I'd bought Tian Yi a fold-up sandalwood fan in the craft shop next door to the restaurant. I'd remembered A-Mei had bought a similar fan in the Friendship Store in Guangzhou. She'd told me they were worth a lot of money abroad. I pulled the present out of my bag and placed it on the table. Tian Yi tore open the wrapping paper, sniffed the fan and said, 'Well, I suppose it's the thought that counts.'

I noticed a glazed expression on Bai Ling's face. It was the look girls adopt when they feel embarrassed and want to avoid attention. Trying to alleviate her discomfort, I said jokingly, 'I wonder what Wang Fei will give you for your birthday. Go on, ask him!' At this, Wang Fei leaned over and kissed her on the cheek. Bai Ling smiled coyly. They clasped hands under the table. Although streaked with dirt, Bai Ling's calves looked smooth and rosy.

Tian Yi ruffled her fingers through my hair and said, 'I hope that on my next birthday we can all go for a picnic in the Fragrant Hills.'

'Yes, as long as we're not in prison,' Bai Ling said, curling a finger behind her sunglasses and rubbing the corner of her eye. 'A student from Shanghai told me that his classmates are very disillusioned with our movement. Six hundred students from his university travelled up to Beijing, and only ten of them are still here.'

'Many of the provincial students have left now,' I said. 'The ones who've remained have lost their enthusiasm, and are worried about what will happen next. I spend most of my time trying to break up fights. I really think it's time we withdrew.'

'Retreat would be tantamount to capitulation,' Wang Fei said. He puffed his cigarette, then picked up a peanut with his chopsticks and put it into his mouth.

'I agree. We must bide our time and wait until the government resorts to using force. We must let the people see the true face of this government.' Bai Ling's fingers were almost as slender as the chopsticks she was holding. She glanced at Wang Fei and added, 'The hunger strike declaration I read out made a big impact on the students. It's my responsibility to carry on.' She put a small bundle of vermicelli into her mouth and slowly chewed on it.

'The Square is our only home now,' said Wang Fei. 'There's nowhere left for us to go. If we went back to our parents, they'd hand us over to the police.'

'Yes, Mao destroyed the traditional family system so that we'd all have to depend on the Party,' Tian Yi said. 'We're a generation of orphans. Our parents gave us no emotional support. As soon as we were born, they handed us over to the Party and let it control our lives.' She paused for a moment to swallow some food. The straps of her denim dress were constantly slipping off her shoulders. I kept having to push them up again for her. Having drunk some beer and eaten a few mouthfuls of hot food, I began to break out in a sweat. Tian Yi's neck was covered with perspiration as well. I picked up a dumpling and put it on her plate.

'If we were to fail now, our parents would side with the government and demand that we be punished,' Bai Ling said. 'I joined the Party on my eighteenth birthday. My father said to me, "From this day on, you belong to the Party. You must devote your life to the Party." How could I go home now? Orphans must learn to forge their own paths in life.' Bai Ling seemed very downcast.

'Yes, we must remain firm and do our best to defend the Square,' Wang Fei said. As soon as he began swigging back the beer, his face became as pink as Bai Ling's.

Tian Yi whisked some flies away with her hand then raised her eyebrows approvingly as a plate of fried pig's liver I'd just ordered was placed on the table. 'Eat up!' she said. 'Look, they've put some peanuts in there as well.'

'Local residents are distributing food and water to the soldiers who are surrounding the city,' Bai Ling said. She bit into a piece of liver. 'Mmm, tastes much better than the liver they serve us in the university canteen . . .' Then she removed her sunglasses and said forlornly, 'I don't want to die.' The rims of her eyes were red.

'It's still not clear who will win this battle.' Wang Fei stubbed out his cigarette and picked up a piece of fried egg.

'Deep down, I'd like to leave the Square, because that would be the safest option,' Bai Ling said. 'But I know that if I leave, I will spend the rest of my life living in fear.' She twisted a paper napkin nervously.

'I want to launch a campaign to press for regional autonomy,' Wang Fei said, placing his hands flat on the table.

'I only joined this movement to make sure Dai Wei didn't do anything rash,' said Tian Yi. 'But as soon as I got involved, I knew that no matter what happened, I'd have to stay with it to the end.'

'This is beginning to sound like one of your psychology tutorials,' Wang Fei complained.

'Pu Wenhua and Hai Feng have been passing information to the military to safeguard their futures,' Bai Ling said. 'The government won't need to communicate with us any longer. Those two guys have effectively destroyed our movement. What we need now is bloodshed. Only when rivers of blood flow through Tiananmen Square will the eyes of the Chinese people finally be opened.' She knitted her eyebrows together and burst into tears.

'Not again! You promised you wouldn't cry again,' Wang Fei whispered, patting Bai Ling's back. Her small delicate ears trembled as her head juddered.

We put down our chopsticks. There were few customers in the restaurant, but many flies. Whenever they settled on the table or a plate of food, Tian Yi would whisk them away with her sandalwood fan. The screeches and roars of the trolleybuses, cars and bicycles outside merged into one large clamour.

'I'm on the government's blacklist,' Bai Ling muttered. 'I want to run away. I don't care if people think I'm selfish. I want to live. Oh, I'm so confused . . .' She dissolved into tears again, her jet-black hair dangling over the fried tomatoes in her bowl.

Wang Fei shifted his stool closer to her and propped her up with his shoulder. Tian Yi pressed another paper napkin into Bai Ling's hand.

This young woman who was so resolute and determined in public was now sobbing like a child. Since the launch of the hunger strike, she'd been pushed to the front line, and to stay there for so long required nerves of steel. Before she started crying, I'd thought of telling her that it was unfortunate she'd approved Mou Sen's resignation, but seeing her distress, I decided not to.

'Hey, it's Tian Yi's birthday,' said Wang Fei. 'Let's not talk about the Square. Tian Yi, I wish you all the happiness and success in the world!' He pulled his hand away from Bai Ling's back and raised his glass of beer.

'I've developed a bad case of war fatigue!' Bai Ling rubbed the tears from her eyes and lifted her glass. 'Tell us what your birthday wish is,' she said, not daring to lift her gaze from Tian Yi's hands.

'My wish is to have freedom of thought and to see an end to this political dictatorship,' Tian Yi said. 'I don't want to have to live in fear.'

'That's easy. All you need to do is go abroad with Dai Wei.' Wang Fei stuffed a paper napkin under his armpit to mop up the sweat then tossed it onto the ground.

'I'm a Chinese citizen,' she replied. 'I don't want to devote my youth to a foreign country.' She turned to Wang Fei and Bai Ling. 'Come on, you two. I'd like to toast to your happiness as well. May all your wishes come true!'

Tian Yi put down her sandalwood fan and poured some more Coke into Bai Ling's glass. I was struck by how self-assured and resolute she'd become over the last few weeks. My mother had sent me a message saying my cousin Kenneth and his wife had arrived in Beijing. I wanted to ask Tian Yi to accompany us on a trip to the Great Wall the next day, but was afraid she'd accuse me of deserting my duties.

'Thank you, thank you,' Bai Ling said, smiling. 'In fact, my only wish is to have an ordinary life. I'd like to have children and watch them grow up. Come on, cheers!' She glanced at Wang Fei and clinked her glass against his. He put his arm around her and downed the beer in one gulp.

The restaurant manager walked over with a cigarette dangling from his mouth and said, 'There's a rumour going round that those new canvas tents you've put up in the Square are part of an empty-fort strategy, a ploy to scare off the government, giving you time to make a quick retreat.'

'We won't retreat,' Wang Fei said. 'We'll stay in the Square until the bitter end. Look, the commander-in-chief is sitting right here.' He patted Bai Ling's shoulder proudly.

'Oh, it's Bai Ling! I've seen your photograph in the newspapers!' The manager was taken aback.

As Bai Ling gave a reluctant smile, the insect bites on her forehead turned redder. 'Well, you can call the police now, if you want, and tell them to come and arrest us,' she said.

'No, no, I'd never do that. I wouldn't want any plain-clothes cops coming round here again. A couple of days ago, two foreigners came in for a meal. As soon as they left, a secret-police officer walked in and asked me what they'd said. There are only four tables in this restaurant, so I can hear everything. But the foreigners were speaking English. How was I to know what they were saying? So I'm not cut out to be a government spy, you see. Come on, have a cigarette!'

You want to stop the glucose solution entering your vein and slowly die of starvation.

My ears are like air vents. I can't choose which noises enter them. What is more frustrating is that my urine has now become a focus of media interest. For the last five days, reporters have been streaming into our flat to interview my mother and take photographs of me.

Yesterday, a man with a squawking voice said, 'Look how translucent his skin is! It's a sign that his years of fasting have transported him to a higher plane.'

'You can tell from his facial features that he's destined to live a long life,' his colleague said.

'He looks just like that qigong master, Kong Hai, who has the most miraculous urine of all the Taoist masters.'

'Master Kong Hai hasn't eaten or slept for thirteen years,' someone else concurred.

'Yes, Kong Hai's urine has been declared a national treasure. Only the Premier's wife is allowed to drink it.'

How could these strange men imagine that my urine has magical properties? What sort of tonic could a corpse like mine produce?

My mother is playing Mahjong with four other women. When they shuffle the plastic pieces it sounds as though they're scattering pebbles onto the table.

'We've uncovered another two fatalities,' Fan Jing says quietly. 'That brings the number of dead to 155.'

The women are skimming through the latest list of casualties of the crackdown and their relatives.

'I know this woman Zhang Li. Her husband was beaten to death on Fuxingmen Street on 6 June. She was sacked from her government job afterwards. She's destitute. All she owns is a bed and a chair. Her mental state is very unstable. She doesn't like staying in her flat when it gets dark, so she spends all night wandering through the lanes.'

'There were still people being killed on 6 June?' my mother asks.

'Yes, the massacre that took place in Fuxingmen has been dubbed a "mini 4 June". Tanks rolled through the street and fired at the crowd indiscriminately. Look, Professor Ding has got details of three people who were killed there. See here – "a boy, just thirteen years old, lay on the street, his guts splayed over his stomach, and the soldiers refused to let anyone go to his rescue."'

'Look at this. I was the one who found out about this guy,' Fan Jing says. 'His wife lives in a tiny shack in the suburbs. She farms twenty mu of land all by herself. No one ever visits her, except the police, who come every anniversary of the crackdown to warn her not to speak to journalists.'

'We should invite her over one day,' my mother says. 'She must get tired of being alone all the time.'

'She wouldn't be able to afford the bus trip. She doesn't even have money to buy herself clothes. She wears a man's army uniform she picked up on the street.'

'See these photographs,' Gui Lan says. 'This girl was called Zhang Chu. She was only nineteen. She's the one in the red shirt leaning against the foreigner. Such a pretty smile. When the bullet struck her head, blood spurted from her ears . . . Someone gave me her parents' address. I went to the flat, but discovered they'd moved out ages ago.'

'Where did she die?'

'In Qianmen, on the main road, in her boyfriend's arms . . .'

These women sound like a band of underground activists as they chat away, playing Mahjong.

'It's amazing to think your son's piss can be used as medicine,' An Qi says, grabbing the copy of the *Beijing Evening Star* that Fan Jing brought with her. 'Look at this headline: "Urine of comatose man cures terminal cancer patient".'

'So it really can cure people?' Gui Lan says, clacking her Mahjong pieces together. 'You should open a urine bank, Huizhen. You could make a fortune.'

'Your husband was shot in the kidneys, wasn't he, An Qi?' my mother says. 'Perhaps his urine has special qualities too.'

'He's got type 4 diabetes now, so I don't think his urine would do anyone much good,' An Qi says.

I still don't understand how urine can be used medicinally. It contains urea, sodium and chromium, which are toxic in high doses. My mother bottles all my piss now and keeps it in the fridge, ready to sell to the urine drinkers who visit us.

'One reporter said she'll get in touch with the producers of *Real Life Contest*, and see if they'd be interested in featuring Dai Wei in one of their shows,' my mother says proudly.

'I've seen that show. Last week, they had a paralysed old man competing against a young girl with liver cancer. After they'd both had a chance to describe their ailments, the audience decided the old man was the sickest and awarded him the 7,000-yuan prize.'

'It's inhuman, making sick people compete for money like that. And the prize money isn't nearly enough to save their lives.'

'They wouldn't dare feature Dai Wei in their show, though,' An Qi says. 'Not after they find out he was shot during the crackdown.'

'My qigong friend, Master Yao, is learning Falun Gong now,' my mother says. 'He told me that if you do the exercises daily, all your diseases will disappear. I'm thinking of giving it a go.' This is surprising, because when Master Yao urged her to try out the routines the other day, she flatly refused.

Strands of rain smelling of dusty roof-tiles splatter against the window-pane. A few drops of water trickle through the cracks in the wooden frame, then fall onto the stack of newspapers on the ground underneath.

'Most of the old courtyard houses in our district have been pulled down,' Gui Lan says. 'Our lane is due to be demolished in a couple of weeks. No one's bothering to collect money for the electricity and water any more.'

'If you can't afford a newly built flat, buy one in an old block. It will save you from having to pay the expensive concierge fees that are levied in the new developments.'

'I think you should wait until the government builds the affordable housing they keep talking about,' my mother says, walking into my room and closing the door to the covered balcony. 'I've heard there's a block going up near here soon.'

'How come the other side of the street has been torn down but this side has been left untouched?' An Qi asks, spitting out a sunflower-seed husk.

'I asked the neighbourhood committee. Apparently, this side belongs to several different work units, and they've had trouble sorting out the property rights.'

I can still hear the rain pattering against the window. Although the sound is much fainter now that the door to the balcony has been shut, it still conjures up memories of walking through the rain in wet shoes.

Drops of urine slowly accumulate in your kidneys' collecting ducts, whose forest of tubules spreads deep into the medulla like fungus sprouting in the rain.

At around six o'clock, someone knocks on the door.

Old Huang, the urine connoisseur, has brought some fellow enthusiasts with him. 'I've invited Director Zhou from the public health bureau,' he says to my mother. 'If he puts in a word for you, you won't need to worry about getting your former work unit to reimburse Dai Wei's medical expenses.'

My mother shows the guests into my room and turns the bedside lamp on. There are four or five people speaking. I recognise one of them as the ill woman who visited us last week. After she'd drunk a glass of my urine, she said, 'It's very sweet. It tastes a little like lemonade that's past its sell-by date.' My mother forgot to give me my antibiotics that day, so the urine the woman drank would have been pure glucose oxidase.

I can feel eyes and noses gather around my penis, inspecting the urine flowing from the tip.

The urine I passed this afternoon, and which is now in a cup on top of the wardrobe, smells of vitamin K. But perhaps the strong scent of rubber from the feeding pipe in my nose is affecting my judgement.

More visitors come and go, bringing smells of dust from the landing into the room. One man's footsteps are so heavy, they make the floor shake. He must be very fat. And there are two women. One of them hobbles about like my mother, the other is wearing high-heeled shoes and always walks close to the wall.

'It's coming out faster than it did yesterday.'

'It's dark red today. The colour of black tea. Even when I eat red chillies, my piss never gets as red as that.'

'I always stick to plain food. I have a cup of milk and an apple every night before I go to bed. The urine I pass in the morning is the sweetest of the day. After I drink my first cup of it, I feel my whole body is cleansed.'

'Look, it's going hard. I didn't know coma patients could get erections.'

I can feel my penis rising. My mother quickly pushes it down again with a cold wet towel, and says, 'Don't worry, if I cool it down like this it will shrivel up again in no time.'

'That shows there's still a chance he might wake up,' Old Huang says. 'It's a good sign.'

My mother presses down on the wet towel and gives my penis a hard pinch. I've made her lose face again.

My brain feels as clogged and muddled as a mud pit being stirred with a wooden stick.

'It tastes like beer,' the fat man says. 'It's strange. For the last couple of days my urine has tasted of aubergine. I'll fill a glass for you in a minute and you can smell for yourself.'

'If you eat white gourd for lunch, your afternoon urine will be much clearer,' Old Huang says. 'But don't drink the first drops or the last drops. Mid-flow urine always tastes the best.'

'Those look like strands of blood,' someone standing on my right says, tapping the side of the cup.

'It's dripping out very slowly,' a woman says to my mother. 'How many glasses does he fill a day?' My mother used to give me two bottles of glucose solution every day, but she's now stepped up the dose to four.

'That glass will give you the same benefits as a month's prescription of herbal medicine,' Old Huang says authoritatively.

The communal central heating is switched off, and a smell of warm urine drifts through the air. The world outside slips away from me as the sky darkens.

I long to leave this urine-producing machine that I've become, and run outside and feel the cold wind brush across my face. Although it's the end of spring now, the wind is still dry and cold enough to raise goosebumps on one's skin . . . 110 li further north lies Mount Spring. There is a beast there that resembles an ape, but its fur is spotted with markings. When it sees a man approach, it pretends to be dead . . .

'This glass is full!' Old Huang shouts. 'Bring me another one.'

The group gathers round me again. I'm lying with my legs splayed open, like a woman about to give birth. I wish I could sit up and kick this band of urine enthusiasts out of the flat.

Someone lifts my penis out of the full glass, lets it rest on my left testicle then places it inside an empty cup. I feel the cold ceramic against my skin.

'Where do you work?'

'At the Number Two Pharmaceutical Factory.'

'I developed paralysis of the left side of my body six months ago, but look, after just three doses of his urine, I'm almost cured. The first time I came here, I had to be carried in. I couldn't move my left leg or arm. Now, see, I can wriggle all my fingers . . .'

'You should change the needle every day, or the insertion hole will become infected,' someone advises my mother.

'This is a glass of his morning urine,' my mother says. 'I've kept it in the fridge for you.'

'Do I look like a man of sixty?' This man has come to drink my urine several times. He must have just arrived. I hear him dump his bag on the sofa then I hear the bag drop to the ground.

'I first started drinking urine after reading a Japanese book called *Urine: The Cure for One Hundred Illnesses*.'

'What are you doing reading Japanese books? The Chinese have been using urine therapy for more than a thousand years.'

'I had shingles. My feet were in so much pain, I couldn't walk. I drank my urine for a week, but nothing happened. But after just one cup of this guy's urine, I'm completely cured.'

'No, you drink this cup. I'll have the next one. I've heard you've applied for authorisation to set up a urine drinkers' association.'

'His condition is stable now. I give him glucose and vitamin formulas every day. Please, help yourself.'

They continue to chat away as they sip. The telephone rings for a long time, but no one goes to answer it.

'In the late Qing Dynasty, herbal medicines were infused in the urine of infant boys.'

'It will take ten years off you, I promise. At ten yuan a cup, it's a bargain.'

'My appetite has improved so much since I've been drinking it. I had four steamed dumplings for lunch today, and a bowl of hot-sour soup.'

'It's very salty. It tastes like sea water.'

I picture a trail of my footprints in the snow outside. What does it feel like to stand upright? I stood for over twenty years, but still have difficulty remembering the sensation. I imagine walking along the snowy path, effortlessly raising my knees. The snow is unmarked now, apart from some paw prints leading to the dustbins. I walk faster and my body becomes as light as a sheet of paper. I start running in time with my panting breath. My feet leave the ground and I fly into a bright light. There are people chasing after me, shooting arrows at my back. Below me, I see a mountain valley and soft white clouds. The arrows are flying as fast as me. As they draw closer, they transform into hypodermic syringes. The needles are infected. My skin tightens and my pores dilate.

A glass falls to the ground. A few people move away while others kick the broken shards into the corner.

'Hold the tube up for me,' a man on my left says. He's pouring milk into my feeding tube, hoping it will sweeten my urine.

'Has the milk been boiled?' a woman standing next to him asks.

'I boiled it this morning,' my mother says.

'*I beseech you, Emperor . . .*' Someone has inadvertently turned up the volume of the television. The actor's loud cry is followed by the high-pitched screech of a two-stringed lute.

I want to recite to myself another passage from *The Book of Mountains and Seas*, but my mind has gone blank. All I can see is a shallow river running through a flat yellow expanse . . . Now I see one of A-Mei's leather shoes. I washed the yellow mud from the sole for her. The wrinkles in the leather resemble lines on the palm of a hand. The outline of her big toe is visible on the shoe's scuffed tip. The two straps cross over the front at the same angle that she crosses her arms over her chest. Some of the holes in the straps are more elongated than others. Looking inside, I can see the shiny print her heel has made in the leather insole and the mysterious darkness where her toes rest. I remember holding her foot in my hand and gazing at her toes splaying softly between my fingers.

Where is she now? I see a faint smile spread across her lips. Whenever her image appears in my mind, a stream of pain pours into my heart through the inferior vena cava, then the left ventricle contracts and the pain is pumped into the rest of my body.

'Look! His face has gone red! Did someone rub oil onto his eyelids, or are those tears I see?'

'How long has he been like this?' I haven't heard this voice before.

'Since 4 June 1989. He was shot in the head during the crackdown. He was studying for a PhD.'

'Huh, this pager never stops bleeping. Can I borrow your phone, Auntie?'

'Look at this article. It says that Mr Desai, the Prime Minister of India, drinks a cup of urine every day.'

A light flits through the darkness. My heart begins to beat faster. I look out of a train window and see yellow mudflats stretching to the horizon and the grey sky reflected in pools of rainwater. A-Mei pulls down the window, wipes the dust from her fingers and says, 'I love the smell of the air after a rainstorm.' As the wind hits my face, I catch whiffs of her lipstick, hair lotion, hand cream and the chicken in soybean sauce she ate in the dining car. The train is heading for Guangxi Province. A sheet of rain and mist flashes past in the distance.

The milk that was poured into me has coated the walls of my stomach and blended with my gastric juices. As the stomach walls contract, drops of the semi-digested liquid flow into my duodenum. The urine discharged by my kidneys collects in my bladder and flows through the prostate gland.

'Does he never open his eyes?' rasps a woman who has just come in.

'If you poured some of his own urine down his tube, perhaps it might bring him out of his coma,' another woman says, placing her clammy hand on my face.

My urine trickles down the urethra then drips into the glass cup. The mouse under my bed has been frightened by our visitors' footsteps, and has hidden itself in the box my mother bought for my ashes.

'He never fills more than seven glasses a day, I'm afraid,' my mother says to the last woman to arrive. 'Come again tomorrow. I'll keep his morning urine in the fridge for you.'

I remember the dream I had last night. A doctor brought me a syringe and said, 'Give yourself the injection. If you do it correctly, you'll wake up from your coma.' But when I took the syringe it turned into a bicycle chain which dragged me off into a glass corridor. I tried to scream for help, but no sound came out of my mouth. Outside the corridor lay a scorching desert. I flung myself against the glass walls like a trapped bird then slowly suffocated to death.

Trapped like a frog inside a glass jar, you wish your scream could light up the night sky.

The Square was bustling again. Residents stood chatting with their friends, enjoying the cool of the evening. Children ran around playing hide-and-seek. Street hawkers pushed their carts along shouting 'Ice lollies for sale!' Further away, a column of marchers arrived waving red banners.

Mou Sen walked up. 'So I hear you went out for supper in Qianmen,' he said, fixing his intense gaze on me.

'It's Tian Yi's birthday. I invited Wang Fei along too. You weren't around.'

'Bai Ling was there as well, wasn't she? You know, Nuwa has guessed that Wang Fei's having an affair with her. He seems serious this time. I don't think it will last, though. Bai Ling has such a fierce temper. She's a Shandong girl, after all. I might as well tell you. Nuwa and I are in love. It was she who chased after me, I promise you. Don't tell anyone. At least, don't tell Yanyan.' His nose twitched awkwardly.

'I see. "The lazy toad dares taste the meat of the swan", as the saying goes!' I looked down at Mou Sen and felt peeved that someone so much shorter than me could seduce a beautiful girl like Nuwa.

'*You're* the bloody toad, Dai Wei!' he said, punching me in the chest.

'All right, your secret's safe. Hey, how are things progressing with your Democracy University?' I didn't want to discuss Nuwa with him. In my mind's eye, I saw her tight denim skirt swaying from side to side, her bottom jutting out a little each time she shifted her weight from one leg to the other.

He told me that forty people had already signed up to join his Democracy University. I warned him I couldn't help organise his preliminary meeting because my cousin Kenneth and his wife had arrived in Beijing, and I had to show them around.

'The spirit of the Square is dying,' Mou Sen said. 'It's up to me to bring it back to life!'

'I really don't understand you. You resigned from the Headquarters because you thought we should withdraw from the Square. Now you're urging everyone to stay here and join your university. Have you gone mad?'

'I just have a gut feeling that if we don't do something dramatic now, our movement will collapse,' he said, gazing into the distance.

'I think the best plan is to withdraw from the Square on 30 May, as Han Dan is suggesting, then continue our campaign back on the campuses.'

As I was about to walk away, he grabbed my shirt, stared at me unblinkingly and said, 'Dai Wei, if either of us is arrested, we must be strong and refuse to surrender.'

'Don't be so melodramatic,' I said, pushing him away.

Sister Gao spotted us and came over. 'The people on the streets were very cold towards us on the march today,' she said. 'They didn't cheer or clap, or offer us any food.' Then she turned to me and said, 'Dai Wei, there's a press conference taking place on the Monument. Zhuzi's looking for you.'

A refreshing drizzle fell from the night sky. Beijing residents were beginning to drift back to their homes. I wanted to find Tian Yi and ask her to go back to the flat with me, but I had no choice but to turn round and head for the Monument.

Han Dan was reading out a ten-point declaration. Yang Tao was standing next him, holding up the megaphone. The journalists had stacked their tape recorders and microphones on the school desk in front of them.

'We propose that the students withdraw from the Square on 30 May, bringing this stage of the movement to a close . . .' Han Dan said. As soon as he'd delivered the declaration, he left before anyone had time to protest.

The *Democracy Forum* discussion that Old Fu began chairing in the broadcast station soon degenerated into an argument. Students and Beijing residents stormed into the tent, grabbed the microphone from the table and shouted their opposition to the proposed withdrawal. Old Fu ran away, fearing for his safety, leaving Chen Di and me to get rid of the intruders.

I searched for Tian Yi, and at last spotted her sitting by the trees near the Museum of Chinese History.

'This is the first day of my twentieth year,' she said, not looking up at me.

'My cousin Kenneth and his wife arrived in Beijing today for their honeymoon. Will you help me show them the sights tomorrow? Your

English is much better than mine. My mother wants us to go and see her tonight to discuss where we'll take them.' I caught a whiff of the scraps of discarded food rotting on the ground beneath the trees.

'Seems like a strange place to spend one's honeymoon. Don't they know there's a revolution going on here?'

'Apparently they booked the holiday months ago and couldn't change it. And anyway, neither of them has been to China before, so they're very excited.'

'Hey, did you see the National Opera Company's orchestra?' she said, as we headed for Changan Avenue.

'No, where?'

'They came here about an hour ago to show their support. They performed the final movement of Beethoven's Eroica. Just there by the national flag.'

'Was my mother with them?'

'No, none of the choir came. Just the conductor and about thirty musicians.'

'They played the Eroica, you said? I wonder what my father would make of that if he were alive . . .'

You want to search for the way out, but you can't move. Your wet flesh envelops you like a dank pelt.

'Looking back at the Beijing fashion trends of 1996, we've seen a big drift towards relaxed, casual clothing, with baggy shirts and short waistcoats . . .' My mother switches off the radio then pulls out the syringe from my arm and lowers my hand onto the bed. Blood rushes to my fingertips. She places my right hand on my thigh and pushes me onto my side. She forgot to move my left hand out of the way, so my hip is now digging into it.

'If only you could die in your sleep . . .' she wheezes, wedging her knee behind my back. With all her might, she pulls me into a sitting position. When she's confident I'm stable, she slowly rotates my head from side to side. It's drooping down, so when it turns, the veins on my face become compressed and bulge out. But at least my blood is flowing smoothly through my back now.

Someone knocks on the door. My mother rests my head on the pillow. 'Hello!' she says, opening the front door. 'You're the first to arrive.'

'Are you alone then, Auntie?'

'What do you mean? There's always the two of us in this flat.'

'Of course. How thoughtless of me. I'm sorry. I came here straight from work. I thought I could help you out before the others arrive. Have one of these fruits I've brought you. They only grow in the south.' It's Mimi. She visited a few months ago. Perhaps Tian Yi told her to come today. She and my mother sit on the sofa.

A fly that has been trapped in this room for months buzzes around my head, then settles on my hair and lays eggs on my scalp.

'Let me take a look at Dai Wei first,' Mimi says, getting up and heading for my room.

There's no sheet covering my naked body. My penis is resting on my thigh. She walks in and yelps.

'Oh, I bet that frightened you!' my mother says, rushing in and flinging a sheet over me. 'I'm sorry. I forgot to cover him. I've just turned him over. He's as thin as a rake, but he still weighs a ton. He needs to be turned over every day, like a leg of ham drying in the sun. Hold his arm, will you, and I'll push him onto his stomach again.'

Mimi grasps my arm. I can feel her breath on my cheek. Her fingers are small and warm.

'I turn him three times a day. Turn around, turn around . . . After Liberation, we were always singing: "*The poor of the world have had their lives turned around!*" But my life hasn't turned round yet. See that bedsore on his shoulder. It was raw and infected for a year. It only healed over last winter.'

'The lives of the government officials have turned around, though. They've made fortunes from all their corrupt profiteering. Do you want to give him a wash?'

'I cleaned him this morning,' my mother lies. 'Does it smell in here? I've got used to it over the years.'

'It smells like a . . . hospital,' Mimi says tactfully.

They roll me onto my back again then shake my quilt and place it over me as they would a sheet over a corpse.

A news presenter's voice drones from the television in the sitting room. 'The family planning authorities' policy of compelling all women who apply for birth permits to swallow an iodised oil capsule has been a great success. In the four years since the scheme was introduced, 17.7 million married women of childbearing age have taken the capsules . . .'

I suddenly remember how my cousin Dai Dongsheng pinned a Red Flag Watch Factory badge onto his lapel when he came to Beijing, hoping he could pass himself off as a city resident. I presume his mad wife is still pacing around their shack, threatening to take her case to the emperor.

'He's so thin now, he barely looks human,' my mother says.

'Go on, try some fruit, Auntie.' Mimi doesn't seem to be too disturbed by my condition.

The telephone rings. My mother picks up the receiver. '. . . Yes, all your old classmates will be here. No problem. Bring her along too. It would be nice to see you.' She hangs up, cracks her knuckles and goes into the kitchen.

Mimi joins her there. I wonder how she's managed to squeeze herself in. I hear oil bubbling in the wok, but the fumes haven't reached me yet.

The late autumn days are turning damper now, but my skin is still dry. Each time a draught blows in from the landing, dead skin cells lift from my body, fly into my nostrils then swirl down through my trachea into my lungs.

My skin is as scaly as the pink, blue and gold angelfish that swam in the tanks of Beijing University's biology lab. From glands beneath their scales, they'd secrete tiny drops of nourishing microbial slime that would fall straight into the mouths of their young.

I hear crackling and spitting as food is plunged into the hot oil. It smells like they're making deep-fried carrot meatballs. I used to love eating those. I liked deep-fried aubergine as well, stuffed with ground pork and coriander. But my favourite of all was deep-fried sea bass that was crisp on the outside but still soft and moist inside. Even the left-over scraps of batter that were ladled out at the end were delicious. In fact, almost everything tastes good when it's deep-fried. I feel a faint pang of hunger, but it remains in my brain and doesn't travel to my mouth or stomach.

In the sitting room, the news presenter prattles on. '. . . China has become infatuated with football. This game is more than just a sport. It can lift the spirit of a nation. But the continual failure of our teams to make any significant mark in the international arena has been a great humiliation to our race . . .'

'Many retired people go to parks in the morning to practise traditional Yangge fan dancing,' Mimi says. 'You should give it a try, Auntie.' She still has the same husky, wavering voice she did at university. It sounds like an out-of-tune viola.

'I'm learning Falun Gong,' my mother says as they return to my room. 'I'm taking lessons from a teacher called Master Yao. The meditation exercises can cure any illness. It's much easier than standard qigong, or the traditional Fragrant Qigong school.'

'Look at this article, Auntie. It's about a British man who woke up recently after being in a coma for nine years. That's his photograph. He said that although he couldn't speak or open his eyes while he was in the coma, he could hear everything that was going on around him. Perhaps Dai Wei can hear our conversation now. You never know . . . I'll read out the article to him in a minute. Shall we rub some more cream on his legs?'

'I have to admit, I've sworn at him a few times these last years. He's put me through hell . . .'

'Not many people could have endured what you've been through. I think you're amazing, looking after him like this for all these years. Have you had any news from his brother?'

'Yes, he phones me from England quite often. But he doesn't dare speak for long in case the police have tapped our line.'

'Do they still come round here?'

'They take us away now each anniversary of 4 June, but otherwise they usually only visit every two or three months. And they're less officious than they used to be. They sit down and have a cup of tea, warn me not to speak to foreign journalists, then get up and leave. Look, he's almost dead now. It's unlikely he's going to start a revolution, isn't it?'

My mother is fifty-eight now. Her voice is warmer and fuzzier than Mimi's. It sounds like a hammer dulcimer. A-Mei's voice sounded like a violin, Tian Yi's like a flute.

'Are you still going out with that boy, what's his name – Yu Jin?'

'Of course! Boyfriends aren't shirts – I don't change them every day. The securities company he was working for in Shanghai has just transferred him to Beijing.'

'Yes – Yu Jin. What a nice boy. The first time he came to see me, he gave me a thousand yuan. You're lucky to be young now. You can go out dancing, go to nice restaurants . . .'

'To be honest, I don't go out much,' she says sombrely. 'I suffer from anxiety. I'm afraid of the dark, I'm afraid of crossing the road. I've stopped using a pager because the electronic beeps make me jump.'

I hear footsteps coming up the stairs. The others have arrived. The prospect of noise and chatter excites me.

Mimi goes to open the door. 'Hey! Chen Di!'

A draught blows the clamour into the flat. Everyone is speaking at once.

'You look like an Italian gangster in that hat, Yu Jin. Where did you buy it?'

'I didn't know you wore glasses, Chen Di!'

'Hey, Yu Jin and Mimi, when are you going to tie the knot? It's always the same with you two: all thunder and no rain!'

'This is for you, Auntie,' Yu Jin says. 'It's Jinhua ham. Dai Wei's still on hunger strike, I presume, so you'd better eat it yourself.'

'What a beautiful box,' my mother says. 'It looks like a Japanese import.'

'Don't talk to me about Japanese imports!' says Yu Jin. 'Our office was given some Japanese biscuits the other day. Each one came in a plastic wrapper with a sachet of drying agents. The office maid assumed the sachets contained flavourings, so she opened them and sprinkled the tiny granules over the biscuits before she served them to us. We all ended up with swollen mouths and had to be rushed to hospital!'

'Auntie, I haven't introduced you yet,' Chen Di says. 'This is my girlfriend, Bingbing.'

'Hello, Auntie,' the girl says. She has a southern accent.

'She's so pretty,' my mother says. 'And even taller than Tian Yi.'

'I came here straight from work. I couldn't reach Wang Fei on his pager. I heard he's gone back to Hainan Island. Look, I've brought a cake.'

'I bumped into Yanyan in the Shangri-la Hotel last night. She was very offhand. She didn't even bother to give me her card. She acted like some hotshot journalist, but she's still only working for the *Workers' Daily*, for God's sake.'

'Yanyan came here for a meal once,' my mother says. 'Come on, give me your jackets and sit down. You can watch the television. The food will be ready in a minute.'

They file into my room. Two, four, six – eight eyes stare down at me. If only I could open mine and look up at them.

'He looks like Chairman Mao lying in the Mausoleum,' says Yu Jin. 'He has that same serene look on his face. "Remain unchanging in changing circumstances." Do you remember saying that to me once, Dai Wei? I'll never forget it.'

'He led our student marshal team in the Square, Bingbing,' Chen Di says. 'He was great. So big and tough. He could even scare off our university's boxing team.'

'Really? But look how skinny he is now.'

There hasn't been so much noise here since the police came and drove away the urine drinkers from our flat.

I remember waking Chen Di one afternoon when he was having a nap in the tent and saying, 'It's time for your broadcast, my friend.' He'd stripped down to his Y-fronts. I could see his penis hanging out. He stared up at me blankly and said, 'I'm so bloody knackered. As soon as this movement's over, I'm going to cuddle up with a girl and sleep for a week.' Although Bingbing probably is taller than Tian Yi, I doubt she's pretty. I imagine she looks similar to the tall girl who drew us a map of Tiananmen Square.

'He seems to have shrunk. He can't be more than 1.7 metres now. He used to be 1.83. The tallest guy in the Science Department.'

'I read that your urine sold for ten yuan a cup, Dai Wei. It's incredible! A man was cured of chronic arthritis after drinking just one cup.'

'Who drank urine?' Bingbing asks.

'Haven't you heard the story? There was even an article about it in *Le Monde*. "Urine of Chinese Coma Patient Cures Cancer". You can look it up on the internet.'

'Only the urine of infant boys was drunk in the past,' Chen Di says. 'So if they're drinking Dai Wei's piss now, perhaps that means he's returned to his infancy!'

It makes me happy to hear them joke and laugh like this. Chen Di has visited several times before, but this is the first time he's stayed for a meal. His girlfriend is wearing expensive perfume. She probably works for a foreign company.

Someone switches off the radio. Someone else bumps their knee against the bed. I feel everyone's gaze move up and down my body.

'Dai Wei, your old classmates have come to celebrate your birthday,' my mother says, coming in to collect my urine bottle. 'You're very lucky to have so many good friends.'

The room falls silent. All I hear is the sound of people breathing. Then Chen Di says, 'Dai Wei, if you can hear me, you'll know who I am. You've been lying here for six years – no, seven. It's your thirtieth birthday today. Confucius said that a man of thirty must take his stand in life. We all hope you'll be able to stand up again one day. I want to hear you explain all those strange theories you had about plant respiration. I want to see you awarded your PhD.'

'Don't make fun of him,' Bingbing says, turning her back to him.

'I'm not making fun of him. He was researching plant cell biology.'

'I hope the government will have reversed its verdict on the student movement by the time you wake up,' Yu Jin says. 'We'll appoint you commander-in-chief of the Square.'

'Let's not talk about the past,' Mimi says, leaning against Yu Jin. 'We should all just wish him a happy birthday.'

I find it hard to believe that Mimi is going out with Yu Jin. They hardly spoke to each other in the Square. I bet she'll tell Yu Jin that she saw my penis. How humiliating. My mother has gone back to the kitchen to chop up bean sprouts. Her life has improved a lot since she met Master Yao. He visits her once a week now.

'Can he hear us?' Bingbing asks.

'I'm sure he can,' Chen Di says. 'He's particularly sensitive to women's voices. When you spoke just now, his eyelids trembled.' Chen

Di is wearing a prosthetic foot. I can hear it squeak when he walks about.

'He's probably just excited to have us all here,' Mimi says. 'Dai Wei, Yu Jin has bought you a special qigong waist belt. It's stuffed with more than thirty different medicinal herbs. Apparently it can cure many afflictions. We'll put it on you in a minute.'

'Since when did you start believing in Chinese medicine, Yu Jin?' Chen Di asks.

'The factory sent marketing agents round to our office. They wouldn't leave until we bought some.'

'I bet they were pretty girls,' Chen Di says. 'You probably sat them down and gave them cups of tea. How many belts did you buy?'

'Stop teasing him! Yu Jin may be guilty of many things, but one thing I'm sure of is that he's no philanderer.'

'Supper's ready!' my mother shouts, laying the chopsticks on the table in the sitting room. 'Come and sit down.'

'Let's give old Chairman Mao here a rest, and go and celebrate his birthday for him,' Chen Di says.

There's another knock on the door.

It's Mao Da and Zhang Jie. They sit at the table without bothering to come in and see me. Wafts of alcohol blow into my room.

'The Tiananmen Mothers group has made a big impact,' Mao Da says to my mother. 'I heard that your leader has been nominated for the Nobel Peace Prize.'

'The whole world knows about your group now, Auntie. You should be proud of yourselves.' As soon as Zhang Jie finishes speaking, his pager rings. He gets up and makes a call on my mother's telephone.

'Poor Professor Ding has been persecuted relentlessly for her activities,' my mother says. 'She's been sacked from her job, arrested, detained. She's under constant surveillance now. There's always a police car parked outside her home.'

'When my colleagues find out I was involved in the Tiananmen Square movement, they treat me like a leper. No one wants to talk about those events.'

Zhang Jie says into the phone, 'All right, we know the pros and cons . . . We'll need a certificate from the Ministry of Information before we can apply for an internet service licence. We must find someone with high-level connections or we'll never get anywhere.' There's a new tone of confidence in his voice.

'None of his old professors have ever visited him.'

'They'd lose their jobs if they did. That Granny Pang downstairs would report them to the police.'

'Granny Pang's taken up Falun Gong. It's completely changed her. She wouldn't dream of reporting anyone to the police now.'

My mother takes her cassette player out to the yard every day and practises Falun Gong exercises with a few other women in the compound. Granny Pang often comes up for a chat now. She told my mother that she realises it was wrong to pass information to the police, and that from now on she will cultivate truth, compassion and tolerance to ensure she doesn't come back as an animal in the next life.

'Get off the phone, Zhang Jie. It's not often we all get a chance to sit down together like this.'

'All right, all right. When I bought this pager three months ago, I was told it would give me daily share-price information, but the service still hasn't been set up. When I ask the girl on the switchboard about it, she always promises to get it sorted, but she never does, of course . . .'

'Yes, that girl on the switchboard sounds like she's on drugs. When I call the number to leave you a message she whines, "Hello. Whoya calling? Got it. Hang up!" in an annoying robotic twang.' Everyone chuckles at Yu Jin's impersonation. 'Why do all young women seem to speak like that these days? Come on now, let's raise our glasses to our old classmate, and wish him a speedy recovery. Cheers!'

'Guess who I bumped into yesterday!' says Chen Di. 'You could say it was someone from our dorm block . . .'

'Little Chan, Liu Gang?'

'Shao Jian . . . Dong Rong?'

'I'd better tell you – you'll never guess. The drifter! He's got a job now, working on a construction site. I bumped into him in my local market.'

My mother interrupts. 'I've got a letter here. Perhaps one of you can make out what it says. I found it in Dai Wei's jacket.'

'Show me!'

My heart stops for a second. Perhaps at last I'll be able to find out some news about A-Mei.

'It looks like a piece of notepaper. The blood has blurred the characters. I can't read any of them . . .'

'It's a pamphlet. No, it's a handwritten letter . . . It was in his pocket, you said?'

'Don't worry, it doesn't matter. I've kept this bloodstained jacket all these years inside the box I bought for his ashes. I'll put it in the furnace with him when he's cremated.' She comes into my room and puts the jacket and bloodstained letter back into the box under my bed.

'Grave plots aren't that expensive any more. Wouldn't you prefer to have him buried?'

'Don't talk about that now. It's his birthday. Come on, let's cut the cake. On behalf of Tian Yi, I'd like to wish Dai Wei a very happy . . .'

At the place where the moon and sun set is the Mountain of the Moon and the Sun. There is a girl there, bathing a baby moon. This is the twelfth moon she has given birth to.

When I first set eyes on my cousin Kenneth in Yanjing Hotel, I found it hard to believe we shared a genetic bond. Although his hair was jet-black like mine, he had pale skin, round eyes and a big nose. His father was my father's uncle and his mother was a white American. He didn't speak a word of Chinese, and since my spoken English was poor, we could only have the most basic conversation. He was in his forties, and played the cello in the Boston Philharmonic Orchestra.

When I offered him a cigarette, he pushed it away and said that smoking was forbidden in the hotel, and that I'd have to go to the forecourt if I wanted a cigarette. The truth is, I hadn't wanted a cigarette. I'd only offered him one out of politeness.

His new wife, Mabel, was a second-generation Chinese American. She was twelve years younger than him and had the small, round face typical of women from southern China. Her parents were born in Fujian Province. She spoke some Fujianese but very little Mandarin.

After a brief exchange of civilities, I went down to wait in the lobby with my brother, mother and Tian Yi, while Mabel had a shower and changed into clean clothes. I flicked through the photocopied documents Kenneth had brought to support my American visa application. He'd included some recent bank statements and a copy of his passport.

My mother wandered through the hotel's gift shops. This was the first time she'd visited a luxury hotel. Tian Yi was wearing the same clothes she'd worn for the last week. When we'd walked into Kenneth and Mabel's room, she'd apologised for looking so scruffy and then scurried into their bathroom. When she came out again, I noticed she'd washed her face and combed her hair into a neat ponytail. The dirt under her fingernails had vanished and there was lipstick on her lips. I didn't know she owned a lipstick. Perhaps she'd borrowed one from Mimi.

The hour we waited in the elegant lobby passed quickly. After Kenneth and Mabel came down, we all crammed into a taxi which delivered us to the Forbidden City. The ticket office was in the courtyard behind Tiananmen Gate. There was a long queue outside it. Tian

Yi and I were dismayed to see a large number of provincial students among the crowd.

'They came to Beijing saying they wanted to join our movement, but they spend all their time sightseeing,' Tian Yi said angrily. 'Where do they get all the money from?'

My brother had travelled up from Sichuan the day before. He said he'd gone straight to the Square when he arrived, but couldn't find me, so had spent the night at the flat. Tian Yi linked arms with my mother and stood with her in the queue. She didn't want to speak English with Mabel. She told me she found her American accent hard to understand.

Mabel gawped up at the majestic walls flanking the Forbidden City's main southern entrance, and repeated in English, '*It's amazing, amazing* . . .' The yells and cries from the crowds and loudspeakers in Tiananmen Square four hundred metres to the south echoed faintly against the huge red walls. I could just about pick out Chen Di's voice, reading out an announcement. Mimi's wavering voice also cut through the din.

When we reached the front of the queue, we huddled around Mabel, trying to pass her off as a local so she could get a Chinese ticket. Kenneth, whose foreign features were impossible to hide, had to buy a foreigner's ticket, which was double the price.

Kenneth and Mabel walked ahead of us, swinging their arms merrily. Mabel stood out from the crowd in her organza knickerbockers and white vest.

'Why do Overseas Chinese women walk around in their underwear?' my mother whispered to Tian Yi as we followed them through the central arch of the ancient entrance gate. 'In China only men strip to their vests.'

'Foreign men go around bare-chested when it's hot, so vests aren't considered to be particularly revealing,' said Tian Yi. Then she turned to me and said, 'Dai Wei, shouldn't you go and get everyone something to drink? Your cousin paid for our drinks at the hotel.'

'Yes, go and buy some cartons of orange juice,' my mother said. 'They've already spent a hundred Foreign Exchange Certificates on us. Don't get one for me, though. I've brought a jar of tea with me.' She took out a ten-yuan bill and pressed it into my palm.

'I don't want orange juice, thank you,' Mabel said to me before going off to take some photographs. 'Just some water.' I felt embarrassed. I assumed she was trying to save us some money, then I remembered that A-Mei didn't drink orange juice either. She said it was bad for her teeth.

'Foreigners like to choose what they want themselves,' my brother said to Tian Yi. 'There are some foreign students at my university. When they have a cigarette, they never offer one to anyone else.'

On a vast marble terrace before us rose the red pillars and two-tiered golden roof of the Hall of Supreme Harmony. Tourists streamed in and out of its central doorway like ants scavenging for food. Kenneth and Mabel kept stopping to hug or kiss each other, which made the Chinese tourists around them step back in fright.

'This was a terrible idea of yours, Mum,' my brother said. 'Foreigners like to visit places on their own. They don't want us tagging along.'

I was carrying the cartons of orange juice that no one wanted to drink. The memory of Mou Sen's unblinking gaze suddenly flashed into my mind.

'Go and tell them a bit about the history of the Forbidden City,' I said to Tian Yi. My brother was too embarrassed to speak to them, and I didn't know much about the place. So Tian Yi walked over to Kenneth and Mabel and said, 'The Forbidden City was completed in 1420, and was home to twenty-four successive emperors of the Ming and Qing Dynasties. We are now standing in the Outer Court, which is known as the "sea of flagstones". This is where the emperors held grand ceremonies and reviewed their troops. Inside the Hall of Supreme Harmony up there is the Dragon Throne, on which the emperors would sit every morning to discuss matters of state . . . There are 9,999 rooms within these palace walls. Most of them were occupied by the emperors' numerous concubines . . .'

Mabel took off her sunglasses and wiped the sweat from her forehead. There was a look of astonishment on her face. Her gold earrings swung back and forth.

Throngs of tourists swarmed through the vast, stone-paved courtyard, buying trinkets from souvenir stalls and taking photographs. Kenneth gave Tian Yi his camera and asked her to take a photo of him and Mabel.

We headed north through the Gate of Heavenly Purity. Tian Yi was now happily babbling away in English to Mabel. I stood beside her, and caught the gist of what she was saying. 'We've now entered the Inner Court, which was the emperors' private quarters. In the Hall of Earthly Tranquillity over there is the red bridal room where the emperor and empress would retire for three days after their wedding. The concubines lived in these chambers on the west and east. And those halls are the Treasure Houses. They house thousands of imperial relics and artefacts. All the foreign tourists like to visit them. We should take a look. The tickets aren't too expensive . . .'

'It's so uncouth, carrying your jar of tea around like that, Mum,' Dai Ru whispered. 'Look how grubby the plastic holder is.' My brother had picked up some foreign affectations since I'd last seen him. He was continually running his fingers through his hair or rubbing his sideburns pensively. My mother had always clipped his hair when he was younger, but he wouldn't have dreamed of letting her touch it now.

'What do you mean, uncouth? These plastic covers are all the rage. Didn't you see that stall at the entrance? It was selling them in four different colours.'

'Those emperors really knew how to live,' Kenneth said with a smile. 'Imagine lying in these sumptuous halls, surrounded by thousands of beautiful concubines . . .'

'Emperor Shizong kept the largest harem,' said Tian Yi. 'He had nine thousand concubines, some were as young as ten years old. Hardly any of them ever got a chance to meet him. Many ended up starving to death in their chambers. When Emperor Chengzu suspected a few of his concubines of disloyalty, he had all 2,800 members of his harem executed.'

'What? Right here?' Mabel's eyes widened in disbelief.

'All the women who lived in these chambers were killed.'

'That's a huge massacre!' Kenneth no longer had that carefree air of a tourist.

'What a gruesome history China has.' Mabel was grimacing too.

'That's why we've occupied the Square. We want to put an end to millennia of autocratic rule.' The pitch of Tian Yi's voice always seemed to rise when she spoke in English.

When we reached the rockery outside the Hall of Mental Cultivation, we asked someone to take a group photograph of us. I then suggested that we leave the Forbidden City from the north exit and take a bus to the Great Wall. Mabel and Kenneth only had three days in Beijing, so I told them they'd have to speed up a little if they were going to see all the sights.

It was already three in the afternoon by the time we made it to the Great Wall's ticket office. My brother said he'd stay with my mother in the car park. Since Tian Yi and I had been up the Great Wall once before, I was reluctant to go a second time and pay for another expensive entrance ticket. But Tian Yi persuaded me to go up with her. She said she wanted to take some photographs. By the time we'd walked through the entrance gate, the happy newly-weds had already climbed halfway up the mountain. Mabel was trotting beside Kenneth, the camera that hung from her shoulder swinging from side to side.

'Come on, take out your camera, then,' I said to Tian Yi.

'Mabel's camera is very sophisticated. She has three different lenses in that bag. My one's got a fixed lens. I'm too embarrassed to bring it out.'

'But yours was made by China's first joint-venture camera company,' I said, trying to reassure her. I gazed at her hair blowing in the wind, and promised that when I had some money, I'd buy her a professional kit.

She hadn't let me touch her in the two weeks since the hunger strike had ended, so as soon as I squeezed her hand, I could feel myself getting an erection. It became uncomfortable walking up the steep path. I leaned against her and whispered, 'Do you want to sneak off behind those trees with me?' Without answering, she shot me a sideways glance then allowed me to lead her away from the path towards the wooded hill to the east.

'Let's not go too far,' she said, her hand sweating in mine. 'There might be plain-clothes policemen about.'

'Those guys who caught us in the grounds of the Old Summer Palace weren't police officers. They were a band of thugs. They paid off the local public security bureau so they could prowl the grounds and exhort fines from couples they found having sex. They were bicycle menders, apparently. I'm sure I saw one of them in the Flying Tigers brigade.'

Tian Yi stood still, her nostrils flaring with rage. 'Why are there so many corrupt people in this world? How could anyone be so evil?'

'They aren't evil, they're just products of an evil system,' I said, wrapping my arms around her. 'Corruption breeds corruption. That's why I want to go abroad after this movement is over. You will come with me, won't you? Kenneth said he'd be happy to be your financial guarantor as well, and give you all the documents you need.' I glanced up at the top of the mountain ridge and saw streams of heads moving behind the crenellated ramparts of the Great Wall.

We continued walking hand in hand towards the wooded hill. Soon the Great Wall faded from view and we found ourselves in a sunny glade.

'What a wonderful view!' Tian Yi said, pulling her camera out from her bag. 'Look at those blue layers of mountains unfolding into the distance.'

'The ridges at the horizon are even paler than the sky.' I stood behind her and put my arms around her waist. She lowered her head. I kissed her neck and her chin. She closed her eyes and opened her mouth.

'Be careful . . .' she whispered, trying to push my hand away, but I moved it down into her knickers and touched the dampness between her legs. Her knees buckled a little, allowing my fingers to move inside her. I glanced around. There was no one about. All I could hear was the wind in the trees and a few car horns beeping at the foot of the mountain. I held her closer to me, lowered her onto the ground, then entered her from behind. After six or seven thrusts I ejaculated. Her hand and cheek were still pressed against the tree trunk. I looked down at her pale buttocks and immediately wanted to make love to her again. I thought how wonderful it was to have a woman by my side.

But when I drew her close to me again, she shouted, 'Get your hands off me,' then pulled up her trousers and walked away.

I lay on my back and stared into the blue sky, struck by the feeling of emptiness that always follows physical bliss.

She came back, kneeled down beside me and stared into my eyes. 'I'm in the middle of my cycle now. What would we do if I got pregnant?'

'We'd get married, of course. It would be fun to have a child of our own, don't you think? You and me combined in one person.'

'I thought you said you were going to leave the country.'

'Well, if you decided not to come with me, I'd marry you before I left. Anyway, I'm not even sure I'm going. I'm not a deserter like Shu Tong.'

'What do you mean?'

I hadn't wanted to tell her, but it had slipped out. 'He flew off to America this morning.'

'What? I don't believe it. He wouldn't desert us at a time like this!' The serious expression she always wore in the Square suddenly returned to her face.

'Would I lie to you about such a thing?' I glanced at my watch. We'd been away for almost an hour. I took her hand and said, 'Let's go back. They've probably returned to the car park by now.' There was a small piece of bark stuck to her palm.

'I don't believe Shu Tong has left. How could you lie to me? You're horrible.' She pulled her hand away and strode out ahead.

I stared at her back as I followed behind her. It's always difficult speaking to a woman after you've just pulled your shrivelled penis from her body.

'Have you gone home to see your father lately?' I said, searching for something to say.

'Shut up!' she snapped, staring at the ground as she marched on.

Fragments of your past drift through your lymph fluid like scraps of an exploded firecracker.

My mother hasn't come back yet. She's probably gone to the market to return some unwanted goods.

There are lots of people walking down the street outside. Their footsteps shake the walls so much that the light bulb above me flickers. Children whose voices I don't recognise shout out to each other in the stairwell. Although there have been rumours that the buildings along this side of the street are going to be demolished soon, shops and restaurants are still springing up every day. Many migrant workers who've found jobs in them have moved into the compound with their families. My mother is always reading out notes that are stuffed under our door by workers looking for rooms or flats to rent.

I wait for Wen Niao's footsteps. Last time she came, she wore a pair of soft, rubber-soled shoes, so I only heard her footsteps when she reached the second-floor landing. She brought a smell of snow into the flat that day. I smelt it on the woollen scarf she dropped on my shoulder. When I inhaled, I also caught the urban smell of residential compounds and bustling crowds. The outside world seemed so close at hand that for a second I experienced a glimmer of the joy one feels when one walks down a busy street.

My mother has run out of money. She's planning to sell one of my kidneys to pay for the medication I need. For some reason, my brother has stopped sending her cash every month.

Wen Niao still works at the Beijing Pharmaceutical Research Institute. When I met her in the Square after Tian Yi fainted, I couldn't have guessed that all these years later she'd turn up at my flat to attend to my comatose body. She comes here twice a week to give me injections. Sometimes she brings new drugs the institute has developed and administers them to me free of charge.

How annoying that my mother isn't here to let her in. She knocks on the door, pauses, then knocks again. She continues to knock for several minutes, then turns round and leaves.

Damn! I wish she'd come back. I always seem to breathe more easily when she's in the flat. After living in the dark for so long, I yearn for people to visit and bring me news from the world outside.

A few minutes later, I hear Wen Niao return with my mother.

'I'll give you my spare set of keys,' my mother says, opening the front door. 'I wouldn't want this to happen again. You must be freezing.'

'No, I'm fine. I'm used to the cold. Back in Changsha, the winters are much colder than this.'

She and my mother take off their coats and sit on the sofa.

'Look at this jumper I bought the other day,' my mother says. 'The stallholder told me it was 100 per cent lambswool. But when I brought it home, I saw the label says: lambswool, angora and nylon. I hate angora. The whole flat's covered in rabbit hairs now. I just went to ask him for a refund, but he refused to give me one.' My mother pushes the box of sunflower seeds across the table and says, 'Help yourself. These jumpers they sell now, they may look nice, but the quality is terrible.'

I hope Wen Niao doesn't eat any of those five-spiced sunflower seeds. They smell disgusting.

'Does your mother still work?' asks my mother, forgetting she already asked her this last week.

'She died a long time ago. She was publicly denounced during the Cultural Revolution. They shaved her hair on one side, in the yin-yang style. She felt so humiliated, she swallowed a bottle of pesticide the next day.' Wen Niao speaks very casually about her mother's death. It's strange to think that Tian Yi's mother committed suicide for the same reason.

'We survivors of the Cultural Revolution were lucky to escape with our lives.'

'I see you've made a little altar there. Are you a Buddhist?'

'Well, I've taken up Falun Gong. It's a form of qigong which combines some of the philosophies of Buddhism and Taoism. I had this book, *Falun Practice*, lying around for ages, but I only started reading it properly last month. It's very interesting. I bought an instruction tape and have been practising the meditation exercises with some other women in the compound. It's had a miraculous effect. I hadn't realised how many little ailments I've developed over the years: headaches, chest pain, backache, arthritis. They all seem to have disappeared since I've been doing the exercises.'

'It looks as if Falun Gong might put us pharmacists out of a job!'

'Why not give it a go? It's very simple. There are only five sets of exercises, four standing, one sitting. You can start with the first exercise. It will help open up your channels.'

'I'm in good health – I don't need to do qigong. But I often visit Buddhist temples and read the Buddhist scriptures.'

'Look, I'll show you the pose. Make a circle with your index and thumb, and let your arms relax . . .'

My mother is probably feeling the qi flow through her channels by now. A few days ago, she practised the exercises for half an hour then slept for a whole day and night. When she woke up, she got straight on the phone to Master Yao.

'I was very downcast a few months ago, Nurse Wen. I'd decided that if my son died, I'd jump into the grave with him. I'd reached the end. But when I started reading the Falun Gong texts, I suddenly understood why my life has been so difficult. All hardships you encounter result from bad deeds committed in past lives . . . We've now entered the era of chaos that precedes the end of the world. The Buddha won't be able to save everyone. When the earth is destroyed, only the souls of Falun Gong practitioners will be admitted into Heaven . . .' My mother is repeating what Master Yao told her, but has strayed a little from his version.

Wen Niao taps my knee. I can sense that her body temperature is higher than mine. She slips a thermometer into my mouth. When her fingers brush against my nose I see a momentary vision of her face.

'You should try it. You won't have to bother taking medicine again.'

'But I'm a Buddhist, Auntie . . .'

'Huh. The Buddha only looks after the next world, but Falun Gong takes care of the present world as well. Anyway, the more gods you believe in the better. Who knows which one might turn up to help you next time you find yourself in trouble?'

'You must look out for signs of him wanting to swallow,' Wen Niao says, eager to change the subject. 'It would indicate nerve cell repair or regeneration.'

'You really seem to care about my son. I must admit, I'm afraid of him waking up, because if he did, the police would storm in and start asking questions. Sometimes I just wish he'd hurry up and die.'

'Don't say that, Auntie. A company in Guangzhou is developing a drug from cows' brains that will help stimulate brain-cell regeneration. Once it's in production, I'll try to get hold of some for you.'

'Huh! Those drug companies send salesmen to every hospital to bully doctors into prescribing their drugs. They work on commission. If you go to hospital these days, the doctors won't let you leave until you've bought several hundred yuan's worth of medicine.'

'I've told many pharmaceutical research institutes about Dai Wei's condition, but unfortunately, as soon as they find out he was involved in the Tiananmen Square protests, they refuse to help.'

Wen Niao opens her case and prepares a syringe of the drug she's brought today.

'You're so kind, Nurse Wen,' my mother says, walking in from the kitchen. 'The nurses who came before weren't nearly as diligent as you. Here, have a cup of tea. It's freshly brewed. Whatever happens, I insist you have some lunch before you leave. I've bought some garlic shoots and pork ribs especially.'

'Thank you,' she says, sliding the needle into my vein. 'It still seems so strange that I met your son in the Square, and here I am seven years later, looking after him. It must have been fate. I even saw him in the early hours of 4 June. He helped me lift dead bodies into the ambulance. Why did he have to end up with a bullet in the head? It's so unfair . . .'

'So you were in the Square that night?' my mother asks, taken aback.

'I was in the emergency tent, near the Goddess of Democracy. I saw students being killed right in front of me. There were corpses under Mao's portrait, near the flagpole on the north side of the Square, and in front of the Museum of Chinese History. I managed to get a lift on an ambulance that was taking casualties to the Children's Hospital. I was relieved to leave the Square. But when I walked into the hospital's emergency room, I saw pools of blood everywhere. I had blood up to my ankles . . . The colleagues of mine who remained in the Square were herded into an enclosure in front of the Museum of Chinese History, and were only released at seven in the morning. They were all sent to work in other cities after that, to ensure they didn't speak to any foreign journalists.'

'Did the police interrogate you afterwards?' They're sitting on the sofa now.

'They wanted me to give them the emergency tent's registration book. They came to my flat many times. One of the officers even became my boyfriend for a while.'

'A boy called Wang Nan was shot during the crackdown. The soldiers hid his body in a flower bed just east of the Zhongnanhai government compound. But the grave was so shallow that his body started poking up from the soil a few days later. Fortunately he was wearing an army uniform, so the authorities assumed he was an injured soldier. Otherwise, they would have sent his body to a secret crematorium, and his mother would never have found out what happened to him.'

They both fall silent. Wen Niao takes a sip of tea. I can smell jasmine in the steam rising from her teacup and in the air she exhales. I inhale, and feel her breath enter my lungs.

'You forgot your watch here last time.' My mother goes into the kitchen. 'I'll just fry this up. It won't take long.'

'I'm always mislaying that watch,' Wen Niao says, walking into my room. 'I'm so scatterbrained.'

I hear her swallow. I know she's looking at me, scrutinising me as she would a caged rabbit in her research lab.

She takes my blood pressure, inspects the skin on my legs then carefully removes a few flakes of skin from behind my ears and places them in a screw-top jar to analyse later.

I hear her breathe in and out as she flicks through some sheets of paper. The air is as smooth as silk.

Her fingers move over my chest. They are warm, as warm as the breath she exhales. Her nails press into my skin for moment, then she pulls her hand away. My penis immediately stiffens. I want her to touch me again. She's the first girl since Tian Yi to show any concern for me.

She notices my erection, lifts the sheet and observes it for some time. 'It seems this vegetable has quite a healthy sexual appetite,' she whispers.

I wish it would go down.

Then she says into my ear, 'Don't worry. I'm sure you'll wake up one day. The drugs I'm giving you are imported. Do you hear me, wooden man? And I've told your mother lots of things she can do to speed up your recovery. I looked after many coma patients during my internship.'

This is the sixth time you've visited me, Wen Niao. One time you came on a Saturday. You said you hadn't anything else to do that weekend.

'You were very handsome seven years ago. There was always a crowd of people milling around you. I never dared look you straight in the eye.'

And I remember that your face was similar to Tian Yi's: oval, and lightly freckled, but with thicker eyebrows and a higher-bridged nose.

'At least you're better off than those students who were sent to the Martial Law Headquarters and tortured so badly they went insane. They're the ones I feel sorry for.'

Yes. I heard Shao Jian was detained at the Martial Law Headquarters after saying he'd seen students killed in Tiananmen Square, which the government still refuses to acknowledge. He was tortured for days until he finally agreed to write a statement refuting what he'd said. But he was sent to jail nevertheless.

'If you wake up, we might make a good couple. So try a bit harder, will you?'

You told me that when you joined the research institute, you felt as though you were slipping into your grave. You don't realise that the body itself is a grave. I dreamed about you the other night. You were locked in a drawer. I tried to pull it out, but it wouldn't budge.

'You're a miracle. If you were in a foreign country, you'd be famous by now.'

Your voice keeps flitting up and down. I remember what a slender neck you have, and how I thought when I first met you that you must have a narrow larynx. I asked you which work unit you belonged to, and you glanced up at me and said, 'You sound like a policeman.'

She wipes my eyes with a ball of cotton wool dipped in eye lotion. The little finger pressing against my face feels as though it's entering my flesh.

'Your corneas are infected. Even if you were to open your eyes one day, you probably wouldn't be able to see much. Your mother should sew the lids together to prevent them getting reinfected.' Her fingertips are cooler than her palm. Her sleeve brushes over my face as she moves her arm.

'Your heart's beating faster. You know that someone's speaking to you, don't you? What are you thinking?'

I'm thinking that whenever you walk into this flat, everything seems to come alive . . . Do you remember my girlfriend? She's getting married. She's set the date already: Christmas Day, 1999. She's marrying a German architect. She says she'll never come back to China again. She doesn't want to live in a country where the police knock on your door every day.

All the windows are shut. You swelter in the heated flat like a half-steamed fish.

Mou Sen and I walked over to the Goddess of Democracy. We'd helped carry pieces of the statue into the Square the night before.

'Someone climbed onto the scaffolding last night and tried to knock the statue over,' Mou Sen says. 'The students pulled him down, but let him go after a few minutes.' As he spoke, he took off his imported beige jacket that I assumed Nuwa had bought for him.

'What's the matter with us?' I said, 'If someone vandalises the portrait of a tyrant, we arrest them, but if they try to destroy a symbol of democracy we let them go.'

Zhang Jie walked up and said, 'Have you heard? Taiwanese students want to get a million people to link hands across Taiwan in solidarity with us . . . What happened to your cheek, Dai Wei?' It was already very hot now, but he was still wearing his black leather jacket. I hadn't seen him in the Square much since he'd returned to the campus after the hunger strike.

'We broke up another coup last night,' I explained. 'The guy who punched me was wearing a ring with a hidden spike.' I kicked aside an empty lemonade bottle lying in my path. The white polystyrene lunch boxes littering the ground were irritatingly bright. The night before, a student had stormed onto the Monument's upper terrace with a group of friends and declared himself commander-in-chief. We had to use force to get them to leave. During the fight, Chen Di's binoculars fell on the ground and smashed into pieces.

Zhang Jie smirked awkwardly, uncertain how to respond. He was the kind of aloof, insecure guy that girls find least attractive.

Mou Sen had persuaded Tang Guoxian and Wu Bin to help set up his Democracy University. During the preparatory meeting the day before, he'd appointed himself chancellor, made Nuwa general secretary, Tang Guoxian admissions officer, Old Fu vice chancellor and Little Chan head of public relations.

We soon found ourselves crushed in the excited crowd that had gathered around the statue. The white goddess, constructed of styrofoam and papier mâché, towered above us, her hands raising a torch towards the blue sky. She was as tall as a three-storey building. Her face was still concealed beneath a sheet of red silk.

'So they managed to put it up in the end!' Mou Sen cried. 'Those art students must have worked through the night. Many Beijing residents came to help after you left. They were amazing. When the students were building the pedestal, they called for some saws, and immediately four or five saws appeared from nowhere. A few hours later, they said they were tired and could do with some congee, and within minutes, the residents wheeled over a trolley with enough congee to feed an army.' Mou Sen was very excited. Tian Yi's camera was hanging around his neck.

The crowd grew impatient. Students were setting up microphones and speakers at the foot of the statue. I spotted Wu Bin over there, supervising the security cordon that circled the base. He allowed us through the cordon and let us sit with the journalists. Student representatives from eight Beijing art colleges sat nearby, waiting to take part in the unveiling ceremony.

A girl even more graceful and slender than Nuwa stood up and announced that the ceremony was about to begin. If she'd been wearing a white dress, she would have looked like a goddess herself. Mou Sen told me she was a film actress.

The art students stood up, and together with a few Beijing citizens pulled the red silk sheet from the statue's face and released balloons into the air. All eyes in the Square gazed up at the Goddess.

'She looks like Tian Yi,' Zhang Jie said, craning his neck. 'Her hair's a bit shorter, that's all.'

Although the features were a little coarse, she was a good replica of New York's Statue of Liberty. She rose majestically from the middle of the Square, directly opposite Chairman Mao's portrait, staring resolutely into the distance, her mouth tightly pursed. When I looked up at her, I felt a renewed sense of courage.

Students from the Academy of Music stood up and sang 'The Blood-stained Spirit' and Beethoven's 'Ode to Joy'. Bare-chested boys from the Dance Academy performed a Shaanxi Province folk-dance, beating drums tied to their waists. The jubilant ceremony then came to an end and the crowds began to scatter.

'Today's paper says the authorities have called the erecting of the Goddess of Democracy an illegal act, and an affront to China's national pride and democratic image,' Hai Feng said, walking up with a newspaper in his hand. He too had been going back to the campus every night, and usually only turned up at the Square in the afternoon.

'Look, the peasant marchers from Daxing County have arrived!' Zhang Jie said. The huge parade of marchers poured into the Square chanting 'Support Li Peng!' and 'Down with Professor Fang Li!'

'So they're attacking the astrophysicist Fang Li,' Hai Feng laughed. 'I bet none of those peasants can even read.'

'The Daxing County propaganda department bribed them into joining the march with the promise of free boxed lunches,' I said, feeling a sudden wave of hunger.

You lie impatiently inside your seminal ducts, waiting for your chance to burst out.

'Your mother's gone to do her Falun Gong exercises in the yard outside,' Wen Niao says. 'Can you hear the music?'

She turns up the radio and starts to dance to the love song that's playing. I hear her feet twisting, her bracelets clinking against her watch and her soft humming echoing in the back of her throat.

'So, is it nice, having a woman dance for you? Are you happy now?' She's breathing faster.

The jasmine tea has cooled down, so now I can smell her hair and the feminine scent of her neck as she pulls off her muslin scarf.

'*You arrived in my life like a beautiful mistake. I still don't know who you are. Your tenderness confuses me. I'm lost in a maze of mist . . .*' She swirls about as she sings. She's very happy, and so am I. I've almost forgotten I'm in a coma.

'*I offered you my love, but you said you didn't want it. Did I upset you in some way?*' She lies down on my bed, takes a deep breath, then moves on top of me. '*Now you are mine, but I'm still not happy. If you love me, say it to my face . . .*' She leans down and whispers into my ear, 'If only all men were like you. You're wonderful. You never go out to night-clubs or play around with other women.' She lets out a long sigh then continues, 'What's going through your mind, wooden man? I want to tell you a secret. I was a Living Buddha in my past life. Ever since I was a child, I've been looking out of my window, waiting for the Tibetan lamas to turn up and take me back to my old monastery . . .'

I can feel her eyes staring at me. She breathes over my face. The smell of tobacco and alcohol on her warm breath excites the nerve cells in my nose as I inhale. I sense my breath enter her nostrils then flow out again as she exhales. My breath smells different when it emerges from her body. I can smell us both in that single outbreath. The blend of male and female scents is as arousing to me as a kiss.

'It's a shame you couldn't see me dance just now,' she says quietly, then begins to sing to me again. '*Don't tell me you don't understand. I've poured my heart out to you* . . . Karaoke bars have sprung up all over the city. If you feel a bit low, you can get a group of friends together and sing the whole night away. It's wonderful. Can you hear me?' Wen Niao's voice seems to have suddenly acquired a beautiful, angelic tone.

She takes off her watch and tucks it under my pillow.

Her hand is cooler than my skin. When it sweeps across my stomach, it feels like rain falling on a hot, dry field.

She lifts the quilt that's draped over me. I sense her staring at my penis, then touching it with her fingers. 'It's as hard as an obelisk. You don't mind if I touch it, do you, young man? You want me, don't you?'

It must be sticking up in the air now, stiff and erect.

She turns the light out. I hear her unbuckle her belt and take off her trousers and shoes. Then she lies on top of me, holds my penis in one hand and strokes herself with the other. Moaning softly, she rises into a squat then sits down on me. I feel myself enter her soft flesh. She lets out a gasp, then swerves from side to side, squeezing me tightly between her warm, damp walls. I feel myself becoming hotter and hotter until at last my sperm spills out. Some of it drips down between her legs, the rest begins to slowly die inside her.

At last I've left my body. I can hear her watch still ticking beneath my pillow.

My penis shrinks away from the pool of sperm, but her warm flesh still holds me within its grip, assuaging the feeling of emptiness that wells up inside me.

I inhale the smell of the sperm that's been locked inside me for so long, the smell of the sheet our warm bodies rubbed against and the scent of sesame-seed paste on her breath, and feel my organs become more vigorous. While the spongeous tissue of my penis is still pulsating, Wen Niao gets dressed and leaves the flat.

My mother returns, switches the radio back on and says, 'Where's Wen Niao? She said she'd wait here until I came back.'

I wish she'd shut up and leave me in peace. I don't want this moment of bliss to slip away. It may never return again.

I see a gleaming expanse of snow marked with a trail of Wen Niao's footprints.

Wen Niao's parting words echo through my mind. 'You're wonderful,' she said. 'I can't believe your mother's thinking of selling one of your kidneys.'

Now that you've been compressed by her body and cleansed by her breath, your thoughts seem much clearer.

'If the government reforms the health insurance system, I'll be in terrible trouble. Most of Dai Wei's medication costs are reimbursed by the opera company I used to belong to. I just ask the pharmacists to put my name on the receipt instead of his. Do you think the reforms are really going to go ahead?' My mother is in the sitting room, talking to Auntie Hao from the neighbourhood committee.

'Well, it says so in today's *People's Daily*. We're going to be hit hard too. My husband gets three hundred yuan of his medication costs reimbursed every month. If the government cuts the subsidies by 70 per cent, I don't know how we'll cope.' Until a month ago, Auntie Hao had only been to our flat twice, but now she drops by three times a week. The neighbourhood committee is going to turn from a volunteer organisation into a proper work unit with a salaried staff. She's probably trying to increase her popularity in the compound, hoping it will help her gain a permanent position on the committee.

'Old Wang's son has opened a video room near my old opera company,' says my mother. 'Apparently, he makes three hundred yuan a day showing pirate videos.'

'I doubt he's making as much as that,' Auntie Hao says. 'Videos are old hat. Everyone's switched to VCDs. The machines only cost four hundred yuan, and you can buy pirated VCDs for just five yuan, so who would want to pay three yuan to watch a film in his grubby video room? Anyway, he won't be there much longer. That area is going to be demolished soon. They're going to build a big commercial residential estate there.'

'When do you think our compound will be demolished?'

'I doubt they'll pull this place down. Some of the blocks in this compound were built in the eighties, but most are 1950s Soviet-style buildings. They're very sturdy. They could last another hundred years.'

'I haven't been to the cinema for ages. I don't even watch television much. They always repeat the same programmes.'

'Haven't you been watching that new series, *The Incorruptible Director General*? It's great. No one has dared make a drama about high-level corruption before. Even the provincial governor is shown to be a crook.'

'The governor was criticising his son for corrupt practices, he wasn't guilty of corruption himself.'

'Well, you must have missed the last episode, then. It revealed that the governor was involved in the fraud too. The police took him away in handcuffs.'

'That drama series *Black Screen* last year had a corrupt city mayor.'

'We're surrounded by corruption these days. All the new casinos and nightclubs that are springing up everywhere are financed by the expense accounts of corrupt officials. They're packed with high-ranking cadres, blowing away public money on expensive food and drink.'

They stop talking for a while and crack melon seeds between their teeth.

When we demonstrated against official profiteering in 1989, only a few cases of corruption had come to light. But now the problem seems to have become endemic.

My mind turns to Wen Niao again. Two weeks after she made love to me, she stopped visiting. During Spring Festival she telephoned my mother to wish us a happy Chinese New Year and said she couldn't make the next appointment because she was going sales shopping at Guiyou Department Store. Perhaps she's already moved into the staff apartment building her institute has built beyond the third ring road. She's been allocated an eighty-square-metre flat. She said it's close to the ring road, so it's very noisy, but she can see the White Dagoba Temple from the windows, so she believes it's her karmic destiny to live there.

On her last visit, she said to me, 'I was on a train one night. The other passengers around me were sprawled over the wooden seats fast asleep. I got up and walked to the end of the carriage. When I looked out of the back window and saw the moon floating above the black horizon a terrible sadness came over me. I finally accepted that I'd been reborn as a woman and the lamas would never come to fetch me . . . When I was fifteen, I went to Tibet and visited all the monasteries, but never found the one my previous incarnation died in.'

She's about the same age as me, so her previous incarnation would have died in the late sixties. He couldn't have died in a monastery. By that time, all the religious buildings in Tibet had been destroyed by the Chinese army, and any incarnate lama would have been languishing in jail or toiling in the fields.

She wiped my face with mineral water and said, 'Then I visited the Forbidden City a few years ago, and I knew I'd once lived there too. I saw the comb I used, the pillow I rested my head on. I tell you, everything looked so familiar to me. I leaned against a pillar and cried my heart out. I didn't want to leave the palace compound. When they closed at five o'clock, the stewards had to drag me out. I did a little research, and realised that I was Empress Wencheng in a past life. She died in Tibet, which explains why I was later reincarnated as a Tibetan lama . . . The spirits of my past lives often visit me, and tell me I must achieve something great. But what can a frail woman like me hope to achieve? My policeman boyfriend was a Buddhist. When I first met him, I knew at once he'd worn the dragon robes of an emperor in his previous life. I realised my role in this incarnation was to make sure he became President of China. I thought that with the power of all my past lives to propel him forward, he was bound to succeed. Unfortunately, he turned out to be a playboy. I had to break up with him. He went to nightclubs and saunas almost every night . . .'

She wrapped her fingers in muslin, then rubbed each of my teeth individually and wiped my tongue clean. It felt wonderful. When my mother scrubs my teeth with cotton earbuds she always makes my gums bleed.

I wish Wen Niao would walk through the door again and bring me some sunlight and fresh air. But I doubt she'd want to repeat what some people might consider a perverse sexual act. She probably thinks her behaviour that afternoon was caused by a temporary lapse of sanity.

She once said to me, 'Everyone out there is sick in the head. Who knows, perhaps you're the only sane person left in this city.'

It's been thirty days since her last visit. My mother tried to reach her on her pager last week but she never replied.

I can hear my mother grumbling, 'What did we do to upset Nurse Wen? Why doesn't she come round any more? Was it because I asked her to empty the urine bottle last time she was here? But she's a trained nurse. She's had to do many worse things than that.'

When the telephone rings, she rushes to the sitting room. A few days ago, a buyer was found for my kidney. A provisional price of eight thousand yuan has been agreed, with the middleman taking a thousand-yuan cut.

'All right . . . You can come and do the blood test tomorrow. When will he hand over the cash? I was wondering if he might be able to give me a bit more . . .'

The voice on the other end says, 'The transplant won't be happening for at least two months. The middleman must make sure your son is compatible with the patient before he can confirm a date. And as for the price, I think you've already got a very good deal. If you'd sold just before Spring Festival you probably wouldn't have got more than two thousand yuan. That's when most of the prisoners are executed, so there's always a glut of available organs . . .'

'I'll need to warn the police station that I'll be away for a while, or they'll presume I've gone on the run.'

'I'll get the middleman to have a word with them. They have strong connections with the police. That's how they manage to get hold of the lists of prisoners on death row.'

My mother has told me she can't do anything more for me, and that my body will have to fend for itself from now on. I hope that I die during the operation. How wonderful that would be.

Although I know Wen Niao will never return, I'm still wallowing in the blissful memories of her visits. Every word she said soothed my nerves. When she leaned over me and I smelt on her shirt collar the scent of grilled chicken livers from the street stall she'd passed on her way to the flat, I almost fainted with pleasure.

She won't come back. She's sitting in a room somewhere in this big city, unaware that my body yearns for her to make love to me again so that I can die in one last burst of ecstasy.

Blood gushes through your body like water from a hot spring. The seeds that Wen Niao buried in your flesh begin to germinate.

A Bangladeshi boy is singing 'Beautiful Lake Tai' in a televised song competition for foreign students. Just as the final round is about to begin, An Qi arrives with her invalid husband. He's been here once before. He's able to walk up to the third floor with the aid of crutches. The cigarettes he smokes smell of hospital wards.

'You should ask your foreign relatives to make enquiries for you,' he says in his native Beijing accent. 'Perhaps they can track down some specialists who are researching conditions like Dai Wei's. If they carry out research on him, you wouldn't have to pay any medical fees.'

'He's always coming up with good ideas,' An Qi says proudly.

'Why didn't I think of that before?' my mother says. 'I should ask my son Dai Ru to see if he can find any specialists in England.'

On the telephone yesterday, my brother said he wouldn't be able to return to China until he graduates. He's working part-time in a Chinese restaurant, and is going out with an English girl. In his half-hour conversation with my mother, he never once asked about me.

They're sitting on the sofa now, drinking tea.

'We made contact with another victim of the crackdown yesterday,' An Qi's husband says. 'He was shot in the head, just like Dai Wei. He's paralysed from the chest down. He spends all day in bed. We sat beside him for half an hour and asked him questions, but he didn't say a word. When we came out, his wife told us that last year he tried to kill himself by swallowing sixty sleeping pills.'

'It can't be easy for you two, tracking down all those injured people. How many have you found so far?'

'Forty-nine, if you include the ones that Professor Ding found . . .'

'He's in great pain but he insists on continuing the search,' An Qi chips in. 'His pelvic inflammation flared up again last month. The old wound became septic. If we had some money, we could pay for him to have steel rods inserted into the damaged joints so that he could walk unaided.'

'I move faster with these two crutches than I did on my own two feet!' he says, tapping his crutches on the ground. 'And besides, if I could throw them away, I might go out to nightclubs every night, and you wouldn't be happy about that!'

'Don't talk nonsense! You've no idea what those places are like now. Those young women from Sichuan smother themselves with make-up, then prance around in tiny bikinis that leave nothing to the imagination. It's so crude.'

'Sounds like a lot of fun to me!' he laughs, tapping his crutches on the floor again.

'We've taken up Falun Gong too, now,' An Qi says. 'But we still haven't felt the Falun wheel of law spinning in our abdomens. Hey, next time Master Li Hongzhi gives a public lecture, you should go along and ask him to install a Falun wheel inside Dai Wei.'

'If you persevere with the meditation exercises, your wheel of law will eventually be awakened,' my mother says. 'When it spins clockwise it will absorb energy from the universe, and when it spins anti-clockwise it will dispel bad karma and illness from your body. You'll never have to waste money on expensive medication again. When you go to hospital these days, the doctors force you to have hundreds of unnecessary blood tests and X-rays, trying to get as much money as they can from you before you leave.'

'They work on commission. They need to prescribe three thousand yuan's worth of medication a day to get a bonus at the end of the month. And if you don't settle your bill every morning, they kick you out onto the street. You can't reason with them.'

'They don't care about saving lives. All they care about is money.'

I suddenly remember an ancient copy of *The Book of Mountains and Seas* I leafed through in a second-hand bookshop in Guangzhou. It had a fold-out map at the back. When I tried to open it, it crumbled into pieces.

Beyond Qizhou Mountain live the People With No Descendants. They all share the surname Ren, and are themselves the descendants of the People With No Bones. They eat only fish and air.

'Only forty people have enrolled so far,' Mou Sen said to Tang Guoxian as he drafted his speech for the Democracy University's opening ceremony. 'We need at least four thousand. If you can't recruit that many, I'll have to find a new admissions officer.'

'Don't talk down to me like that,' Tang Guoxian said, not looking up from the list of contacts he was copying out. 'You just wait and see.

One day I'll be more famous than any of you!' He'd been sacked from the Provincial Students' Federation the previous week for supporting Han Dan's proposal to withdraw from the Square.

'Can you help us out, Dai Ru?' Tian Yi said, handing my brother some name cards. 'Phone these people and see if you can persuade them to enrol.'

My brother seemed distracted. Earlier that day, he'd asked if I had any spare red armbands. We'd run out of them, so I gave him some baseball caps instead. I didn't ask him what he was up to. My mother had stopped interfering in his life, so I thought I should too.

It was stiflingly hot inside the broadcast tent. I'd made a hundred posters publicising the opening ceremony. Xiao Li and Zhang Jie took them from me and went to paste them up around the Square. Everyone was working hard to ensure the Democracy University would be a success.

'I heard your father telephoned you and begged you to leave the Square,' I said to Tian Yi.

'Did you say "father"? That word sounds very unfamiliar to me.'

'Can't we move into another tent, Dai Wei?' Nuwa said. 'It stinks in here.'

'There isn't another one as big as this,' I said.

'It wouldn't smell so bad if you lot stubbed out your cigarettes in a cup rather than in those ink pots,' Tian Yi said, glaring at Mou Sen.

'Who dropped those dumplings?' said Shi Ye, the bespectacled girl who used to share a dorm with A-Mei at Southern University. 'They've been trodden into the ground now. It's disgusting!' She'd arrived in Beijing a few days before. She was waiting to take Mou Sen to meet a student delegation from Hong Kong. She spoke Cantonese, so was going to help translate.

'Be quiet everyone,' Nuwa said, wiping beads of sweat from her brow. 'The Voice of America is broadcasting a news story about us. Shall we relay it to the Square, Mou Sen?'

'You seem to have forgotten I'm not in charge here any more,' he said.

'. . . Fear has descended on the Chinese capital. Liberal intellectuals and progressive Party leaders who discussed democratic reform with such excitement two weeks ago are nowhere to be seen. Beijing citizens are avoiding contact with foreigners. Those with passports are beginning to flee the country. The dissident astrophysicist Fang Li and his wife are believed to have gone into hiding in the outskirts of Beijing . . .'

'What does he mean "fear has descended on the Chinese capital"?' Tang Guoxian said derisively. 'What crap!'

'Did you hear what he said? A million people in Taiwan linked arms and formed a 400-kilometre human chain across the island. And in the pouring rain, too! *Fantastic, fantastic!*' Nuwa said, exclaiming the last words in English.

'The world is watching our every move,' my brother said excitedly. Then he and a couple of his friends walked over to Tang Guoxian and said conspiratorially, 'You really should join forces with us.'

'Do you have anything to eat, Dai Ru?' Tian Yi asked. 'I'm famished.'

'I never keep snacks on me,' he said, turning to her. 'When we were kids, Dai Wei would always rifle through my pockets and steal whatever he found.' Whenever I heard my brother speak, I'd always be reminded of the musty smell of our flat.

I suspected that my brother was attempting to form a new national student organisation, so I tried to dampen his zeal. 'I had a chat with a plain-clothes policeman this morning,' I said, glancing at him. 'He told me that students who cause disturbances are usually sent to a re-education camp for two years, but our protests amount to a counter-revolutionary rebellion, and he thinks we'll get locked away for at least ten. None of us will be able to escape. They have the names and photographs of every student who's stepped into the Square.'

'You once told me that if you're afraid of being sent to jail, you shouldn't join the revolution,' he said.

'We didn't manage to depose Deng Xiaoping in '87,' Mou Sen said. 'This time we mustn't give up until he steps down.' Then he turned to Shi Ye and said, 'Sorry, I won't be long. I just need to write the last paragraph.'

'The word "jail" makes my blood run cold,' Nuwa said. She switched on the light. The naked light bulb's soft glimmer had the same calming effect on us as Nuwa's beauty.

'Being sent to prison isn't that bad,' Tang Guoxian said. 'You get let out in the end, after all. It's capital punishment I'm afraid of. Before the police execute a convict, they tie him to the back of a motorbike and drag him through the streets until all the flesh has been torn from his arse.'

'That's horrible!' Nuwa shrieked, then glanced at Mou Sen, a little embarrassed by the noise she'd made.

'What's the matter with you, Tang Guoxian?' Tian Yi said. 'Stop scaring everyone.'

'Hey, Dai Wei, I spoke to A-Mei on the phone last night,' Shi Ye said. 'She's been appointed general secretary of the Association of Chinese Students in Canada. She said she'll be coming to Beijing in a few days. She wanted me to let you know.'

I felt very awkward. Shi Ye didn't know that Tian Yi was my girlfriend. As I'd expected, Tian Yi looked up and shot me a suspicious glance.

'If she's coming, she's coming. What's it got to do with me?' My expression didn't feel right. I wanted to run away.

'But you specifically asked me to get in touch with her,' Shi Ye said, eyeing me over the top of her glasses.

Mou Sen rushed over and said, 'Let's be off, Shi Ye!', pinching my arm furtively as he dragged her outside.

I tried to dig myself out of the hole. 'I haven't heard from A-Mei since we broke up, Tian Yi,' I said. 'I was only wondering what had happened to her. Don't read anything into it.' As I'd hoped, she didn't want to make a scene in front of the others, so she kept her eyes fixed on the script on her lap and said nothing. I mumbled that I needed to fetch some more ink and quickly left the tent.

You wander across the wastes, searching for a patch of earth in which to bury yourself. You can no longer resist the desire to let your body disintegrate into dust.

'He died five days ago, but the funeral dirges are still being played over the radio,' my mother says into the telephone.

Deng Xiaoping has died. The man who robbed me of my life is dead. But my hatred for him died long ago.

The twelfth episode of a documentary series on Deng Xiaoping's career is booming from the television. I wish my mother would turn it off. My old dorm mate Mao Da has telephoned to tell her that Han Dan has been released from prison and is planning to move to America.

Last week, she read out a letter from Wang Fei that had news of my old classmates. I learned that, since escaping to Hong Kong together, Wu Bin and Sun Chunlin have gained political asylum in France. I wonder how Sun Chunlin managed to convince the French authorities that he was an activist. He was never interested in politics. His contribution to our movement was purely financial. Wu Bin didn't have many friends. I suppose Sun Chunlin was the only guy willing to escape the country with him.

Tang Guoxian was one of the twenty-one student leaders on the government's most-wanted list. To evade arrest, he spent a year as a fugitive, living among peasants in northern China. Then he fled over the Soviet border, crossed the frozen wastes of Siberia and Eastern Europe until eventually finding refuge in Germany. His years of marathon training were probably a good preparation for this epic journey.

'Perhaps after the tenth anniversary of the crackdown, the political climate will relax a little,' my mother says to Mao Da. 'But for the moment, it's probably best if you didn't visit. Since Tian Yi spoke to the American press about what happened to Dai Wei, I haven't been allowed to remove him from the flat. I've only just managed to get special dispensation to take him to a hospital in Hebei.'

She puts down the phone then dials another number. I can't work out who she's speaking to this time. '. . . I know, those wedding photography studios are popping up everywhere now. A former colleague of mine from the opera company has opened one. She's invested 200,000 yuan. I went by the other day. She's employed a photographer with a long ponytail. He really looks the part. The studio's in a prime spot on Wangfujing Street. Huh! If I didn't have to look after this wooden son of mine, I could work there as a make-up artist. It would be nice to be able to earn some money. I don't know how we'll survive when my cash runs out. We'll just have to drink the north-east wind, as they say . . .'

Like a thick cotton thread caught in the eye of a needle, you remain trapped inside your skin.

The floor of the hospital room has been sprinkled with disinfectant, but I can still smell the odour of sickness from the previous patient.

This military hospital is on the outskirts of a town in Hebei Province. Hot gusts of wind blow out from between the town's tall buildings and rush through the hospital corridors, while humid air from the irrigated fields beyond drifts sluggishly into the room. It's early May, but the heat is already stultifying.

Whenever it rains, my skin remembers Wen Niao, and the sour scent she left in the flat after each visit. When she was with me, I felt I could see the sky and the earth and everything in between: houses, bookshops, cinemas. I could touch things, taste them, hear them. I could even run down Changan Avenue again and get struck in the head by a bullet.

The room my mother and I are staying in is on the ground floor. The wealthy colliery boss who will receive my kidney is in a room further down the corridor. He's paying the hospital 150,000 yuan for the transplant, and my mother 8,500 yuan for the kidney – only five hundred yuan more than the provisionally agreed price.

I can hear nurses pacing across the floor above. Their rubber soles make a horrible squelching noise. It sounds as though they're treading on rotten cabbage leaves. A nurse comes in every night to give me an injection. I have to lie here and submit myself to fate, just like the executed convict we dissected at Southern University. The necessary tests have been completed. All I can do now is wait for the surgeons to wheel me into the operating room and cut me open.

At night, when everyone has gone to sleep, I can hear gnats and mosquitoes fluttering around the light bulb or crashing repeatedly against the windowpane.

I hear a plane slicing noisily through the sky.

My mother walks in with a group of people who smell of alcohol solution.

'Does he have a blood donor card?'

'No.'

'If he did, the blood would only cost you three hundred yuan a bag instead of five hundred.'

'How many bags will he need for this operation?'

'At least four . . .'

The nurses take off my clothes and lift me onto a wheeled stretcher. I can feel the cool canvas against my bare skin. Two or three pairs of hands prod my stomach and the small of my back. Then a sheet is draped over me and I'm wheeled out of the building. The sheet slips to the side, exposing my face and chest to the sunlight. My pores quickly open and soak up the fresh air.

But I'm soon taken into another corridor. My senses seem more alive now. I can picture the wooden door my stretcher bangs into and the smooth concrete floor. The images are so vivid I almost feel as if I'm walking along the corridor with my eyes open.

When I'm wheeled into the air-conditioned operating room, my pores quickly close up again. A nurse takes out my medical records. 'It says here he was first admitted to hospital on – I can't make out the date – suffering from a blood clot in the brain. He had a slow pulse and low skin temperature . . . After the clot was surgically removed, the head wound became infected . . .'

'Skip that,' a doctor says through his surgical mask. 'Just check his most recent reports.'

These records are forged, of course. My mother asked Wen Niao to write them.

I'm turned onto my side. There are three or four people surrounding me, assessing my physical condition.

'Is there any evidence of past pressure ulceration on the small of his back?'

'No, the skin there looks healthy . . .'

'This page says, "Insufficient growth of granulation tissue over head wound, shattered skull". The next line is illegible . . .'

'Are you taking out the left one or right one?'

Someone is now rubbing alcohol solution onto my back and legs.

'Do you want me to shave him?'

'No. Just rub him all over with the solution. Make sure he's clean.'

A nurse grabs my penis and cleans it brusquely, as though it were a dirty beer bottle. Another pair of hands wedges some pillows around me to keep me in place. My thoughts return to the executed convict we dissected. I'm now lying in the same position as he did in our lab.

'He's as thin as a rake . . . Have you double-checked his blood group?'

'Yes, it's definitely O positive.'

'Shall I get the anaesthetic ready?'

'I think he's sufficiently unconscious as it is!'

'. . . Is there any hope for that man in a coma next door? He got run over by a car, didn't he?'

'It's been a week since the accident. If he dies now, the cause of death will be recorded as medical mistreatment, instead of road injuries, and we'll all lose our bonuses.'

'No one's come to claim him. The authorities will stop paying for his treatment tomorrow. I think we should dump him outside the hospital gates.'

'Let's put him in the incinerator. We can say he died of septicaemia.'

'No, you can't do that. It's not right. He might be a successful businessman, for all we know, and could reimburse us when he wakes up.'

'So you've taken a fancy to him? Well, he's the right age for you.'

'Shut up! I'm sick of you sticking your nose where it doesn't belong. You'd be better off keeping an eye on that unfaithful wife of yours!'

'Hey, calm down, I was only joking . . .'

Another alcohol swab is wiped across my lower back, then a knife pierces my skin and digs through the superficial fascia and muscle tissue. Balls of medicated cotton wool are wedged inside the incision. A pain signal shoots to the postcentral gyrus of my brain. If my neurons were functioning properly, the pain would be intolerable. Small drops of blood reach the wound through a web of capillaries and escape into the outside world.

The cold metal knife cruises through my warm, soft flesh. As it penetrates deeper, the blade becomes warmer, and the dissected muscles fall neatly to either side.

Clamps are quickly attached to the ends of the severed veins. But I've lost so much blood already that my vessels have slackened. There's not enough oxygen reaching my brain. I see a blurred haze before me, like the fuzzy whiteness on the screen of a broken television set.

The blade reaches the fascia transversalis. Death is close at hand.

Soon I'll be able to leave my body and let my soul drift into the ether . . . I see a rabbit shivering on a frosty street. The kerb behind it is covered with frozen wastewater. Cabbage stalks, cigarette stubs, newspapers, frayed rags and empty pill bottles lie trapped within the frozen mass.

'Be careful not to cut his subcostal nerve.'

'If I resign due to illness, I'll still get 45 per cent of my salary.'

'This vein here, clamp it tight, tight as you can.'

'I could work in a private clinic, or a Sino-foreign hospital. The salaries are much higher there.'

'And now . . .'

My energy suddenly drains from my body, like air from a burst balloon. After the renal fascia is punctured, I see the face of my dead father. I quickly try to erase it from my mind. I want the last image I see before I die to be poetic and uplifting. A car speeding off down a long, empty road, for example, like the closing shot of a film.

'We can leave the fat on for the moment. Clamp that one, no – that one.'

'They've opened up the other patient, Doctor. You must get this kidney to them within the next five minutes.'

'Tell Dr Zhou it'll be there in a minute. Get the tape ready . . .'

A cold pair of scissors is inserted between the renal pelvis and the urethra. There are no more vessels to cut. My renal vein and artery have been severed and clamped. My kidney can now be removed and transferred into the body of the patient next door.

'Does it look healthy?'

'Yes, the outer membrane seems fine. We can use it.'

My urethra is pulled out onto my stomach. It's tugged so hard, my bladder shudders. Everything suddenly goes black. I try to scream for help. The nerves in my oesophagus instruct my throat muscles to contract. Blood rushes to my face. I'm ready to shout, but the connections to the language area of my brain have been damaged so severely, they're unable to transmit the correct signal.

The blood around my wound begins to oxidise and coagulate . . . I see my skeleton walking down the street now. I'm walking behind it. Our feet touch the ground at the same time. I am my own shadow. The road we're walking along looks familiar. The trees lining the pavement have been bleached white by the sun. There are stone steps on my left. I climb them. This is the route home I used to take after school. There's a deep ditch in front of me. I jump across it and walk towards the entrance of the opera company's dormitory block. I'm in the corridor now. It's very dark. The skeleton has disappeared.

'What's this book doing here? Throw it out!'

'It's called *China Can Say No*. It's a bestseller. It's about how we must learn to stand up to the United States.'

'Everyone ready now? Cut it, then! Good! Leave enough length on it.'

My kidney is pulled out from its warm, fatty cocoon and whisked away. In a few seconds, it will sink like a submarine into the body of the wealthy colliery boss.

'It looks a bit smaller than the receiver's kidney we just removed.'

'Careful, don't drop it.'

The hole is empty now. At last my soul can leave my body. But just as it's about to slip out, a nurse quickly sews up the incision. Death eludes me once more. My heartbeat returns to normal. This heap of living flesh refuses to let me die.

'Make sure you've removed all the clamps before you finish sewing it up!'

I keep seeing myself chasing after my father then falling into a ditch. The fluorescent light in operating rooms makes the faces of dead people, or of people who are about to die, look flat and mundane. It's impossible to feel a sense of transcendence here, or gain an intimation of a higher realm. In these rooms, both life and death appear sordid and banal.

'The operation went well. Just wait outside. We'll call you if we need you.'

'Oh . . .' My mother seems to want to ask a question, but before she has a chance to, the door is shut in her face.

You drift through an ocean of thoughts like a silent submarine. No one can hear you breathing.

'A mob stormed in here and shoved a flannel in my mouth,' Wang Fei panted. 'Then one of them said, "Sorry mate, it's not you we're after, it's *her*!" Luckily, we managed to break free and run away.'

'Dai Wei, you're supposed to be in charge of security,' Bai Ling said, straightening her collar. 'We were nearly kidnapped just now. How did they know we were sleeping in this tent?'

'Sorry. I had a beer and dozed off. What happened to your bodyguards?'

'I told them to get some rest and come back in the morning.' Wang Fei was wearing nylon shorts. His skinny legs looked very pale.

A few hours before, Yu Jin and I had escorted Bai Ling to this secret tent so that she could get some sleep. Chen Di and Dong Rong were in the science students' tent behind it, so I thought it would be safe. Yu Jin bought some beer and dried tofu. He and I downed a couple of bottles then fell asleep. No one outside our group knew that Bai Ling was in the tent. I wondered how the mob had tracked her down.

'Did you see their faces?' Dong Rong asked. He never took his designer sunglasses off, even at night. During the day, he spent most of his time showing his girlfriend the sights of Beijing. She came from a small town in Zhejiang, and wore tight clothes and heavy make-up.

'One of them was about thirty,' Wang Fei said, taking out a cigarette. 'He looked like a factory worker.'

'Someone's cut the cables of our loudspeakers on the Monument,' Chen Di said, flashing his torch about nervously. The bright beam illuminated his scuffed white trainers.

'We must hold a press conference,' Wang Fei said, lighting his cigarette then taking a puff. A voice came over his walkie-talkie: 'Zhuzi, Zhuzi. If you can hear me, pick up . . . We have an emergency situation. There are thirty empty army trucks parked on the street and the local residents want to set fire to them . . .'

'There's no need for a press conference,' Bai Ling said, passing a comb through her short hair. 'Let's just keep this episode to ourselves.'

'They must have heard your walkie-talkie going off, Wang Fei!' I said. 'That's how they found you.'

Yu Jin strutted into the tent like a proud little rooster, his open shirt flapping at his sides like wings. 'Many of the leaders seem to have scarpered,' he said. 'I haven't seen Han Dan, Yang Tao or Pu Wenhua since last night. Or Zhou Suo and Fan Yuan, for that matter. We need to get everyone back here. I've just circled Beijing on my bike. There's a huge banner outside Jianguo Hotel that says "Oppose bourgeois liberalism, support the great Chinese Communist Party!" It doesn't bode well . . .'

No one had made any broadcasts that night. It felt as though our movement was fizzling out.

A voice shouted through Wang Fei's walkie-talkie again. 'There's a crowd of about a hundred guys here. They're dressed like civilians, but I suspect they're PLA soldiers in disguise. They're holding chopping knives and metal rods, and they're heading for the Square . . .'

The morning races towards noon, while you still cling to the shadows of your past.

'It stinks in here!' my mother grumbles, opening a window. Immediately a current of warm evening air flows through the window of her bedroom, moves into the sitting room, picking up smells of burnt food, brushes past my nose and escapes through the window of the covered balcony.

She wanders off to the toilet. I haven't heard the plastic fly-swatter that hangs from the doorknob rattle, so I know she hasn't shut the door. It saves her having to turn on the light.

I wonder if the toilet has been redecorated. When I last saw it, there was a carcass of a half-eaten fly suspended in a spider's web above the door. The toothbrushes and toothpaste were kept in a ceramic cup on a wooden shelf, next to a small tub of scouring powder. It had been so long since I'd used the toothbrush that it was caked in dust. The mirror above the shelf was splattered with water and toothpaste residue and still had a rectangle of glue in the corner where a sticky label had been. I looked out of the tiny window. There was an electric cable hanging out of a window of the building behind. When the cable moved, its shadow moved too.

My mother spoke to Tian Yi on the phone yesterday. I heard her say, 'The police took us on our "annual trip". They remove us from Beijing each anniversary of the crackdown and lock us in a hotel in the suburbs for a few days. They say it's part of their yearly "cleansing of the capital's political environment" . . . Huh, it's not Dai Wei they're afraid of – he hasn't the strength even to fart – they just want to make sure I don't talk to any foreign journalists . . . No, there's still no sign of any improvement. I doubt he'll wake up before I die . . . You're coming back to China? You must come and see him, then. I warn you, he's not a pretty sight. He's so skinny, you can see his heart and veins pumping under his skin. He's like one of those transparent watches they sell in the markets now . . .'

In the summer heat, my skin has become as putrid as a hemp sack of rotting rubbish. My back smells the worst. The medicinal powder my mother sprinkled over it a few days ago has soaked into the raw bedsores, which now smell as caustic as insecticide.

'Apparently scientists have developed a new drug from cows' brains that can help repair damaged neurons,' my mother said to Tian Yi. 'I know I shouldn't raise my hopes . . . Tian Yi, you're an adult. You understand that everyone needs money to get by in life. Well, I ran out of cash a while ago and had to sell one of his kidneys. But the money I got for it only paid for three months' worth of medication. I can't afford to buy him proper medicine now, so I go to the country markets and buy antibiotic solutions that have passed their sell-by date. They're cheaper, but the quality's unreliable. Sometimes when I inject them into him, he breaks out in red blotches . . . Oh, if only he'd just hurry up and die . . .'

'Can I say a few words to him?'

'All right. I'll put the receiver next to his ear.'

My mother was perched beside me on the bed. She tugged the telephone lead, then shifted towards me, making the metal bedstead squeak.

Tian Yi's nose was blocked. I could tell she'd been crying. 'Dai Wei, can you hear me? It's ten in the morning here. . . . I feel so guilty. I shouldn't have asked you to come to the Square with me when I joined the hunger strike. I'm the one who should have been shot . . . Do you want to hear the noises outside?' She opened her window, and I heard a roar of cars and motorbikes and wind blowing through trees. I could tell it was a big, noisy city.

'Did he hear it all?' Tian Yi said to my mother.

'Yes, all of it. It's nice of you to still be thinking of him.' In fact, my mother hadn't bothered to place the receiver next to my ear, but I was still able to hear everything Tian Yi said.

'Will you take a photo of him and send it to me? I didn't bring any of our photographs with me.'

'His skin is like tree bark. It flakes off in thick layers. How can I photograph him in such a state?'

Tian Yi laughed. 'Your descriptions are very vivid, Auntie! I must go to work now . . .' I knew she'd only laughed to conceal her sobs.

Her voice faded, like a torch whose batteries were dying. Underneath my pillow, I could hear Wen Niao's watch quietly ticking.

My mother seldom brings the telephone into my room these days. Last week, she started renting out the single bed in the covered balcony to a young graduate called Xue Qin. She's afraid he might use the phone when she's out, so she keeps it in her bedroom most of the time. But Xue Qin has made a copy of my mother's bedroom key. If his pager bleeps while she's out, he unlocks her door and makes a telephone call. He has rifled through all the drawers in the flat, read my father's journals, and taken a swig from each of the bottles of rice wine my mother keeps in the cabinet.

'She's got a foreign fiancé,' my mother grumbled when she put down the receiver. 'What's she doing asking for photographs of you? If she's so concerned about your condition, why doesn't she send us some money? She's living a nice life abroad, but she's forgotten we helped her to get there. She hasn't thanked us once . . .'

My mother flushes the toilet with some old washing-up water, then goes to her bedroom to get changed. The Yangge fan dance troupe she's joined is going to perform at a street party to celebrate the Hong Kong Handover. I know she'll put on a lot of make-up. I remember the colourful make-up she wore on stage. When she carried me home after a performance, I'd rest my head on her shoulders and inhale the sweet scent of her face powder.

'Will you change the drip bag when it runs out, Xue Qin, and remember to turn him onto his side?'

'Don't worry, I'll look after him. You go out and have fun.'

An hour after my mother has left, Xue Qin is still in the sitting room, drinking beer and watching television. My mother was introduced to him by the community service centre. He pays only fifty yuan a month in rent, which is very little, on the understanding that he looks after me two nights a week so that my mother can go out if she wants to.

The phone rings. My brother's voice comes over the answer machine. He says he's going to book his plane tickets to Beijing tomorrow and a hotel room as well. I don't blame him for deciding to stay in a hotel. He wouldn't want his English girlfriend to have to sleep in this putrid-smelling flat.

You wander through your cerebral cortex, trying to find the exact location of your wound.

Distant strains of a female choir waft from my temporal lobe. Their serene voices seem to float to the heavens. But the image that accompanies the music is of a dilapidated shack with a dirty grey door that has the words ELECTRICAL REPAIR SHOP painted in red on its three upper panes of glass. The threshold of the door is marked with bicycle wheel tracks. I can't think where I've seen this shop before. While the choir continues to sing in the distance, the cells in which the music is stored gradually come into view. I watch them vibrate. Not having used my eyes for so many years, my auditory memories often return to me before my visual ones.

My mind has attached the wrong image to the music. I didn't hear that song in a shop. I heard it on the radio in my dorm at Southern University. No, I heard it with A-Mei, the first time I went to her dorm. I remember looking at this girl from Hong Kong sitting opposite me and wondering what I could do to make her like me. I wasn't paying attention to the music she'd put on, but my auditory cortex recorded every note of it, together with the noise of her pouring out tea for me and of my knuckles cracking as I closed my fist . . .

I try not to think about A-Mei, but I can't stop myself, and each time she returns to my thoughts the neurons that hold information about her multiply and spread deeper into my brain. I remember one muggy, overcast day in the room we later rented in the Overseas Chinese block. She was feeling depressed. I stood at the window and watched a beggar with stringy white hair walking slowly along the street. The eucalyptus tree he passed was still damp from the rain that had fallen a few hours before. Some of its leaves shone like shards of broken mirror as they reflected the light of the sky. A-Mei looked down and said, 'I've had enough of this place. Enough! I can't take it any more.' Then she said, in Cantonese, 'Did you bring in those clothes you hung out on the balcony? And don't smoke in here. I hate it. If you want a cigarette, go out into the corridor. Go on, get out. I'm sick of you . . .'

The love you felt for her is still buried inside you, deep within the marrow of your bones.

It's 30 June 1997. A few seconds before midnight, Xue Qin puts down his glass of beer and turns up the volume of the television. 'Five, four, three, two, one . . . Yeah!' he shouts in unison with the crowds on the TV screen. 'We've turfed those bloody Brits out at last!'

I remember picking up one of A-Mei's newspapers and seeing a photograph of Hong Kong citizens burning copies of the mini-constitution that would govern the territory after its handover to China. 'Aren't they pleased that Hong Kong will be returned to the motherland?' I said. She glanced at me coldly. 'Pleased? They feel like a wife who's been abducted from her husband and forced to live with a brute.'

'At last Hong Kong has returned to the bosom of the motherland!' the television presenter emotes. But her voice is soon drowned by the cheers of the hordes surrounding her and by the firecrackers exploding outside my window.

Beijing begins to shake as crowds flood onto the streets, screaming and cheering, their cries rebounding against the night sky. The mice under my bed scuttle for cover into the box of my father's ashes and the other box my mother bought for mine. I can't understand why everyone in this city is so happy. When my brother phoned up last week, he said that most people in Britain couldn't care less which country governs Hong Kong.

Xue Qin, who was sitting on the sofa a few moments ago, is now standing beside my bed. He lifts the sheet. I can tell he's staring at my genitals. He crunches noisily on a boiled sweet, then leans down, wraps his hands around my penis and moves them up and down. My body shakes; the iron bed squeaks. On the floor below, everyone shouts jubilantly: 'The Chinese have washed away a hundred years of national humiliation!'

Xue Qin's arms are pressing against my stomach. The erectile tissue of my penis begins to swell. I'm powerless to defend myself against this lout.

Blood rushes to my groin. I try to divert my mind, hoping to stem the flow, but the testosterone pouring into my bloodstream keeps dragging my thoughts back to my penis. It's stiff now. He moves his hands faster. I focus on the noises outside. There are people singing and dancing, banging drums and gongs. A window is flung open. As the roar from the television inside blasts out, he puts his mouth around my penis. My flesh squashes against his teeth and tongue. Feelings of anguish and pleasure collide inside me. Bright sparks dart through my mind. Sometimes they look like shiny pebbles hurtling towards my testicles. The bastard is now rubbing his teeth over my foreskin. A wave of restlessness sweeps through me. My muscles contract for a second, then I'm propelled like a bullet into his rotten mouth along with a stream of sperm.

President Jiang Zemin's voice bellows from the television: 'After years of abuse at the hands of foreign powers, the Chinese have at last regained their self-respect!'

The crowds outside yell, 'We've kicked the Brits out at last!' Waves of noise from buildings, streets and public squares rise into the sky.

Xue Qin swallows my sperm, jumps to his feet and shouts, 'Yes, we've kicked the bastards out!'

My penis is limp and shrivelled. I wish he'd bugger off now.

He turns on the light, pushes the metal basin back between my legs, and says, 'That was bloody amazing! I didn't know vegetables could get hard-ons. I'll blow you every day from now on.' Then he drapes the cotton sheet over me, switches off the light and leaves.

Fortunately, he didn't see the watch Wen Niao left under my pillow. If he had, I'm sure he would have nicked it.

The wild screams of the crowds are still tearing through the night. Flashes of light from the fireworks and firecrackers exploding outside the window waver across my dry and wrinkled eyelids.

Wen Niao is still ticking away under the pillow. Through the clean plastic drip attached my arm, glucose, vitamins C and E, and antibiotics flow slowly into my veins.

Although my body is no more than a decaying carcass, it continues to cling to this world. Death has become an eternal road whose end I will never reach. My sperm, which is my only proof of vitality, both excites and humiliates me. It has left my body and is now trapped in the gaps between Xue Qin's teeth . . . What a wretched day this has been.

The sky used to have nine suns, but the God of the Sky fired arrows at them and shot eight of them down.

On 1 June, primary school kids flocked to the Square to celebrate Children's Day. They stood in scattered groups around the base of the Monument like clumps of flowers. When I looked at the sky, it seemed bluer and more transparent. The Goddess of Democracy statue was as white as untouched snow.

'It's nice to have these kids here, don't you think?' I said to Tian Yi. 'They give the Square a homely feeling.'

'I pity them, having to grow up under Communism,' she said. 'This country only allows children's bodies to grow, not their minds.'

Although we'd cleared the Monument's lower terrace to give the children some space to run around, the rest of the Square looked a mess. We'd removed all the equipment, furniture and documents from the Headquarters' various offices and dumped them temporarily outside our old broadcast station, but I hadn't managed to find any marshals to protect the muddled heap. The only volunteers I could have called upon were busy on the north side of the Square, erecting the hundreds of blue nylon tents we'd received that morning from Hong Kong. About twenty of the shiny tents had already sprung up among the red banners and flags. That patch looked like a luxurious holiday camp when compared to the shanty town of makeshift shelters that covered the rest of the Square.

'It's strange how these vast crowds lull one into a sense of security,' said Sister Gao. 'They make one feel unassailable.' Her eyes were hidden under the shade of her straw hat. She looked like a friendly nursery school teacher. She and Tian Yi had returned to the campus the previous night to invite some professors to join the Democracy University.

Tian Yi squinted into the sunlight, then looked through the lens of her camera at a kite flying high above us. It was a red goldfish with a long streaming tail.

I asked if she had any food on her. I was famished. I'd spent all morning helping Mou Sen erect a shelter below the Goddess of Democracy and set up a public address system.

She unzipped her rucksack and pulled out an opened pack of instant noodles.

'I like that brand. You can eat them raw. They're nice and chewy.' As I looked down at the pack, I saw her clean toes peeping out of her sandals. I could tell she'd taken a shower the previous night.

'Hey, Dai Wei,' said Sister Gao. 'I've heard the student leaders have been given secret phone numbers they can dial if they get into trouble, and someone will turn up and whisk them away to Hong Kong. What are the rest of us supposed to do? Just stay here and wait until we're flung into jail?' Sister Gao had a rosy glow on her cheeks. Perhaps it was the light bouncing off her red sleeveless shirt. I'd never bothered to ask her whether she had a boyfriend. I didn't tend to pay much attention to women who were older than me. But in fact she was only a few years older. We still belonged to the same generation.

'They're not secret numbers,' I said. 'They're just business cards that Chen Di collected from some Hong Kong tourists. He gave us two each. I doubt they'll be of any use.'

'After Mou Sen's Democracy University gets going, the Headquarters should disband,' Sister Gao said. No one answered. When it wasn't clear to whom she was addressing her comments, we seldom bothered to reply.

A throng of little girls in flowery skirts ran up onto the lower terrace and began hoola-hooping in front of us, while a revolutionary song blared from the loudspeakers on a truck driving through the dense crowds below. '*If we fall down and never get up again, if the flag of the Republic is stained with our blood . . .*'

'I wish I could describe this scene,' Tian Yi said. 'It's like a wedding and a funeral rolled together.'

'Or a song-and-dance show in a battlefield . . .' I said.

'The Square is so squalid now. In our meetings, I have to stand next to sweaty guys who haven't washed or brushed their teeth for ten days . . .' Sister Gao said.

Chen Di approached holding a newspaper. 'Look at today's *News Herald*. It says the police dragged a Japanese journalist off the Square yesterday and punched him in the face.' He was wearing a T-shirt on which he'd drawn large question marks in felt-tip pen. He turned to me and said, 'Liu Gang is planning to give a speech later on. Can you find a team of marshals to help protect him?'

'You'd better go back to the campus and recruit more volunteers,' I said. 'Look, there are no marshals guarding this Monument. If the citizens weren't blocking the intersections, the army tanks would be able to roll straight in here.'

Tian Yi took the newspaper from Chen Di. There was a poem by Mou Sen on the front page. Its title – 'The Blue Skies and Rifle Butts of May' – was printed in large black type.

'It feels as though we're on holiday,' Sister Gao said.

'Yes, our movement has taken a day off. It's like when the government stops shelling Taiwan's Jinmen Island for one day during Spring Festival every year.'

'Who's supposed to be in charge of the Square now?' Sister Gao asked Chen Di. 'We've got 200,000 soldiers surrounding the city ready to launch a crackdown, and here we are sauntering about as though we didn't have a care in the world.'

'The only leader left here now is deputy commander-in-chief Wang Fei,' Chen Di said. 'But no one will follow his orders, apart from Bai Ling.'

'We need someone to take charge. A bird without a head can't fly.' Sister Gao took off her straw hat, scratched her head, then put it on again.

'What do you mean we need leader?' I said, after swallowing a mouthful of dry instant noodles. 'Our problem is that we've got too many. A bird with nine heads can't fly either.'

'Look at Mou Sen!' Chen Di said. 'He gave me loads of jobs to do, just so that he could come up here with Nuwa and re-enact the love scene between Robert Taylor and Vivien Leigh in *Waterloo Bridge*.' Chen Di never took off his baseball cap, so although his nose was sunburnt, the rest of his face was pale.

'This is the Monument to the People's Heroes,' Sister Gao said disapprovingly. 'He shouldn't be canoodling with her like that in the full view of the Square. It's no way for a student leader to behave.'

Mou Sen was leaning against the marble balustrade on the other side of the terrace, his hand on Nuwa's waist. They were looking into each other's eyes and taking gulps from the same bottle of mineral water. Nuwa lowered her head. It looked as though she was waiting for Mou Sen to kiss her. A crowd of kids half their height were skipping around them, wearing brightly coloured clothes and red neck scarves.

Tian Yi told me to call Mou Sen over, then said to Sister Gao, 'Don't look so shocked! Didn't you hear that Wang Fei dumped Nuwa and is going out with Bai Ling now?'

I shouted out to Mou Sen. He and Nuwa glanced round and walked over to us. I felt another pang of hunger.

'Ah! Young love amid the revolution!' Chen Di laughed. 'You're like those two activists in the 1930s who married each other on the execution ground before the Guomingdang shot them dead.'

'If I'm going to be a rebel, I might as well go the whole way!' Mou Sen said. 'The enemy has surrounded the city. There's not much hope for us now.'

'Yes, you look like you're acting out the tragic love scene from that Beijing opera, *King Ba Bids Farewell to his Concubine*,' Sister Gao said in a disapproving tone.

I remembered A-Mei telling me she disliked boisterous, muscular men. The girls that I liked always seemed to be attracted to frail, bookish guys like Mou Sen.

'As long as we're still in the Square, we must continue to fight and to love!' Mou Sen exclaimed, his sun-scorched face dripping with sweat. 'Why did you call me over?'

'Here's your great masterpiece, on the front page!' Tian Yi said. As soon as she showed him the newspaper, Nuwa snatched it from her hands.

'Hey, let me see it! . . . "Here is the blue sky of May, the white dress of spring . . ."' Nuwa read out the first line of the poem then smiled at Mou Sen adoringly.

Sister Gao cleared her throat and laughed. 'You two should hurry up and get married! You can't go on smooching around like this.'

'That's a great idea!' Mou Sen said excitedly. 'Dai Wei can be our best man, Tian Yi can be the bridesmaid, Sister Gao can be the maid of honour and Chen Di – you can be the witness. Everything's set, then. Let's have the wedding right away!' Mou Sen turned round and kissed Nuwa on the lips, right in front of me. The light shining from Nuwa's lipstick contorted the shape of her mouth. I began to feel dizzy.

Chen Di shouted through his megaphone: 'Everyone gather round. We're about to have a wedding!'

A crowd of students and residents rushed up to the lower terrace and formed a circle around us. The children shouted, 'When are the bride and groom going to hand out the sweets?' The bright sunlight shone down on us benevolently. It felt as though we were attending a wedding ceremony on the green lawn of some beautiful estate. The people at the front of the crowd pushed back the people behind. I pushed them back too, then shouted for everyone to stay still. Chen Di announced that it was time for the groom to put a ring onto his bride's finger. With a blush rising to his cheeks, Mou Sen pulled out a ballpoint pen from his pocket, got down on his knees, then took Nuwa's finger and carefully drew a ring around it. Tian Yi quickly adjusted the aperture and shutter speed of her camera and began snapping away. I gripped her hot shoulders. Sister Gao hadn't had time to squeeze her way out of the crowd, so she had to stand beside them, smiling awkwardly.

'Wonderful! Now, let's ask the groom to tell us the story of this beautiful love affair! A round of applause, please, everyone!'

Mou Sen stood up again, his face now completely red. 'I . . . I think I'll just recite a poem, if that's all right.' He picked up the newspaper Tian Yi had given him. He'd removed his glasses, so I knew he wouldn't be able to see properly. Undeterred, he peered at the page and began to recite: '"Our souls belong to the sun. / The sky is our eternal cradle . . ."'

Seeing him begin to struggle, Nuwa edged closer to him, lifted Chen Di's megaphone to her red lips and continued: '"We the people stand in the People's Square, while a thousand rifles point at our heads. / We will never abandon the Monument to the People's Heroes. / We will guard it for ever, as solemnly as a terracotta army . . ."'

I could see her pale finger, marked with the black-ink ring, resting inside Mou Sen's palm. A golden light shone from the megaphone as she waved it in the air.

'". . . Let the bullets fly. / We are the suns that can never be shot down . . ."'

When she came to the end, the crowd applauded rapturously. She and Mou Sen clasped hands and said, 'Thank you! Thank you!'

Chen Di took the megaphone from them and said, 'Great! I now pronounce Mou Sen and Nuwa man and wife. Let's wish them a lifetime of happiness. Please kiss the bride!'

Nuwa kept having to wipe away the tears that clung to her lashes. Mou Sen's shirt was drenched in sweat. He grabbed my megaphone and said, 'Thank you for your applause. I never imagined that I'd get married in Tiananmen Square. I'm so happy! When we're all free, I'll invite you to come and share some Maotai wine with us!'

Tian Yi put down her camera and joined the applause. I grabbed her hand and squeezed it tightly.

Yu Jin pushed his way to the front of the crowd, waved his cap and shouted, 'That's enough, Mou Sen. Now let the bride say a few words!' Everyone pulled out their cameras. Someone put a tape in the cassette player and told the newly-wed couple to dance.

'I'd just like to thank Premier Li Peng,' said Nuwa. 'If it weren't for him, Mou Sen and I would never have met! That's all I've got to say . . .' She wiped the sweat from her forehead and smiled at Mou Sen. Then she swirled around him, her red skirt and black hair twirling like a paintbrush across a page. Mou Sen couldn't dance, so he just jigged about stiffly. Their hands would lock briefly, then separate as she twirled round again. The crowd of children and adults began to dance too. The air and sunlight seemed to move to the rhythm. As the crowd spread out, the paved terrace began to shake.

'*This is the season of love. You can smell the love in the air. Everyone needs to fall in love . . .*' Soon everyone on the Square was dancing. Tens of thousands of people were singing, clapping and stamping their feet. The Goddess of Democracy's upheld arms looked like a flock of white doves soaring into the blue sky.

In the Land of Hidden Thoughts, men and women are able to conceive a child merely by yearning for one another.

My mother has woken up. The sun is rising. She walks into my room and turns on the light. Her footsteps sound aged and weary.

As soon as the light is switched on, flecks dart before my eyes. They look like splinters of electroplated metal.

She turns on the radio next to me, lowers the volume, then switches to a different station. '. . . The song-and-dance epic, *The Glorious History*, is one of the most . . .' In the morning, every noise grates on my nerves.

My mother asked Xue Qin to leave last week, so that there would be room for my brother if he decides to stay here. Thank God he's gone. What sort of society produces scum like that?

She goes into the kitchen, the toilet, then back to the kitchen again. It sounds as though she's sleepwalking. She still hasn't taken away my bedpan.

My brother arrived in Beijing last night. It's the first time he's brought his British girlfriend to China. They spoke to each other in English. I could only pick out a few words, such as: *we*, *room*, *this smell*, *horrible*, *tonight*, *tomorrow*, *eat*, *mother*, *want*, *good*, *yes*, *too tired*, *no*, *bank*, *cash*, *travel*.

I don't know what he looks like now. But I envy him. I'd give anything to swap places with him for one day.

On his way out, he said to my mother, 'Ask Master Yao to join us for lunch tomorrow at the Beijing duck restaurant. Helen said she'd like to try some traditional Chinese food.'

They only stayed for half an hour. They were probably driven away by the stench of my room and the smell of the disinfectant my mother had sprinkled on the floor.

If I were to die now, my mother would be able to relax and enjoy the remaining years of her life in peace. On our train journey to the hospital in Hebei where my kidney was removed, my mother said to the passenger sitting next to her, 'My youngest son has an English girlfriend. They're getting married soon. They want me to go and live with them. They've got a two-storey house with gardens at the front and back. Huh! If I didn't have to look after this other son of mine, I'd be living there now.'

I know I'm a burden to my family. Before Dai Ru moved to England, he said to his old classmate, 'As a child, I used to worship my brother. When the kids in our compound had competitions to see who could flick apricot stones the furthest, he always won. He was a skilled flicker. He'd put his index finger over his third finger, then snap it down onto the edge of the apricot stone with such force that it would fly right over the kerb. None of the other kids could beat him.' I know I'll never be able to make him proud of me again. Last night he asked my mother if she'd ever thought of sending me to a rest home.

I remember what a goofy little kid he was. When I went to collect him from nursery school, his bespectacled teacher would frown and say, 'Your father is a rightist. You must teach your little brother not to smile so much. He always has a grin on his face, even when I make him stand in the corner.'

You see an expanse of dry, heart-shaped leaves glimmering in the sun.

In the afternoon, Tian Yi and I sat on the east viewing stand of Tiananmen Gate, directly opposite the Goddess of Democracy, and watched a crowd of schoolgirls sing songs from the revolution. A soloist stepped forward and gazed up at the portrait of Mao that hung above us. Her white dress was as bright as the Goddess behind her. She opened her mouth and sang: '*Great Helmsman, Chairman Mao, lead us onwards like a guiding star . . .*'

'I hope those girls don't grow up feeling like orphans too,' Tian Yi said morosely.

It did feel unsettling, watching these schoolgirls stand below the Goddess of Democracy singing songs in praise of Mao. Their voices blared from the loudspeakers their teachers had attached to the scaffolding at the base of the statue. The ground below was piled with electric cables, crates of apples, barrels of disinfectant, metal rods and rope. I knew we'd have to clear all that junk away, because that was where we'd planned to build the stage for the Democracy University's opening ceremony.

We were alone on the viewing stand. I stared at the hundreds of thousands of people in the Square below, standing among the red banners and flags or sitting inside the blue nylon tents. Everything suddenly looked orderly and disciplined. For a second, I thought I was daydreaming. The strongly contrasted blues and reds made the scene look like a colourised version of an old black-and-white documentary.

'It doesn't look real, does it?' Tian Yi said, putting her arm around me. 'How did this movement get so vast? . . . I'm exhausted. I'm tired of living like a tramp. I wish I had a safe home to curl up in.'

'No home is safe. I remember when I was a kid, an old neighbour of ours called Granny Li was dragged out of her room by the Red Guards and made to kneel in the yard outside. They tied her up and poured ten thermoses of boiling water over her head. She gripped the branches of the grapevine in front of her and howled in pain.'

'How do you manage to remember all those horrible details?' she muttered. 'I was at home when my mother committed suicide. All I remember is being woken up by a loud thud. It was her body falling to the ground.'

'Even if you did have a home to go to, the Party would always have a key to the door.'

I sat further back in my seat so that she could rest her head on my lap. I too longed to lie down.

'The air up here smells of leaves,' she said. 'It makes me think of fields and forests.'

'Perhaps we should introduce your father to my mother. They're both widowed.'

'No, I doubt they'd get on.'

A column of marchers entered the Square. They looked like government functionaries. Some of them had red headbands, a few were pushing bicycles. I inhaled a deep breath of air and thought about mountains and trees, the forests of Yunnan, and the rivers of *The Book of Mountains and Seas*. 'Still, everyone needs a home,' I said. 'It's where we store all our emotions.'

'My dad doesn't have many friends, apart from the old guys he plays chess with in the yard outside our block,' she said.

'My mother is quite easy-going. Her politics are a little too rigid, that's all.' Then I stroked her hair and said, 'Let's go back to the campus tonight.'

'Our dorms are full. All the beds have been taken by the provincial students. I've no idea where they've put my stuff.'

'We'll snuggle up in a quiet corner. It will be just like Yunnan.' Her body softened after I said this, and she nestled closer to me like a little bird.

'I'd like to go home and have a shower,' she said. Before Mabel and Kenneth left Beijing, Tian Yi had gone to visit them again in their hotel, and had used their en suite bathroom. It was the first time in her life that she'd taken a bath. When she came back, she said, 'The bathroom had a huge mirror, and big white towels folded neatly on a shelf. It was so luxurious.'

With her head still nestled in my lap, she closed her eyes and sang softly, '*In years from now, will you still think of me? Will our paths ever cross again? . . .*'

'We can go to Beixin Bridge public bathhouse on our way back to the campus. It doesn't shut until ten.'

'It's already seven now. Let's go to the bathhouse tomorrow. It's so nice up here. I want to stay a little longer.'

In the three weeks we'd been camping in the Square, this was almost the first time we'd been able to have a quiet moment alone together.

'Mou Sen made a bit of a fool of himself at that fake wedding this morning,' she said, tugging down her skirt to cover her knees. 'He's a student leader. He should behave with more dignity.'

'That was true love, though,' I said, stroking her leg.

'You wouldn't dump me, would you, like he dumped Yanyan?' She gazed over at the Square again. 'That old girlfriend of yours A-Mei will be turning up in Beijing any day now, won't she? Are you hoping to rekindle the flame with her?'

'Don't be silly,' I said, my heart starting to beat faster. 'I can't even remember what she looks like. When she gets here, I'll introduce you to her.'

Tian Yi twisted her head round and stared up at me. 'Haven't you ever thought about what's going to happen to us, Dai Wei?' She seldom used the word 'us' in our conversations.

'I'll ask you to marry me, we'll have a big wedding, then we'll travel around America together and live happily ever after. You can be a journalist, or a writer, or a teacher – whatever you want – and I will be a biologist and write a scientific tome on *The Book of Mountains and Seas*.'

'If you want to marry me you'll have to give me a bathroom with a huge mirror.'

'And I'll give you a big wardrobe to hang your clothes in too, and a garden with a reclining chair . . .' I said, remembering a photograph I'd seen in a foreign magazine.

'Don't get carried away! As long as our salaries can buy us a colour television and a fridge, I'll be satisfied. In fact, all I really want is to own a clean bath. I'll fill it with hot water every night and soak in it for hours.' She closed her eyes. I remembered that A-Mei insisted on showering every day. I guessed that women must have a natural affinity for water. 'You're not one of those unfaithful types, are you?' she said, her eyes still closed.

'Don't be silly. You're everything I could want. Why would I look elsewhere?' I stroked her hair and her ear. She was wearing the necklace with the silver heart pendant that Mabel had given her. I didn't dare tell her that A-Mei used to have one exactly like it. I looked up again and gazed out at the colourful banners and crowds swaying in the slanting light of the evening sun. I fell into a daze again, and for a moment I forgot the Square and the situation we were in. Then my stomach rumbled loudly. 'Hmm, I'd love a bowl of instant noodle soup.'

Tian Yi sat up and smoothed her hair back. 'It's so hot today. Why don't we go and have some cold Korean noodles?'

'I've been eating cold bread and cold dumplings for days. I'd like to have something hot for a change . . .'

'You're so contrary. You always want something different from everyone else . . .'

A pigeon sweeps through the air, the tiny wooden flute attached to its tail whistling sorrowfully.

'How does massaging his feet have any effect on his brain, Master Yao?' my brother asks, rubbing more oil into my freshly washed feet.

Since Master Yao took up Falun Gong, he's spent a lot of time giving public displays of the exercise routines. He used to come here twice a week, but he now only visits twice a month.

'Each acupuncture point on the foot is connected to a specific body part or internal organ. If any part of the body is unwell, the pressure point that corresponds to it will feel sore when pressed, or will change colour. This area below the big toe corresponds to his head. This point here corresponds specifically to the cerebellum. Look, this is the point connected to his injury. Do you see? It's darker than the surrounding skin.'

'Yes, it is a bit darker.' The day before yesterday, my brother took Master Yao and my mother out for lunch at the Beijing duck restaurant. He's probably accepted that this qigong master might one day become our stepfather.

'If he develops a temperature in the next twenty-four hours, it will prove his body is trying to fight his disease and bring down the inflammation.' Master Yao is sitting on the ground below my feet, breathing loudly.

'Have a rest, Old Yao,' my mother says. 'Master Li Hongzhi said that the purpose of cultivation is not to heal people. I wouldn't want him to remove your powers.'

'I'm only trying to help. I often used to heal people when I practised qigong. Anyway, if I do lose my wheel of law, I'll just ask Master Li to install another one in me.'

My blood seems to be circulating more smoothly. A stream of energy flows through my body. Master Yao's thumb is pressing into the arch of my foot. 'This is his kidney point. I will release the pressure in a second, then press down again three more times.'

'But his left kidney has been removed,' my mother says.

'I'm pressing the point on the left foot which is connected to the right kidney.'

'I wish you hadn't sold Dai Wei's kidney, Mum. I told you on the phone that you should let me know if you were short of money.'

'Well at least he's helped save someone's life. Dai Wei lies in bed all day. He doesn't need more than one kidney. When I spoke to you on the phone, I asked you to track down some specialists who were researching conditions like his, but you never did.'

'I didn't approve of your mother's decision either,' Master Yao says. 'You shouldn't remove organs from living people. It upsets the body's primordial qi. Can you pass me that towel, please?' He takes the towel and wraps it around my shrivelled feet. After the half-hour foot massage, my head feels warmer and lighter.

'I wrote to a neuroscience research centre, but never heard back,' my brother says, then coughs into his sleeve. 'Mum, you'll have to reinsert the needle. Look, the skin's inflamed.' Someone knocked the IV tube attached to my right arm and the needle has become dislodged.

'Both his arms are covered in needle pricks. I've had to insert so many drips, his veins must be like sieves now.' My mother walks over and pulls out the needle. 'I won't bother putting it back in. He's already had half a bottle.'

They turn off the light and carry the electric fan with them into the sitting room. My mother has cooked braised pork and bought a bottle of Erguotou distilled wine especially for my brother. Master Yao has given up alcohol and meat.

Since my mother has been having private Falun Gong lessons from Master Yao, she has become much more conscientious. She plays the exercise tapes all the time, and spends hours sitting on her bed meditating. She has also taken to calling him Old Yao now, instead of Master Yao.

'Eat up, Old Yao. Whatever you may say about this government, at least there's enough food to go around now. Back in the famine years, the wind musicians of our opera company's orchestra were classified as "heavy labourers", but we chorus members, who worked just as hard, were classified as "normal workers" and got eight jin less rice a month. And I had to send twenty jin's worth of my monthly ration coupons to my husband, otherwise he would have starved to death in the labour camp.'

'The food we were served in our staff canteen during those years was watery and tasteless,' says Master Yao. 'Occasionally, when I couldn't stomach it any longer, I'd sneak off to a restaurant. But I'd choose one that was a half-hour walk away, to make sure no one from work saw me. I'd sit with the other nervous customers and gorge myself. I'd take a few pieces of duck back home, so that my family could have a taste. But I always felt guilty afterwards. One meal cost half my month's wages . . . A few years later, after my unit was restructured, I was sent to work in the countryside. Life was so hard there, I lost all interest in food.'

'My husband and I never once went out to a restaurant together,' my mother sighs. Before Liberation, her family often dined at expensive restaurants. I'm sure she's thinking back to those days now.

'The Communist Party is more callous than any of the Chinese emperors of the past,' Dai Ru says. 'Dai Wei can't move or talk, but the government still keeps him under constant surveillance.' I remember how my brother jumped to his feet after reading a few pages of my father's journal and vowed to avenge the injustices done to him.

'You're right. They even made me turn my back on my ancestors . . . Go on, eat up, Old Yao.' This is the first time I've heard my mother mention her ancestors.

'So do you see now, Mum? Your beloved Party destroyed your husband and then your son. They have torn our family apart.' My brother sounds just like I used to.

'Perhaps I was too leftist in my young days, but I stuck by your father. I never once considered divorcing him. If you were married to a rightist back then, you were treated like dirt. Most women in my situation would have abandoned him. Huh, if Dai Wei hadn't got into this state, I could have pulled myself up again after your father died. I might have made a career for myself as a duettist.'

'You're so lucky to have been born with a beautiful voice,' Master Yao says,

'What's all this "huh, huh", Mum? Whenever I sighed as a child, you'd clip me round the ear. You said it was unlucky. But now you seem to sigh all the time.'

'I'm frustrated, I suppose. I used to be a professional singer. I should start practising again. Perhaps that would raise my spirits a little. Huh. Before Liberation, my family owned a three-storey house. My father had many American friends, and would hold dance parties for them in our home. We owned a camera, and had albums filled with photographs . . . Eat up, Old Yao!'

'You've been living in the free world for several years, Dai Ru,' Master Yao says. 'You must remember to take care what you say now you're back.'

'Helen and I went to the Square yesterday and laid a bouquet at the foot of the Monument to the People's Heroes. It had six red roses and four white roses to commemorate the students who were killed on 6/4.' I keep hearing my brother putting his tumbler of Erguotou back down on the table. It appears he's become quite a hard drinker.

'You could have got yourself arrested! A woman called Wang Xing went to the Square a while ago and unfurled a banner that said "Reverse the verdict on the Tiananmen Movement". She was arrested, declared "criminally insane" and sent to one of those Ankang mental hospitals that are run by the police. They only release you from those places once they've tortured you so badly that you really have gone insane.'

Dai Ru sighs and says quietly, 'If I hadn't left the intersection to take a message back to the Square, I would probably have got caught in the crossfire too. Four students from my college were shot that night . . . I met up with some old classmates the other day. None of them wanted to talk about Tiananmen. All they're interested in is doing business and making money.'

'You haven't got any cleverer since you've been abroad. I've warned you countless times to stay away from politics, but you never listen to me . . . How much are you paying for your hotel room?'

'Don't ask, Mum. I'm going to give you £800 before I go, so you can buy what you need. This flat is like a scrapyard. No normal person would dare set foot in here.'

'What time does your hotel lock its front door? Your girlfriend will be waiting up for you. You'd better go back.'

'Don't worry. I bought her a ticket for a Beijing opera performance. It doesn't end until eleven. It's so hot in this flat, Mum. I'd like to get some air conditioning installed for you.' My brother bought a microwave oven for my mother yesterday, so that she can have hot food whenever she likes. But she discovered that it's a 100-watt machine, so I know she'll never use it.

After my brother leaves, Master Yao performs a few Falun Gong routines with my mother, then takes a quick shower.

'You pick things up so quickly,' Master Yao says, sitting down on the sofa. 'I suppose artists must have a natural aptitude for spiritual cultivation . . . I have a ceramic figurine of Bodhisattva Guanyin at home. I'll give it to you next time I come. The only thing I keep on my walls now is a photograph of Master Li Hongzhi.'

'This flat is so cramped. I wouldn't want the figurine to get knocked over. Where could I display it?'

'On that side wall of the covered balcony. I'll put up a wooden shelf for you, and give you a photograph of Master Li Hongzhi to hang above it. That way, when you burn the incense, both Guanyin and Master Li will be able to enjoy the sacred smoke while they meditate in the Falun paradise.'

'Tell me, what does the Falun paradise look like?'

'Once Master Li has installed a wheel of law inside you, you will see it for yourself. It's a beautiful, golden realm. There are pavilions made of gold and agate, and emerald ponds covered with lotus flowers. You never have to worry about material concerns. You can pluck whatever food or clothes you need from the trees. It's even better than the Buddhist realm of Utmost Bliss.'

'And what happens when you achieve enlightenment?'

'The soul escapes its fleshy prison. Some enlightened beings are able to climb onto the backs of white cranes and fly into the clouds.'

'Yes, the body *is* a prison. As soon as it falls sick, you have to visit doctors and buy expensive medication.'

'If you continue with the exercises, you will never need to see a doctor again.'

'I understand the medical benefits of Falun Gong, but I have to admit, I still find the mystical elements a little confusing.' My mother has also taken a shower. She's sitting on the sofa now next to Old Yao. The electric fan is purring away beside them.

'Some people believe that Master Li is the reincarnation of Buddha Sakyamuni. While I was meditating one day, he appeared to me as an old man with a long white beard. He looked just like the Taoist sage, Zhuangzi . . .'

'Is Master Li on a higher plane than Buddha Sakyamuni?' My mother puts down her cup. There's water on the glass top of the table. The cup squeaks as it slips across it.

'Master Li exists in many different forms. Sometimes he appears to me as a luminous golden Buddha. When I reach higher states of consciousness, his expression becomes cold and stony.'

'So, you've managed to open your Third Eye,' my mother whispers.

'My Falun wheel rotates constantly, even when I'm asleep. If you stand close to me, you can feel it moving.'

'I used to take sleeping pills, but I haven't needed to since I started the exercises. Even when I get up in the middle of the night to empty Dai Wei's bedpan, I'm able to go straight back to sleep again afterwards. Come on, let me put my ear on your stomach and see if I can hear your Falun wheel turning.' My mother rests her head on Master Yao's stomach. Smells of male and female perspiration mingle in the air.

'I wish I wasn't so uncultured. I know nothing about music or opera . . .'

'Let's climb onto the back of a white crane and fly into the clouds! We don't have to wait until we're immortals . . .'

You're a fish that has been tossed onto a riverbank, a bird that has been plunged into the sea.

My mother is on the phone again. 'She's invested a million yuan in it. It's called the Paris Wedding Photo Studio, I think. Lots of people have copied her idea. There are at least five other studios on the street now. They're very stylish. The managers redecorate every two or three months, trying to outdo each other . . . Most of the customers are from the provinces. They come up to Beijing on honeymoon and have their photos done while they're here. You can choose whatever backdrop you want: a shot of Sydney Harbour, the Eiffel Tower or a traditional Chinese courtyard, and you're allowed six changes of costume. If you choose the 10,000-yuan package you can have exterior shots taken in front of Tiananmen Gate or outside the church on Wangfujing Street.'

Earlier this morning, Wen Niao phoned up to wish my mother happy Chinese New Year. She said she has a four-month-old son now, and has moved to Guangzhou. She doesn't like it down there. It's too hot for her. Our television was on very loud, so that was about all I could gather.

I was shocked to hear she's had a son. Could it be possible that I am the father?

'There's so much infidelity about. All the men seem to be having affairs with those girls from the provinces who work in hair salons and nightclubs . . . Their wives? They just stay at home playing Mahjong and pretend not to know. What else can they do? . . . I've taken up Falun Gong. I do the meditation exercises every day, trying to rectify my heart and cultivate my character.' I don't know who my mother is speaking to. She's been on the phone with this person for half an hour.

Wen Niao promised that next time she comes to Beijing she'll visit us and show us her son. I can still feel her presence ticking away inside me.

I hear a bicycle being hauled up the stairwell, and people on the ground floor stamping the snow off their shoes. The government has forbidden people to let off fireworks tonight. But occasionally I hear one exploding then whizzing through the sky.

'. . . No, I won't be making dumplings tonight. The municipal propaganda bureau has told us to celebrate Spring Festival in a "modern, civilised style" this year. So I'm going to have lunch in a restaurant tomorrow, with my younger son and my daughter-in-law. It will make a nice change.'

The truth is, Dai Ru and his girlfriend aren't in Beijing. They returned to England in September. My mother doesn't want to admit that she'll be spending Spring Festival alone.

She dials another number. '. . . I know, isn't it ridiculous? The bureau said, "Let a thousand shops hang red lanterns and a thousand restaurants serve Spring Festival feasts! Everyone must celebrate Chinese New Year in a modern style this year!" What a joke! I'll be spending it alone in the flat, staring at my comatose son . . . Huh, the chairman of the neighbourhood committee told me the mayor would visit our district over the holiday to hand out bags of American rice to families who are in difficulty. He said I was bound to get a bag. But in the end, the Tuanjiehu committee managed to persuade the mayor to visit their district instead. They told him there's a building in Tuanjiehu which houses five disadvantaged families, including two elderly couples, a widow and an orphaned child. So if he visited it, he'd be able to distribute all the rice in one go, which would save him a lot of trouble.' My mother doesn't put on a front when she's speaking to An Qi.

The windows on each landing of the stairwell are broken. Gusts of wind blow straight through, carrying smells of gunpowder and cigarette-lighter fumes straight into my nose. When the wind is strong, I can hear the rustling of plastic bags or plastic sheeting.

I feel at once tender towards my mother and repelled by her. We live together in this small flat, both discarded by society, trying to ignore each other's presence. We're like scraps of paper lying in a dark corner of the street, being tossed back and forth by the wind.

My mother sits on her bed, puts on a Falun Gong instruction tape and mutters to herself, 'The fortune teller told me I'd travel abroad soon, but I don't believe him, because I keep dreaming of packing my bags and boarding a plane, and everyone knows that dreams always mean the opposite of what they suggest. In my dreams, I often see the Falun wheel rotating inside me, but as soon as I wake up, it vanishes . . . Oh Master Li Hongzhi, I beg you to install one inside my abdomen. When someone gains the Falun wheel, the energy it emits can heal their entire family . . .'

I remember how A-Mei liked to fiddle with her hair, examining the ends of each strand. She often did this before she went to sleep. As she fiddled away, she'd mutter to herself inconsequentially, just like my mother is doing now. Tian Yi also liked to talk to herself while scrutinising a lock of her hair. I think I heard Wen Niao playing with her hair as well a few times. Perhaps it's just something that women like to do. But Lulu never had that habit. She braided her hair into a neat plait which she'd let dangle over her shoulder for a minute before flicking it back with a toss of her head.

At the moment of death, my spirit will escape. But what will it look like and where will it go? Although I long to leave this decaying body of mine, I cannot imagine a life beyond it. Wen Niao seems to have invaded my mind, pushing thoughts of Tian Yi to the side. Perhaps emotional attachments are formed only to satisfy physical needs, and there is nothing particularly sacred about them.

The telephone rings again. My mother goes to pick it up, mumbling that the Spring Festival Televised Gala is about to start and she doesn't want to miss it.

'. . . Yes! I wish you good fortune and prosperity too! . . . Don't worry. A friend brought me a box of food. I've got instant noodles, milk and American ginseng . . . Dai Ru's not here, so I won't bother making any dumplings. I'll buy some frozen ones from the supermarket . . . Come and play Mahjong with you? No, no. Thank you for asking, but this is a time when people should be with their families. I wouldn't want to intrude. Besides, I can't leave Dai Wei on his own . . .'

She puts down the phone and sighs, 'What's there to celebrate? Life just gets worse and worse with every year that passes.'

As society changes, new words and terms keep popping up, such as: sauna, private car ownership, property developer, mortgage and personal instalment loan. Apparently, most businesses have computers now, and there's an 'Electronics Street' in the university district lined with shops selling personal computers and software. No one talks about the Tiananmen protests any more, or about official corruption. The Chinese are very adept at 'reducing big problems to small problems, then reducing small problems to nothing at all', as the saying goes. It's a survival skill they've developed over millennia.

There's not much longer to wait now. My body will soon disintegrate, and then at last I will meet my soul . . .

Your tongue longs to reach into the marrow or veins that are only a few millimetres away.

'An army tank has run over a citizen near the Military Museum,' I announced on entering the broadcast tent. 'The soldier driving it was dressed as a civilian.' It was stiflingly hot inside.

Shao Jian was talking to Tian Yi. 'When Wang Fei ordered everyone to gather round the Monument, a band of students arrived waving tent poles. They looked ready for battle.' He picked up a newspaper to fan his bare chest then slammed it down on a mosquito.

'Don't tell anyone about the tank, Dai Wei,' Tian Yi said, turning to me. 'The students might panic.'

'The Ministry of State Security has put Pu Wenhua up in a hotel room, and ordered him to sabotage our movement,' I said.

'Get Zhuzi to send reinforcements,' Tian Yi said anxiously.

'He's been out with the student marshals supervising the blockades. He's exhausted.'

Shao Jian was sitting on the camp bed, preparing a list of topics for the *Student Forum* debate he was about to chair.

'Where did Nuwa put those instructions about how to defend ourselves against poison gas?' asked Mimi.

A middle-aged man walked into the tent and asked quietly who was in charge. Despite the heat, he was wearing a thick black raincoat.

Tian Yi looked up from her desk and said, 'Why, what do you want?'

'I'm a delegate of the National People's Congress. Some of my colleagues and I would like to have a meeting with you. There's something we need to discuss.'

'If you want to talk, you'll have to go outside,' I said. 'This is the broadcast station.' I suspected he was yet another plain-clothes policeman. But Tian Yi courteously took his business card, then said, 'Mimi, come with me. We'll talk to them outside.'

'I'm no negotiator,' Mimi said. 'You go ahead without me.' She didn't like being bossed about by Tian Yi.

Tian Yi looked embarrassed, so I relented. 'All right, then, you can talk in here, if you want. But make it quick.'

'My colleagues aren't here,' the man said. 'They're waiting for us at a restaurant.'

'I'll go and meet them,' Tian Yi said. 'Shao Jian – don't let your debate overrun.'

I felt obliged to accompany her. We followed the man in the black raincoat across the Square. It was nearing dusk. Groups of students in vests and shorts were playing cards under the street lamps. I whispered to Tian Yi that we shouldn't follow him into any dark, empty lanes.

But it wasn't a kidnap. Before long, he brought us to a restaurant on Changan Avenue.

'We'd like you to have a meal with us,' he said. 'Please sit down.' There were two middle-aged men waiting at the table.

'There's not much point in talking to me,' Tian Yi said. 'Although I'm in charge of the broadcast station, all the important decisions in the Square are made by Bai Ling.'

It was a nice restaurant, with clean white walls, white tablecloths and a delicious aroma of braised beef. Behind our table stood a metre-high cooling fan.

'We have a proposal,' said the man sitting opposite us. He had dyed hair and a southern accent. 'If the students announce that they will withdraw from the Square tomorrow, we will convene an emergency session of the National People's Congress tonight and get the Party leaders' assurance that they will not persecute you after you return to the campuses. We hope very much that you allow us to broadcast this proposal to the Square.'

'I'm sorry, but that won't be possible,' Tian Yi said, her gaze shifting to the dish of stir-fried pork and green peppers the waitress had just brought to the table. 'The broadcast station is controlled by the Defend Tiananmen Square Headquarters. We can only take orders from them.'

'We've spoken to them, but they refused to help,' said the third man, who was wearing a checked shirt. He served us some of the pork. 'Eat up, eat up! It can't have been easy for you, camping in the Square for so long.'

'What positions do you hold, exactly?' I asked, picking up my chopsticks. These three middle-aged men didn't look like secret agents, but they didn't look like government leaders, either.

'We're not able to disclose that information,' said the man with dyed hair. 'But we assure you, we are influential members of the Party's reformist camp, and have access to information at the highest level. You have only twelve hours left. Maximum. If you don't withdraw from the Square before the deadline, it will be a disaster, not only for you, but for your supporters in the intellectual and political elite.'

'Bai Ling, Wang Fei and Lin Lu are too radical,' said the man who'd brought us to the restaurant. 'We've tried to speak to them, but they wouldn't listen. Han Dan and Ke Xi are well-known among the students, but have little power. The Square is in turmoil. Only the broadcast station can influence events.' Tian Yi had shown me our host's business card. He was not only a National People's Congress delegate, but a consultant to a state-owned investment company with a branch in Hong Kong.

'Your decision to stay in the Square until 26 June is absurd,' said the man with dyed hair. 'The government will have crushed you long before that. Remember, you only have until tomorrow morning, at the latest.'

'This is the twelfth day of martial law,' said the man in the checked shirt. 'I understand your fervour and determination. But you must step back and look at the broader picture and also think of your personal safety.'

'I give you my word of honour that we will make sure you won't be persecuted after you withdraw.' Now that he'd removed his raincoat, our host looked more like a cadre.

Tian Yi took a small mouthful of food, then said, 'Personally, I would favour a withdrawal, but I doubt whether any of our leaders could persuade the students to leave.'

'Which is why the broadcast station is so important. If you broadcast our proposal, it could have a huge impact.'

'I'm afraid you three gentlemen are out of touch with the mood in the Square,' I said. 'The students wouldn't want to listen to your proposal. You're Party members, after all. We hold meetings every day to debate whether to stay or withdraw. Nothing you could say would change their minds.'

'Our proposal will benefit both the government and the students. They're bound to support it.' The man's dyed hair was stirred by the air from the fan.

'If you're as persuasive as you claim, why don't you get the government to make some concessions?' Tian Yi said, her gaze shifting to the window. She was probably thinking of the work waiting for her back at the broadcast station.

'We can't negotiate with them until you leave the Square,' said the man in the checked shirt. 'If you don't withdraw, we reformers will very soon be thrown into jail. Millions of officials who've expressed support for you will be purged from the government.'

'The troops that were pushed back by the citizens have been recalled and replaced by more ruthless regiments. They're going through their drills now on the city outskirts. They're armed with live ammunition. The order they will receive will be very simple: crush the rebellion and protect the motherland.' I could see from his expression that he was telling the truth, but I didn't want to face up to it.

Tian Yi put down her chopsticks and got up from the table. 'Sorry, I can't help you. I must go now. Four prominent intellectuals will shortly arrive in the Square to start a hunger strike.'

I got up too, but before leaving, I turned to the three men and said, 'If you were really on our side, you would have insisted that your chairman, Wan Li, be allowed to return to Beijing. Without him here, you won't be able to convene any emergency meeting.'

We walked out. The air was hot and muggy. I told Tian Yi I was still hungry, but she pretended not to hear.

'I wonder how we'll get anyone excited about the opening ceremony of the Democracy University,' I said. 'Mou Sen and Nuwa's wedding has stolen the thunder.'

She gazed at the Square looking sad and worried. 'I wish I understood politics better,' she said. 'I don't know who's right and who's wrong any more.'

'Liu Gang, Han Dan and Shu Tong understood politics, but they never managed to take control. The running of the Square has been monopolised by angry radicals like Ke Xi.'

'How did we get into this mess? We're like a flock of wild geese with no leader to guide us.'

'Everything went wrong when the hunger strike began. That's when the divisions deepened.'

'Did you get those films developed for me?' she said abruptly. She never liked me criticising the hunger strike.

'The prints won't be ready until 4 June.'

'I'm looking forward to seeing how the photos of the Forbidden City turn out. Are Mabel and Kenneth in Shanghai now?'

'Yes, they're going to Yunnan tomorrow, and will be back in Beijing on the 10th. You must make sure you have all your documents ready by the time they return. Kenneth will help you choose a university. Once you receive a letter of acceptance, you'll be able to get a passport very quickly.'

'What about this new regulation that insists students must work for two years before applying for a passport?' Over the weeks, Tian Yi's skin had turned dark brown. I'd been going out with her for nine months, but suddenly she looked like a stranger.

'Don't worry,' I said. 'You can pay someone to forge an employment certificate. That's what I did.'

'This city makes me claustrophobic. I want to fly away.'

'I know what you mean,' I said, trying to share her mood. 'I feel like doing something reckless, like setting fire to those boxes over there.'

'Mabel said that when people march through the streets in America, no one bothers to stop and look. Perhaps living in a country like that would be even worse.' Then she looked at me and said, 'My stomach always clenches when I hear the words "military crackdown". I don't want to die . . .'

A large Yellow River truck trundled past us. Hundreds of factory workers were standing on its open back. A few were sitting on top of the driver's compartment waving red flags. It headed slowly towards the Square. The large paper banners stuck to its side had been shredded by the wind.

You swelter in a bamboo steamer, death crackling through your body like electricity.

The wooden wardrobe begins to creak and moan, just like it did this time last June, as the horizontal strip of wood inside expands in the hot, humid air. I nailed that loose strip back myself. When autumn comes, cool breezes will expel the moisture from the wood, and the strip will contract again. The locust tree outside the window has grown even taller. Its shadow shifts slowly across my face, allowing me to sense I'm still alive.

Every year, at around the time of Tian Yi's birthday, the police turn up and drag us out of Beijing for a few days. Last year, we went to a guest house in Miyun County. The air was fresh and cool. My mother insisted on going for a walk. She put me on a wheeled stretcher and pushed me around the Miyun reservoir, with the two plain-clothes policemen tagging along behind. Everyone we passed assumed we were a family on an afternoon stroll, and that I was a sick relative receiving care at a nearby rest home. This year, my mother demanded to be taken to an area of natural beauty. So the public security bureau allocated us a police car that drove us all the way to Mount Wutai, which my mother had always dreamed of visiting. For a week, she was able to worship in the ancient Buddhist temples and practise Falun Gong in the clean mountain air. She slept soundly at night, and by the end of our stay managed to feel a Falun wheel spinning inside her abdomen. Having not heard from us, Master Yao was sick with worry. My mother phoned him as soon as we got back this morning, and he has rushed over to see us.

'. . . As soon as I stepped inside the Grand Hall of Xiantong monastery, I felt the Falun wheel turning just behind my navel,' my mother tells him. 'I wonder if Master Li Honzhi placed it inside me.'

'Of course he did. It was he who led you to the temple and dispelled the karma from your body. All those who oppose Falun Gong will be destroyed in the end.' Master Yao sits down on the sofa. I catch the smell of his scalp as he removes his hat.

I wish my mother would open a window. This flat is so stuffy. My mother's room is barely larger than her double bed. There's hardly any room to stand. My room is a little bigger, but it feels cramped and airless when the window of the adjacent balcony room is shut. The sitting room is a windowless passageway. But if you open the windows in the toilet and kitchen and keep the front door ajar, a small breeze can pass through it.

The rat poison Master Yao laid out a couple of weeks ago has killed all the mice in the flat. But my mother still hasn't found the dead mouse that's lying inside my father's box of ashes. The smell of its decomposing corpse is disgusting. It makes me think of the frog I buried alive in the glass jar. Why does flesh take so long to disintegrate into dust?

'There was a programme on Beijing TV attacking Falun Gong the other night,' Master Yao says. 'It's a sign that the government has decided to suppress us. I wouldn't be surprised if they're tapping my phone.'

'You must be careful,' my mother sighs.

'It's too hot in here. Let's open the door. Everyone's having their afternoon nap now. No one will disturb us.'

My mother rams her shoulder against the heavy metal front door a couple of times, and finally manages to shove it open. A Taiwanese song floats up from a flat downstairs. '*I'm a tiny, tiny, tiny little bird. I try to fly, but I never get very high-igh-igh . . .*'

'The steel security doors they're making now have little windows at the top that let air flow in and out,' Master Yao says. 'If you want to buy one, I can arrange to have it installed for you.'

'I don't want to make any changes to this flat right now. I'll wait until Dai Wei's situation is resolved.' What she means is that she'll wait until I've died.

My mother usually keeps the door shut, because whenever she opens it, the neighbours complain about the stench that pours out from our flat. They tell her it brings down the value of their property. Everyone in this building, apart from us, has taken advantage of the new policy allowing urban residents to buy their state-owned flats from the government. So our neighbours are homeowners now, with official property ownership certificates. But because my mother resigned from her job, she's not eligible to buy the flat, and has to continue renting it from the National Opera Company. When the authorities demolish this compound, she will only get 10,000 yuan compensation, which isn't nearly enough to buy her a flat in the new estate that most of our neighbours are moving to.

'So you were here all the time! I knocked on your door earlier, but there was no answer. You're sensible to stay indoors on a hot day like this. As soon as I step outside, my clothes become drenched in sweat. Then I have to take a shower when I get home, which wastes so much water . . .'

As usual, opening the front door has brought trouble. The woman from the flat upstairs, who is a sales agent for a fitness equipment company, wants to come in for a chat.

'Sit down, sit down,' my mother says reluctantly.

'This tall gentleman here looks like a company director. Am I right?'

'No. I used to be an accountant. I got laid off.'

'I was laid off too. But I've turned my misfortune into good fortune. I work in direct sales now. I can make at least a thousand yuan a month, which is five times the subsistence salary my former work unit pays me. You look in good shape. I could recommend you to my boss, if you like. We sell exercise bikes. You get a 200-yuan commission for each one you sell. By the end of the year you could make enough money to buy yourself a house, or a car. It's a fantastic scheme . . .'

This new neighbour has tried to persuade my mother to join her pyramid sales group three or four times already. Although my mother has never agreed, she's picked out numbers from the telephone directory and phoned up strangers to test whether she could do the job.

'The bikes are very expensive,' my mother says. 'And they take up a lot of room. You could only sell them to those rich people who live in the big new apartment blocks.'

'But if people have some money to spend, they'd buy themselves a computer, not sports equipment,' Master Yao says.

'No, when people get rich, they start eating too much, and then they start wanting to lose weight,' the woman says. 'Fitness clubs make more money than computer training centres these days. You should look at our website and check out our products. This company has got a great future.'

'I can't afford to use the internet,' Master Yao says. 'It costs twenty yuan an hour. It would be cheaper for me to take a taxi to your warehouse and see the products in person.'

'I like this movie star wall calendar you've got here. Look, this is the actress who did those TV adverts for diet pills.'

From a radio upstairs, a newsreader drones, 'In advance of President Clinton's historic visit to China later this month, President Jiang Zemin expressed his hope that the United States will conduct an honest and purposeful dialogue with China, and will take full advantage of the trading opportunities afforded by our nation's growth . . .'

The world I used to live in has been transformed, like flour that has been baked into bread. I have to chew on it very slowly before I can recapture any sense of what it once was.

You are a passenger on a stricken plane, hurtling towards death at a terrifying speed.

'The martial law troops have begun to force their way through the barricades!' Wang Fei shouted into his walkie-talkie as he headed off with some students to the Liubukou intersection just west of the Zhongnanhai compound. I'd been there an hour before, constructing a roadblock of cement bollards and empty buses. The Beijing Students' Federation had been urging students who'd returned to the campuses to come out onto the streets and help the citizens man the barricades.

Lin Lu ran into the broadcast station and shouted into the microphone: 'This is an emergency! We need more students to go to the intersections immediately and help block the army's advance!' He then turned to Yu Jin and told him to take the few marshals remaining in the Square to the Jianguomen intersection in the east. He'd just received a report that an army truck there had been overturned and set on fire.

All the telephones lines we'd been using had been cut off, and most of the journalists and television crews had left the Square. The festive, carefree atmosphere of the previous few days had gone.

The announcements broadcast from the Beijing Workers' Federation's tent on the other side of Changan Avenue were usually drowned out by louder noises, but now I could hear their leaders calling out for Beijing citizens to join their Dare-to-Die Squad. 'The situation has taken a grave turn for the worse. The military are tightening their circle around Beijing . . .'

'Dai Wei, muster your marshals and set up a security line,' Old Fu said. 'The four intellectuals want to enter the Square and start their hunger strike. I've just found out that one of them is the Taiwanese rock star Hou Dejian. He's a university graduate, so I suppose that makes him an intellectual. The crowds will go mad when they see him.'

'You sort it out,' I said. 'I'm looking after the broadcast station. And anyway, all my marshals have gone to the intersections.'

'Ke Xi mentioned they were coming yesterday, but I forgot all about it,' said Lin Lu. 'We should erect a hunger strike tent for them up on the Monument.' He then began gabbling into his walkie-talkie, trying to muster more reinforcements.

'You're supposed to be in charge of crowd control, Dai Wei,' Old Fu said, popping a stomach pill into his mouth. 'I can't set up the security line. I'm in the middle of moving my finance office into another tent. This couldn't be worse timing.'

'The only marshals still here are a small group from Lanzhou University. I'll see if Tang Guoxian will let us borrow them. He's asked them to man the security cordons during the Democracy University's opening ceremony.'

The four intellectuals walked into the Square. Lin Lu shook hands with one of them and said, 'Welcome! We're just getting someone to put up a tent for you. Come and wait inside our broadcast station.' It was Shan Bo, the Beijing Normal teacher and literary critic who'd been active in the Capital Joint Liaison Group. Behind him was Gao Xin, another lecturer from Beijing Normal, the economist Zi Duo and the rock star Hou Dejian, who was dressed in faded jeans and a white T-shirt.

All the students in the Square were desperate to catch a glimpse of Hou Dejian, so after the four men entered our tent, I quickly blocked the entrance. The only marshals guarding us now were twelve social science students Hai Feng had sent from the campus. Five of them were girls.

A huge crowd surrounded the broadcast station. A pack of journalists appeared from nowhere, waving their reporters' cards and requesting to interview Hou Dejian.

When we received word that the hunger strike tent had been erected, Shao Jian, a student marshal and I linked hands around the four men and pushed them through the excited crowds to the Monument's upper terrace. Lin Lu hurried them into the tent then told the student officials to sit in a protective circle around it.

'My ribs feel as though they've been crushed to pieces,' Shao Jian moaned as we leaned against the balustrades, trying to catch our breath. My shirt was soaking wet. It was a designer one that I'd borrowed from Dong Rong. I noticed that the top button had been ripped off in the scrum.

The arrival of the hunger strikers had sent a wave of excitement through the Square. The students below stood about expectantly, like a crowd outside a cinema the night a new film is released. Books, T-shirts and hats were passed up continually for the men to sign. The crowd was now larger than it had been the day the Beijing rock star Cui Jian came to sing in the Square. Hundreds of people tried to squeeze their way onto the Monument shouting, 'Come out of your tent, Hou Dejian! Sing us a song!'

The terrace below was now packed. A student in a T-shirt that said I LOVE TIANANMEN! climbed up and swung himself over the balustrades, almost kicking me in the face. A stream of people followed behind him. The student officials around the tent jumped up and were immediately shoved back by the invading hordes. The tent wobbled. Fearing it was about to collapse, I squeezed through and said to the intellectuals, 'I think you'd better come out. We can't hold the crowds back any longer.'

Zi Duo sat up, readjusted his glasses and said, 'It's you they want to see, Hou Dejian, not us. You go outside. We'll stay here.'

Shan Bo took an anxious drag from his cigarette and stuttered, 'Wh-what's the point of coming here if we're just going to s-s-stay in the tent?'

'Well, come out too, if you want,' I said. Then I stepped outside and shouted through the megaphone: 'Fellow students, please stop pushing. Step back a few metres. Our guests are coming out to greet you.' The crowd fell silent.

As soon as Hou Dejian stepped out, everyone applauded. Someone shouted, 'Hou Dejian! You're great! Sing us a song!'

I looked down at the crowds that were scrambling towards the Monument, knocking down banners and flags on their way. Hou Dejian held hands with Shan Bo and Gao Xin and began singing his most famous anthem, 'Children of the Dragon'.

I passed my megaphone to Shao Jian, and seized my chance to sneak off to the toilets. I wasn't in the mood to listen to the song.

The song seemed to bring the Square back to life. The banners, flags and students swayed in time to the music.

As I was pushing my way across the Square, I bumped into Mou Sen and Nuwa. 'Look what a reaction your two lecturers up there are getting!' I said grumpily. 'When twenty Beijing University professors joined our hunger strike, no one paid them any attention. They forgot to bring a rock star with them, that's why!'

'*Hurry up, my darling*!' Nuwa said to Mou Sen in English. 'I want to see Hou Dejian!' Mou Sen was hoping to push Nuwa to the front so that she could get a better view, but I knew he wouldn't be strong enough to propel her through that crowd.

As I moved away, I could hear Shan Bo in the distance, shouting through my megaphone: 'We'll get you in the end, Li Peng! You bastard! We'll get you! . . .'

I continued north towards Tiananmen Gate. The dirty paper and fruit-peel trampled onto the paving stones smelt only of dust. All odours of rot and decay had dissipated in the hot air. Chairman Mao was smiling wryly at the Goddess of Democracy, whose eyes were at the same level and were staring straight back at him.

Like an old-fashioned radar receiver, your wound picks up electromagnetic waves reflected by the bird as it flutters past.

The sparrow's arrival has given me a clearer sense of where I am. Perhaps the bird is A-Mei's soul come to visit me. It reminds me of the sacred bird in *The Book of Mountains and Seas* which lays square eggs and resembles a flame of fire when it flies through the sky. Ever since it first landed on my head, I have felt the warmth of its glow.

For days, it has hopped up and down my body. Sometimes it flies around the room. I've dreamed about flying all my life, but with just a flap of its wings and a jump, this creature can make the dream a reality. I can tell from its chirp that it's a sparrow. I imagine that it has tawny grey feathers and yellow claws. It's waiting for me to wake up, so that we can fly away together. A-Mei once said that she wanted to come back as a bird in the next life.

The slightest noise – even the sound of a mung bean rolling onto the floor – will cause its claws to tremble.

My mother has tried many times to flick it out of the room with a feather duster, but it always manages to flap its wings just in time and fly through the duster's feathers. After every narrow escape, I catch a whiff of fresh bird shit.

'All right, stay in the flat if you want!' my mother grumbles. 'This building's going to be pulled down soon, so enjoy it while you can.' A few moments ago, she pinched some of the acupuncture points on my feet that Master Yao told her about, but I didn't feel a thing.

On the phone, Master Yao explained to my mother that the bird was perhaps a reincarnated soul sent by the Buddha to watch over me, and that she shouldn't harm it. He's been very busy recently. A few days ago, forty-five practitioners were arrested during a protest staged outside the offices of a Tianjin magazine which published an article critical of Falun Gong. Master Yao is now helping to organise a demonstration, demanding the release of those detained in Tianjin and official recognition of their movement.

The noises the sparrow makes as it moves through my room allow me to form a picture of my surroundings. When it hops along the windowsill of the covered balcony, I feel I'm touching everything it treads on. I discover there's a row of empty beer bottles on the sill, as well as my old chess set and a shoebox that contains a hammer and screwdriver. The sparrow is under my bed now, trying to peck out the herbs from the medicinal waist belt Yu Jin gave me for my thirtieth birthday. I hear it trip on some pills that have fallen down the side of the bed. When its wings brush over the table in the sitting room, I can hear there's a pile of newspapers on top of it, as well as a telephone directory. It knocks over a teacup, which smashes to the ground. I touch whatever the bird hits. My memories are scratched awake by its claws.

Is it really A-Mei's spirit, visiting me from another realm? I regret that she and I never entered those seven interconnected caves in Guangxi Province. Perhaps if I'd walked through them, I would have achieved enlightenment by now, and been able to tap into the secrets of the spirit world.

I feel a change taking place.

Before the sparrow arrived, I was scattered around the room – over the fibres of my quilt, the ashtray on the table and the metal bowl under the radiator. I had dreams of being crushed between two moving walls, and of a swathe of toppled bicycles glinting in the sun like a wheat field. I even dreamed of glueing my shattered skull back together, taking a bath, then boarding a slow train to death. I'd separated myself from my body, or perhaps my body had separated itself from me. But then the bird arrived and dragged me back into my fleshy tomb.

You lie on your bed like a stone on a riverbed, while time flows past above you.

'Dai Wei! Are you still playing dead?' This is Wang Fei's voice. I haven't heard it for ten years.

'That can't be Dai Wei,' Liu Gang gasps. 'It can't be . . .'

'He looks even thinner than the last time I saw him,' Mao Da says.

Wang Fei grabs my hand and starts trembling. 'He's just a heap of bones. He's skinnier than a mummified corpse. That fucking Premier Li Peng! If I had a gun, I'd shoot the bastard dead!'

Mao Da and Liu Gang are still catching their breath. It can't have been easy hauling Wang Fei and his wheelchair up six flights of stairs.

'I'm sorry the flat's in such a mess,' my mother says, walking in. 'I keep meaning to tidy it up, but I never have time. What prompted you to visit me all of a sudden? Has the sun gone to your heads?'

'What do you mean?' Wang Fei says, tapping the side of his wheelchair. 'I've been writing to you and phoning you for years, Auntie. You look very well. You haven't changed a bit.'

'How are your parents?' my mother asks.

'My father was persecuted so badly during the Cultural Revolution, he went insane. He spends most of his time in a mental hospital.'

In all our days together, Wang Fei never mentioned this to me.

'Sorry, I shouldn't have asked. Now, this man looks very familiar to me.'

'My name's Liu Gang. I was in Wang Fei's dorm at Beijing University. I'm a book trader now. I live in Hefei.'

'Oh, I remember. Your name was on the most-wanted list. I saw your photo on TV. Your hair's turned grey. That's why I didn't recognise you. You were sentenced to seven years in prison . . .'

'So you keep birds now, do you?' Mao Da says, sitting down.

'Huh! It flew in one day and refuses to leave. I'm a Buddhist, so I can't kill it . . . I'll get you something to drink. Do you have any siblings, Liu Gang?'

'Yes. They still live at home. But I don't see them. Since I've been released from prison, my parents haven't let me back into the flat.' Liu Gang's voice sounds very frail.

'Pass me a cigarette,' Wang Fei says, pulling his hand away from mine. A smell of tobacco rises from the impressions his fingers left on my skin.

Wang Fei has lost both his legs, but at least he's alive. I've been half dead for almost ten years. I'm worse off than Shao Jian. Although the beatings he suffered damaged his brain, at least he's now able to use computers and hold down a job.

'What does he eat, Auntie?'

'See those plastic tubes? I pour his food down them: vegetable broth, milk, fruit juice, that kind of thing.'

'Careful you don't give him any of the fake milk that's being sold now,' Wang Fei says. 'I drank some fake rice wine recently. It gave me a terrible rash.' His Sichuan accent sounds less pronounced now.

'Where do you put the tubes?' Liu Gang asks. 'Can he open his mouth?'

'I usually put them into his nose.'

'If he could open his mouth, he wouldn't be in a coma, you fool!' Mao Da says.

'I haven't had time to wash those tubes yet. They've been soaking in that bowl for two days. Look at all those glasses, syringes, feeding tubes – I have to sterilise them every day.' My mother always moans about these things when visitors come round.

'Where have you been this last year, Wang Fei?' Mao Da asks. 'You didn't phone us once.'

'I went to Hainan Island again, and Shenzhen, to help a friend set up an advertising business. But I'm determined to stay in Beijing now, at least until the police find me and send me back to Sichuan. The Beijing Handicapped Centre has picked me for their wheelchair basketball team. The government has put a lot of money into it. It's part of their new bid to host the Olympics. I paid someone in Shenzhen to make me a fake identity card. I've kept my name but have changed my place of birth.'

I wonder how he made it into the team. The only sport he ever played at university was ping-pong.

'I'd heard that Shao Jian's condition had improved. But I bumped into him in Electronics Street the other day. He didn't seem to recognise me when I said hello. He just stared at me blankly and nodded his head up and down.'

'Guess who I met the other day? Do you remember that skinny guy called Zhang Rui who ran the Qinghua broadcast station? He's a property developer now, a multi-millionaire. He's got a huge villa with twelve cars in the garage . . .'

'No, I don't remember him . . .'

'Shu Tong sneaked back to China last month,' Mao Da says. 'You remember him, Auntie.'

'Yes,' my mother says, standing in the doorway. 'Tian Yi sees quite a lot of him in New York.'

'He's formed an US-based Chinese dissident organisation called the Freedom Club,' Mao Da says. 'He's lying low in Sichuan at the moment, but we had a secret meeting with him in Beijing last week. We're planning to do something in the Square to mark the tenth anniversary of the 4 June crackdown.'

'It will give us an opportunity to mourn the dead,' Wang Fei says. 'Perhaps we could carry Dai Wei through the Square and let him revisit his old haunt.'

'If you carry him out of this flat, don't bother bringing him back again,' my mother splutters, as the air fills with tobacco smoke.

'We'll ask Little Chan to stand in front of the tanks again, like he did in '89.' Wang Fei seems to move his hands around much more now that he's lost his legs.

'What? That young man who blocked the army tanks was a friend of yours?'

'Yes. Thanks to the photo the foreigner took, he's become an icon around the world, apparently – a symbol of human courage and defiance.'

'No, that "Tank Man" wasn't Little Chan, he was a factory worker from the provinces.'

'I heard that Little Chan's living in Yunnan now, teaching at a small primary school in the mountains.'

'The Tank Man got a lot of attention, but no one talks about those three guys from Hunan who threw ink on Mao's portrait,' Liu Gang says. 'They're the forgotten heroes of our movement. One of them got a life sentence, the others got sixteen years and eighteen years. I only spent seven years in jail, but it nearly destroyed me. I don't know how they'll manage.'

'But the truth is we were protesting against corruption,' Mao Da says. 'We weren't trying to overthrow the Party or attack Mao. I think they took things too far.'

'Well, *I* was attacking Mao,' Wang Fei says loudly. 'We had guts back then, but we lacked political foresight.'

'I heard the guy who got life – Yu Dongyue – has been tortured very badly. He was tied to a pole in the prison yard and left out there for days, and was then put in solitary confinement for two years. He's a broken man now. When his parents go to visit him in jail, he doesn't recognise them.'

'Do any of you know what's happened to Yang Tao?'

'Our great military strategist? He's a taxi driver now. I've read some articles he's posted on the internet . . .'

'Fan Yuan is a lost cause. There's no point asking him to join us. He runs a tour company now. Can you believe it?'

'I'm sure we'll manage to get at least a thousand people together,' Liu Gang says. 'We'll just walk through the streets. No banners.'

'Yu Jin works for the Global Education Network now. We can ask him to help pass on information about the march. Zhuzi is head of security at an expensive nightclub. He's in contact with several old classmates who now have high-ranking jobs in the Party.'

'Did you hear that Zhang Jie is a delegate of a municipal People's Congress?' Wang Fei says disdainfully. 'That oily wretch. Back in the Square, he was one of my bloody foot soldiers!'

'If you can call it a municipality! It's more like a small country town. He took over a failing state-owned cotton factory, cut the staff, turned it into a joint stock company and made a profit in the first year. He's been named a "model manager".'

The sparrow has flown off into the covered balcony to escape the noise in the room. My mother has put a cardboard box in there for it to sleep in and a bowl of millet.

'And Hai Feng – has anyone heard from him?' Mao Da asks.

'He was in prison for five years and had a nervous breakdown when he came out. He's doing manual work in his uncle's printing factory now. Who else is there in Beijing we can get in touch with?' Liu Gang's voice is very calm. He's sitting on a stool, smoking a cigarette.

'Cheng Bing's got married. I suppose Sister Gao's still around . . . Why don't you open the window and let the bird out, Auntie? The poor creature . . .'

The sparrow isn't used to me having so many visitors. It's flown onto the Bodhisattva Guanyin figurine on the wooden shelf and is chirping loudly.

'I keep the window open all day but it doesn't want to leave. Look, it shits all over the flat, but it has never once shat on Dai Wei.'

'Many students dropped out of university after the crackdown, so it's difficult to find them,' Mao Da says. 'Chen Di's still in Beijing. He's sold the bookshop and set up an interior design company. Then there's Mimi, of course. After she divorced Yu Jin, she opened an etiquette school for girls in the Qianmen district. I can't think of anyone else . . .'

'What's Dong Rong up to? When I phoned his number, a secretary answered and said, "Chairman Dong isn't in his office at this moment."'

'He's loaded. He's bought his mistress a luxury apartment near the International Trade Centre. She's that girl from Hunan who used to hang around with all the painters and movie stars.'

'He keeps a low profile. I think he's set up a fibre-optic cable company that has connections with the Ministry of Foreign Trade. He's always travelling abroad.'

'We must take advantage of Shu Tong's return to China,' Wang Fei says. 'The international community will be watching to see how President Jiang Zemin deals with the tenth anniversary of 4 June. We must do something symbolic to mark the occasion. If we march through the streets, the worst that will happen is that we'll be sent to prison for a few years.'

'Political activists aren't sent to jail now, they're detained in Ankang mental hospitals. You'll end up in one if you're not careful, Wang Fei. They'll get a psychiatrist to diagnose you as a political maniac then imprison you for five years. All the staff are employees of the public security bureau, even the doctors and nurses.'

'We should adopt a moderate strategy, and focus on pushing for gradual democratisation,' Liu Gang says.

'I'm not suggesting we launch another mass movement,' says Wang Fei. 'But as survivors of the massacre we have a duty to hold the government to account. We must demand they reverse their verdict on the student movement and issue a public apology to all the victims of the crackdown and their families.' Wang Fei spits out a cloud of smoke. There's a smell of cat piss wafting from his wheelchair.

'Don't start plotting any more campaigns,' my mother moans. 'Enough people have been killed and injured already. Fighting the government will get you nowhere. It's as pointless as throwing eggs at rocks.'

'It was the demonstration you Falun Gong practitioners staged outside Zhongnanhai that inspired us to get together again, Auntie.'

'That wasn't a demonstration, it was an appeal. None of us sat down, in case the government accused us of staging a sit-in. We didn't even speak. We just stood quietly on the street meditating.'

'If the government is making another bid to host the Olympics, it might allow our march to go ahead, to trick the foreign community into believing that it's turned over a new leaf . . .'

'We're the "Tiananmen Generation", but no one dares call us that,' Wang Fei says. 'It's taboo. We've been crushed and silenced. If we don't take a stand now, we will be erased from the history books. The economy is developing at a frantic pace. In a few more years the country will be so strong, the government will have nothing to fear, and no need or desire to listen to us. So if we want to change our lives, we must take action now. This is our last chance. The Party is begging the world to give China the Olympics. We must beg the Party to give us basic human rights.' Wang Fei's wheelchair rattles and squeaks as he twists from side to side.

Time overlaps before your eyes. The past spreads through your flesh like a maze of blood vessels.

Liu Gang rode up on his bike, having just returned from the Fuxingmen intersection. There were bloodstains on his shirt. 'Cao Ming's afraid that our phone lines are being tapped, so he's gone back to the campus to tell the organising committee that the army has been given orders to clear the Square.'

Bai Ling screeched hoarsely into her megaphone, 'Fellow students, this is Bai Ling speaking . . . The martial law troops have begun forcing their way through the barricades, and they're heading for the Square. There has been bloodshed at most of the major intersections. Fellow students, citizens, we will remain in the Square until the bitter end! Please find yourselves some weapons. You will need to defend yourselves . . .'

'That must be another of Wang Fei's stupid ideas! What weapons do they expect the students to find here that will be the slightest use against tanks?' Hai Feng stamped on some boxes of leftover food. Lin Lu's walkie-talkie was clucking in the background.

'Xiao Li's been injured, Dai Wei,' Yu Jin said, taking off his cap to wipe the sweat from his brow. 'He's in the broadcast station.'

I walked in and saw that the scarf wrapped around Xiao Li's head was soaked in blood. He said that martial law troops had used tear gas to try to disperse the crowd at the barricades, but when that hadn't worked, they'd attacked the crowd with their rifle butts. I told him to lie down on the floor and stay still.

A retired soldier was explaining to the students how to disable army tanks and prepare Molotov cocktails. He'd utter a few sentences into the microphone, then turn to the side and gesticulate with his hands to clarify what he was saying. But each time he turned away, his voice became inaudible. An announcement came over the government speakers fixed to the lamp posts, saying that a counter-revolutionary riot had erupted in Beijing, and that everyone should leave the Square immediately.

Big Chan and Little Chan rushed over with an injured foreign reporter, but there was no room left inside the tent. Big Chan said that if he and Little Chan hadn't pulled the reporter out of the way in time, he would have got crushed under the wheels of a tank. Little Chan had cut his fingers. His nails were covered in blood. Streams of people kept turning up to show us the cartridge cases, steel helmets and compasses they'd pilfered from abandoned army tanks.

'Where's Wang Fei?' Bai Ling asked anxiously. Her skin was sallow and her eyes were red. Having seen the blood-soaked cloth around Xiao Li's head, she was probably afraid that Wang Fei might get injured too.

'Don't worry,' I said. 'Chen Di's gone to fetch him.'

'Send some students to the intersections to remind the citizens not to use violence,' Hai Feng said. 'If the soldiers are attacked, they'll treat us all as the enemy, and none of us will come out of this alive.'

Lin Lu glanced at him angrily and said, 'Everyone's pretty disgusted that Shu Tong ran away to America. I think you Beijing University students should keep quiet from now on.'

'Stop bickering!' Bai Ling said. 'This is the time to show what we're made of!' Perhaps because she spoke so softly and was the only girl in the tent, we all deferred to her.

'Everything here will be razed to the ground,' Zhuzi said, walking up. A continual crackle of commands and reports was coming over the walkie-talkie fixed to his waist.

'My intelligence unit has drawn up a diagram of the situation,' Lin Lu said, pulling out the annotated map. 'Look, we're done for. The 27th Army is moving in from the west, with a unit that's been given specific orders to arrest the student leaders. I've just heard on the walkie-talkie that a secret unit is now guarding the intersections on all the roads leading back to the university district. The soldiers have photographs of each one of us. If we tried to return to the campuses now, they'd seize us and put us in jail. It would be better to let them come into the Square and arrest us in full view of the public.'

'Shao Jian, get your policy implementation unit to tell everyone to leave their tents and gather round the Monument,' Bai Ling said. 'Everyone must stay awake tonight and wait for further orders.'

'There are 200,000 troops heading our way, but there are only 10,000 of us left in the Square,' Liu Gang said, his face deathly pale. 'The citizens are still managing to hold the army back, but they won't be able to do so for much longer.'

I removed my sunglasses then quickly put them back on again. Although everything looked darker through the lenses, they blocked out some of the frenetic dread in the atmosphere.

The sky darkened suddenly and a heavy rain began to fall, accompanied by strong gusts of wind. I thought of Tian Yi, who'd gone to telephone various professors to invite them to the Democracy University's opening ceremony, and of my brother, who was helping her out, cycling through the back lanes to press bureaus across the city to remind the journalists to come. Tian Yi was determined that, whatever happened, the Democracy University's opening ceremony would still go ahead that night.

Only the living have the right to die. You must climb back onto their riverbank before you can throw yourself into the water again.

This 1950s red-brick apartment building has thick, sturdy walls, as do the buildings that surround it on either side. At dawn, the compound is as quiet as the graveyard in my ancestral village. Whenever I think of that place, I smell the earthworms squashed on the stone path.

The migrant labourer who's renting the flat below has stopped shouting and swearing. A few days ago, the police dragged his wife away because she wasn't able to produce a marriage certificate or birth permit.

My mother forgot to close the window of the covered balcony last night, so my nostrils are filled with a green, tranquil scent. It's coming from the old locust tree outside. Its blossom must have fallen by now. There's dust on its branches. The fresh coat of whitewash around its trunk smells like the yolk of a hard-boiled egg.

I remember that there's a building with a steel cooling tower at the end of the compound. In winter, it looks like an ice sculpture. The iron chimneys of the boiler room behind it often spew rusty debris into the air.

The sparrow has been lulled to sleep by the ticking of my heart. Its wings are splayed softly over my chest. Its presence seems to have breathed some life into my stinking corpse.

After my mother gave birth to me, she lay in this bed for six days. I've been lying in it for almost ten years. When my mother came in last night to remove my bedpan before she went to sleep, she mumbled, 'When I brought you back from hospital, you sucked my nipple all night and wouldn't let go . . .' She tried out the special massage technique that Master Yao taught her, but I didn't feel her qi. As she rubbed the arch of my foot, she sighed, 'How many years will I have to practise these exercises before I can heal you?'

The most solid object in this room is the iron bed I'm lying on. It's so heavy, you can hardly lift it. It's as sturdy and durable as this brick apartment block. The khaki-coloured paint has chipped in a few places, revealing the rusty metal beneath, as well as the underlying coats of maroon, blue and brown paint. The lowest coat is white. It covers the orange anti-rust primer like a layer of white underwear. My mother said that her parents bought the bed when they got married. It had belonged to an English family whose textile factory in Tianjin went bankrupt in the 1930s crash. Since white is considered inauspicious, my grandparents repainted it maroon. After my grandfather committed suicide in 1951 following the confiscation of his factory, my grandmother painted it sky-blue. When she died, the bed was passed down to my mother, who covered it in brown emulsion to hide all traces of her dead parents. When my father died, I painted it a dark khaki colour that was popular at the time.

During the day, the little sparrow hops around the bed. Sometimes it flies up and circles the room; then, when it's tired, it settles on my chest and grips my skin with its shaking claws. Since it arrived, the room seems to have grown much larger. I follow it as it flutters through the air. It has given me back a sense of night and day.

I imagine slowly lifting my hands then bringing them down to touch the feathery warmth of its body. It pecks out a hair from my nostrils, rubs its beak against my cheek, and chirps. An episode from my past suddenly returns to me. It's so vivid, my whole body seems to clench. I see A-Mei look up at me and say: 'If you could have one wish, what would it be?'

'To travel the country and climb Mount Everest. And you?'

'That sounds too tiring for me. My wish would be to come back as a bird in the next life and fly through the sky.'

'I often have flying dreams, but when I reach the clouds, I start feeling cold and have to come down again.'

She looked into the sky and said, 'In the next life, I'll be your love-bird and keep you warm. We can fly off to the heavens together . . .'

You are a bird's skeleton drifting on the cold wind.

'Open up! Open up!' There are people banging on our front door. I can tell at once that it's the police. They always turn up at dawn. It's 2 June today. I wonder where they're planning to hide us this year.

'I'm coming,' my mother croaks sleepily, turning on a light.

'Are you – Chen Huizhen?' This man's voice is unfamiliar. He hasn't visited the flat before.

'You've come to drag us out of the city before the tenth anniversary of 4 June, haven't you? So I'm sure you know who I am.'

'You took part in the Falun Gong siege of Zhongnanhai on 25 April.'

'It wasn't a siege, comrade. All we were doing was trying to lodge a complaint at the Central Appeals Office.'

'Ten thousand people surrounding the residential compound of our top government leaders! If that isn't an attempt to subvert state power, then what is?'

'We're a timid lot. We don't dare march through the streets, or even stick up posters. How could we possibly topple the state?'

'Haven't you read the newspapers? Falun Gong is a deceitful, dangerous organisation. 1,400 practitioners have died as a result of refusing medical treatment. Some followers have become so unhinged that they've committed suicide. One woman even strangled her own daughter.'

'Falun Gong fosters the cultivation of truth, compassion and tolerance. What's evil about that? If it opposed the Party, I wouldn't have joined it. I'm stuck at home all day with this mute son of mine. As soon as I step outside, my every move is monitored by the police. When I fall ill, there's no one to help me. Why shouldn't I do a little meditation to help release my tension? And I'm not just doing it for myself, I'm doing it for my son as well. I can't afford to buy him any more medication. If I continue to practise the exercises, my energy field is bound to have a beneficial effect on his health.'

'You think your meditation can heal him?' says a female officer. 'If you're not careful, you'll end up a vegetable yourself.' She walks in and rifles through the drawers, then frisks my mother's mattress. The police always bring a female officer with them. This one has been here twice before.

'You went to the People's University to speak to Ding Zilin.'

'Of course I did. She asked the international community to provide humanitarian assistance to the relatives of the 4 June victims. I wanted to thank her. But that was three years ago now.'

'You know that you're strictly forbidden to have contact with such people. And what about those other women from the Tiananmen Mothers group? They come here every week. What have you been plotting?' This policeman speaking is the officer who interrogated me when I was fifteen. He is now the head of our local public security bureau.

'They only come here for a chat. Aren't we allowed to have a bit of companionship? Do you really think that a few old ladies like us could bring down the government?'

'Just a chat, you say? You can't fool us.'

'I wrote a statement supporting the government crackdown nine years ago. What more do you want?'

'We want to know why you joined the siege of Zhongnanhai. Tell us who sent you there.'

'No one sent us. I was practising my routines in the yard with my neighbours that morning. We were upset about the arrests of those Tianjin practitioners. After our session, we decided to go to Zhongnanhai to appeal for their release. We didn't know that so many other practitioners would have the same idea. It wasn't a siege. All we did was stand on the street meditating. No one is giving us orders. You must believe me. Falun Gong practitioners never lie.'

'We are high-ranking officers, so you'd better watch how you speak to us.'

'We were afraid the government would accuse us of staging a demonstration. That's why none of us sat down, apart from Granny Pang. After standing up for a few hours, her legs began to shake, so she had to rest on her knees for a while.'

'Don't give us any more lies. We're treating this matter very seriously. Pack your bags now. We're taking you and your son away from Beijing for a few days. We don't want you causing any trouble during the 4 June anniversary.' I remember this officer shouting to me in exactly the same way when he kicked me in the shins nearly twenty years ago.

'I'm a law-abiding citizen. You have no right to take me away.'

'If you're so law-abiding, what were you doing demonstrating outside Zhongnanhai?'

'This is my home. You don't have an arrest warrant. I refuse to leave.'

'I warn you, things are going to turn nasty. The government will pronounce its official verdict on Falun Gong soon. If a religion that causes the death of 1,400 people isn't an evil cult, I don't know what is.'

'You can knock me to the ground, but I will crawl back up again, and the Falun wheel will still be spinning inside me. Arrest me, if you want! I don't care. What difference will it make? China is one huge prison. Whether we're in a jail or in our homes, every one of us is a prisoner!' She turns abruptly and storms off to her bedroom.

I've never heard her so enraged before. She certainly didn't react so angrily the last two times the police came to take us away for 4 June. Six weeks ago, she stood outside the Zhongnanhai government compound with 10,000 fellow practitioners for six hours, and returned a different person. She probably feels just like we did at the beginning of the student movement. When people become part of a group, they find a courage they never knew they possessed before.

'In fact, the clampdown on Falun Gong has already begun,' the female officer says, following my mother into the bedroom. 'The police have begun scouring the city's hotels, rounding up Falun Gong members who've travelled up from the provinces. We'll be turning on the Beijing practitioners soon. We've placed you under surveillance all these years because of your son's involvement in the student movement. But this time it's your membership of the cult that worries us . . . We've heard that Falun Gong members are planning to stage a mass suicide in the Fragrant Hills on the birthday of your leader, Li Hongzhi. You can't expect the government to sit back and do nothing.'

'A mass suicide? That's absurd! All we Falun Gong practitioners want is to cultivate our energies so that one day we'll achieve immortality and fly into the sky. None of us wants to kill ourselves.' My mother moves closer to the woman and asks, 'Who are those two male officers? I haven't seen them before.'

'They've been sent by the municipal public security bureau. They're dealing with your files now . . .'

'A nurse comes twice a week to look after my son. I've already paid her fees upfront. You can't expect us to leave like this at the drop of a hat . . .'

While I listen to the commotion, I see Nuwa standing at the foot of the national flagpole on Tiananmen Square, commanding us all to sing along with her: '*Don't be sad! The flag of the Republic will be stained with our blood* . . .' She was wearing a thin white T-shirt. You could see her red bra underneath. It was dawn, and a crowd had gathered round the pole to watch the daily flag-raising ceremony. We didn't feel the cold of the morning air. During those last few days in the Square, we always seemed to be singing 'The Bloodstained Spirit'. There was a large vat of egg soup on the back of a tricycle cart beside me. A woman was ladling out bowls to a long queue of students. She'd come to the Square with the motorcyclists of the Flying Tigers brigade. At first glance, I thought she was Lulu. She had the same short, permed hair and flowery nylon shirt. Perhaps that's why the smell of her egg soup remains so vivid in my mind.

The sparrow suddenly plops onto my chest, digs its claws into my skin and lets out a shrill cry.

'. . . The army's about to roll in and you're still worrying about your stupid opening ceremony. It's too late for that now.' This was Big Chan speaking. His feminine mouth was rosy and his eyes were sparkling. He was wearing a cotton glove on his left hand to protect his long nails. He would only remove the glove when he went into his tent to strum a few tunes on his guitar. He was very popular. Even when he was asleep, there was always a cluster of friends around him. He and I were walking towards the Goddess of Democracy. If we'd known the dawn that was breaking was the last one we'd ever see, perhaps we would have looked a little longer at the beautiful grey glow in the distance.

The officers have carried me downstairs and put me in the back of their van. My mother jumps up and says, 'Wait a minute. His bedpan! I forgot it last time, and had to put him in nappies every day.'

'Follow her up, Xiao Hu. Make sure she doesn't fling herself from the top of the building. That old bag's very devious . . .'

'We're going to be stuck with them for five days! I hope we get a bloody big bonus.'

They light their cigarettes. The van stinks of petrol. The engine begins to rumble.

Damn. Who's going to look after my sparrow?

The emperor tied the God of Twin Burdens to the trunk of a tree, binding his hands together with strands of his own hair. As the years passed, the god slowly solidified into a rock.

The police took us to a small guest house near the Great Wall. Every day, the female officer read out articles to my mother on the evils of Falun Gong. In the month since we've returned, the police have visited twice a week. My mother was told to stay in the flat, but today she went out, leaving me to listen to callers talk into the answer machine.

'It's terrible!' shouts the voice on the other end of the line. 'The police are knocking on every door in the city, rounding up Falun Gong members. Two officers came to our flat last night, dragged my father out by his hair and forced him into a police van. They arrested about thirty people from our compound . . .'

My mother set off with Granny Pang this morning to meet Master Yao outside the Central Appeals Office. He wanted to submit a petition. It's evening now, and she still hasn't returned. I presume she's been arrested. The government appears to have launched a large-scale manhunt.

There is a sinister atmosphere in the air. Two police officers suddenly break into the flat and begin searching through my mother's belongings. One of them comes over and slaps me on both cheeks. 'My God, look what I've found. Is he dead or alive?'

'He's the vegetable. Everyone round here knows about him. He's been like this for ten years. We thought he was putting on an act at first, so we planted a nurse here for a few days, but she confirmed that his coma was genuine. If he'd been faking, we would have flung him in jail. He was one of the student leaders of the Tiananmen movement.'

'So mother and son are both counter-revolutionaries, then.'

'Let's hurry up and see if we can find any incriminating letters or Falun Gong tapes.'

They pull the quilt, sheets and pillowcases off my mother's bed and empty her drawers onto the floor. A third officer pulls out the sofa in the sitting room and rips off the fake leather cover. Then they unhook the mirror from the wall and smash it to check whether there's anything hidden inside the frame. The television set has been wheeled into the middle of the room and is also being smashed open.

'Hey, look at this book: *The Great Law of Falun*. I found it hidden in her kitchen drawer.'

'Well done, Inspector Holmes!'

'It wasn't difficult. She lined a filthy drawer with a clean sheet of newspaper. Any fool could have guessed there was something hidden underneath.'

I feared something like this might happen. Master Yao has been put under house arrest. He phoned my mother several times this week. He told her there are two armed police officers guarding his front door and a police van parked outside his block. At night its headlights shine straight into his flat. He said everyone who petitioned outside Zhongnanhai in April is going to be arrested. 10,000 armed police officers have been mobilised to carry out the job.

At the end of the phone conversation he had with her this morning, he said, 'The government feels we made them lose face in April, and they want to punish us. But they shouldn't slander Master Li Hongzhi. He has never tried to stop any members from seeking medical treatment, and he has no intention of usurping the Communist Party. Falun Gong isn't a political organisation or a religion. It's a cultivation practice that promotes well-being through meditation exercises and good morals. There's no foreign force manipulating us behind the scenes. The government's accusations are unjust. When the guards have their lunch today, I'm going to sneak out of the flat and go to Zhongnanhai to submit a petition to the Central Appeals Office.'

'I'll go with you,' my mother said. 'And I'll get Granny Pang downstairs to come too. I don't care if they arrest me. The police came round last night and told me not to leave the flat. What are they afraid of, for God's sake? I'm not likely to go very far, am I, as long as Dai Wei is still alive. They're forcing us to renounce our movement, just as they forced the students to renounce theirs after the 4 June crackdown.'

But after she put the phone down, my mother squatted on the floor and sighed, 'Huh, I've had to live through so many political campaigns. Is this the one that's finally going to break me?'

She removed the photograph of Li Honzhi from the wall, gathered all her books and instruction tapes together and began concealing them around the flat. She switched on the radio and tuned into each station, searching for the latest updates. Every station was broadcasting the same pre-recorded reading of the *People's Daily* article entitled 'The Truth about Li Hongzhi'. 'Are we going to have to be subjected to another Cultural Revolution?' she muttered to herself. 'Has President Jiang Zemin lost his mind?'

I'm afraid that my mother will be physically punished for her thoughts and actions, just as I was. In this police state, I've managed to gain freedom of thought by pretending to be dead. My muteness is a protective cloak.

You lie hidden inside your body, like a stowaway concealing himself in the hold of a ship.

'Mum? Are you there? Please pick up the phone. It's me! I remember you mentioning that you've taken up Falun Gong. I heard on the BBC today that 10,000 practitioners have been arrested. The Chinese government has jammed the internet. None of the emails I've been sending my old classmates have been getting through. Are you there, Mum? Please pick up . . .'

The sparrow flies around the room all day. Sometimes it goes to the kitchen to drink some water or peck at the bag of millet. In the last few days, it's taken to shitting on my bed. I remember dissecting a sparrow when I was at Southern University. Its feathers had been plucked off. Through the thin, purplish-red skin, I could see its translucent stomach, suspended inside its abdomen like a small sausage.

Before I slowly die of starvation, I must try to take stock of my predicament.

My pulse is stable, my organs are functioning well. If someone were to pour milk or vegetable soup down my feeding tube, I would be able to produce some urine.

Although my motor cortex has atrophied, my synapses have been strengthened through continual use. My cognitive ability has improved and my memories have been consolidated. The plain-clothes officer who shot me destroyed my body, but he didn't destroy my mind. I'm probably the only citizen still alive in this country who hasn't yet signed a statement supporting the government crackdown.

If I were to wake from this hibernation, perhaps I'd become the manager of a computer company or a nightclub security guard. Or maybe I'd take up Falun Gong and end up dying in jail. Do I really want to wake from this deep sleep and rejoin the comatose crowds outside? I withdrew from society and retreated into my bedroom, then from my bedroom I retreated into my body. Eventually, I will leave my body behind and retreat into the earth. When seen from this perspective, death looks like an easy escape route. But although I'm tempted to take it, something pulls me back. I still want to read the *Illustrated Edition of The Book of Mountains and Seas* one more time, then travel through the landscapes it describes, and write a scientific treatise elucidating every geographical, botanical, zoological . . .

A stone smashes through the window of the covered balcony. A kid in the yard probably threw it in an attempt to kill the sparrow. A gust of hot, dry air rushes into the room.

The Arrogant Father chases after the sun. Just as he's about to catch it, he collapses, faint from lack of water. He drinks the Yellow River, then drinks the Wei River, but still dies of thirst.

As well as the sparrow, there is now a mouse in the room. A couple of nights ago, when everything was quiet, I heard it nibbling a bag of flour in the kitchen. Now, it skips and leaps around the flat all day. When the sparrow leaves my room, the mouse climbs onto my bed and nibbles at my cheek.

I haven't had any food poured into me for four days. If my mother doesn't return soon, I'll rot to death. If I was buried under rubble after an earthquake, I could command my body to dig me out. But since I'm buried inside my flesh, all I can do is wait patiently until the bacteria consume me from within.

A light so bright that it's almost black hovers above my bed. I've been lying here for ten years. I have retrieved every detail of my life. There is nothing left for me to remember. If I'm to die now, I won't feel many regrets, only grief and guilt about the students who died before me.

I don't want to see Tian Yi again. She is now no more than a bundle of memories I will take with me to my grave. At this moment, she's probably lying next to her fiancé, about to crawl out of bed.

What torments me is that I have no way of finding out what happened to A-Mei, even though her bloodstained letter is lying under my bed, inside the box my mother bought for my ashes. I've never heard any mention of a foreign student being injured or killed during the crackdown. I remember standing at the window of our room at Southern University, watching her walk down a paved path. She kept stopping in her tracks. I didn't know why at the time, but now I understand. She could never do two things at once. When a thought came to her mind, her feet would forget to move. I watched her walk under the large banyan tree. Her beautiful image flitted in and out of view behind the branches and green leaves. When she emerged from the other side I had a clear view of her again. I watched her bare knees move like two shiny pebbles under her smooth skin, then looked at her thighs and thought about the warm, damp space hidden between them . . .

Only now do I understand that, while I watched A-Mei being embraced by the arms of the banyan tree, I felt an irrational jealousy, and worried about who else or what else might want to wrap their arms around her. So when she walked through the door, I shot her an angry frown. 'You walk as slowly as a cow.'

'It's such a lovely day,' she said breezily. 'I was just taking my time. It's not as if I had a lecture to run to.'

'Well, I've been waiting here for twenty minutes,' I barked.

If I'd realised that my anger was fuelled by self-doubt, I would have made an effort to control myself.

Another image comes to mind. I see her open mouth and the green pak-choi leaf I'd just placed inside it with my chopsticks glinting between her red-painted lips.

That's enough. Everyone feels nostalgia for things they have lost. Memories are no more than regurgitations of the past. They can't lead you anywhere new. I can tell the sunlight is about to leave the far corner of the window. When it has gone, the room will fall dark.

The heavy rainstorm two nights ago soaked the covered balcony's windowsill and the cotton sheets lying on the ground below it. The air smells dank and mouldy. I myself am soaking in my own urine and excrement. My skin is beginning to decay. Swarms of mosquitoes are sucking at my blood. Flies are crawling into my mouth and nostrils. The moment my heart stops beating, my internal bacteria will multiply and begin to ingest me from within. A few days later, I will be no more than a heap of maggots and bones.

Chemical changes are beginning to take place. I see A-Mei reflected in a distorted mirror. Her face grows longer, splits into two, then disperses like paint in a pool of water. Then I see Tian Yi, Nuwa, Mou Sen and Sister Gao standing close together with big grins on their faces, waiting for me to take a group photograph. Chen Di and Yu Jin are standing behind them. The scarlet Tiananmen Gate in the background becomes a black silhouette which slowly melts like a scorched negative. That shot was on a roll of film I never got developed. Before the negative completely melts away, the image flashes before me one last time. Those memories that seem so sacred will all vanish in the end . . .

I'd like to go to a hotel bathroom, fill a clean bath with hot water and soak in it until I die . . . As my mind begins to empty, the mouse suddenly jumps off the chest of drawers that's crammed with medicine bottles and lands noisily on the ground. It leaps onto my bed, darts up my thigh and stomach and settles on my shoulder. As it flicks its head from side to side in trepidation, its skin rubs against the base of my neck. The sparrow hops off my chest, perches on the bedstead and chirps angrily. The mouse isn't frightened away, though. It nibbles at my sheet for a while then sinks its teeth into my right earlobe. How wonderful. If it bites through a few blood vessels, I will be dead within a matter of hours. When the police took us to Mount Wutai last year during the 4 June anniversary, a mouse bit my finger and the wound didn't heal for two months.

Your brain cells course through your dead flesh like streams of lava spewing down a volcano.

A cool draught blows into the room. It feels as though the front door has been opened, but I didn't hear any noise.

A kid in the yard outside shouts, 'It's snowing, Mum. It's snowing!' He's the son of the migrant labourer who's renting the flat below. I often hear him in the early evening. But it's morning now. He should be at school.

'Snow in July! It must be a show of anger from the gods. How can the police lock people in jail for days without notifying their families?' The man speaking now is the kid's father. He has a southern accent.

'I thought someone was blowing soap bubbles,' another voice says. 'The flakes are tiny. They melt as soon as they touch the ground. But look, the sky over there is still blue.'

'The heavens are showing their anger!' the man says.

'I've heard of snows in August in ancient history. They were seen as signs of the gods' anger at cases of injustice. But I've never heard of it snowing in July before.'

'It's uncanny though, that it should snow now, just a few days after the mass arrest of Falun Gong practitioners.'

'When I went into my kitchen a minute ago, I saw the spring-onion cake I bought this morning was covered in ants. There's definitely something strange going on.'

'The government has outlawed Falun Gong. They've declared it an evil cult and a threat to social stability. So be careful what you say . . . The air really does feel unnaturally cool now.'

'Think about it. In May, the Americans bombed the Chinese Embassy in Belgrade. In June – well we all know what 4 June is the anniversary of. And now in July, Falun Gong has been suppressed. All these events are connected with injustice and death.'

'I wonder what's happened to that vegetable upstairs since his mother got arrested. Has anyone been looking after him?'

'That's the government's business, not ours. It's best if you keep your mouth shut and don't ask any questions. Look, the snowflakes vanish as soon as they touch the ground.'

'But he's been alone for a week now. If he's dead, we'll have to report it to the authorities.'

'Go and tell the public security bureau, then, if you're feeling so brave.'

'Look, that bird keeps flying into their window,' the kid says. 'It must have built a nest in there.'

'Why isn't your son at school today?'

'The school he went to was for children of migrant workers. It was unlicensed and run by volunteers. We don't have a Beijing residency permit, so no state school would accept him. When China's Olympic Bid Committee visited the area last week, they came across the school and told the police to close it down. They're proposing to build a huge "Bird's Nest" sports stadium near here. This whole neighbourhood is going to be razed to the ground.'

'The entire city is being demolished and rebuilt. It's all part of the government's "New Beijing, New Olympic Bid" concept. Our compound will be pulled down soon.'

'The snow's stopped! I barely got a chance to cool down, and already it's getting hot again.'

'The state schools are so expensive now. The one my son goes to is middle-ranking, but the fees are 10,000 yuan a year. I only earn 11,000. How can the government expect people like us to fork out that amount of money? . . .'

The snow gave my neighbours a brief respite from the summer heat, but my room is still swelteringly hot. In the afternoon, the sun beats down on the covered balcony and the temperature rises even higher. When I sense my body start to evaporate at last, I feel as relieved as I did whenever I left the stuffy hospital ward in which my father was dying.

A picture comes to mind. I see a woman in blue trousers standing in our flat with her young child. I think it's a boy. There's a yellow star on his cap, and a dog's face embroidered on the knee of his trousers. The fake leather shoes the woman is wearing are cracked and covered in dust. The woman has no face. All I can see is her claw-like hand touching her son's head. Who is she? The mad wife of my cousin, Dai Dongsheng? Perhaps it's an image cobbled together from scraps of other memories. I have no control over my mind any longer. As I slip into unconsciousness, a series of random scenes flicker before my eyes . . . In the north region of the Great Wastes stands Mount Zhangwei. A giant god with a human face and a snake's body lives on its summit. When he closes his vertical eyes, it's night; when he opens them, it's day. He doesn't eat or sleep or breathe. All he feeds on is the wind and the rain. He shines his light over the dark lands, so they call him the Torch Dragon . . .

Both night and death are approaching. The mosquitoes continue to suck my blood while the internal bacteria start to attack my flesh. The sparrow nestled in my armpit shakes its feathers and prepares to sleep.

I hear two men enter the flat. A beam of torchlight moves across my room.

'Careful, there's a corpse in that room. Come on, let's see what we can find!' It sounds like Gouzi, the electrician who works in the restaurant across the road.

'How could anyone bear to live in this squalor? You said her TV had stereo speakers. Where are they? God, this flat's a tip. What a stench!'

'Look at all these newspapers stacked on her table. This one must be two years old, already. It's got a photograph of Deng Xiaoping's corpse on the front.'

'Search through that pile of cardboard boxes then take a look at the bicycle.'

'Hey, a modem! So the old lady wants to join the internet age, does she?'

'What's in all those plastic bags over there?'

'This book is huge. It's called *Illustrated Edition of The Book of Mountains and Seas*. Do you think it's worth anything?'

'You won't get any money for a book, unless it's a business directory.'

'Aiyaa! There's a mouse under that bed!'

'Here's the microwave oven I was looking for. So this is where she put it . . .'

'Have you got everything? Great. Let's get out of here . . .'

They've probably taken all the goods my mother bought when she was collecting lottery tickets. I can smell, too, that the box of soap powder which has been standing in the corner of the sitting room for the last six years, is no longer here. After they flicked through the *Illustrated Edition of The Book of Mountains and Seas* and my mother's *Mysteries of the World*, they tossed them onto the chest of drawers.

The room is quiet again. If I've remembered correctly, today is my seventh day without food. A small distance separates me from death. I am still living in what Buddhists refer to as the stinking skin-bag of the human body.

I remember one night when my mother tried to shoo the sparrow away, it flew out of the window in terror, and I felt myself break free and drift into the locust tree outside. I was too light to fall to the ground, and not strong enough to fly into the sky, so I just hovered in mid-air, caught like a balloon between two branches.

If anyone were to spend a week locked inside his own body, he would choose to run away, even if the only escape route available was death.

Flesh-eating cells gnaw at you. Your organs disconnect and drift apart.

My mother must have been released from detention an hour or so before dawn. She plods back into the flat in a daze and throws herself onto the sofa, without bothering to turn on the light or even shut the door.

She is as silent as a corpse. A sour, grimy smell wafts from her hair. I think she's passed out.

When the sun begins to light up the sky, the sparrow chirrups. My mother stirs and lets out a deep sigh. She walks into my room, stands silently at the door like a stranger, then walks out again.

I've been alone for a week, but am still not dead. I feel guilty for having let my mother down.

There is a mountain called Mount Wilderness, where the sun and the moon set. The people who live there have three faces: one at the front and one on either side. These three-faced people never die.

After the rain, the sky cleared.

The crowd outside the broadcast tent became agitated. Shan Bo, the Beijing Normal teacher, stepped out of the hunger strike tent and squeezed through the throng holding an open letter he wanted to read out. Wang Fei followed behind him, with a megaphone in one hand and a walkie-talkie in the other.

'The broadcast station is the command centre now,' Lin Lu whispered to Bai Ling, switching off his walkie-talkie. 'We can't allow the intellectuals to jump up and say what they want.'

'Why not?' Zhou Suo asked.

'They have no idea how volatile the mood is in the Square. If he reads out his letter, it might trigger a riot.' Lin Lu's mouth twisted into a worried smirk.

'Let him say what he has to say, then take him straight back to the hunger strike tent,' Bai Ling said.

Mimi dragged the three microphones outside and handed them to Shan Bo.

Shan Bo held up the letter and began reading it out: 'We four intellectuals came to the Square to show the world that we too are prepared to put our lives on the line to fight for democracy. We oppose martial law and support your demands for an equal dialogue with the government. But recently we have noticed that despite your good intentions, your movement has become riven with division. It is now badly organised and dangerously undemocratic. If military dictatorship is replaced by student dictatorship, the Democracy Movement will have come to nothing . . .' Wu Bin jumped onto a box and shouted through a megaphone, 'Teacher Shan Bo, we admire you for going on hunger strike. But how can you come here, at this crucial moment, and try to sow discord among the students?'

'Lin Lu, quickly tell Shan Bo to return to his tent,' Bai Ling said crossly.

Before Wu Bin had finished speaking, voices in the crowd shouted,

'Spineless intellectuals! Traitors! If you don't have the balls to continue your hunger strike get out of the Square!'

At this, Shan Bo angrily rolled up his letter, threw it over to Lin Lu and stuttered, 'You will, re-re-regret not listening to me!' then stormed back to his tent.

Lin Lu grabbed a microphone and said, 'Fellow students, in this final hour, let us gather round the Monument to the People's Heroes and allow history to pass its judgement on us. When the army comes to attack us, we will remain peaceful and non-violent . . .'

In the distance, Ke Xi was moving through a crowd on the shoulders of his bodyguard, shouting, 'Fellow students and Beijing citizens! This is our bleakest moment. We can't give up now! In perseverance lies victory!' The crowd roared in support. An hour before, he'd been advocating a mass withdrawal.

The student marshals who'd been guarding the base of the Monument began to disperse. Some went to stand in a protective circle around the hunger strike tent. Apart from the broadcast station and the Taiwanese rock star, Hou Dejian, there wasn't much else left in the Square that needed to be cordoned off.

Wang Fei suggested we hold one final press conference urging the foreign media to stay in the Square to witness the crackdown. Old Fu walked over with some students from his finance office. He agreed to stay, but said we should persuade the girls to leave.

As I set off to go and find Mou Sen, Yanyan walked up to me and said that Ge You, our old friend from Southern University, had travelled up from Shenzhen to give us another big donation.

'That's good news,' I said. 'Mou Sen will need more money for his Democracy University.'

She forced a smile then walked away and disappeared down the pedestrian underpass. I wondered if Mou Sen had spoken to her about Nuwa yet. She'd probably seen the photograph of their Tiananmen Square wedding. It had been printed in all the newspapers.

The broadcast station played a tape of the Internationale. The sound was louder and cracklier than usual. Everyone in the Square sang along. The announcements blaring from the government speakers on the lamp posts had become louder too, and the echoes added to the din.

'Where can I get my batteries recharged?' Wang Fei asked, walking into the tent. 'My walkie-talkie isn't working.'

'Don't use it, then!' I said. 'And keep it in your pocket. If the soldiers see you carrying it, they'll shoot you!'

'They can shoot me if they like. I don't care! My body is made of steel.' The black paint of his megaphone was badly chipped.

Bai Ling sat down and spoke into the microphone. 'This is commander-in-chief Bai Ling speaking. On behalf of the Defend Tiananmen Square Headquarters, I would like to ask everyone who is committed to defending the Square to stand up now.'

Everyone fell silent. The students sitting in the plastic shelters stepped outside to see what was going on. The atmosphere was very tense.

'. . . Please raise your right hands, face the Monument to the People's Heroes and say after me: "They may cut off our heads and make us bleed to death, but we will never give up our fight for democracy!" Although surrounded by residents, tourists and even plain-clothes policemen, the students who raised their right hands ignored all distractions and focused on the solemn oath.

In the last glow before dark, I watched the crowds rush frantically back and forth between Chairman Mao's portrait and the white Goddess of Democracy. They looked like swarms of nervous ants sensing the impending approach of a tidal wave.

West of the Beast With Nine Heads is a tree that never dies. If a man eats it, he will live a long life. There is another sacred tree that, when eaten, can bestow wisdom.

When dusk falls, the noises outside drift towards my iron bed, then everything goes dark.

My mother drags herself like an old cloth bag from the sitting room into the bedroom and slumps onto her bed. There's a lot of phlegm in her throat. I can hear it move when she breathes. She's fallen asleep now. Apart from an occasional crinkling of a plastic bag in the kitchen, the flat is deathly silent.

It's the same kind of silence that pervaded the flat when we returned home from the cemetery after my father was cremated. Dusk had fallen, just like now. I hadn't heard any noise from my mother for a long time, so I quietly opened her door and peeped inside. She was sitting on the chair, fast asleep, her hands hanging limply on either side. A slanting beam of light from the lamp beside her illuminated the wrinkles around her eyes. Her brightly patterned shirt didn't match the look of despair on her face. She was perfectly still. For a moment I thought she'd followed my father into the netherworld.

The room is pitch black now. The last gleams of light have left the windows.

Nights without birdsong feel empty . . . Tian Yi often talked about the red-breasted cuckoo we saw flitting through the rainforest in

Yunnan. 'Why didn't I take a photo of it,' she would say to me. 'I had my camera in my hand . . .'

Today is 1 October 1999 – the fiftieth anniversary of the founding of the People's Republic of China. So as to ensure the celebrations are clean and orderly, the police have arrested thousands of illegal migrant workers and scruffy-looking peasants who've travelled to the capital to lodge complaints, and have locked them in detention centres in the suburbs. The restaurants in this street were raided, and they have now lost half their staff. Every flat in the compound has been inundated with leaflets from the National Day Organising Committee telling the occupants not to accommodate guests from other provinces during the week of the celebrations.

When the parade passed through the city today, no one in the flats, restaurants or shops lining the route was allowed to look out of their windows. If anyone was spotted even standing by a window, they were arrested immediately. So that the government leaders can view tonight's Tiananmen Square pageant in safety, all residents have been asked to stay at home and watch the event on television.

This morning, the municipal government sent a team of workers to spray green paint over any bare patches in the grassed areas along the route. The only people in the yard outside now are the policemen guarding the entrances to the apartment buildings. Our phone was cut off three days ago. My mother visited the caretaker countless times asking for it be reconnected, but he told her there was nothing he could do. I presume it won't get reconnected until after midnight, when the fireworks have been let off and the celebrations have come to an end.

'His armpits are completely rotten,' my mother mutters in her sleep. 'I've run out of alcohol swabs.'

In the two months since my mother was released from the detention centre, her voice seems to have aged a lot. Instead of offering her a path to salvation, Falun Gong has sucked her life force away. She hardly says a word to me any more. Occasionally I'm able to glean some information from her telephone conversations. I know that, in order to be allowed to return home to look after me, she wrote a statement renouncing Falun Gong and gave the police the names of her Falun Gong friends. I also know that while she was in detention, she was unable to sleep, and that her left arm broke when the police attacked her with electric batons. She's still unable to lift it up.

When she turned on the radio yesterday and heard the sentences that have been issued to a group of key Falun Gong practitioners following a trial at the Beijing Intermediate People's Court, my mother's opera-trained voice howled with despair. Among the names listed was Master Yao. He's been sentenced to a fixed term of eighteen years' imprisonment, with deprivation of political rights for a subsequent ten years.

She often paces nervously around the flat, especially late at night. Sometimes she stands at the window and gazes out, listening to the distant roar of machinery as buildings are demolished or constructed, and mumbles, 'They'll be here any minute. They're coming to arrest us. It won't be long now . . .' Then she turns off the dripping tap in the kitchen and sneaks outside into the corridor to see if there's anyone coming.

When my brother phoned the other day, she kept repeating that Falun Gong is evil and dangerous and that she will never practise it again, and that all she wants now is to be a good mother and upstanding citizen.

My brother didn't detect the change in my mother's voice. He just told her to take care of herself, and promised to send another £500 at the end of the month. He doesn't know that in two months' time, this flat will no longer be here.

She often shouts at the sparrow, scolding it for eating too much millet or for dropping its shit on her bed. Sometimes she tells it that, when its feathers regrow in spring, it should fly away to America. Occasionally, she proclaims that the sparrow is a reincarnated Bodhisattva endowed with the roots of goodness, then she lights a stick of incense and prostrates herself at its feet.

In the north of the Land Beyond The Seas, a female rainbow and a male rainbow are locked in an embrace. Both have human heads at each end.

My mother and I listen to the commotion outside while we hide in our flat like snails in their shells.

The Handover of Macao is just two days away now, but the neighbourhood committee hasn't invited my mother's fan-dance troupe to perform in the street party. Six Falun Gong practitioners in the neighbourhood have been sent to re-education-through-labour camps. Granny Pang was released from the detention centre at the same time as my mother. Her family have kept her locked inside her flat ever since.

My mother doesn't bother to speak to me. She's come to the conclusion that I'm incapable of reacting to outside stimuli. I'm not sure if I'm able to react to internal stimuli any more either. My body chemistry no longer seems to respond to my emotional moods. If plants were capable of having thoughts, I wonder if they'd be able to sense the sadness of their roots and branches.

My mother has shut herself in the flat, and is secretly going through a Falun Gong exercise routine. Before she comes to the end of it, she chants quietly: 'Sentient beings have been destroyed by their corrupt ways. Only the Great Law can save them from the chaos. They confuse good and evil as they slander heaven. The autumn winds will sweep them away . . .'

Granny Pang has finally found a chance to slip out of her flat. Since she took up Falun Gong, she's been able to climb the stairs much more quickly.

'Let me in, Huizhen . . .' she whispers. 'Thank you. I can't take it any more. My family watches me the whole time. If I so much as lift my hand, my son thinks I'm about to start a Falun Gong exercise and beats it down again. What can I do? You're so lucky to live alone. You can meditate whenever you want . . .'

'They've confiscated all my instruction tapes and books, so I can only repeat the routines I remember.'

'My son's wife has stuck the Ministry of State Security's "Six Rules" notice above my bed. It says that no one's allowed to display Falun Gong symbols, perform the exercises in public, gather in groups or petition the authorities. She's told me to learn it off by heart. My family is worse than the police. Still, when I close my eyes, I can practise the routines in my mind, and they have no idea what I'm up to.' Granny Pang spent her life reporting people to the police, but she's become a much kinder person since she's taken up Falun Gong.

She moves closer to my mother and whispers, 'I think my Third Eye has opened. Yesterday, this spot between my eyebrows became like a chimney. I looked through it and saw Master Li Hongzhi sitting on a lotus flower, then rising into the sky. Then I saw the construction workers walking around the room on the other side of my wall.'

'Yes, that's definitely your Third Eye. You can see the future through it as well. Quickly, tell me what my son's future is.'

'He – he seems to be sitting up with his eyes closed.'

'He's not flying into the sky on the back of a sparrow, is he?'

'The future is hard to see . . . That Bodhisattva figurine is shaking. I think you should put it away. Master Li Hongzhi said that Falun Gong practitioners shouldn't worship the Buddha. I can't look at that figurine any longer. It's giving me a headache . . .'

'It's the noise of the construction work that's giving you the headache, not the figurine. Old Yao gave it to me. I can't move it . . . Someone's just given me a video called *Five Falun Gong Routines*.

Do you want to watch it with me? I haven't felt my Falun wheel turn for some time.'

'No, I must go. My daughter-in-law will be returning from the shops soon. She thought I was having a nap. If she finds out I've come up here, she'll be furious.'

'Huh! We never get to see each other any more. When I do phone someone from our group, all I hear about is who's been arrested, or who's just died in prison. There's never any good news. It's not the same doing the routines on my own. But if I don't do them every day, my body doesn't feel right.'

'The weather's turning cold. I made these padded trousers for myself, but since my family won't let me out of the flat, they're no use to me now, so I thought you might like them. If you get a chance to go to the park to practise some routines, they might come in handy. Has Officer Liu come up today?'

'No. What questions has he been asking you?'

'All the usual ones: who have I been in contact with, who do I know who took part in the 25 April Zhongnanhai siege and the 20 July protests, am I hiding any Falun Gong banners . . . Before he left, he mentioned that lots of people from out of town have been demonstrating in Tiananmen Square these past few days, and that I shouldn't leave my flat or accommodate any practitioners who've travelled up from the provinces . . .' Granny Pang is still a little out of breath. 'Stay on your guard tonight. I've heard there's going to be another spate of arrests.'

'It's worse than the Cultural Revolution. If more than five Falun Gong practitioners of a province travel to Beijing to complain to the central authorities, the provincial governor is sacked. So the provincial authorities send police to the train stations to stop anyone suspected of being a Falun Gong member from boarding the trains. If the practitioners resist, the police beat them to death. My son Dai Ru phoned me the other day and told me many such stories he'd read in the British press . . . Huh, there's nothing we can do. We just have to be careful.'

'I've been careful all my life. How is it that, just by practising a few meditation exercises, I've got myself into so much trouble with the government?'

'My life has been dogged by one political campaign after another, so I'm used to it. Old Yao's in prison now. He'll probably stay there until the day he dies . . .' My mother starts sobbing quietly then breaks into floods of tears. 'We really have reached the "End Time"!' she cries. 'There's no Pure Land on this earth. We must strive for spiritual perfection so that we can leave this world behind and fly into the sky . . .' She goes to the kitchen to wash her face, then returns to the sofa and changes the subject. 'Your son's bar in the Sanlitun embassy area must be doing very well. Foreigners like to spend a lot of money.'

'No, that street is crammed with bars now, so there's a lot of competition,' Granny Pang says. 'He's poured all 30,000 yuan of his redundancy money into his bar, but it still isn't making a profit . . . They're pulling down this building next month. Have you found a cheap place to move into yet?'

'I haven't bothered to look for one. Dai Wei and I won't be alive for much longer. What difference does it make where we live?'

Two hundred li further north stands Mount Guyao, on which the Lord of Heaven's daughter died. Her name was Female Corpse. After she was buried, she became a plant that has dense foliage and yellow flowers. If a woman eats the fruit of the plant, her face will become more beautiful.

'Let's hold the opening ceremony straight away. We can't wait for the stage to arrive. The reporters and guests are all here.' It was evening now, but Mou Sen's face was covered in sweat. His long hair looked freshly washed.

'The factory you commissioned to make the stage is probably too scared to deliver it,' I said. 'Let's just pull some tables over here and make a temporary stage. The martial law troops have already reached the western end of Changan Avenue. Where have you been, by the way? Ge You has been looking for you. He's got another donation to give you.'

'Nuwa and I went to a hotel to take a shower,' he said, raising his eyebrows suggestively, wanting us all to know that he'd just made love to his new bride.

'You bastard. So, how was it?' I could smell a scent of soap wafting from his goatee.

'I tell you, I could die a happy man now! I'm starving! Is there anything to eat?'

I finished painting the words DEMOCRACY UNIVERSITY'S OPENING CEREMONY on a long white banner, then went off with Tang Guoxian to lug some tables over from the Monument. We wanted to set up the stage at the foot of the Goddess of Democracy, but some provincial students had put up a tent there.

I went inside and asked them to budge. They were drinking and smoking.

'Move our tent for you? Of course it's not all right with us!' they said, then pushed me out as though I was a trespasser.

'I gave you this tent!' I shouted. 'I'm head of security. We want to hold the Democracy University's opening ceremony here tonight. Can't you please just shift your tent over to the right a bit?'

'You think that just because you're some high official you can push the rest of us around! Go and read up a bit on democracy before you come in here again. You don't offer us anything to eat or drink. You just expect us to move our tent out of the goodness of our hearts. Well, it's not going to happen!' They pushed me out again and zipped up their nylon door.

'This is too much!' Mou Sen shouted, having joined me outside their tent. 'If you want something to eat, go to the Hong Kong students' provisions stall. They've got bread and cartons of soft drink. All I can give you are pamphlets.'

'You can say what you like, Mr Security Chief. I'm the tent chief, and I tell you, we're not moving!'

'You'll move pretty fast when the martial law troops turn up!' Tang Guoxian said, squatting down outside the tent's door. 'And besides, the Headquarters has asked everyone to leave their tents now and stay on the Monument.'

'We won't run away when the army turns up!' one of the guys inside shouted. 'We're here now, and we're not moving.'

'Don't waste your time arguing with them,' Nuwa said to Mou Sen, rushing over in a fluster. 'Let's put the stage up on the east side of the Goddess instead. The reporters keep asking me whether the ceremony's going ahead or not. I can't make them wait any longer.'

Xiao Li was setting up the amplifiers and diesel generator. I asked him how his head was, and he said the wound had stopped bleeding and he felt much better. Then he picked up a radio cassette player and said, 'Look what we've just been given! It's got a double cassette deck, a digital display and an automatic tuner. Even the Voice of America sounds crystal clear on it.'

I'd seen cassette players like that three years before in Guangzhou. Xiao Li had never had a chance to travel. The only places he knew were his home village and Beijing.

'Here's the red sash and the scissors for the opening ceremony,' Tian Yi said, handing them to Nuwa. She was still busy trying to find some last-minute guests to attend the event.

I fetched the banner I'd just made and tied one end to the scaffolding at the base of the Goddess of Democracy and the other to a lamp post.

The recorded announcement came over the government speakers

once more: 'A counter-revolutionary riot has broken out in Beijing tonight. Everyone in the Square must leave immediately. If you fail to leave, the martial law troops will have to remove you by force!'

'Where's this counter-revolutionary riot they're talking about?' Tian Yi asked, looking up at me.

'The government has probably given guns to the students and citizens, then taken photographs of them, so they can claim there's been an armed rebellion,' I said.

'Stop trying to frighten me,' she said.

'It's nine o'clock already, and Professor Yan Jia still hasn't turned up,' Nuwa said. 'What are we going to do?' Her cheeks were red and there was a smudge of black ink at the edge of her mouth.

'Go and talk to the other guests,' Tian Yi replied. 'See if any of them will stand in for him. They only need to say a few words.'

'Wasn't Yan Jia the guy who told us that Deng Xiaoping had resigned?' Xiao Li said. 'Why has he been made honorary president?'

'His sources had been mistaken,' Tian Yi said. 'It wasn't his fault. He's a well-respected political scientist. We're lucky that he's agreed to get involved.'

At last everything was ready. The guests and reporters were invited to gather round the stage we'd constructed from the eight tables. The red sash, which we'd tied in the middle in a decorative knot, was lying at the front of the stage, ready to be cut.

Tian Yi stood on a chair and shouted, 'Please can all the students who've enrolled in the Democracy University come and take your places. The opening ceremony is about to start . . .'

A crowd slowly assembled behind the guests and journalists in the large cordoned-off area in front of the stage. The huge Goddess of Democracy towering above us made me feel as though we were making history.

The only student marshals left in the Square belonged to Tang Guoxian's small security squad. Fortunately, everyone was behaving in an orderly manner. No outsiders attempted to climb over the security cordon.

'Is Bai Ling coming?' Tian Yi asked, beads of sweat breaking out on her forehead.

'Liu Gang's gone to fetch her. Why? What's the matter?'

'I overheard that journalist in the black T-shirt say that soldiers in the western districts have opened fire. He's photographed the corpses of students and citizens. The army is shooting to kill!' Tian Yi bit her lower lip. There was terror in her eyes.

'We've got a huge crowd standing here. If panic breaks out and there's a sudden stampede, people will get trampled to death. We must tell Mou Sen to hurry up and get the ceremony over with. As soon as it's finished, we'll move everyone back to the Monument. Most of this crowd are standing on Changan Avenue. The army tanks will be rolling straight down there in a couple of hours . . . Don't worry, Tian Yi. I'll look after you.' I took her hand. It was as cold and clammy as it had been when the thugs found us in the woods of the Summer Palace. There was a damp, scrunched-up tissue in her palm.

'I want a drink of water. I feel sick.' She looked up and removed the sunglasses from my face. She hated me wearing them when it was dark.

I ran over to Mou Sen and said that any guests who hadn't turned up yet were probably trapped behind the roadblocks, so he should stop waiting for them and get on with the ceremony.

Bai Ling hurried over with Old Fu, and said, 'We've just gone through the latest reports we've received from the intersections. The army are coming to clear the Square. They're shooting their way through the city, crashing over the barricades in armoured personnel carriers.'

'Whatever happens, this ceremony must go ahead!' Mou Sen said, his eyes blazing with determination.

Yu Jin ran up to us. His clothes were splattered with blood. 'Look, I picked up this bullet cartridge myself. The soldiers are shooting to kill. They lifted their guns and sprayed the streets with bullets, then tens of bodies dropped to the ground. My racing bike was crushed flat by the wheels of a tank.'

We stared at him in disbelief, and he stared back at me, his eyes wide open.

'If you see any student marshals, tell them to go to the Monument,' I said to him. I searched my pockets for my sunglasses, then remembered that Tian Yi had taken them.

Mou Sen walked up to Bai Ling and said, 'Professor Yan Jia still hasn't turned up yet. Would you stand in for him and cut our red sash?' Then he said to Tian Yi, 'Quickly, make a final announcement calling all those students in the trucks blocking Changan Avenue to come and attend the Democracy University's opening ceremony.'

Tian Yi stepped onto the stage, gripping a microphone nervously in her hand and said, 'Please will all the students come to the Democracy University to attend the trucks blocking Changan Avenue.'

'Oh, that's too much!' hissed Mou Sen, annoyed at her slip-up. He went over and whispered to her, 'I said: attend the opening ceremony, not the trucks!'

Tian Yi put the microphone to her lips again and blurted out, 'I mean, everyone must go to the trucks, not attend them!'

Mou Sen jumped onto the stage and took the microphone from her. I went over and helped Tian Yi down. Her legs were shaking. She looked as though she was about to faint. 'Give me some water,' she said, closing her eyes.

Mou Sen lifted the microphone, and in his loudest voice, cried, 'We don't want you to go to the trucks. We want everyone to come here and enrol in our University of Democracy. We will defend Tiananmen Square to the end, and continue our campaign of peaceful resistance. I now declare the Democracy University officially open. Can I ask Bai Ling to step up and cut the sash? Come on, Bai Ling!'

Bai Ling straightened her back and stepped up onto the stage, her small breasts shaking as she moved. She wrapped her hands around the scissors Mou Sen was holding, and together they cut through the decorative knot of the red silk sash. As they raised the severed sash into the air, the crowd burst into applause and a thousand camera flashes went off.

Tian Yi had calmed down a little. She squeezed my hand and said, 'Promise you won't leave me.'

'Don't worry. If the enemy advances, we'll retreat. We don't have to throw ourselves onto the machine guns like that patriotic Chinese soldier in the Korean War.' There were at least 10,000 people crowded around the stage now. Nuwa was standing beside Mou Sen, translating into Chinese the speech a foreign guest was giving. The high-heeled red leather sandals she was wearing made her legs look elegant.

'And now let our classes begin!' Mou Sen said, smoothing back his long sweaty hair.

As the crowd roared their applause again, a stern announcement blasted from every government speaker in the Square. 'We repeat again, the inauguration of the Democracy University has not been approved by the State Education Committee. The instigators must be prepared to take legal responsibility for their actions . . .' The voice echoed menacingly through the Square, seemingly trying to prove that even the air above us belonged to the Party.

The distant gunfire sounded like a string of firecrackers exploding. I felt as though we were live crabs being tossed inside a scorching wok.

Mou Sen was still delivering his speech. '. . . Chairman Mao said that the People's Liberation Army is a school, but did the State Education Committee approve its inauguration? The Party trains the army to suppress the people. We will train democrats to serve the nation! Tiananmen Square is our lecture hall. The rest of this vast nation is our campus. We don't need the approval of any bloody education committee to establish our university!' The crowd laughed approvingly.

'All right, fellow students,' Nuwa said. 'Now I will ask Bai Ling to read out a message of congratulations from the Defend Tiananmen Square Headquarters. Let's all give her another round of applause!' She looked like a television presenter as she paced gracefully across the stage. The high heels of her red sandals were causing the skin at the back of her feet to wrinkle.

The longer Bai Ling spoke, the wider her eyes became. 'Once this period of darkness is over, we will witness the emergence of a democratic republic, and all our efforts will come to fruition . . .'

As soon as Mou Sen stepped off the stage, Yan Jia, the Democracy University's honorary president, turned up with his wife. Nuwa was so relieved she burst into tears. 'We sent three people out to look for you. How wonderful that you made it! Once the representatives from the intellectual circles have read out their messages of congratulations, we'd like to invite you to give our first lecture!'

The light from the two spotlights powered by the diesel generator was dazzlingly bright one minute and a dim glow the next. The generator we'd used a couple of days before for the unveiling ceremony of the Goddess of Democracy had been much better.

Although people were frantically rushing across the rest of the Square, the audience in front of the stage listened quietly to Yan Jia's lecture, breaking into respectful applause from time to time.

Whenever a flash went off, everyone tensed up, mistaking it for a gunshot. I stood at a distance from the crowd and kept an eye on the four corners of the Square, watching for any signs of trouble.

By the time Mou Sen announced that the opening ceremony was over, there were still more than two thousand people crowded around the stage.

I helped Xiao Li remove the spotlights and generator and roll up my banner. The city residents who were reluctant to leave converged in small groups to discuss what they'd heard. 'So *that's* what democracy is about,' one man said. 'I didn't realise we'd have to overthrow the Communist Party to achieve it . . .'

'They stand here and talk about democracy while the army tanks are rolling towards them. They think they can change this country. They're so naïve. We told them to leave the Square weeks ago, but they wouldn't listen . . .'

A few members of the Workers' Federation's Dare-to-Die Squad, all wearing red armbands, ran over to us and shouted, 'The soldiers are killing people in West Changan Avenue. The citizens need our help. Come on, everyone, let's go. We'll fight those bastards to the death . . .'

You look down at your bed, as though observing the earth from space.

'Wake up! Open your eyes!' my mother cries, banging my iron bedstead. 'I can't go on like this! I've had enough. Enough! I can't take it any more. If you don't hurry up and die, I'll kill myself. I'll jump off the roof. I'll gas myself, hang myself, swallow a bottle of pesticide. I'll cut my wrists . . .' She grabs my sheet and buries her head in it. I hear a muffled scream that sounds like straw crackling in a cotton bag.

Then she stands up and lets out wild, warbling howls. She inhales a breath of air, rasping, 'Will you never die?' then on her outbreath wails, 'You useless lump of wood . . .' Her words float through the dust that's blowing in from the demolition site outside. 'I'll burn this flat down, I'll . . .'

A neighbour bangs on the door. 'Auntie, let me in . . .'

The sparrow is startled. It snuggles into the nape of my neck. It has rubbed itself against my skin so often over the last days that many of its feathers have fallen off, and it now has difficulty flying.

There are three people yelling on the landing. Their cries echo through the stairwell. Still sobbing and shaking, my mother slowly opens the door.

'. . . You must face up to reality, Auntie. Stop burying your head in the sand. Ask your younger son to come back and look after you. It's not his money you need now, it's his help.' This is the neighbour who sells exercise equipment. My mother takes her into her bedroom. The two other neighbours who followed her in are standing in the sitting room.

'Why not pay someone to look after him? Or send him to a care home?'

'I employed a girl to help out, but she left after two days. She said he looked like a corpse and was afraid to touch him.'

'This is a two-bedroom flat, isn't it? Why is it in such a state? It looks like a junk shop.'

Police officers used to raid this flat all the time. But it's so squalid now, they refuse to come, even if they're bribed with large bonuses. They say the flat smells so bad that for days after they visit, they can't wash the stench of it from their skin.

'I'm fine,' my mother says quietly. 'Just a little fed up, that's all.'

'You must take care of yourself. That younger son of yours is so selfish. How could he move abroad and leave you to cope with all this?'

'I haven't told him about the demolition yet.'

'You should have. It won't be easy, buying a new flat and moving house on your own.'

'I'm not moving. If the government doesn't give me proper compensation, I won't budge. I've given fifty years of my life to the Party. They can't turn me out onto the streets.'

'Listen, Auntie. You and I are just ordinary citizens. You can't refuse to move. Government officials will turn up here and squash you like a fly. And anyway, this demolition is important for our Olympic bid. If the old buildings aren't torn down, the new ones can't go up.'

'What have the bloody Olympics got to do with me? . . . I'm getting old now. There's nothing left for me to live for . . .'

'You've been through worse than this, Auntie . . . Once that plank of wood has died, you can apply for a passport and go abroad.'

The two other neighbours walk into my room and look at me. 'It's incredible to think that this vegetable's urine was able to cure so many sick people . . .'

'He looks dead! He's lost all his hair.'

'It's a crime to keep him alive. She should send him to the crematorium and be done with it.'

'Don't say that. It will bring you bad luck. And besides, who knows, if the government rehabilitates him one day, he might become some kind of hero.'

'When are you moving out? Did you end up buying that flat in the Fragrant Garden compound?'

'No, it was too expensive. I've heard the government is planning to build some cheap flats for low-income families not far from here, so I'll wait and buy one of those.'

'Well, you won't be able to afford even them. Property prices between the second and third ring roads have risen to six thousand yuan a square meter. This compound is inside the second ring road, but the Hong Kong developer is only giving us five thousand yuan a square metre. He's very crafty. He's put his Chinese wife in charge of the project. She grew up in this district, apparently, and has connections with top officials. A lot of the money that should have gone to us has been spent on bribes. They cut off the electricity and water in the west side of the compound yesterday, and have started pulling down the buildings over there. The provisions store has already been demolished.'

'I've seen the plans. They're going to raze the compound to the ground and build a huge shopping centre. There'll be an open square, right where this building is, with trees around the perimeter and a tall fountain in the middle. It will be the most luxurious shopping centre in Beijing. They're such crooks, fobbing us off with just five thousand yuan a square metre.'

'You should pop up for a chat some time. My husband often goes away on business. I've got a Mahjong set. We could ask two other neighbours to join us and have a game . . .'

'. . . I'm fine, really, there's no need to worry . . .' my mother says, walking into the sitting room. She sounds much calmer now.

They leave the flat and close the door behind them, cutting out some of the loud chugging noise from the diesel generator that's powering the machines outside. My mother sits down. In the distance, I hear bulldozers thud into the brick apartment blocks.

The black sky drags me out of the window . . . So this building will become a public square. Ten years ago, I escaped from the nation's political centre and retreated into my home. But soon my home will become a shopping centre. Where can I retreat to then?

You wade towards the middle of a lake. The water is getting deeper and deeper.

'Where are you thinking of taking me?' Tian Yi asked. 'I'm not leaving the Square.' Her face was pale.

I took some string from my pocket. 'If there's a stampede, we could lose our shoes. Let's tie them on with this.'

'No, don't bother. That string won't keep them on.' She looked down at her black court shoes. She was probably afraid that the string would make her look foolish. She tightened her ponytail and pulled it through the hole at the back of her baseball cap.

There was a distant sound of gunfire in the east and west. Mou Sen asked some Beijing Normal students to take most of our electrical equipment back to their campus. Then he and Nuwa sat on the stage and stared at the scattered crowds.

Two foreign journalists began to interview Nuwa in English. While answering their questions, she looked into the distance and fiddled with a lock of her hair.

'You must burn the Democracy University's enrolment list,' I said to Mou Sen. 'The troops moving in from the east and west will converge here soon. You should take Nuwa and Tian Yi back to Beijing Normal. The roads to Beijing University have probably been sealed by now.' Then I asked Tian Yi to give me my sunglasses, but she said she didn't have them.

Mou Sen pulled his cigarette pack from his coat pocket, found it was empty and flung it on the ground. 'I can't leave the Square while the

Beijing Normal flag is still flying. But I'll get someone to take our minutes and scripts back to my dorm. I'll need them when I'm writing my novel.'

When the interview was over, Nuwa turned to Mou Sen and said, 'You shouldn't throw your rubbish on the ground like that.' Then she leaned against him and whispered, 'I can see you're anxious. Don't worry. I'll stay with you. If they put you in jail, I'll sit outside the prison gates and go on hunger strike . . . What were you doing with that pack of cigarettes, anyway? I thought you'd given up smoking.'

'I'm not anxious. I'm disappointed. The Democracy University has only just got off the ground and now I have to close it down.'

Nuwa ran her fingers through his hair and said in English, '*Your speech was wonderful, my darling. You are a hero. I love you.*' When Nuwa smiled, my eyes were always drawn to the red curve of her mouth.

'We've had it,' he said, his shoulders hunched forward in despair. 'The soldiers are firing bullets. Real bullets.'

'Don't worry, this is the darkness before dawn,' Nuwa said. 'Good always prevails over evil.'

Mou Sen swept back his sweaty fringe and said, 'You and Tian Yi should leave now and go back to my campus.'

'I'm not going – *if you're not afraid, then neither am I*,' Nuwa said, slipping into English again.

Zhang Jie and Xiao Li came over and told us that Tang Guoxian had gone to the Workers' Federation's tent to join the Dare-to-Die Squad.

'I now officially declare the Democracy University dissolved,' Mou Sen said. Then he looked at Xiao Li and said, 'Go and join Bai Ling on the upper terrace. It's safer there.'

'No, I want to stay down here and keep an eye on things.' Xiao Li was now wearing a baseball cap over the bloodstained cloth tied around his wounded head.

'Shu Tong shouldn't have deserted us,' Mou Sen said. 'He'll regret it for the rest of his life.'

'Come on, let's go to the Monument,' I said, taking Tian Yi's hand. 'We can't stay out here like disbanded soldiers. Come with us, Mou Sen. The army tanks will be rolling up here any minute.'

'It's too much. Has anyone got any fags?' When Mou Sen looked up at me, his forehead became lined with wrinkles.

I reached into my pocket and gave him my packet of filter cigarettes. 'There are only two left. Don't smoke them all at once.' Then I grabbed Tian Yi's hand again and took her back to the Monument.

On the Mountain of the Empty Mulberry Tree two hundred li north lives a wild beast that resembles an ox, but has the markings of a tiger. Its roar sounds like a human groaning in pain. Whenever this beast appears, a disaster will befall the land.

Almost everyone had retreated onto the Monument now. The rest of the Square was empty. I wondered where my brother was. I was worried. I didn't want anything to happen to him.

A large mob had surrounded Bai Ling and Old Fu at the base of the Monument and had pushed Bai Ling's two bodyguards away.

'Dai Wei! Help me pull Bai Ling out!' Big Chan yelled, waving to me.

I squeezed my way through. Angry students were pointing knives, guns and metal rods at Bai Ling's face and shouting, 'You want us to withdraw? We'll kill you first! Do you know how many people have already sacrificed their lives for us tonight?'

A guy in a black vest was holding a gun to Bai Ling's head. 'Don't listen to them. Tell the students to withdraw from the Square now, or I'll shoot you. Enough people have died already.'

I had no weapons on me, so I didn't dare fight them. All I said was, 'There's no use attacking Bai Ling. The decision about whether to remain or withdraw won't be hers alone.'

A factory worker who had a wooden stick in his hand and a knife stuck in his belt said, 'I'll slit the throat of anyone who dares leave the Square!'

Tian Yi squeezed through, grabbed Bai Ling's hand and shouted, 'What are you thinking of, pointing a gun at a woman? Get out of here!'

'Instead of attacking us, why not go and help the students who are getting injured at the barricades?' Old Fu shouted.

The mob fell silent. As we pushed our way out, they cleared a path for us. Once we were free, we raced to the Monument's upper terrace. When we got there, Bai Ling and Tian Yi slumped to the ground and burst into tears.

'Where've you been, you two?' Mimi said to them, stamping her foot in anger. 'The Monument's in chaos.'

'We'll have to do our broadcasts from up here now,' Chen Di said, tugging the long lead of the microphone he'd just brought up. The broadcast station tent below was now surrounded by an impenetrable crowd.

'Where can we escape to when the army arrives?' Big Chan and Little Chan asked, walking over to me

I glanced around the terrace. A few foreign journalists were still milling about taking photographs of us. The students had instinctively huddled together, like fish that form a tight shoal when they sense the approach of a shark. The hunger strike tent stood in the centre of the terrace, peaceful as the eye of a storm. Everyone had forgotten about the three intellectuals and the famous rock star who were inside it.

I walked over to the tent, lifted the plastic curtain and peeped in. Shan Bo was lying down, his head resting on his girlfriend's lap. The economist Zi Duo was lying flat on his stomach, while his girlfriend massaged his back. I couldn't understand how they could lie so calmly while the sound of distant gunfire echoed through the Square.

Liu Gang was standing with Hai Feng and some other Beijing University students near the sculptured frieze at the base of the obelisk. 'We're enclosed within an outer circle of soldiers who want to drive us from the Square, and an inner circle of students and residents who refuse to let us leave. We're trapped. All we can do now is wait here until the soldiers drag us away.' He stamped on a basket of fresh flowers that had been crushed into the paving stones.

'Let's see what the four intellectuals think we should do,' Hai Feng said, walking over to the hunger strike tent.

Wu Bin was with a gang of six or seven guys, all wearing red armbands and holding metal rods or wooden sticks. They looked like a special action squad. 'The troops who've been sent to clear the Square have fought in Vietnam,' I heard one of them say. 'They're wearing camouflage. They're expert marksmen.'

'If only we had some bayonets . . .' said a small muscular guy in a white vest. He had a knife in his hand.

'Are you crazy?' I butted in. 'The soldiers would shoot you dead if they saw you with one.'

'And who do you think *you* are?' the guy in the vest shouted, striding up to me.

'I'm head of the student marshals,' I said calmly. 'I'm responsible for security in the Square. If you want to fight, go to the front line and help defend the barricades. The Square is the rear area of the battle. We don't need military force here.'

'I'm not leaving the Square! Do you have any idea of how many people have been killed tonight while trying to protect you?' He waved his knife threateningly then turned round and rejoined Wu Bin. Another member of their gang was lifting a machine gun onto a marble balustrade. A crowd quickly gathered round them to see what they were up to.

Fan Yuan waved a bottle of petrol at the crowd and shouted, 'All unarmed students must leave the Monument now.' The bandanna he'd tied around his baseball cap said GIVE ME LIBERTY OR GIVE ME DEATH!

Two female marshals from the Workers' Federation broke into tears and said, 'We can't wait here for the army to kill us. Come on! Let's go onto the streets and fight them.'

Shan Bo rushed out of the tent and shouted, 'Put down your weapons! How can you hope to bring about democracy with knives and guns in your hands?'

A doctor followed Shan Bo out of the tent and said, 'Calm down! You're still on hunger strike.'

My brother suddenly appeared with a group of friends. 'Anyone who's afraid to fight should leave the Square at once!' they shouted. 'The rest of you must pledge to defend the Square to the death.' They were armed with broken-off table legs. I told him to put down the weapons, but he ignored me. I remembered how once, when we were kids, he pounced on me and punched my jaw to pay me back for pinching his ear after he stole one of my biscuits.

'You might have been able to fight off the armed police with those table legs,' I said, 'but PLA soldiers are surrounding us now. They have guns and live ammunition, and can shoot you dead from a hundred metres.'

'If we're armed, the soldiers won't dare storm into the Square.' My brother had spent most of the previous day hanging out with Wu Bin. After just three days in the Square, he'd become much more radical.

'Don't assume you're invincible,' I said to my brother. 'Remember: bullets have no eyes. We can't both stay in the Square. I'm head of security here, and if trouble breaks out, the students will need my help. You go home now. If we don't resist, we'll be able to return to the campuses or, at worst, we'll get flung in jail. But if we attack, the army will shoot into the crowd and rivers of blood will flow through the city. One of us has to stay alive and look after Mum.'

'You think you can persuade me to be a deserter?' my brother said, walking away. 'No chance!'

'Stay then, if you want,' I said, pulling him back. 'But put down that stick. You have no right to drag the rest of us into a violent conflict.' When I'd argued with him in the past, I only had to kick him in the shins and he'd do as I asked. But he was a young man now, a slightly smaller version of myself, and was no longer willing to take orders from me.

'Dai Wai, Shi Ye's looking for you,' Chen Di said, spotting me as he walked past. 'She's with a pretty girl in a white dress.'

'Really?' I glanced around and wondered whether the girl might be A-Mei. My mind clouded over. I wanted to see her.

Shan Bo shouted that we should confiscate the machine gun. Hou Dejian and Zi Duo came out of the tent to help.

'You must stop your hunger strike,' Zhuzi said to them. 'The army are coming. Listen to the gunfire. Those are real bullets!' He turned on his walkie-talkie and pressed the buttons so that they could hear the noises of gunfire and screaming being transmitted from the major intersections around the city.

'They're shooting at everyone in sight,' Chen Di said. 'Every bulletin we receive brings news of more deaths and injuries.'

'Yes, we must end the hunger strike,' Zi Duo said.

'The army would only shoot people who are brandishing weapons,' Hou Dejian said. 'My hands are empty. They wouldn't attack me.' He was trying to speak loudly, but he was very weak. None of the four men had eaten anything for almost thirty hours.

'I've just been told that my friend Wu Guofeng has been killed,' Fan Yuan shouted out to us. 'He was shot in the stomach with an exploding bullet. His guts are splayed all over the ground! I'm going over there now. Will any of you join me?'

'There's no point fighting them, you'll never win.' As soon as Zi Duo said this, his girlfriend walked over and put a piece of bread into his mouth.

I could hear Hai Feng nearby, shouting through a megaphone: 'We will never bow down before the executioners!'

Mimi and Tian Yi began reading out the battle commands Old Fu had handed them. But the amplifiers weren't working properly, so no one could make out what they were saying.

'This is a message to all Qinghua University students,' Zhou Suo shouted through his megaphone. 'Our university has sent vans to take us back to the campus. If any of you want to leave, go and board them now.'

'Tell them to let the girls go first,' Zhuzi said, rushing over to Mimi. Tian Yi was running around frantically behind them. I felt I was watching a video on fast-forward.

'What's this talk about leaving?' Big Chan shouted. 'We must stay in the Square until dawn. There's no need to be afraid. I've heard that when the citizens at the barricades throw stones at the troops, the young soldiers run away in terror.'

'Help me extend this cable, Dai Wei,' Old Fu said. 'And Bai Ling, stay in the tent and don't move. The students need to know that you're here, or they will lose morale.'

'Why have you stationed marshals up here at a time like this?' Sister Gao shouted out as she and Shao Jian pushed past a student who was trying to block their way. The brown shirt she was wearing made her face look pale.

'They're not marshals,' I said. 'They're just some students from the Politics and Law University who volunteered to protect the hunger strike tent.'

'Where've you been?' Old Fu asked Shao Jian.

'The troops are forcing their way down West Changan Avenue, spraying bullets into the crowds,' Shao Jian said, trudging over to Zi Duo, his face dripping with sweat and a rucksack slung over his shoulder.

'Tell the students to hand in their weapons,' Old Fu said to me. 'We can't allow them to be armed.'

'Ask Bai Ling to make the announcement,' I said. 'She was the one who told everyone to arm themselves.'

'Well, it was Wang Fei's stupid idea, not hers,' Old Fu said.

'We must stick to our policy of non-violence,' Sister Gao said. 'If we use weapons, we'll all end up dead.' There was a look of despair on her face that I hadn't seen before.

As I helped Chen Di carry more broadcast equipment over to the hunger strike tent, I glanced around, looking for my brother, but couldn't see him anywhere.

'Lin Lu has sent the Dare-to-Die Squad to block the convoys in the east,' Dong Rong said, climbing onto the upper terrace. 'But there are only twelve of them. What use is that? The troops are opening fire now, shooting randomly into the crowds. They've already reached the Jianguomen intersection.' His designer shirt was torn at the collar. He looked like an extra in a fight scene.

The upper terrace was packed. We were like refugees penned inside a fence. We would babble at each other feverishly, then walk off before anyone had a chance to answer. As soon as someone joined our throng, we surrounded them and launched into a new debate.

I saw Big Chan, with his guitar slung from a strap around his neck, rush back into the Square with Qiu Fa and Wang Fei. All three were pushing bicycles.

As soon as Wang Fei stepped onto the terrace, he switched on his black megaphone and yelled, 'The troops opened fire! At first they aimed at the ground, then a few soldiers lifted their guns and shot indiscriminately at the crowd . . .' I gave him a leg up so that he could stand on the edge of the sculptured frieze, then I put my hand on his thigh to stop him falling off. Everyone could see him now. 'After that, tanks, armoured vehicles and army trucks crashed over the barricades . . . Look at this towel!' He pulled a towel from his trouser pocket. 'A student called Zhou Jiang got a bullet in his stomach and died right before my eyes. I tried to smother the wound with this towel, but the blood just kept spurting out.' He pointed to his navel. Without his glasses on, his eyes looked blank. I could feel his thigh begin to shake. He'd slipped into his Sichuan dialect, and not many people understood what he said. I told him to pass his megaphone to Qiu Fa.

I knew the student he mentioned. He'd joined my student marshal team the night we went to Wangfujing Street to protect the shops from looters. He was Zhuzi's secret intelligence officer. He had a walkie-talkie. Cao Ming had told me that everyone issued with walkie-talkies was bound to get tailed by government agents.

Qiu Fa stared into the night sky and said, 'Troops armed with live ammunition ran up onto the overpass and shot at the crowd in the street below, yelling at the top of their voices. I took cover behind a telegraph pole . . . One of the soldiers looked like he was on drugs. Whenever he heard someone cry "Down with Fascism!" he'd point his machine gun at them and unleash a barrage of bullets. Sometimes the soldiers shot at the buildings, killing people who were leaning out of the windows. A teacher from People's University climbed into an army truck to speak to the troops, but as he got on, a soldier pushed him off and stabbed him in the chest with a bayonet.'

Everyone fell silent. I could hear a walkie-talkie crackling nearby.

I helped Wang Fei down and we went off with Old Fu to join our gang outside the hunger strike tent. Old Fu turned to Bai Ling, Wang Fei and Lin Lu, and said, 'As commanders of the Square, you must tell all students who are holding sticks, bricks or Molotov cocktails to put them down at once!'

'And we must persuade all female students to return to the campuses,' Sister Gao said. 'They will be safer there, and it will help break up the troops. I'm going to try to sneak through the army lines and fetch reinforcements from the Business and Economics University.'

Bai Ling had changed into a yellow and white striped T-shirt. She was pacing around distractedly like a patient in a mental asylum. Tian Yi was helping Mimi and Chen Di drag a table over to the tent. The few girls still remaining on the terrace looked tiny compared to the guys standing around them. I wished A-Mei hadn't chosen to arrive in Beijing now, just as the army was shooting its way into the city.

Chen Di put a chair in front of the table outside the tent, asked Bai Ling to sit down, then handed her the microphone.

Annoyed that no one had responded to her, Sister Gao walked off with two journalists. Soldiers were shooting into the air now. Glowing tracer bullets arced through the night sky then exploded with a brilliant white flash. When I glanced at Sister Gao, I thought I saw a bullet enter her back.

Bai Ling looked up at Wang Fei. The passion and resolve she'd shown during the twenty days we'd been in the Square had gone. She'd led the students to a precipice, and now they were trying to push her over the edge. But somehow she found the strength to open her mouth and say, 'I am Bai Ling, commander-in-chief. I am asking all of you to put down your weapons, and for the girls to return to the campuses at once . . . Fellow students, the black day has finally arrived. At this final moment, I would like to read out a poem by Li Qingzhao, a female writer of the Song Dynasty: "In life, we should be heroes among the living. / In death, let us be heroes among the ghosts. / To this day we mourn Xiang Yu, / Who chose to stay and die rather than cross the Yangste River!" When General Xiang Yu was surrounded by enemy troops, he stood firm and chose not to escape to his family on the other side of the river. Fellow students! We are still young, and perhaps we might lack courage when we come face to face with a ruthless army that has shot its way through the city. But we are honourable and upstanding citizens. Whatever happens, we must stay firm and not let our families down . . . Let us use our idealism to wake the Chinese people from their slumber!' By the end of her speech, she was forcing the words out through sobs.

Everyone on the terrace stood still. Tian Yi and Mimi were wiping away tears. I edged over to them and said, 'If you start crying, everyone will, and the mood could get dangerously volatile.'

'Nonsense!' Tian Yi said, pushing me away, her face as white as paper.

Through Wang Fei's walkie-talkie, a voice crackled, 'The tanks are coming! . . .' then broke off. Wang Fei frantically pressed the buttons but couldn't regain the connection.

I became anxious. I wanted to find a safe hiding place for Tian Yi before the army came. I could see she had no strength left.

On the slopes of Mount Shamen grows the herb of immortality. A large bird sits on the summit, keeping watch over a black snake that lives in the dark river below.

'Where is it, where is it?' my mother screams, banging her head against the wardrobe. She gnashes her teeth and cries in pain. She often has screaming fits, but usually manages to lower her professionally trained voice to a deep howl that's inaudible to the neighbours.

My mother hasn't thrown anything out of the flat for years, so she has trouble finding things. I imagine the flat is so crammed now that there isn't much room to stand.

She goes to the sofa, which is piled with biscuit tins, paper boxes, and the letters, bills and leaflets that get stuffed into her mailbox downstairs. As she kicks some cardboard boxes to the ground, her stomach rumbles. I hear her jangling her keys.

She is continually changing our locks, but forgets to throw away the old keys, so they stay on the same ring with the new ones, together with the keys to her leather suitcase, bicycle, and to the small shed outside in which she stores cabbages and charcoal briquettes. Sometimes she sits down and goes through each key, telling herself which one is for what, but then loses track halfway and has to start over again. She'll begin by saying, 'Bathroom, front door, window,' but will soon make do with, 'Big, small, copper, aluminium . . .'

When she can't find space in the sitting room for something, she'll toss it into my room. The empty milk cartons, pill bottles and food packaging she's flung under my bed have attracted colonies of ants. She doesn't bother to cook any more. She eats instant noodles for breakfast, lunch and dinner. She must have got through six big boxes of them in the last few months. She throws the paper packaging onto my bed. I imagine that the only clean objects in the flat are the many calendars hanging on the wall. Her collection continues to grow. The calendar she bought this year has twelve photographs of America's Grand Canyon.

Finding she couldn't switch on my bedside lamp because the socket was buried under a pile of rubbish, she went out and bought a new lamp. Unable to locate another socket for it, she let it lie in the corner for a couple of weeks. Yesterday, she placed it on a cardboard box at the end of my bed and plugged its lead into a portable socket she'd pulled over from the sitting room. This means that my door can't be closed now. The lamp is buzzing. Its light shines on my left cheek. I can smell its plastic shade getting hotter and hotter.

The nurse who visits every week is scolding my mother as if she were one of her patients. She sounds younger than Wen Niao. 'When did you last check his blood pressure? Pass me his medical notes. These are from last year. Why do you Falun Gong practitioners always seem to be in such a daze? . . . It's on the low side – just 50 mmHg. Yes, put it there, where I can see it. Where are the kidney-function test forms I gave you? . . . I'll take this urine sample with me and give you the results next week.'

The nurse doesn't offer to help my mother turn me over or wash me. She performs her duties perfunctorily then leaves, slamming the door shut behind her. As she walks down the stairs, I hear her mutter, 'A perfectly good flat, and she's turned it into a rubbish tip!'

Since Master Yao got arrested, my mother often screams in her sleep. If she hears someone walking up the stairs, she grabs her keys and checks that all the bolts are double-locked.

Three hundred li further south is Mount Luminous. There are crystals and snakes on its slopes. A wild beast that looks like a fox lives on the mountain. It cries out its own name. Whenever it appears, a panic will engulf the land.

Wang Fei was sitting inside the tent, his arms wrapped tightly around Bai Ling. 'Don't be afraid,' he said to her. 'You have your ideals to hang onto.' His eyes were red. Now that she was hidden from the crowd, Bai Ling looked like a frightened rabbit. Between sobs, she gulped a breath of air and said, 'I'm not afraid. Just full of despair. I can't breathe.'

Lin Lu grabbed Old Fu's hand and said, 'If they arrest us, we mustn't capitulate. One day, victory will be ours.'

Hou Dejian was sitting outside. A few journalists shone their torches on his face, and asked him to comment on the situation. Instead of replying, he picked up his guitar and sang: '*All freedom-loving people, throw your shoulders back and stand up straight* . . .' The song only intensified the feeling of impending doom. Down by the broadcast station below, Ke Xi shouted through his megaphone, 'I will die in this Square if I have to, but I will never desert it . . .'

'That's the first time I've heard Ke Xi argue to stay in the Square,' Yu Jin said, walking into the tent. Seeing that Wang Fei had his arms around Bai Ling, he turned instead to me and said, 'The army has encircled us. We must come to a decision.'

Zhuzi returned from Beijing University with fifty new marshals dressed in white T-shirts. Lin Lu told them to stand around the base of the Monument. He said that he would take charge of the east side of the Monument, Zhuzi would look after the west, I would be stationed at the north and Zhang Jie at the south. 'The strongest guys must stand on the outside and stay there, even if they're shot at or injured.' He took a drag from his cigarette. The glowing tip made his face shine red. Bai Ling had just criticised him for having sent hundreds of marshals to the barricades, leaving us vulnerable at this critical moment.

'We are standing on the front line now, and we're not afraid to die!' Wang Fei shouted into the air.

'Mou Sen is over by the Goddess of Democracy with Nuwa, Zhang Jie and Xiao Li,' Qiu Fa said walking over to me, his curly hair falling over his face. 'He refuses to abandon it. I begged him to come to the Monument, but he says he's only two hundred metres away, and can still see us from over there.'

Zhuzi and I went to the balustrades and surveyed the scene. In the west, a small group had set light to some canvas sheets, quilts and wooden sticks. We could hear the rumble of army tanks now, as well as gunfire. We knew that, very soon, troops would appear on all four sides of the Square.

I hurried to the north side of the Monument. I didn't have a megaphone, so I shouted at the top of my voice for the boys to move to the outer edge of the crowd. Within ten minutes, most of them did as they were asked and linked hands, forming a protective cordon around the girls, apart from a few boys who remained seated on the steps with their arms around their girlfriends. Someone began singing along to the Internationale that was playing over the loudspeakers, then everyone joined in, crying out in unison: '*The hot blood that fills our chests is seething. We will struggle for the truth . . .*'

'We will defend Tiananmen Square to the death! We will defend the People's Republic of China!' Mimi shouted into the microphone.

'They can cut off our heads and let us bleed to death, but we will never let them take the People's Square!' Chen Di cried theatrically.

I asked a couple of the guys in red armbands to take over from me, then I wove a path through the crowd of seated students and returned to the hunger strike tent.

'Everyone must cover their mouths with a face mask or wet towel,' Bai Ling said into the microphone, making final preparations for the battle ahead. There was black ink on her shirt. In the darkness it looked like blood.

Old Fu was guarding the microphone. When Bai Ling had finished speaking, he saw that Chen Di hadn't got the next tape ready yet, so he added a few comments of his own. 'When the army arrives, we will show patience, firmness and self-control. We will stay here, hand in hand, shoulder to shoulder. Let the army come and crush us, if they want. We will not move.'

Ke Xi was standing between two Hong Kong students who'd asked to have a photograph taken with him. After the flash went off, he shouted, 'When I'm dead, you must carry my coffin through the streets, then bring it here so that I can have one last look at the Square!' Then he walked over to Bai Ling and said, 'I want to take over as commander-in-chief for the rest of the night.'

Bai Ling cast him a disdainful look. 'The enemy is already at our gates. What would you do as commander-in-chief?'

'I know what needs to be done,' Ke Xi said.

'I will only hand over control to you if you have a workable plan,' Bai Ling said, looking away.

'Don't be so arrogant. Remember: you started out as my secretary!' As soon as Ke Xi said this, Wang Fei jumped up and grabbed him by the collar. He was about to punch him in the face, but Ke Xi's bodyguards pushed him away just in time. Yu Jin grabbed a wooden stick and ran over, waving it at Ke Xi's head. Zhuzi came in and said angrily, 'The students manning the barricades are sacrificing their lives for us. If you don't stop these stupid power struggles, I'll beat you up.'

Chen Di led an injured student to the table and pressed the microphone to his lips. 'My classmate Zhang Han has been shot dead!' the student sobbed. 'I've got his blood all over my body. It's fresh blood. All over me . . .' Zhang Han was another of the student marshals who'd been issued with walkie-talkies.

I told Zhuzi to tell anyone who had a walkie-talkie to discard it immediately.

Ke Xi snatched the microphone from the student's hands and said, 'We will defend Tiananmen Square to the death! We will stay on the Monument to the People's Heroes until the bitter end . . .' He worked himself up into such a frenzy that he fainted into the arms of his bodyguard.

Chen Di took the microphone. 'We need an ambulance and an oxygen canister. Ke Xi has fainted again.'

'Fellow students, you must stay awake and make sure you all have wet towels to hand,' Old Fu announced. 'Don't leave the Monument. Everyone must stay in the centre of the Square.' His calm, mature voice eased the mood.

'We must concentrate our forces in the north side of the Square,' I said to Lin Lu, taking more red armbands from his bag. 'That's where the troops from the east and west will converge. Go and position some more guys over there.'

'Let's do a last circuit of the Square, Dai Wei, and make sure everyone is gathered round the Monument,' Old Fu said.

'Has anyone got a bicycle I can use?' I shouted, but no one could hear me. I wanted to go to the Goddess of Democracy and persuade Mou Sen and Nuwa to come back to the Monument, then I wanted to find Tian Yi a hiding place in the Museum of Chinese History. It was an important national monument. I was sure the army wouldn't dare fire bullets at it.

A small group of students were smashing up weapons on the stone steps at the edge of the terrace. Shan Bo and Fan Yuan, who was still wearing a red armband, were taking it in turns to bash the machine gun. Others were dismantling crude Molotov cocktails. A strong smell of petrol wafted through the air.

Malignant cells gnaw at the lining of your stomach. The tissue looks as ravaged as the walls of a ruined city.

'Where is it, where is it?' my mother groans, rifling through sheets of paper.

She has begun to lose her memory. When Master Yao's son knocked on the door and called out to her, she didn't let him in. I presumed she didn't recognise his voice. But maybe she did, and she didn't want to have to talk about the upsetting matter of Master Yao's arrest. Or perhaps she thought it was the relocation officer come to persuade her to move out.

I suddenly remember an argument my parents once had.

'. . . Where have you hidden my photographs?' my father said angrily.

I was ten years old at the time, and had just come home from school. My elasticated trousers were too big for me. My classmates had pulled them down twice to embarrass me. I was very upset.

'I want a belt!' I said, interrupting their argument.

'If your trousers are loose, it's easier to pull them down when you need to pee,' my mother said, then turned back to my father. 'I burnt the photographs years ago.'

'They ran up behind me and pulled my trousers down. Dad, I want a belt!'

'You haven't got a belly. What do you need a belt for?' My father looked down at me and puffed on his cigarette. His face was as mottled as the old mirror hanging on our wall.

'Go and play in the yard with your brother,' my mother said, walking out of the kitchen in her green slippers.

'I'm sick of wearing elasticated trousers. Can't you buy me some proper ones?'

My mother grabbed me by the collar and spanked me hard, then pushed me out onto the landing.

That father of mine, who entered the crematorium's furnace holding a wall calendar of foreign landscapes, never once applied to join the Party after he returned from America. That showed what a courageous man he was.

Three hundred li south across the shifting sands lie the Ge Mountains. Their bare slopes are scattered with stones that can be used to sharpen knives. With just one of these stones you can sharpen all the knives in the land.

It was about one in the morning already. Most of the girls had gone off to Qinghua University in the vans, but about a hundred had chosen to remain in the Square. I returned to the upper terrace. I wanted to fetch Tian Yi and take her to a safe place. I knew she wouldn't come with me if I told her my plan, so I said, 'My old Southern University classmate, Shi Ye, wants to speak to me. Will you help me find her?'

'Shi Ye is A-Mei's old classmate, not yours,' she said, following me back down to the Square. Big Chan and Little Chan were dunking brushes into a bowl of ink and painting onto the stone wall of the Monument: 4 JUNE IS THE BLACKEST DAY IN CHINESE HISTORY . . .

Tian Yi gripped my arm. I could tell she was as afraid as Bai Ling.

Suddenly, in the north-western corner of the Square, I caught sight of an armoured vehicle. It was ramming into a wall of bollards that residents had placed across Changan Avenue, a few metres from where Mou Sen had staged the Democracy University's opening ceremony. A small crowd of students ran over and tossed stones and petrol bombs at it, and soon flames darted across its roof as it continued to bash into the barricade. Reflected firelight danced across the Goddess of Democracy and the rows of nylon tents nearby.

'Hurry! There's an armoured vehicle trying to force its way into the Square.' I grabbed Tian Yi's arm and we sprinted off in the opposite direction. Before we'd gone very far, I looked up and saw a black mass of soldiers in combat gear, armed with long truncheons, line up on the steps of the Museum of Chinese History.

Tian Yi stood still. 'Stop!' she cried, pulling me back. 'Don't go any further.'

It suddenly occurred to me that the soldiers must having been lurking inside the Museum of Chinese History all along.

I tried to think of somewhere else for Tian Yi to hide, but realised it would be too dangerous to go running through the Square now.

Some of the Beijing residents scattered around us were holding metal rods and beer bottles, and were about to hurl them at the soldiers on the steps. I rushed over and said, 'I'm Dai Wei, head of security. The Defend Tiananmen Square Headquarters has requested that everyone discard their weapons and maintain our policy of peaceful resistance.' Then I told Tian Yi to return to the Monument and tell Bai Ling that the army was now standing right opposite us.

As she turned to leave, she saw a girl sitting under a lamp post reading a book. 'What are you doing?' Tian Yi cried. 'Can't you see the army's here?'

'If they turf us out of the Square, we'll go back to the campus,' the girl said, looking up. 'What's the big deal?'

'Look, this is a bullet cartridge,' Tian Yi said. 'The army are shooting to kill. I need you to help me. Go and tell the Headquarters that there's a huge battalion of troops standing on the steps of the Museum of Chinese History. Give the message to Bai Ling. Say it's from Tian Yi.'

The girl got up reluctantly and stared at the cartridge in Tian Yi's hand.

Tian Yi then came back to my side and shouted, 'Fellow students, let's sing the PLA song, "Three Rules of Discipline and Eight Points of Attention".'

Just at that moment, a signal flare shot through the sky. Its pale glow looked like the ghostly light that illuminates the dead souls' path to hell.

A sound of gunfire rang out from the north-east corner of the Square. The bangs echoed against the northern walls of the Museum of Chinese History. The thousands of soldiers outside the Museum could hear it too, but they remained completely still, standing packed on the steps like a swarm of green bats.

'We're done for, we're done for,' I muttered to myself, my body clenching with fear. I thought of taking Tian Yi down into the underpass below Changan Avenue, but before I had time to move, a frantic crowd came running down from the north-east corner and raced to the ambulance parked outside the Square's emergency tent. A wounded man, covered in blood from head to toe, was being wheeled along on a bicycle. A younger man with blood pouring from his thigh walked beside him. As he was carried onto the ambulance, he shook his head from side to side and shouted, 'Did you see that? Did you see that?' then closed his eyes and fell silent.

Someone shouted madly, 'You butchers! How could you turn your guns on the people! The gods will punish you!' Others ran over to the Museum to hurl stones and beer bottles at the soldiers sitting on the steps. The soldiers jumped to their feet and looked as though they were about to strike back, but the colonel standing in front waved his hand, and they all stood still. Then three soldiers in Changan Avenue ran towards us, pursued by an enraged crowd. One of them was knocked to the ground, the other two sprinted over to the Museum's steps. The troops were furious, and seemed ready to attack. Four students went to help the fallen soldier. As they lifted him to his feet, some angry civilians leaned down, punched the soldier's face and pulled off his helmet.

A boy who looked about ten years old ran past us. Tian Yi tried to grab hold of him, but he slipped through her fingers and ran off towards the Museum. 'My brother has been killed!' he shouted, then raced towards the troops on the steps. A small crowd wielding branches and metal rods followed behind him. Tian Yi caught up with him and managed to hold him back. A few female students surrounded the colonel and pleaded with him to tell the soldiers not to shoot. A short student from Hong Kong fell to her knees and sobbed, 'You can't fire your guns at the students!'

I got everyone to cry out to the troops, 'The People's Army loves the people! The Chinese people don't shoot their fellow countrymen!'

Tian Yi went over to the colonel, pointed to her university badge and said, 'I'm a Beijing University student. We follow a policy of non-resistance. You saw how we went to the aid of that soldier just now.'

'If you shoot us, history will never forgive you!' I butted in. The colonel lowered his head and remained silent. The boy saw a tricycle cart pass by and chased after it.

'That kid has gone mad . . .'

'Perhaps that was his brother's cart,' I said. 'Tian Yi, we must go back and tell Bai Ling what's happening.' Wang Fei had got hold of an army machine gun and had hidden it in one of the tents. He had set up his own secret suicide squad. I knew that if he got out the gun and deployed the squad, it would provoke a massacre.

Tian Yi and I ran towards the Monument. Students holding wooden sticks ran past us, heading for an armoured vehicle that had caught fire. An old man was shouting out to some members of the Workers' Federation's Dare-to-Die Squad, 'Do as the students have asked and put down your weapons . . .' Then he knelt on the ground and wept.

Another prolonged burst of machine-gun fire erupted in Changan Avenue. The noise numbed my ears. Tian Yi and I stood still. The gunfire stopped. I heard a crowd yelling angry slogans, then saw someone carrying the limp body of the young boy we'd just seen. There was blood dripping from him. It looked like he'd been shot dead.

I broke into a cold sweat. 'It's too dangerous out here!' I said, pulling Tian Yi towards the underpass. I thought we'd be safer in there. But as we approached the entrance, another round of gunfire rang out, and in a panic we threw ourselves to the ground.

I looked up to see what was going on. The troops and tanks had sealed Changan Avenue at the north-east corner of the Square. A small crowd of people were crouching behind the low cement wall of the underpass's entrance. I couldn't tell whether they were civilians or students. I guessed they were within range of the machine guns' bullets, and were too afraid to move.

Two workers holding metal rods crept over to us and said, 'You'll be killed if you lie here any longer. Those bastards are shooting everyone in sight! If you don't have weapons, get out of here!'

'Is there anyone in the underpass?' I asked.

'If you go inside, you'll never get out again. There are thousands of people down there already. Run south to Qianmen Road. The army hasn't sealed it off yet.'

I couldn't believe it. This was one of the thugs who'd swindled us in the woods of the Old Summer Palace. I recognised his voice instantly, but fortunately Tian Yi didn't. I stared at his back as he walked away.

That expression, caught in mid-flow, lies immersed in coagulated blood.

More tanks approached the Square from the east, followed by line after line of soldiers advancing like rows of moving walls.

I saw a girl who looked like Nuwa walk towards the martial law troops, her red skirt fluttering behind her as she went. The people squatting behind the cement wall of the underpass entrance stood up and followed her, shouting, 'The People's Army loves the people!' There were now twenty or thirty people standing in front of the troops in the north-east corner of the Square. Among the crowd, I spotted a gangly Provincial Students' Federation marshal who'd attempted to depose Tang Guoxian the day before. His fist was raised high in the air.

The gunfire resumed again. Several people were hit. Some of them staggered backwards, some fell and rolled about in agony. Others dropped flat on their stomachs and lay still. But the girl in the red skirt was unscathed. She continued to walk towards the guns that were pointing straight at her. Then, when she was just two or three metres away from them, a shot was fired . . . Her left foot stepped backwards, her arms and body tilted forward, then she lost balance and crumpled onto the ground.

'Fucking hell! They're executing people in cold blood!' I looked away. I couldn't bear to watch. My heart was thumping. I turned to look at Tian Yi. She was sitting down, her eyes tightly closed and her teeth clamped over her lower lip. She looked as though she was about to faint. I knelt down and put my arm around her.

'I'll take you over to the Red Cross tent. It's just over there.' I wanted to find a doctor and ask him to give her a tranquilliser.

'The monsters! They're killing people!' she said, her body trembling all over.

Nurses in white coats ran past us to tend to the students lying on Changan Avenue. I pulled Tian Yi up and tried to drag her towards the Red Cross tent, but she couldn't move her legs, so I heaved her onto my back and carried her. A wailing ambulance was parked outside the tent. The blue-and-white light of its rotating beacon dazzled my eyes. When we got there, two nurses and a student arrived carrying the girl in the red skirt by her arms and legs. I looked down. It was Nuwa. She'd been shot in the thigh. Blood was gushing from the wound. Her blood-drenched toes were as clenched as bird claws. One of her red sandals was dangling from her foot by a thin leather strap.

A nurse squatted on the ground and shouted, 'Quick, bandage her leg! We must get her into the ambulance as soon as possible! Put her down. She needs to lie flat on her back.'

Tian Yi pushed me away, untied the towel from her arm, leaned down and put it over Nuwa's thigh. The nurse pressed the towel deep into the bullet wound and wrapped a long strip of gauze around it to hold it in place. Then Tian Yi and I took Nuwa's feet, the nurse took her arms and we carefully lifted her up. Steam rose from the drops of blood that dripped onto the concrete paving stones.

'Don't let her die!' Tian Yi cried out suddenly.

'She wanted to tell the soldiers to stop shooting,' the nurse said. 'The guns were pointing straight at her, but she kept walking towards them. She was helping me drag away the wounded just a few minutes before.'

When the nurse looked up, I realised it was Wen Niao. The cap above her thick eyebrows was smeared with blood. She wiped the blood from her hands onto her white coat. 'Quickly, let's put her into the ambulance. You're the security chief, aren't you? Tell your student marshals to move away from the troops. There's a massacre taking place!'

'We know this girl. She's a Beijing University student.' I could hardly breathe. My vision blurred. We carried Nuwa into the ambulance and tied her to a stretcher. 'What about him?' I said, spotting another body lying outside the rescue tent.

'He's dead already,' Wen Niao said, breathing heavily. 'He got hit by two bullets.'

I knelt down and took a closer look. A jolt of horror ran through me. He looked like Mou Sen, but I didn't dare believe it was him. One of his eyes had been blown out and his face was covered in hair and blood. I slipped my hand into his pocket and found my packet of cigarettes.

'Mou Sen! Mou Sen! It's too much!' I howled at the top of my voice. My legs shook as though struck by bullets.

I heard Wen Niao shouting, 'Hurry up, we're leaving!' I turned round and saw her pushing Tian Yi into the ambulance. She banged twice on the door and shouted, 'Go, go!'

'Take care, Dai Wei . . .' Tian Yi said, stretching her hand towards me. As she unfurled her fingers, the shiny bullet cartridge she'd been clasping flew into the night sky. I watched the ambulance speed off, its siren wailing loudly again, and felt my chest tighten.

'That's probably the last trip it will make tonight,' Wen Niao said.

'It might get to the hospital, but I doubt it will be allowed back again.'

'This guy here was my best friend. The girl who got shot is his girlfriend – no, his wife.' My mouth was so dry, I could hardly speak. I stared at the blood on Mou Sen's hair, which I'd cut myself, and thought about how, a few moments before, he'd been alive and in love. I couldn't understand how he could be dead so suddenly.

'That wound in her thigh was deep. It was haemorrhaging badly. She won't survive.' After Wen Niao said this, she turned and pushed her way into the Red Cross tent.

Blood rushed to my head. Everything went dark. I looked down again at Mou Sen. His red eyeball gleamed with reflected light. I crouched down and rubbed his chest, trying to shake him awake. 'Are you really dead? It's too much, Mou Sen. I won't let you die like this.' I opened the cigarette pack. There were still two cigarettes inside.

I sat down beside him. The glint in his eye was strange and unfamiliar. He looked nothing like my father did when he died. His face, teeth, hair, neck and goatee were covered in blood. I had his blood and Nuwa's blood all over my hands.

My mind went blank. I didn't know what to think any more or where to look.

Inside the emergency tent, the nurses were packing away the medical supplies into cardboard boxes and getting ready to carry out the wounded. They pushed everyone with minor injuries out of the tent and said, 'Hurry up and leave the Square!'

On Fajiu Mountain lives a bird with a white beak and red claws. It is the reincarnation of Emperor Yandi's daughter who drowned in the East Sea. It cries out 'Jingwei, jingwei', so people call it the jingwei bird. Every day, it picks up twigs and stones from the mountain and drops them into the East Sea, trying in vain to fill it up.

A student who'd just had his arm bandaged ran towards the troops shouting, 'You'll pay for this, you murderers!' I grabbed him and said, 'Go back to the Monument, my friend, and tell everyone what's happened. Hurry!'

The government loudspeakers overhead were still droning the same announcements. 'A serious counter-revolutionary riot has broken out in Beijing. Thugs have stolen the army's ammunition and set fire to army trucks. Their aim is to destroy the People's Republic of China. We must launch a resolute counter-attack . . .' An armoured personnel carrier careered past the Great Hall of the People, knocking over a man pushing a bicycle. I left Mou Sen's corpse, ran over to where the man had fallen and helped the crowd rebuild the roadblock that the armoured carrier had rammed through. A few workers tossed petrol bombs onto the vehicle's roof.

It came to a large blockade further down the road that it was unable to breach. Its engine roared as it struggled in vain to push through it. A mob raced over and attacked it with more Molotov cocktails. I spotted a quilt lying on the ground, so I picked it up, ran over to the vehicle and tossed it onto the bottles burning on the roof. The quilt immediately caught fire. A few moments later, the armoured carrier finally managed to break through the roadblock and escape west down Changan Avenue, the quilt on its roof still blazing. Marshals from the Workers' Federation chased after it, shouting, 'What the fuck are you doing driving into people like that?' Others ran over with metal rods which they stuck into the tracks, bringing the vehicle to a halt once more. Soon hundreds of people surrounded it and attacked it with metal rods and wooden sticks. Some people even punched the metal sides with their fists. I too went over and kicked it a few times, but the thick smoke pouring from its exhaust pipe made my eyes water, so I ran back to the middle of the Square. Bullets were still arcing through the night sky, accompanied by a continuous sound of gunfire.

Just as I was about to make my way through the rows of nylon tents, a man walked up to me, pulled me aside and told me he was an undercover agent. He urged me to tell the students to leave the Square immediately, as the soldiers were about to move in and clear it by force, and would kill anyone who resisted them. To prove his identity, he pulled a walkie-talkie from his pocket. It was a model used only by the government's security force.

'What difference will it make if we leave now or get driven out in a couple of hours?' I said blankly, then walked off to fetch my backpack from my tent. But when I got there, my mind was so muddled, I forgot what I was looking for. I saw a student in a tent opposite mine scribbling into his journal by torchlight. 'The troops are coming to clear the Square!' I shouted. 'Hurry up and get out of here!'

'I'm writing my will,' he said without looking up. Then he switched off his torch and lay down on his camp bed.

'You will – you will regret this!' A fire was raging in my head. I couldn't think straight.

Five hundred li downriver, you come to Mount Plenty. The River Li rises from the foothills and flows west to empty into the Yellow River. Poisonous fish inhabit its waters. If a man eats them, he will die.

My mother is searching for something again. She's in her bedroom. She always seems to be looking for something or other, but what she is really looking for is herself. She no longer turns on the radio, so most of the noises I hear now are either from her or from the bulldozers which are edging closer and closer to our building.

She must be leaning down. She kicks away a pile of plastic bags. I can hear there's a swelling at the base of her oesophagus. It lies at the opening to her stomach like a rotten potato and gives her breath a smell of sickness.

She survives on a diet of raw cucumber, celery and small snacks that are sold wrapped in cellophane. She often wakes up in the middle of the night, groaning with stomach pain, then turns on the television and watches it until dawn.

The nurse who comes to bring me medicine every week pushes a thermometer into my mouth and says, 'Why don't you open the windows and tidy this flat up a little? It smells worse than a public toilet in here.'

'I don't want the sparrow to fly out,' my mother answers.

'No wonder no one wants to come round here. You really are a strange woman. You have this vegetable to keep you company, and now you want a sparrow as well!'

'I'm sorry . . .'

'There's a new drug you should buy for him. Our clinic has just received a batch. It's synthesised from fresh placenta cells, and helps stimulate cell regeneration. You inject it straight into the blood. As a regular customer, you can have it at a discount rate of just two hundred yuan a box.'

'I don't think I'll bother. There's nothing much wrong with him. All the tests he's been having these last years show that his condition is stable.'

'He's your own son. What's two hundred yuan to you? What a miser you are! You can't be short of money. All the residents of this compound have made a fortune from the demolition compensation fees.'

'Huh, even if I were to get 200,000 yuan, I couldn't buy another flat around here. The smallest flats in the new commercial block round the corner cost at least three times that much.'

'Well, you can rent then. You'll have enough money to cover the rent bills for the rest of your life.'

'No I won't. Everyone in this building has done well, apart from me. Because I took early retirement, my work unit refuses to give me a property ownership certificate, so I'm only eligible for tenants' compensation, which is a tenth of what everyone else is getting. I've told the Hong Kong developers that unless they pay me the full amount, I won't budge.'

'They've daubed the word "demolish" all over this building. Most of the shops and restaurants outside have closed down. It's like a ghost town. I don't want to come here again. Even during the day, I feel frightened walking down that street. I'll come next week, but if you want any more medicine for your son after that, you'll have to visit the clinic.'

'It's a building site outside. There are bulldozers everywhere and mountains of debris. Even the roads are filled with rubble. How can you expect me to leave the flat?'

'Ha! You mad old lady. I've heard that you wander through the streets all the time!' She walks out, shutting the front door behind her.

My mother is getting frail. Over the years, her life has gradually become even worse than mine. Neither her son who's far away in England, nor the comatose son who's lying by her side can help her now.

She checks the radiator, sits on a sunny patch of the bed and takes my hand in hers. 'How strange! The red spots on your fingernails have disappeared! When did that happen? Does it mean you're going to wake up, my son? You'll have to do your hand exercises yourself, now, I'm afraid. I don't have the strength to bend your fingers back . . .' Yesterday, my mother read a book called *The Medicinal Benefits of Palmistry*, which An Qi gave her. Her husband finally died a few weeks ago. His old bullet wound flared up again and he contracted septicaemia.

My mother shuffles off into the sitting room to rummage through a pile of old belongings. Smells of dust and bird droppings waft through the air again.

She has become nostalgic in her old age. She's telephoned some former colleagues at the National Opera Company and asked whether they have photographs of the performance she gave in Moscow. She's even phoned her younger sister, with whom she'd broken contact, and asked her how she is. Master Yao is still in prison, but she seems to have blotted him from her memory.

The sparrow climbs back onto my chest and sits down. The evening light filtering through the window turns my thoughts to death. If my body comes back to life, will my soul return to its previous comatose state?

Your spirit moves restlessly through your flesh. Your heart has been crushed.

'Where is it?' my mother says, taking a brief rest from her rummaging. 'I'm sure I put it between the pages of a book . . .'

I suspect she's searching for the postcard she was sent by a Russian man she met while touring in the Soviet Union with the opera company.

Its disappearance perplexed her for years. It was probably the only love letter she ever received. She gets up, walks into my room and says dreamily, 'His eyes were blue. He was a bit taller than your father.'

She will never know that the postcard with its message written in Cyrillic script was burnt by me.

When I think of that card now, I still feel a glimmer of fear. Three opera company singers in red armbands turned up at our room in the dormitory block one evening and ordered my mother to hand over the postcard she received from the Soviet Union. My mother told me to go into the yard, so I didn't hear what else was said. But I could tell they suspected her of being a spy.

For a few months after that visit, I didn't dare go outside to play, because as soon as the other kids in the yard saw me, they'd shout, '"What's that book you're holding?" "It's a libretto." "Of what?" "*The Tale of Natasha.*"' They were quoting dialogue from a Russian film that was popular at the time. In that particular scene, a female spy made herself known to a government agent.

It was only when I started going to primary school that I realised my mother couldn't have been spying for the Soviet Union, because she didn't speak a word of Russian.

Although my mother's colleagues didn't find the postcard, they confiscated other Russian letters they found in the flat. A few years later, I came across a postcard of Moscow's Red Square while I was flicking through my mother's journal. When no one was looking, I tossed it into the burning embers of our charcoal stove.

My mother had a distant cousin called Dr Wan. She visited him once seeking treatment for a chest infection, and ended up staying with him for almost a month. She said he prepared herbal medicines for her every day. They wrote to each other a lot after she returned. Perhaps that was another brief romantic episode in her life.

After the day shift of demolition workers clocks off, the sparrow sings for a while, then everything becomes so still that I can hear insects nibbling the mung beans in the kitchen. Although the sound each individual insect makes is tiny, when multiplied by 10,000, it amplifies into a loud munch that rumbles through the air. The insects have very hard shells. My mother skims off the insects that float to the surface when she puts the mung beans in a pan of water, but some drown and sink to the bottom. After their little corpses are poured down my throat along with my mother's soup, I can feel them stick to the walls of my stomach. They're harder than the mung beans' indigestible skins.

The night workers begin their shift, and the noise from the demolition sites that surround us on all sides makes the night air shake.

Since my mother lost enthusiasm for life, her days have become tedious and wretched, which is probably why the postcard has assumed such importance. People only escape into the past when they have nowhere left to go. I've had to flee down this backward path for the last ten years.

When dawn breaks, my mother drags a chair out onto the landing, climbs onto it and tries to pull down one of the many objects she's hung outside the front door. There are bundles of flattened cardboard boxes out there, as well as rusty cigarette tins and the bamboo bicycle seat that my brother used to sit in when he was a child. A cold draught blows in. As she taps the objects, I catch a smell of old dust. It's more refined than the smells of mouldering onions, human faeces and bird shit that fill this flat.

'What a cold wind,' she says, dragging the chair back into the room. Then she picks up a leaflet from the floor. 'What? They're turning off the central heating next week? But I've paid for the heating until March next year . . . And what's this? They're cutting off the water and electricity too next month? Ha! Those corrupt officials are colluding with the rich businessmen . . .'

She hasn't begun to look for a flat for us to move into. All she's done is collect a few notices advertising rooms to rent. Since she's still refused to sign the contract, she hasn't received any compensation money yet. In fact, she read the leaflets about the heating, electricity and water last week, but she's forgotten all about them.

Two hundred li further north is the Mountain of the Triumphant Horse. A winged horse with a black head and white body stands on its summit. When it sees a human approach, it flies away.

'Ke Xi is a piece of s-scum!' I heard Shan Bo say to Bai Ling as I squeezed back into the hunger strike tent. 'At the critical moment, he plays sick and runs away!'

Bai Ling's face was blank. Lin Lu was sitting with his legs crossed, smoking a cigarette. Old Fu was having a heated discussion with the rock star Hou Dejian.

I decided against telling Bai Ling that Mou Sen and Nuwa had been shot. I was afraid she'd pass out if she heard the news. But I couldn't bottle up the pain, so I pulled Old Fu outside and said, 'Mou Sen's been hit!'

'Did you see it happen?' Old Fu asked, the glowing streaks of the tracer bullets reflected in his eyes.

'He's dead. The bullet ripped up half his face. Nuwa was shot too.

She's been taken to hospital. Look at my hands. There was a massacre in the north-east corner! I saw seven or eight people killed up there.' I looked down at the blood coagulated on my arms. I couldn't tell which patch of blood belonged to whom.

Old Fu wrung his hands nervously. 'Don't let's broadcast this news yet. We haven't got any funeral music to hand.'

'The Workers' Federation's Dare-to-Die Squad went to repel the troops in the east. I'm sure most of them have been killed by now.'

'If my binoculars hadn't been smashed, I'd be able to see what was going on over there,' Chen Di said. He'd lost his powerful army torch too.

The sound of gunfire intensified on all sides. The student standing next to me had spent some time in the army. 'Those shots are from automatic rifles and machine guns,' he said authoritatively. 'The troops are firing horizontally into the crowds. Only a few of them are shooting into the air. They must have killed a lot of people by now.'

It felt as though we were standing behind the scenes in a theatre, overhearing the noisy commotion taking place on the stage. The students and civilians listened to the gunfire, clutching their masks, waiting for the soldiers to flood onto the Square. A few couples had wrapped themselves tightly together in blankets and had lain down on the ground to sleep. Friends were helping each other pin their student identity cards to the insides of their pockets. Foreign reporters and press photographers gripped their cameras, but didn't know where to point them. In the spot where I'd gone to block the armoured personnel carrier, I could see a bus in flames. Thick clouds of smoke swirled up and scattered into the night sky. Several armoured personnel carriers and tanks were now zipping back and forth along Changan Avenue.

My fingers remembered the warmth of Nuwa's blood. Mou Sen's blood was already cold by the time I touched it. Were those two people really no longer alive? I still couldn't accept it. I knew Tian Yi must have arrived at the hospital by now. Even if she'd wanted to return to the Square, she would have had difficulty breaking back through the ring of encirclement. I knew she would live, and that I would perhaps end up dead, like Mou Sen. For a moment, I considered running away, but the thought filled me with shame.

'Go and fetch Wang Fei,' Hai Feng said, arriving with Shao Jian and Cao Ming.

'We've just received some inside information that General Secretary Zhao Ziyang wants us to stay here until dawn,' Cao Ming said. 'If we stand our ground, the reformers will be able to regain the upper hand. Don't forget, Zhao Ziyang is Deputy Chairman of the Central Military

Commission as well as General Secretary, so he has some control over the army. But we need to give him time to mobilise his troops.'

'All right, we'll stay in the Square,' Lin Lu said, forgetting that only Bai Ling could make this decision. 'Make an announcement asking everyone to form a human wall. There are 10,000 of us here now. If the soldiers want to drag us out one by one, it will take them at least until dawn.'

'We can't stay here,' I said. 'The north-eastern corner of the Square has been sealed. When the troops arrive from the west, they will launch the crackdown.' I still didn't dare mention that Mou Sen had been killed.

'Yes, we must leave,' Zi Duo concurred, rising feebly to his feet. 'I don't care whether the information you received about Zhao Ziyang is true or not. You have no right to put the students' lives at risk!'

'This discussion is for members of the Defend Tiananmen Square Headquarters only, Sir,' Old Fu said. 'You aren't entitled to take part.'

'We've spent the last three weeks debating whether to leave or stay,' Shao Jian said, his usually mild voice rising in pitch. 'We must come to a decision now!'

'Hou Dejian and I want to speak to the martial law troops,' Zi Duo said. 'We'll ask them to give you time to vacate the Square.'

'You must return to the campuses and keep the flame of your movement burning,' Hou Dejian said, walking over. 'You can't just sit here and wait for them to arrest you.'

'If you go and negotiate with the army, you'll be on your own,' Old Fu said. 'You can't speak on behalf of the Headquarters.'

'The army has already pulled down the Workers' Federation's tent,' Tang Guoxian said, squeezing over to us with Zhang Jie. 'The north side of Changan Avenue is packed with martial law troops now.'

I pulled Tang Guoxian to the side and whispered in his ear: 'Mou Sen's been killed.'

'I heard he was hit by a bullet and was taken to the emergency tent. He's dead? My God . . .' His expression froze in disbelief.

I looked over at Tiananmen Gate and saw thousands of soldiers pouring out from the black arch beneath Chairman Mao's portrait. Reflected firelight flickered across their metal helmets. The fires blazing in the distance looked like funeral pyres burning in a graveyard.

After the god Zi You was killed by the emperor, he turned into a maple tree. A red snake lies coiled beneath the tree, keeping watch over it.

'. . . I beg you to sign the contract. I have an invalid wife at home who's waiting for me to bring her some medicine.'

'I'll only agree to move if you give me the same compensation my neighbours received. Why should I be punished for my son's mistake? I've devoted my life to the Party, and now that I'm old and frail, they want to take away my flat. So much for their so-called "Three Represents" policy . . .'

'It's not easy being a relocation officer. I only earn a base salary of three hundred yuan a month. I have to rely on my bonuses to get by. If you sign this contract, my job will be done and I'll leave you in peace . . .'

'You're wasting your time. I'll never sign it. If they attempt to drag me out of here, I'll throw myself off Tiananmen Gate, or I'll jump out of this window.' When my mother's mind is clear, her voice becomes much louder.

'It's not like the old days. The government won't forcibly evict you. But think things through. If you stay here over winter, how will you survive without water, electricity or heating? And besides, the Hong Kong developers have promised to offer you a reward if you agree to move out in time . . .'

'You'd better go now. My phone is ringing . . .' She pushes the officer out of the door, then answers the phone. 'Hello! Really? That's wonderful. Congratulations! . . . The compound is being pulled down. All the roads have been blocked off. Most of the residents have moved out . . . I don't know yet. The new flats around here are so expensive . . .' I don't hear the phone click after my mother hangs up. She probably hasn't put the receiver down properly. I hear her mutter, 'What's wrong with that girl? She's about to marry her foreign fiancé, but she's still thinking about you. That's so bourgeois!'

That must have been Tian Yi on the phone. She will be marrying her boyfriend this Christmas.

When my mother leaves the flat these days, she often ends up sitting outside for hours. If anyone asks her what she's doing, she'll say, 'I'm going to the airport. I'm just waiting for a car to pick me up . . .' In the afternoon, she'll forget what she did in the morning. She has locked herself out of the flat several times. She tells people she is going to move to England, and is just waiting for her visa to be issued. She often mixes up Master Yao and my father, and asks why every man she's known has ended up in jail. She says that her dead father's soul has laid a curse on her.

Sometimes she comes over to me and says, 'I'm going to look at a flat. It's got three bedrooms and two bathrooms . . .' Before she leaves, she makes me a bowl of maize congee and sprinkles some dried shredded pork over the top. Then she inserts the feeding tube into my nose, attaches the funnel to the end and pours the congee in. When the bowl's empty, she mutters, 'I know you're only pretending to be dead,' or 'I'm going away with your father now. He's taking me to America to meet his old college friends . . .' Sometimes she says very softly, 'Look at your skin. It's much smoother. That's a sign you're going to come back to life again soon, my son . . .' Then she says goodbye and leaves.

A few minutes later, she'll be on the street corner outside, sitting on her packed suitcase, staring at the trucks driving through the demolition site loaded with discarded door frames, window frames and concrete flights of steps. She always puts on a lot of make-up before she leaves. I imagine it's the same make-up she wore when she sang on the stage. She liked to draw two fine black arches a little above where her eyebrows should be.

My mother has a quick doze on the sofa. When she wakes up, she turns off the television then switches it on again. It's another programme examining the proposed logos for Beijing's Olympic bid. She tries to shut the door to my room, but there's too much stuff in the way. Like me, the flat has become a corpse that's rotting from within.

She whisks off some nail clippings, or crumbs, from the sofa, then goes into her bedroom. For some reason, she shuts the door behind her. She hasn't done that for years.

You move through the fleshy layers of streets and buildings outside, watching tiny microbes darting restlessly back and forth.

Now that the telephone line has been cut, the flat feels dead. My mother dials the same number again and again, until she finally guesses what has happened.

The last call she received before the line was disconnected was from Mao Da. He said that Liu Gang was detained for working in Beijing without a residency permit. A few days after he was released, he got run over by a police car and died in hospital. He also told her that Wang Fei has been arrested and locked up in an Ankang mental asylum. When she heard this, my mother said, 'A mental asylum? How nice. I wouldn't mind going in for a bit of treatment myself . . .'

I hear her brush her hair. It's caked in so much dust and lacquer that it crackles when the bristles move through it.

The dust and mist outside have tinted the sky yellow. All those solid, fifty-year-old buildings, all those layers of red brick, are crumbling to the ground one by one. My body is being demolished and rebuilt as well. Since my gastric glands stopped secreting digestive enzymes, cells have been flooding in my stomach as though it were a public square. My redundant sperm has been moved into my bone marrow. The cone cells on my neglected retinas have relocated to a newly developed district in my brain's frontal lobe, and have reorganised themselves in such a way that I am now able to sense the world as a bat might do. My superfluous jejunum has also been repositioned. While this commotion takes place inside me, I remain motionless, flat on my back on the iron bed.

The old locust tree outside our building was bulldozed to the ground yesterday. It's probably lying amid the rubble now, covered in grey dust, or perhaps a truck has already taken it away. In my childhood, that tree was my only safe haven. My mother will soon don her red-and-yellow baseball cap, then take her gold ring from her drawer and slip it on her finger. She will then cover the ring with her right hand, to hide it from any thieves that might be prowling outside.

My body has become much more efficient. Through a process of energy conversion, I can now survive for a week on just one glass of milk. My skin has learned to absorb as many ultraviolet rays from one small beam of sunlight as most people absorb during an entire summer. My mother, however, is getting stiffer and frailer by the day. She seems to be slipping into a trance.

She switches on the television. '. . . St Mary's Hospital in Hong Kong has begun to use deep brain stimulation of the thalamus to treat Parkinson's disease. The symptoms of Parkinson's include stiffness and rigidity, a blank facial expression . . .' She quickly turns up the volume. '. . . The procedure involves screwing a metal frame to the head, inserting fine needles into the brain to locate the thalamus, then drilling a hole about the width of a finger into the skull . . .' She turns the volume right down again and mutters, 'Huh! As if that will do any good!'

'Huizhen! It's me – Granny Pang. Will you let me in?'

'What a terrible sandstorm we're having,' my mother says, opening the door.

'It's not sand, it's dust from the demolition site. Look. The stairwell is covered in it. The workers should sprinkle water on the ground to keep the dust under control . . . I've come up to tell you that I'm moving out this afternoon. I'll come back and visit you, when I have time.'

'I still don't know where I'm moving to . . .' When her mind is clear, she forgets how she often talks about moving to England or America.

'You're the last person left in this building. You'd better hurry up and move out. They're going to cut off the electricity soon.'

The sparrow walks up the side of my chest and nuzzles itself into my armpit, to shelter itself from the cold draught. It has lost so many of its feathers that all it can do is skip and scurry over my body. My mother has picked it up a few times and taken it to the window, but just as she's on the point of throwing it out, she always changes her mind and says, 'I'll let you wait until my son wakes up, then you can fly into the sky together . . .'

'I haven't dared open my window,' Granny Pang continues. 'There's so much dust out there. They're working overtime to make sure the project is completed before the millennium. It's been so noisy at night, I haven't slept a wink.'

'They can pull everything down and cut off the electricity, I don't care! I've brought out my old charcoal stove so I can cook on that if I need to. I will stand up to them. Even a rabbit can bite if it's pushed into a corner.'

'To be fair, we should be pleased that the government is finally building new flats for us . . .'

'Auntie Hao from the neighbourhood committee came over yesterday with Officer Liu and tried to persuade me to move out. But I'm not budging. I'm like the turtle in the fable, which swallows a lead weight when someone comes to remove it from its pond. I will stand firm.'

'A Bodhisattva appeared before me yesterday. It looked just like your Guanyin figurine. How do you explain that?'

'Old Yao said that during the early stages of cultivation, the gods that appear to you are as small as a grain of rice, but they grow larger the longer you practise. If you saw a Bodhisattva as large as my figurine, it shows that you have almost reached the stage of Buddha yourself.'

'Really? That means I'll be able to fly into the sky soon . . . The Falun paradise is superior even to the Buddha Realm. It's a land of eternal spring, with golden mountains and silver streams . . .'

Have I now explored all 5,370 mountains of *The Book of Mountains and Seas*? On my travels through my body, I've discovered that all the wonders described in the book exist within me: the peaks and marshes, the buried ores, the trees that grow in the clouds and the birds with nine heads. I know now that to reach the soul, you must travel backwards. But only people who are asleep have time to tread that backward path. Those who are awake must hurtle blindly onwards until the day they die . . .

Dusk is falling. In the darkness, my mother removes the bedpan from between my thighs and empties it into the toilet hole. She hardly ever cleans me any more. Since Gouzi the electrician made this specially shaped bedpan, she hasn't had to wash any of my sheets and blankets.

She's taken to eating her meals in the dark. She seldom turns on the light to read a book or a newspaper. I imagine that the ten volumes of *Mysteries of the World* she used to treasure so much, and keep neatly lined up on the cabinet are now buried under a mound of plastic bags. The photograph of my father playing the violin is probably still hanging on the wall above them. Those objects authenticate my memories. They will survive in my mind, whether they still exist or not, but everything else will slip away.

The sparrow chirps softly. When it's asleep, it clings to me with its claws and warms my skin. It should be living in the sky now, flying so high that people have to lift their heads to see it.

My bed shakes as the piledrivers outside ram steel bars deep into the ground. The thuds seem to pound in time with my heartbeat. I remember the heartbeats of A-Mei and Tian Yi. Everyone else seems distant from me. The hole where my left kidney used to be begins to tremble. Perhaps my left urethra is full of urine, or a few drops of blood have dripped into my bladder. I feel a change taking place. My organs seem to have received some secret signal. They appear to be preparing for something – either death or a return to consciousness . . . My thoughts go back to Wen Niao and the bliss I felt that afternoon she made love to me.

I hear people climbing up the stairwell. They're not removal men or migrant labourers. These footsteps are light. They ascend to the third-floor landing and come to a halt outside our front door.

'You're an illegal resident here,' a voice shouts. 'Everyone else in this building has moved out. We're telling you this for the last time. This building will be pulled down in the next three days. If you don't move out now, you will have to take responsibility for the consequences.'

The pounding thuds of the piledrivers outside echo through the stairwell.

'Who are you? Another bunch of relocation officers trying to pass yourselves off as government officials? I haven't signed the demolition agreement. You have no right to order me to move out.'

'I know you haven't signed it. We're from the demolition and relocation office. Every building has the odd stubborn resident like you. In the end, we have to remove them by force. If you resist us, you will not only forfeit any claim to compensation, you will also be breaking the law. The company has been granted a demolition licence by the public security bureau. When the building is demolished in three days' time, the police will be present to make sure that everything goes smoothly.'

'What a stench! It smells like a chicken hut in here. How can she bear to live like this?'

'You businessmen are colluding with the government to oppress us ordinary citizens. But I'm not afraid of you! Go ahead and build your shopping centre, your public square, your Bird's Nest stadium, but don't push me out of my little nest.'

'This is your last warning!' They walk out without closing the door. I can hear bulldozers thud in the distance and walls topple to the ground.

On the north face of the mountain, the earth is red. A bird with six eyes lives there. Whenever it appears, a calamity will befall the land.

The tanks and armoured personnel carriers lined up on the north side of the Square began rumbling towards us, followed by a huge mass of helmeted soldiers. My head was juddering so much I couldn't see clearly.

Wang Fei, Tang Guoxian and I sat at the front of the crowd and watched the vehicles get into line, and the sea of troops behind them organise themselves into neat columns.

I regretted not carrying Mou Sen's corpse out of the way. A tank had already flattened the emergency tent.

Hou Dejian and Zi Duo went to negotiate with the martial law troops. When they came back, the crowd cleared a path for them allowing them to return to the upper terrace.

Soon, the students' loudspeakers came on. 'This is Hou Dejian speaking. We've just had a private discussion with the army officials. They say that, as long as you all withdraw from the Square now, they will guarantee that no one will come to harm. The four of us entreat you to leave. You can't fool yourselves any longer. If you don't leave now, no one will come out of this alive . . .' Although his voice wasn't very loud, everyone could hear it. 'I know that the students who are still here in the Square aren't afraid of dying. But you can't give up your lives like this, for nothing! There is still so much you can achieve . . .' His hoarse cry was swallowed by the night.

Suddenly all the lights went out. The Square and the sky were pitch black. The only specks of light were from the fires still flickering in the distance.

'Fuck it! If I'd known they'd do this I would have brought a torch.'

'The bastards! They don't have the guts to launch the crackdown with the lights on!'

The crowd became agitated. A few girls began to shriek in panic.

'Fellow students! Please don't stand up or move around!' Old Fu shouted through a megaphone. 'We don't want anyone to get trampled on.'

I got up and shouted, 'Student marshals, this is Dai Wei speaking, head of security. This is it. The moment has come. You must all stand up now and link arms, and protect the crowds behind you.'

At that moment, thousands of helmeted soldiers came running out from the Great Hall of the People in the west and moved towards us. Wu Bin jumped up, pulled out a petrol bomb from his jacket and unscrewed the top. 'If anyone dares come near me we will go up in flames together! I am doing this to avenge Mou Sen's death!' Before he had a chance to reach for his lighter, Tang Guoxian pounced on top of him and grabbed his hands. I smelt the petrol spilling onto the ground.

'Where's the lighter?' I said, trying to snatch the bottle from Wu Bin's hand. Everyone around us panicked and pushed back into the crowd behind, trying to edge away from the smell of petrol.

In the darkness I heard a voice cry, 'Dai Wei? Is there anyone called Dai Wei here?'

A student handed me a letter and said that someone at the back of the crowd had passed it down. The paper felt smooth between my fingers, but it was too dark for me to read what it said, so I put it in my pocket.

Tang Guoxian managed to grab the cigarette lighter and bottle from Wu Bin's hands. Someone in the distance lit a fire. The red flames made my blood run faster.

'Throw away your walkie-talkie, Wang Fei,' I said, spotting a red light glinting on its metallic cover.

'I'm not using it. Anyway, the batteries have run out.'

The national anthem blared out again from the loudspeakers on the Monument. '*Arise, ye who refuse to be slaves! With our flesh and blood, let us build a new Great Wall!*' As we sang along, we began to relax a little. It occurred to me that most of the people who'd been shot by the Party since 1949 had shouted 'Long live the Communist Party!' when the bullets were fired. I wondered whether I, too, was going to die singing the national anthem beneath the national flag. I thought about A-Mei and wondered whether she was in the Square, and whether the letter I'd been handed was from her. I hoped she was sitting safely in a hotel room.

In the distance, we heard the Goddess of Democracy crash to the ground. Everyone yelled, 'Down with Fascism!' Red signal flares shot into the sky, and suddenly the troops lined up directly opposite us. A dozen soldiers lay down on their stomachs, pointed machine guns at us and placed their fingers on the triggers.

The muzzles were black holes. I knew that if they lit up, I would share the same fate as Mou Sen. My veins started throbbing. Everyone linked arms. Our limbs tensed as the roar of the tanks grew louder.

Hou Dejian cried through the loudspeakers, 'Your lives are precious. Don't throw them away needlessly!'

Then Old Fu shouted, 'It's too dark for a show of hands. Let's take a voice vote. If you think we should stay in the Square, shout "stay"!'

'Stay!' The bellowing cries made the crowd seem united.

'If you think we should go, shout "go"!'

'Go!' Although this response was softer, it was produced by more voices.

'Why did you shout "stay" then shout "go"?' Tang Guoxian asked Wang Fei, who was sitting beside him.

'I just needed to shout,' Wang Fei said. 'I can't hold my anger in any longer. Those fucking bastards!'

After the vote, Old Fu said, 'The response for us to go was louder. So I now declare that we will withdraw from the Square! Everyone must file out through the south-east corner . . .'

The lights in the Square came back on. A second later, the machine guns opened fire, spraying rounds of bullets at the loudspeakers above us. The bullets screeched past our heads, hit the Monument's obelisk and showered the cement ground with chips of stone. The students packed on the upper terrace screamed. Now that the loudspeakers had been silenced, the soldiers set to work. Some went to smash the shelters, others knelt down and aimed their rifles at us. The rest moved forward, skirting the spilt petrol that Tang Guoxian had just set light to.

Then a detachment of helmeted soldiers and armed police charged towards us wielding electric batons. They kicked and pushed their way to the top terrace and began driving everyone off the Monument. Soldiers with bayonets rushed up there too, and stared menacingly at the students climbing down to the lower terrace, prodding with their bayonets anyone who moved too slowly. They clubbed the students who were sitting on the steps. A few guys were beaten so badly their faces were covered in blood.

'They've gone up to arrest the ringleaders,' Wu Bin shouted. 'Quickly, let's go and protect Bai Ling.' He and Tang Guoxian ran up the steps. Wang Fei followed behind. But without his glasses, he couldn't see a thing, and he soon tripped and fell. I hurried over and pulled him to his feet. But as I stood up again, a soldier behind me knocked me to the ground . . .

The past surges forward like white waves crashing into a bay.

It's the evening of Christmas Day. My thoughts are racing about wildly, because at this very moment, on the other side of the world, Tian Yi is about to get married.

My mother packed her suitcase and left home again this afternoon. A migrant labourer has just brought her back. He found her lying on the ground fast asleep, clutching her suitcase to her chest, while the bulldozers and trucks roared around her.

The communal heating has been turned off. This building is like an empty rubbish bin standing in the snow.

The only warm patch of skin on my body now is the place over my heart where the sparrow is sitting. I think of the freezing concrete pipe in which I hid with Lulu. I think of my father picking up his violin as he lay on his deathbed and playing a hymn. Although two of the strings screeched a little, he played with great earnestness. The last few notes seemed to hover between earth and heaven.

It is morning in America now. Perhaps there will be bells ringing in the church. Tian Yi will wear a white wedding dress and have her photograph taken surrounded by bouquets of flowers. I'm sure she will be clutching a few petals in her palm. I once promised I would give her a house, and a garden with a reclining chair . . .

I wonder if any of our old classmates will be attending the wedding. Ke Xi left America a couple of years ago, and has moved to Taiwan. He's opened two small snack bars that sell spiced lamb skewers. Han Dan moved to America after he was released from prison, and is doing a PhD in political science, and Shu Tong and Lin Lu are in Boston, so those three will probably be at the wedding. No one has heard from Wu Bin and Sun Chunlin since they sought asylum in France. Perhaps they've met up with Tang Guoxian. After his epic journey across Siberia, he found God, settled in Marseille, and is now a Catholic priest.

Wang Fei's fate is the reverse of mine. His body is alive, but his spirit has been killed. When he's released from the Ankang mental hospital, perhaps he can go back to playing basketball. Maybe, by then, he will have lost all capacity to feel pain.

The headlamps of a passing vehicle fill this cold flat with a snowy-white light. They are probably illuminating the half-dead streets, telegraph poles and the mounds of concrete slabs on the construction site as well, and making the eyes of the cats crouched on the steel girders shine gold. I remember the bright patches of unmelted snow that would dot the compound in late December. You could spot them no matter where they were hidden. Girls in thin jackets would stand shivering under the locust tree, stamping their feet to warm themselves up, letting out an occasional shriek that made the cold air shudder.

'Look what I just found among last year's bills. I wonder who sent it. There's a foreign address on the back.' My mother comes into my room, tosses an envelope onto the pile of junk at the bottom of my bed and walks out again.

My hearts jumps. Perhaps it's a letter from A-Mei. I think of the bloodstained letter lying in the box for my ashes and wonder what it might have said . . . On a mountain seventy li north grow red flowers that can cure sadness and nightmares . . . I want to go to that mountain. But what is its name, and where is it?

The noise of crashing walls and bricks moves closer and closer . . .

In the mounting chaos, the tanks and armoured personnel carriers moved closer, shaking the ground so much that my head bobbed up and down.

They continued to push forward, forcing the students to the east of the Monument to begin evacuating the Square. The remaining crowds at the base shrieked in panic and retreated back onto the Monument. Thousands of students were still packed on the lower terrace. There were loud screams as people were knocked over or trampled underfoot. A few students who were being crushed against the balustrades at the edge of the terrace climbed over and jumped off.

I watched tanks driving back and forth across the nylon tents in the north, and wondered whether the boy I'd seen writing out his will had escaped. I never found my backpack. The thermos cup that Ge You brought me from Shenzhen had presumably been flattened by now. Two foreign journalists took flash photographs as more students began to file out towards the south-east. A band of plain-clothes policemen dressed like reporters snatched the cameras from the journalists, twisted their arms back and dragged them off into the bushes. One of my shoes had been pulled off during the stampede. I took off the other one and flung it at the battalion of soldiers behind us. They were forcing us forward, striking us over the heads with the butts of their guns as though they were driving out a pack of dogs.

We continued south across the Square along a route lined with armed police. A student at the front of our column began shouting slogans through a loudspeaker. The crowd became restive. A voice yelled, 'I'm not leaving. I want to die here in the Square!' Another cried, 'Someone help me! I can't walk!' The soldiers behind us were clutching guns, the butts pointing in the air, ready to attack us if we stepped out of line. Wang Fei glanced back and shouted, 'Down with Fascism!' and was immediately struck across the face. The butt of the soldier's gun hit my shoulder as it swung past. A girl who was being kicked ferociously by an armed police officer screamed, 'Mum, help me . . .'

At last we squeezed our way out of the encirclement. As we walked away, we broke into the chorus of the Internationale, glanced back at the Square and flashed the victory sign. The noise of gunfire and screaming seemed to light up the sky.

One guy bravely unfurled a banner that said ALL DICTATORS WILL PERISH! I too felt my fear slip away as we moved further from the Square.

I looked back again. About three hundred students were still sitting on the south side of the Monument, refusing to move. The soldiers and policemen surrounding them were kicking and clubbing them. I spotted Zhang Jie among the crowd. He stood up and waved a flag but was quickly struck down by a rifle butt.

Xiao Li appeared in front of me. He looked smaller. His eyes were red. His shirt was torn at the shoulder, and the skin underneath was ripped open. He was covered in dirt and blood.

Qiu Fa grabbed his arm and said, 'Where've you been?'

'They killed Mou Sen,' he replied blankly. 'I was right next to him when it happened. We were in the north-east corner . . .'

'Did you see whether there were any students left in the underpass?' I was relieved I hadn't hidden Tian Yi down there.

'We walked towards the troops shouting "The People's Army love the people!" They opened fire, and Mou Sen was struck by two bullets . . . Hai Feng and I jumped onto a bus with some other students and drove it down Changan Avenue to block the troops. But as the bus swivelled round, the soldiers showered us with bullets. The guy who was driving got hit. The bus was a wreck. Hai Feng and I jumped off. A soldier grabbed Hai Feng by the hair and flung him to the ground. I went down on my knees and held up my hands. The troops marched straight past me.' His eyes glazed over.

'One day we'll get our revenge for this. I fucking swear it!' Qiu Fa was usually immaculately groomed, but now the only clean part of him was his left ear. Both his shoes had been dragged off in the rushed evacuation. His feet were bleeding.

Xiao Li squatted down on the ground and stared blankly at the road ahead.

Wang Fei pressed the buttons of his walkie-talkie even though he knew the batteries were dead.

Hou Dejian staggered towards us, a student supporting him on either side. He looked shell-shocked. We stood scattered like detritus across the wide empty road on the south of the Square.

'Down with Fascism! Down with Li Peng!' someone shouted through a megaphone.

A Beijing resident walked up with a large basket of trainers and handed them out to students who'd lost their shoes. I checked the sizes. They were all too small for me. I went back into the bushes that some of the students had escaped through, picked up a plimsoll and a flip-flop that were nearer my size, and made do with those.

Bai Ling's eyes were so swollen, they were now just two narrow slits. Wang Fei walked beside her, gripping her shoulders.

We began to rearrange ourselves into university groups. Flags and banners were brought out again and held aloft. Many of the girls were sobbing. The boys took their hands and led them on. Mimi was crying uncontrollably. Yu Jin heaved her onto his back and carried her. Old Fu shouted into his megaphone, 'We will be back. Tiananmen Square belongs to the people!'

We walked west past Qianmen Gate, skirting the southern edge of the Square. Wu Bin's eyes were blood red. He tied a bullet belt he'd stolen from a soldier to the end of a wooden stick and marched in the middle of our procession, waving it above his head. Big Chan was limping in front of me. His feet were badly cut too. Little Chan was holding his guitar for him, as the shoulder strap had broken. Mimi went over to walk beside Bai Ling. Her pale-blue dress was filthy.

'They make us buy state bonds, and then spend the funds on ammunition to kill us with!' Big Chan shouted. It looked as though he'd had to crawl through the bushes during the evacuation. His short-sleeved shirt had large green stains. The words HEIR OF THE DRAGON, which Hou Dejian had calligraphed across the back, were smeared with soil.

'Fucking bastards!' Little Chan shouted, lifting Big Chan's guitar into the air. 'I'll go to the mountains of Yunnan and return with an army of peasants who will rid us of these bloody tyrants.'

'Be careful,' Dong Rong said, rushing up to us. 'The army fired a round of shots at the public toilets back there a moment ago, after they saw someone take a flash photograph from the roof.' He swept his hair back. He'd lost his sunglasses.

'Butchers! Butchers!' everyone shouted in unison as an army truck approached.

We walked slowly, in scattered ranks, occupying only one side of the road. Soon, we came to a stop to inspect a pool of blood on the ground. A pair of trainers lay in the sticky fluid that was bisected by a thick red wheel mark. Local residents told us that tanks had driven down this road shooting randomly into the crowd and that a young man was hit. His blood was spurting everywhere, but the army wouldn't let anyone go to his rescue. If his wife hadn't got on her knees and begged them to let her go to him, he would have died there on the street . . .

The floodlight shining outside makes the night as bright as day. The labourers are trying to demolish the balcony of the flat next door. There's a deafening noise of drilling and hammering. The whole building shakes, then seconds later, I hear the balcony crash to the ground. The steel bars that run through to our balcony are bent so badly that the metal window frames twist, shattering the glass panes. Clouds of dust shoot into my room. 'That's my balcony!' my mother yells. 'You've no right to touch it!' She coughs into her sleeve, grabs a torch and opens the front door. When she steps outside, the labourers shout, 'Get back in! The roof's about to come down. Get back into your flat now!'

'How dare you take that roof down! My son is still lying in bed . . .'

'We're leaving the section of roof that covers your flat,' the head labourer says. 'Now go back inside. It's not safe to stand there. Look, the landing's been removed . . .'

Now my mother won't be able to fetch any more of the flattened boxes she hangs outside the front door and uses to fuel the stove.

They start drilling into the water and sewer pipes. The noise is unbearable. The building judders so much that my body is tossed up and down. The iron bed slowly slides across the floor. I feel my eardrums are about to explode . . . Ten years ago, I promised my mother I'd take her to America and fulfil my father's wish to be buried in free soil. She should be spending her days in the sunlight, chatting with her retired or laid-off friends, performing fan dances with her neighbours in the park . . . When the sun shines, even the dust is transparent. I want ultraviolet waves to fall on my face, on the palms and backs of my hands, on my clothes, my hair, my shoes. I don't care if I'm inside a cage or outside, as long as the sunlight can reach me. When the sun comes out, there will be a warm breeze. A few leaves will fall from the trees. It will be the beginning of a new day . . .

'Do you dare violate the rights of a Chinese citizen when the national flag is flying?' I imagine she's brought out the national flag I took on a march ten years ago and is waving it at them. She must have put it on a pole some time ago, waiting for this moment to arrive.

'Put that flag down and get back inside! You're illegally occupying state property. And you have no right to fly the national flag . . .'

'The people will be victorious!' my mother yells. 'Down with Fascism!'

In the Land of the Nobles there is a plant called the xunhua. Its life is very short. It sprouts in the morning and dies the same evening.

As dawn approached, the air filled with a smell of scorched tyres and khaki uniforms.

A huge convoy of army trucks drove past, packed with soldiers. A crowd of about thirty men in white underwear passed us on the opposite side of the street and gave us the victory sign. Tang Guoxian said they were armed police who had thrown away their uniforms and refused to follow government orders.

Big Chan and Little Chan attached our university banner to some twigs and held it aloft, which made our group seem a little less bedraggled. But I was so exhausted by now I could hardly walk, let alone find the energy to cry out slogans. One restaurant we passed had already hung up a banner that said RESOLUTELY PROTECT THE GREAT LEADERS OF THE PARTY'S CENTRAL COMMITTEE. When Wu Bin saw it, he snatched his cigarette lighter from Tang Guoxian's pocket, rushed over and set it alight.

About two thousand of us had left the Square, but our crowd seemed to dwindle the further we went, like a stream of water flowing into dry land. Yu Jin was carrying Mimi's backpack. Mimi and Bai Ling were walking hand in hand. Xiao Li was traipsing barefoot behind Chen Di. The flags we'd brought with us from the Square were tattered and torn.

Heading north, we reached the Liubukou intersection. We were back on Changan Avenue again, having looped round from the west. We stood still and stared at the red walls of Zhongnanhai, knowing that behind them, the leaders who'd ordered this massacre were relaxing in their luxurious villas. Thousands of soldiers stood triumphantly outside the walls, rifles at the ready. A long line of tanks and armoured carriers had formed a solid blockade, screening off the view to the Square. Behind them, a green sun hovered at the horizon.

Wang Fei switched on his black megaphone and shouted, 'The people will be victorious! Down with Fascism!'

Tang Guoxian waved our university flag in the air, and everyone shouted Wang Fei's slogans, repeating them faster and faster. But as soon as the girls began shouting, they burst into tears.

Bai Ling borrowed Wang Fei's megaphone and cried, 'Don't look at the soldiers. They're trying to intimidate us. Ignore them.' Her voice was hoarse. She was straining so hard to produce a noise, the tendons on her neck were bulging.

One of the tanks suddenly left the blockade, roared towards us and shot a canister of tear gas which exploded with a great bang in the middle of our crowd. A cloud of yellow smoke engulfed us. My throat burned and my eyes stung. I felt dizzy and couldn't stand straight. Mimi fainted. As I tried to drag her over to the side of the road, I stumbled and fell.

While we were still trying to crawl our way out of the acrid smoke, I heard another tank roar towards us. It paused for a moment in the middle of the road, then rumbled forward again and circled us. As it swerved round, its large central gun swung over my head and knocked down a few students standing beside me. I got up and ran onto the pavement. An armoured personnel carrier drove forward too, and discharged a round of bullets. Everyone searched for cover. I heard Wang Fei scream. I looked back, but the yellow smoke was still too thick to see anything clearly. I waited. I knew the tank must have driven over some people. As the smoke cleared, a scene appeared before me that singed the retinas of my eyes. On the strip of road which the tank had just rolled over, between a few crushed bicycles, lay a mass of silent, flattened bodies. I could see Bai Ling's yellow and white striped T-shirt and red banner drenched in blood. Her face was completely flat. A mess of black hair obscured her elongated mouth. An eyeball was floating in the pool of blood beside her. Wang Fei's flattened black megaphone lay on her chest, next to a coil of steaming intestine. Her right arm and hand were intact. Slowly two of the fingers clenched, testifying that a few moments before, she'd been alive.

Wang Fei was lying next to her. He propped himself up on his elbow, tugged the strap he was holding and dragged his flattened megaphone away from Bai Ling's chest. The bones of his legs were splayed open like flattened sticks of bamboo. His blood-soaked trousers and lumps of his crushed leg were stuck to parts of Bai Ling. I glanced at the stationary tank and saw pieces of Wang Fei's trousers and leg caught in its metal tracks.

Tang Guoxian and I rushed to Wang Fei, lifted him up and shouted, 'Someone get some help!'

As a few local residents ran over, the tank drove away, taking Wang Fei's flesh with it and leaving two trails of blood on the road.

Tang Guoxian took off his shirt and tore it in two, then pulled down Wang Fei's tattered jeans and tied the strips of shirt tightly around the bleeding thighs. Dong Rong flung off his jacket and draped it over Wang Fei's chest. Wang Fei had lost consciousness by now. We dragged him onto the pavement. His trembling mouth stiffened. A red light flashed from the walkie-talkie he was still gripping. A voice cried out through the speaker, 'Down with Fascism! Long live . . .'

Then I spotted Chen Di. He was clutching the metal railings along the side of the road, his left foot crushed to a pulp. The questions marks on his T-shirt seemed to be screaming in anguish. Next to him, Qiu Fa was lying motionless in a pool of blood. When Yu Jin and Old Fu pulled him up, they discovered he'd been hit by one of the bullets discharged by the armoured personnel carrier. Blood was pouring from a wound in his back.

Students hugged each other and wept. Mimi knelt on the road and howled with grief. Old Fu pulled off his red headband and used it to wipe his tears.

Big Chan's body had been pulverised. It was now little more than a bloody tank-track mark. A few white teeth lay on the ground where his head had been. When Little Chan caught sight of the body, he dropped the guitar he was holding and ran over. As he drew near, he slipped in a puddle of crushed flesh, and fell to the ground. Blood splattered onto his face. He picked up Big Chan's left hand, which was still intact, pulled off the cotton glove and stared at the digital watch attached to the wrist.

Tang Guoxian yelled, 'Someone help me lift Wang Fei!' I realised suddenly that we might be able to save Wang Fei. I helped Tang Guoxian lift him onto a wooden handcart, then I grabbed the handles and we ran as fast as we could.

'Where's the nearest hospital?' we shouted as we ran. Someone yelled back, 'Go to Fuxing Hospital. Lots of the injured have been taken there already.'

We kept running. I couldn't make out what the bright or dark objects were that flashed before me. My mind was numb. I felt as though I was wading through knee-deep water.

When we reached the hospital entrance, I walked to the front of the cart to pull Wang Fei onto my back, but there was so much blood on the ground, I slipped and fell.

Tang Guoxian and Wu Bin dragged Wang Fei into the entrance hall and screamed for help.

The doctor who came forward looked as though he'd just crawled out of a river of blood. His gloves and face mask were bright red. 'Lie him flat on the stretcher and wait here!' he shouted. 'There's no more room in the wards.'

The bulldozer charges into the building like an army tank, making our walls shake and our floor-beams tremble and crack. It moves back, its tracks screeching over shattered glass and planks of wood. Beside it, a digger is shovelling broken tiles and metal frames into an open-back truck. The bulldozer rams again and our walls shudder. Unable to take the strain any longer, our balcony suddenly gives way and crashes to the ground, taking our outer wall and the sparrow's nest with it. As the bricks and cement hurtle down, I can hear the Bodhisattva figurine shatter into tiny pieces. Petrol fumes from the machines outside pour into the room together with the stench from broken sewer pipes. A heavy-goods vehicle rumbles past in the distance.

My mother roars like an angry tigress. 'This is my home! You fascists! If you come any nearer, I will jump!'

'Go on, jump then, old lady! Then the bulldozer can scoop you up from the ground and take you away. It will save us a lot of trouble!' This labourer's voice is very familiar. It's the drifter. I'm sure it's him. Mao Da mentioned he was working on construction sites now. I wonder why he still hasn't gone back to Sichuan.

'Get back to your work. The sun is almost up. Don't waste your time pestering that madwoman. You two, go and lean that flight of stairs against her front door, so that she'll be able to climb down if she wants to.'

'What does "fascist" mean?'

'Are you stupid? *Fa-shi-si*: It means "punish-you-with-death".' The drifter hasn't lost any of his Sichuan accent.

A cold, dusty wind sweeps up the pile of receipts and medical records from the chest of drawers, and blows all the calendars off the walls. I hear the pages rustle as they swirl through the air.

'Be careful, there's a strong wind,' a voice shouts up from the ground floor. 'Don't stand by your door. There's no landing left. If you have something to say, climb down tomorrow and speak to the Hong Kong developer.'

'I won't jump,' my mother shouts to a bulldozer's headlamps. 'I want to live!'

'Punish-you-with-death, old lady! If you don't move out, none of us will get our annual bonuses . . .'

The covered balcony and most of the outer walls and windows of the rest of the flat have fallen down. All the flats to our left and right have been demolished, as have the stairwell and landing behind us. Our flat is now no more than a windy corridor. It's like a bird's nest hanging in a tree. I can feel it shaking in the wind.

The cuckoo wept tears of blood, and the world was stained red.

The hospital corridor stretching before me looked like an abattoir. Everywhere there was dark, clotted blood, freshly splattered red blood, the stench of blood, mud and urine. People were weeping and cursing. Doctors and nurses shouted commands as they darted back and forth.

There were ten or so motionless bodies lying on the blood-soaked floor. I couldn't tell whether they were alive or dead.

Wang Fei was taken to a ward at last. We weren't allowed inside. Another casualty was brought in. He had to be put down in the entrance hall because there was no more room in the corridor. A nurse went out to him, squatted down and shone a torch at the bullet wound beneath his chin. It was a very small hole, with only a few specks of blood around it, but when she checked his pulse she found it had stopped. She turned his head round. There was a huge hole at the back of his neck.

A local resident went over and had a look. 'He must have been hit by an exploding bullet. They make a small hole when they enter the body, but explode as they exit, leaving behind large wounds like this. Those bullets have been banned by the international community for decades. The animals!'

'We've run out of blood!' a nurse yelled. Immediately, the twenty or so people milling about rushed over to her and stretched out their arms, all desperate to give blood.

'I'm O positive ,' I said.

'If you know your blood group please stand over there,' the nurse said.

'How could they have done this? They're insane, insane!' A young doctor ran out of a ward, sat on the ground and sobbed into his sleeve. A woman standing at the door knelt down beside him and cried, 'Help him, please! He's my brother! I beg you!'

After Wu Bin and I had finished giving blood, I tapped Tang Guoxian, who was leaning against the wall in a daze, and said, 'Let's count the bodies and try to draw up a list of names.' A soldier was lying on the floor next to him. His eyes were closed. I assumed he was dead.

'Yes, we must do it now before the bodies are taken away,' said Wu Bin. 'Let's split forces. I'll check if there are any bodies outside.' He rolled up his sleeves and went to find a pen and paper.

'You check the morgue, the operating theatre and the wards upstairs,' I said. 'I'll stay down here in outpatients.' I stared at the blood-soaked corridor. I felt so penned in, I could hardly breathe. I saw another injured person lying on a bench, lifting his hand in the air. I went over to him.

His eyes were open. He'd lost half a leg and his chest was wrapped in bandages. I asked him to give me the name of his university and his parents' address.

'Don't tell my mum, whatever you do. I – I was born in this hospital. My name's Tao. I'm a high school student.'

'Where were you hurt?' The bandages around his chest looked very tight. His left leg, which had been severed at the knee, was also covered in bandages.

'My leg was crushed and I got two bullets in the . . . chest. The doctor said . . . I'll be fine. But I know . . . I won't live.' His face was smaller than my brother's. His voice hadn't broken yet. I was about to tell him that he shouldn't have come out onto the streets but stopped myself just in time.

I fumbled through my pockets, searching for a piece of paper to write his address on, and finally pulled something out. It was the letter that had been handed to me in the Square. My fingers had smeared it with so much blood that I couldn't make out what it said.

An elderly female doctor shouted, 'If any of you are with people who have minor injuries, take them home now! The army will be turning up here soon to arrest the injured.'

'I'm a Beijing University student,' I said. 'I want to make a record of the dead and wounded. Can you lend me a pen?'

'Look, we've written their names and work units here,' she said. 'There are students, workers and even government cadres. People from every walk of life.' I looked at the sheets of paper pinned to the corridor wall and realised that it was a list of the dead. The names were numbered. The number of the latest name recorded was 281. The man next to me said, 'There was an hour or so when we didn't have time to record all the names. You'd better go to the morgue and the other rooms in the basement to double-check there. People are dying so fast, we can't keep up.'

I saw Tang Guoxian at the other end of the corridor, leaning his face against the wall and weeping uncontrollably. The muscles of his back shuddered and twitched. A woman in her late thirties walked over to the list. When she saw the name of a loved one on it, she gasped and fainted. The infant at her feet sat wailing on the blood-drenched floor. All the lights overhead seemed to be shaking.

Another casualty was brought in by an old man in his sixties. Everyone moved out of the way to let them through. 'She's been shot in the knee,' the old man said, holding the blood-splattered girl in his arms. 'She needs an operation immediately.'

'Someone get me a torch!' a doctor said, brushing past me.

I borrowed a pen and went back to speak to the boy called Tao. He was lying on the ground now. I knelt down and looked at him. His glazed eyes were staring at the fluorescent-light tubes on the corridor's ceiling. A nurse was crouched by his side, writing some notes on a piece of paper.

'Is he dead?' I asked, my heart thumping.

'His pupils are fully dilated,' she said, continuing to scribble her notes without pausing to look up at me. 'Help me carry him out, will you?'

A wave of nausea swept through me. I wanted to scream. The inside of my mouth twitched. I wanted to put my hand down my throat and wrench my stomach out.

The nurse removed her face mask and said to me, 'Go on. You take the head.'

I had no choice but to place my hands underneath the boy's neck. It felt as though he'd broken out in a cold sweat before he died. The back of his head was wet.

The nurse lifted his leg and we carried him to the bicycle shed in the yard outside. There were already about twenty corpses lying there. The white bandages covering their faces, limbs or chests were stained with red or black blood. Some of the corpses had no shoes.

'Put him down here, quickly!' The nurse was about to topple over. She was exhausted. We lowered Tao's body onto the ground. The corpse next to him had a student identity card on his chest. I could see from the cover that it was a Beijing University card. I picked it up and looked at the name. It said CAO MING . . . I turned away. All I could see was blood. The kind of blood that can never be wiped away. I got up, ran to the wall and retched.

My mother walks to the edge of the room to look at our balcony which is lying in the rubble on the ground. Her shadow sways before my eyes. A loud bang from the bulldozer below frightens her back inside. She grips the frame of my iron bed, squats down and, bursting into tears, pulls out the box of my father's ashes, and the one she bought for mine. She moves to the edge of the room again, hurls the boxes into the floodlight's beam and, in her clearest, most resonant tone, sings out, '*You are liberated at last! Quickly,run away . . .*' As she drops to her knees, the sparrow shrieks. It sounds as though it's fallen off the bed and broken a wing.

A labourer who's knocking down a wall next door teeters across a broken beam and peers into my room. 'Bloody hell! The Fascist has gone mad. Call the foreman. If she kills herself, they'll dock our pay . . .'

Two or three of them sneak over into my room and shine their torches on the floor. 'Look – she's become a vegetable too, now. You can send her off to hospital, and take the other one who's lying on the bed as well, while you're about it.'

'I want to submit a petition! I want go on a march,' she mumbles. 'Down with corruption!'

'Don't poke her with that stick. If you injure her, you'll have to pay compensation . . .'

'Look, there's white foam coming out of her mouth . . .'

'Down with . . . Down with . . . Down . . . Down . . .'

'Be sensible, old lady. Those Hong Kong developers have got the backing of the government. You're just digging your own grave, acting like this.'

'I heard that the chairwoman of the company – Zhang Lulu, I think her name is – used to live in this district as a child,' the drifter says. 'That's how the company managed to buy such a bloody big plot of land. They used all her back-door connections.'

So it's Lulu who is building this shopping centre . . . My mind returns to those winding lanes we used to wander through together. The ancient trees, the sunlight . . .

'I want to go to the Square. I want to go on a hunger strike . . .' my mother says blankly.

You are as brave as a solitary red-billed lovebird that flies out alone, gripping tightly to the wind.

I went to sit on the kerb outside the hospital. I looked across the street and saw a restaurant with a sign above it that said LULU'S CAFÉ. I remembered Lulu mentioning that her restaurant was opposite Fuxing Hospital. The door was locked. The painted characters of her name looked like strings of raw bacon. I looked down and saw blood trapped between my toes. I gagged and retched again.

'If any of you have got any balls, come back to the Square with me and help me rescue some injured people,' a middle-aged man shouted. I got up and walked over to him. A group of provincial students stumbled towards us, looking dishevelled and exhausted. A few of them had lost their shoes and had wrapped strips of cloth around their feet.

'Where have you just come from?' I asked.

'We were with the last group of students who stayed on the Monument. There's a massacre taking place in the Square. Don't go.'

It suddenly occurred to me that I should return to the Liubukou intersection and see if anyone there needed help. I set off, but just before I reached the intersection, a group of residents blocked my path and said, 'Don't go any further. Run away, quickly. They've just let off another smoke bomb. They don't want anyone to see the bodies.'

'The animals!' said an old man in a long cotton shirt. 'They must be on drugs. They're shooting everyone in sight. They've got big grins on their faces.'

A woman walked out in her slippers, tears streaming down her face. 'The soldiers stormed into our courtyard. They said there was a violent thug hiding on our roof and sprayed it with bullets. Fangfang was only ten years old. He was petrified. He'd never seen anything like it. He tried to escape into the back yard, but as soon as he ran, they mowed him down. How could they fire so many bullets at a child? His poor grandfather is so distraught, he can't speak.'

'You haven't got any shoes on, young man. Your feet are bleeding. You should go to the hospital and have them seen to.'

I looked down. My feet were drenched in blood, just as they were when I emerged from my mother's womb.

Through the gaps between these people's heads, I could see Bai Ling's flattened corpse in the distance. As if refusing to be crushed, the flesh and bones had risen a fraction from the tarmac.

I thought about A-Mei and wondered where she was. I wanted to find her . . . I had visions of her moist eyes, and of her glancing round and smiling at me before walking naked into the bathroom . . . Then I heard the tanks start to move again. Everyone around me turned and fled. A woman shouted, 'That tank's number is 107. Someone write that down!'

I stayed where I was. There was no one else around now.

I stepped onto Changan Avenue, and saw the long wall of green soldiers again. Everything was green: the soldiers, the tanks behind them, the buildings on either side. The sky was green, and the sun was greener still . . . Then I saw her: it was A-Mei, in a long white dress, her freshly washed hair floating softly around her shoulders. Why was she standing in the line of fire like that? I pulled the bloodstained letter from my pocket, waved it in the air and ran towards her . . . I remembered going for a stroll with her one day and being irritated at how slowly she walked. I began to imitate her gait, which annoyed her so much, she pushed me off the pavement . . . There was a loud gunshot, flecks of black light, then I saw her fall to her knees.

Did the bullet hit her? As the question came to my mind, my head exploded. My skeleton was shaken by a bolt of pain. I'd been struck too. I was going to die. Hot, sticky blood poured down my face. My hand reached out to touch my head, but couldn't find it . . .

A-Mei is still living inside me. When my soul detaches from my body, I will have to leave her behind . . . But none of that is important any more. I am ready at last to break out of this fleshy tomb, and let my spirit scatter into the light . . .

There is a species of bird that has only one wing and one eye. It must pair up with its mate if it wants to fly.

I feel a wisp of dawn light fall on my eyelids. My body is like a bird's nest that's fallen to the ground. All that remains of me is a cage of ribs propping up a rough sack of skin that allows my organs to retain what little moisture they have left.

The sparrow has rubbed off its last feather. It creeps about like a snail that has lost its shell, trying to return to the spot that it fell from last night. It pauses for a moment, its one remaining wing scratching at my stomach like a claw. Then it crawls up onto my pillow, slips down my neck and squats on my chest. Slowly, it transforms into a red-billed lovebird with dark brown wings and a golden breast. It chirps loudly, as though something has caught its notice. The skin on my stomach that it scratched a few moments ago begins to sting a little. Perhaps my nervous system is about to start functioning properly again . . . I'm not sure whether my eyes are open yet or not. All I can see are splinters of light, like those that scatter across a lake when you try to scoop out the reflection of the moon.

I see a public square. It's a flattened expanse of broken bricks, shattered tiles, sand, dust and earth. Positioned at its centre is not a memorial, but me and my iron bed, lying inside this building that's been carved away like a pear eaten to its core. On the ground below, I spot the frog I buried in a glass jar. Its delicate white skeleton has a divine quality, and conveys much more than its skin and flesh ever could.

Through the gaping hole where the covered balcony used to be, you see the bulldozed locust tree slowly begin to rise again. This is a clear sign that from now on you're going to have to take your life seriously.

You reach for a pillow and tuck it under your shoulders, propping up your head so that the blood in your brain can flow back down into your heart, allowing your thoughts to clear a little. Your mother used to prop you up like that from time to time.

Silvery mornings are always filled with new intentions. But today is the first day of the new millennium, so the dawn is thicker with them than ever.

Although the winter frosts haven't set in yet, the soft breeze blowing on your face feels very cold.

A smell of urine still hangs in the room. It seeps from your pores when the sunlight falls on your skin.

You gaze outside. The morning air isn't rising from the ground as it did yesterday. Instead, it's falling from the sky onto the treetops, then moving slowly through the leaves, brushing past the bloodstained letter caught in the branches, absorbing moisture as it falls.

Before the sparrow arrived, you had almost stopped thinking about flight. Then, last winter, it soared through the sky and landed in front of you, or more precisely on the windowsill of the covered balcony adjoining your bedroom. You knew the grimy windowpanes were caked with dead ants and dust, and smelt as sour as the curtains. But the sparrow wasn't put off. It jumped inside the covered balcony and ruffled its feathers, releasing a sweet smell of tree bark into the air. Then it flew into your bedroom, landed on your chest and stayed there like a cold egg.

Your blood is getting warmer. The muscles of your eye sockets quiver. Your eyes will soon fill with tears. Saliva drips onto the soft palate at the back of your mouth. A reflex is triggered, and the palate rises, closing off the nasal passage and allowing the saliva to flow into your pharynx. The muscles of the oesophagus, which have been dormant for so many years, contract, projecting the saliva down into your stomach. A bioelectrical signal darts like a spark of light from the neurons in your motor cortex, down the spinal cord to a muscle fibre at the tip of your finger.

You will no longer have to rely on your memories to get through the day. This is not a momentary flash of life before death. This is a new beginning.

But once you've climbed out of this fleshy tomb, where is there left for you to go?